*Joseph Sheridan LeFanu. From an ink drawing by the
novelist's son, Brinsley Lefanu, 1916.*

BEST GHOST STORIES OF
J. S. Le Fanu

Edited and with an Introduction by

E. F. BLEILER

Dover Publications, Inc., New York

Bibliographical Note

This Dover edition, first published in 1964, is a new selection of fifteen stories and one essay, taken from the sources indicated on page 467. This material has been reprinted without abridgment or alteration, except for minor changes in "The Familiar," as described on page 467.

The selection was made by E. F. Bleiler, who also wrote the Introduction.

International Standard Book Number

ISBN-13: 978-0-486-20415-4
ISBN-10: 0-486-20415-4

Library of Congress Catalog Card Number: 64-13463

Manufactured in the United States by LSC Communications
20415426   2019
www.doverpublications.com

Introduction to Dover Edition

I

It is now very fashionable to think of the Victorian era as the hey-day of the ghost story. Tenuous ladies in crinoline, sweeping through gingerbread houses or visible from afar on the turrets of neo-Gothic roofs, are extremely appealing to the imagination and much more interesting than the grimy ghosts of a twentieth-century city. Unfortunately, the literature does not support the opinion, and a sampling of Victorian supernatural fiction is very likely to disillusion a reader who is even mildly critical. It would be more truthful to say that the high Victorian era was probably the weakest moment of supernaturalism in the past two hundred years, and that our high estimation of it is due more to our projection of period nostalgia than to the quality of the stories.

I am speaking of the averages, of course, rather than of individuals, for the Victorians did have four excellent practitioners in the ghost story. Three of them were women, and three of them were Irish. There was Miss Rhoda Broughton, who brought a brisk, nervously electrical manner into imaginative situations; Mrs. Charlotte Riddell, who could create a detailed, convincingly realistic background into which the supernatural obtruded; Miss Amelia B. Edwards, amateur archeologist and founder of the Egypt Exploration Fund, whose stories of apparitions and revenants are outstanding for their travel and folkloristic background; and, of course, J. S. LeFanu, the greatest of the four, whose work has been praised highly by critics as varied as M. R. James, Elizabeth Bowen, V. S. Pritchett, and Henry James.

Joseph Sheridan LeFanu (1814–1873) was a Dubliner, born to a moderately well-to-do family of Huguenot descent who had emigrated to Ireland in the 1730's. On his mother's side he was the grandnephew of Richard Brinsley Sheridan, the dramatist. A graduate of Trinity College in Dublin, he first studied for the bar, but soon renounced law for journalism and became the editor and publisher of several newspapers and periodicals in the Dublin area. Of these the *Dublin University Magazine* (which at that time had no more connection with the University) was the most widely known and the highest in quality. Under LeFanu's editorship, from 1856 to 1869, it was one of the leading European journals.

LeFanu's adult life was uneventful externally, although as a child he had had at least one dangerous moment during a race riot outside Dublin. He does not seem to have left Dublin, beyond occasional trips, and during his later life his quiet, shy personality changed to deep melancholy. After the death of his wife he withdrew almost completely from social life and became a recluse, refusing to see even close friends. He died rather suddenly in 1873.

LeFanu was a prolific and successful author, with fourteen novels and many articles, short stories, and ballads to his credit. Most of his novels are now forgotten and almost impossible to find, even in the largest libraries, but he is still remembered for the great mystery novel *Uncle Silas,* which has remained in print since its first appearance in 1864. *Uncle Silas* has been translated into several continental languages, and not too many years ago it was filmed in England under the title *The Inheritor.* In many ways *Uncle Silas* is the Victorian mystery story par excellence, for it is equal in narrative skill to *The Woman in White* and *The Moonstone* and is superior to both in atmosphere, intelligence, and emotional power. *Uncle Silas* is still a living novel, and it may well be one of the scant half-dozen nineteenth-century novels that are still honestly read for pleasure rather than as a school exercise. Henry James may well have had it in mind when he wrote in "The Liar": "There was the customary novel of Mr. LeFanu for the bed-table; the ideal reading in a country house for the hours after midnight."

Most of LeFanu's other novels, however, are pedestrian, inferior to the short stories out of which he often developed them. It is only fair to say, though, that there have always been champions for *The House by the Churchyard* (which M. R. James considered LeFanu's best work) and *Wylder's Hand.* It is as a writer of nouvelles and short stories that LeFanu excels.

LeFanu wrote, in all, some thirty supernatural stories; the exact number will vary according to the reader's definition of supernaturalism. They usually appeared first in periodicals—sometimes in his own *Dublin University Magazine,* sometimes in Dickens's *All the Year Round,* sometimes in Mrs. Braddon's *Belgravia.* They were later gathered together in book form. Of these book publications the most important are the impossibly rare *Ghost Stories and Tales of Mystery* (Dublin and London, 1851) and *Chronicles of Golden Friars* (London, 1871) ; *The Purcell Papers* (London, 1880) , edited by Alfred P. Graves; the collection of hitherto unreprinted material gathered by M. R. James, *Madam Crowl's Ghost and Other Stories* (London, 1923) ; and *In a Glass Darkly* (London, 1872) , his finest collection, which fortunately is easily available second-hand in many reprint editions.

II

Of all the Victorian authors who wrote ghost stories, only LeFanu seems to have recognized that there must be an aesthetic of supernatural terror. He obviously thought deeply about the nature of fictional supernaturalism and was aware of the implications that supernaturalism would have for the other dynamics of the story. Most of his fellow authors felt that they had done enough if they declared a house haunted; from this there followed automatically ghosts dragging chains, shrieking phantoms, or spirits of the dead who made actual physical attacks upon the stalwart hero or fainting heroine. Or they thought of a ghost as a compulsive personality fragment that insisted upon reenacting (often to sad music and pallid lighting) the murders or other crimes that it had committed; or else they peopled the countryside with spirits of missing persons who stalked around evenings, pointing out to the curious the places where their bodies had been hidden. LeFanu seems to have been alone in rejecting these crudities; to him alone it occurred that the personality of the beholder could be just as important and perhaps just as supernatural as the manifestation itself.

In his best work LeFanu was primarily a psychologist, although not in the modern understanding of the term. His mode of thought hearkened back to the earlier nineteenth century, where theorists like Schubert and Carus were dividing the mind into conscious and unconscious levels, and seeing in dream, madness, and vision emergences of both a hidden "nightside of nature" and the supernatural. And like the early nineteenth-century philosophers he was greatly interested in the barrier between the ego and the non-ego, in the manner that each creates the other, and in the osmotic process which can penetrate the seal between the two areas of existence. LeFanu was concerned with penetrating the hidden recesses of the psyches of his characters and mapping out the strange areas where the sense of reality can manifest itself to cover equally what is perceived and not-perceived. Within his better fiction LeFanu so blended and intertwined the natural and the supernatural that his work is a fugue of strange states of consciousness, linkages between the outside world and man, and a hidden, often diabolic morality, that will not suffer evil to go unavenged or unbetrayed. As a result there is nothing else in contemporary literature quite like the effects and symbolism that sweep through "Green Tea," "The Haunted Baronet," or "Squire Toby's Will," just as there is nothing comparable to the perverse eroticism of "Carmilla" or the strange sexuality of "Schalken the Painter."

Within his later work LeFanu developed ever more strongly a rationale of supernaturalism that permitted him to invade both the mind and the manifestation. In the tales grouped together loosely by the analytical lens of Dr. Hesselius in *In a Glass Darkly* the supernatural is an unconscious element in the mind and it may leap into emergence when the barriers protecting the conscious ego are temporarily broken down, in one case by a drug, in another case by a sense of guilt. Yet this is not all, for the larger implications of the mind as a microcosm of the universe also loom out, and potentially evil mental fragments may become hypostatized into semi-independent existence, to ally themselves with larger evil forces of which we are fortunately unaware. Obviously, such concepts are likely to strain the fabric of a story, and in some of LeFanu's later work, like "The Haunted Baronet," the story becomes almost a symbolic organism or passion, in which the characters, instead of being people, are forces or small nodes and concentrations in a larger fabric which twists and strains through a uniquely haunted universe. It is probably significant that "The Haunted Baronet," together with Hoffmann's *Devil's Elixir* (where the concept of dissociated psychological components is even more strongly developed), in the final, typologically extreme spiritualization of the basic Gothic and Romantic plot of the disinherited hero.

In all this LeFanu took, essentially, the opposite road from his contemporaries. He strove to create an artistically consistent world where the supernatural was a natural manifestation; sometimes this was the world of philosophical and psychological speculation; sometimes it was a folkloristic world where faith in the Devil and his workings can account for his presence. LeFanu's fellow writers (if the crude followers of Victor Hugo are ignored), on the other hand, usually dragged occasional and erratic supernaturalism into our everyday life. On a lower level the occasional contributors to the childish Christmas annuals that were printed for many periodicals projected revenants of the dead into melodramatic situations; on the side of quality, the situation is much the same. For example, Charles Dickens's few true supernatural stories (as distinguished from allegories and humor) —"The Bridal Chamber," "The Signal Man," and "The Trial for Murder"—all concern spirits of the dead who are compelled to invade the land of life and give information. The best work of the three lady novelists follows Dickens's pattern. *Weird Tales* and *The Uninhabited House* by Mrs. Riddell, *Tales for Christmas Eve* by Miss Broughton, and *Miss Carew* and *A Night on the Border of the Black Forest* by Miss Edwards all show the same classical separation of the real and unreal. Only LeFanu seems to have equated the haunted swamps and strange fluttering birds and fierce ancestral portraits with the guilt layers of a man's mind.

Why did LeFanu differ so greatly from his fellows? The difference is not just a matter of quality, for the writers I have named were all very competent. It is more a matter of an attitude, a point of view, and a quality of emotion. Obviously, the answer lies in part in LeFanu's own unusual personality, which combined the gentle weaknesses and terrible dreams of the visionary with the strengths of the very competent business man. Both the sensitivity to perceive an emotion and the strength and rigor to analyze and reproduce it were present. Partly, it may have been a matter of personal belief. The supernatural had a personal meaning for LeFanu which did not exist for his more or less orthodox fellow writers. Partly, it was a question of literary origins and antecedents. The supernatural fiction of Madames Riddell, Broughton, and Edwards, all of whom are typically Victorian, was a perfection and refinement of the contemporary story which appeared in all its crudity in the popular periodicals and ephemeral novels of the day. Between Mrs. Riddell of *The Haunted River* and James Murphy of *The Haunted Church*, for example, there is only the gulf of quality; one is competent, the other is rubbish, but there is little or no difference in point of view. LeFanu, on the other hand, is often writing a story of the early nineteenth century, and paradoxically, because of his peculiar time lag is often quite modern.

There is also the question of cultural origins. While three of our four are Irish, LeFanu heard most strongly the creaking of the Anglo-Irish structure. (Miss Broughton, LeFanu's niece, and

Mrs. Riddell left Ireland when young.) He was born into a society that was being fragmented by emergent nationalism and was beginning to collapse; he lived in a culture that had great nostalgia for the past—a very unusual trait for the present-centered Victorians. LeFanu seems to have recognized a parallel between his own life situation and the world that was dying about him. It is recorded in his later days, when his health began to fail, that he suffered from a repetitive dream of a house that threatened to collapse upon him. When he was found dead, his doctor mused, "At last, the house has fallen."

LeFanu was also a scholar and an omnivorous reader. He saturated himself in the religious, theosophical, occult and magical thought of his time and of the past. Indeed, the very title "Green Tea" and the basic concept of the story is taken from an essay about the German ghost-hunters Kerner and Jung-Stilling which had appeared in an early number of the *Dublin University Magazine*. Perhaps this essay was written by LeFanu. In later life, like Henry James, Sr., LeFanu read deeply in Swedenborg, and there are unquestionably traces of the mystical Swede's doctrine of parallels to be found in LeFanu's literary practice.

Much of LeFanu's fiction is based on folklore, and one need only contrast his masterful "Carmilla" with the crude horrors of Prest's *Varney the Vampire* of only twenty years earlier, to see how personal LeFanu made his sources. Yet, despite his Irish background, native Irish folklore seems to have meant little to him. Perhaps his Protestant heritage and his philosophical bent of mind cut him off from the wonder worlds of fairies and enchantments, or perhaps his sensitivity revolted at the ridicule and condescension which formed part of the literary tradition that used Irish folklore.

The few stories in which LeFanu used true Irish folklore are much his weakest work, and have for the most part been omitted from this collection. I have included only "The White Cat of Drumgunniol" as the best of these stories; even here, though, it can be seen that there are worlds of difference between LeFanu's use of the supernatural and parallel material by Lover or Croker.

III

The stories in this present collection range from 1837 to 1871, two years before LeFanu's death. As would be expected from such a long time-span, they vary quite a bit in style and perhaps in quality. LeFanu started his writing career as a follower of Lever, Carleton, and other Irish regionalists; he ended as an independent writer, with a position of his own. His techniques and purposes, too, changed with the years, and if the powerful later work occasionally makes the earlier look crude and unsubtle, the earlier work nevertheless retains the breath of horror and strangeness that was LeFanu's own personality.

About half the material in this selection has never been printed in America before, and several stories have never been reprinted previously. Perhaps I have cheated a little, but in addition to the obvious fiction I have included an essay, "An Authentic Narrative of a Haunted House." Personally, I am inclined to accept LeFanu's strong statement that he was not writing fiction in the guise of fact, and that he is simply reproducing what others had told him. Defoe's "Mrs. Veal" would have been too tawdry a trick for LeFanu. But this essay or whatever one chooses to call it shows LeFanu's narrative touches and can be read as a very unusual story.

I must indicate indebtedness to the researches of S. M. Ellis and M. R. James, who have established most of what is known about LeFanu, and must recall, gratefully, correspondence and conversation, many years ago, with Professor Frederick Shroyer of Los Angeles State College.

E. F. BLEILER

New York, June, 1963

Contents

List of Illustrations

BEST GHOST STORIES OF
J.S.LeFanu

Squire Toby's Will

A Ghost Story

Many persons accustomed to travel the old York and London road, in the days of stage-coaches, will remember passing, in the afternoon, say, of an autumn day, in their journey to the capital, about three miles south of the town of Applebury, and a mile and a half before you reach the Old Angel Inn, a large black-and-white house, as those old-fashioned cage-work habitations are termed, dilapidated and weather-stained, with broad lattice windows glimmering all over in the evening sun with little diamond panes, and thrown into relief by a dense background of ancient elms. A wide avenue, now overgrown like a churchyard with grass and weeds, and flanked by double rows of the same dark trees, old and gigantic, with here and there a gap in their solemn files, and sometimes a fallen tree lying across on the avenue, leads up to the halldoor.

Looking up its sombre and lifeless avenue from the top of the London coach, as I have often done, you are struck with so many signs of desertion and decay,—the tufted grass sprouting in the chinks of the steps and window-stones, the smokeless chimneys over which the jackdaws are wheeling, the absence of human life and all its evidence, that you conclude at once that the place is uninhabited and abandoned to decay. The name of this ancient house is Gylingden Hall. Tall hedges and old timber quickly shroud the old place from view, and about a quarter of a mile further on your pass, embowered in melancholy trees, a small and ruinous Saxon chapel, which, time out of mind, has been the burying-place of the family of Marston, and partakes of the neglect and desolation which brood over their ancient dwelling-place.

The grand melancholy of the secluded valley of Gylingden, lonely as an enchanted forest, in which the crows returning to their roosts among the trees, and the straggling deer who peep from beneath their branches, seem to hold a wild and undisturbed dominion, heightens the forlorn aspect of Gylingden Hall.

1

Of late years repairs have been neglected, and here and there the roof is stripped, and "the stitch in time" has been wanting. At the side of the house exposed to the gales that sweep through the valley like a torrent through its channel, there is not a perfect window left, and the shutters but imperfectly exclude the rain. The ceilings and walls are mildewed and green with damp stains. Here and there, where the drip falls from the ceiling, the floors are rotting. On stormy nights, as the guard described, you can hear the doors clapping in the old house, as far away as old Gryston bridge, and the howl and sobbing of the wind through its empty galleries.

About seventy years ago died the old Squire, Toby Marston, famous in that part of the world for his hounds, his hospitality, and his vices. He had done kind things, and he had fought duels: he had given away money and he had horse-whipped people. He carried with him some blessings and a good many curses, and left behind him an amount of debts and charges upon the estates which appalled his two sons, who had no taste for business or accounts, and had never suspected, till that wicked, openhanded, and swearing old gentleman died, how very nearly he had run the estates into insolvency.

They met at Gylingden Hall. They had the will before them, and lawyers to interpret, and information without stint, as to the encumbrances with which the deceased had saddled them. The will was so framed as to set the two brothers instantly at deadly feud.

These brothers differed in some points; but in one material characteristic they resembled one another, and also their departed father. They never went into a quarrel by halves, and once in, they did not stick at trifles.

The elder, Scroope Marston, the more dangerous man of the two, had never been a favourite of the old Squire. He had no taste for the sports of the field and the pleasures of a rustic life. He was no athlete, and he certainly was not handsome. All this the Squire resented. The young man, who had no respect for him, and outgrew his fear of his violence as he came to manhood, retorted. This aversion, therefore, in the ill-conditioned old man grew into positive hatred. He used to wish that d——d pippinsqueezing, humpbacked rascal Scroope, out of the way of better men—meaning his younger son Charles; and in his cups would talk in a way which even the old and young fellows who followed his hounds, and drank his port, and could stand a reasonable amount of brutality, did not like.

Scroope Marston was slightly deformed, and he had the lean sallow face, piercing black eyes, and black lank hair, which sometimes accompany deformity.

"I'm no feyther o' that hog-backed creature. I'm no sire of hisn, d——n him! I'd as soon call that tongs son o' mine," the old man used to bawl, in allusion to his son's long, lank limbs: "Charlie's a man, but that's a jack-an-ape. He has no good-nature; there's nothing handy, nor manly, nor no one turn of a Marston in him."

And when he was pretty drunk, the old Squire used to swear he should never "sit at the head o' that board; nor frighten away folk from Gylingden Hall wi' his d——d hatchet face—the black loon!"

"Handsome Charlie was the man for his money. He knew what a horse was, and could sit to his bottle; and the lasses were all clean *wad* about him. He was a Marston every inch of his six foot two."

Handsome Charlie and he, however, had also had a row or two. The old Squire was free with his horsewhip as with his tongue, and on occasion when neither weapon was quite practicable, had been known to give a fellow "a tap o' his knuckles." Handsome Charlie, however, thought there was a period at which personal chastisement should cease; and one night, when the port was flowing, there was some allusion to Marion Hayward, the miller's daughter, which for some reason the old gentleman did not like. Being "in liquor," and having clearer ideas about pugilism than self-government, he struck out, to the surprise of all present, at Handsome Charlie. The youth threw back his head scientifically, and nothing followed but the crash of a decanter on the floor. But the old Squire's blood was up, and he bounced from his chair. Up jumped Handsome Charlie, resolved to stand no nonsense. Drunken Squire Lilbourne, intending to mediate, fell flat on the floor, and cut his ear among the glasses. Handsome Charlie caught the thump which the old Squire discharged at him upon his open hand, and catching him by the cravat, swung him with his back to the wall. They said the old man never looked so purple, nor his eyes so goggle before; and then Handsome Charlie pinioned him tight to the wall by both arms.

"Well, I say—come, don't you talk no more nonsense o' that sort, and I won't lick you," croaked the old Squire. "You stopped that un clever, you did. Didn't he? Come, Charlie, man, gie us your hand, I say, and sit down again, lad." And so the battle ended; and I believe it was the last time the Squire raised his hand to Handsome Charlie.

But those days were over. Old Toby Marston lay cold and quiet enough now, under the drip of the mighty ash-tree within the Saxon ruin where so many of the old Marston race returned to dust, and were forgotten. The weather-stained top-boots and leather-breeches, the three-cornered cocked hat to which old gentlemen of that day still clung, and the well-known red waistcoat that reached below his hips, and the fierce pug face of the old Squire, were now but a picture of memory. And the brothers between whom he had planted an irreconcilable quarrel, were now in their new mourning suits, with the gloss still on, debating furiously across the table in the great oak parlour, which had so often resounded to the banter and coarse songs, the oaths and laughter of the congenial neighbours whom the old Squire of Gylingden Hall loved to assemble there.

These young gentlemen, who had grown up in Gylingden Hall, were not accustomed to bridle their tongues, nor, if need be, to hesitate about a blow. Neither had been at the old man's funeral. His death had been sudden. Having been helped to his bed in that hilarious and quarrelsome state which was induced by port and punch, he was found dead in the morning,—his head hanging over the side of the bed, and his face very black and swollen.

Now the Squire's will despoiled his eldest son of Gylingden, which had descended to the heir time out of mind. Scroope Marston was furious. His deep stern voice was heard inveighing against his dead father and living brother, and the heavy thumps on the table with which he enforced his stormy recriminations resounded through the large chamber. Then broke in Charlie's rougher voice, and then came a quick alternation of short sentences, and then both voices together in growing loudness and anger, and at last, swelling the tumult, the expostulations of pacific and frightened lawyers, and at last a sudden break up of the conference. Scroope broke out of the room, his pale furious face showing whiter against his long black hair, his dark fierce eyes blazing, his hands clenched, and looking more ungainly and deformed than ever in the convulsions of his fury.

Very violent words must have passed between them; for Charlie, though he was the winning man, was almost as angry as Scroope. The elder brother was for holding possession of the house, and putting his rival to legal process to oust him. But his legal advisers were clearly against it. So, with a heart boiling over with gall, up he went to London, and found the firm who had managed his father's business fair and communicative enough. They looked into the settlements, and found that Gylingden was excepted. It was very odd, but so it was, specially excepted; so that the right of the old Squire to deal with it by his will could not be questioned.

Notwithstanding all this, Scroope, breathing vengeance and aggression, and quite willing to wreck himself provided he could run his brother down, assailed Handsome Charlie, and battered old Squire Toby's will in the Prerogative Court and also at common law, and the feud between the brothers was knit, and every month their exasperation was heightened.

Scroope was beaten, and defeat did not soften him. Charlie might have forgiven hard words; but he had been himself worsted during the long campaign in some of those skirmishes, special motions. and so forth, that constitute the episodes of a legal epic like that in which the Marston brothers figured as opposing combatants; and the blight of the law-costs had touched him, too, with the usual effect upon the temper of a man of embarrassed means.

Years flew, and brought no healing on their wings. On the contrary, the deep corrosion of this hatred bit deeper by time. Neither brother married. But an accident of a different kind befell the younger, Charles Marston, which abridged his enjoyments very materially.

This was a bad fall from his hunter. There were severe fractures, and there was concussion of the brain. For some time it was thought that he could not recover. He disappointed these evil auguries, however. He did recover, but changed in two essential particulars. He had received an injury to his hip, which doomed him never more to sit in the saddle. And the rollicking animal spirits which hitherto had never failed him, had now taken flight for ever.

He had been for five days in a state of coma—absolute insensibility—and when he recovered consciousness he was haunted by an indescribable anxiety.

Tom Cooper, who had been butler in the palmy days of Gylingden Hall, under old Squire Toby, still maintained his post with old-fashioned fidelity, in these days of faded splendour and frugal housekeeping. Twenty years had passed since the death of his old master. He had grown lean, and stooped, and his face, dark with the peculiar brown of age, furrowed and gnarled, and his temper, except with his master, had waxed surly.

His master had visited Bath and Buxton, and came back, as he went, lame, and halting gloomily about with the aid of a stick. When the hunter was sold, the last tradition of the old life at Gylingden disappeared. The young Squire, as he was still called, excluded by his mischance from the hunting-field, dropped into a solitary way of life, and halted slowly and solitarily about the old place, seldom raising his eyes, and with an appearance of indescribable gloom.

Old Cooper could talk freely on occasion with his master; and one day he said, as he handed him his hat and stick in the hall:

"You should rouse yourself up a bit, Master Charles!"

"It's past rousing with me, old Cooper."

"It's just this, I'm thinking: there's something on your mind, and you won't tell no one. There's no good keeping it on your stomach. You'll be a deal lighter if you tell it. Come, now, what is it, Master Charlie?"

The Squire looked with his round grey eyes straight into Cooper's eyes. He felt that there was a sort of spell broken. It was like the old rule of the ghost who can't speak till it is spoken to. He looked earnestly into old Cooper's face for some seconds, and sighed deeply.

"It ain't the first good guess you've made in your day, old Cooper, and I'm glad you've spoke. It's bin on my mind, sure enough, ever since I had that fall. Come in here after me, and shut the door."

The Squire pushed open the door of the oak parlour, and looked round on the pictures abstractedly. He had not been there for some time, and seating himself on the table, he looked again for a while in Cooper's face before he spoke.

"It's not a great deal, Cooper, but it troubles me, and I would not tell it to the parson nor the doctor; for, God knows what they'd say, though there's nothing to signify in it. But you were always true to the family, and I don't mind if I tell you."

" 'Tis as safe with Cooper, Master Charles, as if 'twas locked in a chest, and sunk in a well."

"It's only this," said Charles Marston, looking down on the end of his stick, with which he was tracing lines and circles, "all the time I was lying like dead, as you thought, after that fall, I was with the old master." He raised his eyes to Cooper's again as he spoke, and with an awful oath he repeated—"I was with him, Cooper!"

"He was a good man, sir, in his way," repeated old Cooper, returning his gaze with awe. "He was a good master to me, and a good father to you, and I hope he's happy. May God rest him!"

"Well," said Squire Charles, "it's only this: the whole of that time I was with him, or he was with me—I don't know which.

The upshot is, we were together, and I thought I'd never get out of his hands again, and all the time he was bullying me about some one thing; and if it was to save my life, Tom Cooper, by—— from the time I waked I never could call to mind what it was; and I think I'd give that hand to know; and if you can think of any- thing it might be—for God's sake! don't be afraid, Tom Cooper, but speak it out, for he threatened me hard, and it was surely him."

Here ensued a silence.

"And what did you think it might be yourself, Master Charles?" said Cooper.

"I han't thought of aught that's likely. I'll never hit on't— *never*. I thought it might happen he knew something about that d—— hump-backed villain, Scroope, that swore before Lawyer Gingham I made away with a paper of settlements—me and father; and, as I hope to be saved, Tom Cooper, there never was a bigger lie! I'd a had the law of him for them identical words, and cast him for more than he's worth; only Lawyer Gingham never goes into nothing for me since money grew scarce in Gylingden; and I can't change my lawyer, I owe him such a hatful of money. But he did, he swore he'd hang me yet for it. He said it in them identical words—he'd never rest till he *hanged* me for it, and I think it was, like enough, something about *that,* the old master was troubled; but it's enough to drive a man mad. I *can't* bring it to mind—I can't remember a word he said, only he threatened awful, and looked—Lord 'a mercy on us!—frightful bad."

"There's no need he should. May the Lord a-mercy on him!" said the old butler.

"No, of course; and you're not to tell a soul, Cooper—not a liv- ing soul, mind, that I said he looked bad, nor nothing about it."

"God forbid!" said old Cooper, shaking his head. "But I was thinking, sir, it might ha' been about the slight that's bin so long put on him by having no stone over him, and never a scratch o' a chisel to say who he is."

"Ay! Well, I didn't think o' that. Put on your hat, old Cooper, and come down wi' me; for I'll look after that, at any rate."

There is a bye-path leading by a turnstile to the park, and thence to the picturesque old burying-place, which lies in a nook by the roadside, embowered in ancient trees. It was a fine autumnal sun- set, and melancholy lights and long shadows spread their peculiar effects over the landscape as "Handsome Charlie" and the old butler made their way slowly toward the place where Handsome Charlie was himself to lie at last.

"Which of the dogs made that howling all last night?" asked the Squire, when they had got on a little way.

" 'Twas a strange dog, Master Charlie, in front of the house; ours was all in the yard—a white dog wi' a black head, he looked to be, and he was smelling round them mounting-steps the old master, God be wi' him! set up, the time his knee was bad. When the tyke got up a' top of them, howlin' up at the windows, I'd a liked to shy something at him."

"Hullo! Is that like him?" said the Squire, stopping short, and pointing with his stick at a dirty-white dog, with a large black head, which was scampering round them in a wide circle, half crouching with that air of uncertainty and deprecation which dogs so well know how to assume.

He whistled the dog up. He was a large, half-starved bull-dog.

"That fellow has made a long journey—thin as a whipping-post, and stained all over, and his claws worn to the stumps," said the Squire, musingly. "He isn't a bad dog, Cooper. My father liked a good bull-dog, and knew a cur from a good 'un."

The dog was looking up into the Squire's face with the peculiar grim visage of his kind, and the Squire was thinking irreverently how strong a likeness it presented to the character of his father's fierce pug features when he was clutching his horsewhip and swearing at a keeper.

"If I did right I'd shoot him. He'll worry the cattle, and kill our dogs," said the Squire. "Hey, Cooper? I'll tell the keeper to look after him. That fellow could pull down a sheep, and he shan't live on my mutton."

But the dog was not to be shaken off. He looked wistfully after the Squire, and after they had got a little way on, he followed timidly.

It was vain trying to drive him off. The dog ran round them in wide circles, like the infernal dog in "Faust"; only he left no track of thin flame behind him. These manoeuvres were executed with a sort of beseeching air, which flattered and touched the object of this odd preference. So he called him up again, patted him, and then and there in a manner adopted him.

The dog now followed their steps dutifully, as if he had belonged to Handsome Charlie all his days. Cooper unlocked the little iron door, and the dog walked in close behind their heels, and followed them as they visited the roofless chapel.

The Marstons were lying under the floor of this little building in rows. There is not a vault. Each has his distinct grave enclosed in a lining of masonry. Each is surmounted by a stone kist, on the upper flag of which is enclosed his epitaph, except that of poor old Squire Toby. Over him was nothing but the grass and the line of masonry which indicate the site of the kist, whenever his family should afford him one like the rest.

"Well, it does look shabby. It's the elder brother's business; but if he won't, I'll see to it myself, and I'll take care, old boy, to cut sharp and deep in it, that the elder son having refused to lend a hand the stone was put there by the younger."

They strolled round this little burial ground. The sun was now below the horizon, and the red metallic glow from the clouds, still illuminated by the departed sun, mingled luridity with the twilight. When Charlie peeped again into the little chapel, he saw the ugly dog streched upon Squire Toby's grave, looking at least twice his natural length, and performing such antics as made the young Squire stare. If you have ever seen a cat streched on the floor, with a bunch of Valerian, straining, writhing, rubbing its jaws in long-drawn caresses, and in the absorption of a sensual ecstasy, you have seen a phenomenon resembling that which Handsome Charlie witnessed on looking in.

The head of the brute looked so large, its body long and thin, and its joints so ungainly and dislocated, that the Squire, with old Cooper beside him, looked on with a feeling of disgust and astonishment, which, in a moment or two more, brought the Squire's stick down upon him with a couple of heavy thumps. The beast awakened from his ecstasy, sprang to the head of the grave, and there on a sudden, thick and bandy as before, confronted the Squire, who stood at its foot, with a terrible grin, and eyes that glared with the peculiar green of canine fury.

The next moment the dog was crouching abjectly at the Squire's feet.

"Well, he's a rum 'un!" said old Cooper, looking hard at him.

"I like him," said the Squire.

"I don't," said Cooper.

"But he shan't come in here again," said the Squire.

"I shouldn't wonder if he was a witch," said old Cooper, who remembered more tales of witchcraft than are now current in that part of the world.

"He's a good dog," said the Squire, dreamily. "I remember the time I'd a given a handful for him—but I'll never be good for nothing again. Come along."

And he stooped down and patted him. So up jumped the dog and looked up in his face, as if watching for some sign, ever so slight, which he might obey.

Cooper did not like a bone under that dog's skin. He could not imagine what his master saw to admire in him. He kept him all night in the gun-room, and the dog accompanied him in his halting rambles about the place. The fonder his master grew of him, the less did Cooper and the other servants like him.

"He hasn't a point of a good dog about him," Cooper would growl. "I think Master Charlie be blind. And old Captain (an old red parrot, who sat chained to a perch in the oak parlour, and conversed with himself, and nibbled at his claws and bit his perch all day),—old Captain, the only living thing, except one or two of us, and the Squire himself, that remembers the old master, the minute he saw the dog, screeched as if he was struck, shakin' his feathers out quite wild, and drops down, poor old soul, a-hangin' by his foot, in a fit."

But there is no accounting for fancies, and the Squire was one of those dogged persons who persist more obstinately in their whims the more they are opposed. But Charles Marston's health suffered by his lameness. The transition from habitual and violent exercise to such a life as his privation now consigned him to, was never made without a risk to health; and a host of dyspeptic annoyances, the existence of which he had never dreamed of before, now beset him in sad earnest. Among these was the now not unfrequent troubling of his sleep with dreams and nightmares. In these his canine favourite invariably had a part and was generally a central, and sometimes a solitary figure. In these visions the dog seemed to stretch himself up the side of the Squire's bed, and in dilated proportions to sit at his feet, with a horrible likeness to the pug features of old Squire Toby, with tricks of wagging his head and throwing up his chin; and then he would talk to him about Scroope, and tell him "all wasn't straight," and that he "must make it up wi' Scroope," that he, the old Squire, had "served him an ill turn," that "time was nigh up," and that "fair was fair,' and he was "troubled where he was, about Scroope."

Then in his dream this semi-human brute would approach his face to his, crawling and crouching up his body, heavy as lead, till the face of the beast was laid on his, with the same odious caresses and stretchings and writhings which he had seen over the old Squire's grave. Then Charlie would wake up with a gasp and a howl, and start upright in the bed, bathed in a cold moisture, and fancy he saw something white sliding off the foot of the bed. Sometimes he thought it might be the curtain with white lining that slipped down, or the coverlet disturbed by his uneasy turnings; but he always fancied, at such moments, that he saw something white sliding hastily off the bed; and always when he had been visited by such dreams the dog next morning was more than usually caressing and servile, as if to obliterate, by a more than ordinary welcome, the sentiment of disgust which the horror of the night had left behind it.

The doctor half-satisfied the Squire that there was nothing in these dreams, which, in one shape or another, invariably attended forms of indigestion such as he was suffering from.

For a while, as if to corroborate this theory, the dog ceased altogether to figure in them. But at last there came a vision in which, more unpleasantly than before, he did resume his old place.

In his nightmare the room seemed all but dark; he heard what he knew to be the dog walking from the door round his bed slowly, to the side from which he always had come upon it. A portion of the room was uncarpeted, and he said he distinctly heard the peculiar tread of a dog, in which the faint clatter of the claws is audible. It was a light stealthy step, but at every tread the whole room shook heavily; he felt something place itself at the foot of his bed, and saw a pair of green eyes staring at him in the dark, from which he could not remove his own. Then he heard, as he thought, the old Squire Toby say—"The eleventh hour be passed, Charlie, and ye've done nothing—you and I 'a done Scroope a wrong!" and then came a good deal more, and then—"The time's nigh up, it's going to strike." And with a long low growl, the thing began to creep up upon his feet; the growl continued, and he saw the reflection of the up-turned green eyes upon the bed-clothes, as it began slowly to stretch itself up his body towards his face. With a loud scream, he waked. The light, which of late the Squire was accustomed to have in his bed-room, had accidentally gone out. He was afraid to get up, or even to look about the room for some time; so sure did he feel of seeing the green eyes in the dark fixed on him from some corner. He had hardly recovered from his first agony which nightmare leaves behind it, and was beginning to collect his thoughts, when he heard the clock strike twelve. And he bethought him of the words "the eleventh hour be passed—time's nigh up—it's going to strike!" and he almost feared that he would hear the voice reopening the subject.

Next morning the Squire came down looking ill.

"Do you know a room, old Cooper," said he, "they used to call King Herod's Chamber?"

"Ay, sir; the story of King Herod was on the walls o't when I was a boy."

"There's a closet off it—is there?"

"I can't be sure o' that; but 'tisn't worth your looking at, now; the hangings was rotten, and took off the walls, before you was born; and there's nou't there but some old broken things and lumber. I seed them put there myself by poor Twinks; he was blind of an eye, and footman afterwards. You'll remember Twinks? He died here, about the time o' the great snow. There was a deal o' work to bury him, poor fellow!"

"Get the key, old Cooper; I'll look at the room," said the Squire.

"And what the devil can you want to look at it for?" said Cooper, with the old-world privilege of a rustic butler.

"And what the devil's that to you? But I don't mind if I tell you. I don't want that dog in the gun-room, and I'll put him somewhere else; and I don't care if I put him there."

"A bull-dog in a bedroom! Oons, sir! the folks 'ill say you're clean mad!"

"Well, let them; get you the key, and let us look at the room."

"You'd shoot him if you did right, Master Charlie. You never heard what a noise he kept up all last night in the gun-room, walking to and fro growling like a tiger in a show; and, say what you like, the dog's not worth his feed; he hasn't a point of a dog; he's a bad dog."

"I know a dog better than you—and he's a good dog!" said the Squire, testily.

"If you was a judge of a dog you'd hang that 'un," said Cooper.

"I'm not going to hang him, so there's an end. Go you, and get the key; and don't be talking, mind, when you go down. I may change my mind."

Now this freak of visiting King Herod's room had, in truth, a totally different object from that pretended by the Squire. The voice in his nightmare had uttered a particular direction, which haunted him, and would give him no peace until he had tested it. So far from liking that dog to-day, he was beginning to regard it with a horrible suspicion; and if old Cooper had not stirred his obstinate temper by seeming to dictate, I dare say he would have got rid of that inmate effectually before evening.

Up to the third storey, long disused, he and old Cooper mounted. At the end of a dusty gallery, the room lay. The old tapestry, from which the spacious chamber had taken its name, had long given place to modern paper, and this was mildewed, and in some places hanging from the walls. A thick mantle of dust lay over the floor. Some broken chairs and boards, thick with dust, lay, along with other lumber, piled together at one end of the room.

They entered the closet, which was quite empty. The Squire looked round, and you could hardly have said whether he was relieved or disappointed.

"No furniture here," said the Squire, and looked through the dusty window. "Did you say anything to me lately—I don't mean this morning—about this room, or the closet—or anything—I forget—"

"Lor' bless you! Not I. I han't been thinkin' o' this room this forty year."

"Is there any sort of old furniture called a *buffet*—do you remember?" asked the Squire.

"A buffet? why, yes—to be sure—there was a buffet, sure enough, in this closet, now you bring it to mind," said Cooper. "But it's papered over."

"And what is it?"

"A little cupboard in the wall," answered the old man.

"Ho—I see—and there's such a thing here, is there, under the paper? Show me whereabouts it was."

"Well—I think it was somewhere about here," answered he, rapping his knuckles along the wall opposite the window. "Ay, there it is," he added, as the hollow sound of a wooden door was returned to his knock.

The Squire pulled the loose paper from the wall, and disclosed the doors of a small press, about two feet square, fixed in the wall.

"The very thing for my buckles and pistols, and the rest of my gimcracks," said the Squire. "Come away, we'll leave the dog where he is. Have you the key of that little press?"

No, he had not. The old master had emptied and locked it up, and desired that it should be papered over, and that was the history of it.

Down came the Squire, and took a strong turn-screw from his gun-case; and quietly reascended to King Herod's room, and with little trouble, forced the door of the small press in the closet wall. There were in it some letters and cancelled leases, and also a parchment deed which he took to the window and read with much agitation. It was a supplemental deed executed about a fortnight after the others, and previously to his father's marriage, placing Gylingden under strict settlement to the elder son, in what is called "tail male." Handsome Charlie, in his fraternal litigation, had acquired a smattering of technical knowledge, and he perfectly well knew that the effect of this would be not only to transfer the house and lands to his brother Scroope, but to leave him at the mercy of that exasperated brother, who might recover from him personally every guinea he had ever received by way of rent, from the date of his father's death.

It was a dismal, clouded day, with something threatening in its aspect, and the darkness, where he stood, was made deeper by the top of one of the huge old trees overhanging the window.

In a state of awful confusion he attempted to think over his position. He placed the deed in his pocket, and nearly made up his mind to destroy it. A short time ago he would not have hesitated for a moment under such circumstances; but now his health and his nerves were shattered, and he was under a supernatural alarm which the strange discovery of his deed had powerfully confirmed.

In this state of profound agitation he heard a sniffing at the closet-door, and then an impatient scratch and a long low growl. He screwed his courage up, and, not knowing what to expect, threw the door open and saw the dog, not in his dream-shape, but wriggling with joy, and crouching and fawning with eager submission; and then wandering about the closet, the brute growled awfully into the corners of it, and seemed in an unappeasable agitation.

Then the dog returned and fawned and crouched again at his feet.

After the first moment was over, the sensations of abhorrence and fear began to subside, and he almost reproached himself for requiting the affection of this poor friendless brute with the antipathy which he had really done nothing to earn.

The dog pattered after him down the stairs. Oddly enough, the sight of this animal, after the first revulsion, reassured him; in his eyes, so attached, so good-natured, and palpably so mere a dog.

By the hour of evening the Squire had resolved on a middle course; he would not inform his brother of his discovery, nor yet would he destroy the deed. He would never marry. He was past that time. He would leave a letter, explaining the discovery of the deed, addressed to the only surviving trustee—who had probably forgotten everything about it—and having seen out his own tenure, he would provide that all should be set right after his death. Was not that fair? At all events it quite satisfied what he called his conscience, and he thought it a devilish good compromise for his brother; and he went out, towards sunset, to take his usual walk.

Returning in the darkening twilight, the dog, as usual attending him, began to grow frisky and wild, at first scampering round him in great circles, as before, nearly at the top of his speed, his

great head between his paws as he raced. Gradually more excited
grew the pace and narrower his circuit, louder and fiercer his continuous growl, and the Squire stopped and grasped his stick hard,
for the lurid eyes and grin of the brute threatened an attack. Turning round and round as the excited brute encircled him, and striking vainly at him with his stick, he grew at last so tired that he
almost despaired of keeping him longer at bay; when on a sudden
the dog stopped short and crawled up to his feet wriggling and
crouching submissively.

Nothing could be more apologetic and abject; and when the
Squire dealt him two heavy thumps with his stick, the dog whim-
pered only, and writhed and licked his feet. The Squire sat down
on a prostrate tree; and his dumb companion, recovering his
wonted spirits immediately, began to sniff and nuzzle among the
roots. The Squire felt in his breast-pocket for the deed—it was
safe; and again he pondered, in this loneliest of spots, on the question whether he should preserve it for restoration after his death
to his brother, or destroy it forthwith. He began rather to lean toward the latter solution, when the long low growl of the dog not
far off startled him.

He was sitting in a melancholy grove of old trees, that slants
gently westward. Exactly the same odd effect of light I have before described—a faint red glow reflected downward from the
upper sky, after the sun had set, now gave to the growing darkness
a lurid uncertainty. This grove, which lies in a gentle hollow, owing to its circumscribed horizon on all but one side, has a peculiar
character of loneliness.

He got up and peeped over a sort of barrier, accidentally formed
of the trunks of felled trees laid one over the other, and saw the
dog straining up the other side of it, and hideously stretched out,
his ugly head looking in consequence twice the natural size. His
dream was coming over him again. And now between the trunks
the brute's ungainly head was thrust, and the long neck came
straining through, and the body, twining after it like a huge white
lizard; and as it came striving and twisting through, it growled
and glared as if it would devour him.

As swiftly as his lameness would allow, the Squire hurried from
this solitary spot towards the house. What thoughts exactly passed
through his mind as he did so, I am sure he could not have told.
But when the dog came up with him it seemed appeased, and
even in high good humor, and no longer resembled the brute that
haunted his dreams.

That night, near ten o'clock, the Squire, a good deal agitated, sent for the keeper, and told him that he believed the dog was mad, and that he must shoot him. He might shoot the dog in the gun-room, where he was—a grain of shot or two in the wainscot did not matter, and the dog must not have a chance of getting out.

The Squire gave the gamekeeper his double-barrelled gun, loaded with heavy shot. He did not go with him beyond the hall. He placed his hand on the keeper's arm; the keeper said his hand trembled, and that he looked "as white as curds."

"Listen a bit!" said the Squire under his breath.

They heard the dog in a state of high excitement in the room—growling ominously, jumping on the window-stool and down again, and running round the room.

"You'll need to be sharp, mind—don't give him a chance—slip in edgeways, d'ye see? and give him both barrels!"

"Not the first mad dog I've knocked over, sir," said the man, looking very serious as he cocked the gun.

As the keeper opened the door, the dog had sprung into the empty grate. He said he "never see sich a stark, staring devil." The beast made a twist round, as if, he thought, to jump up the chimney—"but that wasn't to be done at no price,"—and he made a yell—not like a dog—like a man caught in a mill-crank, and before he could spring, the keeper fired one barrel into him. The dog leaped towards him, and rolled over, receiving the second barrel in his head, as he lay snorting at the keeper's feet!

"I never seed the like; I never heard a screech like that!" said the keeper, recoiling. "It makes a fellow feel queer."

"Quite dead?" asked the Squire.

"Not a stir in him, sir," said the man, pulling him along the floor by the neck.

"Throw him outside the hall-door now," said the Squire; "and mind you pitch him outside the gate to-night—old Cooper says he's a witch," and the pale Squire smiled, "so he shan't lie in Gylingden."

Never was man more relieved than the Squire, and he slept better for a week after this than he had done for many weeks before.

It behooves us all to act promptly on our good resolutions. There is a determined gravitation towards evil, which, if left to itself, will bear down first intentions. If at one moment of superstitious fear, the Squire had made up his mind to a great sacrifice, and resolved in the matter of that deed so strangely recovered, to act honestly by his brother, that resolution very soon gave place to the compromise with fraud, which so conveniently postponed the restitution to the period when further enjoyment on his part was impossible. Then came more tidings of Scroope's violent and minatory language, with always the same burthen—that he would leave no stone unturned to show that there had existed a deed which Charles had either secreted or destroyed, and that he would never rest till he had hanged him.

This of course was wild talk. At first it had only enraged him; but, with his recent guilty knowledge and suppression, had come fear. His danger was the existence of the deed, and little by little he brought himself to a resolution to destroy it. There were many falterings and recoils before he could bring himself to commit this crime. At length, however, he did it, and got rid of the custody of that which at any time might become the instrument of disgrace and ruin. There was relief in this, but also the new and terrible sense of actual guilt.

He had got pretty well rid of his supernatural qualms. It was a different kind of trouble that agitated him now.

But this night, he imagined, he was awakened by a violent shaking of his bed. He could see, in the very imperfect light, two figures at the foot of it, holding each a bed-post. One of these he half-fancied was his brother Scroope, but the other was the old Squire—of that he was sure—and he fancied that they had shaken him up from his sleep. Squire Toby was talking as Charlie wakened, and he heard him say:

"Put out of our own house by you! It won't hold for long. We'll come in together, friendly, and stay. Forewarned, wi' yer eyes open, ye did it; and now Scroope 'll hang you! We'll hang you together! Look at me, you devil's limb."

And the old Squire tremblingly stretched his face, torn with shot and bloody, and growing every moment more and more into the likeness of the dog, and began to stretch himself out and climb the bed over the foot-board, and he saw the figure at the other side, little more than a black shadow, begin also to scale the bed; and there was instantly a dreadful confusion and uproar in the room, and such a grabbling and laughing; he could not catch the words; but, with a scream he woke, and found himself standing on the floor. The phantoms and the clamour were gone, but a crash and ringing of fragments was in his ears. The great china bowl, from which for generations the Marstons of Gylingden had been baptized, had fallen from the mantlepiece, and was smashed on the hearth-stone.

"I've bin dreamin' all night about Mr. Scroope, and I wouldn't wonder, old Cooper, if he was dead," said the Squire, when he came down in the morning.

"God forbid! I was adreamed about him, too, sir: I dreamed he was dammin' and sinkin' about a hole was burnt in his coat, and the old master, God be wi' him! said—quite plain—I'd 'a swore 'twas himself—'Cooper, get up, ye d——d land-loupin' thief, and lend a hand to hang him—for he's a daft cur, and no dog o' mine.' 'Twas the dog shot over night, I do suppose, as was runnin' in my old head. I thought old master gied me a punch wi' his knuckles, and says I, wakenin' up, 'At yer service, sir'; and for a while I couldn't get it out o' my head, master was in the room still."

Letters from town soon convinced the Squire that his brother Scroope, so far from being dead, was particularly active; and Charlie's attorney wrote to say, in serious alarm, that he had heard, accidentally, that he intended setting up a case, of a supplementary deed of settlement, of which he had secondary evidence, which would give him Gylingden. And at this menace Handsome Charlie snapped his fingers, and wrote courageously to his attorney; abiding what might follow with, however, a secret foreboding.

Scroope threatened loudly now, and swore after his bitter fashion, and reiterated his old promise of hanging that cheat at last. In the midst of these menaces and preparations, however, a sudden peace proclaimed itself: Scroope died, without time even to make provisions for a posthumous attack upon his brother. It was one of those cases of disease of the heart in which death is as sudden as a bullet.

Charlie's exultation was undisguised. It was shocking. Not, of course, altogether malignant. For there was the expansion consequent on the removal of a secret fear. There was also the comic piece of luck, that only the day before Scroope had destroyed his old will, which left to a stranger every farthing he possessed, intending in a day or two to execute another to the same person, charged with the express condition of prosecuting the suit against Charlie.

The result was, that all his possessions went unconditionally to his brother Charles as his heir. Here were grounds for abundance of savage elation. But there was also the deep-seated hatred of half a life of mutual and persistent aggression and revilings; and Handsome Charlie was capable of nursing a grudge, and enjoying a revenge with his whole heart.

He would gladly have prevented his brother's being buried in the old Gylingden chapel, where he wished to lie; but his lawyers doubted his power, and he was not quite proof against the scandal which would attend his turning back the funeral, which would, he knew, be attended by some of the country gentry and others, with an hereditary regard for the Marstons.

But he warned his servants that not one of them were to attend it; promising, with oaths and curses not to be disregarded, that any one of them who did so, should find the door shut in his face on his return.

I don't think, with the exception of old Cooper, that the servants cared for this prohibition, except as it baulked a curiosity always strong in the solitude of the country. Cooper was very much vexed that the eldest son of the old Squire should be buried in the old family chapel, and no sign of decent respect from Gylingden Hall. He asked his master, whether he would not, at least, have some wine and refreshments in the oak parlour, in case any of the country gentlemen who paid this respect to the old family should come up to the house? But the Squire only swore at him, told him to mind his own business, and ordered him to say, if such a thing happened, that he was out, and no preparations made, and, in fact, to send them away as they came. Cooper expostulated stoutly, and the Squire grew angrier; and after a tempestuous scene, took his hat and stick and walked out, just as the funeral descending the valley from the direction of the "Old Angel Inn" came in sight.

Old Cooper prowled about disconsolately, and counted the carriages as well as he could from the gate. When the funeral was over, and they began to drive away, he returned to the hall, the door of which lay open, and as usual deserted. Before he reached it quite, a mourning coach drove up, and two gentlemen in black cloaks, and crapes to their hats, got out, and without looking to the right or the left, went up the steps into the house. Cooper followed them slowly. The carriage had, he supposed, gone round to the yard, for, when he reached the door, it was no longer there.

So he followed the two mourners into the house. In the hall he found a fellow-servant, who said he had seen two gentlemen, in black cloaks, pass through the hall, and go up the stairs without removing their hats, or asking leave of anyone. This was very odd, old Cooper thought, and a great liberty; so upstairs he went to make them out.

But he could not find them then, nor ever. And from that hour the house was troubled.

In a little time there was not one of the servants who had not something to tell. Steps and voices followed them sometimes in the passages, and tittering whispers, always minatory, scared them at corners of the galleries, or from dark recesses; so that they would return panic-stricken to be rebuked by thin Mrs. Beckett, who looked on such stories as worse than idle. But Mrs. Beckett herself, a short time after, took a very different view of the matter.

She had herself begun to hear these voices, and with this formidable aggravation, that they came always when she was at her prayers, which she had been punctual in saying all her life, and utterly interrupted them. She was scared at such moments by dropping words and sentences, which grew, as she persisted, into threats and blasphemies.

These voices were not always in the room. They called, as she fancied, through the walls, very thick in that old house, from the neighbouring apartments, sometimes on one side, sometimes on the other; sometimes they seemed to holloa from distant lobbies, and came muffled, but threateningly, through the long panelled passages. As they approached they grew furious, as if several voices were speaking together. Whenever, as I said, this worthy woman applied herself to her devotions, these horrible sentences came hurrying towards the door, and, in panic, she would start from her knees, and all then would subside except the thumping of her heart against her stays, and the dreadful tremors of her nerves.

What these voices said, Mrs. Beckett never could quite remember one minute after they had ceased speaking; one sentence chased another away; gibe and menace and impious denunciation, each hideously articulate, were lost as soon as heard. And this added to the effect of these terrifying mockeries and invectives, that she could not, by any effort, retain their exact import, although their horrible character remained vividly present in her mind.

For a long time the Squire seemed to be the only person in the house absolutely unconscious of these annoyances. Mrs. Beckett had twice made up her mind within the week to leave. A prudent woman, however, who has been comfortable for more than twenty years in a place, thinks oftener than twice before she leaves it. She and old Cooper were the only servants in the house who remembered the good old housekeeping in Squire Toby's day. The others were few, and such as could hardly be accounted regular servants. Meg Dobbs, who acted as housemaid, would not sleep in the house, but walked home in trepidation, to her father's, at the gatehouse, under the escort of her little brother, every night. Old Mrs. Beckett, who was high and mighty with the make-shift servants of fallen Gylingden, let herself down all at once, and made Mrs. Kymes and the kitchen-maid move their beds into her large and faded room, and there, very frankly, shared her nightly terrors with them.

Old Cooper was testy and captious about these stories. He was already uncomfortable enough by reason of the entrance of the two muffled figures into the house, about which there could be no mistake. His own eyes had seen them. He refused to credit the stories of the women, and affected to think that the two mourners might have left the house and driven away, on finding no one to receive them.

Old Cooper was summoned at night to the oak parlour, where the Squire was smoking.

"I say, Cooper," said the Squire, looking pale and angry, "what for ha' you been frightenin' they crazy women wi' your plaguy stories? d—— me, if you see ghosts here it's no place for you, and it's time you should pack. I won't be left without servants. Here has been old Beckett wi' the cook and the kitchenmaid, as white as pipe clay, all in a row, to tell me I must have a parson to sleep among them, and preach down the devil! Upon my soul, you're a wise old body, filling their heads wi' maggots! and Meg goes down to the lodge every night, afeared to lie in the house—all your doing, wi' your old wives stories,—ye withered old Tom o' Bedlam!"

"I'm not to blame, Master Charles. 'Tisn't along o' no stories o' mine, for I'm never done telling 'em it's all vanity and vapours. Mrs. Beckett 'ill tell you that, and there's been many a wry word betwixt us on the head o't. Whate'er I may *think*," said old Cooper, significantly, and looking askance, with the sternness of fear in the Squire's face.

The Squire averted his eyes, and muttered angrily to himself, and turned away to knock the ashes out of his pipe on the hob, and then turning suddenly round upon Cooper again, he spoke, with a pale face, but not quite so angrily as before.

"I know you're no fool, old Cooper, when you like. Suppose there was such a thing as a ghost here, don't you see, it ain't to them snipe-headed women it 'id go to tell its story. What ails you, man, that you should think ought about it, but just what *I* think? You had a good headpiece o' yer own once, Cooper, don't be you clappin' a goosecap over it, as my poor father used to say; d—— it, old boy, you mustn't let 'em be fools, settin' one another wild wi' their blether, and makin' the folks talk what they shouldn't, about Gylingden and the family. I don't think ye'd like that, old Cooper, I'm sure ye wouldn't. The women has gone out o' the kitchen, make up a bit o' fire, and get your pipe. I'll go to you, when I finish this one, and we'll smoke a bit together, and a glass o' brandy and water."

Down went the old butler, not altogether unused to such condescensions in that disorderly and lonely household; and let not those who can choose their company, be too hard on the Squire who couldn't.

When he got things tidy, as he said, he sat down in that big old kitchen, with his feet on the fender, the kitchen candle burning in a great brass candlestick, which stood on the deal table at his elbow, with the brandy bottle and tumblers beside it, and Cooper's pipe also in readiness. And these preparations completed, the old butler, who had remembered other generations and better times, fell into rumination, and so, gradually, into a deep sleep.

Old Cooper was half awakened by some one laughing low, near his head. He was dreaming of old times in the Hall, and fancied one of "the young gentlemen" going to play him a trick, and he mumbled something in his sleep, from which he was awakened by a stern deep voice, saying, "You wern't at the funeral; I might take your life, I'll take your ear." At the same moment, the side of his head received a violent push, and he started to his feet. The fire had gone down, and he was chilled. The candle was expiring in the socket, and threw on the white wall long shadows, that danced up and down from the ceiling to the ground, and their black outlines he fancied resembled the two men in cloaks, whom he remembered with a profound horror.

He took the candle, with all the haste he could, getting along the passage, on whose walls the same dance of black shadows was continued, very anxious to reach his room before the light should go out. He was startled half out of his wits by the sudden clang of his master's bell, close over his head, ringing furiously.

"Ha, ha! There it goes—yes, sure enough," said Cooper, reassuring himself with the sound of his own voice, as he hastened on, hearing more and more distinct every moment the same furious ringing. "He's fell asleep, like me; that's it, and his lights is out, I lay you fifty—"

When he turned the handle of the door of the oak parlour, the Squire wildly called, "Who's *there?*" in the tone of a man who expects a robber.

"It's me, old Cooper, all right, Master Charlie, you didn't come to the kitchen after all, sir."

"I'm very bad, Cooper; I don't know how I've been. Did you meet anything?" asked the Squire.

"No," said Cooper.

They stared on one another.

"Come here—stay here! Don't you leave me! Look round the room, and say is all right; and gie us your hand, old Cooper, for I must hold it." The Squire's was damp and cold, and trembled very much. It was not very far from day-break now.

After a time he spoke again: "I 'a done many a thing I shouldn't; I'm not fit to go, and wi' God's blessin' I'll look to it—why shouldn't I? I'm as lame as old Billy—I'll never be able to do any good no more, and I'll give over drinking, and marry, as I ought to 'a done long ago—none o' yer fine ladies, but a good homely wench; there's Farmer Crump's youngest daughter, a good lass, and discreet. What for shouldn't I take her? She'd take care o' me and wouldn't bring a head full o' romances here, and mantua-makers' trumpery, and I'll talk with the parson, and I'll do what's fair wi' everyone; and mind, I said I'm sorry for many a thing I 'a done."

A wild cold dawn had by this time broken. The Squire, Cooper said, looked "awful bad," as he got his hat and stick, and sallied out for a walk, instead of going to his bed, as Cooper besought him, looking so wild and distracted, that it was plain his object was simply to escape from the house. It was twelve o'clock when the Squire walked into the kitchen, where he was sure of finding some of the servants, looking as if ten years had passed over him since yesterday. He pulled a stool by the fire, without speaking a word, and sat down. Cooper had sent to Applebury for the doctor, who had just arrived, but the Squire would not go to him. "If he wants to see me, he may come here," he muttered as often as Cooper urged him. So the doctor did come, charily enough, and found the Squire very much worse than he had expected.

The Squire resisted the order to get to his bed. But the doctor insisted under a threat of death, at which his patient quailed.

"Well, I'll do what you say—only this—you must let old Cooper and Dick Keeper stay wi' me. I mustn't be left alone, and they must keep awake o' nights; and stay a while, do you. When I get round a bit, I'll go and live in a town. It's dull livin' here, now that I can't do nou't as I used, and I'll live a better life, mind ye; ye heard me say that, and I don't care who laughs, and I'll talk wi' the parson. I like 'em to laugh, hang 'em, it's a sign I'm doin' right, at last."

The doctor sent a couple of nurses from the County Hospital, not choosing to trust his patient to the management he had selected, and he went down himself to Gylingden to meet them in the evening. Old Cooper was ordered to occupy the dressing-room, and sit up at night, which satisfied the Squire, who was in a strangely excited state, very low, and threatened, the doctor said, with fever.

The clergyman came, an old, gentle, "book-learned" man, and talked and prayed with him late that evening. After he had gone the Squire called the nurses to his bedside, and said:

"There's a fellow sometimes comes; you'll never mind him. He looks in at the door and beckons,—a thin, hump-backed chap in mourning, wi' black gloves on; ye'll know him by his lean face, as brown as the wainscot: don't ye mind his smilin'. You don't go out to him, nor ask him in; he won't say nout; and if he grows anger'd and looks awry at ye, don't ye be afeared, for he can't hurt ye, and he'll grow tired waitin', and go away; and for God's sake mind ye don't ask him in, nor go out after him!"

The nurses put their heads together when this was over, and held afterwards a whispering conference with old Cooper. "Law bless ye!—no, there's no madman in the house," he protested; "not a soul but what ye saw,—it's just a trifle o' the fever in his head—no more."

The Squire grew worse as the night wore on. He was heavy and delirious, talking of all sorts of things—of wine, and dogs, and lawyers; and then he began to talk, as it were, to his brother Scroope. As he did so, Mrs. Oliver, the nurse, who was sitting up alone with him, heard, as she thought, a hand softly laid on the door-handle outside, and a stealthy attempt to turn it. "Lord bless us! who's there?" she cried, and her heart jumped into her mouth, as she thought of the hump-backed man in black, who was to put in his head smiling and beckoning—"Mr. Cooper! sir! are you there?" she cried. "Come here, Mr. Cooper, please—do, sir, quick!"

Old Cooper, called up from his doze by the fire, stumbled in from the dressing-room, and Mrs. Oliver seized him tightly as he emerged.

"The man with the hump has been atryin' the door, Mr. Cooper, as sure as I am here." The Squire was moaning and mumbling in his fever, understanding nothing, as she spoke. "No, no! Mrs. Oliver, ma'am, it's impossible, for there's no sich man in the house: what is Master Charlie sayin'?"

"He's saying *Scroope* every minute, whatever he means by that, and—and—hisht!—listen—there's the handle again," and, with a loud scream, she added—"Look at his head and neck in at the door!" and in her tremour she strained old Cooper in an agonizing embrace.

The candle was flaring, and there was a wavering shadow at the door that looked like the head of a man with a long neck, and a longish sharp nose, peeping in and drawing back.

"Don't be a d—— fool, ma'am!" cried Cooper, very white, and shaking her with all his might. "It's only the candle, I tell you— nothing in life but that. Don't you see?" and he raised the light; "and I'm sure there was no one at the door, and I'll try, if you let me go."

The other nurse was asleep on the sofa, and Mrs. Oliver called her up in a panic, for company, as old Cooper opened the door. There was no one near it, but at the angle of the gallery was a shadow resembling that which he had seen in the room. He raised the candle a little, and it seemed to beckon with a long hand as the head drew back. "Shadow from the candle!" exclaimed Cooper aloud, resolved not to yield to Mrs. Oliver's panic; and, candle in hand, he walked to the corner. There was nothing. He could not forbear peeping down the long gallery from this point, and as he moved the light, he saw precisely the same sort of shadow, a little further down, and as he advanced the same withdrawal, and beckon. "Gammon!" said he; "it is nout but the candle." And on he went, growing half angry and half frightened at the persistency with which this ugly shadow—a literal shadow he was sure it was—presented itself. As he drew near the point where it now appeared, it seemed to collect itself, and nearly dissolve in the central panel of an old carved cabinet which he was now approaching.

In the centre panel of this is a sort of boss carved into a wolf's head. The light fell oddly upon this, and the fugitive shadow seemed to be breaking up, and re-arranging itself as oddly. The eye-ball gleamed with a point of reflected light, which glittered also upon the grinning mouth, and he saw the long, sharp nose of Scroope Marston, and his fierce eye looking at him, he thought, with a steadfast meaning.

Old Cooper stood gazing upon this sight, unable to move, till he saw the face, and the figure that belonged to it, begin gradually to emerge from the wood. At the same time he heard voices approaching rapidly up a side gallery, and Cooper, with a loud "Lord a-mercy on us!" turned and ran back again, pursued by a sound that seemed to shake the old house like a mighty gust of wind.

Into his master's room burst old Cooper, half wild with fear, and clapped the door and turned the key in a twinkling, looking as if he had been pursued by murderers.

"Did you hear it?" whispered Cooper, now standing near the dressing-room door. They all listened, but not a sound from without disturbed the utter stillness of night. "God bless us! I doubt it's my old head that's gone crazy!" exclaimed Cooper.

He would tell them nothing but that he was himself "an old fool," to be frightened by their talk, and that "the rattle of a window, or the dropping o' a pin" was enough to scare him now; and so he helped himself through the night with brandy, and sat up talking by his master's fire.

The Squire recovered slowly from his brain fever, but not perfectly. A very little thing, the doctor said, would suffice to upset him. He was not yet sufficiently strong to remove for change of scene and air, which were necessary for his complete restoration.

Cooper slept in the dressing-room, and was now his only nightly attendant. The ways of the invalid were odd: he liked, half sitting up in his bed, to smoke his churchwarden o' nights, and made old Cooper smoke, for company, at the fire-side. As the Squire and his humble friend indulged in it, smoking is a taciturn pleasure, and it was not until the Master of Gylingden had finished his third pipe that he essayed conversation, and when he did, the subject was not such as Cooper would have chosen.

"I say, old Cooper, look in my face, and don't be afeared to speak out," said the Squire, looking at him with a steady, cunning smile; "you know all this time, as well as I do, who's in the house. You needn't deny—hey?—Scroope and my father?"

"Don't you be talking like that, Charlie," said old Cooper, rather sternly and frightened, after a long silence; still looking in his face, which did not change.

"What's the good of shammin', Cooper? Scroope's took the hearin' o' yer right ear—you know he did. He's looking angry. He's nigh took my life wi' this fever. But he's not done wi' me yet, and he looks awful wicked. Ye saw him—ye know ye did."

Cooper was awfully frightened, and the odd smile on the Squire's lips frightened him still more. He dropped his pipe, and stood gazing in silence at his master, and feeling as if he were in a dream.

"If ye think so, ye should not be smiling like that," said Cooper, grimly.

"I'm tired, Cooper, and it's as well to smile as t'other thing; so I'll even smile while I can. You know what they mean to do wi' me. That's all I wanted to say. Now, lad, go on wi' yer pipe—I'm goin' asleep."

So the Squire turned over in his bed, and lay down serenely, with his head on the pillow. Old Cooper looked at him, and glanced at the door, and then half-filled his tumbler with brandy, and drank it off, and felt better, and got to his bed in the dressing-room.

In the dead of night he was suddenly awakened by the Squire, who was standing, in his dressing-gown and slippers, by his bed.

"I've brought you a bit o' a present. I got the rents o' Hazelden yesterday, and ye'll keep that for yourself—it's a fifty—and give t'other to Nelly Carwell to-morrow; I'll sleep the sounder; and I saw Scroope since; he's not such a bad 'un after all, old fellow! He's got a crape over his face—for I told him I couldn't bear it; and I'd do many a thing for him now. I never could stand shilly-shally. Good-night, old Cooper!"

And the Squire laid his trembling hand kindly on the old man's shoulder, and returned to his own room.

"I don't half like how he is. Doctor don't come half often enough. I don't like that queer smile o' his, and his hand was as cold as death. I hope in God his brain's not a-turnin'!" With these reflections, Cooper turned to the pleasanter subject of his present, and at last fell asleep.

In the morning, when he went into the Squire's room, the Squire had left his bed. "Never mind; he'll come back, like a bad shillin'," thought old Cooper, preparing the room as usual. But he did not return. Then began an uneasiness, succeeded by a panic, when it began to be plain that the Squire was not in the house. What had become of him? None of his clothes, but his dressing-gown and slippers were missing. Had he left the house, in his present sickly state, in that garb? and, if so, could he be in his right senses; and was there a chance of his surviving a cold, damp night, so passed, in the open air?

Tom Edwards was up to the house, and told them, that, walking a mile or so that morning, at four o'clock—there being no moon—along with Farmer Nokes, who was driving his cart to market, in the dark, three men walked, in front of the horse, not twenty yards before them, all the way from near Gylingden Lodge to the burial ground, the gate of which was opened for them from within, and the three men entered, and the gate was shut. Tom Edwards thought they were gone in to make preparations for a funeral of some member of the Marston family. But the occurrence seemed to Cooper, who knew there was no such thing, horribly ominous.

He now commenced a careful search, and at last bethought him of the lonely upper storey, and King Herod's chamber. He saw nothing changed there, but the closet door was shut, and, dark as was the morning, something, like a large white knot sticking out over the door, caught his eye.

The door resisted his efforts to open it for a time; some great weight forced it down against the floor; at length, however, it did yield a little, and a heavy crash, shaking the whole floor, and sending an echo flying through all the silent corridors, with a sound like receding laughter, half stunned him.

When he pushed open the door, his master was lying dead upon the floor. His cravat was drawn halter-wise tight round his throat, and had done its work well. The body was cold, and had been long dead.

In due course the coroner held his inquest, and the jury pronounced, "that the deceased, Charles Marston, had died by his own hand, in a state of temporary insanity." But old Cooper had his own opinion about the Squire's death, though his lips were sealed, and he never spoke about it. He went and lived for the residue of his days in York, where there are still people who remember him, a taciturn and surly old man, who attended church regularly, and also drank a little, and was known to have saved some money.

Schalken the Painter

"For he is not a man as I am that we
should come together; neither is there any
that might lay his hand upon us both. Let
him, therefore, take his rod away from me,
and let not his fear terrify me."

THERE exists, at this moment, in good preservation a remarkable work of Schalken's. The curious management of its lights constitutes, as usual in his pieces, the chief apparent merit of the picture. I say *apparent*, for in its subject, and not in its handling, however exquisite, consists its real value. The picture represents the interior of what might be a chamber in some antique religious building; and its foreground is occupied by a female figure, in a species of white robe, part of which is arranged so as to form a veil. The dress, however, is not that of any religious order. In her hand the figure bears a lamp, by which alone her figure and face are illuminated; and her features wear such an arch smile, as well becomes a pretty woman when practising some prankish roguery; in the background, and, excepting where the dim red light of an expiring fire serves to define the form, in total shadow, stands the figure of a man dressed in the old Flemish fashion, in an attitude of alarm, his hand being placed upon the hilt of his sword, which he appears to be in the act of drawing.

There are some pictures, which impress one, I know not how, with a conviction that they represent not the mere ideal shapes and combinations which have floated through the imagination of the artist, but scenes, faces, and situations which have actually existed. There is in that strange picture, something that stamps it as the representation of a reality.

And such in truth it is, for it faithfully records a remarkable and mysterious occurrence, and perpetuates, in the face of the female figure, which occupies the most prominent place in the design, an accurate portrait of Rose Velderkaust, the niece of Gerard Douw, the first, and, I believe, the only love of Godfrey Schalken.

My great grandfather knew the painter well; and from Schalken himself he learned the fearful story of the painting, and from him too he ultimately received the picture itself as a bequest. The story and the picture have become heir-looms in my family, and having described the latter, I shall, if you please, attempt to relate the tradition which has descended with the canvas.

There are few forms on which the mantle of romance hangs more ungracefully than upon that of the uncouth Schalken—the boorish but most cunning worker in oils, whose pieces delight the critics of our day almost as much as his manners disgusted the refined of his own; and yet this man, so rude, so dogged, so slovenly, in the midst of his celebrity, had in his obscure, but happier days, played the hero in a wild romance of mystery and passion.

When Schalken studied under the immortal Gerard Douw, he was a very young man; and in spite of his phlegmatic temperament, he at once fell over head and ears in love with the beautiful niece of his wealthy master. Rose Velderkaust was still younger than he, having not yet attained her seventeenth year, and, if tradition speaks truth, possessed all the soft and dimpling charms of the fair, light-haired Flemish maidens. The young painter loved honestly and fervently. His frank adoration was rewarded. He declared his love, and extracted a faltering confession in return. He was the happiest and proudest painter in all Christendom. But there was somewhat to dash his elation; he was poor and undistinguished. He dared not ask old Gerard for the hand of his sweet ward. He must first win a reputation and a competence.

There were, therefore, many dread uncertainties and cold days before him; he had to fight his way against sore odds. But he had won the heart of dear Rose Velderkaust, and that was half the battle. It is needless to say his exertions were redoubled, and his lasting celebrity proves that his industry was not unrewarded by success.

These ardent labours, and worse still, the hopes that elevated and beguiled them, were however, destined to experience a sudden interruption—of a character so strange and mysterious as to baffle all inquiry and to throw over the events themselves a shadow of preternatural horror.

Schalken had one evening outstayed all his fellow-pupils, and still pursued his work in the deserted room. As the daylight was fast falling, he laid aside his colours, and applied himself to the completion of a sketch on which he had expressed extraordinary pains. It was a religious composition, and represented the temptations of a pot-bellied Saint Anthony. The young artist, however destitute of elevation, had, nevertheless, discernment enough to be dissatisfied with his own work, and many were the patient erasures and improvements which saint and devil underwent, yet all in vain. The large, old-fashioned room was silent, and, with the exception of himself, quite emptied of its usual inmates. An hour had thus passed away, nearly two, without any improved result. Daylight had already declined, and twilight was deepening into the darkness of night. The patience of the young painter was exhausted, and he stood before his unfinished production, angry and mortified, one hand buried in the folds of his long hair, and the other holding the piece of charcoal which had so ill-performed its office, and which he now rubbed, without much regard to the sable streaks it produced, with irritable pressure upon his ample Flemish inexpressibles. "Curse the subject!" said the young man aloud; "curse the picture, the devils, the saint—"

At this moment a short, sudden sniff uttered close beside him made the artist turn sharply round, and he now, for the first time, became aware that his labours had been overlooked by a stranger. Within about a yard and half, and rather behind him, there stood the figure of an elderly man in a cloak and broad-brimmed, conical hat; in his hand, which was protected with a heavy gauntlet-shaped glove, he carried a long ebony walking-stick, surmounted with what appeared, as it glittered dimly in the twilight, to be a massive head of gold, and upon his breast, through the folds of the cloak, there shone the links of a rich chain of the same metal. The room was so obscure that nothing further of the appearance of the figure could be ascertained, and his hat threw his features into profound shadow. It would not have been easy to conjecture the age of the intruder; but a quantity of dark hair escaping from beneath this sombre hat, as well as his firm and upright carriage served to indicate that his years could not yet exceed threescore, or thereabouts. There was an air of gravity and importance about the garb of the person, and something indescribably odd, I might say awful, in the perfect, stone-like stillness of the figure, that effectually checked the testy comment which had at once risen to the lips of the irritated artist. He, therefore, as soon as he had sufficiently recovered his surprise, asked the stranger, civilly, to be seated, and desired to know if he had any message to leave for his master.

"Tell Gerard Douw," said the unknown, without altering his attitude in the smallest degree, "that Minheer Vanderhausen, of Rotterdam, desires to speak with him on tomorrow evening at this hour, and if he please, in this room, upon matters of weight; that is all."

The stranger, having finished this message, turned abruptly, and, with a quick, but silent step quitted the room, before Schalken had time to say a word in reply. The young man felt a curiosity to see in what direction the burgher of Rotterdam would turn, on quitting the *studio,* and for that purpose he went directly to the window which commanded the door. A lobby of considerable extent intervened between the inner door of the painter's room and the street entrance, so that Schalken occupied the post of observation before the old man could possibly have reached the street. He watched in vain, however. There was no other mode of exit. Had the queer old man vanished, or was he lurking about the recesses of the lobby for some sinister purpose? This last suggestion filled the mind of Schalken with a vague uneasiness, which was so unaccountably intense as to make him alike afraid to remain in the room alone, and reluctant to pass through the lobby. However, with an effort which appeared very disproportioned to the occasion, he summoned resolution to leave the room, and, having locked the door and thrust the key in his pocket, without looking to the right or left, he traversed the passage which had so recently, perhaps still, contained the person of his mysterious visitant, scarcely venturing to breathe till he had arrived in the open street.

"Minheer Vanderhausen!" said Gerard Douw within himself, as the appointed hour approached, 'Minheer Vanderhausen, of Rotterdam! I never heard of the man till yesterday. What can he want of me? A portrait, perhaps, to be painted; or a poor relation to be apprenticed; or a collection to be valued; or—pshaw! there's no one in Rotterdam to leave me a legacy. Well, whatever the business may be, we shall soon know it all."

It was now the close of day, and again every easel, except that of Schalken, was deserted. Gerard Douw was pacing the apartment with the restless step of impatient expectation, sometimes pausing to glance over the work of one of his absent pupils, but more frequently placing himself at the window, from whence he might observe the passengers who threaded the obscure by-street in which his studio was placed.

"Said you not, Godfrey," exclaimed Douw, after a long and fruitful gaze from his post of observation, and turning to Schalken, "that the hour he appointed was about seven by the clock of the Stadhouse?"

"It had just told seven when I first saw him, sir," answered the student.

"The hour is close at hand, then," said the master, consulting a horologe as large and as round as an orange. "Minheer Vander-hausen from Rotterdam—is it not so?

"Such was the name."

"And an elderly man, richly clad?" pursued Douw, musingly.

"As well as I might see," replied his pupil; "he could not be young, nor yet very old, neither; and his dress was rich and grave, as might become a citizen of wealth and consideration."

At this moment the sonorous boom of the Stadhouse clock told, stroke after stroke, the hour of seven; the eyes of both master and student were directed to the door; and it was not until the last peal of the bell had ceased to vibrate, that Douw exclaimed—

"So, so; we shall have his worship presently, that is, if he means to keep his hour; if not, you may wait for him, Godfrey, if you court his acquaintance. But what, after all, if it should prove but a mummery got up by Vankarp, or some such wag? I wish you had run all risks, and cudgelled the old burgomaster soundly. I'd wager a dozen of Rhenish, his worship would have unmasked, and pleaded old acquaintance in a trice."

"Here he comes, sir," said Schalken, in a low monitory tone; and instantly, upon turning towards the door, Gerard Douw observed the same figure which had, on the day before, so unexpectedly greeted his pupil Schalken.

There was something in the air of the figure which at once satisfied the painter that there was no masquerading in the case, and that he really stood in the presence of a man of worship; and so, without hesitation, he doffed his cap, and courteously saluting the stranger, requested him to be seated. The visitor waved his hand slightly, as if in acknowledgment of the courtesy, but remained standing.

"I have the honour to see Minheer Vanderhausen of Rotterdam?" said Gerard Douw.

"The same," was the laconic reply of his visitor.

"I understand your worship desires to speak with me," continued Douw, "and I am here by appointment to wait your commands."

"Is that a man of trust?" said Vanderhausen, turning towards Schalken, who stood at a little distance behind his master.

"Certainly," replied Gerard.

"Then let him take this box, and get the nearest jeweller or goldsmith to value its contents, and let him return hither with a certificate of the valuation."

At the same time, he placed a small case about nine inches square in the hands of Gerard Douw, who was as much amazed at its weight as at the strange abruptness with which it was handed to him. In accordance with the wishes of the stranger, he delivered it into the hands of Schalken, and repeating his direction, despatched him upon the mission.

Schalken disposed his precious charge securely beneath the folds of his cloak, and rapidly traversing two or three narrow streets, he stopped at a corner house, the lower part of which was then occupied by the shop of a Jewish goldsmith. He entered the shop, and calling the little Hebrew into the obscurity of its back recesses, he proceeded to lay before him Vanderhausen's casket. On being examined by the light of a lamp, it appeared entirely cased with lead, the outer surface of which was much scraped and soiled, and nearly white with age. This having been partially removed, there appeared beneath a box of some hard wood; which also they forced open and after the removal of two or three folds of linen, they discovered its contents to be a mass of golden ingots, closely packed, and, as the Jew declared, of the most perfect quality. Every ingot underwent the scrutiny of the little Jew, who seemed to feel an epicurean delight in touching and testing these morsels of the glorious metal; and each one of them was replaced in its berth with the exclamation: "*Mein Gott,* how very perfect! not one grain of alloy—beautiful, beautiful!" The task was at length finished, and the Jew certified under his hand the value of the ingots submitted to his examination, to amount to many thousand rix-dollars. With the desired document in his pocket, and the rich box of gold carefully pressed under his arm, and concealed by his cloak, he retraced his way, and entering the studio, found his master and the stranger in close conference. Schalken had no sooner left the room, in order to execute the commission he had taken in charge, than Vanderhausen addressed Gerard Douw in the following terms:—

"I cannot tarry with you to-night more than a few minutes, and so I shall shortly tell you the matter upon which I come. You visited the town of Rotterdam some four months ago, and then I saw in the church of St. Lawrence your niece, Rose Velderkaust. I desire to marry her; and if I satisfy you that I am wealthier than any husband you can dream of for her, I expect that you will forward my suit with your authority. If you approve my proposal, you must close with it here and now, for I cannot wait for calculations and delays."

Gerard Douw was hugely astonished by the nature of Minheer Vanderhausen's communication, but he did not venture to express surprise; for besides the motives supplied by prudence and politeness, the painter experienced a kind of chill and oppression like that which is said to intervene when one is placed in unconscious proximity with the object of a natural antipathy—an undefined but overpowering sensation, while standing in the presence of the eccentric stranger, which made him very unwilling to say anything which might reasonably offend him.

"I have no doubt," said Gerard, after two or three prefatory hems, "that the alliance which you propose would prove alike advantageous and honourable to my niece; but you must be aware that she has a will of her own, and may not acquiesce in what *we* may design for her advantage."

"Do not seek to deceive me, sir painter," said Vanderhausen; "you are her guardian—she is your ward—she is mine if *you* like to make her so."

The man of Rotterdam moved forward a little as he spoke, and Gerard Douw, he scarce knew why, inwardly prayed for the speedy return of Schalken.

"I desire," said the mysterious gentleman, "to place in your hands at once an evidence of my wealth, and a security for my liberal dealing with your niece. The lad will return in a minute or two with a sum in value five times the fortune which she has a right to expect from her husband. This shall lie in your hands, together with her dowry, and you may apply the united sum as suits her interest best; it shall be all exclusively hers while she lives: is that liberal?"

Douw assented, and inwardly acknowledged that fortune had been extraordinarily kind to his niece; the stranger, he thought, must be both wealthy and generous, and such an offer was not to be despised, though made by a humourist, and one of no very prepossessing presence. Rose had no very high pretensions for she had but a modest dowry, which she owed entirely to the generosity of her uncle; neither had she any right to raise exceptions on the score of birth, for her own origin was far from splendid, and as the other objections, Gerald resolved, and indeed, by the usages of the time, was warranted in resolving, not to listen to them for a moment.

"Sir" said he, addressing the stranger, "your offer is liberal, and whatever hesitation I may feel in closing with it immediately, arises solely from my not having the honour of knowing anything of your family or station. Upon these points you can, of course, satisfy me without difficulty?'

"As to my respectability," said the stranger, drily, "you must take that for granted at present; pester me with no inquiries; you can discover nothing more about me than I choose to make known. You shall have sufficient security for my respectability—my word, if you are honourable: if you are sordid, my gold."

"A testy old gentleman," thought Douw, "he must have his own way; but, all things considered, I am not justified to declining his offer. I will not pledge myself unnecessarily, however."

"You will not pledge yourself unnecessarily," said Vanderhausen, strangely uttering the very words which had just floated through the mind of his companion; "but you will do so if it *is* necessary, I presume; and I will show you that I consider it indispensable. If the gold I mean to leave in your hands satisfy you, and if you don't wish my proposal to be at once withdrawn, you must, before I leave this room, write your name to this engagement."

Having thus spoken, he placed a paper in the hands of the master, the contents of which expressed an engagement entered into by Gerard Douw, to give to Wilken Vanderhausen of Rotterdam, in marriage, Rose Velderkaust, and so forth, within one week of the date thereof. While the painter was employed in reading this covenant, by the light of a twinkling oil lamp in the far wall of the room, Schalken, as we have stated, entered the studio, and having delivered the box and the valuation of the Jew, into the hands of the stranger, he was about to retire, when Vanderhausen called to him to wait; and, presenting the case and the certificate to Gerard Douw, he paused in silence until he had satisfied himself, by an inspection of both, respecting the value of the pledge left in his hands. At length he said—

"Are you content?"

The painter said he would fain have another day to consider.

"Not an hour," said the suitor, apathetically.

"Well then," said Douw, with a sore effort, "I *am* content, it is a bargain."

"Then sign at once," said Vanderhausen, "for I am weary."

At the same time he produced a small case of writing materials, and Gerard signed the important document.

"Let this youth witness the covenant," said the old man; and Godfrey Schalken unconsciously attested the instrument which for ever bereft him of his dear Rose Velderkaust.

The compact being thus completed, the strange visitor folded up the paper, and stowed it safely in an inner pocket.

"I will visit you to-morrow night at nine o'clock, at your own house, Gerard Douw, and will see the object of our contract;" and so saying Wilken Vanderhausen moved stiffly, but rapidly, out of the room.

Schalken, eager to resolve his doubts, had placed himself by the window, in order to watch the street entrance; but the experiment served only to support his suspicions, for the old man did not issue from the door. This was *very* strange, odd, nay fearful. He and his master returned together, and talked but little on the way, for each had his own subjects of reflection, of anxiety, and of hope. Schalken, however, did not know the ruin which menaced his dearest projects.

Gerard Douw knew nothing of the attachment which had sprung up between his pupil and his niece; and even if he had, it is doubtful whether he would have regarded its existence as any serious obstruction to the wishes of Minheer Vanderhausen. Marriages were then and there matters of traffic and calculation; and it would have appeared as absurd in the eyes of the guardian to make a mutual attachment an essential element in a contract of the sort, as it would have been to draw up his bonds and receipts in the language of romance.

The painter, however, did not communicate to his niece the important step which he had taken in her behalf, a forebearance caused not by any anticipated opposition on her part, but solely by a ludicrous consciousness that if she were to ask him for a description of her destined bridegroom, he would be forced to confess that he had not once seen his face, and if called upon, would find it absolutely impossible to identify him. Upon the next day, Gerard Douw, after dinner, called his niece to him and having scanned her person with an air of satisfaction, he took her hand, and looking upon her pretty innocent face with a smile of kindness, he said:—

"Rose, my girl, that face of yours will make your fortune." Rose blushed and smiled. "Such faces and such tempers seldom go together, and when they do, the compound is a love charm, few heads or hearts can resist; trust me, you will soon be a bride, girl. But this is trifling, and I am pressed for time, so make ready the large room by eight o'clock to-night, and give directions for supper at nine. I expect a friend; and observe me, child, do you trick yourself out handsomely. I will not have him think us poor or sluttish."

With these words he left her, and took his way to the room in which his pupils worked.

When the evening closed in, Gerard called Schalken, who was about to take his departure to his own obscure and comfortless lodgings, and asked him to come home and sup with Rose and Vanderhausen. The invitation was, of course, accepted and Gerard Douw and his pupil soon found themselves in the handsome and, even then, antique chamber, which had been prepared for the reception of the stranger. A cheerful wood fire blazed in the hearth, a little at one side of which an old-fashioned table, which shone in the fire-light like burnished gold, was awaiting the supper, for which preparations were going forward; and ranged with exact regularity, stood the tall-backed chairs, whose ungracefulness was more than compensated by their comfort. The little party, consisting of Rose, her uncle, and the artist, awaited the arrival of the expected visitor with considerable impatience. Nine o'clock at length came, and with it a summons at the street door, which being speedily answered, was followed by a slow and emphatic tread upon the staircase; the steps moved heavily across the lobby, the door of the room in which the party we have described were assembled slowly opened, and there entered a figure which startled, almost appalled, the phlegmatic Dutchmen, and nearly made Rose scream with terror. It was the form, and arrayed in the garb of Minheer Vanderhausen; the air, the gait, the height were the same, but the features had never been seen by any of the party before. The stranger stopped at the door of the room, and displayed his form and face completely. He wore a dark-coloured cloth cloak, which was short and full, not falling quite to his knees; his legs were cased in dark purple silk stockings, and his shoes were adorned with roses of the same colour. The opening of the cloak in front showed the under-suit to consist of some very dark, perhaps sable material, and his hands were enclosed in a pair of heavy leather gloves, which ran up considerably above the wrist, in the manner of a gauntlet. In one hand he carried his walking-stick and his hat, which he had removed, and the other hung heavily by his side. A quantity of grizzled hair descended in long tresses from his head, and rested upon the plaits of a stiff ruff, which effectually concealed his neck. So far all was well; but the face!—all the flesh of the face was coloured with the bluish leaden hue, which is sometimes produced by metallic medicines, administered in excessive quantities; the eyes showed an undue proportion of muddy white, and had a certain indefinable character of insanity; the hue of the lips bearing the usual relation to that of the face, was, consequently, nearly black; and the entire character of the face was sensual, malignant, and even satanic. It was remarkable that the worshipful stranger suffered as little as possible of his flesh to appear, and that during his visit he did not once remove his gloves. Having stood for some moments at the door, Gerard Douw at length found breath and collectedness to bid him welcome, and with a mute inclination of the head, the stranger stepped forward into the room. There was something indescribably odd, even horrible, about all his motions, something undefinable, that was unnatural, unhuman; it was as if the limbs were guided and directed by a spirit unused to the management of bodily machinery. The stranger spoke hardly at all during his visit, which did not exceed half an hour; and the host himself could scarcely muster courage enough to utter the few necessary salutations and courtesies; and, indeed, such was the nervous terror which the presence of Vanderhausen inspired, that very little would have made all his entertainers fly in downright panic from the room. They had not so far lost all self-possession, however, as to fail to observe two strange peculiarities of their visitor. During his stay his eyelids did not once close, or, indeed, move in the slightest degree; and farther, there was a deathlike stillness in his whole person, owing to the absence of the heaving motion of the chest, caused by the process of respiration. These two peculiarities, though when told they may appear trifling, produced a very striking and unpleasant effect when seen and observed. Vanderhausen at length relieved the painter of Leyden of his inauspicious presence; and with no trifling sense of relief the little party heard the street door close after him.

"Dear uncle," said Rose, "what a frightful man! I would not see him again for the wealth of the States."

"Tush, foolish girl," said Douw, whose sensations were anything but comfortable. "A man may be as ugly as the devil, and yet, if his heart and actions are good, he is worth all the pretty-faced perfumed puppies that walk the Mall. Rose, my girl, it is very true he has not thy pretty face, but I know him to be wealthy and liberal; and were he ten times more ugly, these two virtues would be enough to counterbalance all his deformity, and if not sufficient actually to alter the shape and hue of his features, at least enough to prevent one thinking them so much amiss."

"Do you know, uncle," said Rose, "when I saw him standing at the door, I could not get it out of my head that I saw the old painted wooden figure that used to frighten me so much in the Church of St. Laurence at Rotterdam."

Gerard laughed, though he could not help inwardly acknowledging the justness of the comparison. He was resolved, however, as far as he could, to check his niece's disposition to dilate upon the ugliness of her intended bridegroom, although he was not a little pleased, as well as puzzled, to observe that she appeared totally exempt from that mysterious dread of the stranger which, he could not disguise it from himself, considerably affected him, as also his pupil Godfrey Schalken.

Early on the next day there arrived, from various quarters of the town, rich presents of silks, velvets, jewellery, and so forth, for Rose; and also a packet directed to Gerard Douw, which on being opened, was found to contain a contract of marriage, formally drawn up, between Wilken Vanderhausen of the *Boom-quay,* in Rotterdam, and Rose Velderkaust of Leyden, niece to Gerard Douw, master in the art of painting, also of the same city; and containing engagements on the part of Vanderhausen to make settlements upon his bride, far more splendid than he had before led her guardian to believe likely, and which were to be secured to her use in the most unexceptionable manner possible—the money being placed in the hand of Gerard Douw himself.

I have no sentimental scenes to describe, no cruelty of guardians, no magnanimity of wards, no agonies, or transport of lovers. The record I have to make is one of sordidness, levity, and heartlessness. In less than a week after the first interview which we have just described, the contract of marriage was fulfilled, and Schalken saw the prize which he would have risked existence to secure, carried off in solemn pomp by his repulsive rival. For two or three days he absented himself from the school; he then returned and worked, if with less cheerfulness, with far more dogged resolution than before; the stimulus of love had given place to that of ambition. Months passed away, and, contrary to his expectation, and, indeed, to the direct promise of the parties, Gerard Douw heard nothing of his niece or her worshipful spouse. The interest of the money, which was to have been demanded in quarterly sums, lay unclaimed in his hands.

He began to grow extremely uneasy. Minheer Vanderhausen's direction in Rotterdam he was fully possessed of; after some irresolution he finally determined to journey thither—a trifling undertaking, and easily accomplished—and thus to satisfy himself of the safety and comfort of his ward, for whom he entertained an honest and strong affection. His search was in vain, however; no one in Rotterdam had ever heard of Minheer Vanderhausen. Gerard Douw left not a house in the Boom-quay untried, but all in vain. No one could give him any information whatever touching the object of his inquiry, and he was obliged to return to Leyden nothing wiser and far more anxious, than when he had left it.

On his arrival he hastened to the establishment from which

Vanderhausen had hired the lumbering, though, considering the times, most luxurious vehicle, which the bridal party had employed to convey them to Rotterdam. From the driver of this machine he learned, that having proceeded by slow stages, they had late in the evening approached Rotterdam; but that before they entered the city, and while yet nearly a mile from it, a small party of men, soberly clad, and after the old fashion, with peaked beards and moustaches, standing in the centre of the road, obstructed the further progress of the carriage. The driver reined in his horses, much fearing, from the obscurity of the hour, and the loneliness, of the road, that some mischief was intended. His fears were, however, somewhat allayed by his observing that these strange men carried a large litter, of an antique shape, and which they immediately set down upon the pavement, whereupon the bridegroom, having opened the coach-door from within, descended, and having assisted his bride to do likewise, led her, weeping bitterly, and wringing her hands, to the litter, which they both entered. It was then raised by the men who surrounded it, and speedily carried towards the city, and before it had proceeded very far, the darkness concealed it from the view of the Dutch coachman. In the inside of the vehicle he found a purse, whose contents more than thrice paid the hire of the carriage and man. He saw and could tell nothing more of Minheer Vanderhausen and his beautiful lady.

This mystery was a source of profound anxiety and even grief to Gerard Douw. There was evidently fraud in the dealing of Vanderhausen with him, though for what purpose committed he could not imagine. He greatly doubted how far it was possible for a man possessing such a countenance to be anything but a villain, and every day that passed without his hearing from or of his niece, instead of inducing him to forget his fears, on the contrary tended more and more to aggravate them. The loss of her cheerful society tended also to depress his spirits; and in order to dispel the gloom, which often crept upon his mind after his daily occupations were over, he was wont frequently to ask Schalken to accompany him home, and share his otherwise solitary supper.

One evening, the painter and his pupil were sitting by the fire, having accomplished a comfortable meal, and had yielded to the silent and delicous melancholy of digestion, when their ruminations were disturbed by a loud sound at the street door, as if occasioned by some person rushing and scrambling vehemently against it. A domestic had run without delay to ascertain the cause of the disturbance, and they heard him twice or thrice interrogate the applicant for admission, but without eliciting any other answer but a sustained reiteration of the sounds. They heard him then open the hall-door, and immediately there followed a light and rapid tread on the staircase. Schalken advanced towards the door. It opened before he reached it, and Rose rushed into the room. She looked wild, fierce and haggard with terror and exhaustion, but her dress surprised them as much as even her unexpected appearance. It consisted of a kind of white woollen wrapper, made close about the neck, and descending to the very ground. It was much deranged and travel-soiled. The poor creature had hardly entered the chamber when she fell senseless on the floor. With some difficulty they succeeded in reviving her, and on recovering her senses, she instantly exclaimed, in a tone of terror rather than mere impatience:—

"Wine! wine! quickly, or I'm lost!"

Astonished and almost scared at the strange agitation in which the call was made, they at once administered to her wishes, and she drank some wine with a haste and eagerness which surprised them. She had hardly swallowed it, when she exclaimed, with the same urgency:

"Food, for God's sake, food, at once, or I perish."

A considerable fragment of a roast joint was upon the table, and Schalken immediately began to cut some, but he was anticipated, for no sooner did she see it than she caught it, a more than mortal image of famine, and with her hands, and even with her teeth, she tore off the flesh, and swallowed it. When the paroxysm of hunger had been a little appeased, she appeared on a sudden overcome with shame, or it may have been that other more agitating thoughts overpowered and scared her, for she began to weep bitterly and to wring her hands.

"Oh, send for a minister of God," said she; "I am not safe till he comes; send for him speedily."

Gerard Douw despatched a messenger instantly, and prevailed on his niece to allow him to surrender his bed chamber to her use. He also persuaded her to retire to it at once to rest; her consent was extorted upon the condition that they would not leave her for a moment.

"Oh that the holy man were here," she said; "he can deliver me: the dead and the living can never be one: God has forbidden it."

With these mysterious words she surrendered herself to their guidance, and they proceeded to the chamber which Gerard Douw had assigned to her use.

"Do not, do not leave me for a moment," said she; "I am lost for ever if you do."

Gerard Douw's chamber was approached through a spacious apartment, which they were now about to enter. He and Schalken each carried a candle, so that a sufficiency of light was cast upon all surrounding objects. They were now entering the large chamber, which as I have said, communicated with Douw's apartment, when Rose suddenly stopped, and, in a whisper which thrilled them both with horror, she said:—

"Oh, God! he is here! he is here! See, see! there he goes!"

She pointed towards the door of the inner room, and Schalken thought he saw a shadowy and ill-defined form gliding into that apartment. He drew his sword, and, raising the candle so as to throw its light with increased distinctness upon the objects in the room, he entered the chamber into which the shadow had glided. No figure was there—nothing but the furniture which belonged to the room, and yet he could not be deceived as to the fact that something had moved before them into the chamber. A sickening dread came upon him, and the cold perspiration broke out in heavy drops upon his forehead; nor was he more composed, when he heard the increased urgency and agony of entreaty, with which Rose implored them not to leave her for a moment.

"I saw him," said she; "he's here. I cannot be deceived; I know him; he's by me; he is with me; he's in the room. Then, for God's sake, as you would save me, do not stir from beside me."

They at length prevailed upon her to lie down upon the bed, where she continued to urge them to stay by her. She frequently uttered incoherent sentences, repeating, again and again, "the dead and the living cannot be one: God has forbidden it." And then again, "Rest to the wakeful—sleep to the sleep-walkers." These and such mysterious and broken sentences, she continued to utter until the clergyman arrived. Gerard Douw began to fear, naturally enough, that terror or ill-treatment, had unsettled the poor girl's intellect, and he half suspected, by the suddenness of her appearance, the unseasonableness of the hour, and above all, from the wildness and terror of her manner, that she had made her escape from some place of confinement for lunatics, and was in imminent fear of pursuit. He resolved to summon medical advice as soon as the mind of his niece had been in some measure set at rest by the offices of the clergyman whose attendance she had so earnestly desired; and until this object had been attained, he did not venture to put any questions to her, which might possibly, by reviving painful or horrible recollections, increase her agitation. The clergyman soon arrived—a man of ascetic countenance and venerable age—one whom Gerard Douw respected very much, forasmuch as he was a veteran polemic, though one perhaps more dreaded as a combatant than beloved as a Christian—of pure morality, subtle brain, and frozen heart. He entered the chamber which communicated with that in which Rose reclined and immediately on his arrival, she requested him to pray for her, as for one who lay in the hands of Satan, and who could hope for deliverance only from heaven.

That you may distinctly understand all the circumstances of the event which I am going to describe, it is necessary to state the relative position of the parties who were engaged in it. The old clergyman and Schalken were in the anteroom of which I have already spoken; Rose lay in the inner chamber, the door of which was open; and by the side of the bed, at her urgent desire, stood her guardian; a candle burned in the bedchamber, and three were lighted in the outer apartment. The old man now cleared his voice as if about to commence, but before he had time to begin, a sudden gust of air blew out the candle which served to illuminate the room in which the poor girl lay, and she, with hurried alarm, exclaimed:—

"Godfrey, bring in another candle; the darkness is unsafe."

Gerard Douw forgetting for the moment her repeated injunctions, in the immediate impulse, stepped from the bedchamber into the other, in order to supply what she desired.

"Oh God! do not go, dear uncle," shrieked the unhappy girl—and at the same time she sprung from the bed, and darted after him, in order, by her grasp, to detain him. But the warning came too late, for scarcely had he passed the threshold, and hardly had his niece had time to utter the startling exclamation, when the door which divided the two rooms closed violently after him, as if swung by a strong blast of wind. Schalken and he both rushed to the door, but their united and desperate efforts could not avail so much as to shake it. Shriek after shriek burst from the inner chamber, with all the piercing loudness of despairing terror. Schalken and Douw applied every nerve to force open the door; but all in vain. There was no sound of struggling from within, but the screams seemed to increase in loudness, and at the same time they heard the bolts of the latticed window withdrawn, and the window itself grated upon the sill as if thrown open. One *last* shriek, so long and piercing and agonized as to be scarcely human, swelled from the room, and suddenly there followed a death-like silence. A light step was heard crossing the floor, as if from the bed to the window; and almost at the same instant the door gave way, and, yielding to the pressure of the external applicants, nearly precipitated them into the room. It was empty. The window was open, and Schalken sprung to a chair and gazed out upon the street and canal below. He saw no form, but he saw, or thought he saw, the waters of the broad canal beneath settling ring after ring in heavy circles, as if a moment before disturbed by the submission of some ponderous body.

No trace of Rose was ever after found, nor was anything certain respecting her mysterious wooer discovered or even suspected —no clue whereby to trace the intricacies of the labyrinth and to arrive at its solution, presented itself. But an incident occurred, which, though it will not be received by our rational readers in lieu of evidence, produced nevertheless a strong and a lasting impression upon the mind of Schalken. Many years after the events which we have detailed, Schalken, then residing far away received an intimation of his father's death, and of his intended burial upon a fixed day in the church of Rotterdam. It was necessary that a very considerable journey should be performed by the funeral procession, which as it will be readily believed, was not very numerously attended. Schalken with difficulty arrived in Rotterdam late in the day upon which the funeral was appointed to take place. It had not then arrived. Evening closed in, and still it did not appear.

Schalken strolled down to the church; he found it open; notice of the arrival of the funeral had been given, and the vault in which the body was to be laid had been opened. The sexton, on seeing a well-dressed gentleman, whose object was to attend the expected obsequies, pacing the aisle of the church, hospitably invited him to share with him the comforts of a blazing fire, which, as was his custom in winter time upon such occasions, he had kindled in the hearth of a chamber in which he was accustomed to await the arrival of such grisly guests and which communicated, by a flight of steps, with the vault below. In this chamber, Schalken and his entertainer seated themselves; and the sexton, after some fruitless attempts to engage his guest in conversation, was obliged to apply himself to his tobacco-pipe and can, to solace his solitude. In spite of his grief and cares, the fatigues of a rapid journey of nearly forty hours gradually overcame the mind and body of Godfrey Schalken, and he sank into a deep sleep, from which he awakened by someone's shaking him gently by the shoulder. He first thought that the old sexton had called him, but *he* was no longer in the room. He roused himself, and as soon as he could clearly see what was around him, he perceived a female form, clothed in a kind of light robe of white, part of which was so disposed as to form a veil, and in her hand she carried a lamp. She was moving rather away from him, in the direction of the flight of steps which conducted towards the vaults. Schalken felt a vague alarm at the sight of this figure and at the same time an irresistible impulse to follow its guidance. He followed it towards the vaults, but when it reached the head of the stairs, he paused; the figure paused also, and, turning gently round, displayed, by the light of the lamp it carried, the face and features of his first love, Rose Velderkaust. There was nothing horrible, or even sad, in the countenance. On the contrary, it wore the same arch smile which used to enchant the artist long before in his happy days. A feeling of awe and interest, too intense to be resisted, prompted him to follow the spectre, if spectre it were. She descended the stairs—he followed—and turning to the left, through a narrow passage, she led him, to his infinite surprise, into what appeared to be an old-fashioned Dutch apartment, such as the pictures of Gerard Douw have served to immortalize. Abundance of costly antique furniture was disposed about the room, and in one corner stood a four-post bed, with heavy black cloth curtains around it; the figure frequently turned towards him with the same arch smile; and when she came to the side of the bed, she drew the curtains, and, by the light of the lamp, which she held towards its contents, she disclosed to the horror-stricken painter, sitting bolt upright in the bed, the livid and demoniac form of Vanderhausen. Schalken had hardly seen him, when he fell senseless upon the floor, where he lay until discovered, on the next morning, by persons employed in closing the passages into the vaults. He was lying in a cell of considerable size, which had not been disturbed for a long time, and he had fallen beside a large coffin, which was supported upon small pillars, a security against the attacks of vermin.

To his dying day Schalken was satisfied of the reality of the vision which he had witnessed, and he has left behind him a curious evidence of the impression which it wrought upon his fancy, in a painting executed shortly after the event I have narrated, and which is valuable as exhibiting not only the peculiarities which have made Schalken's pictures sought after, but even more so as presenting a portrait of his early love, Rose Velderkaust, whose mysterious fate must always remain matter of speculation.

Madam Crowl's Ghost

Twenty years have passed since you last saw Mrs. Jolliffe's tall slim figure. She is now past seventy, and can't have many mile-stones more to count on the journey that will bring her to her long home. The hair has grown white as snow, that is parted under her cap, over her shrewd, but kindly face. But her figure is still straight, and her step light and active.

She has taken of late years to the care of adult invalids, having surrendered to younger hands the little people who inhabit cradles, and crawl on all-fours. Those who remember that good-natured face among the earliest that emerge from the darkness of non-entity, and who owe to their first lessons in the accomplishment of walking, and a delighted appreciation of their first babblings and earliest teeth, have "spired up" into tall lads and lasses, now. Some of them shew streaks of white by this time, in brown locks, "the bonny gouden" hair, that she was so proud to brush and shew to admiring mothers, who are seen no more on the green of Golden Friars, and whose names are traced now on the flat grey stones in the church-yard.

So the time is ripening some, and searing others; and the saddening and tender sunset hour has come; and it is evening with the kind old north-country dame, who nursed pretty Laura Mildmay, who now stepping into the room, smiles so gladly, and throws her arms round the old woman's neck, and kisses her twice.

"Now, this is so lucky!" said Mrs. Jenner, "you have just come in time to hear a story."

"Really! That's delightful."

"Na, na, od wite it! no story, ouer true for that, I sid it a wi my aan eyen. But the barn here, would not like, at these hours, just goin' to her bed, to hear tell of freets and boggarts."

"Ghosts? The very thing of all others I should most likely to hear of."

"Well, dear," said Mrs. Jenner, "if you are not afraid, sit ye down here, with us."

"She was just going to tell me all about her first engagement to

47

attend a dying old woman," says Mrs. Jenner, "and of the ghost she saw there. Now, Mrs. Jolliffe, make your tea first, and then begin."

The good woman obeyed, and having prepared a cup of that companionable nectar, she sipped a little, drew her brows slightly together to collect her thoughts, and then looked up with a wondrous solemn face to begin.

Good Mrs. Jenner, and the pretty girl, each gazed with eyes of solemn expectation in the face of the old woman, who seemed to gather awe from the recollections she was summoning.

The old room was a good scene for such a narrative, with the oak-wainscoting, quaint, and clumsy furniture, the heavy beams that crossed its ceiling, and the tall four-post bed, with dark curtains, within which you might imagine what shadows you please.

Mrs. Jolliffe cleared her voice, rolled her eyes slowly round, and began her tale in these words:—

MADAM CROWL'S GHOST

"I'm an ald woman now, and I was but thirteen, my last birthday, the night I came to Applewale House. My aunt was the housekeeper there, and a sort o' one-horse carriage was down at Lexhoe waitin' to take me and my box up to Applewale.

"I was a bit frightened by the time I got to Lexhoe, and when I saw the carriage and horse, I wished myself back again with my mother at Hazelden. I was crying when I got into the 'shay'—that's what we used to call it—and old John Mulbery that drove it, and was a good-natured fellow, bought me a handful of apples at the Golden Lion to cheer me up a bit; and he told me that there was a currant-cake, and tea, and pork-chops, waiting for me, all hot, in my aunt's room at the great house. It was a fine moonlight night, and I eat the apples, lookin' out o' the shay winda.

"It's a shame for gentlemen to frighten a poor foolish child like I was. I sometimes think it might be tricks. There was two on 'em on the tap o' the coach beside me. And they began to question me after nightfall, when the moon rose, where I was going to. Well, I told them it was to wait on Dame Arabella Crowl, of Applewale House, near by Lexhoe.

" 'Ho, then,' says one of them, 'you'll not be long there!'

"And I looked at him as much as to say 'Why not?' for I had spoken out when I told them where I was goin', as if 'twas something clever I hed to say.

" 'Because,' says he, 'and don't you for your life tell no one, only watch her and see—she's possessed by the devil, and more an half a ghost. Have you got a Bible?'

" 'Yes, sir,' says I. For my mother put my little Bible in my box, and I knew it was there: and by the same token, though the print's too small for my ald eyes, I have it in my press to this hour.

"As I looked up at him saying 'Yes, sir,' I thought I saw him winkin' at his friend; but I could not be sure.

" 'Well,' says he, 'be sure you put it under your bolster every night, it will keep the ald girl's claws aff ye.'

"And I got such a fright when he said that, you wouldn't fancy! And I'd a liked to ask him a lot about the ald lady, but I was too shy, and he and his friend began talkin' together about their own consarns, and dowly enough I got down, as I told ye, at Lexhoe. My heart sank as I drove into the dark avenue. The trees stand very thick and big, as ald as the ald house almost, and four people, with their arms out and finger-tips touchin', barely girds round some of them.

"Well my neck was stretched out o' the winda, looking for the first view o' the great house; and all at once we pulled up in front of it.

"A great white-and-black house it is, wi' great black beams across and right up it, and gables lookin' out, as white as a sheet, to the moon, and the shadows o' the trees, two or three up and down in front, you could count the leaves on them, and all the little diamond-shaped winda-panes, glimmering on the great hall winda, and great shutters, in the old fashion, hinged on the wall outside, boulted across all the rest o' the windas in front, for there was but three or four servants, and the old lady in the house, and most o' t'rooms was locked up.

"My heart was in my mouth when I sid the journey was over, and this the great house afoore me, and I sa near my aunt that I never sid till noo, and Dame Crowl, that I was come to wait upon, and was afeard on already.

"My aunt kissed me in the hall, and brought me to her room. She was tall and thin, wi' a pale face and black eyes, and long thin hands wi' black mittins on. She was past fifty, and her word was short; but her word was law. I hev no complaints to make of her; but she was a hard woman, and I think she would hev bin kinder to me if I had bin her sister's child in place of her brother's. But all that's o' no consequence noo.

"The squire—his name was Mr. Chevenix Crowl, he was Dame Crowl's grandson—came down there, by way of seeing that the old lady was well treated, about twice or thrice in the year. I sid him but twice all the time I was at Applewale House.

"I can't say but she was well taken care of, notwithstanding; but that was because my aunt and Meg Wyvern, that was her maid, had a conscience, and did their duty by her.

"Mrs. Wyvern—Meg Wyvern my aunt called her to herself, and Mrs. Wyvern to me— was a fat, jolly lass of fifty, a good height and a good breadth, always good-humoured and walked slow. She had fine wages, but she was a bit stingy, and kept all her fine clothes under lock and key, and wore, mostly, a twilled chocolate cotton, wi' red, and yellow, and green sprigs and balls on it, and it lasted wonderful.

"She never gave me nout, not the vally o' a brass thimble, all the time I was there; but she was good-humoured, and always laughin', and she talked no end o' proas over her tea; and, seeing me sa sackless and dowly, she roused me up wi' her laughin' and stories; and I think I liked her better than my aunt—children is so taken wi' a bit o' fun or a story—though my aunt was very good to me, but a hard woman about some things, and silent always.

"My aunt took me into her bed-chamber, that I might rest myself a bit while she was settin' the tea in her room. But first, she patted me on the shouther, and said I was a tall lass o' my years, and had spired up well, and asked me if I could do plain work and stitchin'; and she looked in my face, and said I was like my father, her brother, that was dead and gone, and she hoped I was a better Christian, and wad na du a' that lids (would not do anything of that sort).

"It was a hard sayin' the first time I set foot in her room, I thought.

"When I went into the next room, the housekeeper's room—very comfortable, yak (oak) all round—there was a fine fire blazin' away, wi' coal, and peat, and wood, all in a low together, and tea on the table, and hot cake, and smokin' meat; and there was Mrs. Wyvern, fat, jolly, and talkin' away, more in an hour than my aunt would in a year.

"While I was still at my tea my aunt went up-stairs to see Madam Crowl.

" 'She's agone up to see that old Judith Squailes is awake,' says Mrs. Wyvern. 'Judith sits with Madam Crowl when me and Mrs. Shutters'—that was my aunt's name—'is away. She's a troublesome old lady. Ye'll hev to be sharp wi' her, or she'll be into the fire, or out o' t' winda. She goes on wires, she does, old though she be.'

" 'How old, ma'am?' says I.

" 'Ninety-three her last birthday, and that's eight months gone,'
says she; and she laughed. 'And don't be askin' questions about
her before your aunt—mind, I tell ye; just take her as you find
her, and that's all.'

" 'And what's to be my business about her, please, ma'am?' says I.

" 'About the old lady? Well,' says she, 'your aunt, Mrs. Shutters,
will tell you that; but I suppose you'll hev to sit in the room with
your work, and see she's at no mischief, and let her amuse herself
with her things on the table, and get her her food or drink as she
calls for it, and keep her out o' mischief, and ring the bell hard
if she's troublesome.'

" 'Is she deaf, ma'am?'

" 'No, nor blind,' says she; 'as sharp as a needle, but she's gone
quite aupy, and can't remember nout rightly; and Jack the Giant
Killer, or Goody Twoshoes will please her as well as the king's
court, or the affairs of the nation.'

" 'And what did the little girl go away for, ma'am, that went
on Friday last? My aunt wrote to my mother she was to go.'

" 'Yes; she's gone.'

" 'What for?' says I again.

" 'She didn't answer Mrs. Shutters, I do suppose,' says she. 'I
don't know. Don't be talkin'; your aunt can't abide a talkin' child.'

" 'And please, ma'am, is the old lady well in health?' says I.

" 'It ain't no harm to ask that,' says she. 'She's torflin a bit lately,
but better this week past, and I dare say she'll last out her hundred
years yet. Hish! Here's your aunt coming down the passage.'

In comes my aunt, and begins talkin' to Mrs. Wyvern, and I,
beginnin' to feel more comfortable and at home like, was walkin'
about the room lookin' at this thing and at that. There was pretty
old china things on the cupboard, and pictures again the wall;
and there was a door open in the wainscot, and I sees a queer old
leathern jacket, wi' straps and buckles to it, and sleeves as long as
the bed-post hangin' up inside.

" 'What's that you're at, child?' says my aunt, sharp enough,
turning about when I thought she least minded. 'What's that in
your hand?'

" 'This, ma'am?' says I, turning about with the leathern jacket.
'I don't know what it is, ma'am.'

"Pale as she was, the red came up in her cheeks, and her eyes
flashed wi' anger, and I think only she had half a dozen steps to
take, between her and me, she'd a gev me a sizzup. But she did gie
me a shake by the shouther, and she plucked the thing out o' my
hand, and says she, 'While ever you stay here, don't ye meddle

wi' nout that don't belong to ye,' and she hung it up on the pin
that was there, and shut the door wi' a bang and locked it fast.

"Mrs. Wyvern was liftin' up her hands and laughin' all this
time, quietly, in her chair, rolling herself a bit in it, as she used
when she was kinkin'.

"The tears was in my eyes, and she winked at my aunt, and says
she, dryin' her own eyes that was wet wi' the laughin', 'Tut, the
child meant no harm—come here to me, child. It's only a pair o'
crutches for lame ducks, and ask us no questions mind, and we'll
tell ye no lies; and come here and sit down, and drink a mug o'
beer before ye go to your bed.'

"My room, mind ye, was upstairs, next to the old lady's, and
Mrs. Wyvern's bed was near hers in her room, and I was to be
ready at call, if need should be.

"The old lady was in one of her tantrums that night and part
of the day before. She used to take fits o' the sulks. Sometimes she
would not let them dress her, and at other times she would not
let them take her clothes off. She was a great beauty, they said, in
her day. But there was no one about Applewale that remembered
her in her prime. And she was dreadful fond o' dress, and had
thick silks, and stiff satins, and velvets, and laces, and all sorts,
enough to set up seven shops at the least. All her dresses was old-
fashioned and queer, but worth a fortune.

"Well, I went to my bed. I lay for a while awake; for a' things
was new to me; and I think the tea was in my nerves, too, for I
wasn't used to it, except now and then on a holiday, or the like.
And I heard Mrs. Wyvern talkin', and I listened with my hand to
my ear; but I could not hear Mrs. Crowl, and I don't think she
said a word.

"There was great care took of her. The people at Applewale
knew that when she died they would every one get the sack; and
their situations was well paid and easy.

"The doctor came twice a week to see the old lady, and you may
be sure they all did as he bid them. One thing was the same every
time; they were never to cross or frump her, any way, but to humour and please her in everything.

"So she lay in her clothes all that night, and next day, not a
word she said, and I was at my needlework all that day, in my
own room, except when I went down to my dinner.

"I would a liked to see the ald lady, and even to hear her speak.
But she might as well a' bin in Lunnon a' the time for me.

"When I had my dinner my aunt sent me out for a walk for an

hour. I was glad when I came back, the trees was so big, and the place so dark and lonesome, and 'twas a cloudy day, and I cried a deal, thinkin' of home, while I was walkin' alone there. That evening, the candles bein' alight, I was sittin' in my room, and the door was open into Madam Crowl's chamber, where my aunt was. It was, then, for the first time I heard what I suppose was the ald lady talking.

"It was a queer noise like, I couldn't well say which, a bird, or a beast, only it had a bleatin' sound in it, and was very small.

"I pricked my ears to hear all I could. But I could not make out one word she said. And my aunt answered:

" 'The evil one can't hurt no one, ma'am, bout the Lord permits.'

"Then the same queer voice from the bed says something more that I couldn't make head nor tail on.

"And my aunt med answer again: 'Let them pull faces, ma'am, and say what they will; if the Lord be for us, who can be against us?'

"I kept listenin' with my ear turned to the door, holdin' my breath, but not another word or sound came in from the room. In about twenty minutes, as I was sittin' by the table, lookin' at the pictures in the old Aesop's Fables, I was aware o' something moving at the door, and lookin' up I sid my aunt's face lookin' in at the door, and her hand raised.

" 'Hish!' says she, very soft, and comes over to me on tiptoe, and she says in a whisper: 'Thank God, she's asleep at last, and don't ye make no noise till I come back, for I'm goin' down to take my cup o' tea, and I'll be back i' noo—me and Mrs. Wyvern, and she'll be sleepin' in the room, and you can run down when we come up, and Judith will gie ye yaur supper in my room.'

"And with that she goes.

"I kep' looking at the picture-book, as before, listenin' every noo and then, but there was no sound, not a breath, that I could hear; an' I began whisperin' to the pictures and talkin' to myself to keep my heart up, for I was growin' feared in that big room.

"And at last up I got, and began walkin' about the room, lookin' at this and peepin' at that, to amuse my mind, ye'll understand. And at last what sud I do but peeps into Madam Crowl's bedchamber.

"A grand chamber it was, wi' a great four-poster, wi' flowered silk curtains as tall as the ceilin', and foldin' down on the floor, and drawn close all round. There was a lookin'-glass, the biggest

I ever sid before, and the room was a blaze o' light. I counted twenty-two wax candles, all alight. Such was her fancy, and no one dared say her nay.

"I listened at the door, and gaped and wondered all round. When I heard there was not a breath, and did not see so much as a stir in the curtains, I took heart, and walked into the room on tiptoe, and looked round again. Then I takes a keek at myself in the big glass; and at last it came in my head, 'Why couldn't I ha' a keek at the ald lady herself in the bed?'

"Ye'd think me a fule if ye knew half how I longed to see Dame Crowl, and I thought to myself if I didn't peep now I might wait many a day before I got so gude a chance again.

"Well, my dear, I came to the side o' the bed, the curtains bein' close, and my heart a'most failed me. But I took courage, and I slips my finger in between the thick curtains, and then my hand. So I waits a bit, but all was still as death. So, softly, softly I draws the curtain, and there, sure enough, I sid before me, stretched out like the painted lady on the tomb-stean in Lexhoe Church, the famous Dame Crowl, of Applewale House. There she was, dressed out. You never sid the like in they days. Satin and silk, and scarlet and green, and gold and pint lace; by Jen! 'twas a sight! A big powdered wig, half as high as herself, was a-top o' her head, and, wow!—was ever such wrinkles?—and her old baggy throat all powdered white, and her cheeks rouged, and mouse-skin eybrows, that Mrs. Wyvern used to stick on, and there she lay proud and stark, wi' a pair o' clocked silk hose on, and heels to her shoon as tall as nine-pins. Lawk! But her nose was crooked and thin, and half the whites o' her eyes was open. She used to stand, dressed as she was, gigglin' and dribblin' before the lookin'-glass, wi' a fan in her hand and a big nosegay in her bodice. Her wrinkled little hands was stretched down by her sides, and such long nails, all cut into points, I never sid in my days. Could it even a bin the fashion for grit fowk to wear their fingernails so?

"Well, I think ye'd a-bin frightened yourself if ye'd a sid such a sight. I couldn't let go the curtain, nor move an inch, nor take my eyes off her; my very heart stood still. And in an instant she opens her eyes and up she sits, and spins herself round, and down wi' her, wi' a clack on her two tall heels on the floor, facin' me, ogglin' in my face wi' her two great glassy eyes, and a wicked simper wi' her wrinkled lips, and lang fause teeth.

"Well, a corpse is a natural thing; but this was the dreadfullest sight I ever sid. She had her fingers straight out pointin' at me, and her back was crooked, round again wi' age. Says she:

" 'Ye little limb! what for did ye say I killed the boy? I'll tickle ye till ye're stiff!'

"If I'd a thought an instant, I'd a turned about and run. But I couldn't take my eyes off her, and I backed from her as soon as I could; and she came clatterin' after like a thing on wires, with her fingers pointing to my throat, and she makin' all the time a sound with her tongue like zizz-zizz-zizz.

"I kept backin' and backin' as quick as I could, and her fingers was only a few inches away from my throat, and I felt I'd lose my wits if she touched me.

"I went back this way, right into the corner, and I gev a yellock, ye'd think saul and body was partin', and that minute my aunt, from the door, calls out wi' a blare, and the ald lady turns round on her, and I turns about, and ran through my room, and down the stairs, as hard as my legs could carry me.

"I cried hearty, I can tell you, when I got down to the house-keeper's room. Mrs. Wyvern laughed a deal when I told her what happened. But she changed her key when she heard the ald lady's words.

" 'Say them again,' says she.

"So I told her.

" 'Ye little limb! What for did ye say I killed the boy? I'll tickle ye till ye're stiff.'

" 'And did ye say she killed a boy?' says she.

" 'Not I, ma'am,' says I.

Judith was always up with me, after that, when the two elder women was away from her. I would a jumped out at winda, rather than stay alone in the same room wi' her.

"It was about a week after, as well as I can remember, Mrs. Wyvern, one day when me and her was alone, told me a thing about Madam Crowl that I did not know before.

"She being young and a great beauty, full seventy year before, had married Squire Crowl, of Applewale. But he was a widower, and had a son about nine years old.

"There never was tale or tidings of this boy after one mornin'. No one could say where he went to. He was allowed too much liberty, and used to be off in the morning, one day, to the keeper's cottage and breakfast wi' him, and away to the warren, and not home, mayhap, till evening; and another time down to the lake, and bathe there, and spend the day fishin' there, or paddlin' about in the boat. Well, no one could say what was gone wi' him; only this, that his hat was found by the lake, under a haathorn that grows thar to this day, and 'twas thought he was drowned bathin'.

And the squire's son, by his second marriage, with this Madam Crowl that lived sa dreadful lang, came in far the estates. It was his son, the ald lady's grandson, Squire Chevenix Crowl, that owned the estates at the time I came to Applewale.

"There was a deal o' talk lang before my aunt's time about it; and 'twas said the step-mother knew more than she was like to let out. And she managed her husband, the ald squire, wi' her white-heft and flatteries. And as the boy was never seen more, in course of time the thing died out of fowks' minds.

"I'm goin' to tell ye noo about what I sid wi' my own een.

"I was not there six months, and it was winter time, when the ald lady took her last sickness.

"The doctor was afeard she might a took a fit o' madness, as she did fifteen years befoore, and was buckled up, many a time, in a strait-waistcoat, which was the very leathern jerkin I sid in the closet, off my aunt's room.

"Well, she didn't. She pined, and windered, and went off, torflin', torflin', quiet enough, till a day or two before her flittin', and then she took to rabblin', and sometimes skirlin' in the bed, ye'd think a robber had a knife to her throat, and she used to work out o' the bed, and not being strong enough, then, to walk or stand, she'd fall on the flure, wi' her ald wizened hands stretched before her face, and skirlin' still for mercy.

"Ye may guess I didn't go into the room, and I used to be shiverin' in my bed wi' fear, at her skirlin' and scrafflin' on the flure, and blarin' out words that id make your skin turn blue.

"My aunt, and Mrs. Wyvern, and Judith Squailes, and a woman from Lexhoe, was always about her. At last she took fits, and they wore her out.

"'T' sir was there, and prayed for her; but she was past praying with. I suppose it was right, but none could think there was much good in it, and sa at lang last she made her flittin', and a' was over, and old Dame Crowl was shrouded and coffined, and Squire Chevenix was wrote for. But he was away in France, and the delay was sa lang, that t' sir and doctor both agreed it would not du to keep her langer out o' her place, and no one cared but just them two, and my aunt and the rest o' us, from Applewale, to go to the buryin'. So the old lady of Applewale was laid in the vault under Lexhoe Church; and we lived up at the great house till such time as the squire should come to tell his will about us, and pay off such as he chose to discharge.

"I was put into another room, two doors away from what was

Dame Crowl's chamber, after her death, and this thing happened the night before Squire Chevenix came to Applewale.

"The room I was in now was a large square chamber, covered wi' yak pannels, but unfurnished except for my bed, which had no curtains to it, and a chair and a table, or so, that looked nothing at all in such a big room. And the big looking-glass, that the old lady used to keek into and admire herself from head to heel, now that there was na mair o' that wark, was put out of the way, and stood against the wall in my room, for there was shiftin' o' many things in her chamber ye may suppose, when she came to be coffined.

"The news had come that day that the squire was to be down next morning at Applewale; and not sorry was I, for I thought I was sure to be sent home again to my mother. And right glad was I, and I was thinkin' of a' at hame, and my sister Janet, and the kitten and the pymag, and Trimmer the tike, and all the rest, and I got sa fidgetty, I couldn't sleep, and the clock struck twelve, and me wide awake, and the room as dark as pick. My back was turned to the door, and my eyes toward the wall opposite.

"Well, it could na be a full quarter past twelve, when I sees a lightin' on the wall befoore me, as if something took fire behind, and the shadas o' the bed, and the chair, and my gown, that was hangin' from the wall, was dancin' up and down on the ceilin' beams and the yak pannels; and I turns my head ower my shouther quick, thinkin' something must a gone a' fire.

"And what sud I see, by Jen! but the likeness o' the ald beldame, bedizened out in her satins and velvets, on her dead body, simperin', wi' her eyes as wide as saucers, and her face like the fiend himself. 'Twas a red light that rose about her in a fuffin low, as if her dress round her feet was blazin'. She was drivin' on right for me, wi' her ald shrivelled hands crooked as if she was goin' to claw me. I could not stir, but she passed me straight by, wi' a blast o' cald air, and I sid her, at the wall, in the alcove as my aunt used to call it, which was a recess where the state bed used to stand in ald times wi' a door open wide, and her hands gropin' in at somethin' was there. I never sid that door befoore. And she turned round to me, like a thing on a pivot, flyrin', and all at once the room was dark, and I standin' at the far side o' the bed; I don't know how I got there, and I found my tongue at last, and if I did na blare a yellock, rennin' down the gallery and almost pulled Mrs. Wyvern's door off t' hooks, and frighted her half out o' wits.

"Ye may guess I did na sleep that night; and wi' the first light, down wi' me to my aunt, as fast as my two legs cud carry me.

"Well my aunt did na frump or flite me, as I thought she would, but she held me by the hand, and looked hard in my face all the time. And she telt me not to be feared; and says she:

" 'Hed the appearance a key in its hand?'

" 'Yes,' says I, bringin' it to mind. 'a big key in a queer brass handle.'

" 'Stop a bit,' says she, lettin' go ma hand, and openin' the cupboard-door. 'Was it like this?' says she, takin' one out in her fingers, and showing it to me, with a dark look in my face.

" 'That was it,' says I, quick enough.

" 'Are ye sure?' she says, turnin' it round.

" 'Sart,' says I, and I felt like I was gain' to faint when I sid it.

" 'Well, that will do, child,' says she, saftly thinkin', and she locked it up again.

" 'The squire himself will be here today, before twelve o'clock, and ye must tell him all about it,' says she, thinkin', 'and I suppose I'll be leavin' soon, and so the best thing for the present is, that ye should go home this afternoon, and I'll look out another place for you when I can.'

"Fain was I, ye may guess, at that word.

"My aunt packed up my things for me, and the three pounds that was due to me, to bring home, and Squire Crowl himself came down to Applewale that day, a handsome man, about thirty years ald. It was the second time I sid him. But this was the first time he spoke to me.

"My aunt talked wi' him in the housekeeper's room, and I don't know what they said. I was a bit feared on the squire, he bein' a great gentleman down in Lexhoe, and I darn't go near till I was called. And says he, smilin':

" 'What's a' this ye a sen, child? it mun be a dream, for ye know there's na sic a thing as a bo or a freet in a' the world. But whatever it was, ma little maid, sit ye down and tell all about it from first to last.'

"Well, so soon as I made an end, he thought a bit, and says he to my aunt:

" 'I mind the place well. In old Sir Olivur's time lame Wyndel told me there was a door in that recess, to the left, where the lassie dreamed she saw my grandmother open it. He was past eighty when he told me that, and I but a boy. It's twenty year sen. The plate and jewels used to be kept there, long ago, before the iron closet was made in the arras chamber, and he told me the key had a brass handle, and this ye say was found in the bottom o' the kist where she kept her old fans. Now, would not it be a queer thing if we found some spoons or diamonds forgot there? Ye mun come up wi' us, lassie, and point to the very spot.'

"Loth was I, and my heart in my mouth, and fast I held by my aunt's hand as I stept into that awsome room, and showed them both how she came and passed me by, and the spot where she stood, and where the door seemed to open.

"There was an ald empty press against the wall then, and shoving it aside, sure enough there was the tracing of a door in the wainscot, and a keyhole stopped with wood, and planed across as smooth as the rest, and the joining of the door all stopped wi' putty the colour o' yak, and, but for the hinges that showed a bit when the press was shoved aside, ye would not consayt there was a door there at all.

" 'Ha!' says he, wi' a queer smile, 'this looks like it.'

"It took some minutes wi' a small chisel and hammer to pick the bit o' wood out o' the keyhole. The key fitted, sure enough, and, wi' a strang twist and a lang skreak, the boult went back and he pulled the door open.

"There was another door inside, stranger than the first, but the lacks was gone, and it opened easy. Inside was a narrow floor and walls and vault o' brick; we could not see what was in it, for 'twas dark as pick.

"When my aunt had lighted the candle, the squire held it up and stept in.

"My aunt stood on tiptoe tryin' to look over his shouther, and I did na see nout.

" 'Ha! ha!' says the squire, steppin' backward. 'What's that? Gi' ma the poker—quick!' says he to my aunt. And as she went to the hearth I peeps beside his arm, and I sid squat down in the far corner a monkey or a flayin' on the chest, or else the maist shrivelled up, wizzened ald wife that ever was sen on yearth.

" 'By Jen!' says my aunt, as puttin' the poker in his hand, she keeked by his shouther, and sid the ill-favoured thing, 'hae a care, sir, what ye're doin'. Back wi' ye, and shut to the door!'

"But in place o' that he steps in saftly, wi' the poker pointed like a swoord, and he gies it a poke, and down it a' tumbles together, head and a', in a heap o' bayans and dust, little meyar an' a hatful.

" 'Twas the bayans o' a child; a' the rest went to dust at a touch. They said nout for a while, but he turns round the skull, as it lay on the floor.

"Young as I was, I consayted I knew well enough what they was thinkin' on.

" 'A dead cat!' says he, pushin' back and blowin' out the can'le, and shuttin' to the door. 'We'll come back, you and me, Mrs. Shutters, and look on the shelves by-and-bye. I've other matters first to speak to ye about; and this little girl's goin' hame, ye say. She has her wages, and I mun mak' her a present,' says he, pattin' my shouther wi' his hand.

"And he did gimma a goud pound and I went aff to Lexhoe about an hour after, and sa hame by the stage-coach, and fain was I to be at hame again; and I never sid Dame Crowl o' Applewale, God be thanked, either in appearance or in dream, at-efter. But when I was grown to be a woman, my aunt spent a day and night wi' me at Littleham, and she telt me there was no doubt it was the poor little boy that was missing sa lang sen, that was shut up to die thar in the dark by that wicked beldame, whar his skirls, or his prayers, or his thumpin' cud na be heard, and his hat was left by the water's edge, whoever did it, to mak' belief he was drowned. The clothes, at the first touch, a' ran into a snuff o' dust in the cell whar the bayans was found. But there was a handful o' jet buttons, and a knife with a green heft, together wi' a couple o' pennies the poor little fella had in his pocket, I suppose, when he was decoyed in thar, and sid his last o' the light. And there was, amang the squire's papers, a copy o' the notice that was prented after he was lost, when the ald squire thought he might 'a run away, or bin took by gipsies, and it said he had a green-hefted knife wi' him, and that his buttons were o' cut jet. Sa that is a' I hev to say consarnin' ald Dame Crowl, o' Applewale House."

The Haunted Baronet

CHAPTER I

The George and Dragon

The pretty little town of Golden Friars—standing by the margin
of the lake, hemmed round by an amphitheatre of purple mountain, rich in tint and furrowed by ravines, high in air, when the
tall gables and narrow windows of its ancient graystone houses,
and the tower of the old church, from which every evening the
curfew still rings, show like silver in the moonbeams, and the
black elms that stand round throw moveless shadows upon the
short level grass—is one of the most singular and beautiful sights
I have ever seen.

There it rises, 'as from the stroke of the enchanter's wand,' looking so light and filmy, that you could scarcely believe it more than
a picture reflected on the thin mist of night.

On such a still summer night the moon shone splendidly upon
the front of the George and Dragon, the comfortable graystone
inn of Golden Friars, with the grandest specimen of the old inn-
sign, perhaps, left in England. It looks right across the lake; the
road that skirts its margin running by the steps of the hall-door,
opposite to which, at the other side of the road, between two great
posts, and framed in a fanciful wrought-iron border splendid with
gilding, swings the famous sign of St. George and the Dragon, gorgeous with colour and gold.

In the great room of the George and Dragon, three or four of the
old *habitués* of that cozy lounge were refreshing a little after the
fatigues of the day.

This is a comfortable chamber, with an oak wainscot; and whenever in summer months the air is sharp enough, as on the present
occasion, a fire helped to light it up; which fire, being chiefly wood,

made a pleasant broad flicker on panel and ceiling, and yet did not make the room too hot.

On one side sat Doctor Torvey, the doctor of Golden Friars, who knew the weak point of every man in the town, and what medicine agreed with each inhabitant—a fat gentleman, with a jolly laugh and an appetite for all sorts of news, big and little, and who liked a pipe, and made a tumbler of punch at about this hour, with a bit of lemon-peel in it. Beside him sat William Peers, a thin old gentleman, who had lived for more than thirty years in India, and was quiet and benevolent, and the last man in Golden Friars who wore a pigtail. Old Jack Amerald, an ex-captain of the navy, with his short stout leg on a chair, and its wooden companion beside it, sipped his grog, and bawled in the old-fashioned navy way, and called his friends his 'hearties.' In the middle, opposite the hearth, sat deaf Tom Hollar, always placid, and smoked his pipe, looking serenely at the fire. And the landlord of the George and Dragon every now and then strutted in, and sat down in the high-backed wooden arm-chair, according to the old-fashioned republican ways of the place, and took his share in the talk gravely, and was heartily welcome.

"And so Sir Bale is coming home at last," said the Doctor. "Tell us any more you heard since."

"Nothing," answered Richard Turnbull, the host of the George. "Nothing to speak of; only 'tis certain sure, and so best; the old house won't look so dowly now."

"Twyne says the estate owes a good capful o' money by this time, hey?" said the Doctor, lowering his voice and winking.

"Weel, they do say he's been nout at dow. I don't mind saying so to *you*, mind, sir, where all's friends together; but he'll get that right in time."

"More like to save here than where he is," said the Doctor with another grave nod.

"He does very wisely," said Mr. Peers, having blown out a thin stream of smoke, "and creditably, to pull-up in time. He's coming here to save a little, and perhaps he'll marry; and it is the more creditable, if, as they say, he dislikes the place, and would prefer staying where he is."

And having spoken thus gently, Mr. Peers resumed his pipe cheerfully.

"No, he don't like the place; that is, I'm told he *didn't*," said the innkeeper.

"He *hates* it," said the Doctor with another dark nod.

"And no wonder, if all's true I've heard," cried old Jack Amerald. "Didn't he drown a woman and her child in the lake?"

"Hollo! my dear boy, don't let them hear you say that; you're all in the clouds."

"By Jen!" exclaimed the landlord after an alarmed silence, with his mouth and eyes open, and his pipe in his hand, "why, sir, I pay rent for the house up there. I'm thankful—dear knows, I *am* thankful—we're all to ourselves!"

Jack Amerald put his foot on the floor, leaving his wooden leg in its horizontal position, and looked round a little curiously.

"Well, if it wasn't him, it was some one else. I'm sure it happened up at Mardykes. I took the bearings on the water myself from Glads Scaur to Mardykes Jetty, and from the George and Dragon sign down here—down to the white house under Forrick Fells. I could fix a buoy over the very spot. Some one here told me the bearings, I'd take my oath, where the body was seen; and yet no boat could ever come up with it; and that was queer, you know, so I clapt it down in my log."

"Ay, sir, there *was* some flummery like that, Captain," said Turnbull; "for folk will be gabbin'. But 'twas his grandsire was talked o', not him; and 'twould play the hangment wi' me doun here, if 'twas thought there was stories like that passin' in the George and Dragon.'

"Well, his grandfather; 'twas all one to him, I take it."

"There never was no proof, Captain, no more than smoke; and the family up at Mardykes wouldn't allow the king to talk o' them like that, sir; for though they be lang dead that had most right to be angered in the matter, there's none o' the name but would be half daft to think 'twas still believed, and he full out as mich as any. Not that I need care more than another, though they do say he's a bit frowsy and short-waisted; for he can't shouther me out o' the George while I pay my rent, till nine hundred and ninety-nine year be rin oot; and a man, be he ne'er sa het, has time to cool before then. But there's no good quarrellin' wi' teathy folk; and it may lie in his way to do the George many an ill turn, and mony a gude one; an' it's only fair to say it happened a long way before he was born, and there's no good in vexin' him; and I lay ye a pound, Captain, the Doctor hods wi' me."

The Doctor, whose business was also sensitive, nodded; and then he said, "But for all that, the story's old, Dick Turnbull—older than you or I, my jolly good friend."

"And best forgotten," interposed the host of the George.

"Ay, best forgotten; but that it's not like to be," said the Doctor, plucking up courage. "Here's our friend the Captain has heard it;

and the mistake he has made shows there's one thing worse than its being quite remembered, and that is, its being *half* remembered. We can't stop people talking; and a story like that will see us all off the hooks, and be in folks' mouths, still, as strong as ever."

"Ay; and now I think on it, 'twas Dick Harman that has the boat down there—an old tar like myself—that told me that yarn. I was trying for pike, and he pulled me over the place, and that's how I came to hear it. I say, Tom, my hearty, serve us out another glass of brandy, will you?" shouted the Captain's voice as the waiter crosssed the room; and that florid and grizzled naval hero clapped his leg again on the chair by its wooden companion, which he was wont to call his jury-mast.

"Well, I do believe it will be spoke of longer than we are like to hear," said the host, "and I don't much matter the story, if it baint told o' the wrong man." Here he touched his tumbler with the spoon, indicating by that little ring that Tom, who had returned with the Captain's grog, was to replenish it with punch. "And Sir Bale is like to be a friend to this house. I don't see no reason why he shouldn't. The George and Dragon has bin in our family ever since the reign of King Charles the Second. It was William Turnbull in that time, which they called it the Restoration, he taking the lease from Sir Tony Mardykes that was then. They was but knights then. They was made baronets first in the reign of King George the Second; you may see it in the list of baronets and the nobility. The lease was made to William Turnbull, which came from London; and he built the stables, which they was out o' repair, as you may read to this day in the lease; and the house has never had but one sign since—the George and Dragon, it is pretty well known in England—and one name to its master. It has been owned by a Turnbull from that day to this, and they have not been counted bad men." A murmur of applause testified the assent of his guests. "They has been steady churchgoin' folk, and brewed good drink, and maintained the best o' characters, hereaways and farther off too, though 'tis I, Richard Turnbull, that says it; and while they pay their rent, no man has power to put them out; for their title's as good to the George and Dragon, and the two fields, and the croft, and the grazing o' their kye on the green, as Sir Bale Mardykes to the Hall up there and estate. So 'tis nout to me, except in the way o' friendliness, what the family may think o' me; only the George and they has always been kind and friendly, and I don't want to break the old custom."

"Well said, Dick!" exclaimed Doctor Torvey; "I own to your conclusion; but there ain't a soul here but ourselves—and we're all friends, and you are your own master—and, hang it, you'll tell us that story about the drowned woman, as you heard it from your father long ago."

"Ay, do, and keep us to our liquor, my hearty!" cried the Captain.

Mr. Peers looked his entreaty; and deaf Mr. Hollar, having no interest in the petition, was at least a safe witness, and, with his pipe in his lips, a cozy piece of furniture.

Richard Turnbull had his punch beside him; he looked over his shoulder. The door was closed, the fire was cheery, and the punch was fragrant, and all friendly faces about him. So said he:

"Gentlemen, as you're pleased to wish it, I don't see no great harm in it; and at any rate, 'twill prevent mistakes. It is more than ninety years since. My father was but a boy then; and many a time I have heard him tell it in this very room."

And looking into his glass he mused, and stirred his punch slowly.

CHAPTER II

The Drowned Woman

"It ain't much of a homminy," said the host of the George. "I'll not keep you long over it, gentlemen. There was a handsome young lady, Miss Mary Feltram o' Cloostedd by name. She was the last o' that family; and had gone very poor. There's but the walls o' the house left now; grass growing in the hall, and ivy over the gables; there's no one livin' has ever hard tell o' smoke out o' they chimblies. It stands on t'other side o' the lake, on the level wi' a deal o' a'ad trees behint and aside it at the gap o' the clough, under the pike o' Maiden Fells. Ye may see it wi' a spyin'-glass from the boatbield at Mardykes Hall."

"I've been there fifty times," said the Doctor.

"Well there was dealin's betwixt the two families; and there's good and bad in every family; but the Mardykes, in them days, was a wild lot. And when old Feltram o' Cloostedd died, and the young lady his daughter was left a ward o' Sir Jasper Mardykes— an ill day for her, poor lass!—twenty year older than her he was, an' more; and nothin' about him, they say, to make anyone like or love him, ill-faur'd and little and dow."

"Dow—that's gloomy," Doctor Torvey instructed the Captain aside.

"But they do say, they has an old blud-stean ring in the family that has a charm in't; and happen how it might, the poor lass fell in love wi' him. Some said they was married. Some said it hang'd i' the bell-ropes, and never had the priest's blessing; but anyhow, married or no, there was talk enough amang the folk, and out o' doors she would na budge. And there was two wee barns; and she prayed him hard to confess the marriage, poor thing! But t'was a bootlese bene, and he would not allow they should bear his name, but their mother's; he was a hard man, and hed the bit in his teeth, and went his ain gait. And having tired of her, he took in his head to marry a lady of the Barnets, and it behoved him to be shut o' her and her children; and so she nor them was seen no more at Mardykes Hall. And the eldest, a boy, was left in care of my grandfather's father here in the George."

"That queer Philip Feltram that's travelling with Sir Bale so long is a descendant of his?" said the Doctor.

"Grandson," observed Mr. Peers, removing his pipe for a moment; "and is the last of that stock."

"Well, no one could tell where she had gone to. Some said to distant parts, some said to the madhouse, some one thing, some another; but neither she nor the barn was ever seen or spoke to by the folk at Mardykes in life again. There was one Mr. Wigram that lived in them times down at Moultry, and had sarved, like the Captain here, in the king's navy in his day; and early of a morning down he comes to the town for a boat, sayin' he was looking towards Snakes Island through his spyin'-glass, and he seen a woman about a hundred and fifty yards outside of it; the Captain here has heard the bearings right enough. From her hips upwards she was stark and straight out o' the water, and a baby in her arms. Well, no one else could see it, nor he neither, when they went down to the boat. But next morning he saw the same thing, and the boatman saw it too; and they rowed for it, both pulling might and main; but after a mile or so they could see it no more, and gave over. The next that saw it was the vicar, I forget his name now—but he was up the lake to a funeral at Mortlock Church; and coming back with a bit of a sail up, just passin' Snakes Island, what should they hear on a sudden but a wowl like a death-cry, shrill and bleak, as made the very blood hoot in their veins; and looking along the water not a hundred yards away, saw the same grizzled sight in the moonlight; so they turned the tiller, and came near enough to see her face—blea it was, and drenched wi' water—and she was above the lake to her middle, stiff as a post, holdin' the weeny barn out to them, and flyrin' [smiling scornfully] on them as they drew nigh her. They were half-frighted, not knowing what to make of it; but passing as close as the boatman could bring her side, the vicar stretched over the gunwale to catch her, and she bent forward, pushing the dead bab forward; and as she did, on a sudden she gave a yelloch that scared them, and they saw her no more. 'Twas no livin' woman, for she couldn't rise that height above the water, as they well knew when they came to think; and knew it was a dobby they saw; and ye may be sure they didn't spare prayer and blessin', and went on their course straight before the wind; for neither would a-took the worth o' all the Mardykes to look sich a freetin' i' the face again. 'Twas seen another time by market-folk crossin' fra Gyllenstan in the self-same place; and Snakes Island got a bad neam, and none cared to go nar it after nightfall."

"Do you know anything of that Feltram that has been with him abroad?" asked the Doctor.

"They say he's no good at anything—a harmless mafflin; he was a long gaumless gawky when he went awa," said Richard Turnbull. "The Feltrams and the Mardykes was sib, ye know; and that made what passed in the misfortune o' that young lady spoken of all the harder; and this young man ye speak of is a grandson o' the lad that was put here in care o' my grandfather."

"*Great*-grandson. His father was grandson," said Mr. Peers; "he held a commission in the army and died in the West Indies. This Philip Feltram is the last o' that line—illegitimate, you know, it is held—and the little that remained of the Feltram property went nearly fourscore years ago to the Mardykes, and this Philip is maintained by Sir Bale; it is pleasant, notwithstanding all the stories one hears, gentlemen, that the only thing we know of him for certain should be so creditable to his kindness."

"To be sure," acquiesced Mr. Turnbull.

While they talked the horn sounded, and the mail-coach drew up at the door of the George and Dragon to set down a passenger and his luggage.

Dick Turnbull rose and went out to the hall with careful bustle, and Doctor Torvey followed as far as the door, which commanded a view of it, and saw several trunks cased in canvas pitched into the hall, and by careful Tom and a boy lifted one on top of the other, behind the corner of the banister. It would have been below the dignity of his cloth to go out and read the labels on these, or the Doctor would have done otherwise, so great was his curiosity.

CHAPTER III

Philip Feltram

The new guest was now in the hall of the George, and Doctor Torvey could hear him talking with Mr. Turnbull. Being himself one of the dignitaries of Golden Friars, the Doctor, having regard to first impressions, did not care to be seen in his post of observation; and closing the door gently, returned to his chair by the fire, and in an under-tone informed his cronies that there was a new arrival in the George, and he could not hear, but would not wonder if he were taking a private room; and he seemed to have trunks enough to build a church with.

"Don't be too sure we haven't Sir Bale on board," said Amerald, who would have followed his crony the Doctor to the door—for never was retired naval hero of a village more curious than he— were it not that his wooden leg made a distinct pounding on the floor that was inimical, as experience had taught him, to mystery.

"That can't be," answered the Doctor; "Charley Twyne knows everything about it, and has a letter every second day; and there's no chance of Sir Bale before the tenth; this is a tourist, you'll find. I don't know what the d—l keeps Turnbull; he knows well enough we are all naturally willing to hear who it is."

"Well, he won't trouble us here, I bet ye;" and catching deaf Mr. Hollar's eye, the Captain nodded, and pointed to the little table beside him, and made a gesture imitative of the rattling of a dice-box; at which that quiet old gentleman also nodded sunnily; and up got the Captain and conveyed the backgammon-box to the table, near Hollar's elbow, and the two worthies were soon sinc-ducing and catre-acing, with the pleasant clatter that accompanies that ancient game. Hollar had thrown sizes and made his double point, and the honest Captain, who could stand many things better than Hollar's throwing such throws so early in the evening, cursed his opponent's luck and sneered at his play, and called the company to witness, with a distinctness which a stranger to smiling Hollar's deafness would have thought hardly civil; and just at this moment the door opened, and Richard Turnbull showed his new guest into the room, and ushered him to a vacant seat near the other corner of the table before the fire.

The stranger advanced slowly and shyly, with something a little deprecatory in his air, to which a lathy figure, a slight stoop, and a very gentle and even heartbroken look in his pale long face, gave a more marked character of shrinking and timidity.

He thanked the landlord aside, as it were, and took his seat with a furtive glance round, as if he had no right to come in and intrude upon the happiness of these honest gentlemen.

He saw the Captain scanning him from under his shaggy grey eyebrows while he was pretending to look only at his game; and the Doctor was able to recount to Mrs. Torvey when he went home every article of the stranger's dress.

It was odd and melancholy as his peaked face.

He had come into the room with a short black cloak on, and a rather tall foreign felt hat, and a pair of shiny leather gaiters or leggings on his thin legs; and altogether presented a general resemblance to the conventional figure of Guy Fawkes.

Not one of the company assembled knew the appearance of the Baronet. The Doctor and old Mr. Peers remembered something of his looks; and certainly they had no likeness, but the reverse, to those presented by the new-comer. The Baronet, as now described by people who had chanced to see him, was a dark man, not above the middle size, and with a certain decision in his air and talk; whereas this person was tall, pale, and in air and manner feeble. So this broken trader in the world's commerce, with whom all seemed to have gone wrong, could not possibly be he.

Presently, in one of his stealthy glances, the Doctor's eye encountered that of the stranger, who was by this time drinking his tea—a thin and feminine liquor little used in that room.

The stranger did not seem put out; and the Doctor, interpreting his look as a permission to converse, cleared his voice, and said urbanely,

"We have had a little frost by night, down here, sir, and a little fire is no great harm—it is rather pleasant, don't you think?"

The stranger bowed acquiescence with a transient wintry smile, and looked gratefully on the fire.

"This place is a good deal admired, sir, and people come a good way to see it; you have been here perhaps before?"

"Many years ago."

Here was another pause.

"Places change imperceptibly—in detail, at least—a good deal," said the Doctor, making an effort to keep up a conversation that plainly would not go on of itself; "and people too; population shifts—there's an old fellow, sir, they call *Death*."

"And an old fellow they call the *Doctor*, that helps him," threw in the Captain humorously, allowing his attention to get entangled in the conversation, and treating them to one of his tempestuous ha-ha-ha's.

"We are expecting the return of a gentleman who would be a very leading member of our little society down here," said the Doctor, not noticing the Captain's joke. "I mean Sir Bale Mardykes. Mardykes Hall is a pretty object from the water, sir, and a very fine old place."

The melancholy stranger bowed slightly, but rather in courtesy to the relator, it seemed, than that the Doctor's lore interested him much.

"And on the opposite side of the lake," continued Doctor Torvey, "there is a building that contrasts very well with it—the old house of the Feltrams—quite a ruin now, at the mouth of the glen —Cloostedd House, a very picturesque object."

"Exactly opposite," said the stranger dreamily, but whether in the tone of acquiescence or interrogatory, the Doctor could not be quite sure.

"That was one of our great families down here that has disappeared. It has dwindled down to nothing."

"Duce ace," remarked Mr. Hollar, who was attending to his game.

"While others have mounted more suddenly and amazingly still," observed gentle Mr. Peers, who was great upon county genealogies.

"Sizes!" thundered the Captain, thumping the table with an oath of disgust.

"And Snakes Island is a very pretty object; they say there used to be snakes there," said the Doctor, enlightening the visitor.

"Ah! that's a mistake," said the dejected guest, making his first original observation. "It should be spelt *Snaiks*. In the old papers it is called Sen-aiks Island from the seven oaks that grew in a clump there."

"Hey? that's very curious, egad! I daresay," said the Doctor, set right thus by the stranger, and eyeing him curiously.

"Very true, sir," observed Mr. Peers; "three of those oaks, though, two of them little better than stumps, are there still; and Clewson of Heckleston has an old document—"

Here, unhappily, the landlord entered the room in a fuss, and walking up to the stranger, said, "The chaise is at the door, Mr. Feltram, and the trunks up, sir."

Mr. Feltram rose quietly and took out his purse, and said, "I suppose I had better pay at the bar?"

"As you like best, sir," said Richard Turnbull.

Mr. Feltram bowed all round to the gentlemen, who smiled, ducked or waved their hands; and the Doctor fussily followed him to the hall-door, and welcomed him back to Golden Friars— there was real kindness in this welcome—and proffered his broad brown hand, which Mr. Feltram took; and then he plunged into his chaise, and the door being shut, away he glided, chaise, horses, and driver, like shadows, by the margin of the moonlighted lake, towards Mardykes Hall.

And after a few minutes' stand upon the steps, looking along the shadowy track of the chaise, they returned to the glow of the room, in which a pleasant perfume of punch still prevailed; and beside Mr. Philip Feltram's deserted tea-things, the host of the George enlightened his guests by communicating freely the little he had picked up. The principal fact he had to tell was, that Sir Bale adhered strictly to his original plan, and was to arrive on the tenth. A few days would bring them to that, and the nine-days wonder run its course and lose its interest. But in the meantime, all Golden Friars was anxious to see what Sir Bale Mardykes was like.

CHAPTER IV

The Baronet Appears

As the candles burn blue and the air smells of brimstone at the approach of the Evil One, so, in the quiet and healthy air of Golden Friars, a depressing and agitating influence announced the coming of the long-absent Baronet.

From abroad, no good whatever had been at any time heard of him, and a great deal that was, in the ears of simple folk living in that unsophisticated part of the world, vaguely awful.

Stories that travel so far, however, lose something of their authority, as well as definiteness, on the way; there was always room for charity to suggest a mistake or exaggeration; and if good men turned up their hands and eyes after a new story, and ladies of experience, who knew mankind, held their heads high and looked grim and mysterious at mention of his name, nevertheless an interval of silence softened matters a little, and the sulphureous perfume dissipated itself in time.

Now that Sir Bale Mardykes had arrived at the Hall, there were hurried consultations held in many households. And though he was tried and sentenced by drum-head over some austere hearths, as a rule the law of gravitation prevailed, and the greater house drew the lesser about it, and county people within the visiting radius paid their respects at the Hall.

The Reverend Martin Bedel, the then vicar of Golden Friars, a stout short man, with a mulberry-coloured face and small gray eyes, and taciturn habits, called and entered the drawing-room at Mardykes Hall, with his fat and garrulous wife on his arm.

The drawing-room has a great projecting Tudor window looking out on the lake, with its magnificent background of furrowed and purple mountains.

Sir Bale was not there, and Mrs. Bedel examined the pictures, and ornaments, and the books, making such remarks as she saw fit; and then she looked out of the window, and admired the prospect. She wished to stand well with the Baronet, and was in a mood to praise everything.

You may suppose she was curious to see him, having heard for years such strange tales of his doings.

She expected the hero of a brilliant and wicked romance; and listened for the step of the truant Lovelace who was to fulfil her idea of manly beauty and fascination.

She sustained a slight shock when he did appear.

Sir Bale Mardykes was, as she might easily have remembered, a middle-aged man—and he looked it. He was not even an imposing-looking man for his time of life: he was of about the middle height, slightly made, and dark featured. She had expected something of the gaiety and animation of Versailles, and an evident cultivation of the art of pleasing. What she did see was a remarkable gravity, not to say gloom, of countenance—the only feature of which that struck her being a pair of large dark-gray eyes, that were cold and earnest. His manners had the ease of perfect confidence; and his talk and air were those of a person who might have known how to please, if it were worth the trouble, but who did not care twopence whether he pleased or not.

He made them each a bow, courtly enough, but there was no smile—not even an affectation of cordiality. Sir Bale, however, was chatty, and did not seem to care much what he said, or what people thought of him; and there was a suspicion of sarcasm in what he said that the rustic literality of good Mrs. Bedel did not always detect.

"I believe I have not a clergyman but *you,* sir, within any reasonable distance?"

"Golden Friars *is* the nearest," said Mrs. Bedel, answering, as was her pleasure on all practicable occasions, for her husband. "And southwards, the nearest is Wyllarden—and by a bird's flight that is thirteen miles and a half, and by the road more than nineteen—twenty, I may say, by the road. Ha, ha, ha! it is a long way to look for a clergyman."

"Twenty miles of road to carry you thirteen miles across, hey? The road-makers lead you a pretty dance here; those gentlemen know how to make money, and like to show people the scenery from a variety of points. No one likes a straight road but the man who pays for it, or who, when he travels, is brute enough to wish to get to his journey's end."

"That is so true, Sir Bale; one never cares if one is not in a hurry. That's what Martin thinks—don't we, Martin?—And then, you know, coming home is the time you *are* in a hurry—when you are thinking of your cup of tea and the children; and *then,* you know, you have the fall of the ground all in your favour."

"It's well to have anything in your favour in this place. And so there are children?"

"A good many," said Mrs. Bedel, with a proud and mysterious smile, and a nod; "you wouldn't guess how many."

"Not I; I only wonder you did not bring them all."

"That's very good-natured of you, Sir Bale, but all could not come at one bout; there are—tell him, Martin—ha, ha, ha! there are eleven."

"It must be very cheerful down at the vicarage," said Sir Bale graciously; and turning to the vicar he added, "But how unequally blessings are divided! You have eleven, and I not one—that I'm aware of."

"And then, in that direction straight before you, you have the lake, and then the fells; and five miles from the foot of the mountain at the other side, before you reach Fottrell—and that is twenty-five miles by the road—"

"Dear me! how far apart they are set! My gardener told me this morning that asparagus grows very thinly in this part of the world. How thinly clergymen grow also down here—in one sense," he added politely, for the vicar was stout.

"We were looking out of the window—we amused ourselves that way before you came—and your view is certainly the very best anywhere round this side; your view of the lake and the fells—what mountains they are, Sir Bale!"

" 'Pon my soul, they are! I wish I could blow them asunder with a charge of duck-shot, and I shouldn't be stifled by them long. But I suppose, as we can't get rid of them, the next best thing is to admire them. We are pretty well married to them, and there is no use in quarrelling."

"I know you don't think so, Sir Bale, ha, ha, ha! You wouldn't take a good deal and spoil Mardykes Hall."

"You can't get a mouthful or air, or see the sun of a morning, for those frightful mountains," he said with a peevish frown at them.

"Well, the lake at all events—that you *must* admire, Sir Bale?"

"No ma'am, I don't admire the lake. I'd drain the lake if I could—I hate the lake. There's nothing so gloomy as a lake pent up among barren mountains. I can't conceive what possessed my people to build our house down here, at the edge of a lake; unless it was the fish, and precious fish it is—pike! I don't know how people digest it—*I* can't. I'd as soon think of eating a watchman's pike."

"I thought that having travelled so much abroad, you would have acquired a great liking for that kind of scenery, Sir Bale; there is a great deal of it on the Continent, ain't there?" said Mrs. Bedel. "And the boating."

"Boating, my dear Mrs. Bedel, is the dullest of all things; don't you think so? Because a boat looks very pretty from the shore, we fancy the shore must look very pretty from a boat; and when we try it, we find we have only got down into a pit and can see nothing rightly. For my part I hate boating, and I hate the water; and I'd rather have my house, like Haworth, at the edge of a moss, with good wholesome peat to look at, and an open horizon— savage and stupid and bleak as all that is—than be suffocated among impassable mountains, or upset in a black lake and drowned like a kitten. O, there's luncheon in the next room; won't you take some?"

CHAPTER V

Mrs. Julaper's Room

Sir Bale Mardykes being now established in his ancestral house, people had time to form conclusions respecting him. It must be allowed he was not popular. There was, perhaps, in his conduct something of the caprice of contempt. At all events his temper and conduct were uncertain, and his moods sometimes violent and insulting.

With respect to but one person was his conduct uniform, and that was Philip Feltram. He was a sort of aide-de-camp near Sir Bale's person, and chargeable with all the commissions and offices which could not be suitably intrusted to a mere servant. But in many respects he was treated worse than any servant of the Baronet's. Sir Bale swore at him, and cursed him; laid the blame of everything that went wrong in house, stable, or field upon his shoulders; railed at him, and used him, as people said, worse than a dog.

Why did Feltram endure this contumelious life? What could he do but endure it? was the answer. What was the power that induced strong soldiers to put off their jackets and shirts, and present their hands to be tied up, and tortured for hours, it might be, under the scourge, with an air of ready volition? The moral coercion of despair; the result of an unconscious calculation of chances which satisfies them that it is ultimately better to do all that, bad as it is, than try the alternative. These unconscious calculations are going on every day with each of us, and the results embody themselves in our lives; and no one knows that there has been a process and a balance struck, and that what they see, and very likely blame, is by the fiat of an invisible but quite irresistible power.

A man of spirit would rather break stones on the highway than eat that bitter bread, was the burden of every man's song on Feltram's bondage. But he was not so sure that even the stone-breaker's employment was open to him, or that he could break stones well enough to retain it on a fair trial. And he had other ideas of providing for himself, and a different alternative in his mind.

Good-natured Mrs. Julaper, the old housekeeper at Mardykes Hall, was kind to Feltram, as to all others who lay in her way and were in affliction.

She was one of those good women whom Nature provides to receive the burden of other people's secrets, as the reeds did long ago, only that no chance wind could steal them away, and send them singing into strange ears.

You may still see her snuggery in Mardykes Hall, though the housekeeper's room is now in a different part of the house.

Mrs. Julaper's room was in the oldest quarter of that old house.

It was wainscoted, in black panels, up to the ceiling, which was stuccoed over in the fanciful diagrams of James the First's time. Several dingy portraits, banished from time to time from other statelier rooms, found a temporary abode in this quiet spot, where they had come finally to settle and drop out of remembrance. There is a lady in white satin and a ruff; a gentleman whose legs have faded out of view, with a peaked beard, and a hawk on his wrist. There is another in a black periwig lost in the dark background, and with a steel cuirass, the gleam of which out of the darkness strikes the eye, and a scarf is dimly discoverable across it. This is that foolish Sir Guy Mardykes, who crossed the Border and joined Dundee, and was shot through the temple at Killie-crankie and whom more prudent and whiggish scions of the Mardykes family removed forthwith from his place in the Hall, and found a retirement here, from which he has not since emerged.

At the far end of this snug room is a second door, on opening which you find yourself looking down upon the great kitchen, with a little balcony before you, from which the housekeeper used to issue her commands to the cook, and exercise a sovereign supervision.

There is a shelf on which Mrs. Julaper had her Bible, her *Whole Duty of Man,* and her *Pilgrim's Progress;* and, in a file beside them, her books of housewifery, and among them volumes of MS. recipes, cookery-books, and some too on surgery and medicine, as practised by the Ladies Bountiful of the Elizabethan age, for which an antiquarian would nowadays give an eye or a hand.

Gentle half-foolish Philip Feltram would tell the story of his wrongs, and weep and wish he was dead; and kind Mrs. Julaper, who remembered him a child, would comfort him with cold pie and cherry-brandy, or a cup of coffee, or some little dainty.

"O, ma'am, I'm tired of my life. What's the good of living, if a poor devil is never let alone, and called worse names than a dog? Would not it be better, Mrs. Julaper, to be dead? Wouldn't it be better, ma'am? I think so; I think it night and day. I'm always thinking the same thing. I don't care, I'll just tell him what I think, and have it off my mind. I'll tell him I can't live and bear it longer."

"There now, don't you be frettin'; but just sip this, and remember you're not to judge a friend by a wry word. He does not mean it, not he. They all had a rough side to their tongue now and again; but no one minded that. I don't, nor you needn't, no more than other folk; for the tongue, be it never so bitin', it can't draw blood, mind ye, and hard words break no bones; and I'll

make a cup o' tea—ye like a cup o' tea—and we'll take a cup together, and ye'll chirp up a bit, and see how pleasant and ruddy
the sun shines on the lake this evening."

She was patting him gently on the shoulder, as she stood slim
and stiff in her dark silk by his chair, and her rosy little face
smiled down on him. She was, for an old woman, wonderfully
pretty still. What a delicate skin she must have had! The wrinkles
were etched upon it with so fine a needle, you scarcely could see
them a little way off; and as she smiled her cheeks looked fresh
and smooth as two ruddy little apples.

"Look out, I say," and she nodded towards the window, deep
set in the thick wall. "See how bright and soft everything looks in
that pleasant light; *that's* better, child, than the finest picture
man's hand ever painted yet, and God gives it us for nothing; and
how pretty Snakes Island glows up in that light!"

The dejected man, hardly raising his head, followed with his
eyes the glance of the old woman, and looked mournfully through
the window.

"That island troubles me, Mrs. Julaper."

"Everything troubles you, my poor goose-cap. I'll pull your lug
for ye, child, if ye be so dowly;" and with a mimic pluck the good-
natured old housekeeper pinched his ear and laughed.

"I'll go to the still-room now, where the water's boiling, and I'll
make a cup of tea; and if I find ye so dow when I come back, I'll
throw it all out o' the window, mind."

It was indeed a beautiful picture that Feltram saw in its deep
frame of old masonry. The near part of the lake was flushed all
over with the low western light; the more distant waters lay dark
in the shadow of the mountains; and against this shadow of purple
the rocks on Snakes Island, illuminated by the setting sun, started
into sharp clear yellow.

But this beautiful view had no charm—at least, none powerful
enough to master the latent horror associated with its prettiest
feature—for the weak and dismal man who was looking at it; and
being now alone, he rose and leant on the window, and looked
out, and then with a kind of shudder clutching his hands together,
and walking distractedly about the room.

Without his perceiving, while his back was turned, the housekeeper came back; and seeing him walking in this distracted way,
she thought to herself, as he leant again upon the window:

"Well, it *is* a burning shame to worrit any poor soul into that
state. Sir Bale was always down on someone or something, man
or beast; there always was something he hated, and could never

let alone. It was not pretty; it was his nature. Happen, poor fellow, he could not help it; but so it was."

A maid came in and set the tea-things down; and Mrs. Julaper drew her sad guest over by the arm, and made him sit down, and she said: "What has a man to do, frettin' in that way? By Jen, I'm ashamed o' ye, Master Philip! Ye like three lumps o' sugar, I think, and—look cheerful, ye must!—a good deal o' cream?"

"You're so kind, Mrs. Julaper, you're so cheery. I feel quite comfortable after awhile when I'm with you; I feel quite happy," and he began to cry.

She understood him very well by this time and took no notice, but went on chatting gaily, and made his tea as he liked it; and he dried his tears hastily, thinking she had not observed.

So the clouds began to clear. This innocent fellow liked nothing better than a cup of tea and a chat with gentle and cheery old Mrs. Julaper, and a talk in which the shadowy old times which he remembered as a child emerged into sunlight and lived again.

When he began to feel better, drawn into the kindly old times by the tinkle of that harmless old woman's tongue, he said:

"I sometimes think I would not so much mind—I should not care so much—if my spirits were not so depressed, and I so agitated. I suppose I am not quite well."

"Well, tell me what's wrong, child, and it's odd but I have a recipe on the shelf there that will do you good."

"It is not a matter of that sort I mean; though I'd rather have you than any doctor, if I needed medicine, to prescribe for me."

Mrs. Julaper smiled in spite of herself, well pleased; for her skill in pharmacy was a point on which the good lady prided herself, and was open to flattery, which, without intending it, the simple fellow administered.

"No, I'm well enough; I can't say I ever was better. It is only, ma'am, that I have such dreams—you have no idea."

"There are dreams and dreams, my dear: there's some signifies no more than the babble of the lake down there on the pebbles, and there's others that has a meaning; there's dreams that is but vanity, and there's dreams that is good, and dreams that is bad. Lady Mardykes—heavens be her bed this day! that's his grandmother I mean—was very sharp for reading dreams. Take another cup of tea. Dear me! what a noise the crows keep aboon our heads, going home! and how high they wing it!—that's a sure sign of fine weather. An' what do you dream about? Tell me your dream, and I may show you it's a good one, after all. For many a dream is ugly to see and ugly to tell, and a good dream, with a happy meaning, for all that."

CHAPTER VI

The Intruder

"Well, Mrs. Julaper, dreams I've dreamed like other people, old and young; but this, ma'am, has taken a fast hold of me," said Mr. Feltram dejectedly, leaning back in his chair and looking down with his hands in his pockets. "I think, Mrs. Julaper, it is getting into me. I think it's like possession."

"Possession, child! what do you mean?"

"I think there is something trying to influence me. Perhaps it is the way fellows go mad; but it won't let me alone. I've seen it three times, think of that!"

"Well, dear, and what *have* ye seen?" she asked, with an uneasy cheerfulness, smiling, with eyes fixed steadily upon him; for the idea of a madman—even gentle Philip in that state—was not quieting.

"Do you remember the picture, full-length, that had no frame— the lady in the white-satin saque—she was beautiful, *funeste*," he added, talking more to himself; and then more distinctly to Mrs. Julaper again—"in the white-satin saque; and with the little mob cap and blue ribbons to it, and a bouquet in her fingers; that was —that—you know who she was?"

"That was your great-grandmother, my dear," said Mrs. Julaper, lowering her eyes. "It was a dreadful pity it was spoiled. The boys in the pantry had it for a year there on the table for a tray, to wash the glasses on and the like. It was a shame; that was the prettiest picture in the house, with the gentlest, rosiest face."

"It ain't so gentle or rosy now, I can tell you," said Philip. "As fixed as marble; with thin lips, and a curve at the nostril. Do you remember the woman that was found dead in the clough, when I was a boy, that the gipsies murdered, it was thought,—a cruel-looking woman?"

"Agoy! Master Philip, dear! ye would not name that terrible-looking creature with the pretty, fresh, kindly face!"

"Faces change, you see; no matter what she's like; it's her talk that frightens me. She wants to make use of me; and, you see, it is like getting a share in my mind, and a voice in my thoughts, and a command over me gradually; and it is just one idea, as straight as a line of light across the lake—see what she's come to. O Lord, help me!"

"Well, now, don't you be talkin' like that. It is just a little bit dowly and troubled, because the master says a wry word now and then; and so ye let your spirits go down, don't ye see, and all sorts o' fancies comes into your head."

"There's no fancy in my head," he said with a quick look of suspicion; "only you asked me what I dreamed. I don't care if all the world knew. I dreamed I went down a flight of steps under the lake, and got a message. There are no steps near Snakes Island, we all know that," and he laughed chillily. "I'm out of spirits, as you say; and—and—O dear! I wish—Mrs. Julaper—I wish I was in my coffin, and quiet."

"Now that's very wrong of you, Master Philip; you should think of all the blessings you have, and not be makin' mountains o' molehills; and those little bits o' temper Sir Bale shows, why, no one minds 'em—that is, to take 'em to heart like you do, don't ye see?"

"I daresay; I suppose, Mrs. Julaper, you are right. I'm unreasonable often, I know," said gentle Philip Feltram. "I daresay I make too much of it; I'll try. I'm his secretary, and I know I'm not so bright as he is, and it is natural he should sometimes be a little impatient; I ought to be more reasonable, I'm sure. It is all that thing that has been disturbing me—I mean fretting, and, I think, I'm not quite well; and—and letting myself think too much of vexations. It's my own fault, I'm sure, Mrs. Julaper; and I know I'm to blame."

"That's quite right, that's spoken like a wise lad; only I don't say you're to blame, nor no one; for folk can't help frettin' sometimes, no more than they can help a headache—none but a mafflin would say that—and I'll not deny but he has dowly ways when the fit's on him, and he frumps us all round, if such be his humour. But who is there hasn't his faults? We must bear and forbear, and take what we get and be cheerful. So chirp up, my lad; Philip, didn't I often ring the a'd rhyme in your ear long ago?

> Be always as merry as ever you can,
> For no one delights in a sorrowful man.

So don't ye be gettin' up off your chair like that, and tramping about the room wi' your hands in your pockets, looking out o' this window, and staring out o' that, and sighing and crying, and looking so black-ox-trodden, 'twould break a body's heart to see you. Ye must be cheery; and happen you're hungry, and don't know it. I'll tell the cook to grill a hot bit for ye."

"But I'm not hungry, Mrs. Julaper. How kind you are! dear me, Mrs. Julaper, I'm not worthy of it; I don't deserve half your kindness. I'd have been heartbroken long ago, but for you."

"And I'll make a sup of something hot for you; you'll take a rummer-glass of punch—you must."

"But I like the tea better; I do, indeed, Mrs. Julaper."

"Tea is no drink for a man when his heart's down. It should be something with a leg in it, lad; something hot that will warm your courage for ye, and set your blood a-dancing, and make ye talk brave and merry; and will you have a bit of a broil first? No? Well then, you'll have a drop o' punch?—ye sha'n't say no."

And so, all resistance overpowered, the consolation of Philip Feltram proceeded.

A gentler spirit than poor Feltram, a more good-natured soul than the old housekeeper, were nowhere among the children of earth.

Philip Feltram, who was reserved enough elsewhere, used to come into her room and cry, and take her by both hands piteously, standing before her and looking down in her face, while tears ran deviously down his cheeks.

"Did you ever know such a case? was there ever a fellow like *me?* did you ever *know* such a thing? You know what I am, Mrs. Julaper, and who I am. They call me Feltram; but Sir Bale knows as well as I that my true name is not that. I'm Philip Mardykes; and another fellow would make a row about it, and claim his name and his rights, as she is always croaking in my ear I ought. But you know that is not reasonable. My grandmother was married; she was the true Lady Mardykes; *think* what it was to see a woman like that turned out of doors, and her children robbed of their name. O, ma'am, you *can't* think it; unless you were me, you couldn't—you couldn't—you couldn't!"

"Come, come, Master Philip, don't you be taking on so; and ye mustn't be talking like that, d'ye mind? You know he wouldn't stand that; and it's an old story now, and there's naught can be proved concerning it; and what I think is this—I wouldn't wonder the poor lady was beguiled. But anyhow she surely thought she was his lawful wife; and though the law may hev found a flaw somewhere—and I take it 'twas so—yet sure I am she was an honourable lady. But where's the use of stirring that old sorrow? or how can ye prove aught? and the dead hold their peace, you know; dead mice, they say, feels no cold; and dead folks are past fooling. So don't you talk like that; for stone walls have ears, and ye might say that ye couldn't *un*say; and death's day is doom's day. So leave all in the keeping of God; and, above all, never lift hand when ye can't strike."

"Lift my hand! O, Mrs. Julaper, you couldn't think that; you little know me; I did not mean that; I never dreamed of hurting Sir Bale. Good heavens! Mrs. Julaper, you couldn't think *that!* It all comes of my poor impatient temper, and complaining as I do, and my misery; but O, Mrs. Julaper, you could not think I ever meant to trouble him by law, or any other annoyance! I'd like to see a stain removed from my family, and my name restored; but to touch his property, O, no!—O, no! that never entered my mind, by heaven! that never entered my mind, Mrs. Julaper. I'm not cruel; I'm not rapacious; I don't care for money; don't you know that, Mrs. Julaper? O, surely you won't think me capable of attacking the man whose bread I have eaten so long! I never dreamed of it; I should hate myself. Tell me you don't believe it; O, Mrs. Julaper, say you don't!"

And the gentle feeble creature burst into tears and good Mrs. Julaper comforted him with kind words; and he said,

"Thank you, ma'am; thank you. God knows I would not hurt Bale, nor give him one uneasy hour. It is only this: that I'm—I'm so miserable; and I'm only casting in my mind where to turn to, and what to do. So little a thing would be enough, and then I shall leave Mardykes. I'll go; not in any anger, Mrs. Julaper—don't think that; but I can't stay, I must be gone."

"Well, now, there's nothing yet, Master Philip, to fret you like that. You should not be talking so wild-like. Master Bale has his sharp word and his short temper now and again; but I'm sure he likes you. If he didn't, he'd a-said so to me long ago. I'm sure he likes you well."

"Hollo! I say, who's there? Where the devil's Mr. Feltram?" called the voice of the baronet, at a fierce pitch, along the passage.

"La! Mr. Feltram, it's him! Ye'd better run to him," whispered Mrs. Julaper.

"D—n me! does nobody hear? Mrs. Julaper! Hollo! ho! house, there! ho! D—n me, will nobody answer?"

And Sir Bale began to slap the wainscot fast and furiously with his walking-cane with a clatter like a harlequin's lath in a pantomime.

Mrs. Julaper, a little paler than usual, opened her door, and stood with the handle in her hand, making a little curtsey, enframed in the door-case; and Sir Bale, being in a fume, when he saw her, ceased whacking the panels of the corridor, and stamped on the floor, crying,

"Upon my soul, ma'am, I'm glad to see you! Perhaps you can tell me where Feltram is?"

"He is in my room, Sir Bale. Shall I tell him you want him, please?"

"Never mind; thanks," said the Baronet. "I've a tongue in my head;" marching down the passage to the housekeeper's room, with his cane clutched hard, glaring savagely, and with his teeth fast set, like a fellow advancing to beat a vicious horse that has chafed his temper.

CHAPTER VII

The Bank Note

Sir Bale brushed by the housekeeper as he strode into her sanctuary, and there found Philip Feltram awaiting him dejectedly, but with no signs of agitation.

If one were to judge by the appearance the master of Mardykes presented, very grave surmises as to impending violence would have suggested themselves; but though he clutched his cane so hard that it quivered in his grasp, he had no notion of committing the outrage of a blow. The Baronet was unusually angry notwithstanding, and stopping short about three steps away, addressed Feltram with a pale face and gleaming eyes. It was quite plain that there was something very exciting upon his mind.

"I've been looking for you, Mr. Feltram; I want a word or two, if you have done your—your—whatever it is." He whisked the point of his stick towards the modest tea-tray. "I should like five minutes in the library."

The Baronet was all this time eyeing Feltram with a hard suspicious gaze, as if he expected to read in his face the shrinkings and trepidations of guilt; and then turning suddenly on his heel he led the way to his library—a good long march, with a good many turnings. He walked very fast, and was not long in getting

there. And as Sir Bale reached the hearth, on which was smoulder-
ing a great log of wood, and turned about suddenly, facing the
door, Philip Feltram entered.

The Baronet looked oddly and stern—so oddly, it seemed to
Feltram, that he could not take his eyes off him, and returned his
grim and somewhat embarrassed gaze with a stare of alarm and
speculation.

And so doing, his step was shortened, and grew slow and slower,
and came quite to a stop before he had got far from the door—a
wide stretch of that wide floor still intervening between him and
Sir Bale, who stood upon the hearthrug, with his heels together
and his back to the fire, cane in hand, like a drill-sergeant, facing
him.

"Shut that door, please; that will do; come nearer now. I don't
want to bawl what I have to say. Now listen."

The Baronet cleared his voice and paused, with his eyes upon
Feltram.

"It is only two or three days ago," said he, "that you said you
wished you had a hundred pounds. Am I right?"

"Yes; I think so."

"*Think?* you know it, sir, devilish well. You said that you wished
to get away. I have nothing particular to say against that, more
especially now. Do you understand what I say?"

"Understand, Sir Bale? I do, sir—quite."

"I daresay *quite*," he repeated with an angry sneer. "Here, sir, is
an odd coincidence: you want a hundred pounds, and you can't
earn it, and you can't borrow it—there's another way, it seems—
but I have got it—a Bank-of-England note of £100—locked up in
that desk;" and he poked the end of his cane against the brass lock
of it viciously. "There it is, and there are the papers you work at;
and there are two keys—I've got one and you have the other—and
devil another key in or out of the house has any one living. Well,
do you begin to see? Don't mind. I don't want any d——d lying
about it."

Feltram was indeed beginning to see that he was suspected of
something very bad, but exactly what, he was not yet sure; and
being a man of that unhappy temperament which shrinks from
suspicion, as others do from detection, he looked very much put
out indeed.

"Ha, ha! I think we do begin to see," said Sir Bale savagely. "It's
a bore, I know, troubling a fellow with a story that he knows
before; but I'll make mine short. When I take my key, intending
to send the note to pay the crown and quit-rents that you know —

you—you—no matter—you know well enough must be paid, I open it so—and so—and look *there,* where I left it, for my note; and the note's gone—you understand, the note's *gone!"*

Here was a pause, during which, under the Baronet's hard insulting eye, poor Feltram winced, and cleared his voice, and essayed to speak, but said nothing.

"It's gone, and we know where. Now, Mr. Feltram, *I* did not steal that note, and no one but you and I have access to this desk. You wish to go away, and I have no objection to that—but d—n me if you take away that note with you; and you may as well produce it now and here, as hereafter in a worse place."

"O, my good heaven!" exclaimed poor Feltram at last. "I'm very ill."

"So you are, of course. It takes a stiff emetic to get all that money off a fellow's stomach; and it's like parting with a tooth to give up a bank-note. Of course you're ill, but that's no sign of innocence, and I'm no fool. You had better give the thing up quietly."

"May my Maker strike me—"

"So He will, you d—d rascal, if there's justice in heaven, unless you produce the money. I don't want to hang you. I'm willing to let you off if you'll let me, but I'm cursed if I let my note off along with you; and unless you give it up forthwith, I'll get a warrant and have you searched, pockets, bag, and baggage."

"Lord! am I awake?" exclaimed Philip Feltram.

"Wide awake, and so am I," replied Sir Bale. "You don't happen to have got it about you?"

"God forbid, sir! O, Sir—O, Sir Bale—why, Bale, *Bale,* it's impossible! You *can't* believe it. When did I ever wrong you? You know me since I was not higher than the table, and—and—"

He burst into tears.

"Stop your snivelling, sir, and give up the note. You know devilish well I can't spare it; and I won't spare you if you put me to it. I've said my say."

Sir Bale signed towards the door; and like a somnambulist, with dilated gaze and pale as death, Philip Feltram, at his wit's end, went out of the room. It was not till he had again reached the housekeeper's door that he recollected in what direction he was going. His shut hand was pressed with all his force to his heart, and the first breath he was conscious of was a deep wild sob or two that quivered from his heart as he looked from the lobby-window upon a landscape which he did not see.

All he had ever suffered before was mild in comparison with this dire paroxysm. Now, for the first time, was he made acquainted with his real capacity for pain, and how near he might be to madness and yet retain intellect enough to weigh every scruple, and calculate every chance and consequence, in his torture.

Sir Bale, in the meantime, had walked out a little more excited than he would have allowed. He was still convinced that Feltram had stolen the note, but not quite so certain as he had been. There were things in his manner that confirmed, and others that perplexed, Sir Bale.

The Baronet stood upon the margin of the lake, almost under the evening shadow of the house, looking towards Snakes Island. There were two things about Mardykes he specially disliked.

One was Philip Feltram, who, right or wrong, he fancied knew more than was pleasant of his past life.

The other was the lake. It was a beautiful piece of water, his eye, educated at least in the excellences of landscape-painting, acknowledged. But although he could pull a good oar, and liked other lakes, to this particular sheet of water there lurked within him an insurmountable antipathy. It was engendered by a variety of associations.

There is a faculty in man that will acknowledge the unseen. He may scout and scare religion from him; but if he does, superstition perches near. His boding was made-up of omens, dreams, and such stuff as he most affected to despise, and there fluttered at his heart a presentiment and disgust.

His foot was on the gunwale of the boat, that was chained to its ring at the margin; but he would not have crossed that water in it for any reason that man could urge.

What was the mischief that sooner or later was to befall him from that lake, he could not define; but that some fatal danger lurked there, was the one idea concerning it that had possession of his fancy.

He was now looking along its still waters, towards the copse and rocks of Snakes Island, thinking of Philip Feltram; and the yellow level sunbeams touched his dark features, that bore a saturnine resemblance to those of Charles II, and marked sharply their firm grim lines, and left his deep-set eyes in shadow.

Who has the happy gift to seize the present, as a child does, and live in it? Who is not often looking far off for his happiness, as Sidney Smith says, like a man looking for his hat when it is upon his head? Sir Bale was brooding over his double hatred, of Feltram and of the lake. It would have been better had he struck down the raven that croaked upon his shoulder, and listened to the harmless birds that were whistling all round among the branches in the golden sunset.

CHAPTER VIII

Feltram's Plan

This horror of the beautiful lake, which other people thought so lovely, was, in that mind which affected to scoff at the unseen, a distinct creation of downright superstition.

The nursery tales which had scared him in his childhood were founded on the tragedy of Snakes Island, and haunted him with an unavowed persistence still. Strange dreams untold had visited him, and a German conjuror, who had made some strangely successful vaticinations, had told him that his worst enemy would come up to him from a lake. He had heard very nearly the same thing from a fortune-teller in France; and once at Lucerne, when he was waiting alone in his room for the hour at which he had appointed to go upon the lake, all being quiet, there came to the window, which was open, a sunburnt, lean, wicked face. Its ragged owner leaned his arm on the window-frame, and with his head in the room, said in his patois, "Ho! waiting are you? You'll have enough of the lake one day. Don't you mind watching; they'll send when you're wanted;" and twisting his yellow face into a malicious distortion, he went on.

This thing had occurred so suddenly, and chimed-in so oddly with his thoughts, which were at that moment at distant Mardykes and the haunted lake, that it disconcerted him. He laughed, he looked out of the window. He would have given that fellow money to tell him why he said that. But there was no good in looking for the scamp; he was gone.

A memory not preoccupied with that lake and its omens, and a presentiment about himself, would not have noted such things. But *his* mind they touched indelibly; and he was ashamed of his childish slavery, but could not help it.

The foundation of all this had been laid in the nursery, in the winter's tales told by its fireside, and which seized upon his fancy and his fears with a strange congeniality.

There is a large bedroom at Mardykes Hall, which tradition assigns to the lady who had perished tragically in the lake. Mrs. Julaper was sure of it; for her aunt, who died a very old woman twenty years before, remembered the time of the lady's death, and when she grew to woman's estate had opportunity in abundance; for the old people who surrounded her could remember forty years farther back, and tell everything connected with the old house in beautiful Miss Feltram's time.

This large old-fashioned room, commanding a view of Snakes Island, the fells, and the lake—somewhat vast and gloomy, and furnished in a stately old fashion—was said to be haunted, especially when the wind blew from the direction of Golden Friars, the point from which it blew on the night of her death in the lake; or when the sky was overcast, and thunder rolled among the lofty fells, and lightning gleamed on the wide sheet of water.

It was on a night like this that a lady visitor, who long after that event occupied, in entire ignorance of its supernatural character, that large room; and being herself a lady of a picturesque turn, and loving the grander melodrama of Nature, bid her maid leave the shutters open, and watched the splendid effects from her bed, until, the storm being still distant, she fell asleep.

It was travelling slowly across the lake, and it was the deep-mouthed clangour of its near approach that startled her, at dead of night, from her slumber, to witness the same phenomena in the tremendous loudness and brilliancy of their near approach.

At this magnificent spectacle she was looking with the awful ecstasy of an observer in whom the sense of danger is subordinated to that of the sublime, when she saw suddenly at the window a woman, whose long hair and dress seemed drenched with water. She was gazing in with a look of terror, and was shaking the sash of the window with vehemence. Having stood there for a few seconds, and before the lady, who beheld all this from her bed, could make up her mind what to do, the storm-beaten figure, wringing her hands, seemed to throw herself backward, and was gone.

Possessed with the idea that she had seen some poor woman overtaken in the storm, who, failing to procure admission there, had gone round to some of the many doors of the mansion, and obtained an entry there, she again fell asleep.

It was not till the morning, when she went to her window to look out upon the now tranquil scene, that she discovered what, being a stranger to the house, she had quite forgotten, that this room was at a great height—some thirty feet—from the ground.

Another story was that of good old Mr. Randal Rymer, who was often a visitor at the house in the late Lady Mardykes' day. In his youth he had been a campaigner; and now that he was a preacher he maintained his hardy habits, and always slept, summer and winter, with a bit of his window up. Being in that room in his bed, and after a short sleep lying awake, the moon shining softly through the window, there passed by that aperture into the room a figure dressed, it seemed to him, in gray that was nearly white. It passed straight to the hearth, where was an expiring wood fire; and cowering over it with outstretched hands, it appeared to be gathering what little heat was to be had. Mr. Rymer, amazed and awestruck, made a movement in his bed; and the figure looked round, with large eyes that in the moonlight looked like melting snow, and stretching its long arms up the chimney, they and the figure itself seemed to blend with the smoke, and so pass up and away.

Sir Bale, I have said, did not like Feltram. His father, Sir William, had left a letter creating a trust, it was said, in favour of Philip Feltram. The document had been found with the will, addressed to Sir Bale in the form of a letter.

"That is mine," said the Baronet, when it dropped out of the will; and he slipped it into his pocket, and no one ever saw it after.

But Mr. Charles Twyne, the attorney of Golden Friars, whenever he got drunk, which was pretty often, used to tell his friends with a grave wink that he knew a thing or two about that letter. It gave Philip Feltram two hundred a-year, charged on Harfax. It was only a direction. It made Sir Bale a trustee, however; and having made away with the "letter," the Baronet had been robbing Philip Feltram ever since.

Old Twyne was cautious, even in his cups, in his choice of an audience, and was a little enigmatical in his revelations. For he was afraid of Sir Bale, though he hated him for employing a lawyer who lived seven miles away, and was a rival. So people were not quite sure whether Mr. Twyne was telling lies or truth, and the principal fact that corroborated his story was Sir Bale's manifest hatred of his secretary. In fact, Sir Bale's retaining him in his house, detesting him as he seemed to do, was not easily to be accounted for, except on the principle of a tacit compromise—a miserable compensation for having robbed him of his rights.

The battle about the bank-note proceeded. Sir Bale certainly had doubts, and vacillated; for moral evidence made powerfully in favour of poor Feltram, though the evidence of circumstance made as powerfully against him. But Sir Bale admitted suspicion easily, and in weighing probabilities would count a virtue very lightly against temptation and opportunity; and whatever his doubts might sometimes be, he resisted and quenched them, and never let that ungrateful scoundrel Philip Feltram so much as suspect their existence.

For two days Sir Bale had not spoken to Feltram. He passed by on stair and passage, carrying his head high, and with a thundrous countenance, rolling conclusions and revenges in his soul.

Poor Feltram all this time existed in one long agony. He would have left Mardykes, were it not that he looked vaguely to some just power—to chance itself—against this hideous imputation. To go with this indictment ringing in his ears, would amount to a confession and flight.

Mrs. Julaper consoled him with might and main. She was a sympathetic and trusting spirit, and knew poor Philip Feltram, in her simplicity, better than the shrewdest profligate on earth could have known him. She cried with him in his misery. She was fired with indignation by these suspicions, and still more at what followed.

Sir Bale showed no signs of relenting. It might have been that he was rather glad of so unexceptionable an opportunity of getting rid of Feltram, who, people thought, knew something which it galled the Baronet's pride that he should know.

The Baronet had another shorter and sterner interview with Feltram in his study. The result was, that unless he restored the missing note before ten o'clock next morning, he should leave Mardykes.

To leave Mardykes was no more than Philip Feltram, feeble as he was of will, had already resolved. But what was to become of him? He did not very much care, if he could find any calling, however humble, that would just give him bread.

There was an old fellow and his wife (an ancient dame,) who lived at the other side of the lake, on the old territories of the Feltrams, and who, from some tradition of loyalty, perhaps, were fond of poor Philip Feltram. They lived somewhat high up on the fells—about as high as trees would grow—and those which were clumped about their rude dwelling were nearly the last you passed in your ascent of the mountain. These people had a multitude of sheep and goats, and lived in their airy solitude a pastoral and simple life, and were childless. Philip Feltram was hardy and active, having passed his early days among that arduous scenery. Cold and rain did not trouble him; and these people being wealthy in their way, and loving him, would be glad to find him employment of that desultory pastoral kind which would best suit him.

This vague idea was the only thing resembling a plan in his mind.

When Philip Feltram came to Mrs. Julaper's room, and told her that he had made up his mind to leave the house forthwith—to cross the lake to the Cloostedd side in Tom Marlin's boat, and then to make his way up the hill alone to Trebeck's lonely farmstead, Mrs. Julaper was overwhelmed.

"Ye'll do no such thing to-night, anyhow. You're not to go like that. Ye'll come into the small room here, where he can't follow; and we'll sit down and talk it over a bit, and ye'll find 'twill all come straight; and this will be no night, anyhow, for such a march. Why, man, 'twould take an hour and more to cross the lake, and then a long uphill walk before ye could reach Trebeck's place; and if the night should fall while you were still on the mountain, ye might lose your life among the rocks. It can't be 'tis come to that yet; and the call was in the air, I'm told, all yesterday, and distant thunder to-day, travelling this way over Blarwyn Fells; and 'twill be a night no one will be out, much less on the mountain side."

CHAPTER IX

The Crazy Parson

Mrs. Julaper had grown weather-wise, living for so long among this noble and solitary scenery, where people must observe Nature or else nothing—where signs of coming storm or change are almost local, and record themselves on particular cliffs and mountain-peaks, or in the mists, or in mirrored tints of the familiar lake, and are easily learned or remembered. At all events, her presage proved too true.

The sun had set an hour and more. It was dark; and an awful thunder-storm, whose march, like the distant reverberations of an invading army, had been faintly heard beyond the barriers of Blarwyn Fells throughout the afternoon, was near them now, and had burst in deep-mouthed battle among the ravines at the other side, and over the broad lake, that glared like a sheet of burnished steel under its flashes of dazzling blue. Wild and fitful blasts sweeping down the hollows and cloughs of the fells of Golden Friars agitated the lake, and bent the trees low, and whirled away their sere leaves in melancholy drift in their tremendous gusts. And from the window, looking on a scene enveloped in more than the darkness of the night, you saw in the pulsations of the lightning, before "the speedy gleams the darkness swallowed," the tossing trees and the flying foam and eddies on the lake.

In the midst of the hurlyburly, a loud and long knocking came at the hall-door of Mardykes. How long it had lasted before a chance lull made it audible I do not know.

There was nothing picturesquely poor, any more than there were evidences of wealth, anywhere in Sir Bale Mardykes' household. He had no lack of servants, but they were of an inexpensive and homely sort; and the hall-door being opened by the son of an old tenant on the estate—the tempest beating on the other side of the house, and comparative shelter under the gables at the front— he saw standing before him, in the agitated air, a thin old man, who muttering, it might be, a benediction, stepped into the hall, and displayed long silver tresses, just as the storm had blown them, ascetic and eager features, and a pair of large light eyes that wandered wildly. He was dressed in threadbare black; a pair of long leather gaiters, buckled high above his knee, protecting his thin shanks through moss and pool; and the singularity of his appearance was heightened by a wide-leafed felt hat, over which he had tied his handkerchief, so as to bring the leaf of it over his ears, and to secure it from being whirled from his head by the storm.

This odd and storm-beaten figure—tall, and a little stooping, as well as thin—was not unknown to the servant, who saluted him with something of fear as well as of respect as he bid him reverently welcome, and asked him to come in and sit by the fire.

"Get you to your master, and tell him I have a message to him from one he has not seen for two-and-forty years."

As the old man, with his harsh old voice, thus spoke, he unknotted his handkerchief and bet the rain-drops from his hat upon his knee.

The servant knocked at the library-door, where he found Sir Bale.

"Well, what's the matter?" cried Sir Bale sharply, from his chair before the fire, with angry eyes looking over his shoulder.

"Here's 't sir cumman, Sir Bale," he answered.

"Sir," or "the Sir," is still used as the clergyman's title in the Northumbrian counties.

"What sir?"

"Sir Hugh Creswell, if you please, Sir Bale."

"Ho!—mad Creswell?—O, the crazy parson. Well, tell Mrs.

Julaper to let him have some supper—and—and to let him have a bed in some suitable place. That's what he wants. These mad fellows know what they are about."

"No, Sir Bale Mardykes, that is not what he wants," said the loud wild voice of the daft sir over the servant's shoulder. "Often has Mardykes Hall given me share of its cheer and its shelter and the warmth of its fire; and I bless the house that has been an inn to the wayfarer of the Lord. But to-night I go up the lake to Pindar's Bield, three miles on; and there I rest and refresh—not here."

"And why not *here*, Mr. Creswell?" asked the Baronet; for about this crazy old man, who preached in the fields, and appeared and disappeared so suddenly in the orbit of his wide and unknown perambulations of those northern and border counties, there was that sort of superstitious feeling which attaches to the mysterious and the good—an idea that it was lucky to harbour and dangerous to offend him. No one knew whence he came or whither he went. Once in a year, perhaps, he might appear at a lonely farmstead door among the fells, salute the house, enter, and be gone in the morning. His life was austere; his piety enthusiastic, severe, and tinged with the craze which inspired among the rustic population a sort of awe.

"I'll not sleep at Mardykes to-night; neither will I eat, nor drink, nor sit me down—no, nor so much as stretch my hands to the fire. As the man of God came out of Judah to king Jeroboam, so come I to you, sent by a vision, to bear a warning; and as he said, 'If thou wilt give me half thy house, I will not go in with thee, neither will I eat bread nor drink water in this place,' so also say I."

"Do as you please," said Sir Bale, a little sulkily. "Say your say; and you are welcome to stay or go, if go you will on so mad a night as this."

"Leave us," said Creswell, beckoning the servant back with his thin hands; "what I have to say is to your master."

The servant went, in obedience to a gesture from Sir Bale, and shut the door.

The old man drew nearer to the Baronet, and lowering his loud stern voice a little, and interrupting his discourse from time to time, to allow the near thunder-peals to subside, he said,

"Answer me, Sir Bale—what is this that has chanced between you and Philip Feltram?"

The Baronet, under the influence of that blunt and peremptory demand, told him shortly and sternly enough.

"And of all these facts you are sure, else ye would not blast your early companion and kinsman with the name of thief?"

"I *am* sure," said Sir Bale grimly.

"Unlock that cabinet," said the old man with the long white locks.

"I've no objection," said Sir Bale; and he did unlock an old oak cabinet that stood, carved in high relief with strange figures and gothic grotesques, against the wall, opposite the fireplace. On opening it there were displayed a system of little drawers and pigeon-holes such as we see in more modern escritoires.

"Open that drawer with the red mark of a seal upon it," continued Hugh Creswell, pointing to it with his lank finger.

Sir Bale did so; and to his momentary amazement, and even consternation, there lay the missing note, which now, with one of those sudden caprices of memory which depend on the laws of suggestion and association, he remembered having placed there with his own hand.

"That is it," said old Creswell with a pallid smile, and fixing his wild eyes on the Baronet. The smile subsided into a frown, and said he: "Last night I slept near Haworth Moss; and your father came to me in a dream, and said: 'My son Bale accuses Philip of having stolen a bank-note from his desk. He forgets that he himself placed it in his cabinet. Come with me.' I was, in the spirit, in this room; and he led me to this cabinet, which he opened; and in that drawer he showed me that note. 'Go,' said he, 'and tell him to ask Philip Feltram's pardon, else he will but go in weakness to return in power;' and he said that which it is not lawful to repeat. My message is told. Now a word from myself," he added sternly. "The dead, through my lips, has spoken, and under God's thunder and lightning his words have found ye. Why so uppish wi' Philip Feltram? See how ye threaped, and yet were wrong. He's no tazzle —he's no taggelt. Ask his pardon. Ye must change, or he will change. Go, in weakness, come in power: mark ye the words. 'Twill make a peal that will be heard in toon and desert, in the swirls o' the mountain, through pikes and valleys, and mak' a waaly man o' thee."

The old man with these words, uttered in the broad northern dialect of his common speech, strode from the room and shut the door. In another minute he was forth into the storm, pursuing what remained of his long march to Pindar's Bield.

"Upon my soul!" said Sir Bale, recovering from his sort of stun which the sudden and strange visit had left, "that's a cool old fellow! Come to rate me and teach me my own business in my own house!" and he rapped out a fierce oath. "Change his mind or no, here he sha'n't stay to-night—not an hour."

Sir Bale was in the lobby in a moment, and thundered to his servants:

"I say, put that fool out of the door—put him out by the shoulder, and never let him put his foot inside it more!"

But the old man's yea was yea, and his nay nay. He had quite meant what he said; and, as I related, was beyond the reach of the indignity of extrusion.

Sir Bale on his return shut his door as violently as if it were in the face of the old prophet.

"Ask Feltram's pardon, by Jove! For what? Why, any jury on earth would have hanged him on half the evidence; and I, like a fool, was going to let him off with his liberty and my hundred pound-note! Ask his pardon indeed!"

Still there were misgivings in his mind; a consciousness that he did owe explanation and apology to Feltram, and an insurmountable reluctance to undertake either. The old dislike—a contempt mingled with fear—not any fear of his malevolence, a fear only of his carelessness and folly; for, as I have said, Feltram knew many things, it was believed, of the Baronet's Continental and Asiatic life, and had even gently remonstrated with him upon the dangers into which he was running. A simple fellow like Philip Feltram is a dangerous depository of a secret. This Baronet was proud, too; and the mere possession of his secrets by Feltram was an involuntary insult, which Sir Bale could not forgive. He wished him far away; and except for the recovery of his bank-note, which he could ill spare, he was sorry that this suspicion was cleared up.

The thunder and storm were unabated; it seemed indeed that they were growing wilder and more awful.

He opened the window-shutter and looked out upon that sublimest of scenes; and so intense and magnificent were its phenomena, that Sir Bale, for a while, was absorbed in this contemplation.

When he turned about, the sight of his £100 note, still between his finger and thumb, made him smile grimly.

The more he thought of it, the clearer it was that he could not leave matters exactly as they were. Well, what should he do? He would send for Mrs. Julaper, and tell her vaguely that he had changed his mind about Feltram, and that he might continue to stay at Mardykes Hall as usual. That would suffice. She could speak to Feltram.

He sent for her; and soon, in the lulls of the great uproar without, he could hear the jingle of Mrs. Julaper's keys and her light tread upon the lobby.

"Mrs. Julaper," said the Baronet, in his dry careless way, "Feltram may remain; your eloquence has prevailed. What have you been crying about?" he asked, observing that his housekeeper's usually cheerful face was, in her own phrase, 'all cried.'

"It is too late, sir; he's gone."

"And when did he go?" asked Sir Bale, a little put out. "He chose an odd evening, didn't he? So like him!"

"He went about half an hour ago; and I'm very sorry, sir; it's a sore sight to see the poor lad going from the place he was reared in, and a hard thing, sir; and on such a night, above all."

"No one asked him to go to-night. Where is he gone to?"

"I don't know, I'm sure; he left my room, sir, when I was up-stairs; and Janet saw him pass the window not ten minutes after Mr. Creswell left the house."

"Well, then, there's no good, Mrs. Julaper, in thinking more about it; he has settled the matter his own way; and as he so ordains it—amen, say I. Goodnight."

CHAPTER X

Adventure in Tom Marlin's Boat

Philip Feltram was liked very well—a gentle, kindly, and very timid creature, and, before he became so heart-broken, a fellow who liked a joke or a pleasant story, and could laugh heartily. Where will Sir Bale find so unresisting and respectful a butt and retainer? and whom will he bully now?

Something like remorse was worrying Sir Bale's heart a little; and the more he thought on the strange visit of Hugh Creswell that night, with its unexplained menace, the more uneasy he became.

The storm continued; and even to him there seemed something exaggerated and inhuman in the severity of his expulsion on such a night. It was his own doing, it was true; but would people believe that? and would he have thought of leaving Mardykes at all if it had not been for his kinsman's severity? Nay, was it not certain that if Sir Bale had done as Hugh Creswell had urged him, and sent for Feltram forthwith, and told him how all had been cleared up, and been a little friendly with him, he would have found him still in the house?—for he had not yet gone for ten minutes after Creswell's departure, and thus, all that was to follow might have been averted. But it was too late now, and Sir Bale would let the affair take its own course.

Below him, outside the window at which he stood ruminating, he heard voices mingling with the storm. He could with tolerable certainty perceive, looking into the obscurity, that there were three men passing close under it, carrying some very heavy burden among them.

He did not know what these three black figures in the obscurity were about. He saw them pass round the corner of the building toward the front, and in the lulls of the storm could hear their gruff voices talking.

We have all experienced what a presentiment is, and we all know with what an intuition the faculty of observation is sometimes heightened. It was such an apprehension as sometimes gives its peculiar horror to a dream—a sort of knowledge that what those people were about was in a dreadful way connected with his own fate.

He watched for a time, thinking that they might return; but they did not. He was in a state of uncomfortable suspense.

"If they want me, they won't have much trouble in finding me, nor any scruple, egad, in plaguing me; they never have."

Sir Bale returned to his letters, a score of which he was that night getting off his conscience—an arrear which would not have troubled him had he not ceased, for two or three days, altogether to employ Philip Feltram, who had been accustomed to take all that sort of drudgery off his hands.

All the time he was writing now he had a feeling that the shadows he had seen pass under his window were machinating some trouble for him, and an uneasy suspense made him lift his eyes now and then to the door, fancying sounds and footsteps; and after a resultless wait he would say to himself, "If any one is coming, why the devil don't he come?" and then he would apply himself again to his letters.

But on a sudden he heard good Mrs. Julaper's step trotting along the lobby, and the tiny ringing of her keys.

Here was news coming; and the Baronet stood up looking at the door, on which presently came a hurried rapping; and before he had answered, in the midst of a long thunder-clap that suddenly broke, rattling over the house, the good woman opened the door in great agitation, and cried with a tremulous uplifting of her hands,

"O, Sir Bale! O, la, sir! here's poor dear Philip Feltram come home dead!"

Sir Bale stared at her sternly for some seconds.

"Come, now, do be distinct," said Sir Bale; "what has happened?"

"He's lying on the sofer in the old still-room. You never saw— my God!—O, sir—what is life?"

"D—n it, can't you cry by-and-by, and tell me what's the matter *now?*"

"A bit o' fire there, as luck would have it; but what is hot or cold now? La, sir, they're all doin' what they can; he's drowned, sir, and Tom Warren is on the gallop down to Golden Friars for Doctor Torvey."

"*Is* he drowned, or is it only a ducking? Come, bring me to the place. Dead men don't usually want a fire, or consult doctors. I'll see for myself."

So Sir Bale Mardykes, pale and grim, accompanied by the light-footed Mrs. Julaper, strode along the passages, and was led by her into the old still-room, which had ceased to be used for its original purpose. All the servants in the house were now collected there, and three men also who lived by the margin of the lake; one of them thoroughly drenched, with rivulets of water still trickling from his sleeves, water along the wrinkles and pockets of his waist-coat and from the feet of his trousers, and pumping and oozing from his shoes, and streaming from his hair down the channels of his cheeks like a continuous rain of tears.

The people drew back a little as Sir Bale entered with a quick step and a sharp pallid frown on his face. There was a silence as he stooped over Philip Feltram, who lay on a low bed next the wall, dimly lighted by two or three candles here and there about the room.

He laid his hand, for a moment, on his cold wet breast.

Sir Bale knew what should be done in order to give a man in such a case his last chance for life. Everybody was speedily put in motion. Philip's drenched clothes were removed, hot blankets enveloped him, warming-pans and hot bricks lent their aid; he was placed at the prescribed angle, so that the water flowed freely from his mouth. The old expedient for inducing artificial breathing was employed, and a lusty pair of bellows did duty for his lungs.

But these helps to life, and suggestions to nature, availed not. Forlorn and peaceful lay the features of poor Philip Feltram; cold and dull to the touch; no breath through the blue lips; no sight in the fish-like eyes; pulseless and cold in the midst of all the hot bricks and warming-pans about him.

At length, everything having been tried, Sir Bale, who had been directing, placed his hand within the clothes, and laid it silently on Philip's shoulder and over his heart; and after a little wait, he shook his head, and looking down on his sunken face, he said,

"I am afraid he's gone. Yes, he's gone, poor fellow! And bear you this in mind, all of you; Mrs. Julaper there can tell you more about it. She knows that it was certainly in no compliance with my wish that he left the house to-night: it was his own obstinate perversity, and perhaps—I forgive him for it—a wish in his unreasonable resentment to throw some blame upon this house, as having refused him shelter on such a night; than which imputation nothing can be more utterly false. Mrs. Julaper there knows how welcome he was to stay the night; but he would not; he had made up his mind, it seems, without telling any person. Had he told you, Mrs. Julaper?"

"No, sir," sobbed Mrs. Julaper from the centre of a pocket-handkerchief in which her face was buried.

"Not a human being: an angry whim of his own. Poor Feltram! and here's the result," said the Baronet. "We have done our best—done everything. I don't think the doctor, when he comes, will say that anything has been omitted; but all won't do. Does any one here know how it happened?"

Two men knew very well—the man who had been ducked, and his companion, a younger man, who was also in the still-room, and had lent a hand in carrying Feltram up to the house.

Tom Marlin had a queer old stone tenement by the edge of the lake just under Mardykes Hall. Some people said it was the stump of an old tower that had once belonged to Mardykes Castle, of which in the modern building scarcely a relic was discoverable.

This Tom Marlin had an ancient right of fishing in the lake, where he caught pike enough for all Golden Friars; and keeping a couple of boats, he made money beside by ferrying passengers over now and then. This fellow, with a furrowed face and shaggy eyebrows, bald at top, but with long grizzled locks falling upon his shoulders, said,

"He wer wi' me this mornin', sayin' he'd want t' boat to cross the lake in, but he didn't say what hour; and when it came on to thunder and blow like this, ye guess I did not look to see him to-night. Well, my wife was just lightin' a pig-tail—tho' light enough and to spare there was in the lift already—when who should come clatterin' at the latch-pin in the blow o' thunder and wind but Philip, poor lad, himself; and an ill hour for him it was. He's been some time in ill fettle, though he was never frowsy, not he, but always kind and dooce, and canty once, like anither; and he asked me to tak the boat across the lake at once to the Clough o' Cloostedd at t'other side. The woman took the pet and wodn't hear o't; and, 'Dall me, if I go to-night,' quoth I. But he would not be put off so, not he; and dingdrive he went to it, cryin' and putrein' ye'd a-said, poor fellow, he was wrang i' his garrets a'most. So at long last I bethought me, there's nout o' a sea to the north o' Snakes Island, so I'll pull him by that side—for the storm is blowin' right up by Golden Friars, ye mind—and when we get near the point, thinks I, he'll see wi' his een how the lake is, and gie it up. For I liked him, poor lad; and seein' he'd set his heart on't, I wouldn't vex nor frump him wi' a no. So down we three—myself, and Bill there, and Philip Feltram—come to the boat; and we pulled out, keeping Snakes Island atwixt us and the wind. 'Twas smooth water wi' us, for 'twas a scug there, but white enough was all beyont the point; and passing the finger-stone, not forty fathom from the shore o' the island, Bill and me pullin' and he sittin' in the stern, poor lad, up he rises, a bit rabblin' to himself, wi' his hands lifted so.

" 'Look a-head!' says I, thinkin' something wos comin' atort us.

"But 'twasn't that. The boat was quiet, for while we looked, oo'er our shouthers, oo'er her bows, we didn't pull, so she lay still; and lookin' back again on Philip, he was rabblin' on all the same.

" 'It's nobbut a prass wi' himsel', poor lad,' thinks I.

"But that wasn't it neither; for I sid something white come out o' t' water, by the gunwale, like a hand. By Jen! and he leans oo'er and tuk it; and he sagged like, and so it drew him in, under the mere, before I cud du nout. There was nout to thraa tu him, and no time; down he went, and I followed; and thrice I dived before I found him, and brought him up by the hair at last; and there he is, poor lad! and all one if he lay at the bottom o' t' mere."

As Tom Marlin ended his narrative—often interrupted by the noise of the tempest without, and the peals of thunder that echoed awfully above, like the chorus of a melancholy ballad—the sudden clang of the hall-door bell, and a more faintly-heard knocking, announced a new arrival.

"I sid something white come out o' t' water, by the gunwale, like a hand."

CHAPTER XI

Sir Bale's Dream

It was Doctor Torvey who entered the old still-room now, but-toned-up to the chin in his greatcoat, and with a muffler of many colours wrapped partly over that feature.

"Well!—hey? So poor Feltram's had an accident?"

The Doctor was addressing Sir Bale, and getting to the bedside as he pulled off his gloves.

"I see you've been keeping him warm—that's right; and a considerable flow of water from his mouth; turn him a little that way. Hey? O, ho!" said the Doctor, as he placed his hand upon Philip, and gently stirred his limbs. "It's more than an hour since this happened. I'm afraid there's very little to be done now;" and in a lower tone, with his hand on poor Philip Feltram's arm, and so down to his fingers, he said in Sir Bale Mardykes' ear, with a shake of his head,

"Here, you see, poor fellow, here's the cadaveric stiffness; it's very melancholy, but it's all over, he's gone; there's no good trying any more. Come here, Mrs. Julaper. Did you ever see any one dead? Look at his eyes, look at his mouth. You ought to have known that, with half an eye. And you know," he added again confidentially in Sir Bale's ear, "trying any more *now* is all my eye."

Then after a few more words with the Baronet, and having heard his narrative, he said from time to time, "Quite right; nothing could be better; capital practice, sir," and so forth. And at the close of all this, amid the sobs of kind Mrs. Julaper and the general whimpering of the humbler handmaids, the Doctor standing by the bed, with his knuckles on the coverlet, and a glance now and then on the dead face beside him, said—by way of 'quieting men's minds,' as the old tract-writers used to say—a few words to the following effect:

"Everything has been done here that the most experienced physician could have wished. Everything has been done in the best way. I don't know anything that has not been done, in fact. If I had been here myself, I don't know—hot bricks—salt isn't a bad thing. I don't know, I say, that anything of any consequence has been omitted." And looking at the body, "You see," and he drew the fingers a little this way and that, letting them return, as they stiffly did, to their former attitude, "you may be sure that the poor gentleman was quite dead by the time he arrived here. So, since he was laid there, nothing has been lost by delay. And, Sir Bale, if you have any directions to send to Golden Friars, sir, I shall be most happy to undertake your message."

"Nothing, thanks; it is a melancholy ending, poor fellow! You must come to the study with me, Doctor Torvey, and talk a little bit more; and—very sad, doctor—and you must have a glass of sherry, or some port—the port used not to be bad here; I don't take it—but very melancholy it is—bring some port and sherry; and, Mrs. Julaper, you'll be good enough to see that everything that should be done here is looked to; and let Marlin and the men have supper and something to drink. You have been too long in your wet clothes, Marlin."

So, with gracious words all round, he led the Doctor to the library where he had been sitting, and was affable and hospitable, and told him his own version of all that had passed between him and Philip Feltram, and presented himself in an amiable point of view, and pleased the Doctor with his port and flatteries—for he could not afford to lose anyone's good word just now; and the Doctor was a bit of a gossip, and in most houses in that region, in one character or another, every three months in the year.

So in due time the Doctor drove back to Golden Friars, with a high opinion of Sir Bale, and higher still of his port, and highest of all of himself: in the best possible humour with the world, not minding the storm that blew in his face, and which he defied in good-humoured mock-heroics spoken in somewhat thick accents, and regarding the thunder and lightning as a lively gala of fire-works; and if there had been a chance of finding his cronies still in the George and Dragon, he would have been among them forth-with, to relate the tragedy of the night, and tell what a good fellow, after all, Sir Bale was; and what a fool, at best, poor Philip Feltram.

But the George was quiet for that night. The thunder rolled over voiceless chambers; and the lights had been put out within the windows, on whose multitudinous small panes the lightning glared. So the Doctor went home to Mrs. Torvey, whom he charmed into good-humoured curiosity by the tale of wonder he had to relate.

Sir Bale's qualms were symptomatic of something a little less sublime and more selfish than conscience. He was not sorry that Philip Feltram was out of the way. His lips might begin to babble inconveniently at any time, and why should not his mouth be stopped? and what stopper so effectual as that plug of clay which fate had introduced? But he did not want to be charged with the odium of the catastrophe. Every man cares something for the opinion of his fellows. And seeing that Feltram had been well liked, and that his death had excited a vehement commiseration, Sir Bale did not wish it to be said that he had made the house too hot to hold him, and had so driven him to extremity.

Sir Bale's first agitation had subsided. It was now late, he had written many letters, and he was tired. It was not wonderful, then, that having turned his lounging-chair to the fire, he should have fallen asleep in it, as at last he did.

The storm was passing gradually away by this time. The thunder was now echoing among the distant glens and gorges of Daulness Fells, and the angry roar and gusts of the tempest were subsiding into the melancholy soughing and piping that soothe like a lullaby.

Sir Bale therefore had his unpremeditated sleep very comfortably, except that his head was hanging a little uneasily; which, perhaps, helped him to this dream.

It was one of those dreams in which the continuity of the waking state that immediately preceded it seems unbroken; for he thought that he was sitting in the chair which he occupied, and in the room where he actually was. It seemed to him that he got up, took a candle in his hand, and went through the passages to the old still-room where Philip Feltram lay. The house seemed perfectly still. He could hear the chirp of the crickets faintly from the distant kitchen, and the tick of the clock sounded loud and hollow along the passage. In the old still-room, as he opened the door, was no light, except what was admitted from the candle he carried. He found the body of poor Philip Feltram just as he had left it—his gentle face, saddened by the touch of death, was turned upwards, with white lips: with traces of suffering fixed in its outlines, such as caused Sir Bale, standing by the bed, to draw the coverlet over the dead man's features, which seemed silently to upbraid him. "Gone in weakness!" said Sir Bale, repeating the words of the "daft sir," Hugh Creswell; as he did so, a voice whispered near him, with a great sigh, "Come in power!" He looked round, in his dream, but there was no one; the light seemed to fail, and a horror slowly overcame him, especially as he thought he saw the figure under the coverlet stealthily beginning to move. Backing towards the door, for he could not take his eyes off it, he saw something like a huge black ape creep out at the foot of the bed; and springing at him, it griped him by the throat, so that he could not breathe; and a thousand voices were instantly round him, holloaing, cursing, laughing in his ears; and in this direful plight he waked.

Was it the ring of those voices still in his ears, or a real shriek, and another, and a long peal, shriek after shriek, swelling madly through the distant passages, that held him still, freezing in the horror of his dream?

I will tell you what this noise was.

CHAPTER XII

Marcella Bligh and Judith Wale Keep Watch

After his bottle of port with Sir Bale, the Doctor had gone down again to the room where poor Philip Feltram lay.

Mrs. Julaper had dried her eyes, and was busy by this time; and two old women were making all their arrangements for a night-watch by the body, which they had washed, and, as their phrase goes, 'laid out' in the humble bed where it had lain while there was still a hope that a spark sufficient to rekindle the fire of life might remain. These old women had points of resemblance: they were lean, sallow, and wonderfully wrinkled, and looked each malign and ugly enough for a witch.

Marcella Bligh's thin hooked nose was now like the beak of a bird of prey over the face of the drowned man, upon whose eyelids she was placing penny-pieces, to keep them from opening; and her one eye was fixed on her work, its sightless companion showing white in its socket, with an ugly leer.

Judith Wale was lifting the pail of hot water with which they had just washed the body. She had long lean arms, a hunched back, a great sharp chin sunk on her hollow breast, and small eyes restless as a ferret's; and she clattered about in great bowls of shoes, old and clouted, that were made for a foot as big as two of hers.

The Doctor knew these two old women, who were often employed in such dismal offices.

"How does Mrs. Bligh? See me with half an eye? Hey—that's rhyme, isn't it?—And, Judy lass—why, I thought you lived nearer the town—here making poor Mr. Feltram's last toilet. You have helped to dress many a poor fellow for his last journey. Not a bad notion of drill either—they stand at attention stiff and straight enough in the sentry-box. Your recruits do you credit, Mrs. Wale."

The Doctor stood at the foot of the bed to inspect, breathing forth a vapour of very fine old port, his hands in his pockets, speaking with a lazy thickness, and looking so comfortable and facetious, that Mrs. Julaper would have liked to turn him out of the room.

But the Doctor was not unkind, only extremely comfortable. He was a good-natured fellow, and had thought and care for the living, but not a great deal of sentiment for the dead, whom he had looked in the face too often to be much disturbed by the spectacle.

"You'll have to keep that bandage on. You should be sharp; you should know all about it, girl, by this time, and not let those muscles stiffen. I need not tell you the mouth shuts as easily as this snuff-box, if you only take it in time.—I suppose, Mrs. Julaper, you'll send to Jos Fringer for the poor fellow's outfit. Fringer is a very proper man—there ain't a properer und-aker in England. I always re-mmend Fringer—in Church-street in Golden Friars. You know Fringer, I daresay."

"I can't say, sir, I'm sure. That will be as Sir Bale may please to direct," answered Mrs. Julaper.

"You've got him very straight—straighter than I thought you could; but the large joints were not so stiff. A very little longer wait, and you'd hardly have got him into his coffin. He'll want a vr-r-ry long one, poor lad. Short cake is life, ma'am. Sad thing this. They'll open their eyes, I promise you, down in the town. 'Twill be cool enough, I'd shay, affre all th-thunr-thunnle, you know. I think I'll take a nip, Mrs. Jool-fr, if you wouldn't mine makin' me out a thimmle-ful bran-band-bran-rand-andy, eh, Mishs Joolfr?"

And the Doctor took a chair by the fire; and Mrs. Julaper, with a dubious conscience and dry hospitality, procured the brandy-flask and wine-glass, and helped the physician in a thin hesitating stream, which left him ample opportunity to cry "Hold—enough!" had he been so minded. But that able physician had no confidence, it would seem, in any dose under a bumper, which he sipped with commendation, and then fell asleep with the firelight on his face —to tender-hearted Mrs. Julaper's disgust—and snored with a sensual disregard of the solemnity of his situation; until with a profound nod, or rather dive, toward the fire, he awoke, got up and shook his ears with a kind of start, and standing with his back to the fire, asked for his muffler and horse; and so took his leave also of the weird sisters, who were still pottering about the body, with croak and whisper, and nod and ogle. He took his leave also of good Mrs. Julaper, who was completing arrangements with teapot and kettle, spiced elderberry wine, and other comforts, to support them through their proposed vigil. And finally, in a sort of way, he took his leave of the body, with a long business-like stare, from the foot of the bed, with his short hands stuffed into his pockets.

And so, to Mrs. Julaper's relief, this unseemly doctor, speaking thickly, departed.

And now, the Doctor being gone, and all things prepared for the 'wake' to be observed by withered Mrs. Bligh of the one eye, and yellow Mrs. Wale of the crooked back, the house grew gradually still. The thunder had by this time died into the solid boom of distant battle, and the fury of the gale had subsided to the long sobbing wail that is charged with so eerie a melancholy. Within all was stirless, and the two old women, each a 'Mrs.' by courtesy, who had not much to thank Nature or the world for, sad and cynical, and in a sort outcasts told off by fortune to these sad and grizzly services, sat themselves down by the fire, each perhaps feeling unusually at home in the other's society; and in this soured and forlorn comfort, trimming their fire, quickening the song of the kettle to a boil, and waxing polite and chatty; each treating the other with that deprecatory and formal courtesy which invites a return in kind, and both growing strangely happy in this little world of their own, in the unusual and momentary sense of an importance and consideration which were delightful.

The old still-room of Mardykes Hall is an oblong room wainscoted. From the door you look its full length to the wide stone-shafted Tudor window at the other end. At your left is the ponderous mantelpiece, supported by two spiral stone pillars; and close to the door at the right was the bed in which the two crones had just stretched poor Philip Feltram, who lay as still as an uncoloured wax-work, with a heavy penny-piece on each eye, and a bandage under his jaw, making his mouth look stern. And the two old ladies over their tea by the fire conversed agreeably, compared their rheumatisms and other ailments wordily, and talked of old times, and early recollections, and of sick-beds they had attended, and corpses that "you would not know, so pined and windered" were they; and others so fresh and canny, you'd say the dead had never looked so bonny in life.

Then they began to talk of people who grew tall in their coffins, of others who had been buried alive, and of others who walked after death. Stories as true as holy writ.

"Were you ever down by Hawarth, Mrs. Bligh—hard by Dalworth Moss?" asked crook-backed Mrs. Wale, holding her spoon suspended over her cup.

"Neea whaar sooa far south, Mrs. Wale, ma'am; but ma father was offtimes down thar cuttin' peat."

"Ah, then ye'll not a kenned farmer Dykes that lived by the Lin-tree Scaur. 'Tweer I that laid him out, poor aad fellow, and a dow man he was when aught went cross wi' him; and he cursed and sweared, twad gar ye dodder to hear him. They said he was a hard man wi' some folk; but he kep a good house, and liked to see plenty, and many a time when I was swaimous about my food, he'd clap t' meat on ma plate, and mak' me eat ma fill. Na, na—there was good as well as bad in farmer Dykes. It was a year after he deed, and Tom Ettles was walking home, down by the Birken Stoop one night, and not a soul nigh, when he sees a big ball, as high as his knee, whirlin' and spangin' away before him on the road. What it wer he could not think; but he never consayted there was a freet or a bo thereaway; so he kep near it, watching every spang and turn it took, till it ran into the gripe by the roadside. There was a gravel pit just there, and Tom Ettles wished to take another gliff at it before he went on. But when he keeked into the pit, what should he see but a man attoppa a horse that could not get up or on: and says he, 'I think ye be at a dead-lift there, gaffer.' And wi' the word, up looks the man, and who sud it be but farmer Dykes himsel; and Tom Ettles saw him plain eneugh, and kenned the horse too for Black Captain, the farmer's aad beast, that broke his leg and was shot two years and more before the farmer died. 'Ay,' says farmer Dykes, lookin' very bad; 'forsett-and-backsett, ye'll tak me oot, Tom Ettles, and clap ye doun behint me quick, or I'll claw ho'd o' thee.' Tom felt his hair rislin' stiff on his heed, and his tongue so fast to the roof o' his mouth he could scarce get oot a word; but says he, 'If Black Jack can't do it o' noo, he'll ne'er do't and carry double.' 'I ken my ain business best,' says Dykes. 'If ye gar me gie ye a look, 'twill gie ye the creepin's while ye live; so git ye doun, Tom;' and with that the dobby lifts its neaf, and Tom saw there was a red light round horse and man, like the glow of a peat fire. And says Tom, 'In the name o' God, ye'll let me pass;' and with the word the gooast draws itsel' doun, all a-creaked, like a man wi' a sudden pain; and Tom Ettles took to his heels more deed than alive."

They had approached their heads, and the story had sunk to that mysterious murmur that thrills the listener, when in the brief silence that followed they heard a low odd laugh near the door.

In that direction each lady looked aghast, and saw Feltram sitting straight up in the bed, with the white bandage in his hand, and as it seemed, for one foot was below the coverlet, near the floor, about to glide forth.

Mrs. Bligh, uttering a hideous shriek, clutched Mrs. Wale, and Mrs. Wale, with a scream as dreadful, gripped Mrs. Bligh; and quite forgetting their somewhat formal politeness, they reeled and tugged, wrestling towards the window, each struggling to place her companion between her and the 'dobby,' and both uniting in a direful peal of yells.

This was the uproar which had startled Sir Bale from his dream, and was now startling the servants from theirs.

CHAPTER XIII

The Mist on the Mountain

Doctor Torvey was sent for early next morning, and came full of wonder, learning and scepticism. Seeing is believing, however; and there was Philip Feltram living, and soon to be, in all bodily functions, just as usual.

"Upon my soul, Sir Bale, I couldn't have believed it, if I had not seen it with my eyes," said the Doctor impressively, while sipping a glass of sherry in the 'breakfast parlour,' as the great panelled and pictured room next the dining-room was called. "I don't think there is any similar case on record—no pulse, no more than the poker; no respiration, by Jove, no more than the chimney-piece; as cold as a lead image in the garden there. Well, you'll say all that might possibly be fallacious; but what will you say to the cadaveric stiffness? Old Judy Wale can tell you; and my friend Marcella—Monocula would be nearer the mark—Mrs. Bligh, she knows all those common, and I may say up to this, infallible, signs of death, as well as I do. There is no mystery about them; they'll depose to the literality of the symptoms. You heard how they gave tongue. Upon my honour, I'll send the whole case up to my old chief, Sir Hervey Hansard, to London. You'll hear what a noise it will make among the profession. There never was —and it ain't too much to say there never *will* be—another case like it."

During this lecture, and a great deal more, Sir Bale leaned back in his chair, with his legs extended, his heels on the ground, and his arms folded, looking sourly up in the face of a tall lady in white satin, in a ruff, and with a bird on her hand, who smiled down superciliously from her frame on the Baronet. Sir Bale seemed a little bit high and dry with the Doctor.

"You physicians are unquestionably," he said, "a very learned profession."

The Doctor bowed.

"But there's just one thing you know nothing about—"

"Eh? What's that?" inquired Doctor Torvey.

"Medicine," answered Sir Bale. "I was aware you never knew what was the matter with a sick man; but I didn't know, till now, that you couldn't tell when he was dead."

"Ha, ha!—well—ha, ha!—*yes*—well, you see, you—ha, ha!—you certainly have me there. But it's a case without a parallel—it is, upon my honour. You'll find it will not only be talked about, but written about; and, whatever papers appear upon it, will come to me; and I'll take care, Sir Bale, you shall have an opportunity of reading them."

"Of which I shan't avail myself," answered Sir Bale. "Take another glass of sherry, Doctor."

The Doctor made his acknowledgments and filled his glass, and looked through the wine between him and the window.

"Ha, ha!—see there, your port, Sir Bale, gives a fellow such habits—looking for the beeswing, by Jove. It isn't easy, in one sense at least, to get your port out of a fellow's head when once he has tasted it."

But if the honest Doctor meant a hint for a glass of that admirable bin, it fell pointless; and Sir Bale had no notion of making another libation of that precious fluid in honour of Doctor Torvey.

"And I take it for granted," said Sir Bale, "that Feltram will do very well; and, should anything go wrong, I can send for you—unless he should die again; and in that case I think I shall take my own opinion."

So he and the Doctor parted.

Sir Bale, although he did not consult the Doctor on his own case, was not particularly well. "That lonely place, those frightful mountains, and that damp black lake"—which features in the landscape he cursed all round—"are enough to give any man blue devils; and when a fellow's spirits go, he's all gone. That's why I'm dyspeptic —that and those d—d debts—and the post, with its flight of croaking and screeching letters from London. I wish there was no post here. I wish it was like Sir Amyrald's time, when they shot the York mercer that came to dun him, and no one ever took anyone to task about it; and now they can pelt you at any distance they please through the post; and fellows lose their spirits and their appetite and any sort of miserable comfort that is possible in this odious abyss."

Was there gout in Sir Bale's case, or 'vapours'? I know not what the faculty would have called it; but Sir Bale's mode of treatment was simply to work off the attack by long and laborious walking.

This evening his walk was upon the Fells of Golden Friars— long after the landscape below was in the eclipse of twilight, the broad bare sides and angles of these gigantic uplands were still lighted by the misty western sun.

There is no such sense of solitude as that which we experience upon the silent and vast elevations of great mountains. Lifted high above the level of human sounds and habitations, among the wild expanses and colossal features of Nature, we are thrilled in our loneliness with a strange fear and elation—an ascent above the reach of life's vexations or companionship, and the tremblings of a wild and undefined misgiving. The filmy disc of the moon had risen in the east, and was already faintly silvering the shadowy scenery below, while yet Sir Bale stood in the mellow light of the western sun, which still touched also the summits of the opposite peaks of Morvyn Fells.

Sir Bale Mardykes did not, as a stranger might, in prudence, hasten his descent from the heights at which he stood while yet a gleam of daylight remained to him. For he was, from his boyhood, familiar with those solitary regions; and, beside this, the thin circle of the moon, hung in the eastern sky, would brighten as the sunlight sank, and hang like a lamp above his steps.

There was in the bronzed and resolute face of the Baronet, lighted now in the parting beams of sunset, a resemblance to that of Charles the Second—not our "merry" ideal, but the more energetic and saturnine face which the portraits have preserved to us.

He stood with folded arms on the side of the slope, admiring, in spite of his prejudice, the unusual effects of a view so strangely lighted—the sunset tints on the opposite peaks, lost in the misty twilight, now deepening lower down into a darker shade, through which the outlines of the stone gables and tower of Golden Friars and the light of fire or candle in their windows were dimly visible.

As he stood and looked, his more distant sunset went down, and sudden twilight was upon him, and he began to remember the beautiful Homeric picture of a landscape coming out, rock and headland, in the moonlight.

There had hung upon the higher summits, at his right, a heavy fold of white cloud, which on a sudden broke, and, like the smoke of artillery, came rolling down the slopes toward him. Its principal volume, however, unfolded itself in a mighty flood down the side of the mountain towards the lake; and that which spread towards and soon enveloped the ground on which he stood was by no means so dense a fog. A thick mist enough it was; but still, to a distance of twenty or thirty yards, he could discern the outline of a rock or scaur, but not beyond it.

There are few sensations more intimidating than that of being thus enveloped on a lonely mountain-side, which, like this one, here and there breaks into precipice.

There is another sensation, too, which affects the imagination. Overtaken thus on the solitary expanse, there comes a new chill and tremour as this treacherous medium surrounds us, through which unperceived those shapes which fancy conjures up might approach so near and bar our path.

From the risk of being reduced to an actual standstill he knew he was exempt. The point from which the wind blew, light as it was, assured him of that. Still the mist was thick enough seriously to embarrass him. It had overtaken him as he was looking down upon the lake; and he now looked to his left, to try whether in that direction it was too thick to permit a view of the nearest landmarks. Through this white film he saw a figure standing only about five-and-twenty steps away, looking down, as it seemed, in precisely the same direction as he, quite motionless, and standing like a shadow projected upon the smoky vapour. It was the figure of a slight tall man, with his arm extended, as if pointing to a remote object, which no mortal eye certainly could discern through the mist. Sir Bale gazed at this figure, doubtful whether he were in a waking dream, unable to conjecture whence it had come; and as he looked, it moved, and was almost instantly out of sight.

He descended the mountain cautiously. The mist was now thinner, and through the haze he was beginning to see objects more distinctly, and, without danger, to proceed at a quicker pace. He had still a long walk by the uplands towards Mardykes Hall before he descended to the level of the lake.

The mist was still quite thick enough to circumscribe his view and to hide the general features of the landscape; and well was it, perhaps, for Sir Bale that his boyhood had familiarised him with the landmarks on the mountain-side.

He had made nearly four miles on his solitary homeward way, when, passing under a ledge of rock which bears the name of the Cat's Skaitch, he saw the same figure in the short cloak standing within some thirty or forty yards of him—the thin curtain of mist, through which the moonlight touched it, giving to it an airy and unsubstantial character.

Sir Bale came to a standstill. The man in the short cloak nodded and drew back, and was concealed by the angle of the rock.

Sir Bale was now irritated, as men are after a start, and shouting to the stranger to halt, he 'slapped' after him, as the northern phrase goes, at his best pace. But again he was gone, and nowhere could he see him, the mist favouring his evasion.

Looking down the fells that overhang Mardykes Hall, the mountain-side dips gradually into a glen, which, as it descends, becomes precipitous and wooded. A footpath through this ravine conducts the wayfarer to the level ground that borders the lake; and by this dark pass Sir Bale Mardykes strode, in comparatively clear air, along the rocky path dappled with moonlight.

As he emerged upon the lower ground he again encountered the same figure. It approached. It was Philip Feltram.

CHAPTER XIV

A New Philip Feltram

The Baronet had not seen Feltram since his strange escape from death. His last interview with him had been stern and threatening; Sir Bale dealing with appearances in the spirit of an incensed judge, Philip Feltram lamenting in the submission of a helpless despair.

Feltram was full in the moonlight now, standing erect, and smiling cynically on the Baronet.

There was that in the bearing and countenance of Feltram that disconcerted him more than the surprise of the sudden meeting.

He had determined to meet Feltram in a friendly way, whenever that not very comfortable interview became inevitable. But he was confused by the suddenness of Feltram's appearance; and the tone, cold and stern, in which he had last spoken to him came first, and he spoke in it after a brief silence.

"I fancied, Mr. Feltram, you were in your bed; I little expected to find you here. I think the Doctor gave very particular directions, and said that you were to remain perfectly quiet."

"But I know more than the Doctor," replied Feltram, still smiling unpleasantly.

"I think, sir, you would have been better in your bed," said Sir Bale loftily.

"Come, come, come, come!" exclaimed Philip Feltram contemptuously.

*It was the figure of a slight tall man, with his arm extended,
as if pointing to a remote object.*

"It seems to me," said Sir Bale, a good deal astonished, "you rather forget yourself."

"Easier to forget oneself, Sir Bale, than to forgive others, at times," replied Philip Feltram in his unparalleled mood.

"That's the way fools knock themselves up," continued Sir Bale. "You've been walking ever so far—away to the Fells of Golden Friars. It was you whom I saw there. What d—d folly! What brought you there?"

"To observe you," he replied.

"And have you walked the whole way there and back again? How did you get there?"

"Pooh! how did I come—how did you come—how did the fog come? From the lake, I suppose. We all come up, and then down." So spoke Philip Feltram, with serene insolence.

"You are pleased to talk nonsense," said Sir Bale.

"Because I like it—with a *meaning*."

Sir Bale looked at him, not knowing whether to believe his eyes and ears. He did not know what to make of him.

"I had intended speaking to you in a conciliatory way; you seem to wish to make that impossible"—Philip Feltram's face wore its repulsive smile;—"and in fact I don't know what to make of you, unless you are ill; and ill you well may be. You can't have walked much less than twelve miles."

"Wonderful effort for me!" said Feltram with the same sneer.

"Rather surprising for a man so nearly drowned," answered Sir Bale Mardykes.

"A dip: you don't like the lake, sir; but I do. And so it is: as Antæus touched the earth, so I the water, and rise refreshed."

"I think you'd better get in and refresh there. I meant to tell you that all the unpleasantness about that bank-note is over."

"Is it?"

"Yes. It has been recovered by Mr. Creswell, who came here last night. I've got it, and you're not to blame," said Sir Bale.

"But some one *is* to blame," observed Mr. Feltram, smiling still.

"Well, *you* are not, and that ends it," said the Baronet peremptorily.

"Ends it? Really, how good! how very good!"

Sir Bale looked at him, for there was something ambiguous and even derisive in the tone of Feltram's voice.

But before he could quite make up his mind, Feltram spoke again.

"Everything is settled about you and me?"

"There is nothing to prevent your staying at Mardykes now," said Sir Bale graciously.

"I shall be with you for two years, and then I go on my travels," answered Feltram, with a saturnine and somewhat wild look around him.

"Is he going mad?" thought the Baronet.

"But before I go, I'm to put you in a way of paying off your mortgages. That is my business here."

Sir Bale looked at him sharply. But now there was not the unpleasant smile, but the darkened look of a man in secret pain.

"You shall know it all by and by."

And without more ceremony, and with a darkening face, Philip Feltram made his way under the boughs of the thick oaks that grew there, leaving on Sir Bale's mind an impression that he had been watching some one at a distance, and had gone in consequence of a signal.

In a few seconds he followed in the same direction, halloaing after Feltram; for he did not like the idea of his wandering about the country by moonlight, or possibly losing his life among the precipices, and bringing a new discredit upon his house. But no answer came; nor could he in that thick copse gain sight of him again.

When Sir Bale reached Mardykes Hall he summoned Mrs. Julaper, and had a long talk with her. But she could not say that there appeared anything amiss with Philip Feltram; only he seemed more reserved, and as if he was brooding over something he did not intend to tell.

"But, you know, Sir Bale, what happened might well make a thoughtful man of him. If he's ever to think of Death, it should be after looking him so hard in the face; and I'm not ashamed to say, I'm glad to see he has grace to take the lesson, and I hope his experiences may be sanctified to him, poor fellow! Amen."

"Very good song, and very well sung," said Sir Bale; "but it doesn't seem to me that he has been improved, Mrs. Julaper. He seems, on the contrary, in a queer temper and anything but a heavenly frame of mind; and I thought I'd ask you, because if he is ill—I mean feverish—it might account for his eccentricities, as well as make it necessary to send after him, and bring him home, and put him to bed. But I suppose it is as you say,—his adventure has upset him a little, and he'll sober in a day or two, and return to his old ways."

But this did not happen. A change, more comprehensive than

at first appeared, had taken place, and a singular alteration was gradually established.

He grew thin, his eyes hollow, his face gradually forbidding.

His ways and temper were changed: he was a new man with Sir Bale; and the Baronet after a time, people said, began to grow afraid of him. And certainly Feltram had acquired an extraordinary influence over the Baronet, who a little while ago had regarded and treated him with so much contempt.

CHAPTER XV

The Purse of Gold

The Baronet was very slightly known in his county. He had led a reserved and inhospitable life. He was pressed upon by heavy debts; and being a proud man, held aloof from society and its doings. He wished people to understand that he was nursing his estate; but somehow the estate did not thrive at nurse. In the country other people's business is admirably well known; and the lord of Mardykes was conscious, perhaps, that his neighbours knew as well he did, that the utmost he could do was to pay the interest charged upon it, and to live in a frugal way enough.

The lake measures some four or five miles across, from the little jetty under the walls of Mardykes Hall to Cloostedd.

Philip Feltram, changed and morose, loved a solitary row upon the lake; and sometimes, with no one to aid him in its management, would take the little sailboat and pass the whole day upon those lonely waters.

Frequently he crossed to Cloostedd; and mooring the boat under the solemn trees that stand reflected in that dark mirror, he would disembark and wander among the lonely woodlands, as people thought, cherishing in those ancestral scenes the memory of ineffaceable injuries, and the wrath and revenge that seemed of late to darken his countenance, and to hold him always in a moody silence.

One autumnal evening Sir Bale Mardykes was sourly ruminating after his solitary meal. A very red sun was pouring its last low beams through the valley at the western extremity of the lake, across its elsewhere sombre waters, and touching with a sudden and blood-red tint the sail of the skiff in which Feltram was returning from his lonely cruise.

"Here comes my domestic water-fiend," sneered Sir Bale, as he lay back in his cumbrous arm-chair. "Cheerful place, pleasant people, delicious fate! The place alone has been enough to set that fool out of his little senses, d—n him!"

Sir Bale averted his eyes, and another subject not pleasanter entered his mind. He was thinking of the races that were coming off next week at Heckleston Downs, and what sums of money might be made there, and how hard it was that he should be excluded by fortune from that brilliant lottery.

"Ah, Mrs. Julaper, is that you?"

Mrs. Julaper, who was still at the door, curtsied, and said, "I came, Sir Bale, to see whether you'd please to like a jug of mulled claret, sir."

"Not I, my dear. I'll take a mug of beer and my pipe; that homely solace better befits a ruined gentleman."

"H'm, sir; you're not that, Sir Bale; you're no worse than half the lords and great men that are going. I would not hear another say that of you, sir."

"That's very kind of you, Mrs. Julaper; but you won't call *me* out for backbiting myself, especially as it is true, d—d true, Mrs. Julaper! Look ye; there never was a Mardykes here before but he could lay his hundred or his thousand pounds on the winner of the Heckleston Cup; and what could I bet? Little more than that mug of beer I spoke of. It was my great-grandfather who opened the course on the Downs of Heckleston, and now *I* can't show there! Well, what must I do? Grin and bear it, that's all. If you please, Mrs. Julaper, I will have that jug of claret you offered. I want spice and hot wine to keep me alive; but I'll smoke my pipe first, and in an hour's time it will do."

When Mrs. Julaper was gone, he lighted his pipe, and drew near the window, through which he looked upon the now fading sky and the twilight landscape.

He smoked his pipe out, and by that time it had grown nearly dark. He was still looking out upon the faint outlines of the view, and thinking angrily what a little bit of luck at the races would do for many a man who probably did not want it half so much as he. Vague and sombre as his thoughts were, they had, like the darkening landscape outside, shape enough to define their general character. Bitter and impious they were—as those of egotistic men naturally are in suffering. And after brooding, and muttering by fits and starts, he said:

"How many tens and hundreds of thousands of pounds will change hands at Heckleston next week; and not a shilling in all the change and shuffle will stick to me! How many a fellow would sell himself, like Dr. Faustus, just for the knowledge of the name of the winner! But he's no fool, and does not buy his own."

Something caught his eye; something moving on the wall. The fire was lighted, and cast a flickering and gigantic shadow upward; the figure of a man standing behind Sir Bale Mardykes, on whose shoulder he placed a lean hand. Sir Bale turned suddenly about, and saw Philip Feltram. He was looking dark and stern, and did not remove his hand from his shoulder as he peered into the Baronet's face with his deep-set mad eyes.

"Ha, Philip, upon my soul!" exclaimed Sir Bale, surprised. "How time flies! It seems only this minute since I saw the boat a mile and a half away from the shore. Well—yes; there has been time; it is dark now. Ha, ha! I assure you, you startled me. Won't you take something? Do. Shall I touch the bell?"

"You have been troubled about those mortgages. I told you I should pay them off, I thought."

Here there was a pause, and Sir Bale looked hard in Feltram's face. If he had been in his ordinary spirits, or perhaps in some of his haunts less solitary than Mardykes, he would have laughed; but here he had grown unlike himself, gloomy and credulous, and was, in fact, a nervous man.

Sir Bale smiled, and shook his head dismally.

"It is very kind of you, Feltram; the idea shows a kindly disposition. I know you would do me a kindness if you could."

As Sir Bale, each looking in the other's eyes, repeated in this sentence the words "kind," "kindly," "kindness," a smile lighted Feltram's face with at each word an intenser light; and Sir Bale grew sombre in its glare; and when he had done speaking, Feltram's face also on a sudden darkened.

"I have found a fortune-teller in Cloostedd Wood. Look here."

And he drew from his pocket a leathern purse, which he placed on the table in his hand; and Sir Bale heard the pleasant clink of coin in it.

"A fortune-teller! You don't mean to say she gave you that?" said Sir Bale.

Feltram smiled again, and nodded.

"It was the custom to give the fortuneteller a trifle. It is a great improvement making her fee you," observed Sir Bale, with an approach to his old manner.

"He put that in my hand with a message," said Feltram.

"He? O, then it was a male fortune-teller!"

"Gipsies go in gangs, men and women. *He* might lend, though *she* told fortunes," said Feltram.

"It's the first time I ever heard of gipsies lending money;" and he eyed the purse with a whimsical smile.

With his lean fingers still holding it, Feltram sat down at the table. His face contracted as if in cunning thought, and his chin sank upon his breast as he leaned back.

"I think," continued Sir Bale, "ever since they were spoiled, the Egyptians have been a little shy of lending, and leave that branch of business to the Hebrews."

"What would you give to know, now, the winner at Heckleston races?" said Feltram suddenly, raising his eyes.

"Yes; that would be worth something," answered Sir Bale, looking at him with more interest than the incredulity he affected would quite warrant.

"And this money I have power to lend you, to make your game."

"Do you mean that really?" said Sir Bale, with a new energy in tone, manner, and features.

"That's heavy; there are some guineas there," said Feltram with a dark smile, raising the purse in his hand a little, and letting it drop upon the table with a clang.

"There is *something* there, at all events," said Sir Bale.

Feltram took the purse by the bottom, and poured out on the table a handsome pile of guineas.

"And do you mean to say you got all that from a gipsy in Cloostedd Wood?"

"A friend, who is—*myself,*" answered Philip Feltram.

"Yourself! Then it is yours—*you* lend it?" said the Baronet, amazed; for there was no getting over the heap of guineas, and the wonder was pretty equal whence they had come.

"Myself, and not myself," said Feltram oracularly; "as like as voice and echo, man and shadow."

Had Feltram in some of his solitary wanderings and potterings lighted upon hidden treasure? There was a story of two Feltrams of Cloostedd, brothers, who had joined the king's army and fought at Marston Moor, having buried in Cloostedd Wood a great deal of gold and plate and jewels. They had, it was said, intrusted one tried servant with the secret; and that servant remained at home. But by a perverse fatality the three witnesses had perished within a month: the two brothers at Marston Moor; and the confidant, of fever, at Cloostedd. From that day forth treasure-seekers had from time to time explored the woods of Cloostedd; and many a tree of mark was dug beside, and the earth beneath many a stone and scar and other landmark in that solitary forest was opened by night, until hope gradually died out, and the tradition had long ceased to prompt to action, and had become a story and nothing more.

The image of the nursery-tale had now recurred to Sir Bale after so long a reach of years; and the only imaginable way, in his mind, of accounting for penniless Philip Feltram having all that gold in his possession was that, in some of his lonely wanderings, chance had led him to the undiscovered hoard of the two Feltrams who had died in the great civil wars.

"Perhaps those gipsies you speak of found the money where you found them; and in that case, as Cloostedd Forest, and all that is in it is my property, their sending it to me is more like my servant's handing me my hat and stick when I'm going out, than making me a present."

"You will not be wise to rely upon the law, Sir Bale, and to refuse the help that comes unasked. But if you like your mortgages as they are, keep them; and if you like my terms as they are, take them; and when you have made up your mind, let me know."

Philip Feltram dropped the heavy purse into his capacious coat-pocket, and walked, muttering, out of the room.

CHAPTER XVI

The Message from Cloostedd

"Come back, Feltram; come back, Philip!" cried Sir Bale hastily. "Let us talk, can't we? Come and talk this odd business over a little; you must have mistaken what I meant; I should like to hear all about it."

"All is not much, sir," said Philip Feltram, entering the room again, the door of which he had half closed after him. "In the forest of Cloostedd I met to-day some people, one of whom can foretell events, and told me the names of the winners of the first three races at Heckleston, and gave me this purse, with leave to lend you so much money as you care to stake upon the races. I take no security; you shan't be troubled; and you'll never see the lender, unless you seek him out."

"Well, those are not bad terms," said Sir Bale, smiling wistfully at the purse, which Feltram had again placed upon the table.

"No, not bad," repeated Feltram, in the harsh low tone in which he now habitually spoke.

"You'll tell me what the prophet said about the winners; I should like to hear their names."

"The names I shall tell you if you walk out with me," said Feltram.

"Why not here?" asked Sir Bale.

"My memory does not serve me here so well. Some people, in some places, though they be silent, obstruct thought. Come, let us speak," said Philip Feltram, leading the way.

Sir Bale, with a shrug, followed him.

By this time it was dark. Feltram was walking slowly towards the margin of the lake; and Sir Bale, more curious as the delay increased, followed him, and smiled faintly as he looked after his tall, gaunt figure, as if, even in the dark, expressing a ridicule which he did not honestly feel, and the expression of which, even if there had been light, there was no one near enough to see.

When he reached the edge of the lake, Feltram stooped, and Sir Bale thought that his attitude was that of one who whispers to and caresses a reclining person. What he fancied was a dark figure lying horizontally in the shallow water, near the edge, turned out to be, as he drew near, no more than a shadow on the elsewhere lighter water; and with his change of position it had shifted and was gone, and Philip Feltram was but dabbling his hand this way and that in the water, and muttering faintly to himself. He rose as the Baronet drew near, and standing upright, said,

"I like to listen to the ripple of the water among the grass and pebbles; the tongue and lips of the lake are lapping and whispering all along. It is the merest poetry; but you are so romantic, you excuse me."

There was an angry curve in Feltram's eyebrows, and a cynical smile, and something in the tone which to the satirical Baronet was almost insulting. But even had he been less curious, I don't think he would have betrayed his mortification; for an odd and unavowed influence which he hated was gradually establishing in Feltram an ascendency which sometimes vexed and sometimes cowed him.

"You are not to tell," said Feltram, drawing near him in the dusk. "The secret is yours when you promise."

"Of course I promise," said Sir Bale. "If I believed it, you don't think I could be such an ass as to tell it; and if I didn't believe it, I'd hardly take the trouble."

Feltram stooped, and dipping the hollow of his hand in the water, he raised it full, and said he, "Hold out your hand—the hollow of your hand—like this. I divide the water for a sign—share to me and share to you." And he turned his hand, so as to pour half the water into the hollow palm of Sir Bale, who was smiling, with some uneasiness mixed in his mockery.

"Now, you promise to keep all secrets respecting the teller and the finder, be that who it may?"

"Yes, I promise," said Sir Bale.

"Now do as I do," said Feltram. And he shed the water on the ground, and with his wet fingers touched his forehead and his breast; and then he joined his hand with Sir Bale's, and said, "Now you are my safe man."

Sir Bale laughed. "That's the game they call 'grand mufti,'" said he.

"Exactly; and means nothing," said Feltram, "except that some day it will serve you to remember by. And now the names. Don't speak; listen—you may break the thought else. The winner of the first is *Beeswing;* of the second, *Falcon;* and of the third, *Lightning.*"

He had stood for some seconds in silence before he spoke; his eyes were closed; he seemed to bring up thought and speech with difficulty, and spoke faintly and drowsily, both his hands a little raised, and the fingers extended, with the groping air of a man who moves in the dark. In this odd way, slowly, faintly, with many a sigh and scarcely audible groan, he gradually delivered his message and was silent. He stood, it seemed, scarcely half awake, muttering indistinctly and sighing to himself. You would have said that he was exhausted and suffering, like a man at his last hour resigning himself to death.

At length he opened his eyes, looked round a little wildly and languidly, and with another great sigh sat down on a large rock that lies by the margin of the lake, and sighed heavily again and again. You might have fancied that he was a second time recovering from drowning.

Then he got up, and looked drowsily round again, and sighed like a man worn out with fatigue, and was silent.

Sir Bale did not care to speak until he seemed a little more likely to obtain an answer. When that time came, he said, "I wish, for the sake of my believing, that your list was a little less incredible. Not one of the horses you name is the least likely; not one of them has a chance."

"So much the better for you; you'll get what odds you please.

You had better seize your luck; on Tuesday Beeswing runs," said Feltram. "When you want money for the purpose, I'm your banker —here is your bank."

He touched his breast, where he had placed the purse, and then he turned and walked swiftly away.

Sir Bale looked after him till he disappeared in the dark. He fluctuated among many surmises about Feltram. Was he insane, or was he practising an imposture? or was he fool enough to believe the predictions of some real gipsies? and had he borrowed this money, which in Sir Bale's eyes seemed the greatest miracle in the matter, from those thriving shepherd mountaineers, the old Trebecks, who, he believed, were attached to him? Feltram had, he thought, borrowed it as if for himself; and having, as Sir Bale in his egotism supposed, "a sneaking regard" for him, had meant the loan for his patron, and conceived the idea of his using his revelations for the purpose of making his fortune. So, seeing no risk, and the temptation being strong, Sir Bale resolved to avail himself of the purse, and use his own judgment as to what horse to back.

About eleven o'clock Feltram, unannounced, walked, with his hat still on, into Sir Bale's library, and sat down at the opposite side of his table, looking gloomily into the Baronet's face for a time.

"Shall you want the purse?" he asked at last.

"Certainly; I always want a purse," said Sir Bale energetically.

"The condition is, that you shall back each of the three horses I have named. But you may back them for much or little, as you like, only the sum must not be less than five pounds in each hundred which this purse contains. That is the condition, and if you violate it, you will make some powerful people very angry, and you will feel it. Do you agree?"

"Of course; five pounds in the hundred—certainly; and how many hundreds are there?"

"Three."

"Well, a fellow with luck may win something with three hundred pounds, but it ain't very much."

"Quite enough, if you use it aright."

"Three hundred pounds," repeated the Baronet, as he emptied the purse, which Feltram had just placed in his hand, upon the table; and contemplating them with grave interest, he began telling them off in little heaps of five-and-twenty each. He might have thanked Feltram, but he was thinking more of the guineas than of the grizzly donor.

"Ay," said he, after a second counting, "I think there *are* exactly three hundred. Well, so you say I must apply three times five—fifteen of these. It is an awful pity backing those queer horses you have named; but if I must make the sacrifice, I must, I suppose?" he added, with a hesitating inquiry in the tone.

"If you don't, you'll rue it," said Feltram coldly, and walked away.

"Penny in pocket's a merry companion," says the old English proverb, and Sir Bale felt in better spirits and temper than he had for many a day as he replaced the guineas in the purse.

It was long since he had visited either the race-course or any other place of amusement. Now he might face his kind without fear that his pride should be mortified, and dabble in the fascinating agitations of the turf once more.

"Who knows how this little venture may turn out?" he thought. "It is time the luck should turn. My last summer in Germany, my last winter in Paris—d—n me, I'm owed something. It's time I should win a bit."

Sir Bale had suffered the indolence of a solitary and discontented life imperceptibly to steal upon him. It would not do to appear for the first time on Heckleston Lea with any of those signs of negligence which, in his case, might easily be taken for poverty. All his appointments, therefore, were carefully looked after; and on the Monday following, he, followed by his groom, rode away for the Saracen's Head at Heckleston, where he was to put up, for the races that were to begin on the day following, and presented as handsome an appearance as a peer in those days need have cared to show.

CHAPTER XVII

On the Course—Beeswing, Falcon, and Lightning

As he rode towards Golden Friars, through which his route lay, in the early morning light, in which the mists of night were clearing, he looked back towards Mardykes with a hope of speedy deliverance from that hated imprisonment, and of a return to the continental life in which he took delight. He saw the summits and angles of the old building touched with the cheerful beams, and the grand old trees, and at the opposite side the fells dark, with their backs to wards the east; and down the side of the wooded and precipitous clough of Feltram, the light, with a pleasant contrast against the beetling purple of the fells, was breaking in the faint distance. On the lake he saw the white speck that indicated the sail of Philip Feltram's boat, now midway between Mardykes and the wooded shores of Cloostedd.

"Going on the same errand," thought Sir Bale, "I should not wonder. I wish him the same luck. Yes, he's going to Cloostedd Forest. I hope he may meet his gipsies there—the Trebecks, or whoever they are."

And as a momentary sense of degradation in being thus beholden to such people smote him, "Well," thought he, "who knows? Many a fellow will make a handsome sum of a poorer purse than this at Heckleston. It will be a light matter paying them then."

Through Golden Friars he rode. Some of the spectators who did not like him, wondered audibly at the gallant show, hoped it was paid for, and conjectured that he had ridden out in search of a wife. On the whole, however, the appearance of their Baronet in a smarter style than usual was popular, and accepted as a change to the advantage of the town.

Next morning he was on the race-course of Heckleston, renewing old acquaintance and making himself as agreeable as he could—an object, among some people, of curiosity and even interest. Leaving the carriage-sides, the hoods and bonnets, Sir Bale was soon among the betting men, deep in more serious business.

How did he make his book? He did not break his word. He backed Beeswing, Falcon, and Lightning. But it must be owned not for a shilling more than the five guineas each, to which he stood pledged. The odds were forty-five to one against Beeswing, sixty to one against Lightning, and fifty to one against Falcon.

"A pretty lot to choose!" exclaimed Sir Bale, with vexation. "As if I had money so often, that I should throw it away!"

The Baronet was testy thinking over all this, and looked on Feltram's message as an impertinence and the money as his own.

Let us now see how Sir Bale Mardykes' pocket fared.

Sulkily enough at the close of the week he turned his back on Heckleston racecourse, and took the road to Golden Friars.

He was in a rage with his luck, and by no means satisfied with himself; and yet he had won something. The result of the racing had been curious. In the three principal races the favourites had been beaten: one by an accident, another on a technical point, and the third by fair running. And what horses had won? The names were precisely those which the "fortune-teller" had predicted.

Well, then, how was Sir Bale in pocket as he rode up to his ancestral house of Mardykes, where a few thousand pounds would have been very welcome? He had won exactly 775 guineas; and had he staked a hundred instead of five on each of the names communicated by Feltram, he would have won 15,500 guineas.

He dismounted before his hall-door, therefore, with the discontent of a man who had lost nearly 15,000 pounds. Feltram was upon the steps, and laughed dryly.

"What do you laugh at?" asked Sir Bale tartly.

"You've won, haven't you?"

"Yes, I've won; I've won a trifle."

"On the horses I named?"

"Well, yes; it so turned out, by the merest accident."

Feltram laughed again dryly, and turned away.

Sir Bale entered Mardykes Hall, and was surly. He was in a much worse mood than before he had ridden to Heckleston. But after a week or so ruminating upon the occurrence, he wondered that Feltram spoke no more of it. It was undoubtedly wonderful. There had been no hint of repayment yet, and he had made some hundreds by the loan; and, contrary to all likelihood, the three horses named by the unknown soothsayer had won. Who was this gipsy? It would be worth bringing the soothsayer to Mardykes, and giving his people a camp on the warren, and all the poultry they could catch, and a pig or a sheep every now and then. Why, that seer was worth the philosopher's stone, and could make Sir Bale's fortune in a season. Some one else would be sure to pick him up if *he* did not.

So, tired of waiting for Feltram to begin, he opened the subject one day himself. He had not seen him for two or three days; and in the wood of Mardykes he saw his lank figure standing among the thick trees, upon a little knoll, leaning on a staff which he sometimes carried with him in his excursions up the mountains.

"Feltram!" shouted Sir Bale.

Feltram turned and beckoned. Sir Bale muttered, but obeyed the signal.

"I brought you here, because you can from this point with unusual clearness today see the opening of the Clough of Feltram at the other side, and the clump of trees, where you will find the way to reach the person about whom you are always thinking."

"Who said I am always thinking about him?" said the Baronet angrily; for he felt like a man detected in a weakness, and resented it.

"*I* say it, because I *know* it; and *you* know it also. See that clump of trees standing solitary in the hollow? Among them, to the left, grows an ancient oak. Cut in its bark are two enormous letters H—F; so large and bold, that the rugged furrows of the oak bark fail to obscure them, although they are ancient and spread by time. Standing against the trunk of this great tree, with your back to these letters, you are looking up the Glen or Clough of Feltram, that opens northward, where stands Cloostedd Forest spreading far and thick. Now, how do you find our fortune-teller?"

"That is exactly what I wish to know," answered Sir Bale; "because, although I can't, of course, believe that he's a witch, yet he has either made the most marvellous fluke I've heard of, or else he has got extraordinary sources of information; or perhaps he acts partly on chance, partly on facts. Be it which you please, I say he's a marvellous fellow; and I should like to see him, and have a talk with him; and perhaps he could arrange with me. I should be very glad to make an arrangement with him to give me the benefit of his advice about any matter of the same kind again."

"I think he's willing to see you; but he's a fellow with a queer fancy and a pig-head. He'll not come here; you must go to him; and approach him his own way too, or you may fail to find him. On these terms he invites you."

Sir Bale laughed.

"He knows his value, and means to make his own terms."

"Well, there's nothing unfair in that; and I don't see that I should dispute it. How is one to find him?"

"Stand, as I told you, with your back to those letters cut in the oak. Right before you lies an old Druidic altar-stone. Cast your eye over its surface, and on some part of it you are sure to see a black stain about the size of a man's head. Standing, as I suppose you, against the oak, that stain, which changes its place from day to day, will give you the line you must follow through the forest in order to light upon him. Take carefully from it such trees or objects as will guide you; and when the forest thickens, do the best you can to keep to the same line. You are sure to find him."

"You'll come, Feltram. I should lose myself in that wilderness, and probably fail to discover him," said Sir Bale; "and I really wish to see him."

"When two people wish to meet, it is hard if they don't. I can go with you a bit of the way; I can walk a little through the forest by your side, until I see the small flower that grows peeping here and there, that always springs where those people walk; and when I begin to see that sign, I must leave you. And, first, I'll take you across the lake."

"By Jove, you'll do no such thing!" said Sir Bale hastily.

"But that is the way he chooses to be approached," said Philip Feltram.

"I have a sort of feeling about that lake; it's the one childish spot that is left in my imagination. The nursery is to blame for it—old stories and warnings; and I can't think of that. I should feel I had invoked an evil omen if I did. I know it is all nonsense; but we are queer creatures, Feltram. I must only ride there."

"Why, it is five-and-twenty miles round the lake to that; and after all were done, he would not see you. He knows what he's worth, and he'll have his own way," answered Feltram. "The sun will soon set. See that withered branch, near Snakes Island, that looks like fingers rising from the water? When its points grow tipped with red, the sun has but three minutes to live."

"That is a wonder which I can't see; it is too far away."

"Yes, the lake has many signs; but it needs sight to see them," said Feltram.

"So it does," said the Baronet; "more than most men have got. I'll ride round, I say; and I make my visit, for this time, my own way."

"You'll not find him, then; and he wants his money. It would be a pity to vex him."

"It was to you he lent the money," said Sir Bale.

"Yes."

"Well, you are the proper person to find him out and pay him," urged Sir Bale.

"Perhaps so; but he invites you; and if you don't go, he may be offended, and you may hear no more from him."

"We'll try. When can you go? There are races to come off next week, for once and away, at Langton. I should not mind trying my luck there. What do you say?

"You can go there and pay him, and ask the same question—what horses, I mean, are to win. All the county are to be there; and plenty of money will change hands."

"I'll try," said Feltram.

"When will you go?"

"To-morrow," he answered.

"I have an odd idea, Feltram, that you are really going to pay off those cursed mortgages."

He laid his hand with at least a gesture of kindness on the thin arm of Feltram, who coldly answered,

"So have I;" and walked down the side of the little knoll and away, without another word or look.

CHAPTER XVIII

On the Lake, at Last

Next day Philip Feltram crossed the lake; and Sir Bale, seeing the boat on the water, guessed its destination, and watched its progress with no little interest, until he saw it moored and its sail drop at the rude pier that affords a landing at the Clough of Feltram. He was now satisfied that Philip had actually gone to seek out the 'cunning man,' and gather hints for the next race.

When that evening Feltram returned, and, later still, entered Sir Bale's library, the master of Mardykes was gladder to see his face and more interested about his news than he would have cared to confess.

Philip Feltram did not affect unconsciousness of that anxiety, but, with great directness, proceeded to satisfy it.

"I was in Cloostedd Forest to-day, nearly all day—and found the old gentleman in a wax. He did not ask me to drink, nor show me any kindness. He was huffed because you would not take the trouble to cross the lake to speak to him yourself. He took the money you sent him and counted it over, and dropped it into his pocket; and he called you hard names enough and to spare; but I brought him round, and at last he did talk."

"And what did he say?"

"He said that the estate of Mardykes would belong to a Feltram."

"He might have said something more likely," said Sir Bale sourly. "Did he say anything more?"

"Yes. He said the winner at Langton Lea would be Silver Bell."

"Any other name?"

"No."

"Silver Bell? Well, that's not so odd as the last. Silver Bell stands high in the list. He has a good many backers—long odds in his favour against most of the field. I should not mind backing Silver Bell."

The fact is, that he had no idea of backing any other horse from the moment he heard the soothsayer's prediction. He made up his mind to no half measures this time. He would go in to win something handsome.

He was in great force and full of confidence on the race-course. He had no fears for the result. He bet heavily. There was a good margin still untouched of the Mardykes estate; and Sir Bale was a good old name in the county. He found a ready market for his offers, and had soon staked—such is the growing frenzy of that excitement—about twenty thousand pounds on his favourite, and stood to win seven.

He did not win, however. He lost his twenty thousand pounds.

And now the Mardykes estate was in imminent danger. Sir Bale returned, having distributed I O Us and promissory notes in all directions about him—quite at his wit's end.

Feltram was standing—as on the occasion of his former happier return—on the steps of Mardykes Hall, in the evening sun, throwing eastward a long shadow that was lost in the lake. He received him, as before, with a laugh.

Sir Bale was too much broken to resent this laugh as furiously as he might, had he been a degree less desperate.

He looked at Feltram savagely, and dismounted.

"Last time you would not trust him, and this time he would not trust you. He's huffed, and played you false."

"It was not he. I should have backed that d—d horse in any case," said Sir Bale, grinding his teeth. "What a witch you have discovered! One thing is true, perhaps. If there was a Feltram rich enough, he might have the estate now; but there ain't. They are all beggars. So much for your conjurer."

"He may make amends to you, if you make amends to him."

"He! Why, what can that wretched impostor do? D—n me, I'm past helping now."

"Don't you talk so," said Feltram. "Be civil. You must please the old gentleman. He'll make it up. He's placable when it suits him. Why not go to him his own way? I hear you are nearly ruined. You must go and make it up."

"Make it up! With whom? With a fellow who can't make even a guess at what's coming? Why should I trouble my head about him more?"

"No man, young or old, likes to be frumped. Why did you cross his fancy? He won't see you unless you go to him as he chooses."

"If he waits for that, he may wait till doomsday. I don't choose to go on that water—and cross it I won't," said Sir Bale.

But when his distracting reminders began to pour in upon him, and the idea of dismembering what remained of his property came home to him, his resolution faltered.

"I say, Feltram, what difference can it possibly make to him if I choose to ride round to Cloostedd Forest instead of crossing the lake in a boat?"

Feltram smiled darkly, and answered.

"I can't tell. Can you?"

"Of course I can't—I say I can't; besides, what audacity of a fellow like that presuming to prescribe to me! Utterly ludicrous! And he can't predict—do you really think or believe, Feltram, that he can?"

"I know he can. I know he misled you on purpose. He likes to punish those who don't respect his will; and there is a reason in it, often quite clear—not ill-natured. Now you see he compels you to seek him out, and when you do, I think he'll help you through your trouble. He said he would."

"Then you have seen him since?"

"Yesterday. He has put a pressure on you; but he means to help you."

"If he means to help me, let him remember I want a banker more than a seer. Let him give me a lift, as he did before. He must lend me money."

"He'll not stick at that. When he takes up a man, he carries him through."

"The races of Byermere—I might retrieve at them. But they don't come off for a month nearly; and what is a man like me to do in the meantime?"

"Every man should know his own business best. I'm not like you," said Feltram grimly.

Now Sir Bale's trouble increased, for some people were pressing. Something like panic supervened; for it happened that land was bringing just then a bad price, and more must be sold in consequence.

"All I can tell them is, I am selling land. It can't be done in an hour. I'm selling enough to pay them all twice over. Gentlemen used to be able to wait till a man sold his acres for payment. D—n them! do they want my body, that they can't let me alone for five minutes?"

The end of it was, that before a week Sir Bale told Feltram that he would go by boat, since that fellow insisted on it; and he did not very much care if he were drowned.

It was a beautiful autumnal day. Everything was bright in that mellowed sun, and the deep blue of the lake was tremulous with golden ripples; and crag and peak and scattered wood, faint in the distance, came out with a filmy distinctness on the fells in that pleasant light.

Sir Bale had been ill, and sent down the night before for Doctor Torvey. He was away with a patient. Now, in the morning, he had arrived inopportunely. He met Sir Bale as he issued from the house, and had a word with him in the court, for he would not turn back.

"Well," said the Doctor, after his brief inspection, "you ought to be in your bed; that's all I can say. You are perfectly mad to think of knocking about like this. Your pulse is at a hundred and ten; and, if you go across the lake and walk about Cloostedd, you'll be raving before you come back."

Sir Bale told him, apologetically, as if his life were more to his doctor than to himself, that he would take care not to fatigue himself, and that the air would do him good, and that in any case he could not avoid going; and so they parted.

Sir Bale took his seat beside Feltram in the boat, the sail was spread, and, bending to the light breeze that blew from Golden Friars, she glided from the jetty under Mardykes Hall, and the eventful voyage had begun.

CHAPTER XIX

Mystagogus

The sail was loosed, the boat touched the stone step, and Feltram sprang out and made her fast to the old iron ring. The Baronet followed. So! he had ventured upon that water without being drowned. He looked round him as if in a dream. He had not been there since his childhood. There were no regrets, no sentiment, no remorse; only an odd return of the associations and fresh feelings of boyhood, and a long reach of time suddenly annihilated.

The little hollow in which he stood; the three hawthorn trees at his right; every crease and undulation of the sward, every angle and crack in the lichen-covered rock at his feet, recurred with a sharp and instantaneous recognition to his memory.

"Many a time your brother and I fished for hours together from that bank there, just where the bramble grows. That bramble has not grown an inch ever since, not a leaf altered; we used to pick blackberries off it, with our rods stuck in the bank—it was later in the year than now—till we stript it quite bare after a day or two. The steward used to come over—they were marking timber for cutting and we used to stay here while they rambled through the wood, with an axe marking the trees that were to come down. I wonder whether the big old boat is still anywhere. I suppose she was broken up, or left to rot; I have not seen her since we came

home. It was in the wood that lies at the right—the other wood is
called the forest; they say in old times it was eight miles long,
northward up the shore of the lake, and full of deer; with a forester,
and a reeve, and a verderer, and all that. Your brother was older
than you; he went to India, or the Colonies; is he living still?"

"I care not."

"That's good-natured, at all events; but do you know?"

"Not I; and what matter? If he's living, I warrant he has his
share of the curse, the sweat of his brow and his bitter crust; and if
he is dead, he's dust or worse, he's rotten, and smells accordingly."

Sir Bale looked at him; for this was the brother over whom, only
a year or two ago, Philip used to cry tears of pathetic longing.
Feltram looked darkly in his face, and sneered with a cold laugh.

"I suppose you mean to jest?" said Sir Bale.

"Not I; it is the truth. It is what you'd say, if you were honest.
If he's alive, let him keep where he is; and if he's dead, I'll have
none of him, body or soul. Do you hear that sound?"

"Like the wind moaning in the forest?"

"Yes."

"But I feel no wind. There's hardly a leaf stirring."

"I think so," said Feltram. "Come along."

And he began striding up the gentle slope of the glen, with many
a rock peeping through its sward, and tufted ferns and furze, giving
a wild and neglected character to the scene; the background of
which, where the glen loses itself in a distant turn, is formed by its
craggy and wooded side.

Up they marched, side by side, in silence, towards that irregular
clump of trees, to which Feltram had pointed from the Mardykes
side.

As they approached, it showed more scattered, and two or three
of the trees were of grander dimensions than in the distance they
had appeared; and as they walked, the broad valley of Cloostedd
Forest opened grandly on their left, studding the sides of the valley
with solitary trees or groups, which thickened as it descended to the
broad level, in parts nearly three miles wide, on which stands the
noble forest of Cloostedd, now majestically reposing in the stirless
air, gilded and flushed with the melancholy tints of autumn.

I am now going to relate wonderful things; but they rest on the
report, strangely consistent, it is true, of Sir Bale Mardykes. That
all his senses, however, were sick and feverish, and his brain not
quite to be relied on at that moment, is a fact of which sceptics have
a right to make all they please and can.

Startled at their approach, a bird like a huge mackaw bounced from the boughs of the trees, and sped away, every now and then upon the ground, toward the shelter of the forest, fluttering and hopping close by the side of the little brook which, emerging from the forest, winds into the glen, and beside the course of which Sir Bale and Philip Feltram had ascended from the margin of the lake.

It fluttered on, as if one of its wings were hurt, and kept hopping and bobbing and flying along the grass at its swiftest, screaming all the time discordantly.

"That must be old Mrs. Amerald's bird, that got away a week ago," said Sir Bale, stopping and looking after it. "Was not it a mackaw?"

"No," said Feltram; "that was a gray parrot; but there are stranger birds in Cloostedd Forest, for my ancestors collected all that would live in our climate, and were at pains to find them the food and shelter they were accustomed to until they grew hardy— that is how it happens."

"By Jove, that's a secret worth knowing," said Sir Bale. "That would make quite a feature. What a fat brute that bird was! and green and dusky-crimson and yellow; but its head is white—age, I suspect; and what a broken beak—hideous bird! splendid plumage; something between a mackaw and a vulture."

Sir Bale spoke jocularly, but with the interest of a bird-fancier; a taste which, when young, he had indulged; and for the moment forgot his cares and the object of his unwonted excursion.

A moment after, a lank slim bird, perfectly white, started from the same boughs, and winged its way to the forest.

"A kite, I think; but its body is a little too long, isn't it?" said Sir Bale again, stopping and looking after its flight also.

"A foreign kite, I daresay?" said Feltram.

All this time there was hopping near them a jay, with the tameness of a bird accustomed to these solitudes. It peered over its slender wing curiously at the visitors; pecking here and nodding there; and thus hopping, it made a circle round them more than once. Then it fluttered up, and perched on a bough of the old oak, from the deep labyrinth of whose branches the other birds had emerged; and from thence it flew down and lighted on the broad druidic stone, that stood like a cyclopean table on its sunken stone props, before the snakelike roots of the oak.

Across this it hopped conceitedly, as over a stage on which it figured becomingly; and after a momentary hesitation, with a little spring, it rose and winged its way in the same direction which the other birds had taken, and was quickly lost in thick forest to the left.

"Here," said Feltram, "this is the tree."

"I remember it well! A gigantic trunk; and, yes, those marks; but I never before read them as letters. Yes, H. F., so they are—very odd I should not have remarked them. They are so large, and so strangely drawn-out in some places, and filled-in in others, and distorted, and the moss has grown about them; I don't wonder I took them for natural cracks and chasms in the bark," said Sir Bale.

"Very like," said Feltram.

Sir Bale had remarked, ever since they had begun their walk from the shore, that Feltram seemed to undergo a gloomy change. Sharper, grimmer, wilder grew his features, and shadow after shadow darkened his face wickedly.

The solitude and grandeur of the forest, and the repulsive gloom of his companion's countenance and demeanour, communicated a tone of anxiety to Sir Bale; and they stood still, side by side, in total silence for a time, looking toward the forest glades; between themselves and which, on the level sward of the valley, stood many a noble tree and fantastic group of forked birch and thorn, in the irregular formations into which Nature had thrown them.

"Now you stand between the letters. Cast your eyes on the stone," said Feltram suddenly, and his low stern tones almost startled the Baronet.

Looking round, he perceived that he had so placed himself that his point of vision was exactly from between the two great letters, now half-obliterated, which he had been scrutinizing just as he turned about to look toward the forest of Cloostedd.

"Yes, so I am," said Sir Bale.

There was within him an excitement and misgiving, akin to the sensation of a man going into battle, and which corresponded with the pale and sombre frown which Feltram wore, and the manifest change which had come over him.

"Look on the stone steadily for a time, and tell me if you see a black mark, about the size of your hand, anywhere upon its surface," said Feltram.

Sir Bale affected no airs of scepticism now; his imagination was stirred, and a sense of some unknown reality at the bottom of that which he had affected to treat before as illusion, inspired a strange interest in the experiment.

"Do you see it?" asked Feltram.

Sir Bale was watching patiently, but he had observed nothing of the kind.

Sharper, darker, more eager grew the face of Philip Feltram, as his eyes traversed the surface of that huge horizontal block.

"Now?" asked Feltram again.

No, he had seen nothing.

Feltram was growing manifestly uneasy, angry almost; he walked away a little, and back again, and then two or three times round the tree, with his hands shut, and treading the ground like a man trying to warm his feet, and so impatiently he returned, and looked again on the stone.

Sir Bale was still looking, and very soon said, drawing his brows together and looking hard,

"Ha!—yes—hush. There it is, by Jove!—wait—yes—there; it is growing quite plain."

It seemed not as if a shadow fell upon the stone, but rather as if the stone became semi-transparent, and just under its surface was something dark—a hand, he thought it—and darker and darker it grew, as if coming up toward the surface, and after some little wavering, it fixed itself movelessly, pointing, as he thought, toward the forest.

"It looks like a hand," said he. "By Jove, it *is* a hand—pointing towards the forest with a finger."

"Don't mind the finger; look only on that black blurred mark, and from the point where you stand, taking that point for your direction, look to the forest. Take some tree or other landmark for an object, enter the forest there, and pursue the same line, as well as you can, until you find little flowers with leaves like wood-sorrel, and with tall stems and a red blossom, not larger than a drop, such as you have not seen before, growing among the trees, and follow wherever they seem to grow thickest, and there you will find him."

All the time that Feltram was making this little address, Sir Bale was endeavouring to fix his route by such indications as Feltram described; and when he had succeeded in quite establishing the form of a peculiar tree—a melancholy ash, one huge limb of which had been blasted by lightning, and its partly stricken arm stood high and barkless, stretching its white fingers, as it were, in invitation into the forest, and signing the way for him—

"I have it now," said he. "Come Feltram, you'll come a bit of the way with me."

Feltram made no answer, but slowly shook his head, and turned and walked away, leaving Sir Bale to undertake his adventure alone.

The strange sound they had heard from the midst of the forest, like the rumble of a storm or the far-off trembling of a furnace, had quite ceased. Not a bird was hopping on the grass, or visible on bough or in the sky. Not a living creature was in sight—never was stillness more complete, or silence more oppressive.

It would have been ridiculous to give way to the old reluctance which struggled within him. Feltram had strode down the slope, and was concealed by a screen of bushes from his view. So alone, and full of an interest quite new to him, he set out in quest of his adventures.

CHAPTER XX

The Haunted Forest

Sir Bale Mardykes walked in a straight line, by bush and scaur, over the undulating ground, to the blighted ash-tree; and as he approached it, its withered bough stretched more gigantically into the air, and the forest seemed to open where it pointed.

He passed it by, and in a few minutes had lost sight of it again, and was striding onward under the shadow of the forest, which already enclosed him. He was directing his march with all the care he could, in exactly that line which, according to Feltram's rule, had been laid down for him. Now and then, having, as soldiers say, taken an object, and fixed it well in his memory, he would pause and look about him.

As a boy he had never entered the wood so far; for he was under a prohibition, lest he should lose himself in its intricacies, and be benighted there. He had often heard that it was haunted ground, and that too would, when a boy, have deterred him. It was on this account that the scene was so new to him, and that he cared so often to stop and look about him. Here and there a vista opened, exhibiting the same utter desertion, and opening farther perspectives through the tall stems of the trees faintly visible in the solemn shadow. No flowers could he see, but once or twice a wood anemone, and now and then a tiny grove of wood-sorrel.

Huge oak-trees now began to mingle and show themselves more and more frequently among the other timber; and gradually the forest became a great oak wood unintruded upon by any less noble tree. Vast trunks curving outwards to the roots, and expanding again at the branches, stood like enormous columns, striking out their groining boughs, with the dark vaulting of a crypt.

As he walked under the shadow of these noble trees, suddenly his eye was struck by a strange little flower, nodding quite alone by the knotted root of one of those huge oaks.

He stooped and picked it up, and as he plucked it, with a harsh scream just over his head, a large bird with heavy beating wings broke away from the midst of the branches. He could not see it, but he fancied the scream was like that of the huge mackaw whose ill-poised flight he had watched. This conjecture was but founded on the odd cry he had heard.

The flower was a curious one—a stem fine as a hair supported a little bell, that looked like a drop of blood, and never ceased trembling. He walked on, holding this in his fingers; and soon he saw another of the same odd type, then another at a shorter distance, then one a little to the right and another to the left, and farther on a little group, and at last the dark slope was all over trembling with these little bells, thicker and thicker as he descended a gentle declivity to the bank of the little brook, which flowing through the forest loses itself in the lake. The low murmur of this forest stream was almost the first sound, except the shriek of the bird that startled him a little time ago, which had disturbed the profound silence of the wood since he entered it. Mingling with the faint sound of the brook, he now heard a harsh human voice calling words at intervals, the purport of which he could not yet catch; and walking on, he saw seated upon the grass, a strange figure, corpulent, with a great hanging nose, the whole face glowing like copper. He was dressed in a bottle-green cut-velvet coat, of the style of Queen Anne's reign, with a dusky crimson waistcoat, both overlaid with broad and tarnished gold lace, and his silk stockings on thick swollen legs, with great buckled shoes, straddling on the grass, were rolled up over his knees to his short breeches. This ill-favoured old fellow, with a powdered wig that came down to his shoulders, had a dice-box in each hand, and was apparently playing his left against his right, and calling the throws with a hoarse cawing voice.

Raising his black piggish eyes, he roared to Sir Bale, by name, to come and sit down, raising one of his dice-boxes, and then indicating a place on the grass opposite to him.

Now Sir Bale instantly guessed that this was the man, gipsy, warlock, call him what he might, of whom he had come in search. With a strange feeling of curiosity, disgust, and awe, he drew near. He was resolved to do whatever this old man required of him, and to keep him, this time, in good humour.

Sir Bale did as he bid him, and sat down; and taking the box he presented, they began throwing turn about, with three dice, the copper-faced old man teaching him the value of the throws, as he proceeded, with many a curse and oath; and when he did not like a throw, grinning with a look of such real fury, that the master of Mardykes almost expected him to whip out his sword and prick him through as he sat before him.

After some time spent at this play, in which guineas passed now this way, now that, chucked across the intervening patch of grass, or rather moss, that served them for a green cloth, the old man roared over his shoulder,

"Drink;" and picking up a longstemmed conical glass which Sir Bale had not observed before, he handed it over to the Baronet; and taking another in his fingers, he held it up, while a very tall slim old man, dressed in a white livery, with powdered hair and cadaverous face, which seemed to run out nearly all into a long thin hooked nose, advanced with a flask in each hand. Looking at the unwieldly old man, with his heavy nose, powdered head, and all the bottle-green, crimson, and gold about him, and the long slim serving man, with sharp beak, and white from head to heel, standing by him, Sir Bale was forcibly reminded of the great old macaw and the long and slender kite, whose colours they, after their fashion, reproduced, with something, also indescribable, of the air and character of the birds. Not standing on ceremony, the old fellow held up his own glass first, which the white lackey filled from the flask, and then he filled Sir Bale's glass.

It was a large glass, and might have held about half a pint; and the liquor with which the servant filled it was something of the colour of an opal, and circles of purple and gold seemed to be spreading continually outward from the centre, and running inward from the rim, and crossing one another, so as to form a beautiful rippling net-work.

"I drink to your better luck next time," said the old man, lifting his glass high, and winking with one eye, and leering knowingly with the other; "and you know what I mean."

Sir Bale put the liquor to his lips. Wine? Whatever it was, never had he tasted so delicious a flavour. He drained it to the bottom, and placing it on the grass beside him, and looking again at the old dicer, who was also setting down his glass, he saw, for the first time, the graceful figure of a young woman seated on the grass. She was dressed in deep mourning, had a black hood carelessly over her head, and, strangely, wore a black mask, such as are used at masquerades. So much of her throat and chin as he could see were beautifully white; and there was a prettiness in her air and figure which made him think what a beautiful creature she in all likelihood was. She was reclining slightly against the burly man in bottle-green and gold, and her arm was round his neck, and her slender white hand showed itself over his shoulder.

"Ho! my little Geaiette," cried the old fellow hoarsely; "it will be time that you and I should get home.—So, Bale Mardykes, I have nothing to object to you this time; you've crossed the lake, and you've played with me and won and lost, and drank your glass like a jolly companion, and now we know one another; and an acquaintance is made that will last. I'll let you go, and you'll come when I call for you. And now you'll want to know what horse will win next month at Rindermere races.—Whisper me, lass, and I'll tell him."

So her lips, under the black curtain, crept close to his ear, and she whispered.

"Ay, so it will;" roared the old man, gnashing his teeth; "it will be Rainbow, and now make your best speed out of the forest, or I'll set my black dogs after you, ho, ho, ho! and they may chance to pull you down. Away!"

He cried this last order with a glare so black, and so savage a shake of his huge fist, that Sir Bale, merely making his general bow to the group, clapped his hat on his head, and hastily began his retreat; but the same discordant voice yelled after him:

"You'll want that, you fool; pick it up." And there came hurtling after and beside him a great leather bag, stained, and stuffed with a heavy burden, and bounding by him it stopped with a little wheel that brought it exactly before his feet.

He picked it up, and found it heavy.

Turning about to make his acknowledgments, he saw the two persons in full retreat; the profane old scoundrel in the bottle-green limping and stumbling, yet bowling along at a wonderful rate, with many a jerk and reel, and the slender lady in black gliding away by his side into the inner depths of the forest.

So Sir Bale, with a strange chill, and again in utter solitude, pursued his retreat, with his burden, at a swifter pace, and after an hour or so, had recovered the point where he had entered the forest, and passing by the druidic stone and the mighty oak, saw down the glen at his right, standing by the edge of the lake, Philip Feltram, close to the bow of the boat.

CHAPTER XXI

Rindermere

Feltram looked grim and agitated when Sir Bale came up to him, as he stood on the flat stone by which the boat was moored.

"You found him?" said he.

"Yes."

"The lady in black was there?"

"She was."

"And you played with him?"

"Yes."

"And what is that in your hand?"

"A bag of something, I fancy money; it is heavy; he threw it after me. We shall see just now; let us get away."

"He gave you some of his wine to drink?" said Feltram, looking darkly in his face; but there was a laugh in his eyes.

"Yes; of course I drank it; my object was to please him."

"To be sure."

The faint wind that carried them across the lake had quite subsided by the time they had reached the side where they now were.

There was now not wind enough to fill the sail, and it was already evening.

"Give me an oar; we can pull her over in little more than an hour," said Sir Bale; "only let us get away."

He got into the boat, sat down, and placed the leather bag with its heavy freightage at his feet, and took an oar. Feltram loosed the rope and shoved the boat off; and taking his seat also, they began to pull together, without another word, until, in about ten minutes, they had got a considerable way off the Cloostedd shore.

The leather bag was too clumsy a burden to conceal; besides, Feltram knew all about the transaction, and Sir Bale had no need to make a secret. The bag was old and soiled, and tied about the "neck" with a long leather thong, and it seemed to have been sealed with red wax, fragments of which were still sticking to it.

He got it open, and found it full of guineas.

"Halt!" cried Sir Bale, delighted, for he had half apprehended a trick upon his hopes; "gold it is, and a lot of it, by Jove!"

Feltram did not seem to take the slightest interest in the matter. Sulkily and drowsily he was leaning with his elbow on his knee, and it seemed thinking of something far away. Sir Bale could not wait to count them any longer. He reckoned them on the bench, and found two thousand.

It took some time; and when he had got them back into the leather bag, and tied them up again, Feltram, with a sudden start, said sharply,

"Come, take your oar—unless you like the lake by night; and see, a wind will soon be up from Golden Friars!"

He cast a wild look towards Mardykes Hall and Snakes Island, and applying himself to his oar, told Sir Bale to take his also; and nothing loath, the Baronet did so.

It was slow work, for the boat was not built for speed; and by the time they had got about midway, the sun went down, and twilight and the melancholy flush of the sunset tints were upon the lake and fells.

"Ho! here comes the breeze—up from Golden Friars," said Feltram; "we shall have enough to fill the sails now. If you don't fear spirits and Snakes Island, it is all the better for us it should blow from that point. If it blew from Mardykes now, it would be a stiff pull for you and me to get this tub home."

Talking as if to himself, and laughing low, he adjusted the sail and took the tiller, and so, yielding to the rising breeze, the boat glided slowly toward still distant Mardykes Hall.

The moon came out, and the shore grew misty, and the towering fells rose like sheeted giants; and leaning on the gunwale of the boat, Sir Bale, with the rush and gurgle of the water on the boat's side sounding faintly in his ear, thought of his day's adventure, which seemed to him like a dream—incredible but for the heavy bag that lay between his feet.

As they passed Snakes Island, a little mist, like a fragment of a fog, seemed to drift with them, and Sir Bale fancied that whenever it came near the boat's side she made a dip, as if strained toward the water; and Feltram always put out his hand, as if waving it from him, and the mist seemed to obey the gesture; but returned again and again, and the same thing always happened.

It was three weeks after, that Sir Bale, sitting up in his bed, very pale and wan, with his silk night-cap nodding on one side, and his thin hand extended on the coverlet, where the doctor had been feeling his pulse, in his darkened room, related all the wonders of this day to Doctor Torvey. The doctor had attended him through a fever which followed immediately upon his visit to Cloostedd.

"And, my dear sir, by Jupiter, can you really believe all that delirium to be sober fact?" said the doctor, sitting by the bedside, and actually laughing.

"I can't help believing it, because I can't distinguish in any way between all that and everything else that actually happened, and which I must believe. And, except that this is more wonderful, I can find no reason to reject it, that does not as well apply to all the rest."

"Come, come, my dear sir, this will never do—nothing is more common. These illusions accompanying fever frequently antedate the attack, and the man is actually raving before he knows he is ill."

"But what do you make of that bag of gold?"

"Some one has lent it. You had better ask all about it of Feltram when you can see him; for in speaking to me he seemed to know all about it, and certainly did not seem to think the matter at all out of the commonplace. It is just like that fisherman's story, about the hand that drew Feltram into the water on the night that he was nearly drowned. Every one can see what that was. Why of course it was simply the reflection of his own hand in the water, in that vivid lightning. When you have been out a little and have gained strength you will shake off these dreams."

"I should not wonder," said Sir Bale.

It is not to be supposed that Sir Bale reported all that was in his memory respecting his strange vision, if such it was, at Cloostedd. He made a selection of the incidents, and threw over the whole adventure an entirely accidental character, and described the money which the old man had thrown to him as amounting to a purse of five guineas, and mentioned nothing of the passages which bore on the coming race.

Good Doctor Torvey, therefore, reported only that Sir Bale's delirium had left two or three illusions sticking in his memory.

But if they were illusions, they survived the event of his recovery, and remained impressed on his memory with the sharpness of very recent and accurately observed fact.

He was resolved on going to the races of Rindermere, where, having in his possession so weighty a guarantee as the leather purse, he was determined to stake it all boldly on Rainbow— against which horse he was glad to hear there were very heavy odds.

The race came off. One horse was scratched, another bolted, the rider of a third turned out to have lost a buckle and three half-pence and so was an ounce and a half under weight, a fourth knocked down the post near Rinderness churchyard, and was held to have done it with his left instead of his right knee, and so had run at the wrong side. The result was that Rainbow came in first, and I should be afraid to say how much Sir Bale won. It was a sum that paid off a heavy debt, and left his affairs in a much more manageable state.

From this time Sir Bale prospered. He visited Cloostedd no more; but Feltram often crossed to that lonely shore as heretofore, and it is believed conveyed to him messages which guided his betting. One thing is certain, his luck never deserted him. His debts disappeared; and his love of continental life seemed to have departed. He became content with Mardykes Hall, laid out money on it, and although he never again cared to cross the lake, he seemed to like the scenery.

In some respects, however, he lived exactly the same odd and unpopular life. He saw no one at Mardykes Hall. He practised a very strict reserve. The neighbours laughed at and disliked him, and he was voted, whenever any accidental contact arose, a very disagreeable man; and he had a shrewd and ready sarcasm that made them afraid of him, and himself more disliked.

Odd rumours prevailed about his household. It was said that his old relations with Philip Feltram had become reversed; and that he was as meek as a mouse, and Feltram the bully now. It was also said that Mrs. Julaper had one Sunday evening when she drank tea at the Vicar's, told his good lady very mysteriously, and with many charges of secrecy, that Sir Bale was none the better of his late-found wealth; that he had a load upon his spirits, that he was afraid of Feltram, and so was every one else, more or less, in the house; that he was either mad or worse; and that it was an eerie dwelling, and strange company, and she should be glad herself of a change.

Good Mrs. Bedel told her friend Mrs. Torvey; and all Golden Friars heard all this, and a good deal more, in an incredibly short time.

All kinds of rumours now prevailed in Golden Friars, connecting Sir Bale's successes on the turf with some mysterious doings in Cloostedd Forest. Philip Feltram laughed when he heard these stories—especially when he heard the story that a supernatural personage had lent the Baronet a purse full of money.

"You should not talk to Doctor Torvey so, sir," said he grimly; "he's the greatest tattler in the town. It was old Farmer Trebeck, who could buy and sell us all down here, who lent that money. Partly from good-will, but not without acknowledgment. He has my hand for the first, not worth much, and yours to a bond for the two thousand guineas you brought home with you. It seems strange you should not remember that venerable and kind old farmer whom you talked with so long that day. His grandson, who expects to stand well in his will, being a trainer in Lord Varney's stables, has sometimes a tip to give, and he is the source of your information."

"By Jove, I must be a bit mad, then, that's all," said Sir Bale, with a smile and a shrug.

Philip Feltram moped about the house, and did precisely what he pleased. The change which had taken place in him became more and more pronounced. Dark and stern he always looked, and often malignant. He was like a man possessed of one evil thought which never left him.

There was, besides, the good old Gothic superstition of a bargain or sale of the Baronet's soul to the arch-fiend. This was, of course, very cautiously whispered in a place where he had influence. It was only a coarser and directer version of a suspicion, that in a more credulous generation penetrated a level of society quite exempt from such follies in our day.

One evening at dusk, Sir Bale, sitting after his dinner in his window, saw the tall figure of Feltram, like a dark streak, standing movelessly by the lake. An unpleasant feeling moved him, and then an impatience. He got up, and having primed himself with two glasses of brandy, walked down to the edge of the lake, and placed himself beside Feltram.

"Looking down from the window," said he, nerved with his Dutch courage, "and seeing you standing like a post, do you know what I began to think of?"

Feltram looked at him, but answered nothing.

"I began to think of taking a wife—*marrying*."

Feltram nodded. The announcement had not produced the least effect.

"Why the devil will you make me so uncomfortable! Can't you be like yourself—what you *were*, I mean? I won't go on living here alone with you. I'll take a wife, I tell you. I'll choose a good church-going woman, that will have every man, woman, and child in the house on their marrow-bones twice a day, morning and evening, and three times on Sundays. How will you like that?"

"Yes, you will be married," said Feltram, with a quiet decision which chilled Sir Bale, for he had by no means made up his mind to that desperate step.

Feltram slowly walked away, and that conversation ended.

Now an odd thing happened about this time. There was a family of Feltram—county genealogists could show how related to the vanished family of Cloostedd—living at that time on their estate not far from Carlisle. Three co-heiresses now represented it. They were great beauties—the belles of their county in their day.

One was married to Sir Oliver Haworth of Haworth, a great family in those times. He was a knight of the shire, and had refused a baronetage, and, it was said, had his eye on a peerage. The other sister was married to Sir William Walsingham, a wealthy baronet; and the third and youngest, Miss Janet, was still unmarried, and at home at Cloudesly Hall, where her aunt, Lady Harbottle, lived with her, and made a dignified chaperon.

Now it so fell out that Sir Bale, having business at Carlisle, and knowing old Lady Harbottle, paid his respects at Cloudesly Hall; and being no less than five-and-forty years of age, was for the first time in his life, seriously in love.

Miss Janet was extremely pretty—a fair beauty with brilliant red lips and large blue eyes, and ever so many pretty dimples when she talked and smiled. It was odd, but not perhaps against the course of nature, that a man, though so old as he, and quite *blasé*, should fall at last under that fascination.

But what are we to say of the strange infatuation of the young lady? No one could tell why she liked him. It was a craze. Her family were against it, her intimates, her old nurse—all would not do; and the oddest thing was, that he seemed to take no pains to please her. The end of this strange courtship was that he married her; and she came home to Mardykes Hall, determined to please everybody, and to be the happiest woman in England.

With her came a female cousin, a good deal her senior, past thirty—Gertrude Mainyard, pale and sad, but very gentle, and with all the prettiness that can belong to her years.

This young lady has a romance. Her hero is far away in India; and she, content to await his uncertain return with means to accomplish the hope of their lives, in that frail chance has long embarked all the purpose and love of her life.

When Lady Mardykes came home, a new leaf was, as the phrase is, turned over. The neighbours and all the country people were willing to give the Hall a new trial. There was visiting and returning of visits; and young Lady Mardykes was liked and admired. It could not indeed have been otherwise. But here the improvement in the relations of Mardykes Hall with other homes ceased. On one excuse or another Sir Bale postponed or evaded the hospitalities which establish intimacies. Some people said he was jealous of his young and beautiful wife. But for the most part his reserve was set down to the old inhospitable cause, some ungenial defect in his character; and in a little time the tramp of horses and roll of carriage-wheels were seldom heard up or down the broad avenue of Mardykes Hall.

Sir Bale liked this seclusion; and his wife, "so infatuated with her idolatry of that graceless old man," as surrounding young ladies said, that she was well content to forego the society of the county people for a less interrupted enjoyment of that of her husband. "What she could see in him" to interest or amuse her so, that for his sake she was willing to be "buried alive in that lonely place," the same critics were perpetually wondering.

A year and more passed thus; for the young wife, happily—*very* happily indeed, had it not been for one topic on which she and her husband could not agree. This was Philip Feltram; and an odd quarrel it was.

CHAPTER XXII

Sir Bale is Frightened

To Feltram she had conceived, at first sight, a horror. It was not a mere antipathy; fear mingled largely in it. Although she did not see him often, this restless dread grew upon her so, that she urged his dismissal upon Sir Bale, offering to provide, herself, for him a handsome annuity, charged on that part of her property which, by her marriage settlement, had remained in her power. There was a time when Sir Bale was only too anxious to get rid of him. But that was changed now. Nothing could now induce the Baronet to part with him. He at first evaded and resisted quietly. But, urged with a perseverance to which he was unused, he at last broke into fury that appalled her, and swore that if he was worried more upon the subject, he would leave her and the country, and see neither again. This exhibition of violence affrighted her all the more by reason of the contrast; for up to this he had been an uxorious husband. Lady Mardykes was in hysterics, and thoroughly frightened, and remained in her room for two or three days. Sir Bale went up to London about business, and was not home for more than a week. This was the first little squall that disturbed the serenity of their sky.

This point, therefore, was settled; but soon there came other things to sadden Lady Mardykes. There occurred a little incident, soon after Sir Bale's return from London, which recalled the topic on which they had so nearly quarrelled.

Sir Bale had a dressing-room, remote from the bedrooms, in which he sat and read and sometimes smoked. One night, after the house was all quiet, the Baronet being still up, the bell of this dressing-room rang long and furiously. It was such a peal as a person in extreme terror might ring. Lady Mardykes, with her maid in her room, heard it; and in great alarm she ran in her dressing-gown down the gallery to Sir Bale's room. Mallard the butler had already arrived, and was striving to force the door, which was secured. It gave way just as she reached it, and she rushed through.

Sir Bale was standing with the bell-rope in his hand, in the extremest agitation, looking like a ghost; and Philip Feltram was sitting in his chair, with a dark smile fixed upon him. For a minute she thought he had attempted to assassinate his master. She could not otherwise account for the scene.

There had been nothing of the kind, however; as her husband assured her again and again, as she lay sobbing on his breast, with her arms about his neck.

"To her dying hour," she afterwards said to her cousin, "she never could forget the dreadful look in Feltram's face."

No explanation of that scene did she ever obtain from Sir Bale, nor any clue to the cause of the agony that was so powerfully expressed in his countenance. Thus much only she learned from him, that Feltram had sought that interview for the purpose of announcing his departure, which was to take place within the year.

"You are not sorry to hear that. But if you knew all, you might. Let the curse fly where it may, it will come back to roost. So, darling, let us discuss him no more. Your wish is granted, *dis iratis.*"

Some crisis, during this interview, seemed to have occurred in the relations between Sir Bale and Feltram. Henceforward they seldom exchanged a word; and when they did speak, it was coldly and shortly, like men who were nearly strangers.

One day in the courtyard, Sir Bale seeing Feltram leaning upon the parapet that overlooks the lake, approached him, and said in a low tone,

"I've been thinking if we—that is, I—do owe that money to old Trebeck, it is high time I should pay it. I was ill, and had lost my head at the time; but it turned out luckily, and it ought to be paid. I don't like the idea of a bond turning up, and a lot of interest."

"The old fellow meant it for a present. He is richer than you are; he wished to give the family a lift. He has destroyed the bond, I believe, and in no case will he take payment."

"No fellow has a right to force his money on another," answered Sir Bale. "I never asked him. Besides, as you know, I was not really myself, and the whole thing seems to me quite different from what you say it was; and, so far as my brain is concerned, it was all a phantasmagoria; but, you say, it was he."

"Every man is accountable for what he intends and for what he *thinks* he does," said Feltram cynically.

"Well, I'm accountable for dealing with that wicked old dicer I *thought* I saw—isn't that it? But I must pay old Trebeck all the same, since the money was his. Can you manage a meeting?"

"Look down here. Old Trebeck has just landed; he will sleep to-night at the George and Dragon, to meet his cattle in the morning at Golden Friars fair. You can speak to him yourself."

So saying Feltram glided away, leaving Sir Bale the task of opening the matter to the wealthy farmer of Cloostedd Fells.

A broad flight of steps leads down from the courtyard to the level of the jetty at the lake: and Sir Bale descended, and accosted the venerable farmer, who was bluff, honest, and as frank as a man can be who speaks a *patois* which hardly a living man but himself can understand.

Sir Bale asked him to come to the Hall and take luncheon; but Trebeck was in haste. Cattle had arrived which he wanted to look at, and a pony awaited him on the road, hard by, to Golden Friars; and the old fellow must mount and away.

Then Sir Bale, laying his hand upon his arm in a manner that was at once lofty and affectionate, told in his ears the subject on which he wished to be understood.

The old farmer looked hard at him, and shook his head and laughed in a way that would have been insupportable in a house, and told him, "I hev narra bond o' thoine, mon."

"I know how that is; so does Philip Feltram."

"Well?"

"Well, I must replace the money."

The old man laughed again, and in his outlandish dialect told him to wait till he asked him. Sir Bale pressed it, but the old fellow put it off with outlandish banter; and as the Baronet grew testy, the farmer only waxed more and more hilarious, and at last, mounting his shaggy pony, rode off, still laughing, at a canter to Golden Friars; and when he reached Golden Friars, and got into the hall of the George and Dragon, he asked Richard Turnbull with a chuckle if he ever knew a man refuse an offer of money, or a man want to pay who did not owe; and inquired whether the Squire down at Mardykes Hall mightn't be a bit "wrang in t' garrets." All this, however, other people said, was intended merely to conceal the fact that he really had, through sheer loyalty, lent the money, or rather bestowed it, thinking the old family in jeopardy, and meaning a gift, was determined to hear no more about it. I can't say; I only know people held, some by one interpretation, some by another.

As the caterpillar sickens and changes its hue when it is about to undergo its transformation, so an odd change took place in Feltram. He grew even more silent and morose; he seemed always in an agitation and a secret rage. He used to walk through the woodlands on the slopes of the fells above Mardykes, muttering to himself, picking up the rotten sticks with which the ground was strewn, breaking them in his hands, and hurling them from him, and stamping on the earth as he paced up and down.

One night a thunder-storm came on, the wind blowing gently up from Golden Friars. It was a night black as pitch, illuminated only by the intermittent glare of the lightning. At the foot of the stairs Sir Bale met Feltram, whom he had not seen for some days. He had his cloak and hat on.

"I am going to Cloostedd to-night," he said, "and if all is as I expect, I sha'n't return. We remember all, you and I." And he nodded and walked down the passage.

Sir Bale knew that a crisis had happened in his own life. He felt faint and ill, and returned to the room where he had been sitting. Throughout that melancholy night he did not go to his bed.

In the morning he learned that Marlin, who had been out late, saw Feltram get the boat off, and sail towards the other side. The night was so dark that he could only see him start; but the wind was light and coming up the lake, so that without a tack he could easily make the other side. Feltram did not return. The boat was found fast to the ring at Cloostedd landing place.

Lady Mardykes was relieved, and for a time was happier than ever. It was different with Sir Bale; and afterwards her sky grew dark also.

CHAPTER XXIII
A Lady in Black

Shortly after this, there arrived at the George and Dragon a stranger. He was a man somewhat past forty, embrowned by distant travel, and, his years considered, wonderfully good-looking. He had good eyes; his dark-brown hair had no sprinkling of gray in it; and his kindly smile showed very white and even teeth. He made inquiries about neighbours, especially respecting Mardykes Hall; and the answers seemed to interest him profoundly. He inquired after Philip Feltram, and shed tears when he heard that he was no longer at Mardykes Hall, and that Trebeck or other friends could give him no tidings of him.

And then he asked Richard Turnbull to show him to a quiet room; and so, taking the honest fellow by the hand, he said,

"Mr. Turnbull, don't you know me?"

"No, sir," said the host of the George and Dragon, after a puzzled stare, "I can't say I do, sir."

The stranger smiled a little sadly, and shook his head: and with a gentle laugh, still holding his hand in a very friendly way, he said, "I should have known you anywhere, Mr. Turnbull—anywhere on earth or water. Had you turned up on the Himalayas, or in a junk on the Canton river, or as a dervish in the mosque of St. Sophia, I should have recognised my old friend, and asked what news from Golden Friars. But of course I'm changed. You were a little my senior; and one advantage among many you have over your juniors is that you don't change as we do. I have played many a game of hand-ball in the inn-yard of the George, Mr. Turnbull. You often wagered a pot of ale on my play; you used to say I'd make the best player of fives, and the best singer of a song, within ten miles round the meer. You used to have me behind the bar when I was a boy, with more of an appetite than I have now. I was then at Mardykes Hall, and used to go back in old Marlin's boat. Is old Marlin still alive?"

"Ay, that—he—is," said Turnbull slowly, as he eyed the stranger again carefully. "I don't know who you can be, sir, unless you are —the boy—William Feltram. La! he was seven or eight years younger than Philip. But, lawk!—Well—By Jen, and be you Willie Feltram? But no, you can't!"

"Ay, Mr. Turnbull, that very boy—Willie Feltram—even he, and no other; and now you'll shake hands with me, not so formally, but like an old friend."

"Ay, that I will," said honest Richard Turnbull, with a great smile, and a hearty grasp of his guest's hand; and they both laughed together, and the younger man's eyes, for he was an affectionate fool, filled up with tears.

" And I want you to tell me this," said William, after they had talked a little quietly, "now that there is no one to interrupt us, what has become of my brother Philip? I heard from a friend an account of his health that has caused me unspeakable anxiety."

"His health was not bad; no, he was a hardy lad, and liked a walk over the fells, or a pull on the lake; but he was a bit daft, every one said, and a changed man; and, in troth, they say the air o' Mardykes don't agree with every one, no more than him. But that's a tale that's neither here nor there."

"Yes," said William, "that was what they told me—his mind affected. God help and guard us! I have been unhappy ever since; and if I only knew it was well with poor Philip, I think I should be too happy. And where is Philip now?"

"He crossed the lake one night, having took leave of Sir Bale. They thought he was going to old Trebeck's up the Fells. He likes the Feltrams, and likes the folk at Mardykes Hall—though those two families was not always o'er kind to one another. But Trebeck seed nowt o' him, nor no one else; and what has gone wi' him no one can tell."

"I heard that also," said William with a deep sigh. "But I hoped it had been cleared up by now, and something happier been known of the poor fellow by this time. I'd give a great deal to know—I don't know what I *would* not give to know—I'm so unhappy about him. And now, my good old friend, tell your people to get me a chaise, for I must go to Mardykes Hall; and, first, let me have a room to dress in."

At Mardykes Hall a pale and pretty lady was looking out, alone, from the stone-shafted drawing-room window across the courtyard and the balustrade, on which stood many a great stone cup with flowers, whose leaves were half shed and gone with the winds— emblem of her hopes. The solemn melancholy of the towering fells, the ripple of the lonely lake, deepened her sadness.

The unwonted sound of carriage-wheels awoke her from her reverie.

Before the chaise reached the steps, a hand from its window had seized the handle, the door was thrown open, and William Feltram jumped out.

She was in the hall, she knew not how; and, with a wild scream and a sob, she threw herself into his arms.

Here at last was an end of the long waiting, the dejection which had reached almost the point of despair. And like two rescued from shipwreck, they clung together in an agony of happiness.

William had come back with no very splendid fortune. It was enough, and only enough, to enable them to marry. Prudent people would have thought it, very likely, too little. But he was now home in England, with health unimpaired by his long sojourn in the East, and with intelligence and energies improved by the discipline of his arduous struggle with fortune. He reckoned, therefore, upon one way or other adding something to their income; and he knew that a few hundreds a year would make them happier than hundreds of thousand could other people.

It was five years since they had parted in France, where a journey of importance to the Indian firm, whose right hand he was, had brought him.

The refined tastes that are supposed to accompany gentle blood, his love of art, his talent for music and drawing, had accidentally attracted the attention of the little travelling-party which old Lady Harbottle chaperoned. Miss Janet, now Lady Mardykes, learning that his name was Feltram, made inquiry through a common friend, and learned what interested her still more about him. It ended in an acquaintance, which his manly and gentle nature and his entertaining qualities soon improved into an intimacy.

Feltram had chosen to work his own way, being proud, and also prosperous enough to prevent his pride, in this respect, from being placed under too severe a pressure of temptation. He heard not from but of his brother, through a friend in London, and more lately from Gertrude, whose account of him was sad and even alarming.

When Lady Mardykes came in, her delight knew no bounds. She had already formed a plan for their future, and was not to be put off—William Feltram was to take the great grazing farm that belonged to the Mardykes estate; or, if he preferred it, to farm it for her, sharing the profits. She wanted something to interest her, and this was just the thing. It was hardly half-a-mile away, up the lake, and there was such a comfortable house and garden, and she and Gertrude could be as much together as ever almost; and, in fact, Gertrude and her husband could be nearly always at Mardykes Hall.

So eager and entreating was she, that there was no escape. The plan was adopted immediately on their marriage, and no happier neighbours for a time were ever known.

But was Lady Mardykes content? was she even exempt from the heartache which each mortal thinks he has all to himself? The longing of her life was for children; and again and again had her hopes been disappointed.

One tiny pretty little baby indeed was born, and lived for two years, and then died; and none had come to supply its place and break the childless silence in the great old nursery. That was her sorrow; a greater one than men can understand.

Another source of grief was this: that Sir Bale Mardykes conceived a dislike to William Feltram that was unaccountable. At first suppressed, it betrayed itself negatively only; but with time it increased; and in the end the Baronet made little secret of his wish to get rid of him. Many and ingenious were the annoyances he contrived; and at last he told his wife plainly that he wished William Feltram to find some other abode for himself.

Lady Mardykes pleaded earnestly, and even with tears; for if Gertrude were to leave the neighbourhood, she well knew how utterly solitary her own life would become.

Sir Bale at last vouchsafed some little light as to his motives. There was an old story, he told her, that his estate would go to a Feltram. He had an instinctive distrust of that family. It was a feeling not given him for nothing; it might be the means of defeating their plotting and strategy. Old Trebeck, he fancied, had a finger in it. Philip Feltram had told him that Mardykes was to pass away to a Feltram. Well, they might conspire; but he would take what care he could that the estate should not be stolen from his family. He did not want his wife stript of her jointure, or his children, if he had any, left without bread.

All this sounded very like madness; but the idea was propounded by Philip Feltram. His own jealousy was at bottom founded on superstition which he would not avow and could hardly define. He bitterly blamed himself for having permitted William Feltram to place himself where he was.

In the midst of these annoyances William Feltram was seriously thinking of throwing up the farm, and seeking similar occupation somewhere else.

One day, walking alone in the thick wood that skirts the lake near his farm, he was discussing this problem with himself; and every now and then he repeated his question, "Shall I throw it up, and give him the lease back if he likes?" On a sudden he heard a voice near him say:

"Hold it, you fool!—hold hard, you fool!—hold it, you fool!"

The situation being lonely, he was utterly puzzled to account for the interruption, until on a sudden a huge parrot, green, crimson, and yellow, plunged from among the boughs over his head to the ground, and partly flying, and partly hopping and tumbling along, got lamely, but swiftly, out of sight among the thick underwood; and he could neither start it nor hear it any more. The interruption reminded him of that which befel Robinson Crusoe. It was more singular, however; for he owned no such bird; and its strangeness impressed the omen all the more.

He related it when he got home to his wife; and as people when living a solitary life, and also suffering, are prone to superstition, she did not laugh at the adventure, as in a healthier state of spirits, I suppose, she would.

They continued, however, to discuss the question together; and all the more industriously as a farm of the same kind, only some fifteen miles away, was now offered to all bidders, under another landlord. Gertrude, who felt Sir Bale's unkindness all the more that she was a distant cousin of his, as it had proved on comparing notes, was very strong in favour of the change, and had been urging it with true feminine ingenuity and persistence upon her husband. A very singular dream rather damped her ardour, however, and it appeared thus:

She had gone to her bed full of this subject; and she thought, although she could not remember having done so, had fallen asleep. She was still thinking, as she had been all the day, about leaving the farm. It seemed to her that she was quite awake, and a candle burning all the time in the room, awaiting the return of her husband, who was away at the fair near Haworth; she saw the interior of the room distinctly. It was a sultry night, and a little bit of the window was raised. A very slight sound in that direction attracted her attention; and to her surprise she saw a jay hop upon the window-sill, and into the room.

Up sat Gertrude, surprised and a little startled at the visit of so large a bird, without presence of mind for the moment even to frighten it away, and staring at it, as they say, with all her eyes. A sofa stood at the foot of the bed; and under this the bird swiftly hopped. She extended her hand now to take the bell-rope at the left side of the bed, and in doing so displaced the curtains, which were open only at the foot. She was amazed there to see a lady dressed entirely in black, and with the old-fashioned hood over her head. She was young and pretty, and looked kindly at her, but with now and then a slight contraction of lips and eyebrows that indicates pain. This little twitching was momentary, and recurred, it seemed, about once or twice in a minute.

How it was that she was not frightened on seeing this lady, standing like an old friend at her bedside, she could not afterwards understand. Some influence besides the kindness of her look prevented any sensation of terror at the time. With a very white hand the young lady in black held a white handkerchief pressed to her bosom at the top of her bodice.

"Who are you?" asked Gertrude.

"I am a kinswoman, although you don't know me; and I have come to tell you that you must not leave Faxwell" (the name of the place) "or Janet. If you go, I will go with you; and I can make you fear me."

Her voice was very distinct, but also very faint, with something undulatory in it, that seemed to enter Gertrude's head rather than her ear.

Saying this she smiled horribly, and, lifting her handkerchief, disclosed for a moment a great wound in her breast, deep in which Gertrude saw darkly the head of a snake writhing.

Hereupon she uttered a wild scream of terror, and, diving under the bed-clothes, remained more dead than alive there, until her maid, alarmed by her cry, came in, and having searched the room, and shut the window at her desire, did all in her power to comfort her.

If this was a nightmare and embodied only by a form of expression which in some states belongs to the imagination, a leading idea in the controversy in which her mind had long been employed, it had at least the effect of deciding her against leaving Faxwell. And so that point was settled; and unpleasant relations continued between the tenants of the farm and the master of Mardykes Hall.

To Lady Mardykes all this was very painful, although Sir Bale did not insist upon making a separation between his wife and her cousin. But to Mardykes Hall that cousin came no more. Even Lady Mardykes thought it better to see her at Faxwell than to risk a meeting in the temper in which Sir Bale then was. And thus several years passed.

No tidings of Philip Feltram were heard; and, in fact, none ever reached that part of the world; and if it had not been highly improbable that he could have drowned himself in the lake without his body sooner or later having risen to the surface, it would have been concluded that he had either accidentally or by design made away with himself in its waters.

Over Mardykes Hall there was a gloom—no sound of children's voices was heard there, and even the hope of that merry advent had died out.

This disappointment had no doubt helped to fix in Sir Bale's mind the idea of the insecurity of his property, and the morbid fancy that William Feltram and old Trebeck were conspiring to seize it; than which, I need hardly say, no imagination more insane could have fixed itself in his mind.

In other things, however, Sir Bale was shrewd and sharp, a clear and rapid man of business, and although this was a strange whim, it was not so unnatural in a man who was by nature so prone to suspicion as Sir Bale Mardykes.

During the years, now seven, that had elapsed since the marriage of Sir Bale and Miss Janet Feltram, there had happened but one event, except the death of their only child, to place them in mourning. That was the decease of Sir William Walsingham, the husband of Lady Mardykes' sister. She now lived in a handsome old dowerhouse at Islington, and being wealthy, made now and then an excursion to Mardykes Hall, in which she was sometimes accompanied by her sister Lady Haworth. Sir Oliver being a Parliamentman was much in London and deep in politics and intrigue, and subject, as convivial rogues are, to occasional hard hits from gout.

But change and separation had made no alteration in these ladies' mutual affections, and no three sisters were ever more attached.

Was Lady Mardykes happy with her lord? A woman so gentle and loving as she, is a happy wife with any husband who is not an absolute brute. There must have been, I suppose, some good about Sir Bale. His wife was certainly deeply attached to him. She admired his wisdom, and feared his inflexible will, and altogether made of him a domestic idol. To acquire this enviable position, I suspect there must be something not essentially disagreeable about a man. At all events, what her neighbours good-naturedly termed her infatuation continued, and indeed rather improved by time.

CHAPTER XXIV

An Old Portrait

Sir Bale—whom some remembered a gay and convivial man, not to say a profligate one—had grown to be a very gloomy man indeed. There was something weighing upon his mind; and I daresay some of the good gossips of Golden Friars, had there been any materials for such a case, would have believed that Sir Bale had murdered Philip Feltram, and was now the victim of the worm and fire of remorse.

The gloom of the master of the house made his very servants gloomy, and the house itself looked sombre, as if it had been startled with strange and dismal sights.

Lady Mardykes was something of an artist. She had lighted lately, in an out-of-the-way room, upon a dozen or more old portraits. Several of these were full-lengths; and she was—with the help of her maid, both in long aprons, amid sponges and basins, soft handkerchiefs and varnish-pots and brushes—busy in removing the dust and smoke-stains, and in laying-on the varnish, which brought out the colouring, and made the transparent shadows yield up their long-buried treasures of finished detail.

Against the wall stood a full-length portrait as Sir Bale entered the room; having for a wonder, a word to say to his wife.

"O," said the pretty lady, turning to him in her apron, and with her brush in her hand, "we are in such in pickle, Munnings and I have been cleaning these old pictures. Mrs. Julaper says they are the pictures that came from Cloostedd Hall long ago. They were buried in dust in the dark room in the clock-tower. Here is such a characteristic one. It has a long powdered wig—George the First or Second, I don't know which—and such a combination of colours, and such a face. It seems starting out of the canvas, and all but speaks. Do look; that is, I mean, Bale, if you can spare time."

Sir Bale abstractedly drew near, and looked over his wife's shoulder on the full-length portrait that stood before him; and as he did so a strange expression for a moment passed over his face.

The picture represented a man of swarthy countenance, with signs of the bottle glowing through the dark skin; small fierce pig eyes, a rather flat pendulous nose, and a grim forbidding mouth, with a large wart a little above it. On the head hung one of those full-bottomed powdered wigs that look like a cloud of cotton-wadding; a lace cravat was about his neck; he wore short black-velvet breeches with stockings rolled over them, a bottle-green coat of cut velvet and a crimson waistcoat with long flaps; coat and waistcoat both heavily laced with gold. He wore a sword, and leaned upon a crutch-handled cane, and his figure and aspect indicated a swollen and gouty state. He could not be far from sixty. There was uncommon force in this fierce and forbidding-looking portrait. Lady Mardykes said, "What wonderful dresses they wore! How like a fine magic-lantern figure he looks! What gorgeous colouring! it looks like the plumage of a mackaw; and what a claw his hand is! and that huge broken beak of a nose! Isn't he like a wicked old mackaw?"

"Where did you find that?" asked Sir Bale.

Surprised at his tone, she looked round, and was still more surprised at his looks.

"I told you, dear Bale, I found them in the clock-tower. I hope I did right; it was not wrong bringing them here? I ought to have asked. Are you vexed, Bale?"

"Vexed! not I. I only wish it was in the fire. I must have seen that picture when I was a child. I hate to look at it. I raved about it once, when I was ill. I don't know who it is; I don't remember when I saw it. I wish you'd tell them to burn it."

"It is one of the Feltrams," she answered. " 'Sir Hugh Feltram' is on the frame at the foot; and old Mrs. Julaper says he was the father of the unhappy lady who was said to have been drowned near Snakes Island."

"Well, suppose he is; there's nothing interesting in that. It is a disgusting picture. I connect it with my illness; and I think it is the kind of thing that would make any one half mad, if they only looked at it often enough. Tell them to burn it; and come away, come to the next room; I can't say what I want here."

Sir Bale seemed to grow more and more agitated the longer he remained in the room. He seemed to her both frightened and furious; and taking her a little roughly by the wrist, he led her through the door.

When they were in another apartment alone, he again asked the affrighted lady who had told her that picture was there, and who told her to clean it.

She had only the truth to plead. It was, from beginning to end, the merest accident.

"If I thought, Janet, that you were taking counsel of others, talking me over, and trying clever experiments—" he stopped short with his eyes fixed on hers with black suspicion.

His wife's answer was one pleading look, and to burst into tears.

Sir Bale let-go her wrist, which he had held up to this; and placing his hand gently on her shoulder, he said,

"You must not cry, Janet; I have given you no excuse for tears. I only wished an answer to a very harmless question; and I am sure you would tell me, if by any chance you have lately seen Philip Feltram; he is capable of arranging all that. No one knows him as I do. There, you must not cry any more; but tell me truly, has he turned up? is he at Faxwell?"

She denied all this with perfect truth; and after a hesitation of some time, the matter ended. And as soon as she and he were more themselves, he had something quite different to tell her.

"Sit down, Janet; sit down, and forget that vile picture and all

I have been saying. What I came to tell you, I think you will like; I am sure it will please you."

And with this little preface he placed his arm about her neck, and kissed her tenderly. She certainly was pleased; and when his little speech was over, she, smiling, with her tears still wet upon her cheeks, put her arms round her husband's neck, and in turn kissed him with the ardour of gratitude, kissed him affectionately; again and again thanking him all the time.

It was no great matter, but from Sir Bale Mardykes it was something quite unusual.

Was it a sudden whim? What was it? Something had prompted Sir Bale, early in that dark shrewd month of December, to tell his wife that he wished to call together some of his county acquaintances, and to fill his house for a week or so, as near Christmas as she could get them to come. He wished her sisters—Lady Haworth (with her husband) and the Dowager Lady Walsingham—to be invited for an early day, before the coming of the other guests, so that she might enjoy their society for a little time quietly to herself before the less intimate guests should assemble.

Glad was Lady Mardykes to hear the resolve of her husband, and prompt to obey. She wrote to her sisters to beg them to arrange to come, together, by the tenth or twelfth of the month, which they accordingly arranged to do. Sir Oliver, it was true, could not be of the party. A minister of state was drinking the waters at Bath; and Sir Oliver thought it would do him no harm to sip a little also, and his fashionable doctor politely agreed, and "ordered" to those therapeutic springs the knight of the shire, who was "consumedly vexed" to lose the Christmas with that jolly dog, Bale, down at Mardykes Hall. But a fellow must have a stomach for his Christmas pudding, and politics takes it out of a poor gentleman deucedly; and health's the first thing, egad!

So Sir Oliver went down to Bath, and I don't know that he tippled much of the waters, but he did drink the burgundy of that haunt of the ailing; and he had the honour of making a fourth not unfrequently in the secretary of state's whist-parties.

It was about the 8th of December when, in Lady Walsingham's carriage, intending to post all the way, that lady, still young, and Lady Haworth, with all the servants that were usual in such expeditions in those days, started from the great Dower House at Islington in high spirits.

Lady Haworth had not been very well—low and nervous; but the clear frosty sun, and the pleasant nature of the excursion, raised her spirits to the point of enjoyment; and expecting nothing·

but happiness and gaiety—for, after all, Sir Bale was but one of a large party, and even he could make an effort and be agreeable as well as hospitable on occasion—they set out on their northward expedition. The journey, which is a long one, they had resolved to break into a four days' progress; and the inns had been written to, bespeaking a comfortable reception.

CHAPTER XXV

Through the Wall

On the third night they put-up at the comfortable old inn called the Three Nuns. With an effort they might easily have pushed on to Mardykes Hall that night, for the distance is not more than five-and-thirty miles. But, considering her sister's health, Lady Walsingham in planning their route had resolved against anything like a forced march.

Here the ladies took possession of the best sitting-room; and, notwithstanding the fatigue of the journey, Lady Haworth sat up with her sister till near ten o'clock, chatting gaily about a thousand things.

Of the three sisters, Lady Walsingham was the eldest. She had been in the habit of taking the command at home; and now, for advice and decision, her younger sisters, less prompt and courageous than she, were wont, whenever in her neighbourhood, to throw upon her all the cares and agitations of determining what was best to be done in small things and great. It is only fair to say, in addition, that this submission was not by any means exacted; it was the deference of early habit and feebler will, for she was neither officious nor imperious.

It was now time that Lady Haworth, a good deal more fatigued than her sister, should take leave of her for the night.

Accordingly they kissed and bid each other good-night; and Lady Walsingham, not yet disposed to sleep, sat for some time longer in the comfortable room where they had taken tea, amusing the time with the book that had, when conversation flagged, beguiled the weariness of the journey. Her sister had been in her room nearly an hour, when she became herself a little sleepy. She had lighted her candle, and was going to ring for her maid, when, to her surprise, the door opened, and her sister Lady Haworth entered in a dressing-gown, looking frightened.

"My darling Mary!" exclaimed Lady Walsingham, "what is the matter? Are you well?"

"Yes, darling," she answered, "quite well; that is, I don't know what is the matter—I'm frightened." She paused, listening, with her eyes turned towards the wall. "O, darling Maud, I am so frightened! I don't know what it can be."

"You must not be agitated, darling; there's nothing. You have been asleep, and I suppose you have had a dream. Were you asleep?"

Lady Haworth had caught her sister fast by the arm with both hands, and was looking wildly in her face.

"Have *you* heard nothing?" she asked, again looking towards the wall of the room, as if she expected to hear a voice through it.

"Nonsense, darling; you are dreaming still. Nothing; there has been nothing to hear. I have been awake ever since; if there had been anything to hear, I could not have missed it. Come, sit down. Sip a little of this water; you are nervous, and over-tired; and tell me plainly, like a good little soul, what is the matter; for nothing has happened here; and you ought to know that the Three Nuns is the quietest house in England; and I'm no witch, and if you won't tell me what's the matter, I can't divine it."

"Yes, of course," said Mary, sitting down, and glancing round her wildly. "I don't hear it now; *you* don't?"

"Do, my dear Mary, tell me what you mean," said Lady Walsingham kindly but firmly.

Lady Haworth was holding the still untasted glass of water in her hand.

"Yes, I'll tell you; I have been so frightened! You are right; I had a dream, but I can scarcely remember anything of it, except the very end, when I wakened. But it was not the dream; only it was connected with what terrified me so. I was so tired when I went to bed, I thought I should have slept soundly; and indeed I fell asleep immediately; and I must have slept quietly for a good while. How long is it since I left you?"

"More than an hour."

"Yes, I must have slept a good while; for I don't think I have been ten minutes awake. How my dream began I don't know. I remember only that gradually it came to this: I was standing in a recess in a panelled gallery; it was lofty, and, I thought, belonged to a handsome but old-fashioned house. I was looking straight towards the head of a wide staircase, with a great oak banister.

At the top of the stairs, as near to me, about, as that window there, was a thick short column of oak, on top of which was a candlestick. There was no other light but from that one candle; and there was a lady standing beside it, looking down the stairs, with her back turned towards me; and from her gestures I should have thought speaking to people on a lower lobby, but whom from my place I could not see. I soon perceived that this lady was in great agony of mind; for she beat her breast and wrung her hands every now and then, and wagged her head slightly from side to side, like a person in great distraction. But one word she said I could not hear. Nor when she struck her hand on the banister, or stamped, as she seemed to do in her pain, upon the floor, could I hear any sound. I found myself somehow waiting upon this lady, and was watching her with awe and sympathy. But who she was I knew not, until turning towards me I plainly saw Janet's face, pale and covered with tears, and with such a look of agony as—O God!— I can never forget."

"Pshaw! Mary darling, what is it but a dream! I have had a thousand more startling; it is only that you are so nervous just now."

"But that is not all—nothing; what followed is so dreadful; for either there is something very horrible going on at Mardykes, or else I am losing my reason," said Lady Haworth in increasing agitation. "I wakened instantly in great alarm, but I suppose no more than I have felt a hundred times on awakening from a frightful dream. I sat up in my bed; I was thinking of ringing for Winnefred, my heart was beating so, but feeling better soon I changed my mind. All this time I heard a faint sound of a voice, as if coming through a thick wall. It came from the wall at the left side of my bed, and I fancied was that of some woman lamenting in a room separated from me by that thick partition. I could only perceive that it was a sound of crying mingled with ejaculations of misery, or fear, or entreaty. I listened with a painful curiosity, wondering who it could be, and what could have happened in the neighbouring rooms of the house; and as I looked and listened, I could distinguish my own name, but at first nothing more. That, of course, might have been an accident; and I knew there were many Marys in the world besides myself. But it made me more curious; and a strange thing struck me, for I was now looking at that very wall through which the sounds were coming. I saw that there was a window in it. Thinking that the rest of the wall might nevertheless be covered by another room, I drew the curtain of it and looked out. But there is no such thing. It is the outer wall the entire way along. And it is equally impossible of the other wall, for it is to the front of the house, and has two windows in it; and the wall that the head of my bed stands against has the gallery outside it all the way; for I remarked that as I came to you."

"Tut, tut, Mary darling, nothing on earth is so deceptive as sound; this and fancy account for everything."

"But hear me out; I have not told you all. I began to hear the voice more clearly, and at last quite distinctly. It was Janet's, and she was conjuring you by name, as well as me, to come to her to Mardykes, without delay, in her extremity; yes, *you,* just as vehemently as me. It was Janet's voice. It still seemed separated by the wall, but I heard every syllable now; and I never heard voice or words of such anguish. She was imploring of us to come on, without a moment's delay, to Mardykes; and crying that, if we were not with her, she should go mad."

"Well, darling," said Lady Walsingham, "you see I'm included in this invitation as well as you, and should hate to disappoint Janet just as much; and I do assure you, in the morning you will laugh over this fancy with me; or rather, she will laugh over it with us, when we get to Mardykes. What you do want is rest, and a little sal-volatile."

So saying she rang the bell for Lady Haworth's maid. Having comforted her sister, and made her take the nervous specific she recommended, she went with her to her room; and taking possession of the arm-chair by the fire, she told her that she would keep her company until she was asleep, and remain long enough to be sure that the sleep was not likely to be interrupted. Lady Haworth had not been ten minutes in her bed, when she raised herself with a start to her elbow, listening with parted lips and wild eyes, her trembling fingers behind her ears. With an exclamation of horror, she cried,

"There it is again, upbraiding us! I can't stay longer."

She sprang from the bed, and rang the bell violently.

"Maud," she cried in an ecstasy of horror, "nothing shall keep me here, whether you go or not. I will set out the moment the horses are put to. If you refuse to come, Maud, mind the responsibility is yours—listen!" and with white face and starting eyes she pointed to the wall. "Have you ears; don't you hear?"

The sight of a person in extremity of terror so mysterious, might have unnerved a ruder system than Lady Walsingham's. She was pale as she replied; for under certain circumstances those terrors which deal with the supernatural are more contagious than any others. Lady Walsingham still, in terms, held to her opinion; but although she tried to smile, her face showed that the panic had touched her.

"Well, dear Mary," she said, "as you will have it so, I see no good in resisting you longer. Here, it is plain, your nerves will not suffer you to rest. Let us go then, in heaven's name; and when you get to Mardykes Hall you will be relieved."

All this time Lady Haworth was getting on her things, with the careless hurry of a person about to fly for her life; and Lady Walsingham issued her orders for horses, and the general preparations for resuming the journey.

It was now between ten and eleven; but the servant who rode armed with them, according to the not unnecessary usage of the times, thought that with a little judicious bribing of postboys they might easily reach Mardykes Hall before three o'clock in the morning.

When the party set forward again, Lady Haworth was comparatively tranquil. She no longer heard the unearthly mimickry of her sister's voice; there remained only the fear and suspense which that illusion or visitation had produced.

Her sister, Lady Walsingham, after a brief effort to induce something like conversation, became silent. A thin sheet of snow had covered the darkened landscape, and some light flakes were still dropping. Lady Walsingham struck her repeater often in the dark, and inquired the distances frequently. She was anxious to get over the ground, though by no means fatigued. Something of the anxiety that lay heavy at her sister's heart had touched her own.

CHAPTER XXVI

Perplexed

The roads even then were good, and very good horses the posting-houses turned out; so that by dint of extra pay the rapid rate of travelling undertaken by the servant was fully accomplished in the first two or three stages.

While Lady Walsingham was continually striking her repeater in her ear, and as they neared their destination, growing in spite of herself more anxious, her sister's uneasiness showed itself in a less reserved way; for, cold as it was, with snowflakes actually dropping, Lady Haworth's head was perpetually out at the window, and when she drew it up, sitting again in her place, she would audibly express her alarms, and apply to her sister for consolation and confidence in her suspense.

Under its thin carpet of snow, the pretty village of Golden Friars looked strangely to their eyes. It had long been fast asleep, and both ladies were excited as they drew up at the steps of the George and Dragon, and with bell and knocker roused the slumbering household.

What tidings awaited them here? In a very few minutes the door was opened, and the porter staggered down, after a word with the driver, to the carriage-window, not half awake.

"Is Lady Mardykes well?" demanded Lady Walsingham.

"Is Sir Bale well?"

"Are all the people at Mardykes Hall quite well?"

With clasped hands Lady Haworth listened to the successive answers to these questions which her sister hastily put. The answers were all satisfactory. With a great sigh and a little laugh, Lady Walsingham placed her hand affectionately on that of her sister; who, saying, "God be thanked!" began to weep.

"When had you last news from Mardykes?" asked Lady Walsingham.

"A servant was down here about four o'clock."

"O! no one since?" said she in a disappointed tone.

No one had been from the great house since, but all were well then.

"They are early people, you know, dear; and it is dark at four, and that is as late as they could well have heard, and nothing could have happened since—very unlikely. We have come very fast; it is only a few minutes past two, darling."

But each felt the chill and load of their returning anxiety.

While the people at the George were rapidly getting a team of horses to, Lady Walsingham contrived a moment for an order from the other window to her servant, who knew Golden Friars perfectly, to knock-up the people at Doctor Torvey's, and to inquire whether all were well at Mardykes Hall.

There he learned that a messenger had come for Doctor Torvey at ten o'clock, and that the Doctor had not returned since. There was no news, however, of any one's being ill; and the Doctor himself did not know what he was wanted about. While Lady Haworth was talking to her maid from the window next the steps, Lady

Walsingham was, unobserved, receiving this information at the other.

It made her very uncomfortable.

In a few minutes more, however, with a team of fresh horses, they were again rapidly passing the distance between them and Mardykes Hall.

About two miles on, their drivers pulled-up, and they heard a voice talking with them from the roadside. A servant from the Hall had been sent with a note for Lady Walsingham, and had been ordered, if necessary, to ride the whole way to the Three Nuns to deliver it. The note was already in Lady Walsingham's hand; her sister sat beside her, and with the corner of the open note in her fingers, she read it breathlessly at the same time by the light of a carriage-lamp which the man held to the window. It said:

My dearest love—my darling sister—dear sisters both!—in God's name, lose not a moment. I am so overpowered and *terrified*. I cannot explain; I can only implore of you to come with all the haste you can make. Waste no time, darlings. I hardly understand what I write. Only this, dear sisters; I feel that my reason will desert me, unless you come soon. You will not fail me now. Your poor distracted

JANET

The sisters exchanged a pale glance, and Lady Haworth grasped her sister's hand.

"Where is the messenger?" asked Lady Walsingham.

A mounted servant came to the window.

"Is any one ill at home?" she asked.

"No, all were well—my lady, and Sir Bale—no one sick."

"But the Doctor was sent for; what was that for?"

"I can't say, my lady."

"You are quite certain that no one—think—*no* one is ill?"

"There is no one ill at the Hall, my lady, that I have heard of."

"Is Lady Mardykes, my sister, still up?"

"Yes, my lady; and her maid is with her."

"And Sir Bale, are you certain he is quite well?"

"Sir Bale is quite well, my lady; he has been busy settling papers to-night, and was as well as usual."

"That will do, thanks," said the perplexed lady; and to her own servant she added, "On to Mardykes Hall with all the speed they can make. I'll pay them well, tell them."

And in another minute they were gliding along the road at a pace which the muffled beating of the horses' hoofs on the thin sheet of snow that covered the road showed to have broken out of the conventional trot, and to resemble something more like a gallop.

And now they were under the huge trees, that looked black as hearse-plumes in contrast with the snow. The cold gleam of the lake in the moon which had begun to shine out now met their gaze; and the familiar outline of Snakes Island, its solemn timber bleak and leafless, standing in a group, seemed to watch Mardykes Hall with a dismal observation across the water. Through the gate and between the huge files of trees the carriage seemed to fly; and at last the steaming horses stood panting, nodding and snorting, before the steps in the courtyard.

There was a light in an upper window, and a faint light in the hall, the door of which was opened; and an old servant came down and ushered the ladies into the house.

CHAPTER XXVII

The Hour

Lightly they stepped over the snow that lay upon the broad steps, and entering the door saw the dim figure of their sister, already in the large and faintly-lighted hall. One candle in the hand of her scared maid, and one burning on the table, leaving the distant parts of that great apartment in total darkness, touched the figures with the odd sharp lights in which Schalken delights; and a streak of chilly moonlight, through the open door, fell upon the floor, and was stretched like a white sheet at her feet. Lady Mardykes, with an exclamation of agitated relief, threw her arms, in turn, round the necks of her sisters, and hugging them, kissed them again and again, murmuring her thanks, calling them her "blessed sisters," and praising God for his mercy in having sent them to her in time, and altogether in a rapture of agitation and gratitude.

Taking them each by a hand, she led them into a large room, on whose panels they could see the faint twinkle of the tall gilded frames, and the darker indication of the old portraits, in which that interesting house abounds. The moonbeams, entering obliquely through the Tudor stone-shafts of the window and thrown upon the floor, reflected an imperfect light; and the candle which the maid who followed her mistress held in her hand shone dimly

from the sideboard, where she placed it. Lady Mardykes told her
that she need not wait.

"They don't know; they know only that we are in some great
confusion; but—God have mercy on me!—nothing of the reality.
Sit down, darlings; you are tired."

She sat down between them on a sofa, holding a hand of each.
They sat opposite the window, through which appeared the
magnificent view commanded from the front of the house: in the
foreground the solemn trees of Snakes Island, one great branch
stretching upward, bare and moveless, from the side, like an arm
raised to heaven in wonder or in menace towards the house; the
lake, in part swept by the icy splendour of the moon, trembling
with a dazzling glimmer, and farther off lost in blackness; the Fells
rising from a base of gloom, into ribs and peaks white with snow,
and looking against the pale sky, thin and transparent as a haze.
Right across to the storied woods of Cloostedd, and the old
domains of the Feltrams, this view extended.

Thus alone, their mufflers still on, their hands clasped in hers,
they breathlessly listened to her strange tale.

Connectedly told it amounted to this: Sir Bale seemed to have
been relieved of some great anxiety about the time when, ten days
before, he had told her to invite her friends to Mardykes Hall.
This morning he had gone out for a walk with Trevor, his under-
steward, to talk over some plans about thinning the woods at this
side; and also to discuss practically a proposal, lately made by a
wealthy merchant, to take a very long lease, on advantageous terms
to Sir Bale as he thought, of the old park and chase of Cloostedd,
with the intention of building there, and making it once more a
handsome residence.

In the improved state of his spirits, Sir Bale had taken a shrewd
interest in this negotiation; and was actually persuaded to cross
the lake that morning with his adviser, and to walk over the
grounds with him.

Sir Bale had seemed unusually well, and talked with great
animation. He was more like a young man who had just attained
his majority, and for the first time grasped his estates, than the
grim elderly Baronet who had been moping about Mardykes, and
as much afraid as a cat of the water, for so many years.

As they were returning toward the boat, at the roots of that
same scathed elm whose barkless bough had seemed, in his former
visit to this old wood, to beckon him from a distance, like a
skeleton arm, to enter the forest, he and his companion on a

sudden missed an old map of the grounds which they had been consulting.

"We must have left it in the corner tower of Cloostedd House, which commands that view of the grounds, you remember; it would not do to lose it. It is the most accurate thing we have. I'll sit down here and rest a little till you come back."

The man was absent little more than twenty minutes. When he returned, he found that Sir Bale had changed his position, and was now walking to and fro, around and about, in what, at a distance, he fancied was mere impatience, on the open space a couple of hundred paces nearer to the turn in the valley towards the boat. It was not impatience. He was agitated. He looked pale, and he took his companion's arm—a thing he had never thought of doing before—and said, "Let us away quickly. I've something to tell at home,—and I forgot it."

Not another word did Sir Bale exchange with his companion. He sat in the stern of the boat, gloomy as a man about to glide under traitor's-gate. He entered his house in the same sombre and agitated state. He entered his library, and sat for a long time as if stunned.

At last he seemed to have made-up his mind to something; and applied himself quietly and diligently to arranging papers, and docketing some and burning others. Dinner-time arrived. He sent to tell Lady Mardykes that he should not join her at dinner, but would see her afterwards.

"It was between eight and nine," she continued, "I forget the exact time, when he came to the tower drawing-room where I was. I did not hear his approach. There is a stone stair, with a thick carpet on it. He told me he wished to speak to me there. It is an out-of-the-way place—a small old room with very thick walls, and there is a double door, the inner one of oak—I suppose he wished to guard against being overheard.

"There was a look in his face that frightened me; I saw he had something dreadful to tell. He looked like a man on whom a lot had fallen to put some one to death," said Lady Mardykes. "O, my poor Bale! my husband, my husband! he knew what it would be to me."

Here she broke into the wildest weeping, and it was some time before she resumed.

"He seemed very kind and very calm," she said at last; "he said but little; and, I think, these were his words: 'I find, Janet, I have made a great miscalculation—I thought my hour of danger had passed. We have been many years together, but a parting must sooner or later be, and my time has come.'

"I don't know what I said. I would not have so much minded—for I could not have believed, if I had not seen him—but there was that in his look and tone which no one could doubt.

" 'I shall die before to-morrow morning,' he said. 'You must command yourself, Janet; it can't be altered now.'

" 'O, Bale,' I cried nearly distracted, 'you would not kill your-self!'

" 'Kill myself! poor child! no, indeed,' he said; 'it is simply that I shall die. No violent death—nothing but the common sub-sidence of life—I have made up my mind; what happens to every-body can't be so very bad; and millions of worse men than I die every year. You must not follow me to my room, darling; I shall see you by and by.'

"His language was collected and even cold; but his face looked as if it was cut in stone; you never saw, in a dream, a face like it."

Lady Walsingham here said, "I am certain he is ill; he's in a fever. You must not distract and torture yourself about his pre-dictions. You sent for Doctor Torvey; what did he say?"

"I could not tell him all."

"O, no; I don't mean that; they'd only say he was mad, and we little better for minding what he says. But did the Doctor see him? and what did he say of his health?"

"Yes; he says there is nothing wrong—no fever—nothing what-ever. Poor Bale has been so kind; he saw him to please me," she sobbed again wildly. "I wrote to implore of him. It was my last hope, strange as it seems; and O, would to God I could think it! But there is nothing of that kind. Wait till you have seen him. There is a frightful calmness about all he says and does; and his directions are all so clear, and his mind so perfectly collected, it is quite impossible."

And poor Lady Mardykes again burst into a frantic agony of tears.

CHAPTER XXVIII

Sir Bale in the Gallery

"Now, Janet darling, you are yourself low and nervous, and you treat this fancy of Bale's as seriously as he does himself. The truth is, he is a hypochondriac, as the doctors say; and you will find that I am right; he will be quite well in the morning, and I daresay a little ashamed of himself for having frightened his poor little wife as he has. I will sit up with you. But our poor Mary is not, you know, very strong; and she ought to lie down and rest a little. Suppose you give me a cup of tea in the drawing-room. I will run up to my room and get these things off, and meet you in the drawing-room; or, if you like it better, you can sit with me in my own room; and for goodness' sake let us have candles enough and a bright fire; and I promise you, if you will only exert your own good sense, you shall be a great deal more cheerful in a very little time."

Lady Walsingham's address was kind and cheery, and her air confident. For a moment a ray of hope returned, and her sister Janet acknowledged at least the possibility of her theory. But if confidence is contagious, so also is panic; and Lady Walsingham experienced a sinking of the heart which she dared not confess to her sister, and vainly strove to combat.

Lady Walsingham went up with her sister Mary, and having seen her in her room, and spoken again to her in the same cheery tone in which she had lectured her sister Lady Mardykes, she went on; and having taken possession of her own room, and put off her cloaks and shawls, she was going downstairs again, when she heard Sir Bale's voice, as he approached along the gallery, issuing orders to a servant, as it seemed, exactly in his usual tone.

She turned, with a strange throb at her heart, and met him.

A little sterner, a little paler than usual he looked; she could perceive no other change. He took her hand kindly and held it, as with dilated eyes he looked with a dark inquiry for a moment in her face. He signed to the servant to go on, and said, "I'm glad you have come, Maud. You have heard what is to happen; and I don't know how Janet could have borne it without your support. You did right to come; and you'll stay with her for a day or two, and take her away from this place as soon as you can."

She looked at him with the embarrassment of fear. He was speaking to her with the calmness of a leave-taking in the press-room—the serenity that overlies the greatest awe and agony of which human nature is capable.

"I am glad to see you, Bale," she began, hardly knowing what she said, and she stopped short.

"You are come, it turns out, on a sad mission," he resumed; "you find all about to change. Poor Janet! it is a blow to her. I shall not live to see to-morrow's sun."

"Come," she said, startled, "you must not talk so. No, Bale, you have no right to speak so; you can have no reason to justify it. It is cruel and wicked to trifle with your wife's feelings. If you are under a delusion, you must make an effort and shake it off, or, at least, cease to talk of it. You are not well; I know by your looks you are ill; but I am very certain we shall see you much better by tomorrow, and still better the day following."

"No, I'm not ill, sister. Feel that pulse, if you doubt me; there is no fever in it. I never was more perfectly in health; and yet I know that before the clock, that has just struck three, shall have struck five, I, who am talking to you, shall be dead."

Lady Walsingham was frightened, and her fear irritated her.

"I have told you what I think and believe," she said vehemently. "I think it wrong and cowardly of you to torture my poor sister with your whimsical predictions. Look into your own mind, and you will see you have absolutely no reason to support what you say. How *can* you inflict all this agony upon a poor creature foolish enough to love you as she does, and weak enough to believe in your idle dreams?"

"Stay, sister; it is not a matter to be debated so. If to-morrow I can hear you, it will be time enough to upbraid me. Pray return now to your sister; she needs all you can do for her. She is much to be pitied; her sufferings afflict me. I shall see you and her again before my death. It would have been more cruel to leave her unprepared. Do all in your power to nerve and tranquillise her. What is past cannot now be helped."

He paused, looking hard at her, as if he had half made up his mind to say something more. But if there was a question of the kind, it was determined in favour of silence.

He dropped her hand, turned quickly, and left her.

CHAPTER XXIX

Dr. Torvey's Opinion

When Lady Walsingham reached the head of the stairs, she met her maid, and from her learned that her sister, Lady Mardykes, was downstairs in the same room. On approaching, she heard her sister Mary's voice talking with her, and found them together.

Mary, finding that she could not sleep, had put on her clothes again, and come down to keep her sister company. The room looked more comfortable now. There were candles lighted, and a good fire burnt in the grate; tea-things stood on a little table near the fire, and the two sisters were talking, Lady Mardykes appearing more collected, and only they two in the room.

"Have you seen him, Maud?" cried Lady Mardykes, rising and hastily approaching her the moment she entered.

"Yes, dear; and talked with him, and—"

"Well?"

"And I think very much as I did before. I think he is nervous, he says he is not ill; but he is nervous and whimsical, and as men always are when they happen to be out of sorts, very positive; and of course the only thing that can quite undeceive him is the lapse of the time he has fixed for his prediction, as it is sure to pass without any tragic result of any sort. We shall then all see alike the nature of his delusion."

"O, Maud, if I were only sure you thought so! if I were sure you really had hopes! Tell me, Maud, for God's sake, what you really think."

Lady Walsingham was a little disconcerted by the unexpected directness of her appeal.

"Come, darling, you must not be foolish," she said; "we can only talk of impressions, and we are imposed upon by the solemnity of his manner, and the fact that he evidently believes in his own delusion; every one does believe in his own delusion—there is nothing strange in that."

"O, Maud, I see you are not convinced; you are only trying to comfort me. You have no hope—none, none, none!" and she covered her face with her hands, and wept again convulsively.

Lady Walsingham was silent for a moment, and then with an effort said, as she placed her hand on her sister's arm, "You see, dear Janet, there is no use in my saying the same thing over and over again; an hour or two will show who is right. Sit down again, and be like yourself. My maid told me that you had sent to the parlour for Doctor Torvey; he must not find you so. What would he think? Unless you mean to tell him of Bale's strange fancy; and a pretty story that would be to set afloat in Golden Friars. I think I hear him coming."

So, in effect, he was. Doctor Torvey—with the florid gravity of a man who, having just swallowed a bottle of port, besides some glasses of sherry, is admitted to the presence of ladies whom he respects—entered the room, made what he called his "leg and his compliments," and awaited the ladies' commands.

"Sit down, Doctor Torvey," said Lady Walsingham, who in the incapacity of her sister undertook the doing of the honours. "My sister, Lady Mardykes, has got it into her head somehow that Sir Bale is ill. I have been speaking to him; he certainly does not look very well, but he says he is quite well. Do you think him well?— that is, we know you don't think there is anything of importance amiss—but she wishes to know whether you think him *perfectly* well."

The Doctor cleared his voice and delivered his lecture, a little thickly at some words, upon Sir Bale's case; the result of which was that it was no case at all; and that if he would only live something more of a country gentleman's life, he would be as well as any man could desire—as well as any man, gentle or simple, in the country.

"The utmost I should think of doing for him would be, perhaps, a little quinine, nothing mo'—shurely—he is really and toory a very shoun' shtay of health."

Lady Walsingham looked encouragingly at her sister and nodded.

"I've been shen' for, La'y Walsh—Walse—Walsing—*ham*; old Jack Amerald—he likshe his glass o' port," he said roguishly, "and shuvversh accord'n'ly," he continued, with a compassionating paddle of his right hand; "one of thoshe aw—odd feels in his stomach; and as I have pretty well done all I can man-n'ge down here, I must be off, ye shee. Wind up from Golden Friars, and a little flutter ovv zhnow, thazh all;" and with some remarks about the extreme cold of the weather, and the severity of their night journey, and many respectful and polite parting speeches, the Doctor took his leave; and they soon heard the wheels of his gig and the tread of his horse, faint and muffled from the snow in the court-yard, and the Doctor, who had connected that melancholy and agitated household with the outer circle of humanity, was gone.

There was very little snow falling, half-a-dozen flakes now and again, and their flight across the window showed, as the Doctor had in a manner boasted, that the wind was in his face as he returned to Golden Friars. Even these desultory snow-flakes ceased, at times, altogether; and returning, as they say, "by fits and starts," left for long intervals the landscape, under the brilliant light of the moon, in its wide white shroud. The curtain of the great window had not been drawn. It seemed to Lady Walsingham that the moonbeams had grown more dazzling, that Snakes Island was nearer and more distinct, and the outstretched arm of the old tree looked bigger and angrier, like the uplifted arm of an assassin, who draws silently nearer as the catastrophe approaches.

Cold, dazzling, almost repulsive in this intense moonlight and white sheeting, the familiar landscape looked in the eyes of Lady Walsingham. The sisters gradually grew more and more silent, an unearthly suspense overhung them all, and Lady Mardykes rose every now and then and listened at the open door for step or voice in vain. They all were overpowered by the intenser horror that seemed gathering around them. And thus an hour or more passed.

CHAPTER XXX

Hush!

Pale and silent those three beautiful sisters sat. The horrible quietude of a suspense that had grown all but insupportable oppressed the guests of Lady Mardykes, and something like the numbness of despair had reduced her to silence, the dreadful counterfeit of peace.

Sir Bale Mardykes on a sudden softly entered the room. Reflected from the floor near the window, the white moonlight somehow gave to his fixed features the character of a smile. With a warning gesture, as he came in, he placed his finger to his lips, as if to enjoin silence; and then, having successively pressed the hands of his two sisters-in-law, he stooped over his almost fainting wife, and twice pressed her cold forehead with his lips; and so, without a word, he went softly from the room.

Some seconds elapsed before Lady Walsingham, recovering her presence of mind, with one of the candlesticks from the table in her hand, opened the door and followed.

She saw Sir Bale mount the last stair of the broad flight visible from the hall, and candle in hand turn the corner of the massive banister, and as the light thrown from his candle showed, he continued, without hurry, to ascend the second flight.

With the irrepressible curiosity of horror she continued to follow him at a distance.

She saw him enter his own private room, and close the door. Continuing to follow she placed herself noiselessly at the door of the apartment, and in breathless silence, with a throbbing heart, listened for what should pass.

She distinctly heard Sir Bale pace the floor up and down for some time, and then, after a pause, a sound as if some one had thrown himself heavily on the bed. A silence followed, during which her sisters, who had followed more timidly, joined her. She warned them with a look and gesture to be silent.

Lady Haworth stood a little behind, her white lips moving, and her hands clasped in a silent agony of prayer. Lady Mardykes leaned against the massive oak door-case.

With her hand raised to her ear, and her lips parted, Lady Walsingham listened for some seconds—for a minute, two minutes, three. At last, losing heart, she seized the handle in her panic, and turned it sharply. The door was locked on the inside, but some one close to it said from within, "Hush, hush!"

Much alarmed now, the same lady knocked violently at the door. No answer was returned.

She knocked again more violently, and shook the door with all her fragile force. It was something of horror in her countenance as she did so, that, no doubt, terrified Lady Mardykes, who with a loud and long scream sank in a swoon upon the floor.

The servants, alarmed by these sounds, were speedily in the gallery. Lady Mardykes was carried to her room, and laid upon her bed; her sister, Lady Haworth, accompanying her. In the meantime the door was forced. Sir Bale Mardykes was found stretched upon his bed.

Those who have once seen it, will not mistake the aspect of death. Here, in Sir Bale Mardykes' room, in his bed, in his clothes, is a stranger, grim and awful; in a few days to be insupportable, and to pass alone into the prison-house, and to be seen no more.

Where is Sir Bale Mardykes now, whose roof-tree and whose place at board and bed will know him no more? Here lies a chap-fallen, fish-eyed image, chilling already into clay, and stiffening in every joint.

There is a marble monument in the pretty church of Golden Friars. It stands at the left side of what antiquarians call "the high altar." Two pillars at each end support an arch with several armorial bearings on as many shields sculptured above. Beneath, on a marble flooring raised some four feet, with a cornice round, lies Sir Bale Mardykes, of Mardykes Hall, ninth Baronet of that ancient family, chiseled in marble with knee-breeches and buckled-shoes, and *ailes de pigeon,* and single-breasted coat and long waist-coat, ruffles and sword, such as gentlemen wore about the year 1770, and bearing a strong resemblance to the features of the second Charles. On the broad marble which forms the background is inscribed an epitaph, which has perpetuated to our times the estimate formed by his "inconsolable widow," the Dowager Lady Mardykes, of the virtues and accomplishments of her deceased lord.

Lady Walsingham would have qualified two or three of the more highly-coloured hyperboles, at which the Golden Friars of those days sniffed and tittered. They don't signify now; there is no contemporary left to laugh or whisper. And if there be not much that is true in the letter of that inscription, it at least perpetuates something that *is* true—that wonderful glorificaion of partisan-ship, the affection of an idolising wife.

Lady Mardykes, a few days after the funeral, left Mardykes Hall for ever. She lived a great deal with her sister, Lady Walsingham; and died, as a line cut at the foot of Sir Bale Mardykes' epitaph records, in the year 1790; her remains being laid beside those of her beloved husband in Golden Friars.

The estates had come to Sir Bale Mardykes free of entail. He had been pottering over a will, but it was never completed, nor even quite planned; and after much doubt and scrutiny, it was at last ascertained that, in default of a will and of issue, a clause in the marriage-settlement gave the entire estates to the Dowager Lady Mardykes.

By her will she bequeathed the estates to "her cousin, also a kinsman of the late Sir Bale Mardykes her husband," William Feltram, on condition of his assuming the name and arms of Mardykes, the arms of Feltram being quartered in the shield.

Thus was oddly fulfilled the prediction which Philip Feltram had repeated, that the estates of Mardykes were to pass into the hands of a Feltram.

About the year 1795 the baronetage was revived, and William Feltram enjoyed the title for fifteen years, as Sir William Mardykes.

Green Tea

PROLOGUE

Martin Hesselius, the German Physician

Though carefully educated in medicine and surgery, I have never practised either. The study of each continues, nevertheless, to interest me profoundly. Neither idleness nor caprice caused my secession from the honourable calling which I had just entered. The cause was a very trifling scratch inflicted by a dissecting knife. This trifle cost me the loss of two fingers, amputated promptly, and the more painful loss of my health, for I have never been quite well since, and have seldom been twelve months together in the same place.

In my wanderings I became acquainted with Dr. Martin Hesselius, a wanderer like myself, like me a physician, and like me an enthusiast in his profession. Unlike me in this, that his wanderings were voluntary, and he a man, if not of fortune, as we estimate fortune in England, at least in what our forefathers used to term "easy circumstances." He was an old man when I first saw him; nearly five-and-thirty years my senior.

In Dr. Martin Hesselius, I found my master. His knowledge was immense, his grasp of a case was an intuition. He was the very man to inspire a young enthusiast, like me, with awe and delight. My admiration has stood the test of time and survived the separation of death. I am sure it was well-founded.

For nearly twenty years I acted as his medical secretary. His immense collection of papers he has left in my care, to be arranged, indexed and bound. His treatment of some of these cases is curious. He writes in two distinct characters. He describes what he saw and heard as an intelligent layman might, and when in this style of narrative he had seen the patient either through his own hall-door, to the light of day, or through the gates of darkness to

178

the caverns of the dead, he returns upon the narrative, and in the terms of his art and with all the force and originality of genius, proceeds to the work of analysis, diagnosis and illustration.

Here and there a case strikes me as of a kind to amuse or horrify a lay reader with an interest quite different from the peculiar one which it may possess for an expert. With slight modifications, chiefly of language, and of course a change of names, I copy the following. The narrator is Dr. Martin Hesselius. I find it among the voluminous notes of cases which he made during a tour in England about sixty-four years ago.

It is related in series of letters to his friend Professor Van Loo of Leyden. The professor was not a physician, but a chemist, and a man who read history and metaphysics and medicine, and had, in his day, written a play.

The narrative is therefore, if somewhat less valuable as a medical record, necessarily written in a manner more likely to interest an unlearned reader.

These letters, from a memorandum attached, appear to have been returned on the death of the professor, in 1819, to Dr. Hesselius. They are written, some in English, some in French, but the greater part in German. I am a faithful, though I am conscious, by no means a graceful translator, and although here and there I omit some passages, and shorten others, and disguise names, I have interpolated nothing.

CHAPTER I

Dr. Hesselius Relates How He Met
the Rev. Mr. Jennings

The Rev. Mr. Jennings is tall and thin. He is middle-aged, and dresses with a natty, old-fashioned, high-church precision. He is naturally a little stately, but not at all stiff. His features, without being handsome, are well formed, and their expression extremely kind, but also shy.

I met him one evening at Lady Mary Heyduke's. The modesty and benevolence of his countenance are extremely prepossessing.

We were but a small party, and he joined agreeably enough in the conversation, He seems to enjoy listening very much more than contributing to the talk; but what he says is always to the purpose and well said. He is a great favourite of Lady Mary's, who it seems, consults him upon many things, and thinks him the most happy and blessed person on earth. Little knows she about him.

The Rev. Mr. Jennings is a bachelor, and has, they say sixty thousand pounds in the funds. He is a charitable man. He is most anxious to be actively employed in his sacred profession, and yet though always tolerably well elsewhere, when he goes down to his vicarage in Warwickshire, to engage in the actual duties of his sacred calling, his health soon fails him, and in a very strange way. So says Lady Mary.

There is no doubt that Mr. Jennings' health does break down in, generally, a sudden and mysterious way, sometimes in the very act of officiating in his old and pretty church at Kenlis. It may be his heart, it may be his brain. But so it has happened three or four times, or oftener, that after proceeding a certain way in the service, he has on a sudden stopped short, and after a silence, apparently quite unable to resume, he has fallen into solitary, inaudible prayer, his hands and his eyes uplifted, and then pale as death, and in the agitation of a strange shame and horror, descended trembling, and got into the vestry-room, leaving his congregation, without explanation, to themselves. This occurred when his curate was absent. When he goes down to Kenlis now, he always takes care to provide a clergyman to share his duty, and to supply his place on the instant should he become thus suddenly incapacitated.

When Mr. Jennings breaks down quite, and beats a retreat from the vicarage, and returns to London, where, in a dark street off Piccadilly, he inhabits a very narrow house, Lady Mary says that he is always perfectly well. I have my own opinion about that. There are degrees of course. We shall see.

Mr. Jennings is a perfectly gentlemanlike man. People, however, remark something odd. There is an impression a little ambiguous. One thing which certainly contributes to it, people I think don't remember; or, perhaps, distinctly remark. But I did, almost immediately. Mr. Jennings has a way of looking sidelong upon the carpet, as if his eye followed the movements of something there. This, of course, is not always. It occurs now and then. But often enough to give a certain oddity, as I have said, to his manner, and in this glance travelling along the floor there is something both shy and anxious.

A medical philosopher, as you are good enough to call me, elaborating theories by the aid of cases sought out by himself, and by him watched and scrutinised with more time at command, and consequently infinitely more minuteness than the ordinary practitioner can afford, falls insensibly into habits of observation, which accompany him everywhere, and are exercised, as some people would say, impertinently, upon every subject that presents itself with the least likelihood of rewarding inquiry.

There was a promise of this kind in the slight, timid, kindly, but reserved gentleman, whom I met for the first time at this agreeable little evening gathering. I observed, of course, more than I here set down; but I reserve all that borders on the technical for a strictly scientific paper.

I may remark, that when I here speak of medical science, I do so, as I hope some day to see it more generally understood, in a much more comprehensive sense than its generally material treatment would warrant. I believe the entire natural world is but the ultimate expression of that spiritual world from which, and in which alone, it has its life. I believe that the essential man is a spirit, that the spirit is an organised substance, but as different in point of material from what we ordinarily understand by matter, as light or electricity is; that the material body is, in the most literal sense, a vesture, and death consequently no interruption of the living man's existence, but simply his extrication from the natural body —a process which commences at the moment of what we term death, and the completion of which, at furthest a few days later, is the resurrection "in power."

The person who weighs the consequences of these positions will probably see their practical bearing upon medical science. This is, however, by no means the proper place for displaying the proofs and discussing the consequences of this too generally unrecognized state of facts.

In pursuance of my habit, I was covertly observing Mr. Jennings, with all my caution—I think he perceived it—and I saw plainly that he was as cautiously observing me. Lady Mary happening to address me by my name, as Dr. Hesselius, I saw that he glanced at me more sharply, and then became thoughtful for a few minutes.

After this, as I conversed with a gentleman at the other end of the room, I saw him look at me more steadily, and with an interest which I thought I understood. I then saw him take an opportunity of chatting with Lady Mary, and was, as one always is, perfectly aware of being the subject of a distant inquiry and answer.

This tall clergyman approached me by-and-by; and in a little time we had got into conversation. When two people, who like reading, and know books and places, having travelled, wish to discourse, it is very strange if they can't find topics. It was not accident that brought him near me, and led him into conversation.

He knew German and had read my Essays on Metaphysical Medicine which suggest more than they actually say.

This courteous man, gentle, shy, plainly a man of thought and reading, who moving and talking among us, was not altogether of us, and whom I already suspected of leading a life whose transactions and alarms were carefully concealed, with an impenetrable reserve from, not only the world, but his best beloved friends— was cautiously weighing in his own mind the idea of taking a certain step with regard to me.

I penetrated his thoughts without his being aware of it, and was careful to say nothing which could betray to his sensitive vigilance my suspicions respecting his position, or my surmises about his plans respecting myself.

We chatted upon indifferent subjects for a time but at last he said:

"I was very much interested by some papers of yours, Dr. Hesselius, upon what you term Metaphysical Medicine—I read them in German, ten or twelve years ago—have they been translated?"

"No, I'm sure they have not—I should have heard. They would have asked my leave, I think."

"I asked the publishers here, a few months ago, to get the book for me in the original German; but they tell me it is out of print."

"So it is, and has been for some years; but it flatters me as an author to find that you have not forgotten my little book, although," I added, laughing, "ten or twelve years is a considerable time to have managed without it; but I suppose you have been turning the subject over again in your mind, or something has happened lately to revive your interest in it."

At this remark, accompanied by a glance of inquiry, a sudden embarrassment disturbed Mr. Jennings, analogous to that which makes a young lady blush and look foolish. He dropped his eyes, and folded his hands together uneasily, and looked oddly, and you would have said, guiltily, for a moment.

I helped him out of his awkwardness in the best way, by appearing not to observe it, and going straight on, I said: "Those revivals of interest in a subject happen to me often; one book suggests another, and often sends me back a wild-goose chase over an interval of twenty years. But if you still care to possess a copy, I shall be only too happy to provide you; I have still got two or three by me —and if you allow me to present one I shall be very much honoured."

"You are very good indeed," he said, quite at his ease again, in a moment: "I almost despaired—I don't know how to thank you."

"Pray don't say a word; the thing is really so little worth that I am only ashamed of having offered it, and if you thank me any more I shall throw it into the fire in a fit of modesty."

Mr. Jennings laughed. He inquired where I was staying in London, and after a little more conversation on a variety of subjects, he took his departure.

CHAPTER II

The Doctor Questions Lady Mary and She Answers

"I like your vicar so much, Lady Mary," said I, as soon as he was gone. "He has read, travelled, and thought, and having also suffered, he ought to be an accomplished companion."

"So he is, and, better still, he is a really good man," said she. "His advice is invaluable about my schools, and all my little undertakings at Dawlbridge, and he's so painstaking, he takes so much trouble—you have no idea—wherever he thinks he can be of use: he's so good-natured and so sensible."

"It is pleasant to hear so good an account of his neighbourly virtues. I can only testify to his being an agreeable and gentle companion, and in addition to what you have told me, I think I can tell you two or three things about him," said I.

"Really!"

"Yes, to begin with, he's unmarried."

"Yes, that's right—go on."

"He has been writing, that is he *was*, but for two or three years perhaps, he has not gone on with his work, and the book was upon some rather abstract subject—perhaps theology."

"Well, he was writing a book, as you say; I'm not quite sure what it was about, but only that it was nothing that I cared for; very likely you are right, and he certainly did stop—yes."

"And although he only drank a little coffee here to-night, he likes tea, at least, did like it extravagantly."

"Yes, that's *quite* true."

"He drank green tea, a good deal, didn't he?" I pursued.

"Well, that's very odd! Green tea was a subject on which we used almost to quarrel."

"But he has quite given that up," said I.

"So he has."

"And, now, one more fact. His mother or his father, did you know them?"

"Yes, both; his father is only ten years dead, and their place is near Dawlbridge. We knew them very well," she answered.

"Well, either his mother or his father—I should rather think his father, saw a ghost," said I.

"Well, you really are a conjurer, Dr. Hesselius."

"Conjurer or no, haven't I said right?" I answered merrily.

"You certainly have, and it *was* his father: he was a silent, whimsical man, and he used to bore my father about his dreams, and at last he told him a story about a ghost he had seen and talked with, and a very odd story it was. I remember it particularly, because I was so afraid of him. This story was long before he died—when I was quite a child—and his ways were so silent and moping, and he used to drop in sometimes, in the dusk, when I was alone in the drawing-room, and I used to fancy there were ghosts about him."

I smiled and nodded.

"And now, having established my character as a conjurer, I think I must say good-night," said I.

"But how *did* you find it out?"

"By the planets, of course, as the gipsies do," I answered, and so, gaily we said good-night.

Next morning I sent the little book he had been inquiring after, and a note to Mr. Jennings, and on returning late that evening, I found that he had called at my lodgings, and left his card. He asked whether I was at home, and asked at what hour he would be most likely to find me.

Does he intend opening his case, and consulting me "professionally," as they say? I hope so. I have already conceived a theory about him. It is supported by Lady Mary's answers to my parting questions. I should like much to ascertain from his own lips. But what can I do consistently with good breeding to invite a confession? Nothing. I rather think he meditates one. At all events, my dear Van L., I shan't make myself difficult of access; I mean to return his visit tomorrow. It will be only civil in return for his politeness, to ask to see him. Perhaps something may come of it. Whether much, little, or nothing, my dear Van L., you shall hear.

CHAPTER III

Dr. Hesselius Picks Up Something in Latin Books

Well, I have called at Blank Street.

On inquiring at the door, the servant told me that Mr. Jennings was engaged very particularly with a gentleman, a clergyman from Kenlis, his parish in the country. Intending to reserve my privilege, and to call again, I merely intimated that I should try another time, and had turned to go, when the servant begged my pardon, and asked me, looking at me a little more attentively than well-bred persons of his order usually do, whether I was Dr. Hesselius; and, on learning that I was, he said, "Perhaps then, sir, you would allow me to mention it to Mr. Jennings, for I am sure he wishes to see you."

The servant returned in a moment, with a message from Mr. Jennings, asking me to go into his study, which was in effect his back drawing-room, promising to be with me in a very few minutes.

This was really a study—almost a library. The room was lofty, with two tall slender windows, and rich dark curtains. It was much larger than I had expected, and stored with books on every side, from the floor to the ceiling. The upper carpet—for to my tread it felt that there were two or three—was a Turkey carpet. My steps fell noiselessly. The bookcases standing out, placed the windows, particularly narrow ones, in deep recesses. The effect of the room was, although extremely comfortable, and even luxurious, decidedly gloomy, and aided by the silence, almost oppressive. Perhaps, however, I ought to have allowed something for association. My mind had connected peculiar ideas with Mr. Jennings. I stepped into this perfectly silent room, of a very silent house, with a peculiar foreboding; and its darkness, and solemn clothing of books, for except where two narrow looking-glasses were set in the wall, they were everywhere, helped this somber feeling.

While awaiting Mr. Jennings' arrival, I amused myself by looking into some of the books with which his shelves were laden. Not among these, but immediately under them, with their backs upward, on the floor, I lighted upon a complete set of Swedenborg's "Arcana Cælestia," in the original Latin, a very fine folio set, bound in the natty livery which theology affects, pure vellum, namely, gold letters, and carmine edges. There were paper markers in several of these volumes, I raised and placed them, one after the other, upon the table, and opening where these papers were placed, I read in the solemn Latin phraseology, a series of sentences indicated by a pencilled line at the margin. Of these I copy here a few, translating them into English.

"When man's interior sight is opened, which is that of his spirit, then there appear the things of another life, which cannot possibly be made visible to the bodily sight." . . . .

"By the internal sight it has been granted me to see the things that are in the other life, more clearly than I see those that are in the world. From these considerations, it is evident that external vision exists from interior vision, and this from a vision still more interior, and so on." . . . .

"There are with every man at least two evil spirits." . . . .

"With wicked genii there is also a fluent speech, but harsh and grating. There is also among them a speech which is not fluent, wherein the dissent of the thoughts is perceived as something secretly creeping along within it."

"The evil spirits associated with man are, indeed from the hells, but when with man they are not then in hell, but are taken out thence. The place where they then are, is in the midst between heaven and hell, and is called the world of spirits—when the evil spirits who are with man, are in that world, they are not in any infernal torment, but in every thought and affection of man, and so, in all that the man himself enjoys. But when they are remitted into their hell, they return to their former state." . . . .

"If evil spirits could perceive that they were associated with man, and yet that they were spirits separate from him, and if they could flow in into the things of his body, they would attempt by a thousand means to destroy him; for they hate man with a deadly hatred." . . . .

"Knowing, therefore, that I was a man in the body, they were continually striving to destroy me, not as to the body only, but especially as to the soul; for to destroy any man or spirit is the very delight of the life of all who are in hell; but I have been continually protected by the Lord. Hence it appears how dangerous it is for man to be in a living consort with spirits, unless he be in the good of faith." . . . .

"Nothing is more carefully guarded from the knowledge of associate spirits than their being thus conjoint with a man, for if they knew it they would speak to him, with the intention to destroy him." . . . .

"The delight of hell is to do evil to man, and to hasten his eternal ruin."

A long note, written with a very sharp and fine pencil, in Mr. Jennings' neat hand, at the foot of the page, caught my eye. Expecting his criticism upon the text, I read a word or two, and stopped, for it was something quite different, and began with these words, *Deus misereatur mei*—"May God compassionate me." Thus warned of its private nature, I averted my eyes, and shut the book, replacing all the volumes as I had found them, except one which interested me, and in which, as men studious and solitary in their habits will do, I grew so absorbed as to take no cognisance of the outer world, nor to remember where I was.

I was reading some pages which refer to "representatives" and "correspondents," in the technical language of Swedenborg, and had arrived at a passage, the substance of which is, that evil spirits, when seen by other eyes than those of their infernal associates, present themselves, by "correspondence," in the shape of the beast (*fera*) which represents their particular lust and life, in aspect direful and atrocious. This is a long passage, and particularises a number of those bestial forms.

CHAPTER IV

Four Eyes Were Reading the Passage

I was running the head of my pencil-case along the line as I read it, and something caused me to raise my eyes.

Directly before me was one of the mirrors I have mentioned, in which I saw reflected the tall shape of my friend, Mr. Jennings, leaning over my shoulder, and reading the page at which I was busy, and with a face so dark and wild that I should hardly have known him.

I turned and rose. He stood erect also, and with an effort laughed a little, saying:

"I came in and asked you how you did, but without succeeding in awaking you from your book; so I could not restrain my curiosity, and very impertinently, I'm afraid, peeped over your shoulder. This is not your first time of looking into those pages. You have looked into Swedenborg, no doubt, long ago?"

"Oh dear, yes! I owe Swedenborg a great deal; you will discover traces of him in the little book on Metaphysical Medicine, which you were so good as to remember."

Although my friend affected a gaiety of manner, there was a slight flush in his face, and I could perceive that he was inwardly much perturbed.

"I'm scarcely yet qualified, I know so little of Swedenborg. I've only had them a fortnight," he answered, "and I think they are rather likely to make a solitary man nervous—that is, judging from the very little I have read—I don't say that they have made me so," he laughed; "and I'm so very much obliged for the book. I hope you got my note?"

I made all proper acknowledgments and modest disclaimers.

"I never read a book that I go with, so entirely, as that of yours," he continued. "I saw at once there is more in it than is quite unfolded. Do you know Dr. Harley?" he asked, rather abruptly.

In passing, the editor remarks that the physician here named was one of the most eminent who had ever practised in England.

I did, having had letters to him, and had experienced from him great courtesy and considerable assistance during my visit to England.

"I think that man one of the very greatest fools I ever met in my life," said Mr. Jennings.

This was the first time I had ever heard him say a sharp thing of anybody, and such a term applied to so high a name a little startled me.

"Really! and in what way?" I asked.

"In his profession," he answered.

I smiled.

"I mean this," he said: "he seems to me, one half, blind—I mean one half of all he looks at is dark—preternaturally bright and vivid all the rest; and the worst of it is, it seems *wilful*. I can't get him—I mean he won't—I've had some experience of him as a physician, but I look on him as, in that sense, no better than a paralytic mind, an intellect half dead. I'll tell you—I know I shall some time—all about it," he said, with a little agitation. "You stay some months longer in England. If I should be out of town during your stay for a little time, would you allow me to trouble you with a letter?"

"I should be only too happy," I assured him.

"Very good of you. I am so utterly dissatisfied with Harley."

"A little leaning to the materialistic school," I said.

"A *mere* materialist," he corrected me; "you can't think how that sort of thing worries one who knows better. You won't tell any one—any of my friends you know—that I am hippish; now, for instance, no one knows—not even Lady Mary—that I have seen Dr. Harley, or any other doctor. So pray don't mention it; and, if I should have any threatening of an attack, you'll kindly let me write, or, should I be in town, have a little talk with you."

I was full of conjecture, and unconsciously I found I had fixed my eyes gravely on him, for he lowered his for a moment, and he said:

"I see you think I might as well tell you now, or else you are forming a conjecture; but you may as well give it up. If you were guessing all the rest of your life, you will never hit on it."

He shook his head smiling, and over that wintry sunshine a black cloud suddenly came down, and he drew his breath in, through his teeth as men do in pain.

"Sorry, of course, to learn that you apprehend occasion to consult any of us; but, command me when and how you like, and I need not assure you that your confidence is sacred."

He then talked of quite other things, and in a comparatively cheerful way and after a little time, I took my leave.

CHAPTER V

Dr. Hesselius is Summoned to Richmond

We parted cheerfully, but he was not cheerful, nor was I. There are certain expressions of that powerful organ of spirit—the human face—which, although I have seen them often, and possess a doctor's nerve, yet disturb me profoundly. One look of Mr. Jennings haunted me. It had seized my imagination with so dismal a power that I changed my plans for the evening, and went to the opera, feeling that I wanted a change of ideas.

I heard nothing of or from him for two or three days, when a note in his hand reached me. It was cheerful, and full of hope. He said that he had been for some little time so much better—quite well, in fact—that he was going to make a little experiment, and run down for a month or so to his parish, to try whether a little work might not quite set him up. There was in it a fervent religious expression of gratitude for his restoration, as he now almost hoped he might call it.

A day or two later I saw Lady Mary, who repeated what his note had announced, and told me that he was actually in Warwickshire, having resumed his clerical duties at Kenlis; and she added, "I begin to think that he is really perfectly well, and that there never was anything the matter, more than nerves and fancy; we are all nervous, but I fancy there is nothing like a little hard work for that kind of weakness, and he has made up his mind to try it. I should not be surprised if he did not come back for a year."

Notwithstanding all this confidence, only two days later I had this note, dated from his house off Piccadilly:

DEAR SIR,—I have returned disappointed. If I should feel at all able to see you, I shall write to ask you kindly to call. At present, I am too low, and, in fact, simply unable to say all I wish to say. Pray don't mention my name to my friends. I can see no one. By-and-by, please God, you shall hear from me. I mean to take a run into Shropshire, where some of my people are. God bless you! May we, on my return, meet more happily than I can now write.

About a week after this I saw Lady Mary at her own house, the last person, she said, left in town, and just on the wing for Brighton, for the London season was quite over. She told me that she had heard from Mr. Jenning's niece, Martha, in Shropshire. There was nothing to be gathered from her letter, more than that he was low and nervous. In those words, of which healthy people think so lightly, what a world of suffering is sometimes hidden!

Nearly five weeks had passed without any further news of Mr. Jennings. At the end of that time I received a note from him. He wrote:

"I have been in the country, and have had change of air, change of scene, change of faces, change of everything—and in everything —but *myself*. I have made up my mind, so far as the most irresolute creature on earth can do it, to tell my case fully to you. If your engagements will permit, pray come to me to-day, to-morrow, or the next day; but, pray defer as little as possible. You know not how much I need help. I have a quiet house at Richmond, where I now am. Perhaps you can manage to come to dinner, or to luncheon, or even to tea. You shall have no trouble in finding me out. The servant at Blank Street, who takes this note, will have a carriage at your door at any hour you please; and I am always to be found. You will say that I ought not to be alone. I have tried everything. Come and see."

I called up the servant, and decided on going out the same evening, which accordingly I did.

He would have been much better in a lodging-house, or hotel, I thought, as I drove up through a short double row of sombre elms to a very old-fashioned brick house, darkened by the foliage of these trees, which overtopped, and nearly surrounded it. It was a perverse choice, for nothing could be imagined more triste and silent. The house, I found, belonged to him. He had stayed for a day or two in town, and, finding it for some cause insupportable, had come out here, probably because being furnished and his own, he was relieved of the thought and delay of selection, by coming here.

The sun had already set, and the red reflected light of the western sky illuminated the scene with the peculiar effect with which we are all familiar. The hall seemed very dark, but, getting to the back drawing-room, whose windows command the west, I was again in the same dusky light.

I sat down, looking out upon the richly-wooded landscape that glowed in the grand and melancholy light which was every moment fading. The corners of the room were already dark; all was growing dim, and the gloom was insensibly toning my mind, already prepared for what was sinister. I was waiting alone for his arrival, which soon took place. The door communicating with the front room opened, and the tall figure of Mr. Jennings, faintly seen in the ruddy twilight, came, with quiet stealthy steps, into the room.

We shook hands, and, taking a chair to the window, where there was still light enough to enable us to see each other's faces, he sat down beside me, and, placing his hand upon my arm, with scarcely a word of preface began his narrative.

CHAPTER VI

How Mr. Jennings Met His Companion

The faint glow of the west, the pomp of the then lonely woods of Richmond, were before us, behind and about us the darkening room, and on the stony face of the sufferer—for the character of his face, though still gentle and sweet, was changed—rested that dim, odd glow which seems to descend and produce, where it touches, lights, sudden though faint, which are lost, almost without gradation, in darkness. The silence, too, was utter: not a distant wheel, or bark, or whistle from without; and within the depressing stillness of an invalid bachelor's house.

I guessed well the nature, though not even vaguely the particulars of the revelations I was about to receive, from that fixed face of suffering that so oddly flushed stood out, like a portrait of Schalken's, before its background of darkness.

"It began," he said, "on the 15th of October, three years and eleven weeks ago, and two days—I keep very accurate count, for every day is torment. If I leave anywhere a chasm in my narrative tell me.

"About four years ago I began a work, which had cost me very much thought and reading. It was upon the religious metaphysics of the ancients."

"I know," said I, "the actual religion of educated and thinking paganism, quite apart from symbolic worship? A wide and very interesting field."

"Yes, but not good for the mind—the Christian mind, I mean. Paganism is all bound together in essential unity, and, with evil sympathy, their religion involves their art, and both their manners, and the subject is a degrading fascination and the Nemesis sure. God forgive me!

"I wrote a great deal; I wrote late at night. I was always thinking on the subject, walking about, wherever I was, everywhere. It thoroughly infected me. You are to remember that all the material ideas connected with it were more or less of the beautiful, the subject itself delightfully interesting, and I, then, without a care."

He sighed heavily.

"I believe, that every one who sets about writing in earnest does his work, as a friend of mine phrased it, on something—tea, or coffee, or tobacco. I suppose there is a material waste that must be hourly supplied in such occupations, or that we should grow too abstracted, and the mind, as it were, pass out of the body, unless it were reminded often enough of the connection by actual sensation. At all events, I felt the want, and I supplied it. Tea was my companion—at first the ordinary black tea, made in the usual way, not too strong: but I drank a good deal, and increased its strength as I went on. I never experienced an uncomfortable symptom from it. I began to take a little green tea. I found the effect pleasanter, it cleared and intensified the power of thought so, I had come to take it frequently, but not stronger than one might take it for pleasure. I wrote a great deal out here, it was so quiet, and in this room. I used to sit up very late, and it became a habit with me to sip my tea—green tea—every now and then as my work proceeded. I had a little kettle on my table, that swung over a lamp, and made tea two or three times between eleven o'clock and two or three in the morning, my hours of going to bed. I used to go into town every day. I was not a monk, and, although I spent an hour or two in a library, hunting up authorities and looking out lights upon my theme, I was in no morbid state as far as I can judge. I met my friends pretty much as usual and enjoyed their society, and, on the whole, existence had never been, I think, so pleasant before.

"I had met with a man who had some odd old books, German editions in mediæval Latin, and I was only too happy to be permitted access to them. This obliging person's books were in the City, a very out-of-the-way part of it. I had rather out-stayed my intended hour, and, on coming out, seeing no cab near, I was tempted to get into the omnibus which used to drive past this house. It was darker than this by the time the 'bus had reached an old house, you may have remarked, with four poplars at each side of the door, and there the last passenger but myself got out. We drove along rather faster. It was twilight now. I leaned back in my corner next the door ruminating pleasantly.

"The interior of the omnibus was nearly dark. I had observed in the corner opposite to me at the other side, and at the end next the horses, two small circular reflections, as it seemed to me of a reddish light. They were about two inches apart, and about the size of those small brass buttons that yachting men used to put upon their jackets. I began to speculate, as listless men will, upon this trifle, as it seemed. From what centre did that faint but deep red light come, and from what—glass beads, buttons, toy decorations—was it reflected? We were lumbering along gently, having nearly a mile still to go. I had not solved the puzzle, and it became in another minute more odd, for these two luminous points, with a sudden jerk, descended nearer and nearer the floor, keeping still their relative distance and horizontal position, and then, as suddenly, they rose to the level of the seat on which I was sitting and I saw them no more.

"My curiosity was now really excited, and, before I had time to think, I saw again these two dull lamps, again together near the floor; again they disappeared, and again in their old corner I saw them.

"So, keeping my eyes upon them, I edged quietly up my own side, towards the end at which I still saw these tiny discs of red.

"There was very little light in the 'bus. It was nearly dark. I leaned forward to aid my endeavour to discover what these little circles really were. They shifted position a little as I did so. I began now to perceive an outline of something black, and I soon saw, with tolerable distinctness, the outline of a small black monkey, pushing its face forward in mimicry to meet mine; those were its eyes, and I now dimly saw its teeth grinning at me.

"I drew back, not knowing whether it might not meditate a spring. I fancied that one of the passengers had forgot this ugly pet, and wishing to ascertain something of its temper, though not caring to trust my fingers to it, I poked my umbrella softly towards it. It remained immovable—up to it—*through* it. For through it, and back and forward it passed, without the slightest resistance.

"I can't, in the least, convey to you the kind of horror that I felt. When I had ascertained that the thing was an illusion, as I then supposed, there came a misgiving about myself and a terror that fascinated me in impotence to remove my gaze from the eyes of the brute for some moments. As I looked, it made a little skip back, quite into the corner, and I, in a panic, found myself at the door, having put my head out, drawing deep breaths of the outer air, and staring at the lights and tress we were passing, too glad to reassure myself of reality.

"I stopped the 'bus and got out. I perceived the man look oddly at me as I paid him. I dare say there was something unusual in my looks and manner, for I had never felt so strangely before."

CHAPTER VII

The Journey: First Stage

"When the omnibus drove on, and I was alone upon the road, I looked carefully round to ascertain whether the monkey had followed me. To my indescribable relief I saw it nowhere. I can't describe easily what a shock I had received, and my sense of genuine gratitude on finding myself, as I supposed, quite rid of it.

"I had got out a little before we reached this house, two or three hundred steps. A brick wall runs along the footpath, and inside the wall is a hedge of yew, or some dark evergreen of that kind, and within that again the row of fine trees which you may have remarked as you came.

"This brick wall is about as high as my shoulder, and happening to raise my eyes I saw the monkey, with that stooping gait, on all fours, walking or creeping, close beside me, on top of the wall. I stopped, looking at it with a feeling of loathing and horror. As I stopped so did it. It sat up on the wall with its long hands on its knees looking at me. There was not light enough to see it much more than in outline, nor was it dark enough to bring the peculiar light of its eyes into strong relief. I still saw, however, that red foggy light plainly enough. It did not show its teeth, nor exhibit any sign of irritation, but seemed jaded and sulky, and was observing me steadily.

"I drew back into the middle of the road. It was an unconscious recoil, and there I stood, still looking at it. It did not move.

"With an instinctive determination to try something—anything, I turned about and walked briskly towards town with askance look, all the time, watching the movements of the beast. It crept swiftly along the wall, at exactly my pace.

"Where the wall ends, near the turn of the road, it came down, and with a wiry spring or two brought itself close to my feet, and continued to keep up with me, as I quickened my pace. It was at my left side, so close to my leg that I felt every moment as if I should tread upon it.

"The road was quite deserted and silent, and it was darker every moment. I stopped dismayed and bewildered, turning as I did so, the other way—I mean, towards this house, away from which I had been walking. When I stood still, the monkey drew back to a distance of, I suppose, about five or six yards, and remained stationary, watching me.

"I had been more agitated than I have said. I had read, of course, as everyone has, something about 'spectral illusions,' as you physicians term the phenomena of such cases. I considered my situation, and looked my misfortune in the face.

"These affections, I had read, are sometimes transitory and sometimes obstinate. I had read of cases in which the appearance, at first harmless, had, step by step, degenerated into something direful and insupportable, and ended by wearing its victim out. Still as I stood there, but for my bestial companion, quite alone, I tried to comfort myself by repeating again and again the assurance, 'the thing is purely disease, a well-known physical affection, as distinctly as small-pox or neuralgia. Doctors are all agreed on that, philosophy demonstrates it. I must not be a fool. I've been sitting up too late, and I daresay my digestion is quite wrong, and, with God's help, I shall be all right, and this is but a symptom of nervous dyspepsia.' Did I believe all this? Not one word of it, no more than any other miserable being ever did who is once seized and riveted in this satanic captivity. Against my convictions, I might say my knowledge, I was simply bullying myself into a false courage.

"I now walked homeward. I had only a few hundred yards to go. I had forced myself into a sort of resignation, but I had not got over the sickening shock and the flurry of the first certainty of my misfortune.

"I made up my mind to pass the night at home. The brute moved close beside me, and I fancied there was the sort of anxious drawing toward the house, which one sees in tired horses or dogs, sometimes as they come toward home.

"I was afraid to go into town, I was afraid of any one's seeing and recognizing me. I was conscious of an irrepressible agitation in my manner. Also, I was afraid of any violent change in my habits, such as going to a place of amusement, or walking from home in order to fatigue myself. At the hall door it waited till I mounted the steps, and when the door was opened entered with me.

"I drank no tea that night. I got cigars and some brandy and water. My idea was that I should act upon my material system, and by living for a while in sensation apart from thought, send myself forcibly, as it were, into a new groove. I came up here to this drawing-room. I sat just here. The monkey then got upon a small table that then stood *there*. It looked dazed and languid. An irrepressible uneasiness as to its movements kept my eyes always upon it. Its eyes were half closed, but I could see them glow. It was looking steadily at me. In all situations, at all hours, it is awake and looking at me. That never changes.

"I shall not continue in detail my narrative of this particular night. I shall describe, rather, the phenomena of the first year, which never varied, essentially. I shall describe the monkey as it appeared in daylight. In the dark, as you shall presently hear, there are peculiarities. It is a small monkey, perfectly black. It had only one peculiarity—a character of malignity—unfathomable malignity. During the first year it looked sullen and sick. But this character of intense malice and vigilance was always underlying that surly languor. During all that time it acted as if on a plan of giving me as little trouble as was consistent with watching me. Its eyes were never off me. I have never lost sight of it, except in my sleep, light or dark, day or night, since it came here, excepting when it withdraws for some weeks at a time, unaccountably.

"In total dark it is visible as in daylight. I do not mean merely its eyes. It is *all* visible distinctly in a halo that resembles a glow of red embers, and which accompanies it in all its movements.

"When it leaves me for a time, it is always at night, in the dark, and in the same way. It grows at first uneasy, and then furious, and then advances towards me, grinning and shaking, its paws clenched, and, at the same time, there comes the appearance of fire in the grate. I never have any fire. I can't sleep in the room where there is any, and it draws nearer and nearer to the chimney, quivering, it seems, with rage, and when its fury rises to the highest pitch, it springs into the grate, and up the chimney, and I see it no more.

"When first this happened, I thought I was released. I was now a new man. A day passed—a night—and no return, and a blessed week—a week—another week. I was always on my knees, Dr. Hesselius, always, thanking God and praying. A whole month passed of liberty, but on a sudden, it was with me again."

CHAPTER VIII

The Second Stage

"It was with me, and the malice which before was torpid under a sullen exterior, was now active. It was perfectly unchanged in every other respect. This new energy was apparent in its activity and its looks, and soon in other ways.

"For a time, you will understand, the change was shown only in an increased vivacity, and an air of menace, as if it were always brooding over some atrocious plan. Its eyes, as before, were never off me."

"Is it here now?" I asked.

"No," he replied, "it has been absent exactly a fortnight and a day—fifteen days. It has sometimes been away so long as nearly two months, once for three. Its absence always exceeds a fortnight, although it may be but by a single day. Fifteen days having past since I saw it last, it may return now at any moment."

"Is its return," I asked, "accompanied by any peculiar manifestation?"

"Nothing—no," he said. "It is simply with me again. On lifting my eyes from a book, or turning my head, I see it, as usual, looking at me, and then it remains, as before, for its appointed time. I have never told so much and so minutely before to any one."

I perceived that he was agitated, and looking like death, and he repeatedly applied his handkerchief to his forehead; I suggested that he might be tired, and told him that I would call, with pleasure, in the morning, but he said:

"No, if you don't mind hearing it all now. I have got so far, and I should prefer making one effort of it. When I spoke to Dr. Harley, I had nothing like so much to tell. You are a philosophic physician. You give spirit its proper rank. If this thing is real——"

He paused looking at me with agitated inquiry.

"We can discuss it by-and-by, and very fully. I will give you all I think," I answered, after an interval.

"Well—very well. If it is anything real, I say, it is prevailing, little by little, and drawing me more interiorly into hell. Optic nerves, he talked of. Ah! well—there are other nerves of communication. May God Almighty help me! You shall hear.

"Its power of action, I tell you, had increased. Its malice became, in a way, aggressive. About two years ago, some questions that were pending between me and the bishop having been settled, I went down to my parish in Warwickshire, anxious to find occupation in my profession. I was not prepared for what happened, although I have since thought I might have apprehended something like it. The reason of my saying so is this——"

He was beginning to speak with a great deal more effort and reluctance, and sighed often, and seemed at times nearly overcome. But at this time his manner was not agitated. It was more like that of a sinking patient, who has given himself up.

"Yes, but I will first tell you about Kenlis, my parish.

"It was with me when I left this place for Dawlbridge. It was my silent travelling companion, and it remained with me at the vicarage. When I entered on the discharge of my duties, another change took place. The thing exhibited an atrocious determination to thwart me. It was with me in the church—in the reading-desk—in the pulpit—within the communion rails. At last, it reached this extremity, that while I was reading to the congregation, it would spring upon the book and squat there, so that I was unable to see the page. This happened more than once.

"I left Dawlbridge for a time. I placed myself in Dr. Harley's hands. I did everything he told me. He gave my case a great deal of thought. It interested him, I think. He seemed successful. For nearly three months I was perfectly free from a return. I began to think I was safe. With his full assent I returned to Dawlbridge.

"I travelled in a chaise. I was in good spirits. I was more—I was happy and grateful. I was returning, as I thought, delivered from a dreadful hallucination, to the scene of duties which I longed to enter upon. It was a beautiful sunny evening, everything looked

serene and cheerful, and I was delighted. I remember looking out
of the window to see the spire of my church at Kenlis among the
trees, at the point where one has the earliest view of it. It is exactly
where the little stream that bounds the parish passes under the
road by a culvert, and where it emerges at the road-side, a stone
with an old inscription is placed. As we passed this point, I drew
my head in and sat down, and in the corner of the chaise was the
monkey.

"For a moment I felt faint, and then quite wild with despair
and horror. I called to the driver, and got out, and sat down at the
road-side, and prayed to God silently for mercy. A despairing
resignation supervened. My companion was with me as I re-
entered the vicarage. The same persecution followed. After a short
struggle I submitted, and soon I left the place.

"I told you," he said," that the beast has before this become in
certain ways aggressive. I will explain a little. It seemed to be ac-
tuated by intense and increasing fury, whenever I said my prayers,
or even meditated prayer. It amounted at last to a dreadful interruption. You will ask, how could a silent immaterial phantom
effect that? It was thus, whenever I meditated praying; It was always before me, and nearer and nearer.

"It used to spring on a table, on the back of a chair, on the
chimney-piece, and slowly to swing itself from side to side, looking
at me all the time. There is in its motion an indefinable power to
dissipate thought, and to contract one's attention to that monotony, till the ideas shrink, as it were, to a point, and at last to nothing—and unless I had started up, and shook off the catalepsy I
have felt as if my mind were on the point of losing itself. There
are other ways," he sighed heavily; "thus, for instance, while I
pray with my eyes closed, it comes closer and closer, and I see it. I
know it is not to be accounted for physically, but I do actually see
it, though my lids are closed, and so it rocks my mind, as it were,
and overpowers me, and I am obliged to rise from my knees. If
you had ever yourself known this, you would be acquainted with
desperation."

CHAPTER IX

The Third Stage

"I see, Dr. Hesselius, that you don't lose one word of my statement.

I need not ask you to listen specially to what I am now going to tell you. They talk of the optic nerves, and of spectral illusions, as if the organ of sight was the only point assailable by the influences that have fastened upon me—I know better. For two years in my direful case that limitation prevailed. But as food is taken in softly at the lips, and then brought under the teeth, as the tip of the little finger caught in a mill crank will draw in the hand, and the arm, and the whole body, so the miserable mortal who has been once caught firmly by the end of the finest fibre of his nerve, is drawn in and in, by the enormous machinery of hell, until he is as I am. Yes, Doctor, as *I* am, for a while I talk to you, and implore relief, I feel that my prayer is for the impossible, and my pleading with the inexorable."

I endeavoured to calm his visibly increasing agitation, and told him that he must not despair.

While we talked the night had overtaken us. The filmy moonlight was wide over the scene which the window commanded, and I said:

"Perhaps you would prefer having candles. This light, you know, is odd. I should wish you, as much as possible, under your usual conditions while I make my diagnosis, shall I call it—otherwise I don't care."

"All lights are the same to me," he said; "except when I read or write, I care not if night were perpetual. I am going to tell you what happened about a year ago. The thing began to speak to me."

"Speak! How do you mean—speak as a man does, do you mean?"

"Yes; speak in words and consecutive sentences, with perfect coherence and articulation; but there is a peculiarity. It is not like the tone of a human voice. It is not by my ears it reaches me—it comes like a singing through my head.

"This faculty, the power of speaking to me, will be my undoing. It won't let me pray, it interrupts me with dreadful blasphemies. I dare not go on, I could not. Oh! Doctor, can the skill, and thought, and prayers of man avail me nothing!"

"You must promise me, my dear sir, not to trouble yourself with unnecessarily exciting thoughts; confine yourself strictly to the narrative of *facts;* and recollect, above all, that even if the thing that infests you be, you seem to suppose a reality with an actual independent life and will, yet it can have no power to hurt you, unless it be given from above: its access to your senses depends mainly upon your physical condition—this is, under God, your comfort and reliance: we are all alike environed. It is only that in your case, the *'paries,'* the veil of the flesh, the screen, is a little out of repair, and sights and sounds are transmitted. We must enter on a new course, sir,—be encouraged. I'll give to-night to the careful consideration of the whole case."

"You are very good, sir; you think it worth trying, you don't give me quite up; but, sir, you don't know, it is gaining such an influence over me: it orders me about, it is such a tyrant, and I'm growing so helpless. May God deliver me!"

"It orders you about—of course you mean by speech?"

"Yes, yes; it is always urging me to crimes, to injure others, or myself. You see, Doctor, the situation is urgent, it is indeed. When I was in Shropshire, a few weeks ago" (Mr. Jennings was speaking rapidly and trembling now, holding my arm with one hand, and looking in my face), "I went out one day with a party of friends for a walk: my persecutor, I tell you, was with me at the time. I lagged behind the rest: the country near the Dee, you know, is beautiful. Our path happened to lie near a coal mine, and at the verge of the wood is a perpendicular shaft, they say, a hundred and fifty feet deep. My niece had remained behind with me—she knows, of course nothing of the nature of my sufferings. She knew, however, that I had been ill, and was low, and she remained to prevent my being quite alone. As we loitered slowly on together, the brute that accompanied me was urging me to throw myself down the shaft. I tell you now—oh, sir, think of it!—the one consideration that saved me from that hideous death was the fear lest the shock of witnessing the occurrence should be too much for the poor girl. I asked her to go on and walk with her friends, saying that I could go no further. She made excuses, and the more I urged her the firmer she became. She looked doubtful and frightened. I suppose there was something in my looks or manner that alarmed her; but she would not go, and that literally saved me. You had no idea, sir, that a living man could be made so abject a slave of Satan," he said, with a ghastly groan and a shudder.

There was a pause here, and I said, "You *were* preserved nevertheless. It was the act of God. You are in His hands and in the power of no other being: be therefore confident for the future."

CHAPTER X

Home

I made him have candles lighted, and saw the room looking

cheery and inhabited before I left him. I told him that he must regard his illness strictly as one dependent on physical, though *subtle* physical causes. I told him that he had evidence of God's care and love in the deliverance which he had just described, and that I had perceived with pain that he seemed to regard its peculiar features as indicating that he had been delivered over to spiritual reprobation. Than such a conclusion nothing could be, I insisted, less warranted; and not only so, but more contrary to facts, as disclosed in his mysterious deliverance from that murderous influence during his Shropshire excursion. First, his niece had been retained by his side without his intending to keep her near him; and, secondly, there had been infused into his mind an irresistible repugnance to execute the dreadful suggestion in her presence.

As I reasoned this point with him, Mr. Jennings wept. He seemed comforted. One promise I exacted, which was that should the monkey at any time return, I should be sent for immediately; and, repeating my assurance that I would give neither time nor thought to any other subject until I had thoroughly investigated his case, and that to-morrow he should hear the result, I took my leave.

Before getting into the carriage I told the servant that his master was far from well, and that he should make a point of frequently looking into his room.

My own arrangements I made with a view to being quite secure from interruption.

I merely called at my lodgings, and with a travelling-desk and carpet-bag, set off in a hackney carriage for an inn about two miles out of town, called "The Horns," a very quiet and comfortable house, with good thick walls. And there I resolved, without the possibility of intrusion or distraction, to devote some hours of the the night, in my comfortable sitting-room, to Mr. Jennings' case, and so much of the morning as it might require.

(There occurs here a careful note of Dr. Hesselius' opinion upon the case, and of the habits, dietary, and medicines which he prescribed. It is curious—some persons would say mystical. But, on the whole, I doubt whether it would sufficiently interest a reader of the kind I am likely to meet with, to warrant its being here reprinted. The whole letter was plainly written at the inn where he had hid himself for the occasion. The next letter is dated from his town lodgings.)

I left town for the inn where I slept last night at half-past nine, and did not arrive at my room in town until one o'clock this afternoon. I found a letter in Mr. Jennings' hand upon my table. It had not come by post, and, on inquiry, I learned that Mr. Jennings' servant had brought it, and on learning that I was not to return until to-day, and that no one could tell him my address, he seemed very uncomfortable, and said his orders from his master were that that he was not to return without an answer.

I opened the letter and read:

DEAR DR. HESSELIUS.—It is here. You had not been an hour gone when it returned. It is speaking. It knows all that has happened. It knows every-thing—it knows you, and is frantic and atrocious. It reviles. I send you this. It knows every word I have written—I write. This I promised, and I therefore write, but I fear very confused, very incoherently. I am so inter-rupted, disturbed.

Ever yours, sincerely yours,
ROBERT LYNDER JENNINGS.

"When did this come?" I asked.

"About eleven last night: the man was here again, and has been here three times to-day. The last time is about an hour since."

Thus answered, and with the notes I had made upon his case in my pocket, I was in a few minutes driving towards Richmond, to see Mr. Jennings.

I by no means, as you perceive, despaired of Mr. Jennings' case. He had himself remembered and applied, though quite in a mis-taken way, the principle which I lay down in my Metaphysical Medicine, and which governs all such cases. I was about to apply it in earnest. I was profoundly interested, and very anxious to see and examine him while the "enemy" was actually present.

I drove up to the sombre house, and ran up the steps, and knocked. The door, in a little time, was opened by a tall woman in black silk. She looked ill, and as if she had been crying. She curt-seyed, and heard my question, but she did not answer. She turned her face away, extending her hand towards two men who were coming down-stairs; and thus having, as it were, tacitly made me over to them, she passed through a side-door hastily and shut it.

The man who was nearest the hall, I at once accosted, but being now close to him, I was shocked to see that both his hands were covered with blood.

I drew back a little, and the man, passing downstairs, merely said in a low tone, "Here's the servant, sir."

The servant had stopped on the stairs, confounded and dumb at seeing me. He was rubbing his hands in a handkerchief, and it was steeped in blood.

"Jones, what is it? what has happened?" I asked, while a sicken-ing suspicion overpowered me.

The man asked me to come up to the lobby. I was beside him in a moment, and, frowning and pallid, with contracted eyes, he told me the horror which I already half guessed.

His master had made away with himself.

I went upstairs with him to the room—what I saw there I won't tell you. He had cut his throat with his razor. It was a frightful gash. The two men had laid him on the bed, and composed his limbs. It had happened, as the immense pool of blood on the floor declared, at some distance between the bed and the window. There was carpet round his bed, and a carpet under his dressing-table, but none on the rest of the floor, for the man said he did not like a carpet on his bedroom. In this sombre and now terrible room, one of the great elms that darkened the house was slowly moving the shadow of one of its great boughs upon this dreadful floor.

I beckoned to the servant, and we went downstairs together. I turned off the hall into an old-fashioned panelled room, and there standing, I heard all the servant had to tell. It was not a great deal.

"I concluded, sir, from your words, and looks, sir, as you left last night, that you thought my master was seriously ill. I thought it might be that you were afraid of a fit, or something. So I attended very close to your directions. He sat up late, till past three o'clock. He was not writing or reading. He was talking a great deal to himself, but that was nothing unusual. At about that hour I assisted him to undress, and left him in his slippers and dressing-gown. I went back softly in about half-an-hour. He was in his bed, quite undressed, and a pair of candles lighted on the table beside his bed. He was leaning on his elbow, and looking out at the other side of the bed when I came in. I asked him if he wanted anything, and he said No.

"I don't know whether it was what you said to me, sir, or something a little unusual about him, but I was uneasy, uncommon uneasy about him last night.

"In another half hour, or it might be a little more, I went up again. I did not hear him talking as before. I opened the door a little. The candles were both out, which was not usual. I had a bedroom candle, and I let the light in, a little bit, looking softly round. I saw him sitting in that chair beside the dressing-table with his clothes on again. He turned round and looked at me. I thought it strange he should get up and dress, and put out the candles to sit in the dark, that way. But I only asked him again if I could do anything for him. He said, No, rather sharp, I thought. I asked him if I might light the candles, and he said, 'Do as you like, Jones.' So I lighted them, and I lingered about the room, and he said, 'Tell me truth, Jones; why did you come again—you did not hear anyone cursing?' 'No, sir,' I said, wondering what he could mean.

" 'No,' said he, after me, 'of course, no;' and I said to him, 'Wouldn't it be well, sir, you went to bed? It's just five o'clock;' and he said nothing, but, 'Very likely; good-night, Jones.' So I went, sir, but in less than an hour I came again. The door was fast, and he heard me, and called as I thought from the bed to know what I wanted, and he desired me not to disturb him again. I lay down and slept for a little. It must have been between six and seven when I went up again. The door was still fast, and he made no answer, so I did not like to disturb him, and thinking he was asleep, I left him till nine. It was his custom to ring when he wished me to come, and I had no particular hour for calling him. I tapped very gently, and getting no answer, I stayed away a good while, supposing he was getting some rest then. It was not till eleven o'clock I grew really uncomfortable about him—for at the latest he was never, that I could remember, later than half-past ten. I got no answer. I knocked and called, and still no answer. So not being able to force the door, I called Thomas from the stables, and together we forced it, and found him in the shocking way you saw."

Jones had no more to tell. Poor Mr. Jennings was very gentle, and very kind. All his people were fond of him. I could see that the servant was very much moved.

So, dejected and agitated, I passed from that terrible house, and its dark canopy of elms, and I hope I shall never see it more. While I write to you I feel like a man who has but half waked from a frightful and monotonous dream. My memory rejects the picture with incredulity and horror. Yet I know it is true. It is the story of the process of a poison, a poison which excites the reciprocal action of spirit and nerve, and paralyses the tissue that separates those cognate functions of the senses, the external and the interior. Thus we find strange bed-fellows, and the mortal and immortal prematurely make acquaintance.

CONCLUSION

A Word for Those Who Suffer

My dear Van L—, you have suffered from an affection similar to that which I have just described. You twice complained of a return of it.

Who, under God, cured you? Your humble servant, Martin Hesselius. Let me rather adopt the more emphasised piety of a certain good old French surgeon of three hundred years ago: "I treated, and God cured you."

Come, my friend, you are not to be hippish. Let me tell you a fact.

I have met with, and treated, as my book shows, fifty-seven cases of this kind of vision, which I term indifferently "sublimated," "precocious," and "interior."

There is another class of affections which are truly termed—though commonly confounded with those which I describe—spectral illusions. These latter I look upon as being no less simply curable than a cold in the head or a trifling dyspepsia.

It is those which rank in the first category that test our promptitude of thought. Fifty-seven such cases have I encounteed, neither more nor less. And in how many of these have I failed? In no one single instance.

There is no one affliction of mortality more easily and certainly reducible, with a little patience, and a rational confidence in the physician. With these simple conditions, I look upon the cure as absolutely certain.

You are to remember that I had not even commenced to treat Mr. Jennings' case. I have not any doubt that I should have cured him perfectly in eighteen months, or possibly it might have extended to two years. Some cases are very rapidly curable, others extremely tedious. Every intelligent physician who will give thought and diligence to the task, will effect a cure.

You know my tract on "The Cardinal Functions of the Brain." I there, by the evidence of innumerable facts, prove, as I think, the high probability of a circulation arterial and venous in its mechanism, through the nerves. Of this system, thus considered, the brain is the heart. The fluid, which is propagated hence through one class of nerves, returns in an altered state through another, and the nature of that fluid is spiritual, though not immaterial, any more than, as I before remarked, light or electricity are so.

By various abuses, among which the habitual use of such agents as green tea is one, this fluid may be affected as to its quality, but it is more frequently disturbed as to equilibrium. This fluid being that which we have in common with spirits, a congestion found upon the masses of brain or nerve, connected with the interior sense, forms a surface unduly exposed, on which disembodied spirits may operate: communication is thus more or less effectually established. Between this brain circulation and the heart circulation there is an intimate sympathy. The seat, or rather the instrument of exterior vision, is the eye. The seat of interior vision is the nervous tissue and brain, immediately about and above the eyebrow. You remember how effectually I dissipated your pictures by the simple application of iced eau-de-cologne. Few cases, however, can be treated exactly alike with anything like rapid success. Cold acts powerfully as a repellant of the nervous fluid. Long enough continued it will even produce that permanent insensibility which we call numbness, and a little longer, muscular as well as sensational paralysis.

I have not, I repeat, the slightest doubt that I should have first dimmed and ultimately sealed that inner eye which Mr. Jennings had inadvertently opened. The same senses are opened in delirium tremens, and entirely shut up again when the overaction of the cerebral heart, and the prodigious nervous congestions that attend it, are terminated by a decided change in the state of the body. It is by acting steadily upon the body, by a simple process, that this result is produced—and inevitably produced—I have never yet failed.

Poor Mr. Jennings made away with himself. But that catastrophe was the result of a totally different malady, which, as it were, projected itself upon the disease which was established. His case was in the distinctive manner a complication, and the complaint under which he really succumbed, was hereditary suicidal mania. Poor Mr. Jennings I cannot call a patient of mine, for I had not even begun to treat his case, and he had not yet given me, I am convinced, his full and unreserved confidence. If the patient do not array himself on the side of the disease, his cure is certain.

The Familiar

PROLOGUE

Out of about two hundred and thirty cases, more or less nearly akin to that I have entitled "Green Tea," I select the following, which I call "The Familiar."

To this MS., Doctor Hesselius has, after his wont, attached some sheets of letter-paper, on which are written, in his hand nearly as compact as print, his own remarks upon the case. He says—

"In point of conscience, no more unexceptionable narrator, than the venerable Irish Clergyman who has given me this paper, on Mr. Barton's case, could have been chosen. The statement is, however, medically imperfect. The report of an intelligent physician, who had marked its progress, and attended the patient, from its earlier stages to its close, would have supplied what is wanted to enable me to pronounce with confidence. I should have been acquainted with Mr. Barton's probable hereditary predispositions; I should have known, possibly, by very early indications, something of a remoter origin of the disease that can now be ascertained.

"In a rough way, we may reduce all similar cases to three distinct classes. They are founded on the primary distinction between the subjective and the objective. Of those whose senses are alleged to be subject to supernatural impressions—some are simply visionaries, and propagate the illusions of which they complain, from diseased brain or nerves. Others are, unquestionably, infested by, as we term them, spiritual agencies, exterior to themselves. Others, again, owe their sufferings to a mixed condition. The interior sense, it is true, is opened; but it has been and continues open by the action of disease. This form of disease may, in one sense, be compared to the loss of the scarf-skin, and a consequent exposure of surfaces for whose excessive sensitiveness, nature has provided a muffling. The loss of this covering is attended by an habitual impassibility, by influences against which we were intended to be guarded. But in the case of the brain, and the nerves immediately connected with its functions and its sensuous impressions, the cerebral circulation undergoes periodically that vibratory disturbance, which, I believe, I have satisfactorily examined and demonstrated, in my MS. Essay, A. 17. This vibratory disturbance differs, as I there prove, essentially from congestive disturbance, the phenomena of which are examined in A. 19. It is, when excessive, invariably accompanied by *illusions*.

"Had I seen Mr. Barton, and examined him upon the points, in his case, which need elucidation, I should have without difficulty referred those phenomena to their proper disease. My diagnosis is now, necessarily, conjectural."

Thus writes Doctor Hesselius; and adds a great deal which is of interest only to a scientific physician.

The Narrative of the Rev. Thomas Herbert, which furnishes all that is known of the case, will be found in the chapters that follow.

CHAPTER I

Footsteps

I was a young man at the time, and intimately acquainted with some of the actors in this strange tale; the impression which its incidents made on me, therefore, were deep and lasting. I shall now endeavour, with precision, to relate them all, combining, of course, in the narrative, whatever I have learned from various sources, tending, however imperfectly, to illuminate the darkness which involves its progress and termination.

Somewhere about the year 1794, the younger brother of a certain baronet, whom I shall call Sir James Barton, returned to Dublin. He had served in the navy with some distinction, having commanded one of His Majesty's frigates during the greater part of the American war. Captain Barton was apparently some two or three-and-forty years of age. He was an intelligent and agreeable companion when he pleased it, though generally reserved, and occasionally even moody.

In society, however, he deported himself as a man of the world,

and a gentleman. He had not contracted any of the noisy brusque-
ness sometimes acquired at sea; on the contrary, his manners
were remarkably easy, quiet and even polished. He was in person
about the middle size, and somewhat strongly formed—his countenance was marked with the lines of thought, and on the whole
wore an expression of gravity and melancholy; being, however,
as I have said, a man of perfect breeding, as well as of good family,
and in affluent circumstances, he had, of course, ready access to the
best society of Dublin, without the necessity of any other creden-
tials.

In his personal habits Mr. Barton was unexpensive. He occupied
lodgings in one of the *then* fashionable streets in the south side of
the town—kept but one horse and one servant—and though a re-
puted freethinker, yet lived an orderly and moral life—indulging
neither in gaming, drinking, nor any other vicious pursuit—living
very much to himself, without forming intimacies, or choosing
any companions, and appearing to mix in gay society rather for
the sake of its bustle and distraction, than for any opportunities
it offered of interchanging thought or feeling with its votaries.

Barton was, therefore, pronounced a saving, prudent, unsocial
sort of fellow, who bid fair to maintain his celibacy alike against
stratagem and assault, and was likely to live to a good old age, die
rich, and leave his money to a hospital.

It was now apparent, however, that the nature of Mr. Barton's
plans had been totally misconceived. A young lady, whom I shall
call Miss Montague, was at this time introduced into the gay world
by her aunt, the Dowager Lady Rochdale. Miss Montague was decidedly pretty and accomplished, and having some natural clever-
ness, and a great deal of gaiety, became for a while a reigning
toast.

Her popularity, however, gained her, for a time, nothing more
than that unsubstantial admiration which, however pleasant as an
incense to vanity, is by no means necessarily antecedent to matri-
mony—for, unhappily for the young lady in question, it was an
understood thing, that beyond her personal attractions, she had
no kind of earthly provision. Such being the state of affairs, it will
readily be believed that no little surprise was consequent upon the
appearance of Captain Barton as the avowed lover of the penniless
Miss Montague.

His suit prospered, as might have been expected, and in a short
time it was communicated by old Lady Rochdale to each of her
hundred-and-fifty particular friends in succession, that Captain
Barton had actually tendered proposals of marriage, with her ap-

probation, to her niece, Miss Montague, who had, moreover, accepted the offer of his hand, conditionally upon the consent of her father, who was then upon his homeward voyage from India, and expected in two or three weeks at the furthest.

About this consent there could be no doubt—the delay, therefore, was one merely of form—they were looked upon as absolutely engaged, and Lady Rochdale, with a rigour of old-fashioned decorum with which her niece would, no doubt, gladly have dispensed, withdrew her thenceforward from all further participation in the gaieties of the town.

Captain Barton was a constant visitor, as well as a frequent guest at the house, and was permitted all the privileges of intimacy which a betrothed suitor is usually accorded. Such was the relation of parties, when the mysterious circumstances which darken this narrative first begun to unfold themselves.

Lady Rochdale resided in a handsome mansion at the north side of Dublin, and Captain Barton's lodgings, as we have already said, were situated at the south. The distance intervening was considerable, and it was Captain Barton's habit generally to walk home without an attendant, as often as he passed the evening with the old lady and her fair charge.

His shortest way in such nocturnal walks, lay, for a considerable space, through a line of street which had as yet merely been laid out, and little more than the foundations of the houses constructed.

One night, shortly after his engagement with Miss Montague had commenced, he happened to remain unusually late, in company with her and Lady Rochdale. The conversation had turned upon the evidences of revelation, which he had disputed with the callous scepticism of a confirmed infidel. What were called "French principles," had in those days found their way a good deal into fashionable society, especially that portion of it which professed allegiance to Whiggism, and neither the old lady nor her charge were so perfectly free from the taint, as to look upon Mr. Barton's views as any serious objection to the proposed union.

The discussion had degenerated into one upon the supernatural and the marvellous, in which he had pursued precisely the same line of argument and ridicule. In all this, it is but truth to state, Captain Barton was guilty of no affectation—the doctrines upon which he insisted, were, in reality, but too truly the basis of his own fixed belief, if so it might be called; and perhaps not the least strange of the many strange circumstances connected with my narrative, was the fact that the subject of the fearful influences I am about to describe, was himself, from the deliberate conviction of years, an utter disbeliever in what are usually termed preternatural agencies.

It was considerably past midnight when Mr. Barton took his leave, and set out upon his solitary walk homeward. He had now reached the lonely road, with its unfinished dwarf walls tracing the foundations of the projected row of houses on either side—the moon was shining mistily, and its imperfect light made the road he trod but additionally dreary—that utter silence which has in it something indefinably exciting, reigned there, and made the sound of his steps, which alone broke it, unnaturally loud and distinct.

He had proceeded thus some way, when he, on a sudden, heard other footballs, pattering at a measured pace, and, as it seemed, about two score steps behind him.

The suspicion of being dogged is at all times unpleasant: it is, however, especially so in a spot so lonely: and this suspicion became so strong in the mind of Captain Barton, that he abruptly turned about to confront his pursuer, but, though there was quite sufficient moonlight to disclose any object upon the road he had traversed, no form of any kind was visible there.

The steps he had heard could not have been the reverberation of his own, for he stamped his foot upon the ground, and walked briskly up and down, in the vain attempt to awake an echo; though by no means a fanciful person, therefore, he was at last fain to charge the sounds upon his imagination, and treat them as an illusion. Thus satisfying himself, he resumed his walk, and before he had proceeded a dozen paces, the mysterious footfall was again audible from behind, and this time, as if with the special design of showing that the sounds were not the responses of an echo —the steps sometimes slackened nearly to a halt, and sometimes hurried for six or eight strides to a run, and again abated to a walk.

Captain Barton, as before, turned suddenly round, and with the same result—no object was visible above the deserted level of the road. He walked back over the same ground, determined that, whatever might have been the cause of the sounds which had so disconcerted him, it should not escape his search—the endeavour, however, was unrewarded.

In spite of his scepticism, he felt something like a superstitious fear stealing fast upon him, and with these unwonted and uncomfortable sensations, he once more turned and pursued his way. There was no repetition of these haunting sounds, until he had reached the point where he had last stopped to retrace his steps—

here they were resumed—and with sudden starts of running, which threatened to bring the unseen pursuer up to the alarmed pedestrian.

Captain Barton arrested his course as formerly—the unaccountable nature of the occurrence filled him with vague and disagreeable sensations—and yielding to the excitement that was gaining upon him, he shouted sternly, "Who goes there?" The sound of one's own voice, thus exerted, in utter solitude, and followed by total silence, has in it something unpleasantly dismaying, and he felt a degree of nervousness which, perhaps from no cause had he ever known before.

To the very end of this solitary street the steps pursued him— and it required a strong effort of stubborn pride on his part, to resist the impulse that prompted him every moment to run for safety at the top of his speed. It was not until he had reached his lodging, and sate by his own fireside, that he felt sufficiently reassured to rearrange and reconsider in his own mind the occurrences which had so discomposed him. So little a matter, after all, is sufficient to upset the pride of scepticism and vindicate the old simple laws of nature within us.

CHAPTER II

The Watcher

Mr. Barton was next morning sitting at a late breakfast, reflecting upon the incidents of the previous night, with more of inquisitiveness than awe, so speedily do gloomy impressions upon the fancy disappear under the cheerful influence of day, when a letter just delivered by the postman was placed upon the table before him.

There was nothing remarkable in the address of this missive, except that it was written in a hand which he did not know—perhaps it was disguised—for the tall narrow characters were sloped backward; and with the self-inflicted suspense which we often see practised in such cases, he puzzled over the inscription for a full minute before he broke the seal. When he did so, he read the following words, written in the same hand:—

Mr. Barton, late captain of the "Dolphin," is warned of DANGER. He will do wisely to avoid ——— Street—[here the locality of his last night's adventure was named]—if he walks there as usual he will meet with something unlucky—let him take warning, once for all, for he has reason to dread

THE WATCHER.

Captain Barton read and re-read this strange effusion; in every light and in every direction he turned it over and over; he examined the paper on which it was written, and scrutinized the hand-writing once more. Defeated here, he turned to the seal; it was nothing but a patch of wax, upon which the accidental impression of a thumb was imperfectly visible.

There was not the slightest mark, or clue of any kind, to lead him to even a guess as to its possible origin. The writer's object seemed a friendly one, and yet he subscribed himself as one whom he had "reason to dread." Altogether the letter, its author, and its real purpose were to him an inexplicable puzzle, and one, moreover, unpleasantly suggestive, in his mind, of other associations connected with his last night's adventure.

In obedience to some feeling—perhaps of pride—Mr. Barton did not communicate, even to his intended bride, the occurrences which I have just detailed. Trifling as they might appear, they had in reality most disagreeably affected his imagination, and he cared not to disclose, even to the young lady in question, what she might possibly look upon as evidences of weakness. The letter might very well be but a hoax, and the mysterious footfall but a delusion or a trick. But although he affected to treat the whole affair as unworthy of a thought, it yet haunted him pertinaciously, tormenting him with perplexing doubts, and depressing him with undefined apprehensions. Certain it is, that for a considerable time afterwards he carefully avoided the street indicated in the letter as the scene of danger.

It was not until about a week after the receipt of the letter which I have transcribed, that anything further occurred to remind Captain Barton of its contents, or to counteract the gradual disappearance from his mind of the disagreeable impressions then received.

He was returning one night, after the interval I have stated, from the theatre, which was then situated in Crow Street, and having there seen Miss Montague and Lady Rochdale into their carriage, he loitered for some time with two or three acquaintances.

With these, however, he parted close to the college, and pursued his way alone. It was now fully one o'clock, and the streets were quite deserted. During the whole of his walk with the companions from whom he had just parted, he had been at times painfully aware of the sound of steps, as it seemed, dogging them on their way.

Once or twice he had looked back, in the uneasy anticipation that he was again about to experience the same mysterious annoyances which had so disconcerted him a week before, and earnestly hoping that he might *see* some form to account naturally for the sounds. But the street was deserted—no one was visible.

Proceeding now quite alone upon his homeward way, he grew really nervous and uncomfortable, as he became sensible, with increased distinctness, of the well-known and now absolutely dreaded sounds.

By the side of the dead wall which bounded the college park, the sounds followed, recommencing almost simultaneously with his own steps. The same unequal pace—sometimes slow, sometimes for a score of yards or so, quickened almost to a run—was audible from behind him. Again and again he turned; quickly and stealthily he glanced over his shoulder—almost at every half-dozen steps; but no one was visible.

The irritation of this intangible and unseen pursuit became gradually all but intolerable; and when at last he reached his home, his nerves were strung to such a pitch of excitement that he could not rest, and did not attempt even to lie down until after the daylight had broken.

He was awakened by a knock at his chamber-door, and his servant entering, handed him several letters which had just been received by the penny post. One among them instantly arrested his attention—a single glance at the direction aroused him thoroughly. He at once recognized its character, and read as follows:—

You may as well think, Captain Barton, to escape from your own shadow as from me; do what you may, I will see you as often as I please, and you shall see me, for I do not want to hide myself, as you fancy. Do not let it trouble your rest, Captain Barton; for, with a *good conscience,* what need you fear from the eye of

THE WATCHER.

It is scarcely necessary to dwell upon the feelings that accompanied a perusal of this strange communication. Captain Barton was observed to be unusually absent and out of spirits for several days afterwards, but no one divined the cause.

Whatever he might think as to the phantom steps which followed him, there could be no possible illusion about the letters he had received; and, to say the least, their immediate sequence upon the mysterious sounds which had haunted him, was an odd coincidence.

The whole circumstance was, in his own mind, vaguely and instinctively connected with certain passages in his past life, which, of all others, he hated to remember.

It happened, however, that in addition to his own approaching nuptials, Captain Barton had just then—fortunately, perhaps, for himself—some business of an engrossing kind connected with the adjustment of a large and long-litigated claim upon certain properties.

The hurry and excitement of business had its natural effect in gradually dispelling the gloom which had for a time occasionally oppressed him, and in a little while his spirits had entirely recovered their accustomed tone.

During all this time, however, he was, now and then, dismayed by indistinct and half-heard repetitions of the same annoyance, and that in lonely places, in the day-time as well as after nightfall. These renewals of the strange impressions from which he had suffered so much, were, however, desultory and faint, insomuch that often he really could not, to his own satisfaction, distinguish between them and the mere suggestions of an excited imagination.

One evening he walked down to the House of Commons with a Mr. Norcott, a Member, an acquaintance of his and mine. This was one of the few occasions upon which I have been in company with Captain Barton. As we walked down together, I observed that he became absent and silent, and to a degree that seemed to argue the pressure of some urgent and absorbing anxiety.

I afterwards learned that during the whole of our walk, he had heard the well-known footsteps tracking him as we proceeded.

This, however, was the last time he suffered from this phase of the persecution, of which he was already the anxious victim. A new and a very different one was about to be presented.

CHAPTER III

An Advertisement

Of the new series of impressions which were afterwards gradually to work out his destiny, I that evening witnessed the first; and but for its relation to the train of events which followed, the incident would scarcely have been now remembered by me.

As we were walking in at the passage from College Green, a man, of whom I remember only that he was short in stature, looked like a foreigner, and wore a kind of fur travelling cap, walked very rapidly, and as if under fierce excitement, directly towards us, muttering to himself, fast and vehemently the while.

This odd looking person walked straight toward Barton, who was foremost of the three, and halted, regarding him for a moment or two with a look of maniacal menace and fury; and then turning about as abruptly, he walked before us at the same agitated pace, and disappeared at a side passage. I do distinctly remember being a good deal shocked at the countenance and bearing of this man, which indeed irresistibly impressed me with an undefined sense of danger, such as I have never felt before or since from the presence of anything human; but these sensations were, on my part, far from amounting to anything so disconcerting as to flurry or excite me—I had seen only a singularly evil countenance, agitated, as it seemed, with the excitement of madness.

I was absolutely astonished, however, at the effect of this apparition upon Captain Barton. I knew him to be a man of proud courage and coolness in real danger—a circumstance which made his conduct upon this occasion the more conspicuously odd. He recoiled a step or two as the stranger advanced, and clutched my arm in silence, with what seemed to be a spasm of agony or terror! and then, as the figure disappeared, shoving me roughly back, he followed it for a few paces, stopped in great disorder, and sat down upon a form. I never beheld a countenance more ghastly and haggard.

"For God's sake, Barton, what is the matter?" said Norcott, our companion, really alarmed at his appearance. "You're not hurt are you?—or unwell? What is it?"

"What did he say?—I did not hear it— what was it?" asked Barton, wholly disregarding the question.

"Nonsense," said Norcott, greatly surprised; "who cares what the fellow said. You are unwell, Barton—decidedly unwell; let me call a coach."

"Unwell! No—not unwell," he said, evidently making an effort to recover his self-possession; "but, to say the truth, I am fatigued —a little over-worked—and perhaps over anxious. You know I have been in Chancery, and the winding-up of a suit is always a nervous affair. I have felt uncomfortable all this evening; but I am better now. Come, come—shall we go on?"

"No, no. Take my advice, Barton, and go home; you really do need rest; you are looking quite ill. I really do insist on your allowing me to see you home," replied his friend.

I seconded Norcott's advice, the more readily as it was obvious that Barton was not himself disinclined to be persuaded. He left us, declining our offered escort. I was not sufficiently intimate with Norcott to discuss the scene we had both just witnessed. I was, however, convinced from his manner in the few common-place comments and regrets we exchanged, that he was just as little satisfied as I with the extempore plea of illness with which he had accounted for the strange exhibition, and that we were both agreed in suspecting some lurking mystery in the manner.

I called next day at Barton's lodgings, to inquire for him, and learned from the servant that he had not left his room since his return the night before; but that he was not seriously indisposed, and hoped to be out in a few days. That evening he sent for Dr. Richards, then in large and fashionable practice in Dublin, and their interview was, it is said, an odd one.

He entered into a detail of his symptoms in an abstracted and desultory way, which seemed to argue a strange want of interest in his own cure, and, at all events, made it manifest that there was some topic engaging his mind of more engrossing importance than his present ailment. He complained of occasional palpitations and headache.

Dr. Richards asked him, among other questions, whether there was any irritating circumstance or anxiety then occupying his thoughts. This he denied quickly and almost peevishly; and the physician thereupon declared his opinion that there was nothing amiss except some slight derangement of the digestion, for which he accordingly wrote a prescription, and was about to withdraw, when Mr. Barton, with the air of a man who recollects a topic which had nearly escaped him, recalled him.

"I beg your pardon, Doctor, but I really almost forgot; will you permit me to ask you two or three medical questions—rather odd ones, perhaps, but a wager depends upon their solution, you will, I hope, excuse my unreasonableness?"

The physician readily undertook to satisfy the inquirer.

Barton seemed to have some difficulty about opening the proposed interrogatories, for he was silent for a minute, then walked to his book-case, and returned as he had gone; at last he sat down, and said—

"You'll think them very childish questions, but I can't recover my wager without a decision; so I must put them. I want to know first about lock-jaw. If a man actually has had that complaint, and appears to have died of it—so much so, that a physician of average skill pronounces him actually dead—may he, after all, recover?"

The physician smiled and shook his head.

"But—but a blunder may be made," resumed Barton. "Suppose an ignorant pretender to medical skill; may *he* be so deceived by any stage of the complaint, as to mistake what is only a part of the progress of the disease, for death itself?"

"No one who had ever seen death," answered he, "could mistake it in a case of lock-jaw."

Barton mused for a few minutes. "I am going to ask you a question, perhaps, still more childish; but first, tell me, are the regulations of foreign hospitals, such as that of, let us say, Naples, very lax and bungling? May not all kinds of blunders and slips occur in their entries of names, and so forth?"

Doctor Richards professed his incompetence to answer that query.

"Well, then, Doctor, here is the last of my questions. You will, probably, laugh at it; but it must out nevertheless. Is there any disease, in all the range of human maladies, which would have the effect of perceptibly contracting the stature, and the whole frame—causing the man to shrink in all his proportions, and yet to preserve his exact resemblance to himself in every particular —with the one exception, his height and bulk; *any* disease, mark— no matter how rare—how little believed in, generally—which could possibly result in producing such an effect?"

The physician replied with a smile, and a very decided negative.

"Tell me, then," said Barton, abruptly, "if a man be in reasonable fear of assault from a lunatic who is at large, can he not procure a warrant for his arrest and detention?"

"Really, that is more a lawyer's question than one in my way," replied Doctor Richards; "but I believe, on applying to a magistrate, such a course would be directed."

The physician then took his leave; but, just as he reached the hall-door, remembered that he had left his cane upstairs, and returned. His appearance was awkward, for a piece of paper, which he recognized as his own prescription, was slowly burning upon the fire, and Barton sitting close by with an expression of settled gloom and dismay.

Doctor Richards had too much tact to observe what presented itself; but he had seen quite enough to assure him that the mind, and not the body, of Captain Barton was in reality the seat of suffering.

A few days afterwards, the following advertisement appeared in the Dublin newspapers:—

"If Sylvester Yelland, formerly a foremast man on board His Majesty's frigate 'Dolphin,' or his nearest of kin, will apply to Mr. Hubert Smith, attorney, at his office, Dame Street, he or they may hear something greatly to his or their advantage. Admission may be had at any hour up to twelve o'clock at night, should parties desire to avoid observation; and the strictest secresy, as to all communications intended to be confidential, shall be honourably observed."

The "Dolphin," as I have mentioned, was the vessel which Captain Barton had commanded; and this circumstance, connected with the extraordinary exertions made by the circulation of handbills, etc., as well as by repeated advertisements, to secure for this strange notice the utmost possible publicity, suggested to Dr. Richards the idea that Captain Barton's extreme uneasiness was somehow connected with the individual to whom the advertisement was addressed, and he himself the author of it.

This, however, it is needless to add, was no more than a conjecture. No information, whatsoever, as to the real purpose of the advertisement was divulged by the agent, nor yet any hint as to who his employer might be.

CHAPTER IV

He Talks with a Clergyman

Mr. Barton, although he had latterly begun to earn for himself the character of an hypochondriac, was yet very far from deserving it. Though by no means lively, he had yet, naturally, what are termed "even spirits," and was not subject to undue depressions.

He soon, therefore, began to return to his former habits; and one of the earliest symptoms of this healthier tone of spirits was his appearing at a grand dinner of the Freemasons, of which worthy fraternity he was himself a brother. Barton, who had been at first gloomy and abstracted, drank much more freely than was his wont—possibly with the purpose of dispelling his own secret anxieties—and under the influence of good wine and pleasant company, became gradually (unlike himself) talkative, and even noisy.

It was under this unwonted excitement that he left his company at about half-past ten o'clock; and, as conviviality is a strong incentive to gallantry, it occurred to him to proceed forthwith to Lady Rochdale's, and pass the remainder of the evening with her and his destined bride.

Accordingly, he was soon at —— Street, and chatting gaily with the ladies. It is not to be supposed that Captain Barton had exceeded the limits which propriety prescribes to good fellowship— he had merely taken enough wine to raise his spirits, without, however, in the least degree unsteadying his mind, or affecting his manners.

With this undue elevation of spirits had supervened an entire oblivion or contempt of those undefined apprehensions which had for so long weighed upon his mind, and to a certain extent estranged him from society; but as the night wore away, and his artificial gaiety began to flag, these painful feelings gradually intruded themselves again, and he grew abstracted and anxious as heretofore.

He took his leave at length, with an unpleasant foreboding of some coming mischief, and with a mind haunted with a thousand mysterious apprehensions, such as, even while he acutely felt their pressure, he, nevertheless, inwardly strove, or affected to contemn.

It was this proud defiance of what he regarded as his own weakness, which prompted him upon the present occasion to that course which brought about the adventure I am now about to relate.

Mr. Barton might have easily called a coach, but he was conscious that his strong inclination to do so proceeded from no cause other than what he desperately persisted in representing to himself to be his own superstitious tremors.

He might also have returned home by a *route* different from that against which he had been warned by his mysterious correspondent; but for the same reason he dismissed this idea also, and with a dogged and half desperate resolution to force matters to a crisis of some kind, if there were any reality in the causes of his former suffering, and if not, satisfactorily to bring their delusiveness to the proof, he determined to follow precisely the course which he had trodden upon the night so painfully memorable in his own mind as that on which his strange persecution commenced. Though, sooth to say, the pilot who for the first time steers his vessel under the muzzles of a hostile battery, never felt his resolution more severely tasked than did Captain Barton, as he breathlessly pursued this solitary path—a path which, spite of every effort of scepticism and reason, he felt to be infested by some (as respected *him*) malignant being.

He pursued his way steadily and rapidly, scarcely breathing from intensity of suspense; he, however, was troubled by no renewal of the dreaded footsteps, and was beginning to feel a return of confidence, as more than three-fourths of the way being accomplished with impunity, he approached the long line of twinkling oil lamps which indicated the frequented streets.

This feeling of self-congratulation was, however, but momentary. The report of a musket at some hundred yards behind him, and the whistle of a bullet close to his head, disagreeably and startlingly dispelled it. His first impulse was to retrace his steps in pursuit of the assassin; but the road on either side was, as we have said, embarrassed by the foundations of a street, beyond which extended waste fields, full of rubbish and neglected lime and brick-kilns, and all now as utterly silent as though no sound had ever disturbed their dark and unsightly solitude. The futility of, single-handed, attempting, under such circumstances, a search for the murderer, was apparent especially as no sound, either of retreating steps or any other kind, was audible to direct his pursuit.

With the tumultuous sensations of one whose life has just been exposed to a murderous attempt, and whose escape has been the narrowest possible Captain Barton turned again; and without, however, quickening his pace actually to a run, hurriedly pursued his way.

He had turned, as I have said, after a pause of a few seconds, and had just commenced his rapid retreat, when on a sudden he met the well-remembered little man in the fur cap. The encounter was but momentary. The figure was walking at the same exaggerated pace, and with the same strange air of menace as before; and as it passed him, he thought he heard it say, in a furious whisper, "Still alive—still alive!"

The state of Mr. Barton's spirits began now to work a corresponding alteration in his health and looks, and to such a degree that it was impossible that the change should escape general remark.

For some reasons, known but to himself, he took no steps whatsoever to bring the attempt upon his life, which he had so narrowly escaped, under the notice of the authorities; on the contrary, he kept it jealously to himself; and it was not for many weeks after the occurrence that he mentioned it, and then in strict confidence, to a gentleman, whom the torments of his mind at last compelled him to consult.

Spite of his blue devils, however, poor Barton, having no satisfactory reason to render to the public for any undue remissness in the attentions exacted by the relation existing between him and

Miss Montague, was obliged to exert himself, and present to the world a confident and cheerful bearing.

The true source of his sufferings, and every circumstance connected with them, he guarded with a reserve so jealous, that it seemed dictated by at least a suspicion that the origin of his strange persecution was known to himself, and that it was of a nature which, upon his own account, he could not or dared not disclose.

The mind thus turned in upon itself, and constantly occupied with a haunting anxiety which it dared not reveal or confide to any human breast, became daily more excited, and, of course, more vividly impressible, by a system of attack which operated through the nervous system; and in this state he was destined to sustain, with increasing frequency, the stealthy visitations of that apparition which from the first had seemed to possess so terrible a hold upon his imagination.

      *   *   *   *   *

It was about this time that Captain Barton called upon the then celebrated preacher, Dr. Macklin, with whom he had a slight acquaintance, and an extraordinary conversation ensued.

The divine was seated in his chambers in college, surrounded with works upon his favourite pursuit, and deep in theology, when Barton was announced.

There was something at once embarrassed and excited in his manner, which, along with his wan and haggard countenance, impressed the student with the unpleasant consciousness that his visitor must have recently suffered terribly indeed, to account for an alteration so striking—almost shocking.

After the usual interchange of polite greeting, and a few common-place remarks, Captain Barton, who obviously perceived the surprise which his visit had excited, and which Doctor Macklin was unable wholly to conceal, interrupted a brief pause by remarking—

"This is a strange call, Doctor Macklin, perhaps scarcely warranted by an acquaintance so slight as mine with you. I should not under ordinary circumstances have ventured to disturb you; but my visit is neither an idle nor impertinent intrusion. I am sure you will not so account it, when I tell you how afflicted I am."

Doctor Macklin interrupted him with assurances such as good breeding suggested, and Barton resumed—

"I am come to task your patience by asking your advice. When I say your patience, I might, indeed, say more; I might have said your humanity—your compassion; for I have been and am a great sufferer."

"My dear sir," replied the churchman, "it will, indeed, afford me infinite gratification if I can give you comfort in any distress of mind! but—you know—"

"I know what you would say," resumed Barton, quickly; "I am an unbeliever, and, therefore, incapable of deriving help from religion; but don't take that for granted. At least you must not assume that, however unsettled my convictions may be, I do not feel a deep—a very deep— interest in the subject. Circumstances have lately forced it upon my attention, in such a way as to compel me to review the whole question in a more candid and teachable spirit, I believe, than I ever studied it in before."

"Your difficulties, I take it for granted, refer to the evidences of revelation," suggested the clergyman.

"Why—no—not altogether; in fact, I am ashamed to say I have not considered even my objections sufficiently to state them connectedly; but—but there is one subject on which I feel a peculiar interest."

He paused again and Doctor Macklin pressed him to proceed.

"The fact is," said Barton, "whatever may be my uncertainty as to the authenticity of what we are taught to call revelation, of one fact I am deeply and horribly convinced, that there does exist beyond this a spiritual world—a system whose workings are generally in mercy hidden from us—a system which may be, and which is sometimes, partially and terribly revealed. I am sure—I *know*," continued Barton, with increasing excitement, "that there is a God—a dreadful God—and that retribution follows guilt, in ways the most mysterious and stupendous—by agencies the most inexplicable and terrific;—there is a spiritual system—great God, how I have been convinced!—a system malignant, and implacable, and omnipotent, under whose persecutions I am, and have been, suffering the torments of the damned!—yes, sir—yes—the fires and frenzy of hell!"

As Barton spoke, his agitation became so vehement that the Divine was shocked, and even alarmed. The wild and excited rapidity with which he spoke, and, above all, the indefinable horror that stamped his features, afforded a contrast to his ordinary cool and unimpassioned self-possession striking and painful in the last degree.

CHAPTER V

Mr. Barton States His Case

"My dear sir," said Doctor Macklin, after a brief pause, "I fear you have been very unhappy, indeed; but I venture to predict that the depression under which you labour will be found to originate in purely physical causes, and that with a change of air, and the aid of a few tonics, your spirits will return, and the tone of your mind be once more cheerful and tranquil as heretofore. There was, after all, more truth than we are quite willing to admit in the classic theories which assigned the undue predominance of any one affection of the mind, to the undue action or torpidity of one or other of our bodily organs. Believe me, that a little attention to diet, exercise, and the other essentials of health, under competent direction, will make you as much yourself as you can wish."

"Doctor Macklin," said Barton, with something like a shudder, "I *cannot* delude myself with such a hope. I have no hope to cling to but one, and that is, that by some other spiritual agency more potent than that which tortures me, *it* may be combated, and I delivered. If this may not be, I am lost—now and for ever lost."

"But, Mr. Barton, you must remember," urged his companion, "that others have suffered as you have done, and—"

"No, no, no," interrupted he, with irritability—"no, sir, I am not a credulous—far from a superstitious man. I have been, perhaps, too much the reverse—too sceptical, too slow of belief; but unless I were one whom no amount of evidence could convince, unless I were to contemn the repeated, the *perpetual* evidence of my own senses, I am now—now at last constrained to believe—I have no escape from the conviction—the overwhelming certainty —that I am haunted and dogged, go where I may, by—by a DEMON!"

There was a preternatural energy of horror in Barton's face, as, with its damp and death-like lineaments turned towards his companion, he thus delivered himself.

"God help you, my poor friend," said Doctor Macklin, much shocked, "God help you; for, indeed, you *are* a sufferer, however your sufferings may have been caused."

"Ay, ay, God help me," echoed Barton sternly; "but *will* He help me—will He help me?"

"Pray to Him—pray in an humble and trusting spirit," said he.

"Pray, pray," echoed he again; "I can't pray—I could as easily move a mountain by an effort of my will. I have not belief enough to pray; there is something within me that will not pray. You prescribe impossibilities—literal impossibilities."

"You will not find it so, if you will but try," said Doctor Macklin.

"Try! I *have* tried, and the attempt only fills me with confusion: and, sometimes, terror: I have tried in vain, and more than in vain. The awful, unutterable idea of eternity and infinity oppresses and maddens my brain whenever my mind approaches the contemplation of the Creator: I recoil from the effort scared. I tell you, Doctor Macklin, if I am to be saved, it must be by other means. The idea of an eternal Creator is to me intolerable—my mind cannot support it."

"Say, then, my dear sir," urged he, "say how you would have me serve you—what you would learn of me—what I can do or say to relieve you?"

"Listen to me first," replied Captain Barton, with a subdued air, and an effort to suppress his excitement, "listen to me while I detail the circumstances of the persecution under which my life has become all but intolerable—a persecution which has made me fear *death* and the world beyond the grave as much as I have grown to hate existence."

Barton then proceeded to relate the circumstances which I have already detailed, and then continued:

"This has now become habitual—an accustomed thing. I do not mean the actual seeing him in the flesh—thank God, *that* at least is not permitted daily. Thank God, from the ineffable horrors of that visitation I have been mercifully allowed intervals of repose, though none of security; but from the consciousness that a malignant spirit is following and watching me wherever I go, I have never, for a single instant, a temporary respite. I am pursued with blasphemies, cries of despair, and appalling hatred. I hear those dreadful sounds called after me as I turn the corners of the streets; they come in the night-time, while I sit in my chamber alone; they haunt me everywhere, charging me with hideous crimes, and— great God!—threatening mc with coming vengeance and eternal misery. Hush! do you hear *that?*" he cried, with a horrible smile of triumph; "there—there, will that convince you?"

The clergyman felt a chill of horror steal over him, while, during the wail of a sudden gust of wind, he heard, or fancied he heard, the half-articulate sounds of rage and derision mingling in the sough.

"Well, what do you think of *that?*" at length Barton cried, drawing a long breath through his teeth.

"I heard the wind," said Doctor Macklin. "What should I think of it—what is there remarkable about it?"

"The prince of the powers of the air," muttered Barton, with a shudder.

"Tut, tut! my dear sir," said the student, with an effort to reassure himself; for though it was broad daylight, there was nevertheless something disagreeably contagious in the nervous excitement under which his visitor so miserably suffered. "You must not give way to those wild fancies; you must resist these impulses of the imagination."

"Ay, ay; 'resist the devil and he will flee from thee,' " said Barton, in the same tone; "but *how* resist him? ay, there it is—there is the rub. What—*what* am I to do? what *can* I do?"

"My dear sir, this *is* fancy," said the man of folios; "you are your own tormentor."

"No, no, sir—fancy has no part in it," answered Barton, somewhat sternly. "Fancy! was it that made *you*, as well as me, hear, but this moment, those accents of hell? Fancy indeed! No, no."

"But you have seen this person frequently," said the ecclesiastic; "why have you not accosted or secured him? Is it not a little precipitate, to say no more, to assume, as you have done, the existence of preternatural agency; when, after all, everything may be easily accountable, if only proper means were taken to sift the matter."

"There are circumstances connected with this—this *appearance*," said Barton, "which it is needless to disclose, but which to *me* are proofs of its horrible nature. I know that the being that follows me is not human—I say I *know* this; I could prove it to your own conviction." He paused for a minute, and then added, "And as to accosting it, I dare not, I could not; when I see it I am powerless; I stand in the gaze of death, in the triumphant presence of infernal power and malignity. My strength, and faculties, and memory, all forsake me. O God, I fear, sir, you know not what you speak of. Mercy, mercy; heaven have pity on me!"

He leaned his elbow on the table, and passed his hand across his eyes, as if to exclude some image of horror, muttering the last words of the sentence he had just concluded, again and again.

"Doctor Macklin," he said, abruptly raising himself, and looking full upon the clergyman with an imploring eye, "I know you will do for me whatever may be done. You know now fully the circumstances and the nature of my affliction. I tell you I cannot help myself; I cannot hope to escape; I am utterly passive. I conjure you, then, to weigh my case well, and if anything may be done for me by vicarious supplication—by the intercession of the good—or by any aid or influence whatsoever, I implore of you, I adjure you in the name of the Most High, give me the benefit of that influence—deliver me from the body of this death. Strive for me, pity me; I know you will; you cannot refuse this; it is the purpose and object of my visit. Send me away with some hope—however little—some faint hope of ultimate deliverance, and I will nerve myself to endure, from hour to hour, the hideous dream into which my existence has been transformed."

Doctor Macklin assured him that all he could do was to pray earnestly for him, and that so much he would not fail to do. They parted with a hurried and melancholy valediction. Barton hastened to the carriage that awaited him at the door, drew down the blinds, and drove away, while Doctor Macklin returned to his chamber, to ruminate at leisure upon the strange interview which had just interrupted his studies.

CHAPTER VI

Seen Again

It was not to be expected that Captain Barton's changed and eccentric habits should long escape remark and discussion. Various were the theories suggested to account for it. Some attributed the alteration to the pressure of secret pecuniary embarrassments; others to a repugnance to fulfil an engagement into which he was presumed to have too precipitately entered; and others, again, to the supposed incipiency of mental disease, which latter, indeed, was the most plausible, as well as the most generally received, of the hypotheses circulated in the gossip of the day.

From the very commencement of this change, at first so gradual in its advances, Miss Montague had of course been aware of it. The intimacy involved in their peculiar relation, as well as the near interest which it inspired afforded, in her case, a like opportunity and motive for the successful exercise of that keen and penetrating observation peculiar to her sex.

His visits became, at length, so interrupted, and his manner, while they lasted, so abstracted, strange, and agitated, that Lady Rochdale, after hinting her anxiety and her suspicions more than once, at length distinctly stated her anxiety, and pressed for an explanation.

The explanation was given, and although its nature at first relieved the worst solicitudes of the old lady and her niece, yet the circumstances which attended it, and the really dreadful consequences which it obviously indicated, as regarded the spirits, and indeed the reason of the now wretched man, who made the strange declaration, were enough, upon little reflection, to fill their minds with perturbation and alarm.

General Montague, the young lady's father, at length arrived. He had himself slightly known Barton, some ten or twelve years previously, and being aware of his fortune and connexions, was disposed to regard him as an unexceptionable and indeed a most desirable match for his daughter. He laughed at the story of Barton's supernatural visitations, and lost no time in calling upon his intended son-in-law.

"My dear Barton," he continued, gaily, after a little conversation, "my sister tells me that you are a victim to blue devils, in quite a new and original shape."

Barton changed countenance, and sighed profoundly.

"Come, come; I protest this will never do," continued the General; "you are more like a man on his way to the gallows than to the altar. These devils have made quite a saint of you."

Barton made an effort to change the conversation.

"No, no, it won't do," said his visitor laughing; "I am resolved to say what I have to say upon this magnificent mock mystery of yours. You must not be angry, but really it is too bad to see you at your time of life, absolutely frightened into good behavior, like a naughty child by a bugaboo, and as far as I can learn, a very contemptible one. Seriously, I have been a good deal annoyed at what they tell me; but at the same time thoroughly convinced that there is nothing in the matter that may not be cleared up, with a little attention and management, within a week at furthest."

"Ah, General, you do not know—" he began.

"Yes, but I do know quite enough to warrant my confidence," interrupted the soldier, "don't I know that all your annoyance proceeds from the occasional appearance of a certain little man in a cap and greatcoat, with a red vest and a bad face, who follows you about, and pops upon you at corners of lanes, and throws you into ague fits. Now, my dear fellow, I'll make it my business to *catch* this mischievous little mountebank, and either beat him to a jelly with my own hands, or have him whipped through the town, at the cart's tail, before a month passes."

"If *you* knew what *I* knew," said Barton, with gloomy agitation, "you would speak very differently. Don't imagine that I am so weak as to assume, without proof the most overwhelming, the conclusion to which I have been forced—the proofs are here, locked up here." As he spoke he tapped upon his breast, and with an anxious sigh continued to walk up and down the room.

"Well, well, Barton," said his visitor, "I'll wager a rump and a dozen I collar the ghost, and convince even you before many days are over."

He was running on in the same strain when he was suddenly arrested, and not a little shocked, by observing Barton, who had approached the window, stagger slowly back, like one who had received a stunning blow; his arm extended toward the street—his face and his very lips white as ashes—while he muttered, "There —by heaven!—there—there!"

General Montague started mechanically to his feet, and from the window of the drawing-room, saw a figure corresponding, as well as his hurry would permit him to discern, with the description of the person whose appearance so persistently disturbed the repose of his friend.

The figure was just turning from the rails of the area upon which it had been leaning, and, without waiting to see more, the old gentleman snatched his cane and hat, and rushed down the stairs and into the street, in the furious hope of securing the person, and punishing the audacity of the mysterious stranger.

He looked round him, but in vain, for any trace of the person he had himself distinctly seen. He ran breathlessly to the nearest corner, expecting to see from thence the retiring figure, but no such form was visible. Back and forward, from crossing to crossing, he ran, at fault, and it was not until the curious gaze and laughing countenances of the passers-by reminded him of the absurdity of his pursuit, that he checked his hurried pace, lowered his walking cane from the menacing altitude which he had mechanically given it, adjusted his hat, and walked composedly back again, inwardly vexed and flurried. He found Barton pale and trembling in every joint; they both remained silent, though under emotions very different. At last Barton whispered, "You saw it?"

"*It*—him—some one—you mean—to be sure I did," replied Montague, testily. "But where is the good or the harm of seeing him? The fellow runs like a lamplighter. I wanted to *catch* him, but he had stolen away before I could reach the hall door. However, it is no great matter; next time, I dare say, I'll do better; and, egad, if I once come within reach of him, I'll introduce his shoulders to the weight of my cane."

Notwithstanding General Montague's undertakings and exhortations, however, Barton continued to suffer from the self-same unexplained cause; go how, when, or where he would, he was still constantly dogged or confronted by the being who had established over him so horrible an influence.

Nowhere and at no time was he secure against the odious appearance which haunted him with such diabolic perseverance.

His depression, misery, and excitement became more settled and alarming every day, and the mental agonies that ceaselessly prayed upon him, began at last so sensibly to affect his health, that Lady Rochdale and General Montague succeeded, without, indeed, much difficulty, in persuading him to try a short tour on the Continent, in the hope that an entire change of scene would, at all events, have the effect of breaking through the influences of local association, which the more sceptical of his friends assumed to be by no means inoperative in suggesting and perpetuating what they conceived to be a mere form of nervous illusion.

General Montague indeed was persuaded that the figure which haunted his intended son-in-law was by no means the creation of his imagination, but, on the contrary, a substantial form of flesh and blood, animated by a resolution, perhaps with some murderous object in perspective, to watch and follow the unfortunate gentleman.

Even this hypothesis was not a very pleasant one; yet it was plain that if Barton could ever be convinced that there was nothing preternatural in the phenomenon which he had hitherto regarded in that light, the affair would lose all its terrors in his eyes, and wholly cease to exercise upon his health and spirits the baleful influence which it had hitherto done. He therefore reasoned, that if the annoyance were actually escaped by mere locomotion and change of scene, it obviously could not have originated in any supernatural agency.

CHAPTER VII

Flight

Yielding to their persuasions, Barton left Dublin for England, accompanied by General Montague. They posted rapidly to London, and thence to Dover, whence they took the packet with a fair wind for Calais. The General's confidence in the result of the expedition on Barton's spirits had risen day by day, since their departure from the shores of Ireland; for to the inexpressible relief and delight of the latter, he had not since then, so much as even once fancied a repetition of those impressions which had, when at home, drawn him gradually down to the very depths of despair.

This exemption from what he had begun to regard as the inevitable condition of his existence, and the sense of security which began to pervade his mind, were inexpressibly delightful; and in the exultation of what he considered his deliverance, he indulged in a thousand happy anticipations for a future into which so lately he had hardly dared to look; and, in short, both he and his companion secretly congratulated themselves upon the termination of that persecution which had been to its immediate victim a source of such unspeakable agony.

It was a beautiful day, and a crowd of idlers stood upon the jetty to receive the packet, and enjoy the bustle of the new arrivals. Montague walked a few paces in advance of his friend, and as he made his way through the crowd, a little man touched his arm, and said to him, in a broad provincial *patois*—

"Monsieur is walking too fast; he will lose his sick comrade in the throng, for, by my faith, the poor gentleman seems to be fainting."

Montague turned quickly, and observed that Barton did indeed look deadly pale. He hastened to his side.

"My dear fellow, are you ill?" he asked anxiously.

The question was unheeded, and twice repeated, ere Barton stammered—

"I saw him—by——, I saw him!"

"*Him!*—the wretch—who—where now?—where is he?" cried Montague, looking around him.

"I saw him—but he is gone," repeated Barton, faintly.

"But where—where? For God's sake speak," urged Montague, vehemently.

"It is but this moment—*here*," said he.

"But what did he look like—what had he on—what did he wear —quick, quick," urged his excited companion, ready to dart among the crowd and collar the delinquent on the spot.

"He touched your arm—he spoke to you—he pointed to me. God be merciful to me, there is no escape," said Barton, in the low, subdued tones of despair.

Montague had already bustled away in all the flurry of mingled hope and rage; but though the singular *personnel* of the stranger who had accosted him was vividly impressed upon his recollection, he failed to discover among the crowd even the slightest resemblance to him.

After a fruitless search, in which he enlisted the services of several of the bystanders, who aided all the more zealously, as they believed he had been robbed, he at length, out of breath and baffled, gave over the attempt.

"Ah, my friend, it won't do," said Barton, with the faint voice and bewildered, ghastly look of one who had been stunned by some mortal shock; "there is no use in contending; whatever it is, the dreadful association between me and it is now established—I shall never escape—never!"

"Nonsense, nonsense, my dear Barton; don't talk so," said Montague, with something at once of irritation and dismay; "you must not, I say; we'll jockey the scoundrel yet; never mind, I say—never mind."

It was, however, but labour lost to endeavour henceforward to inspire Barton with one ray of hope; he became desponding.

This intangible, and, as it seemed, utterly inadequate influence was fast destroying his energies of intellect, character, and health. His first object was now to return to Ireland, there, as he believed, and now almost hoped, speedily to die.

To Ireland accordingly he came, and one of the first faces he saw upon the shore, was again that of his implacable and dreaded attendant. Barton seemed at last to have lost not only all enjoyment and every hope in existence, but all independence of will besides. He now submitted himself passively to the management of the friends most nearly interested in his welfare.

With the apathy of entire despair, he implicitly assented to whatever measures they suggested and advised; and as a last resource, it was determined to remove him to a house of Lady Rochdale's, in the neighbourhood of Clontarf, where, with the advice of his medical attendant, who persisted in his opinion that the whole train of consequences resulted merely from some nervous derangement, it was resolved that he was to confine himself strictly to the house, and make use only of those apartments which commanded a view of an enclosed yard, the gates of which were to be kept jealously locked.

Those precautions would certainly secure him against the casual appearance of any living form, that his excited imagination might possibly confound with the spectre which, as it was contended, his fancy recognized in every figure that bore even a distant or general resemblance to the peculiarities with which his fancy had at first invested it.

A month or six weeks' absolute seclusion under these conditions, it was hoped mignt, by interrupting the series of these terrible im pressions, gradually dispel the predisposing apprehensions, and the associations which had confirmed the supposed disease, and rendered recovery hopeless.

Cheerful society and that of his friends was to be constantly supplied, and on the whole, very sanguine expectations were indulged in, that under the treatment thus detailed, the obstinate hypochondria of the patient might at length give way.

Accompanied, therefore, by Lady Rochdale, General Montague and his daughter—his own affianced bride—Poor Barton—himself never daring to cherish a hope of his ultimate emancipation from the horrors under which his life was literally wasting away—took possession of the apartments, whose situation protected him against the intrusions, from which he shrank with such unutterable terror.

After a little time, a steady persistence in this system began to manifest its results, in a very marked though gradual improvement, alike in the health and spirits of the invalid. Not, indeed that anything at all approaching complete recovery was yet discernible. On the contrary, to those who had not seen him since the commencement of his strange sufferings, such an alteration would have been apparent as might well have shocked them.

The improvement, however, such as it was, was welcomed with gratitude and delight, especially by the young lady, whom her attachment to him, as well as her now singularly painful position, consequent on his protracted illness, rendered an object scarcely one degree less to be commiserated than himself.

A week passed—a fortnight—a month—and yet there had been no recurrence of the hated visitation. The treatment had, so far forth, been followed by complete success. The chain of associations was broken. The constant pressure upon the overtasked spirits had been removed, and, under these comparatively favourable circumstances, the sense of social community with the world about him, and something of human interest, if not of enjoyment, began to reanimate him.

It was about this time that Lady Rochdale who, like most old ladies of the day, was deep in family receipts, and a great pretender to medical science, dispatched her own maid to the kitchen garden, with a list of herbs, which were there to be carefully culled, and brought back to her housekeeper for the purpose stated. The handmaiden, however, returned with her task scarce half completed, and a good deal flurried and alarmed. Her mode of accounting for her precipitate retreat and evident agitation was odd, and, to the old lady, startling.

CHAPTER VIII

Softened

It appeared that she had repaired to the kitchen garden, pursuant to her mistress's directions, and had there begun to make the specified election among the rank and neglected herbs which crowded one corner of the enclosure, and while engaged in this pleasant labour, she carelessly sang a fragment of an old song, as she said, "to keep herself company." She was, however, interrupted by a sort of mocking echo of the air she was singing; and, looking up, she saw through the old thorn hedge, which surrounded the garden, a singularly ill-looking little man, whose countenance wore the stamp of menace and malignity, standing close to her, at the other side of the hawthorn screen.

She described herself as utterly unable to move or speak, while he charged her with a message for Captain Barton; the substance of which she distinctly remembered to have been to the effect, that he, Captain Barton, must come abroad as usual, and show himself to his friends, out of doors, or else prepare for a visit in his own chamber.

On concluding this brief message, the stranger had, with a threatening air, got down into the outer ditch, and, seizing the hawthorn stems in his hands, seemed on the point of climbing through the fence— a feat which might have been accomplished without much difficulty.

Without, of course, awaiting this result, the girl—throwing down her treasures of thyme and rosemary—had turned and run, with the swiftness of terror, to the house. Lady Rochdale commanded her, on pain of instant dismissal, to observe an absolute silence respecting all that passed of the incident which related to Captain Barton; and, at the same time, directed instant search to be made by her men, in the garden and the fields adjacent. This measure, however, was as usual, unsuccessful, and, filled with undefinable misgivings, Lady Rochdale communicated the incident to her brother. The story, however, until long afterwards, went no further, and, of course, it was jealously guarded from Barton, who continued to mend though slowly.

Barton now began to walk occasionally in the court-yard which I have mentioned, and which being enclosed by a high wall, commanded no view beyond its own extent. Here he, therefore, considered himself perfectly secure: and, but for a careless violation of orders by one of the grooms, he might have enjoyed, at least for some time longer, his much-prized immunity. Opening upon the public road, this yard was entered by a wooden gate, with a wicket in it, and was further defended by an iron gate upon the outside. Strict orders had been given to keep both carefully locked; but, spite of these, it had happened that one day, as Barton was slowly pacing this narrow enclosure, in his accustomed walk, and reaching the farther extremity, was turning to retrace his steps, he saw the boarded wicket ajar, and the face of his tormentor immovably looking at him through the iron bars. For a few seconds he stood riveted to the earth—breathless and bloodless—in the fascination of that dreaded gaze, and then fell helplessly insensible upon the pavement.

There he was found a few minutes afterwards, and conveyed to his room—the apartment which he was never afterwards to leave alive. Henceforward a marked and unaccountable change was observable in the tone of his mind. Captain Barton was now no longer the excited and despairing man he had been before; a strange alteration had passed upon him—an unearthly tranquillity reigned in his mind—it was the anticipated stillness of the grave.

"Montague, my friend, this struggle is nearly ended now," he said, tranquilly, but with a look of fixed and fearful awe. "I have, at last, some comfort from that world of spirits, from which my punishment has come. I now know that my sufferings will soon be over."

Montague pressed him to speak on.

"Yes," said he, in a softened voice, "my punishment is nearly ended. From sorrow, perhaps, I shall never, in time or eternity, escape; but my *agony* is almost over. Comfort has been revealed to me, and what remains of my allotted struggle I will bear with submission—even with hope."

"I am glad to hear you speak so tranquilly, my dear Barton," said Montague; "peace and cheer of mind are all you need to make you what you were."

"No, no—I never can be that," said he mournfully. "I am no longer fit for life. I am soon to die. I am to see *him* but once again, and then all is ended."

"He said so, then?" suggested Montague.

"*He?*—No, no: good tidings could scarcely come through him; and these were good and welcome; and they came so solemnly and sweetly—with unutterable love and melancholy, such as I could not—without saying more than is needful, or fitting, of other long past scenes and persons—fully explain to you." As Barton said this he shed tears.

"Come, come," said Montague, mistaking the source of his emotions, "you must not give way. What is it, after all, but a pack of dreams and nonsense; or, at worst, the practices of a scheming rascal that enjoys his power of playing upon your nerves, and loves to exert it—a sneaking vagabond that owes you a grudge, and pays it off this way, not daring to try a more manly one."

"A grudge, indeed, he owes me—you say rightly," said Barton, with a sudden shudder; "a grudge as you call it. Oh, my God! when the justice of Heaven permits the Evil one to carry out a scheme of vengeance—when its execution is committed to the lost and terrible victim of sin, who owes his own ruin to the man, the very man, whom he is commissioned to pursue—then, indeed, the torments and terrors of hell are anticipated on earth. But heaven has dealt mercifully with me—hope has opened to me at last; and if death could come without the dreadful sight I am doomed to see, I would gladly close my eyes this moment upon the world. But though death is welcome, I shrink with an agony you cannot understand—an actual frenzy of terror—from the last encounter with that—that DEMON, who has drawn me thus to the verge of the chasm, and who is himself to plunge me down. I am to see him again—once more—but under circumstances unutterably more terrific than ever."

As Barton thus spoke, he trembled so violently that Montague was really alarmed at the extremity of his sudden agitation, and hastened to lead him back to the topic which had before seemed to exert so tranquillizing an effect upon his mind.

"It was not a dream," he said, after a time; "I was in a different state—I felt differently and strangely; and yet it was all as real, as clear, and vivid, as what I now see and hear—it was a reality."

"And what *did* you see and hear?" urged his companion.

"When I wakened from the swoon I fell into on seeing *him*," said Barton, continuing as if he had not heard the question, "it was slowly, very slowly—I was lying by the margin of a broad lake, with misty hills all round, and a soft, melancholy, rose-coloured light illuminated it all. It was unusually sad and lonely, and yet more beautiful than any earthly scene. My head was leaning on the lap of a girl, and she was singing a song, that told, I know not how—whether by words or harmonies—of all my life—all that is past, and all that is still to come; and with the song the old feelings that I thought had perished within me came back, and tears flowed from my eyes—partly for the song and its mysterious beauty, and partly for the unearthly sweetness of her voice; and yet I knew the voice—oh! how well; and I was spellbound as I listened and looked at the solitary scene, without stirring, almost without breathing—and, alas! alas! without turning my eyes towards the face that I knew was near me, so sweetly powerful was the enchantment that held me. And so, slowly, the song and scene grew fainter, and fainter, to my senses, till all was dark and still again. And then I awoke to this world, as you saw, comforted, for I knew that I was forgiven much." Barton wept again long and bitterly.

From this time, as we have said, the prevailing tone of his mind was one of profound and tranquil melancholy. This, however, was not without its interruptions. He was thoroughly impressed with the conviction that he was to experience another and a final visitation, transcending in horror all he had before experienced. From this anticipated and unknown agony, he often shrank in such paroxysms of abject terror and distraction, as filled the whole household with dismay and superstitious panic. Even those among them who affected to discredit the theory of preternatural agency, were often in their secret souls visited during the silence of night with qualms and apprehensions, which they would not have readily confessed; and none of them attempted to dissuade Barton from the resolution on which he now systematically acted, of shutting himself up in his own apartment. The window-blinds of this room were kept jealously down; and his own man was seldom out of his presence, day or night, his bed being placed in the same chamber.

This man was an attached and respectable servant; and his duties, in addition to those ordinarily imposed upon valets, but which Barton's independent habits generally dispensed with, were to attend carefully to the simple precautions by means of which his master hoped to exclude the dreaded intrusion of the "Watcher." And, in addition to attending to those arrangements, which amounted merely to guarding against the possibility of his master's being, through any unscreened window or open door, exposed to the dreaded influence, the valet was never to suffer him to be alone —total solitude, even for a minute, had become to him now almost as intolerable as the idea of going abroad into the public ways— it was an instinctive anticipation of what was coming.

CHAPTER IX

Requiescat

It is needless to say, that under these circumstances, no steps were taken toward the fulfilment of that engagement into which he had entered. There was quite disparity enough in point of years, and indeed of habits, between the young lady and Captain Barton, to have precluded anything like very vehement or romantic attachment on her part. Though grieved and anxious, therefore, she was very far from being heart-broken.

Miss Montague, however, devoted much of her time to the patient but fruitless attempt to cheer the unhappy invalid. She read for him and conversed with him; but it was apparent that whatever exertions he made, the endeavour to escape from the one ever waking fear that preyed upon him, was utterly and miserably unavailing.

Young ladies are much given to the cultivation of pets; and among those who shared the favour of Miss Montague was a fine old owl, which the gardener, who caught him napping among the ivy of a ruined stable, had dutifully presented to that young lady.

The caprice which regulates such preferences was manifested in the extravagant favour with which this grim and ill-favoured bird was at once distinguished by his mistress; and, trifling as this whimsical circumstance may seem, I am forced to mention it, inasmuch as it is connected, oddly enough, with the concluding scene of the story.

Barton, so far from sharing in this liking for the new favourite, regarded it from the first with an antipathy as violent as it was utterly unaccountable. Its very vicinity was unsupportable to him. He seemed to hate and dread it with a vehemence absolutely laughable, and which, to those who have never witnessed the exhibition of antipathies of this kind, would seem all but incredible.

With these few words of preliminary explanation, I shall proceed to state the particulars of the last scene in this strange series of incidents. It was almost two o'clock one winter's night, and Barton was, as usual at that hour, in his bed; the servant we have mentioned occupied a smaller bed in the same room, and a light was burning. The man was on a sudden aroused by his master, who said—

"I can't get it out of my head that that accursed bird has got out somehow, and is lurking in some corner of the room. I have been dreaming about him. Get up, Smith, and look about; search for him. Such hateful dreams!"

The servant rose, and examined the chamber, and while engaged in so doing, he heard the well-known sound, more like a long-drawn gasp than a hiss, with which these birds from their secret haunts affright the quiet of the night.

This ghostly indication of its proximity—for the sound proceeded from the passage upon which Barton's chamber-door opened—determined the search of the servant, who, opening the door, proceeded a step or two forward for the purpose of driving the bird away. He had, however, hardly entered the lobby, when the door behind him slowly swung to under the impulse, as it seemed, of some gentle current of air; but as immediately over the door there was a kind of window, intended in the day time to aid in lighting the passage, and through which at present the rays of the candle were issuing, the valet could see quite enough for his purpose.

As he advanced he heard his master—who, lying in a well-curtained bed, had not, as it seemed, perceived his exit from the room—call him by name, and direct him to place the candle on the table by his bed. The servant, who was now some way in the long passage, and not liking to raise his voice for the purpose of replying, lest he should startle the sleeping inmates of the house, began to walk hurriedly and softly back again, when, to his amazement, he heard a voice in the interior of the chamber answering calmly, and actually saw, through the window which overtopped the door, that the light was slowly shifting, as if carried across the room in answer to his master's call. Palsied by a feeling akin to terror, yet not unmingled with curiosity, he stood breathless and listening at the threshold, unable to summon resolution to push open the door and enter. Then came a rustling of the curtains, and a sound like that of one who in a low voice hushes a child to rest, in the midst of which he heard Barton say, in a tone of stifled horror—"Oh, God—oh, my God!" and repeat the same exclamation several times. Then ensued a silence, which again was broken by the same strange soothing sound; and at last there burst forth, in one swelling peal, a yell of agony so appalling and hideous, that, under some impulse of ungovernable horror, the man rushed to the door, and with his whole strength strove to force it open. Whether it was that, in his agitation, he had himself but imperfectly turned the handle, or that the door was really secured upon the inside, he failed to effect an entrance; and as he tugged and pushed, yell after yell rang louder and wilder through the chamber, accompanied all the while by the same hushed sounds. Actually freezing with terror, and scarce knowing what he did, the man turned and ran down the passage, wringing his hands in the extremity of horror and irresolution. At the stair-head he was encountered by General Montague, scared and eager, and just as they met the fearful sounds had ceased.

"What is it? Who—where is your master?" said Montague, with the incoherence of extreme agitation. "Has anything—for God's sake is anything wrong?"

"Lord have mercy on us, it's all over," said the man, staring wildly towards his master's chamber. "He's dead, sir, I'm sure he's dead."

Without waiting for inquiry or explanation, Montague, closely followed by the servant, hurried to the chamber door, turned the handle, and pushed it open. As the door yielded to his pressure, the ill-omened bird of which the servant had been in search, uttering its spectral warning, started suddenly from the far side of the bed, and flying through the doorway close over their heads, and extinguishing, in his passage, the candle which Montague carried, crashed through the skylight that overlooked the lobby, and sailed away into the darkness of the outer space.

"There it is, God bless us," whispered the man after a breathless pause.

"Curse that bird," muttered the General, startled by the suddenness of the apparition, and unable to conceal his discomposure.

"The candle is moved," said the man, after another breathless pause, pointing to the candle that still burned in the room; "see, they put it by the bed."

"Draw the curtains, fellow, and don't stand gaping there," whispered Montague, sternly.

The man hesitated.

"Hold this, then," said Montague, impatiently thrusting the candlestick into the servant's hand, and himself advancing to the bed-side, he drew the curtains apart. The light of the candle, which was still burning at the bedside, fell upon a figure huddled together, and half upright, at the head of the bed. It seemed as though it had slunk back as far as the solid panelling would allow, and the hands were still clutched in the bed-clothes.

"Barton, Barton, *Barton!*" cried the General, with a strange mixture of awe and vehemence. He took the candle, and held it so that it shone full upon the face. The features were fixed, stern, and white; the jaw was fallen; and the sightless eyes still open, gazed vacantly forward toward the front of the bed. "God Almighty! he's dead," muttered the General, as he looked upon this fearful spectacle. They both continued to gaze upon it in silence for a minute or more. "And cold, too," whispered Montague, withdrawing his hand from that of the dead man.

"And see, see—may I never have life, sir," added the man, after another pause, with a shudder, "but there was something else on the bed with him. Look there—look there—see that, sir."

As the man thus spoke he pointed to a deep indenture as if caused by a heavy pressure, near the foot of the bed.

Montague was silent.

"Come, sir, come away, for God's sake," whispered the man, drawing close up to him, and holding fast by his arm, while he glanced fearfully round; "what good can be done here now—come away, for God's sake!"

At this moment they heard the steps of more than one approaching, and Montague, hastily desiring the servant to arrest their progress, endeavoured to loose the rigid gripe with which the fingers of the dead man were clutched in the bed-clothes, and drew, as well as he was able, the awful figure into a reclining posture; then closing the curtains carefully upon it, he hastened himself to meet those persons that were approaching.

* * * * *

It is needless to follow the personages so slightly connected with this narrative, into the events of their after life; it is enough to say, that no clue to the solution of these mysterious occurrences was ever after discovered; and so long an interval having now passed since the event which I have just described concluded this strange history, it is scarcely to be expected that time can throw any new lights upon its dark and inexplicable outline. Until the secrets of the earth shall be no longer hidden, therefore, these transactions must remain shrouded in their original obscurity.

The only occurrence in Captain Barton's former life to which reference was ever made, as having any possible connection with the sufferings with which his existence closed, and which he himself seemed to regard as working out a retribution for some grievous sin of his past life, was a circumstance which not for several years after his death was brought to light. The nature of this disclosure was painful to his relatives, and discreditable to his memory.

It appeared that some six years before Captain Barton's final return to Dublin, he had formed, in the town of Plymouth, a guilty attachment, the object of which was the daughter of one of the ship's crew under his command. The father had visited the frailty of his unhappy child with extreme harshness, and even brutality, and it was said that she had died heart-broken. Presuming upon Barton's implication in her guilt, this man had conducted himself toward him with marked insolence, and Barton retaliated this, and what he resented with still more exasperated bitterness—his treatment of the unfortunate girl—by a systematic exercise of those terrible and arbitrary severities which the regulations of the navy placed at the command of those who are responsible for its discipline. The man had at length made his escape, while the vessel was in port at Naples, but died as it was said, in an hospital in that town, of the wounds inflicted in one of his recent and sanguinary punishments.

Whether these circumstances in reality bear, or not, upon the occurrences of Barton's after-life, it is, of course, impossible to say. It seems, however, more than probable that they were at least, in his own mind, closely associated with them. But however the truth may be, as to the origin and motives of this mysterious persecution, there can be no doubt that, with respect to the agencies by which it was accomplished, absolute and impenetrable mystery is like to prevail until the day of doom.

POSTSCRIPT BY THE EDITOR

The preceding narrative is given in the *ipsissima verba* of the good old clergyman, under whose hand it was delivered to Doctor Hesselius. Notwithstanding the occasional stiffness and redundancy of his sentences, I thought it better to reserve to myself the power of assuring the reader, that in handing to the printer the MS. of a statement so marvellous, the Editor has not altered one letter of the original text.—[*Ed. Papers of Dr. Hesselius.*]

Mr. Justice Harbottle

PROLOGUE

On this case Doctor Hesselius has inscribed nothing more than the words, "Harman's Report," and a simple reference to his own extraordinary Essay on "The Interior Sense, and the Conditions of the Opening thereof."

The reference is to Vol. I., Section 317, Note Zᵃ. The note to which reference is thus made, simply says: "There are two accounts of the remarkable case of the Honourable Mr. Justice Harbottle, one furnished to me by Mrs. Trimmer, of Tunbridge Wells (June, 1805) ; the other at a much later date, by Anthony Harman, Esq. I much prefer the former; in the first place, because it is minute and detailed, and written, it seems to me, with more caution and knowledge; and in the next, because the letters from Dr. Hedstone, which are embodied in it, furnish matter of the highest value to a right apprehension of the nature of the case. It was one of the best declared cases of an opening of the interior sense, which I have met with. It was affected too, by the phenomenon, which occurs so frequently as to indicate a law of these eccentric conditions; that is to say, it exhibited what I may term, the contagious character of this sort of intrusion of the spirit-world upon the proper domain of matter. So soon as the spirit-action has established itself in the case of one patient, its developed energy begins to radiate, more or less effectually, upon others. The interior vision of the child was opened; as was, also, that of its mother, Mrs. Pyneweck; and both the interior vision and hearing of the scullery-maid, were opened on the same occasion. After-appearances are the result of the law explained in Vol. II., Section 17 to 49. The common centre of association, simultaneously recalled, unites, or *reunites*, as the case may be, for a period measured, as we see, in Section 37. The *maximum* will extend to days, the *minimum* is little more than a

244

second. We see the operation of this principle perfectly displayed, in certain cases of lunacy, of epilepsy, of catalepsy, and of mania, of a peculiar and painful character, though unattended by incapacity of business."

The memorandum of the case of Judge Harbottle, which was written by Mrs. Trimmer, of Tunbridge Wells, which Doctor Hesselius thought the better of the two, I have been unable to discover among his papers. I found in his escritoire a note to the effect that he had lent the Report of Judge Harbottle's case, written by Mrs. Trimmer, to Dr. F. Heyne. To that learned and able gentleman accordingly I wrote, and received from him, in his reply, which was full of alarms and regrets, on account of the uncertain safety of that "valuable MS.," a line written long since by Dr. Hesselius, which completely exonerated him, inasmuch as it acknowledged the safe return of the papers. The narrative of Mr. Harman, is therefore, the only one available for this collection. The late Dr. Hesselius, in another passage of the note that I have cited, says, "As to the facts (non-medical) of the case, the narrative of Mr. Harman exactly tallies with that furnished by Mrs. Trimmer." The strictly scientific view of the case would scarcely interest the popular reader; and, possibly, for the purposes of this selection, I should, even had I both papers to choose between, have preferred that of Mr. Harman, which is given, in full, in the following pages.

CHAPTER I

The Judge's House

Thirty years ago, an elderly man, to whom I paid quarterly a small annuity charged on some property of mine, came on the quarter-day to receive it. He was a dry, sad, quiet man, who had known better days, and had always maintained an unexceptionable character. No better authority could be imagined for a ghost story.

He told me one, though with a manifest reluctance; he was drawn into the narration by his choosing to explain what I should not have remarked, that he had called two days earlier than that week after the strict day of payment, which he had usually allowed to elapse. His reason was a sudden determination to change his lodgings, and the consequent necessity of paying his rent a little before it was due.

He lodged in a dark street in Westminster, in a spacious old house, very warm, being wainscoted from top to bottom, and furnished with no undue abundance of windows, and those fitted with thick sashes and small panes.

This house was, as the bills upon the windows testified, offered to be sold or let. But no one seemed to care to look at it.

A thin matron, in rusty black silk, very taciturn, with large, steady, alarmed eyes, that seemed to look in your face, to read what you might have seen in the dark rooms and passages through which you had passed, was in charge of it, with a solitary "maid-of-all-work" under her command. My poor friend had taken lodgings in this house, on account of their extraordinary cheapness. He had occupied them for nearly a year without the slightest disturbance, and was the only tenant, under rent, in the house. He had two rooms; a sitting-room and a bed-room with a closet opening from it, in which he kept his books and papers locked up. He had gone to his bed, having also locked the outer door. Unable to sleep, he had lighted a candle, and after having read for a time, had laid the book beside him. He heard the old clock at the stair-head strike one; and very shortly after, to his alarm, he saw the closet-door, which he thought he had locked, open stealthily, and a slight dark man, particularly sinister, and somewhere about fifty, dressed in mourning of a very antique fashion, such a suit as we see in Hogarth, entered the room on tip-toe. He was followed by an elder man, stout, and blotched with scurvy, and whose features, fixed as a corpse's, were stamped with dreadful force with a character of sensuality and villany.

This old man wore a flowered silk dressing-gown and ruffles, and he remarked a gold ring on his finger, and on his head a cap of velvet, such as, in the days of perukes, gentlemen wore in undress.

This direful old man carried in his ringed and ruffled hand a coil of rope; and these two figures crossed the floor diagonally, passing the foot of his bed, from the closet door at the farther end of the room, at the left, near the window, to the door opening upon the lobby, close to the bed's head, at his right.

He did not attempt to describe his sensations as these figures passed so near him. He merely said, that so far from sleeping in that room again, no consideration the world could offer would induce him so much as to enter it again alone, even in the daylight. He found both doors, that of the closet, and that of the room opening upon the lobby, in the morning fast locked as he had left them before going to bed.

In answer to a question of mine, he said that neither appeared

These two figures crossed the floor diagonally, passing the foot of the bed.

the least conscious of his presence. They did not seem to glide, but walked as living men do, but without any sound, and he felt a vibration on the floor as they crossed it. He so obviously suffered from speaking about the apparitions, that I asked him no more questions.

There were in his description, however, certain coincidences so very singular, as to induce me, by that very post, to write to a friend much my senior, then living in a remote part of England, for the information which I knew he could give me. He had himself more than once pointed out that old house to my attention, and told me, though very briefly, the strange story which I now asked him to give me in greater detail.

His answer satisfied me; and the following pages convey its substance.

Your letter (he wrote) tells me you desire some particulars about the closing years of the life of Mr. Justice Harbottle, one of the judges of the Court of Common Pleas. You refer, of course, to the extraordinary occurrences that made that period of his life long after a theme for "winter tales" and metaphysical speculation. I happen to know perhaps more than any other man living of those mysterious particulars.

The old family mansion, when I revisited London, more than thirty years ago, I examined for the last time. During the years that have passed since then, I hear that improvement, with its preliminary demolitions, has been doing wonders for the quarter of Westminster in which it stood. If I were quite certain that the house had been taken down, I should have no difficulty about naming the street in which it stood. As what I have to tell, however, is not likely to improve its letting value, and as I should not care to get into trouble, I prefer being silent on that particular point.

How old the house was, I can't tell. People said it was built by Roger Harbottle, a Turkey merchant, in the reign of King James I. I am not a good opinion upon such questions; but having been in it, though in its forlorn and deserted state, I can tell you in a general way what it was like. It was built of dark-red brick, and the door and windows were faced with stone that had turned yellow by time. It receded some feet from the line of the other houses in the street; and it had a florid and fanciful rail of iron about the broad steps that invited your ascent to the hall-door, in which were fixed, under a file of lamps among scrolls and twisted leaves, two immense "extinguishers," like the conical caps of fairies, into which, in old times, the footmen used to thrust their flambeaux when their chairs or coaches had set down their great people, in the hall or at the steps, as the case might be. That hall is panelled up to the ceiling, and has a large fire-place. Two or three stately old rooms open from it at each side. The windows of these are tall, with many small panes. Passing through the arch at the back of the hall, you come upon the wide and heavy well-stair-case. There is a back staircase also. The mansion is large, and has not as much light, by any means, in proportion to its extent, as modern houses enjoy. When I saw it, it had long been untenanted, and had the gloomy reputation beside of a haunted house. Cob-webs floated from the ceilings or spanned the corners of the cornices, and dust lay thick over everything. The windows were stained with the dust and rain of fifty years, and darkness had thus grown darker.

When I made it my first visit, it was in company with my father, when I was still a boy, in the year 1808. I was about twelve years old, and my imagination impressible, as it always is at that age. I looked about me with great awe. I was here in the very centre and scene of those occurrences which I had heard recounted at the fire-side at home, with so delightful a horror.

My father was an old bachelor of nearly sixty when he married. He had, when a child, seen Judge Harbottle on the bench in his robes and wig a dozen times at least before his death, which took place in 1748, and his appearance made a powerful and unpleasant impression, not only on his imagination, but upon his nerves.

The Judge was at that time a man of some sixty-seven years. He had a great mulberry-coloured face, a big, carbuncled nose, fierce eyes, and a grim and brutal mouth. My father, who was young at the time, thought it the most formidable face he had ever seen; for there were evidences of intellectual power in the formation and lines of the forehead. His voice was loud and harsh, and gave effect to the sarcasm which was his habitual weapon on the bench.

This old gentleman had the reputation of being about the wickedest man in England. Even on the bench he now and then showed his scorn of opinion. He had carried cases his own way, it was said, in spite of counsel, authorities, and even of juries, by a sort of cajolery, violence, and bamboozling, that somehow con-fused and overpowered resistance. He had never actually com-mitted himself; he was too cunning to do that. He had the charac-ter of being, however, a dangerous and unscrupulous judge; but his character did not trouble him. The associates he chose for his hours of relaxation cared as little as he did about it.

CHAPTER II

Mr. Peters

One night during the session of 1746 this old Judge went down in his chair to wait in one of the rooms of the House of Lords for the result of a division in which he and his order were interested.

This over, he was about to return to his house close by, in his chair; but the night had become so soft and fine that he changed his mind, sent it home empty, and with two footmen, each with a flambeau, set out on foot in preference. Gout had made him rather a slow pedestrian. It took him some time to get through the two or three streets he had to pass before reaching his house.

In one of those narrow streets of tall houses, perfectly silent at that hour, he overtook, slowly as he was walking, a very singular-looking old gentleman.

He had a bottle-green coat on, with a cape to it, and large stone buttons, a broad-leafed low-crowned hat, from under which a big powdered wig escaped; he stooped very much, and supported his bending knees with the aid of a crutch-handled cane, and so shuffled and tottered along painfully.

"I ask your pardon, sir," said this old man, in a very quavering voice, as the burly Judge came up with him, and he extended his hand feebly towards his arm.

Mr. Justice Harbottle saw that the man was by no means poorly dressed, and his manner that of a gentleman.

The Judge stopped short, and said, in his harsh peremptory tones, "Well, sir, how can I serve you?"

"Can you direct me to Judge Harbottle's house? I have some intelligence of the very last importance to communicate to him."

"Can you tell it before witnesses?" asked the Judge.

"By no means; it must reach *his* ear only," quavered the old man earnestly.

"If that be so, sir, you have only to accompany me a few steps farther to reach my house, and obtain a private audience; for I am Judge Harbottle."

With this invitation the infirm gentleman in the white wig complied very readily; and in another minute the stranger stood in what was then termed the front parlour of the Judge's house, *tête-à-tête* with that shrewd and dangerous functionary.

He had to sit down, being very much exhausted, and unable for a little time to speak; and then he had a fit of coughing, and after that a fit of gasping; and thus two or three minutes passed, during which the Judge dropped his roquelaure on an arm-chair, and threw his cocked-hat over that.

The venerable pedestrian in the white wig quickly recovered his voice. With closed doors they remained together for some time.

There were guests waiting in the drawing-rooms, and the sound of men's voices laughing, and then of a female voice singing to a harpsichord, were heard distinctly in the hall over the stairs; for old Judge Harbottle had arranged one of his dubious jollifications, such as might well make the hair of godly men's heads stand upright for that night.

This old gentleman in the powdered white wig, that rested on his stooped shoulders, must have had something to say that interested the Judge very much; for he would not have parted on easy terms with the ten minutes and upwards which that conference filched from the sort of revelry in which he most delighted, and in which he was the roaring king, and in some sort the tyrant also, of his company.

The footman who showed the aged gentleman out observed that the Judge's mulberry-coloured face, pimples and all, were bleached to a dingy yellow, and there was the abstraction of agitated thought in his manner, as he bid the stranger good-night. The servant saw that the conversation had been of serious import, and that the Judge was frightened.

Instead of stumping upstairs forthwith to his scandalous hilarities, his profane company, and his great china bowl of punch—the identical bowl from which a bygone Bishop of London, good easy man, had baptised this Judge's grandfather, now clinking round the rim with silver ladles, and hung with scrolls of lemon-peel— instead, I say, of stumping and clambering up the great staircase to the cavern of his Circean enchantment, he stood with his big nose flattened against the window-pane, watching the progress of the feeble old man, who clung stiffly to the iron rail as he got down, step by step, to the pavement.

The hall-door had hardly closed, when the old Judge was in the hall bawling hasty orders, with such stimulating expletives as old colonels under excitement sometimes indulge in now-a-days, with a stamp or two of his big foot, and a waving of his clenched fist in the air. He commanded the footman to overtake the old gentleman in the white wig, to offer him his protection on his way home, and in no case to show his face again without having ascertained where he lodged, and who he was, and all about him.

"By——, sirrah! if you fail me in this, you doff my livery to-night!"

Forth bounced the stalwart footman, with his heavy cane under

his arm, and skipped down the steps, and looked up and down the
street after the singular figure, so easy to recognize.

What were his adventures I shall not tell you just now.

The old man, in the conference to which he had been admitted
in that stately panelled room, had just told the Judge a very
strange story. He might be himself a conspirator; he might possibly be crazed; or possibly his whole story was straight and true.

The aged gentleman in the bottle-green coat, in finding himself alone with Mr. Justice Harbottle, had become agitated. He
said,

"There is, perhaps you are not aware, my lord, a prisoner in
Shrewsbury jail, charged with having forged a bill of exchange for
a hundred and twenty pounds, and his name is Lewis Pyneweck, a
grocer of that town."

"Is there?" says the Judge, who knew well that there was.

"Yes, my lord," says the old man.

"Then you had better say nothing to affect this case. If you do,
by —, I'll commit you! for I'm to try it," says the judge, with his
terrible look and tone.

"I am not going to do anything of the kind, my lord; of him or
his case I know nothing, and care nothing. But a fact has come to
my knowledge which it behoves you to well consider."

"And what may that fact be?" inquired the Judge; "I'm in haste,
sir, and beg you will use dispatch."

"It has come to my knowledge, my lord, that a secret tribunal is
in process of formation, the object of which is to take cognisance
of the conduct of the judges; and first, of *your* conduct, my lord; it
is a wicked conspiracy."

"Who are of it?" demands the Judge.

"I know not a single name as yet. I know but the fact, my lord;
it is most certainly true."

"I'll have you before the Privy Council, sir," says the Judge.

"That is what I most desire; but not for a day or two, my lord."

"And why so?"

"I have not as yet a single name, as I told your lordship; but I
expect to have a list of the most forward men in it, and some other
papers connected with the plot, in two or three days."

"You said one or two just now."

"About that time, my lord."

"Is this a Jacobite plot?"

"In the main I think it is, my lord."

"Why, then, it is political. I have tried no State prisoners, nor
am like to try any such. How, then, doth it concern me?"

"From what I can gather, my lord, there are those in it who desire private revenges upon certain judges."

"What do they call their cabal?"

"The High Court of Appeal, my lord."

"Who are you, sir? What is your name?"

"Hugh Peters, my lord."

"That should be a Whig name?"

"It is, my lord."

"Where do you lodge, Mr. Peters?"

"In Thames Street, my lord, over against the sign of the "Three
Kings.' "

" 'Three Kings?' Take care one be not too many for you, Mr.
Peters! How come you, an honest Whig, as you say, to be privy to a
Jacobite plot? Answer me that."

"My lord, a person in whom I take an interest has been seduced
to take a part in it; and being frightened at the unexpected wick-
edness of their plans, he is resolved to become an informer for the
Crown."

"He resolves like a wise man, sir. What does he say of the persons? Who are in the plot? Doth he know them?"

"Only two, my lord; but he will be introduced to the club in a
few days, and he will then have a list, and more exact information
of their plans, and above all of their oaths, and their hours and
places of meeting, with which he wishes to be acquainted before
they can have any suspicions of his intentions. And being so informed, to whom, think you, my lord, had he best go then?"

"To the king's attorney-general straight. But you say this concerns me, sir, in particular? How about this prisoner, Lewis Pyneweck? Is he one of them?"

"I can't tell, my lord; but for some reason, it is thought your
lordship will be well advised if you try him not. For if you do, it is
feared 'twill shorten your days."

"So far as I can learn, Mr. Peters, this business smells pretty
strong of blood and treason. The king's attorney-general will know
how to deal with it. When shall I see you again, sir?"

"If you give me leave, my lord, either before your lordship's
court sits, or after it rises, to-morrow. I should like to come and tell
your lordship what has passed."

"Do so, Mr. Peters, at nine o'clock to-morrow morning. And see
you play me no trick, sir, in this matter; if you do, by —, sir, I'll
lay you by the heels!"

"You need fear no trick from me, my lord; had I not wished to serve you, and acquit my own conscience, I never would have come all this way to talk with your lordship."

"I'm willing to believe you, Mr. Peters; I'm willing to believe you, sir."

And upon this they parted.

"He has either painted his face, or he is consumedly sick," thought the old Judge.

The light had shown more effectually upon his features as he turned to leave the room with a low bow, and they looked, he fancied, unnaturally chalky.

"D— him!" said the Judge ungraciously, as he began to scale the stairs: "he has half-spoiled my supper."

But if he had, no one but the Judge himself perceived it, and the evidence was all, as any one might perceive, the other way.

CHAPTER III

Lewis Pyneweck

In the meantime the footman dispatched in pursuit of Mr. Peters speedily overtook that feeble gentleman. The old man stopped when he heard the sound of pursuing steps, but any alarms that may have crossed his mind seemed to disappear on his recognizing the livery. He very gratefully accepted the proffered assistance, and placed his tremulous arm within the servant's for support. They had not gone far, however, when the old man stopped suddenly, saying,

"Dear me! as I live, I have dropped it. You heard it fall. My eyes, I fear, won't serve me, and I'm unable to stoop low enough; but if you will look, you shall have half the find. It is a guinea; I carried it in my glove."

The street was silent and deserted. The footman had hardly descended to what he termed his "hunkers," and begun to search the pavement about the spot which the old man indicated, when Mr. Peters, who seemed very much exhausted, and breathed with difficulty, struck him a violent blow, from above, over the back of the head with a heavy instrument, and then another; and leaving him bleeding and senseless in the gutter, ran like a lamplighter down a lane to the right, and was gone.

When an hour later, the watchman brought the man in livery home, still stupid and covered with blood, Judge Harbottle cursed his servant roundly, swore he was drunk, threatened him with an indictment for taking bribes to betray his master, and cheered him with a perspective of the broad street leading from the Old Bailey to Tyburn, the cart's tail, and the hangman's lash.

Notwithstanding this demonstration, the Judge was pleased. It was a disguised "affidavit man," or footpad, no doubt, who had been employed to frighten him. The trick had fallen through.

A "court of appeal," such as the false Hugh Peters had indicated, with assassination for its sanction, would be an uncomfortable institution for a "hanging judge" like the Honourable Justice Harbottle. That sarcastic and ferocious administrator of the criminal code of England, at that time a rather pharisaical, bloody and heinous system of justice, had reasons of his own for choosing to try that very Lewis Pyneweck, on whose behalf this audacious trick was devised. Try him he would. No man living should take that morsel out of his mouth.

Of Lewis Pyneweck, of course, so far as the outer world could see, he knew nothing. He would try him after his fashion, without fear, favour, or affection.

But did he not remember a certain thin man, dressed in mourning, in whose house, in Shrewsbury, the Judge's lodgings used to be, until a scandal of ill-treating his wife came suddenly to light? A grocer with a demure look, a soft step, and a lean face as dark as mahogany, with a nose sharp and long, standing ever so little awry, and a pair of dark steady brown eyes under thinly-traced black brows—a man whose thin lips wore always a faint unpleasant smile.

Had not that scoundrel an account to settle with the Judge? had he not been troublesome lately? and was not his name Lewis Pyneweck, some time grocer in Shrewsbury, and now prisoner in the jail of that town?

The reader may take it, if he pleases, as a sign that Judge Harbottle was a good Christian, that he suffered nothing ever from remorse. That was undoubtedly true. He had, nevertheless, done this grocer, forger, what you will, some five or six years before, a grievous wrong; but it was not that, but a possible scandal, and possible complications, that troubled the learned Judge now.

Did he not, as a lawyer, know, that to bring a man from his shop to the dock, the chances must be at least ninety-nine out of a hundred that he is guilty?

A weak man like his learned brother Withershins was not a

judge to keep the high-roads safe, and make crime tremble. Old Judge Harbottle was the man to make the evil-disposed quiver, and to refresh the world with showers of wicked blood, and thus save the innocent, to the refrain of the ancient saw he loved to quote:

> Foolish pity
> Ruins a city.

In hanging that fellow he could not be wrong. The eye of a man accustomed to look upon the dock could not fail to read "villain" written sharp and clear in his plotting face. Of course he would try him, and no one else should.

A saucy-looking woman, still handsome, in a mob-cap gay with blue ribbons, in a saque of flowered silk, with lace and rings on, much too fine for the Judge's housekeeper, which nevertheless she was, peeped into his study next morning, and, seeing the Judge alone, stepped in.

"Here's another letter from him, come by the post this morning. Can't you do nothing for him?" she said wheedlingly, with her arm over his neck, and her delicate finger and thumb fiddling with the lobe of his purple ear.

"I'll try," said Judge Harbottle, not raising his eyes from the paper he was reading.

"I knew you'd do what I asked you," she said.

The Judge clapt his gouty claw over his heart, and made her an ironical bow.

"What," she asked, "will you do?"

"Hang him," said the Judge with a chuckle.

"You don't mean to; no, you don't, my little man," said she, surveying herself in a mirror on the wall.

"I'm d—d but I think you're falling in love with your husband at last!" said Judge Harbottle.

"I'm blest but I think you're growing jealous of him," replied the lady with a laugh. "But no; he was always a bad one to me; I've done with him long ago."

"And he with you, by George! When he took your fortune, and your spoons, and your ear-rings, he had all he wanted of you. He drove you from his house; and when he discovered you had made yourself comfortable, and found a good situation, he'd have taken your guineas, and your silver, and your ear-rings over again, and then allowed you half-a-dozen years more to make a new harvest for his mill. You don't wish him good; if you say you do, you lie."

She laughed a wicked, saucy laugh, and gave the terrible Rhadamanthus a playful tap on the chops.

"He wants me to send him money to fee a counsellor," she said, while her eyes wandered over the pictures on the wall, and back again to the looking-glass; and certainly she did not look as if his jeopardy troubled her very much.

"Confound his impudence, the *scoundrel!*" thundered the old Judge, throwing himself back in his chair, as he used to do *in furore* on the bench, and the lines of his mouth looked brutal, and his eyes ready to leap from their sockets. "If you answer his letter from my house to please yourself, you'll write your next from somebody else's to please me. You understand, my pretty witch, I'll not be pestered. Come, no pouting; whimpering won't do. You don't care a brass farthing for the villain, body or soul. You came here but to make a row. You are one of Mother Carey's chickens; and where you come, the storm is up. Get you gone, baggage! get you *gone!*" he repeated, with a stamp; for a knock at the hall-door made her instantaneous disappearance indispensable.

I need hardly say that the venerable Hugh Peters did not appear again. The Judge never mentioned him. But oddly enough, considering how he laughed to scorn the weak invention which he had blown into dust at the very first puff, his white-wigged visitor and the conference in the dark front parlour were often in his memory.

His shrewd eye told him that allowing for change of tints and such disguises as the playhouse affords every night, the features of this false old man, who had turned out too hard for his tall footman, were identical with those of Lewis Pyneweck.

Judge Harbottle made his registrar call upon the crown solicitor, and tell him that there was a man in town who bore a wonderful resemblance to a prisoner in Shrewsbury jail named Lewis Pyneweck, and to make inquiry through the post forthwith whether any one was personating Pyneweck in prison and whether he had thus or otherwise made his escape.

The prisoner was safe, however, and no question as to his identity.

CHAPTER IV

Interruption in Court

In due time Judge Harbottle went circuit; and in due time the judges were in Shrewsbury. News travelled slowly in those days, and newspapers, like the wagons and stage coaches, took matters easily. Mrs. Pyneweck, in the Judge's house, with a diminished household—the greater part of the Judge's servants having gone with him, for he had given up riding circuit, and travelled in his coach in state—kept house rather solitarily at home.

In spite of quarrels, in spite of mutual injuries—some of them, inflicted by herself, enormous—in spite of a married life of spited bickerings—a life in which there seemed no love or liking or forbearance, for years—now that Pyneweck stood in near danger of death, something like remorse came suddenly upon her. She knew that in Shrewsbury were transacting the scenes which were to determine his fate. She knew she did not love him; but she could not have supposed, even a fortnight before, that the hour of suspense could have affected her so powerfully.

She knew the day on which the trial was expected to take place. She could not get it out of her head for a minute; she felt faint as it drew towards evening.

Two or three days passed; and then she knew that the trial must be over by this time. There were floods between London and Shrewsbury, and news was long delayed. She wished the floods would last forever. It was dreadful waiting to hear; dreadful to know that the event was over, and that she could not hear till self-willed rivers subsided; dreadful to know that they must subside and the news come at last.

She had some vague trust in the Judge's good nature, and much in the resources of chance and accident. She had contrived to send the money he wanted. He would not be without legal advice and energetic and skilled support.

At last the news did come—a long arrear all in a gush: a letter from a female friend in Shrewsbury; a return of the sentences, sent up for the Judge; and most important, because most easily got at, being told with great aplomb and brevity, the long-deferred intelligence of the Shrewsbury Assizes in the *Morning Advertiser*. Like an impatient reader of a novel, who reads the last page first, she read with dizzy eyes the list of the executions.

Two were respited, seven were hanged; and in that capital catalogue was this line:

"Lewis Pyneweck—forgery."

She had to read it a half-a-dozen times over before she was sure she understood it. Here was the paragraph:

Sentence, Death—7.
Executed accordingly, on Friday the 13th instant, to wit:
Thomas Primer, *alias* Duck—highway robbery.
Flora Guy—stealing to the value of 11s. 6d.
Arthur Pounden—burglary.

Matilda Mummery—riot.
Lewis Pyneweck—forgery, bill of exchange.

And when she reached this, she read it over and over, feeling very cold and sick.

This buxom housekeeper was known in the house as Mrs. Carwell—Carwell being her maiden name, which she had resumed.

No one in the house except its master knew her history. Her introduction had been managed craftily. No one suspected that it had been concerted between her and the old reprobate in scarlet and ermine.

Flora Carwell ran up the stairs now, and snatched her little girl, hardly seven years of age, whom she met on the lobby, hurriedly up in her arms, and carried her into her bedroom, without well knowing what she was doing, and sat down, placing the child before her. She was not able to speak. She held the child before her, and looked in the little girl's wondering face, and burst into tears of horror.

She thought the Judge could have saved him. I daresay he could. For a time she was furious with him, and hugged and kissed her bewildered little girl, who returned her gaze with large round eyes.

That little girl had lost her father, and knew nothing of the matter. She had always been told that her father was dead long ago.

A woman, coarse, uneducated, vain, and violent, does not reason, or even feel, very distinctly; but in these tears of consternation were mingling a self-upbraiding. She felt afraid of that little child.

But Mrs. Carwell was a person who lived not upon sentiment, but upon beef and pudding; she consoled herself with punch; she did not trouble herself long even with resentments; she was a gross and material person, and could not mourn over the irrevocable for more than a limited number of hours, even if she would.

Judge Harbottle was soon in London again. Except the gout, this savage old epicurean never knew a day's sickness. He laughed, and coaxed, and bullied away the young woman's faint upbraidings, and in a little time Lewis Pyneweck troubled her no more; and the Judge secretly chuckled over the perfectly fair removal of a bore, who might have grown little by little into something very like a tyrant.

It was the lot of the Judge whose adventures I am now recounting to try criminal cases at the Old Bailey shortly after his return. He had commenced his charge to the jury in a case of forgery, and was, after his wont, thundering dead against the prisoner, with many a hard aggravation and cynical gibe, when suddenly all died away in silence, and, instead of looking at the jury, the eloquent

Judge was gaping at some person in the body of the court.

Among the persons of small importance who stand and listen at the sides was one tall enough to show with a little prominence; a slight mean figure, dressed in seedy black, lean and dark of visage. He had just handed a letter to the crier, before he caught the Judge's eye.

That Judge descried, to his amazement, the features of Lewis Pyneweck. He had the usual faint thin-lipped smile; and with his blue chin raised in air, and as it seemed quite unconscious of the distinguished notice he has attracted, he was stretching his low cravat with his crooked fingers, while he slowly turned his head from side to side—a process which enabled the Judge to see distinctly a stripe of swollen blue round his neck, which indicated, he thought, the grip of the rope.

This man, with a few others, had got a footing on a step, from which he could better see the court. He now stepped down, and the Judge lost sight of him.

His lordship signed energetically with his hand in the direction in which this man had vanished. He turned to the tipstaff. His first effort to speak ended in a gasp. He cleared his throat, and told the astounded official to arrest that man who had interrupted the court.

"He's but this moment gone down *there*. Bring him in custody before me, within ten minutes' time, or I'll strip your gown from your shoulders and fine the sheriff!" he thundered, while his eyes flashed round the court in search of the functionary.

Attorneys, counsellors, idle spectators, gazed in the direction in which Mr. Justice Harbottle had shaken his gnarled old hand. They compared notes. Not one had seen any one making a disturbance. They asked one another if the Judge was losing his head.

Nothing came of the search. His lordship concluded his charge a great deal more tamely; and when the jury retired, he stared round the court with a wandering mind, and looked as if he would not have given sixpence to see the prisoner hanged.

CHAPTER V

Caleb Searcher

The Judge had received the letter; had he known from whom it came, he would no doubt have read it instantaneously. As it was he simply read the direction:

> To the Honourable
> The Lord Justice
> Elijah Harbottle,
> One of his Majesty's Justices of
> the Honourable Court of Common Pleas.

It remained forgotten in his pocket till he reached home.

When he pulled out that and others from the capacious pocket of his coat, it had its turn, as he sat in his library in his thick silk dressing-gown; and then he found its contents to be a closely-written letter, in a clerk's hand, and an enclosure in "secretary hand," as I believe the angular scrivinary of law-writings in those days was termed, engrossed on a bit of parchment about the size of this page. The letter said:

> MR. JUSTICE HARBOTTLE,—MY LORD,
> I am ordered by the High Court of Appeal to acquaint your lordship, in order to your better preparing yourself for your trial, that a true bill hath been sent down, and the indictment lieth against your lordship for the murder of one Lewis Pyneweck of Shrewsbury, citizen, wrongfully executed for the forgery of a bill of exchange, on the —th day of —— last, by reason of the wilful perversion of the evidence, and the undue pressure put upon the jury, together with the illegal admission of evidence by your lordship, well knowing the same to be illegal, by all which the promoter of the prosecution of the said indictment, before the High Court of Appeal, hath lost his life.
> And the trial of the said indictment, I am farther ordered to acquaint your lordship, is fixed for the 10th day of —— next ensuing, by the right honourable the Lord Chief Justice Twofold, of the court aforesaid, to wit, the High Court of Appeal, on which day it will most certainly take place. And I am farther to acquaint your lordship, to prevent any surprise or miscarriage, that your case stands first for the said day, and that the said High Court of Appeal sits day and night, and never rises; and herewith, by order of the said court, I furnish your lordship with a copy (extract) of the record in this case, except of the indictment, whereof, notwithstanding, the substance and effect is supplied to your lordship in this Notice. And farther I am to inform you, that in case the jury then to try your lordship should find you guilty, the right honourable the Lord Chief Justice will, in passing sentence of death upon you, fix the day of execution for the 10th day of ——, being one calendar month from the day of your trial.
> It was signed by
> > CALEB SEARCHER,
> > Officer of the Crown Solicitor in the
> > Kingdom of Life and Death.

The Judge glanced through the parchment.

" 'Sblood! Do they think a man like me is to be bamboozled by their buffoonery?"

The Judge's coarse features were wrung into one of his sneers; but he was pale. Possibly, after all, there was a conspiracy on foot. It was queer. Did they mean to pistol him in his carriage? or did they only aim at frightening him?

Judge Harbottle had more than enough of animal courage. He was not afraid of highwaymen, and he had fought more than his share of duels, being a foul-mouthed advocate while he held briefs at the bar. No one questioned his fighting qualities. But with respect to this particular case of Pyneweck, he lived in a house of glass. Was there not his pretty, dark-eyed, over-dressed housekeeper, Mrs. Flora Carwell? Very easy for people who knew Shrewsbury to identify Mrs. Pyneweck, if once put upon the scent; and had he not stormed and worked hard in that case? Had he not made it hard sailing for the prisoner? Did he not know very well what the bar thought of it? It would be the worst scandal that ever blasted Judge.

So much there was intimidating in the matter but nothing more. The Judge was a little bit gloomy for a day or two after, and more testy with every one than usual.

He locked up the papers; and about a week after he asked his housekeeper, one day, in the library:

"Had your husband never a brother?"

Mrs. Carwell squalled on this sudden introduction of the funereal topic, and cried exemplary "piggins full," as the Judge used pleasantly to say. But he was in no mood for trifling now, and he said sternly:

"Come, madam! this wearies me. Do it another time; and give me an answer to my question." So she did.

Pyneweck had no brother living. He once had one; but he died in Jamaica.

"How do you know he is dead?" asked the Judge.

"Because he told me so."

"Not the dead man."

"Pyneweck told me so."

"Is that all?" sneered the Judge.

He pondered this matter; and time went on. The Judge was growing a little morose, and less enjoying. The subject struck nearer to his thoughts than he fancied it could have done. But so it is with most undivulged vexations, and there was no one to whom he could tell this one.

It was now the ninth; and Mr Justice Harbottle was glad. He knew nothing would come of it. Still it bothered him; and to-morrow would see it well over.

[What of the paper I have cited? No one saw it during his life; no one, after his death. He spoke of it to Dr. Hedstone; and what purported to be "a copy," in the old Judge's handwriting, was found. The original was nowhere. Was it a copy of an illusion, incident to brain disease? Such is my belief.]

CHAPTER VI

Arrested

Judge Harbottle went this night to the play at Drury Lane. He was one of the old fellows who care nothing for late hours, and occasional knocking about in pursuit of pleasure. He had appointed with two cronies of Lincoln's Inn to come home in his coach with him to sup after the play.

They were not in his box, but were to meet him near the entrance, and get into his carriage there; and Mr. Justice Harbottle, who hated waiting, was looking a little impatiently from the window.

The Judge yawned.

He told the footman to watch for Counsellor Thavies and Counsellor Beller, who were coming; and, with another yawn, he laid his cocked hat on his knees, closed his eyes, leaned back in his corner, wrapped his mantle closer about him, and began to think of pretty Mrs. Abington.

And being a man who could sleep like a sailor, at a moment's notice, he was thinking of taking a nap. Those fellows had no business to keep a judge waiting.

He heard their voices now. Those rake-hell counsellors were laughing, and bantering, and sparring after their wont. The carriage swayed and jerked, as one got in, and then again as the other followed. The door clapped, and the coach was now jogging and rumbling over the pavement. The Judge was a little bit sulky. He did not care to sit up and open his eyes. Let them suppose he was asleep. He heard them laugh with more malice than good-humour, he thought, as they observed it. He would give them a d—d hard knock or two when they got to his door, and till then he would counterfeit his nap.

The clocks were chiming twelve. Beller and Thavies were silent as tombstones. They were generally loquacious and merry rascals.

The Judge suddenly felt himself roughly seized and thrust from his corner into the middle of the seat, and opening his eyes, instantly he found himself between his two companions.

Before he could blurt out the oath that was at his lips, he saw that they were two strangers—evil-looking fellows, each with a pistol in his hand, and dressed like Bow Street officers.

The Judge clutched at the check-string. The coach pulled up. He stared about him. They were not among houses; but through the windows, under a broad moonlight, he saw a black moor stretching lifelessly from right to left, with rotting trees, pointing fantastic branches in the air, standing here and there in groups, as if they held up their arms and twigs like fingers, in horrible glee at the Judge's coming.

A footman came to the window. He knew his long face and sunken eyes. He knew it was Dingly Chuff, fifteen years ago a footman in his service, whom he had turned off at a moment's notice, in a burst of jealousy, and indicted for a missing spoon. The man had died in prison of the jail-fever.

The Judge drew back in utter amazement. His armed companions signed mutely; and they were again gliding over this unknown moor.

The bloated and gouty old man, in his horror considered the question of resistance. But his athletic days were long over. This moor was a desert. There was no help to be had. He was in the hands of strange servants, even if his recognition turned out to be a delusion, and they were under the command of his captors. There was nothing for it but submission, for the present.

Suddenly the coach was brought nearly to a standstill, so that the prisoner saw an ominous sight from the window.

It was a gigantic gallows beside the road; it stood three-sided, and from each of its three broad beams at top depended in chains some eight or ten bodies, from several of which the cere-clothes had dropped away, leaving the skeletons swinging lightly by their chains. A tall ladder reached to the summit of the structure, and on the peat beneath lay bones.

On top of the dark transverse beam facing the road, from which, as from the other two completing the triangle of death, dangled a row of these unfortunates in chains, a hangman, with a pipe in his mouth, much as we see him in the famous print of the "Idle Apprentice," though here his perch was ever so much higher, was reclining at his ease and listlessly shying bones, from a little heap at his elbow, at the skeletons that hung round, bringing down now a rib or two, now a hand, now half a leg. A long-sighted man could have discerned that he was a dark fellow, lean; and from continually looking down on the earth from the elevation over which, in another sense, he always hung, his nose, his lips, his chin were pendulous and loose, and drawn down into a monstrous grotesque.

This fellow took his pipe from his mouth on seeing the coach, stood up, and cut some solemn capers high on his beam, and shook a new rope in the air, crying with a voice high and distant as the caw of a raven hovering over a gibbet, "A robe for Judge Harbottle!"

The coach was now driving on at its old swift pace.

So high a gallows as that, the Judge had never, even in his most hilarious moments, dreamed of. He thought he must be raving. And the dead footman! He shook his ears and strained his eyelids; but if he was dreaming, he was unable to awake himself.

There was no good in threatening these scoundrels. A *brutum fulmen* might bring a real one on his head.

Any submission to get out of their hands; and then heaven and earth he would move to unearth and hunt them down.

Suddenly they drove round a corner of a vast white building, and under a *porte-cochère*.

CHAPTER VII

Chief-Justice Twofold

The Judge found himself in a corridor lighted with dingy oil lamps, the walls of bare stone; it looked like a passage in a prison. His guards placed him in the hands of other people. Here and there he saw bony and gigantic soldiers passing to and fro, with muskets over their shoulders. They looked straight before them, grinding their teeth, in bleak fury, with no noise but the clank of their shoes. He saw these by glimpses, round corners, and at the ends of passages, but he did not actually pass them by.

And now, passing under a narrow doorway, he found himself in the dock, confronting a judge in his scarlet robes, in a large courthouse. There was nothing to elevate this Temple of Themis above its vulgar kind elsewhere. Dingy enough it looked, in spite of candles lighted in decent abundance. A case had just closed, and the last juror's back was seen escaping through the door in the wall of the jury-box. There were some dozen barristers, some fiddling with pen and ink, others buried in briefs, some beckoning, with the plumes of their pens, to their attorneys, of whom there were no lack; there were clerks to-ing and fro-ing, and the officers of the court, and the registrar, who was handing up a paper to the judge; and the tipstaff, who was presenting a note at the end of his wand to a king's counsel over the heads of the crowd between. If this was the High Court of Appeal, which never rose day or night, it might account for the pale and jaded aspect of everybody in it. An air of indescribable gloom hung upon the pallid features of all the people here; no one ever smiled; all looked more or less secretly suffering.

"The King against Elijah Harbottle!" shouted the officer.

"Is the appellant Lewis Pyneweck in court?" asked Chief-Justice Twofold, in a voice of thunder, that shook the woodwork of the court, and boomed down the corridors.

Up stood Pyneweck from his place at the table.

"Arraign the prisoner!" roared the Chief: and Judge Harbottle felt the panels of the dock round him, and the floor, and the rails quiver in the vibrations of that tremendous voice.

The prisoner, *in limine*, objected to this pretended court, as being a sham, and non-existent in point of law; and then, that, even if it were a court constituted by law (the Judge was growing dazed), it had not and could not have any jurisdiction to try him for his conduct on the bench.

Whereupon the chief-justice laughed suddenly, and every one in court, turning round upon the prisoner, laughed also, till the laugh grew and roared all round like a deafening acclamation; he saw nothing but glittering eyes and teeth, a universal stare and grin; but though all the voices laughed, not a single face of all those that concentrated their gaze upon him looked like a laughing face. The mirth subsided as suddenly as it began.

The indictment was read. Judge Harbottle actually pleaded! He pleaded "Not Guilty." A jury were sworn. The trial proceeded. Judge Harbottle was bewildered. This could not be real. He must be either mad, or *going* mad, he thought.

One thing could not fail to strike even him. This Chief-Justice Twofold, who was knocking him about at every turn with sneer and gibe, and roaring him down with his tremendous voice, was a dilated effigy of himself; an image of Mr. Justice Harbottle, at least double his size, and with all his fierce colouring, and his ferocity of eye and visage, enhanced awfully.

Nothing the prisoner could argue, cite, or state, was permitted to retard for a moment the march of the case towards its catas-trophe.

The chief-justice seemed to feel his power over the jury, and to exult and riot in the display of it. He glared at them, he nodded to them; he seemed to have established an understanding with them. The lights were faint in that part of the court. The jurors were mere shadows, sitting in rows; the prisoner could see a dozen pair of white eyes shining, coldly, out of the darkness; and when-ever the judge in his charge, which was contemptuously brief, nodded and grinned and gibed, the prisoner could see, in the obscurity, by the dip of all these rows of eyes together, that the jury nodded in acquiescence.

And now the charge was over, the huge chief-justice leaned back panting and gloating on the prisoner. Every one in the court turned about, and gazed with steadfast hatred on the man in the dock. From the jury-box where the twelve sworn brethren were whispering together, a sound in the general stillness like a pro-longed "hiss-s-s!" was heard; and then, in answer to the challenge of the officer, "How say you, gentlemen of the jury, guilty or not guilty?" came in a melancholy voice the finding, "Guilty."

The place seemed to the eyes of the prisoner to grow gradually darker and darker, till he could discern nothing distinctly but the lumen of the eyes that were turned upon him from every bench and side and corner and gallery of the building. The prisoner doubtless thought that he had quite enough to say, and conclusive, why sentence of death should not be pronounced upon him; but the lord chief-justice puffed it contemptuously away, like so much smoke, and proceeded to pass sentence of death upon the prisoner, having named the tenth of the ensuing month for his execution.

Before he had recovered the stun of this ominous farce, in obedi-ence to the mandate, "Remove the prisoner," he was led from the dock. The lamps seemed all to have gone out, and there were stoves and charcoal-fires here and there, that threw a faint crimson light on the walls of the corridors through which he passed. The stones that composed them looked now enormous, cracked and unhewn.

He came into a vaulted smithy, where two men, naked to the waist, with heads like bulls, round shoulders, and the arms of giants, were welding red-hot chains together with hammers that pelted like thunderbolts.

They looked on the prisoner with fierce red eyes, and rested on their hammers for a minute; and said the elder to his companion, "Take out Elijah Harbottle's gyves;" and with a pincers he plucked the end which lay dazzling in the fire from the furnace.

"One end locks," said he, taking the cool end of the iron in one hand, while with the grip of a vice he seized the leg of the Judge, and locked the ring round his ankle. "The other," he said with a grin, "is welded."

The iron band that was to form the ring for the other leg lay still red hot upon the stone floor, with briliant sparks sporting up and down its surface.

His companion, in his gigantic hands, seized the old Judge's other leg, and pressed his foot immovably to the stone floor; while his senior, in a twinkling, with a masterly application of pincers and hammer, sped the glowing bar around his ankle so tight that the skin and sinews smoked and bubbled again, and old Judge Harbottle uttered a yell that seemed to chill the very stones, and make the iron chains quiver on the wall.

Chains, vaults, smiths, and smithy all vanished in a moment; but the pain continued. Mr. Justice Harbottle was suffering torture all round the ankle on which the infernal smiths had just been operating.

His friends, Thavies and Beller, were startled by the Judge's roar in the midst of their elegant trifling about a marriage à-la-mode case which was going on. The Judge was in panic as well as pain. The street lamps and the light of his own hall door restored him.

"I'm very bad," growled he between his set teeth; "my foot's blazing. Who was he that hurt my foot? 'Tis the gout—'tis the gout!" he said, awaking completely. "How many hours have we been coming from the playhouse? 'Sblood, what has happened on the way? I've slept half the night!"

There had been no hitch or delay, and they had driven home at a good pace.

The Judge, however, was in gout; he was feverish too; and the attack, though very short, was sharp; and when, in about a fortnight, it subsided, his ferocious joviality did not return. He could not get this dream, as he chose to call it, out of his head.

CHAPTER VIII

Somebody Has Got Into the House

People remarked that the Judge was in the vapours. His doctor said he should go for a fortnight to Buxton.

Whenever the Judge fell into a brown study, he was always conning over the terms of the sentence pronounced upon him in his vision—"in one calendar month from the date of this day;" and then the usual form, "and you shall be hanged by the neck till you are dead," etc. "That will be the 10th—I'm not much in the way of being hanged. I know what stuff dreams are, and I laugh at them; but this is continually in my thoughts, as if it forecast misfortune of some sort. I wish the day my dream gave me were passed and over. I wish I were well purged of my gout. I wish I were as I used to be. 'Tis nothing but vapours, nothing but a maggot." The copy of the parchment and letter which had announced his trial with many a snort and sneer he would read over and over again, and the scenery and people of his dream would rise about him in places the most unlikely, and steal him in a moment from all that surrounded him into a world of shadows.

The Judge had lost his iron energy and banter. He was growing taciturn and morose. The Bar remarked the change, as well they might. His friends thought him ill. The doctor said he was troubled with hypochondria, and that his gout was still lurking in his system, and ordered him to that ancient haunt of crutches and chalk-stones, Buxton.

The Judge's spirits were very low; he was frightened about himself; and he described to his housekeeper, having sent for her to his study to drink a dish of tea, his strange dream in his drive home from Drury Lane Playhouse. He was sinking into the state of nervous dejection in which men lose their faith in orthodox advice, and in despair consult quacks, astrologers, and nursery storytellers. Could such a dream mean that he was to have a fit, and so die on the 10th? She did not think so. On the contrary, it was certain some good luck must happen on that day.

The Judge kindled; and for the first time for many days, he looked for a minute or two like himself, and he tapped her on the cheek with the hand that was not in flannel.

"Odsbud! odsheart! you dear rogue! I had forgot. There is young Tom—yellow Tom, my nephew, you know, lies sick at Harrogate; why shouldn't he go that day as well as another, and if he does, I get an estate by it? Why, lookee, I asked Doctor Hedstone yesterday if I was like to take a fit any time, and he laughed, and swore I was the last man in town to go off that way."

The Judge sent most of his servants down to Buxton to make his lodgings and all things comfortable for him. He was to follow in a day or two.

It was now the 9th; and the next day well over, he might laugh at his visions and auguries.

On the evening of the 9th, Dr. Hedstone's footman knocked at the Judge's door. The Doctor ran up the dusky stairs to the drawing-room. It was a March evening, near the hour of sunset, with an east wind whistling sharply through the chimney-stacks. A wood fire blazed cheerily on the hearth. And Judge Harbottle, in what was then called a brigadier-wig, with his red roquelaure on, helped the glowing effect of the darkened chamber, which looked red all over like a room on fire.

The Judge had his feet on a stool, and his huge grim purple face confronted the fire, and seemed to pant and swell, as the blaze alternately spread upward and collapsed. He had fallen again among his blue devils, and was thinking of retiring from the Bench, and of fifty other gloomy things.

But the Doctor, who was an energetic son of Aesculapius, would listen to no croaking, told the Judge he was full of gout, and in his present condition no judge even of his own case, but promised him leave to pronounce on all those melancholy questions, a fortnight later.

In the meantime the Judge must be very careful. He was overcharged with gout, and he must not provoke an attack, till the waters of Buxton should do that office for him, in their own salutary way.

The Doctor did not think him perhaps quite so well as he pretended, for he told him he wanted rest, and would be better if he went forthwith to his bed.

Mr. Gerningham, his valet, assisted him, and gave him his drops; and the Judge told him to wait in his bedroom till he should go to sleep.

Three persons that night had specially odd stories to tell.

The housekeeper had got rid of the trouble of amusing her little girl at this anxious time, by giving her leave to run about the sitting-rooms and look at the pictures and china, on the usual condition of touching nothing. It was not until the last gleam of sunset had for some time faded, and the twilight had so deepened that she could no longer discern the colours on the china figures on the chimneypiece or in the cabinets, that the child returned to the housekeeper's room to find her mother.

To her she related, after some prattle about the china, and the pictures, and the Judge's two grand wigs in the dressing-room off the library, an adventure of an extraordinary kind.

In the hall was placed, as was customary in those times, the sedan-chair which the master of the house occasionally used, covered with stamped leather, and studded with gilt nails, and with its red silk blinds down. In this case, the doors of this old-fashioned conveyance were locked, the windows up, and, as I said, the blinds down, but not so closely that the curious child could not peep underneath one of them, and see into the interior.

A parting beam from the setting sun, admitted through the window of a back room, shot obliquely through the open door, and lighting on the chair, shone with a dull transparency through the crimson blind.

To her surprise, the child saw in the shadow a thin man, dressed in black, seated in it; he had sharp dark features; his nose, she fancied, a little awry, and his brown eyes were looking straight before him; his hand was on his thigh, and he stirred no more than the waxen figure she had seen at Southwark fair.

A child is so often lectured for asking questions, and on the propriety of silence, and the superior wisdom of its elders, that it accepts most things at last in good faith; and the little girl acquiesced respectfully in the occupation of the chair by this mahogany-faced person as being all right and proper.

It was not until she asked her mother who this man was, and observed her scared face as she questioned her more minutely upon the appearance of the stranger, that she began to understand that she had seen something unaccountable.

Mrs. Carwell took the key of the chair from its nail over the footman's shelf, and led the child by the hand up to the hall, having a lighted candle in her other hand. She stopped at a distance from the chair, and placed the candlestick in the child's hand.

"Peep in, Margery, again, and try if there's anything there," she whispered; "hold the candle near the blind so as to throw its light through the curtain."

The child peeped, this time with a very solemn face, and intimated at once that he was gone.

"Look again, and be sure," urged her mother.

The little girl was quite certain; and Mrs. Carwell, with her mob-cap of lace and cherry-coloured ribbons, and her dark brown hair, not yet powdered, over a very pale face, unlocked the door, looked in, and beheld emptiness.

"All a mistake, child, you see."

"*There!* ma'am! see there! He's gone round the corner," said the child.

"Where?" said Mrs. Carwell, stepping backward a step.

"Into that room."

"Tut, child! 'twas the shadow," cried Mrs. Carwell, angrily, because she was frightened. "I moved th candle." But she clutched one of the poles of the chair, which leant against the wall in the corner, and pounded the floor furiously with one end of it, being afraid to pass the open door the child had pointed to.

The cook and two kitchen-maids came running upstairs, not knowing what to make of this unwonted alarm.

They all searched the room; but it was still and empty, and no sign of any one's having been there.

Some people may suppose that the direction given to her thoughts by this odd little incident will account for a very strange illusion which Mrs. Carwell herself experienced about two hours later.

CHAPTER IX

The Judge Leaves His House

Mrs. Flora Carwell was going up the great staircase with a posset for the Judge in a china bowl, on a little silver tray.

Across the top of the well-staircase there runs a massive oak rail; and, raising her eyes accidentally, she saw an extremely odd-looking stranger, slim and long, leaning carelessly over with a pipe between his finger and thumb. Nose, lips, and chin seemed all to droop downward into extraordinary length, as he leant his odd peering face over the banister. In his other hand he held a coil of rope, one end of which escaped from under his elbow and hung over the rail.

Mrs. Carwell, who had no suspicion at the moment, that he was not a real person, and fancied that he was some one employed in cording the Judge's luggage, called to know what he was doing there.

Instead of answering, he turned about, and walked across the lobby, at about the same leisurely pace at which she was ascending. and entered a room, into which she followed him. It was an uncarpeted and unfurnished chamber. An open trunk lay upon the floor empty, and beside it the coil of rope; but except herself there was no one in the room. Perhaps, when she was able to think it over, it was a relief to her.

Mrs. Carwell was very much frightened, and now concluded that the child must have seen the same ghost that had just appeared to believe so; for the face, figure, and dress described by the child were awfully like Pyneweck; and this certainly was not he.

Very much scared and very hysterical, Mrs. Carwell ran down to her room, afraid to look over her shoulder, and got some companions about her, and wept, and talked, and drank more than one cordial, and talked and wept again, and so on, until, in those early days, it was ten o'clock, and time to go to bed.

A scullery maid remained up finishing some of her scouring and "scalding" for some time after the other servants—who, as I said, were few in number—that night had got to their beds. This was a low-browed, broad-faced, intrepid wench with black hair, who did not "vally a ghost not a button," and treated the housekeeper's hysterics with measureless scorn.

The old house was quiet now. It was near twelve o'clock, no sounds were audible except the muffled wailing of the wintry winds, piping high among the roofs and chimneys, or rumbling at intervals, in under gusts, through the narrow channels of the street.

The spacious solitudes of the kitchen level were awfully dark, and this sceptical kitchen-wench was the only person now up and about the house. She hummed tunes to herself, for a time; and then stopped and listened; and then resumed her work again. At last, she was destined to be more terrified than even was the housekeeper.

There was a back kitchen in this house, and from this she heard, as if coming from below its foundations, a sound like heavy strokes, that seemed to shake the earth beneath her feet. Sometimes a dozen in sequence, at regular intervals; sometimes fewer. She walked out softly into the passage, and was surprised to see a dusky glow issuing from this room, as if from a charcoal fire.

The room seemed thick with smoke.

Looking in she very dimly beheld a monstrous figure, over a furnace, beating with a mighty hammer the rings and rivets of a chain.

The strokes, swift and heavy as they looked, sounded hollow and distant. The man stopped, and pointed to something on the floor, that, through the smoky haze, looked, the thought, like a dead body. She remarked no more; but the servants in the room close by, startled from their sleep by a hideous scream, found her in a swoon on the flags, close to the door, where she had just witnessed this ghastly vision.

Startled by the girl's incoherent asseverations that she had seen the Judge's corpse on the floor, two servants having first searched the lower part of the house, went rather frightened up-stairs to inquire whether their master was well. They found him, not in his bed, but in his room. He had a table with candles burning at his bedside, and was getting on his clothes again; and he swore and cursed at them roundly in his old style, telling them that he had business, and that he would discharge on the spot any scoundrel who should dare to disturb him again.

So the invalid was left to his quietude.

In the morning it was rumored here and there in the street that the Judge was dead. A servant was sent from the house three doors away, by Counssellor Traverse, to inquire at Judge Harbottle's hall door.

The servant who opened it was pale and reserved, and would only say that the Judge was ill. He had had a dangerous accident; Doctor Hedstone had been with him at seven o'clock in the morning.

There were averted looks, short answers, pale and frowning faces, and all the usual signs that there was a secret that sat heavily upon their minds and the time for disclosing which had not yet come. That time would arrive when the coroner had arrived, and the mortal scandal that had befallen the house could be no longer hidden. For that morning Mr. Justice Harbottle had been found hanging by the neck from the banister at the top of the great staircase, and quite dead.

There was not the smallest sign of any struggle or resistance. There had not been heard a cry or any other noise in the slightest degree indicative of violence. There was medical evidence to show that, in his atrabilious state, it was quite on the cards that he might have made away with himself. The jury found accordingly that it was a case of suicide. But to those who were acquainted with the strange story which Judge Harbottle had related to at least two persons, the fact that the catastrophe occurred on the morning of March 10th seemed a startling coincidence.

A few days after, the pomp of a great funeral attended him to the grave; and so, in the language of Scripture, "the rich man died, and was buried."

Carmilla

PROLOGUE

Upon a paper attached to the Narrative which follows, Doctor Hesselius has written a rather elaborate note, which he accompanies with a reference to his Essay on the strange subject which the MS. illuminates.

This mysterious subject he treats, in that Essay, with his usual learning and acumen, and with remarkable directness and condensation. It will form but one volume of the series of that extraordinary man's collected papers.

As I publish the case, in this volume, simply to interest the "laity," I shall forestal the intelligent lady, who relates it, in nothing; and after due consideration, I have determined, therefore, to abstain from presenting any *précis* of the learned Doctor's reasoning, or extract from his statement on a subject which he describes as "involving, not improbably, some of the profoundest arcana of our dual existence, and its intermediates."

I was anxious on discovering this paper, to reopen the correspondence commenced by Doctor Hesselius, so many years before, with a person so clever and careful as his informant seems to have been. Much to my regret, however, I found that she had died in the interval.

She, probably, could have added little to the Narrative which she communicates in the following pages, with, so far as I can pronounce, such a conscientious particularity.

CHAPTER I

An Early Fright

In Styria, we, though by no means magnificent people, inhabit a castle, or schloss. A small income, in that part of the world, goes a great way. Eight or nine hundred a year does wonders. Scantily enough ours would have answered among wealthy people at home. My father is English, and I bear an English name, although I never saw England. But here, in this lonely and primitive place, where everything is so marvelously cheap, I really don't see how ever so much more money would at all materially add to our comforts, or even luxuries.

My father was in the Austrian service, and retired upon a pension and his patrimony, and purchased this feudal residence, and the small estate on which it stands, a bargain.

Nothing can be more picturesque or solitary. It stands on a slight eminence in a forest. The road, very old and narrow, passes in front of its drawbridge, never raised in my time, and its moat, stocked with perch, and sailed over by many swans, and floating on its surface white fleets of water-lilies.

Over all this the schloss shows its many-windowed front, its towers, and its Gothic chapel.

The forest opens in an irregular and very picturesque glade before its gate, and at the right a steep Gothic bridge carries the road over a stream that winds in deep shadow through the wood.

I have said that this is a very lonely place. Judge whether I say truth. Looking from the hall door towards the road, the forest in which our castle stands extends fifteen miles to the right, and twelve to the left. The nearest inhabited village is about seven of your English miles to the left. The nearest inhabited schloss of any historic associations, is that of old General Spielsdorf, nearly twenty miles away to the right.

I have said "the nearest *inhabited* village," because there is, only three miles westward, that is to say in the direction of General Spielsdorf's schloss, a ruined village, with its quaint little church, now roofless, in the aisle of which are the mouldering tombs of the proud family of Karnstein, now extinct, who once owned the equally-desolate château which, in the thick of the forest, overlooks the silent ruins of the town.

Respecting the cause of the desertion of this striking and melancholy spot, there is a legend which I shall relate to you another time.

I must tell you now, how very small is the party who constitute the inhabitants of our castle. I don't include servants, or those dependants who occupy rooms in the buildings attached to the schloss. Listen, and wonder! My father, who is the kindest man on earth, but growing old; and I, at the date of my story, only nineteen. Eight years have passed since then. I and my father constituted the family at the schloss. My mother, a Styrian lady, died in my infancy, but I had a good-natured governess, who had been with me from, I might almost say, my infancy. I could not remember the time when her fat, benignant face was not a familiar picture in my memory. This was Madame Perrodon, a native of Berne, whose care and good nature in part supplied to me the loss of my mother, whom I do not even remember, so early I lost her. She made a third at our little dinner party. There was a fourth, Mademoiselle De Lafontaine, a lady such as you term, I believe, a "finishing governess." She spoke French and German, Madame Perrodon French and broken English, to which my father and I added English, which, partly to prevent its becoming a lost language among us, and partly from patriotic motives, we spoke every day. The consequence was a Babel, at which strangers used to laugh, and which I shall make no attempt to reproduce in this narrative. And there were two or three young lady friends besides, pretty nearly of my own age, who were occasional visitors, for longer or shorter terms; and these visits I sometimes returned.

These were our regular social resources; but of course there were chance visits from "neighbours" of only five or six leagues' distance. My life was, notwithstanding, rather a solitary one, I can assure you.

My gouvernantes had just so much control over me as you might conjecture such sage persons would have in this case of a rather spoiled girl, whose only parent allowed her pretty nearly her own way in everything.

The first occurrence in my existence, which produced a terrible impression upon my mind, which, in fact, never has been effaced, was one of the very earliest incidents of my life which I can recollect. Some people will think it so trifling that it should not be recorded here. You will see, however, by-and-by, why I mention it. The nursery, as it was called, though I had it all to myself, was a large room in the upper story of the castle, with a steep oak roof. I can't have been more than six years old, when one night I awoke, and looking round the room from my bed, failed to see the nursery-maid. Neither was my nurse there; and I thought myself alone. I was not frightened, for I was one of those happy children who are studiously kept in ignorance of ghost stories, of fairy tales, and of all such lore as makes us cover up our heads when the door creaks suddenly, or the flicker of an expiring candle makes the shadow of a bed-post dance upon the wall, nearer to our faces. I was vexed and insulted at finding myself, as I conceived, neglected, and I began to whimper, preparatory to a hearty bout of roaring; when to my surprise, I saw a solemn, but very pretty face looking at me from the side of the bed. It was that of a young lady who was kneeling, with her hands under the coverlet. I looked at her with a kind of pleased wonder, and ceased whimpering. She caressed me with her hands, and lay down beside me on the bed, and drew me towards her, smiling; I felt immediately delightfully soothed, and fell asleep again. I was wakened by a sensation as if two needles ran into my breast very deep at the same moment, and I cried loudly. The lady started back, with her eyes fixed on me, and then slipped down upon the floor, and, as I thought, hid herself under the bed.

I was now for the first time frightened, and I yelled with all my might and main. Nurse, nursery-maid, housekeeper, all came running in, and hearing my story, they made light of it, soothing me all they could meanwhile. But, child as I was, I could perceive that their faces were pale with an unwonted look of anxiety, and I saw them look under the bed, and about the room, and peep under tables and pluck open cupboards; and the housekeeper whispered to the nurse; "Lay your hand along that hollow in the bed; some one did lie there, so sure as you did not; the place is still warm."

I remember the nursery-maid petting me, and all three examining my chest, where I told them I felt the puncture, and pronouncing that there was no sign visible that any such thing had happened to me.

The housekeeper and the two other servants who were in charge of the nursery, remained sitting up all night; and from that time a servant always sat up in the nursery until I was about fourteen.

I was very nervous for a long time after this. A doctor was called in, he was pallid and elderly. How well I remember his long saturnine face, slightly pitted with small-pox, and his chestnut wig. For a good while, every second day, he came and gave me medicine, which of course I hated.

The morning after I saw this apparition I was in a state of terror, and could not bear to be left alone, daylight though it was, for a moment.

I remember my father coming up and standing at the bedside, and talking cheerfully, and asking the nurse a number of questions, and laughing very heartily at one of the answers; and patting me on the shoulder, and kissing me, and telling me not to be frightened, that it was nothing but a dream and could not hurt me.

But I was not comforted, for I knew the visit of the strange woman was *not* a dream; and I was *awfully* frightened.

I was a little consoled by the nursery-maid's assuring me that it was she who had come and looked at me, and lain down beside me in the bed, and that I must have been half-dreaming not to have known her face. But this, though supported by the nurse, did not quite satisfy me.

I remember, in the course of that day, a venerable old man, in a black cassock, coming into the room with the nurse and housekeeper, and talking a little to them, and very kindly to me; his face was very sweet and gentle, and he told me they were going to pray, and joined my hands together, and desired me to say, softly, while they were praying, "Lord, hear all good prayers for us, for Jesus' sake." I think these were the very words, for I often repeated them to myself, and my nurse used for years to make me say them in my prayers.

I remember so well the thoughtful sweet face of that white-haired old man, in his black cassock, as he stood in that rude, lofty, brown room, with the clumsy furniture of a fashion three hundred years old, about him, and the scanty light entering its shadowy atmosphere through the small lattice. He kneeled, and the three women with him, and he prayed aloud with an earnest quavering voice for, what appeared to me, a long time. I forget all my life preceding that event, and for some time after it is all obscure also; but the scenes I have just described stand out vivid as the isolated pictures of the phantasmagoria surrounded by darkness.

CHAPTER II

A Guest

I am now going to tell you something so strange that it will require all your faith in my veracity to believe my story. It is not only true, nevertheless, but truth of which I have been an eye-witness.

It was a sweet summer evening, and my father asked me, as he sometimes did, to take a little ramble with him along that beautiful forest vista which I have mentioned as lying in front of the schloss.

"General Spielsdorf cannot come to us so soon as I had hoped," said my father, as we pursued our walk.

He was to have paid us a visit of some weeks, and we had expected his arrival next day. He was to have brought with him a young lady, his niece and ward, Mademoiselle Rheinfeldt, whom I had never seen, but whom I had heard described as a very charming girl, and in whose society I had promised myself many happy days. I was more disappointed than a young lady living in a town, or a bustling neighbourhood can possibly imagine. This visit, and the new acquaintance it promised, had furnished my day dream for many weeks.

"And how soon does he come?" I asked.

"Not till autumn. Not for two months, I dare say," he answered. "And I am very glad now, dear, that you never knew Mademoiselle Rheinfeldt."

"And why?" I asked, both mortified and curious.

"Because the poor young lady is dead," he replied. "I quite forgot I had not told you, but you were not in the room when I received the General's letter this evening."

I was very much shocked. General Spielsdorf had mentioned in his first letter, six or seven weeks before, that she was not so well as he would wish her, but there was nothing to suggest the remotest suspicion of danger.

"Here is the General's letter," he said, handing it to me. "I am afraid he is in great affliction; the letter appears to me to have been written very nearly in distraction."

We sat down on a rude bench, under a group of magnificent lime trees. The sun was setting with all its melancholy splendour behind the sylvan horizon, and the stream that flows beside our home, and passes under the steep old bridge I have mentioned, wound through many a group of noble trees, almost at our feet, reflecting in its current the fading crimson of the sky. General Spielsdorf's letter was extraordinary, so vehement, and in some places so self-contradictory, that I read it twice over—the second time aloud to my father—and was still unable to account for it, except by supposing that grief had unsettled his mind.

It said, "I have lost my darling daughter, for as such I loved her. During the last days of dear Bertha's illness I was not able to write to you. Before then I had no idea of her danger. I have lost her, and now learn *all,* too late. She died in the peace of innocence and in the glorious hope of a blessed futurity. The fiend who betrayed our infatuated hospitality has done it all. I thought I was receiving into my house innocence, gaiety, a charming companion for my lost Bertha. Heavens! what a fool I have been! I thank God my child died without a suspicion of the cause of her sufferings. She is gone without so much as conjecturing the nature of her illness, and the accursed passion of the agent of all this misery. I devote my remaining days to tracking and extinguishing a monster. I am told I may hope to accomplish my righteous and merciful purpose. At present there is scarcely a gleam of light to guide me. I curse my conceited incredulity, my despicable affectation of superiority, my blindness, my obstinacy—all—too late. I cannot write or talk collectedly now. I am distracted. So soon as I shall have a little recovered, I mean to devote myself for a time to inquiry, which may possibly lead me as far as Vienna. Some time in the autumn, two months hence, or earlier if I live, I will see you— that is, if you permit me; I will then tell you all that I scarce dare put upon paper now. Farewell. Pray for me, dear friend."

In these terms ended this strange letter. Though I had never seen Bertha Rheinfeldt, my eyes filled with tears at the sudden intelligence; I was startled, as well as profoundly disappointed.

The sun had now set, and it was twilight by the time I had returned the General's letter to my father.

It was a soft clear evening, and we loitered, speculating upon the possible meanings of the violent and incoherent sentences which I had just been reading. We had nearly a mile to walk before reaching the road that passes the schloss in front, and by that time the moon was shining brilliantly. At the drawbridge we met Madame Perrodon and Mademoiselle De Lafontaine, who had come out, without their bonnets, to enjoy the exquisite moonlight.

We heard their voices gabbling in animated dialogue as we approached. We joined them at the drawbridge, and turned about to admire with them the beautiful scene.

The glade through which we had just walked lay before us. At our left the narrow road wound away under clumps of lordly trees, and was lost to sight amid the thickening forest. At the right the same road crosses the steep and picturesque bridge, near which stands a ruined tower, which once guarded that pass; and beyond the bridge an abrupt eminence rises, covered with trees, and showing in the shadow some grey ivy-clustered rocks.

Over the sward and low grounds, a thin film of mist was stealing, like smoke, marking the distances with a transparent veil; and here and there we could see the river faintly flashing in the moonlight. No softer, sweeter scene could be imagined. The news I had just heard made it melancholy; but nothing could disturb its character of profound serenity, and the enchanted glory and vagueness of the prospect.

My father, who enjoyed the picturesque, and I, stood looking in silence over the expanse beneath us. The two good governesses, standing a little way behind us, discoursed upon the scene, and were eloquent upon the moon.

Madame Perrodon was fat, middle-aged, and romantic, and talked and sighed poetically. Mademoiselle De Lafontaine—in right of her father, who was a German, assumed to be psychological, metaphysical, and something of a mystic—now declared that when the moon shone with a light so intense it was well known that it indicated a special spiritual activity. The effect of the full moon in such a state of brilliancy was manifold. It acted on dreams, it acted on lunacy, it acted on nervous people; it had marvellous physical influences connected with life. Mademoiselle related that her cousin, who was mate of a merchant ship, having taken a nap on deck on such a night, lying on his back, with his face full in the light of the moon, had wakened, after a dream of an old woman clawing him by the cheek, with his features horribly drawn to one side; and his countenance had never quite recovered its equilibrium.

"The moon, this night," she said, "is full of odylic and magnetic influence—and see, when you look behind you at the front of the schloss, how all its windows flash and twinkle with that silvery splendour, as if unseen hands had lighted up the rooms to receive fairy guests."

There are indolent states of the spirits in which, indisposed to talk ourselves, the talk of others is pleasant to our listless ears; and I gazed on, pleased with the tinkle of the ladies' conversation.

"I have got into one of my moping moods tonight," said my father, after a silence, and quoting Shakespeare, whom, by way of keeping up our English, he used to read aloud, he said:—

> In truth I know not why I am so sad:
> It wearies me; you say it wearies you;
> But how I got it—came by it.

"I forget the rest. But I feel as if some great misfortune were hanging over us. I suppose the poor general's afflicted letter has had something to do with it."

At this moment the unwonted sound of carriage wheels and many hoofs upon the road, arrested our attention.

They seemed to be approaching from the high ground overlooking the bridge, and very soon the equipage emerged from that point. Two horsemen first crossed the bridge, then came a carriage drawn by four horses, and two men rode behind.

It seemed to be the travelling carriage of a person of rank; and we were all immediately absorbed in watching that very unusual spectacle. It became, in a few moments, greatly more interesting, for just as the carriage had passed the summit of the steep bridge, one of the leaders, taking fright, communicated his panic to the rest, and, after a plunge or two, the whole team broke into a wild gallop together, and dashing between the horsemen who rode in front, came thundering along the road towards us with the speed of a hurricane.

The excitement of the scene was made more painful by the clear, long-drawn screams of a female voice from the carriage window.

We all advanced in curiosity and horror; my father in silence, the rest with various ejaculations of terror.

Our suspense did not last long. Just before you reach the castle drawbridge, on the route they were coming, there stands by the roadside a magnificent lime tree, on the other side stands an ancient stone cross, at sight of which the horses, now going at a pace that was perfectly frightful, swerved so as to bring the wheel over the projecting roots of the tree.

I knew what was coming. I covered my eyes, unable to see it out, and turned my head away; at the same moment I heard a cry from my lady-friends, who had gone on a little.

Curiosity opened my eyes, and I saw a scene of utter confusion. Two of the horses were on the ground, the carriage lay upon its side, with two wheels in the air; the men were busy removing the traces, and a lady, with a commanding air and figure had got out, and stood with clasped hands, raising the handkerchief that was in them every now and then to her eyes. Through the carriage door was now lifted a young lady, who appeared to be lifeless. My dear old father was already beside the elder lady, with his hat in his hand, evidently tendering his aid and the resources of his schloss. The lady did not appear to hear him, or to have eyes for anything but the slender girl who was being placed against the slope of the bank.

I approached; the young lady was apparently stunned, but she was certainly not dead. My father, who piqued himself on being something of a physician, had just had his fingers to her wrist and assured the lady, who declared herself her mother, that her pulse, though faint and irregular, was undoubtedly still distinguishable. The lady clasped her hands and looked upward, as if in a momentary transport of gratitude; but immediately she broke out again in that theatrical way which is, I believe, natural to some people.

She was what is called a fine-looking woman for her time of life, and must have been handsome; she was tall, but not thin, and dressed in black velvet, and looked rather pale, but with a proud and commanding countenance, though now agitated strangely.

"Was ever being so born to calamity?" I heard her say, with clasped hands, as I came up. "Here am I, on a journey of life and death, in prosecuting which to lose an hour is possibly to lose all. My child will not have recovered sufficiently to resume her route for who can say how long. I must leave her; I cannot, dare not, delay. How far on, sir, can you tell, is the nearest village? I must leave her there; and shall not see my darling, or even hear of her till my return, three months hence."

I plucked my father by the coat, and whispered earnestly in his ear, "Oh! papa, pray ask her to let her stay with us—it would be so delightful. Do, pray."

"If Madame will entrust her child to the care of my daughter, and of her good gouvernante, Madame Perrodon, and permit her to remain as our guest, under my charge, until her return, it will confer a distinction and an obligation upon us, and we shall treat her with all the care and devotion which so sacred a trust deserves."

"I cannot do that, sir, it would be to task your kindness and chivalry too cruelly," said the lady, distractedly.

"It would, on the contrary, be to confer on us a very great kindness at the moment when we most need it. My daughter has just been disappointed by a cruel misfortune, in a visit from which she had long anticipated a great deal of happiness. If you confide this young lady to our care it will be her best consolation. The nearest village on your route is distant, and affords no such inn as you could think of placing your daughter at; you cannot allow her to continue her journey for any considerable distance without danger. If, as you say, you cannot suspend your journey, you must part with her to-night, and nowhere could you do so with more honest assurances of care and tenderness than here."

There was something in this lady's air and appearance so distinguished, and even imposing, and in her manner so engaging, as to impress one, quite apart from the dignity of her equipage, with a conviction that she was a person of consequence.

By this time the carriage was replaced in its upright position, and the horses, quite tractable, in the traces again.

The lady threw on her daughter a glance which I fancied was not quite so affectionate as one might have anticipated from the beginning of the scene; then she beckoned slightly to my father, and withdrew two or three steps with him out of hearing; and talked to him with a fixed and stern countenance, not at all like that with which she had hitherto spoken.

I was filled with wonder that my father did not seem to perceive the change, and also unspeakably curious to learn what it could be that she was speaking, almost in his ear, with so much earnestness and rapidity.

Two or three minutes at most, I think, she remained thus employed, then she turned, and a few steps brought her to where her daughter lay, supported by Madame Perrodon. She kneeled beside her for a moment and whispered, as Madame supposed, a little benediction in her ear; then hastily kissing her, she stepped into her carriage, the door was closed, the footmen in stately liveries jumped up behind, the outriders spurred on, the postilions cracked their whips, the horses plunged and broke suddenly into a furious canter that threatened soon again to become a gallop, and the carriage whirled away, followed at the same rapid pace by the two horsemen in the rear.

CHAPTER III

We Compare Notes

We followed the *cortège* with our eyes until it was swiftly lost to sight in the misty wood; and the very sound of the hoofs and wheels died away in the silent night air.

Nothing remained to assure us that the adventure had not been an illusion of a moment but the young lady, who just at that moment opened her eyes. I could not see, for her face was turned from me, but she raised her head, evidently looking about her, and I heard a very sweet voice ask complainingly, "Where is mamma?"

Our good Madame Perrodon answered tenderly, and added some comfortable assurances.

I then heard her ask:

"Where am I? What is this place?" and after that she said, "I don't see the carriage; and Matska, where is she?"

Madame answered all her questions in so far as she understood them; and gradually the young lady remembered how the misadventure came about, and was glad to hear that no one in, or in attendance on, the carriage was hurt; and on learning that her mamma had left her here, till her return in about three months, she wept.

I was going to add my consolations to those of Madame Perrodon when Mademoiselle de Lafontaine placed her hand upon my arm, saying:

"Don't approach, one at a time is as much as she can at present converse with; a very little excitement would possibly overpower her now."

As soon as she is comfortably in bed, I thought, I will run up to her room and see her.

My father in the meantime had sent a servant on horseback for the physician, who lived about two leagues away; and a bedroom was being prepared for the young lady's reception.

The stranger now rose, and leaning on Madame's arm, walked slowly over the drawbridge and into the castle gate.

In the hall, servants waited to receive her, and she was conducted forthwith to her room.

The room we usually sat in as our drawing-room is long, having four windows, that looked over the moat and drawbridge, upon the forest scene I have just described.

It is furnished in old carved oak, with large carved cabinets, and the chairs are cushioned with crimson Utrecht velvet. The walls are covered with tapestry, and surrounded with great gold frames, the figures being as large as life, in ancient and very curious costume, and the subjects represented are hunting, hawking, and generally festive. It is not too stately to be extremely comfortable; and here we had our tea, for with his usual patriotic leanings he insisted that the national beverage should make its appearance regularly with our coffee and chocolate.

We sat here this night, and with candles lighted, were talking over the adventure of the evening.

Madame Perrodon and Mademoiselle De Lafontaine were both of our party. The young stranger had hardly lain down in her bed when she sank into a deep sleep; and those ladies had left her in the care of a servant.

"How do you like our guest?" I asked, as soon as Madame entered. "Tell me all about her?"

"I like her extremely," answered Madame, "she is, I almost think, the prettiest creature I ever saw; about your age, and so gentle and nice."

"She is absolutely beautiful," threw in Mademoiselle, who had peeped for a moment into the stranger's room.

"And such a sweet voice!" added Madame Perrodon.

"Did you remark a woman in the carriage, after it was set up again, who did not get out," inquired Mademoiselle, "but only looked from the window?"

No, we had not seen her.

Then she described a hideous black woman, with a sort of coloured turban on her head, who was gazing all the time from the carriage window, nodding and grinning derisively towards the ladies, with gleaming eyes and large white eye-balls, and her teeth set as if in fury.

"Did you remark what an ill-looking pack of men the servants were?" asked Madame.

"Yes," said my father, who had just come in, "ugly, hang-dog looking fellows, as ever I beheld in my life. I hope they mayn't rob the poor lady in the forest. They are clever rogues, however; they got everything to rights in a minute."

"I dare say they are worn out with too long travelling," said Madame. "Besides looking wicked, their faces were so strangely lean, and dark, and sullen. I am very curious, I own; but I dare say the young lady will tell us all about it to-morrow, if she is sufficiently recovered."

"I don't think she will," said my father, with a mysterious smile, and a little nod of his head, as if he knew more about it than he cared to tell us.

This made me all the more inquisitive as to what had passed between him and the lady in the black velvet, in the brief but earnest interview that had immediately preceded her departure.

We were scarcely alone, when I entreated him to tell me. He did not need much pressing.

"There is no particular reason why I should not tell you. She expressed a reluctance to trouble us with the care of her daughter, saying she was in delicate health, and nervous, but not subject to any kind of seizure—she volunteered that—nor to any illusion; being, in fact, perfectly sane."

"How very odd to say all that!" I interpolated. "It was so unnecessary."

"At all events it *was* said," he laughed, "and as you wish to know all that passed, which was indeed very little, I tell you. She then said, 'I am making a long journey of *vital* importance'—she emphasized the word—'rapid and secret; I shall return for my child in three months; in the meantime, she will be silent as to who we

are, whence we come, and whither we are travelling.' That is all
she said. She spoke very pure French. When she said the word
'secret,' she paused for a few seconds, looking sternly, her eyes fixed
on mine. I fancy she makes a great point of that. You saw how
quickly she was gone. I hope I have not done a very foolish thing,
in taking charge of the young lady."

For my part, I was delighted. I was longing to see and talk to
her; and only waiting till the doctor should give me leave. You,
who live in towns, can have no idea how great an event the introduction of a new friend is, in such a solitude as surrounded us.

The doctor did not arrive till nearly one o'clock; but I could no
more have gone to my bed and slept, than I could have overtaken,
on foot, the carriage in which the princess in black velvet had
driven away.

When the physician came down to the drawing-room, it was to
report very favourably upon his patient. She was now sitting up,
her pulse quite regular, apparently perfectly well. She had sustained no injury, and the little shock to her nerves had passed away
quite harmlessly. There could be no harm certainly in my seeing
her, if we both wished it; and with this permission, I sent, forthwith, to know whether she would allow me to visit her for a few
minutes in her room.

The servant returned immediately to say that she desired
nothing more.

You may be sure I was not long in availing myself of this permission.

Our visitor lay in one of the handsomest rooms in the schloss. It
was, perhaps, a little stately. There was a sombre piece of tapestry
opposite the foot of the bed, representing Cleopatra with the asps
to her bosom; and other solemn classic scenes were displayed, a
little faded, upon the other walls. But there was gold carving, and
rich and varied colour enough in the other decorations of the
room, to more than redeem the gloom of the old tapestry.

There were candles at the bed side. She was sitting up; her
slender pretty figure enveloped in the soft silk dressing-gown, em-
broidered with flowers, and lined with thick quilted silk, which
her mother had thrown over her feet as she lay upon the ground.

What was it that, as I reached the bed side and had just begun
my little greeting, struck me dumb in a moment, and made me recoil a step or two from before her? I will tell you.

I saw the very face which had visited me in my childhood at
night, which remained so fixed in my memory, and on which I had
for so many years so often ruminated with horror, when no one
suspected of what I was thinking.

It was pretty, even beautiful; and when I first beheld it, wore the same melancholy expression.

But this almost instantly lighted into a strange fixed smile of recognition.

There was a silence of fully a minute, and then at length *she* spoke; *I* could not.

"How wonderful!" she exclaimed. "Twelve years ago, I saw your face in a dream, and it has haunted me ever since."

"Wonderful indeed!" I repeated, overcoming with an effort the horror that had for a time suspended my utterances. "Twelve years ago, in vision or reality, *I* certainly saw you. I could not forget your face. It has remained before my eyes ever since."

Her smile had softened. Whatever I had fancied strange in it, was gone, and it and her dimpling cheeks were now delightfully pretty and intelligent.

I felt reassured, and continued more in the vein which hospitality indicated, to bid her welcome, and to tell her how much pleasure her accidental arrival had given us all, and especially what a happiness it was to me.

I took her hand as I spoke. I was a little shy, as lonely people are, but the situation made me eloquent, and even bold. She pressed my hand, she laid hers upon it, and her eyes glowed, as, looking hastily into mine, she smiled again, and blushed.

She answered my welcome very prettily. I sat down beside her, still wondering; and she said:

"I must tell you my vision about you; it is so very strange that you and I should have had, each of the other, so vivid a dream, that each should have seen, I you and you me, looking as we do now, when of course we both were mere children. I was a child, about six years old, and I awoke from a confused and troubled dream, and found myself in a room, unlike my nursery, wainscoted clumsily in some dark wood, and with cupboards and bedsteads, and chairs and benches placed about it. The beds were, I thought, all empty, and the room itself without any one but myself in it; and I, after looking about me for some time, and admiring especially an iron candlestick, with two branches, which I should certainly know again, crept under one of the beds to reach the window; but as I got from under the bed, I heard some one crying; and looking up, while I was still upon my knees, I saw *you*—most assuredly you—as I see you now; a beautiful young lady, with golden hair and large blue eyes, and lips—your lips—you, as you are here. Your looks won me; I climbed on the bed and put my arms about you, and I think we both fell asleep. I was aroused by a scream; you were sitting up screaming. I was frightened, and slipped down upon the ground, and, it seemed to me, lost consciousness for a moment; and when I came to myself, I was again in my nursery at home. Your face I have never forgotten since. I could not be misled by mere resemblance. You *are* the lady whom I then saw."

It was now my turn to relate my corresponding vision, which I did, to the undisguised wonder of my new acquaintance.

"I don't know which should be most afraid of the other," she said, again smiling. "If you were less pretty I think I should be very much afraid of you, but being as you are, and you and I both so young, I feel only that I have made your acquaintance twelve years ago, and have already a right to your intimacy; at all events, it does seem as if we were destined, from our earliest childhood, to be friends. I wonder whether you feel as strangely drawn towards me as I do to you; I have never had a friend—shall I find one now?" She sighed, and her fine dark eyes gazed passionately on me.

Now the truth is, I felt rather unaccountably towards the beautiful stranger. I did feel, as she said, "drawn towards her," but there was also something of repulsion. In this ambiguous feeling, however, the sense of attraction immensely prevailed. She interested and won me; she was so beautiful and so indescribably engaging.

I perceived now something of languor and exhaustion stealing over her, and hastened to bid her good night.

"The doctor thinks," I added, "that you ought to have a maid to sit up with you to-night; one of ours is waiting, and you will find her a very useful and quiet creature."

"How kind of you, but I could not sleep, I never could with an attendant in the room. I shan't require any assistance—and, shall I confess my weakness, I am haunted with a terror of robbers. Our house was robbed once, and two servants murdered, so I always lock my door. It has become a habit—and you look so kind I know you will forgive me. I see there is a key in the lock."

She held me close in her pretty arms for a moment and whispered in my ear, "Good-night, darling, it is very hard to part with you, but good-night; to-morrow, but not early, I shall see you again."

She sank back on the pillow with a sigh, and her fine eyes followed me with a fond and melancholy gaze, and she murmured again, "Good-night, dear friend."

Young people like, and even love, on impulse. I was flattered by the evident, though as yet undeserved, fondness she showed me. I liked the confidence with which she at once received me. She was determined that we should be very dear friends.

Next day came and we met again. I was delighted with my companion; that is to say, in many respects.

Her looks lost nothing in daylight—she was certainly the most beautiful creature I had ever seen, and the unpleasant remembrance of the face presented in my early dream, had lost the effect of the first unexpected recognition.

She confessed that she had experienced a similar shock on seeing me, and precisely the same faint antipathy that had mingled with my admiration of her. We now laughed together over our momentary horrors.

CHAPTER IV

Her Habits—A Saunter

I told you that I was charmed with her in most particulars.

There were some that did not please me so well.

She was above the middle height of women. I shall begin by describing her. She was slender, and wonderfully graceful. Except that her movements were languid—*very* languid—indeed, there was nothing in her appearance to indicate an invalid. Her complexion was rich and brilliant; her features were small and beautifully formed; her eyes large, dark, and lustrous; her hair was quite wonderful, I never saw hair so magnificently thick and long when it was down about her shoulders; I have often placed my hands under it, and laughed with wonder at its weight. It was exquisitely fine and soft, and in colour a rich very dark brown, with something of gold. I loved to let it down, tumbling with its own weight, as, in her room, she lay back in her chair talking in her sweet low voice, I used to fold and braid it, and spread it out and play with it. Heavens! If I had but known all!

I said there were particulars which did not please me. I have told you that her confidence won me the first night I saw her; but I found that she exercised with respect to herself, her mother, her history, everything in fact connected with her life, plans, and people, an ever-wakeful reserve. I dare say I was unreasonable, perhaps I was wrong; I dare say I ought to have respected the solemn injunction laid upon my father by the stately lady in black velvet. But curiosity is a restless and unscrupulous passion, and no one girl can endure, with patience, that hers should be baffled by another. What harm could it do anyone to tell me what I so ardently desired to know? Had she no trust in my good sense or honour? Why would she not believe me when I assured her, so solemnly, that I would not divulge one syllable of what she told me to any mortal breathing?

There was a coldness, it seemed to me, beyond her years, in her smiling melancholy persistent refusal to afford me the least ray of light.

I cannot say we quarrelled upon this point, for she would not quarrel upon any. It was, of course, very unfair of me to press her, very ill-bred, but I really could not help it; and I might just as well have let it alone.

What she did tell me amounted, in my unconscionable estimation—to nothing.

It was all summed up in three very vague disclosures:

First.—Her name was Carmilla.

Second.—Her family was very ancient and noble.

Third.—Her home lay in the direction of the west.

She would not tell me the name of her family, nor their armorial bearings, nor the name of their estate, nor even that of the country they lived in.

You are not to suppose that I worried her incessantly on these subjects. I watched opportunity, and rather insinuated than urged my inquiries. Once or twice, indeed, I did attack her more directly. But no matter what my tactics, utter failure was invariably the result. Reproaches and caresses were all lost upon her. But I must add this, that her evasion was conducted with so pretty a melancholy and deprecation, with so many, and even passionate declarations of her liking for me, and trust in my honour, and with so many promises that I should at last know all, that I could not find it in my heart long to be offended with her.

She used to place her pretty arms about my neck, draw me to her, and laying her cheek to mine, murmur with her lips near my ear, "Dearest, your little heart is wounded; think me not cruel because I obey the irresistible law of my strength and weakness; if your dear heart is wounded, my wild heart bleeds with yours. In the rapture of my enormous humiliation I live in your warm life, and you shall die—die, sweetly die—into mine. I cannot help it; as I draw near to you, you, in your turn, will draw near to others, and learn the rapture of that cruelty, which yet is love; so, for a while, seek to know no more of me and mine, but trust me with all your loving spirit."

And when she had spoken such a rhapsody, she would press me

more closely in her trembling embrace, and her lips in soft kisses gently glow upon my cheek.

Her agitations and her language were unintelligible to me.

From these foolish embraces, which were not of very frequent occurrence, I must allow, I used to wish to extricate myself; but my energies seemed to fail me. Her murmured words sounded like a lullaby in my ear, and soothed my resistance into a trance, from which I only seemed to recover myself when she withdrew her arms.

In these mysterious moods I did not like her. I experienced a strange tumultuous excitement that was pleasurable, ever and anon, mingled with a vague sense of fear and disgust. I had no distinct thoughts about her while such scenes lasted, but I was conscious of a love growing into adoration, and also of abhorrence. This I know is paradox, but I can make no other attempt to explain the feeling.

I now write, after an interval of more than ten years, with a trembling hand, with a confused and horrible recollection of certain occurrences and situations, in the ordeal through which I was unconsciously passing; though with a vivid and very sharp remembrance of the main current of my story. But, I suspect, in all lives there are certain emotional scenes, those in which our passions have been most wildly and terribly roused, that are of all others the most vaguely and dimly remembered.

Sometimes after an hour of apathy, my strange and beautiful companion would take my hand and hold it with a fond pressure, renewed again and again; blushing softly, gazing in my face with languid and burning eyes, and breathing so fast that her dress rose and fell with the tumultuous respiration. It was like the ardour of a lover; it embarrassed me; it was hateful and yet overpowering; and with gloating eyes she drew me to her, and her hot lips travelled along my cheek in kisses; and she would whisper, almost in sobs, "You are mine, you *shall* be mine, and you and I are one for ever." Then she has thrown herself back in her chair, with her small hands over her eyes, leaving me trembling.

"Are we related," I used to ask; "what can you mean by all this? I remind you perhaps of some one whom you love; but you must not, I hate it; I don't know you—I don't know myself when you look so and talk so."

She used to sigh at my vehemence, then turn away and drop my hand.

Respecting these very extraordinary manifestations I strove in vain to form any satisfactory theory—I could not refer them to affectation or trick. It was unmistakably the momentary breaking out of suppressed instinct and emotion. Was she, notwithstanding her mother's volunteered denial, subject to brief visitations of insanity; or was there here a disguise and a romance? I had read in old story books of such things. What if a boyish lover had found his way into the house, and sought to prosecute his suit in masquerade, with the assistance of a clever old adventuress? But there were many things against this hypothesis, highly interesting as it was to my vanity.

I could boast of no little attentions such as masculine gallantry delights to offer. Between these passionate moments there were long intervals of common-place, of gaiety, of brooding melancholy, during which, except that I detected her eyes so full of melancholy fire, following me, at times I might have been as nothing to her. Except in these brief periods of mysterious excitement her ways were girlish; and there was always a languor about her, quite incompatible with a masculine system in a state of health.

In some respects her habits were odd. Perhaps not so singular in the opinion of a town lady like you, as they appeared to us rustic people. She used to come down very late, generally not till one o'clock, she would then take a cup of chocolate, but eat nothing; we then went out for a walk, which was a mere saunter, and she seemed, almost immediately, exhausted, and either returned to the schloss or sat on one of the benches that were placed, here and there, among the trees. This was a bodily languor in which her mind did not sympathise. She was always an animated talker, and very intelligent.

She sometimes alluded for a moment to her own home, or mentioned an adventure or situation, or an early recollection, which indicated a people of strange manners, and described customs of which we knew nothing. I gathered from these chance hints that her native country was much more remote than I had at first fancied.

As we sat thus one afternoon under the trees a funeral passed us by. It was that of a pretty young girl, whom I had often seen, the daughter of one of the rangers of the forest. The poor man was walking behind the coffin of his darling; she was his only child, and he looked quite heartbroken. Peasants walking two-and-two came behind, they were singing a funeral hymn.

I rose to mark my respect as they passed, and joined in the hymn they were very sweetly singing.

My companion shook me a little roughly, and I turned surprised.

She said brusquely, "Don't you perceive how discordant that is?"

"I think it very sweet, on the contrary," I answered, vexed at the interruption, and very uncomfortable, lest the people who composed the little procession should observe and resent what was passing.

I resumed, therefore, instantly, and was again interrupted. "You pierce my ears," said Carmilla, almost angrily, and stopping her ears with her tiny fingers. "Besides, how can you tell that your religion and mine are the same; your forms wound me, and I hate funerals. What a fuss! Why, *you* must die—*everyone* must die; and all are happier when they do. Come home."

"My father has gone on with the clergyman to the churchyard. I thought you knew she was to be buried to-day."

"*She?* I don't trouble my head about peasants. I don't know who she is," answered Carmilla, with a flash from her fine eyes.

"She is the poor girl who fancied she saw a ghost a fortnight ago, and has been dying ever since, till yesterday, when she expired."

"Tell me nothing about ghosts. I shan't sleep to-night if you do."

"I hope there is no plague or fever coming; all this looks very like it," I continued. "The swineherd's young wife died only a week ago, and she thought something seized her by the throat as she lay in her bed, and nearly strangled her. Papa says such horrible fancies do accompany some forms of fever. She was quite well the day before. She sank afterwards, and died before a week."

"Well, *her* funeral is over, I hope, and *her* hymn sung; and our ears shan't be tortured with that discord and jargon. It has made me nervous. Sit down here, beside me; sit close; hold my hand; press it hard—hard—harder."

We had moved a little back, and had come to another seat.

She sat down. Her face underwent a change that alarmed and even terrified me for a moment. It darkened, and became horribly livid; her teeth and hands were clenched, and she frowned and compressed her lips, while she stared down upon the ground at her feet, and trembled all over with a continued shudder as irrepressible as ague. All her energies seemed strained to suppress a fit, with which she was then breathlessly tugging; and at length a low convulsive cry of suffering broke from her, and gradually the hysteria subsided. "There! That comes of strangling people with hymns!" she said at last. "Hold me, hold me still. It is passing away."

And so gradually it did; and perhaps to dissipate the sombre impression which the spectacle had left upon me, she became unusually animated and chatty; and so we got home.

As we sat thus one afternoon under the trees a funeral passed us by.

This was the first time I had seen her exhibit any definable symptoms of that delicacy of health which her mother had spoken of. It was the first time, also, I had seen her exhibit anything like temper.

Both passed away like a summer cloud; and never but once afterwards did I witness on her part a momentary sign of anger. I will tell you how it happened.

She and I were looking out of one of the long drawing-room windows, when there entered the court-yard, over the drawbridge, a figure of a wanderer whom I knew very well. He used to visit the schloss generally twice a year.

It was the figure of a hunchback, with the sharp lean features that generally accompany deformity. He wore a pointed black beard, and he was smiling from ear to ear, showing his white fangs. He was dressed in buff, black, and scarlet, and crossed with more straps and belts than I could count, from which hung all manner of things. Behind, he carried a magic-lantern, and two boxes, which I well knew, in one of which was a salamander, and in the other a mandrake. These monsters used to make my father laugh. They were compounded of parts of monkeys, parrots, squirrels, fish, and hedgehogs, dried and stitched together with great neatness and startling effect. He had a fiddle, a box of conjuring apparatus, a pair of foils and masks attached to his belt, several other mysterious cases dangling about him, and a black staff with copper ferrules in his hand. His companion was a rough spare dog, that followed at his heels, but stopped short, suspiciously at the drawbridge, and in a little while began to howl dismally.

In the meantime, the mountebank, standing in the midst of the court-yard, raised his grotesque hat, and made us a very ceremonious bow, paying his compliments very volubly in execrable French, and German not much better. Then, disengaging his fiddle, he began to scrape a lively air, to which he sang with a merry discord, dancing with ludicrous airs and activity, that made me laugh, in spite of the dog's howling.

Then he advanced to the window with many smiles and salutations, and his hat in his left hand, his fiddle under his arm, and with a fluency that never took breath, he gabbled a long advertisement of all his accomplishments, and the resources of the various arts which he placed at our service, and the curiosities and entertainments which it was in his power, at our bidding to display.

"Will your ladyships be pleased to buy an amulet against the oupire, which is going like the wolf, I hear, through these woods," he said, dropping his hat on the pavement. "They are dying of it right and left, and here is a charm that never fails; only pinned to the pillow, and you may laugh in his face."

These charms consisted of oblong slips of vellum, with cabalistic ciphers and diagrams upon them.

Carmilla instantly purchased one, and so did I.

He was looking up, and we were smiling down upon him, amused; at least, I could answer for myself. His piercing black eye, as he looked up in our faces, seemed to detect something that fixed for a moment his curiosity.

In an instant he unrolled a leather case, full of all manner of odd little steel instruments.

"See here, my lady," he said, displaying it, and addressing me, "I profess, among other things less useful, the art of dentistry. Plague take the dog!" he interpolated. "Silence, beast! He howls so that your ladyships can scarcely hear a word. Your noble friend, the young lady at your right, has the sharpest tooth—long, thin, pointed, like an awl, like a needle; ha, ha! With my sharp and long sight, as I look up, I have seen it distinctly; now if it happens to hurt the young lady, and I think it must, here am I, here are my file, my punch, my nippers; I will make it round and blunt, if her ladyship pleases; no longer the tooth of a fish, but of a beautiful young lady as she is. Hey? Is the young lady displeased? Have I been too bold? Have I offended her?"

The young lady, indeed, looked very angry as she drew back from the window.

"How dares that mountebank insult us so? Where is your father? I shall demand redress from him. My father would have had the wretch tied up to the pump, and flogged with a cart-whip, and burnt to the bones with the castle brand!"

She retired from the window a step or two, and sat down, and had hardly lost sight of the offender, when her wrath subsided as suddenly as it had risen, and she gradually recovered her usual tone, and seemed to forget the little hunchback and his follies.

My father was out of spirits that evening. On coming in he told us that there had been another case very similar to the two fatal ones which had lately occurred. The sister of a young peasant on his estate, only a mile away, was very ill, had been, as she described it, attacked very nearly in the same way, and was now slowly but steadily sinking.

"All this," said my father, "is strictly referable to natural causes. These poor people infect one another with their superstitions, and so repeat in imagination the images of terror that have infested their neighbours."

"But that very circumstance frightens one horribly," said Carmilla.

"How so?" inquired my father.

"I am so afraid of fancying I see such things; I think it would be as bad as reality."

"We are in God's hands; nothing can happen without His permission, and all will end well for those who love Him. He is our faithful creator; He has made us all, and will take care of us."

"Creator! *Nature!*" said the young lady in answer to my gentle father. "And this disease that invades the country is natural. Nature. All things proceed from Nature—don't they? All things in the heaven, in the earth, and under the earth, act and live as Nature ordains? I think so."

"The doctor said he would come here to-day," said my father, after a silence. "I want to know what he thinks about it, and what he thinks we had better do."

"Doctors never did me any good," said Carmilla.

"Then you have been ill?" I asked.

"More ill than ever you were," she answered.

"Long ago?"

"Yes, a long time. I suffered from this very illness; but I forget all but my pain and weakness, and they were not so bad as are suffered in other diseases."

"You were very young then?"

"I dare say; let us talk no more of it. You would not wound a friend?" She looked languidly in my eyes, and passed her arm round my waist lovingly, and led me out of the room. My father was busy over some papers near the window.

"Why does your papa like to frighten us?" said the pretty girl, with a sigh and a little shudder.

"He doesn't, dear Carmilla, it is the very furthest thing from his mind."

"Are you afraid, dearest?"

"I should be very much if I fancied there was any real danger of my being attacked as those poor people were."

"You are afraid to die?"

"Yes, everyone is."

"But to die as lovers may—to die together, so that they may live together. Girls are caterpillars while they live in the world, to be finally butterflies when the summer comes; but in the meantime there are grubs and larvæ, don't you see—each with their peculiar propensities, necessities and structure. So says Monsieur Buffon, in his big book, in the next room."

Later in the day the doctor came, and was closeted with papa for some time. He was a skilful man, of sixty and upwards, he wore powder, and shaved his pale face smooth as a pumpkin. He and papa emerged from the room together, and I heard papa laugh, and say as they came out:

"Well, I do wonder at a wise man like you. What do you say to hippogriffs and dragons?"

The doctor was smiling, and made answer, shaking his head—

"Nevertheless, life and death are mysterious states, and we know little of the resources of either."

And so they walked on, and I heard no more. I did not then know what the doctor had been broaching, but I think I guess it now.

CHAPTER V

A Wonderful Likeness

This evening there arrived from Gratz the grave, dark-faced son of the picture-cleaner, with a horse and cart laden with two large packing-cases, having many pictures in each. It was a journey of ten leagues, and whenever a messenger arrived at the schloss from our little capital of Gratz, we used to crowd about him in the hall, to hear the news.

This arrival created in our secluded quarters quite a sensation. The cases remained in the hall, and the messenger was taken charge of by the servants till he had eaten his supper. Then with assistants, and armed with hammer, ripping chisel, and turnscrew, he met us in the hall, where we had assembled to witness the unpacking of the cases.

Carmilla sat looking listlessly on, while one after the other the old pictures, nearly all portraits, which had undergone the process of renovation, were brought to light. My mother was of an old Hungarian family, and most of these pictures, which were about to be restored to their places, had come to us through her.

My father had a list in his hand, from which he read, as the artist rummaged out the corresponding numbers. I don't know that the pictures were very good, but they were, undoubtedly, very old, and some of them very curious also. They had, for the most part, the merit of being now seen by me, I may say, for the first time; for the smoke and dust of time had all but obliterated them.

"There is a picture that I have not seen yet," said my father. "In one corner, at the top of it, is the name, as well as I could read, 'Marcia Karnstein,' and the date '1698;' and I am curious to see how it has turned out."

I remembered it; it was a small picture, about a foot and a half high, and nearly square, without a frame; but it was so blackened by age that I could not make it out.

The artist now produced it, with evident pride. It was quite beautiful; it was startling; it seemed to live. It was the effigy of Carmilla!

"Carmilla, dear, here is an absolute miracle. Here you are, living, smiling, ready to speak, in this picture. Isn't it beautiful, papa? And see, even the mole on her throat."

My father laughed, and said, "Certainly it is a wonderful likeness," but he looked away, and to my surprise seemed but little struck by it, and went on talking to the picture-cleaner, who was also something of an artist, and discoursed with intelligence about the portraits or other works, which his art had just brought into light and colour, while I was more and more lost in wonder the more I looked at the picture.

"Will you let me hang this picture in my room, papa?" I asked.

"Certainly, dear," said he, smiling, "I'm very glad you think it so like. It must be prettier even than I thought it, if it is."

The young lady did not acknowledge this pretty speech, did not seem to hear it. She was leaning back in her seat, her fine eyes under their long lashes gazing on me in contemplation, and she smiled in a kind of rapture.

"And now you can read quite plainly the name that is written in the corner. It is not Marcia; it looks as if it was done in gold. The name is Mircalla, Countess Karnstein, and this is a little coronet over it, and underneath A. D. 1698. I am descended from the Karnsteins; that is, mamma was."

"Ah!" said the lady, languidly, "so am I, I think, a very long descent, very ancient. Are there any Karnsteins living now?"

"None who bear the name, I believe. The family were ruined, I believe, in some civil wars, long ago but the ruins of the castle are only about three miles away."

"How interesting!" she said, languidly. "But see what beautiful moonlight!" She glanced through the hall door, which stood a little open. "Suppose you take a little ramble round the court, and look down at the road and river."

"It is so like the night you came to us," I said.

She sighed, smiling.

She rose, and each with her arm about the other's waist, we walked out upon the pavement.

In silence, slowly we walked down to the drawbridge, where the beautiful landscape opened before us.

"And so you were thinking of the night I came here?" she almost whispered. "Are you glad I came?"

"Delighted, dear Carmilla," I answered.

"And you ask for a picture you think like me, to hang in your room," she murmured with a sigh, as she drew her arm closer about my waist, and let her pretty head sink upon my shoulder.

"How romantic you are, Carmilla," I said. "Whenever you tell me your story, it will be made up chiefly of some one great romance."

She kissed me silently.

"I am sure, Carmilla, you have been in love; that there is, at this moment, an affair of the heart going on."

"I have been in love with no one, and never shall," she whispered, "unless it should be you."

How beautiful she looked in the moonlight!

Shy and strange was the look with which she quickly hid her face in my neck and hair, with tumultuous sighs, that seemed almost to sob, and pressed in mine a hand that trembled.

Her soft cheek was glowing against mine. "Darling, darling," she murmured, "I live in you; and you would die for me, I love you so."

I started from her.

She was gazing on me with eyes from which all fire, all meaning had flown, and a face colourless and apathetic.

"Is there a chill in the air, dear?" she said drowsily. "I almost shiver; have I been dreaming? Let us come in. Come, come; come in."

"You look ill, Carmilla; a little faint. You certainly must take some wine," I said.

"Yes, I will. I'm better now. I shall be quite well in a few minutes. Yes, do give me a little wine," answered Carmilla, as we approached the door. "Let us look again for a moment; it is the last time, perhaps, I shall see the moonlight with you."

"How do you feel now, dear Carmilla? Are you really better?" I asked.

I was beginning to take alarm, lest she should have been stricken with the strange epidemic that they said had invaded the country about us.

"Papa would be grieved beyond measure," I added, "if he thought you were ever so little ill, without immediately letting us know. We have a very skilful doctor near this, the physician who was with papa to-day."

"I'm sure he is. I know how kind you all are: but, dear child, I am quite well again. There is nothing ever wrong with me, but a little weakness. People say I am languid; I am incapable of exertion; I can scarcely walk as far as a child of three years old; and every now and then the little strength I have falters, and I become as you have just seen me. But after all I am very easily set up again; in a moment I am perfectly myself. See how I have recovered."

So, indeed, she had; and she and I talked a great deal, and very animated she was; and the remainder of that evening passed without any recurrence of what I called her infatuations. I mean her crazy talk and looks, which embarrassed, and even frightened me.

But there occurred that night an event which gave my thoughts quite a new turn, and seemed to startle even Carmilla's languid nature into momentary energy.

CHAPTER VI

A Very Strange Agony

When we got into the drawing-room, and had sat down to our coffee and chocolate, although Carmilla did not take any, she seemed quite herself again, and Madame, and Mademoiselle De Lafontaine, joined us, and made a little card party, in the course of which papa came in for what he called his "dish of tea."

When the game was over he sat down beside Carmilla on the sofa, and asked her, a little anxiously, whether she had heard from her mother since her arrival.

She answered "No."

He then asked her whether she knew where a letter would reach her at present.

"I cannot tell," she answered, ambiguously, "but I have been thinking of leaving you; you have been already too hospitable and too kind to me. I have given you an infinity of trouble, and I should wish to take a carriage to-morrow, and post in pursuit of her; I know where I shall ultimately find her, although I dare not yet tell you."

"But you must not dream of such a thing," exclaimed my father, to my great relief. "We can't afford to lose you so, and I won't consent to your leaving us, except under the care of your mother, who was so good as to consent to your remaining with us till she should herself return. I should be quite happy if I knew that you heard from her; but this evening the accounts of the progress of the mysterious disease that has invaded our neighbourhood, grow even more alarming; and my beautiful guest, I do feel the responsibility, unaided by advice from your mother, very much. But I shall do my best; and one thing is certain, that you must not think of leaving us without her distinct direction to that effect. We should suffer too much in parting from you to consent to it easily."

"Thank you, sir, a thousand times for your hospitality," she answered, smiling bashfully. "You have all been too kind to me; I have seldom been so happy in all my life before, as in your beautiful château, under your care, and in the society of your dear daughter."

So he gallantly, in his old-fashioned way, kissed her hand, smiling, and pleased at her little speech.

I accompanied Carmilla as usual to her room, and sat and chatted with her while she was preparing for bed.

"Do you think," I said, at length, "that you will ever confide fully in me?"

She turned around smiling, but made no answer, only continued to smile on me.

"You won't answer that?" I said. "You can't answer pleasantly; I ought not to have asked you."

"You were quite right to ask me that, or anything. You do not know how dear you are to me, or you could not think any confidence too great to look for. But I am under vows, no nun half so awfully, and I dare not tell my story yet, even to you. The time is very near when you shall know everything. You will think me cruel, very selfish, but love is always selfish; the more ardent the more selfish. How jealous I am you cannot know. You must come with me, loving me, to death; or else hate me, and still come with me, and *hating* me through death and after. There is no such word as indifference in my apathetic nature."

"Now, Carmilla, you are going to talk your wild nonsense again," I said hastily.

"Not I, silly little fool as I am, and full of whims and fancies; for your sake I'll talk like a sage. Were you ever at a ball?"

"No; how you do run on. What is it like? How charming it must be."

"I almost forget, it is years ago."

I laughed.

"You are not so old. Your first ball can hardly be forgotten yet."

"I remember everything about it—with an effort. I see it all, as divers see what is going on above them, through a medium, dense, rippling, but transparent. There occurred that night what has confused the picture, and made its colours faint. I was all but assassinated in my bed, wounded *here*," she touched her breast, "and never was the same since."

"Were you near dying?"

"Yes, a very—cruel love—strange love, that would have taken my life. Love will have its sacrifices. No sacrifice without blood. Let us go to sleep now; I feel lazy. How can I get up just now and lock my door?"

She was lying with her tiny hands buried in her rich wavy hair, under her cheek, her little head upon the pillow, and her glittering eyes followed me wherever I moved, with a kind of shy smile that I could not decipher.

I bid her good-night, and crept from the room with an uncomfortable sensation.

I often wondered whether our pretty guest ever said her prayers. *I* certainly had never seen her upon her knees. In the morning she never came down until long after our family prayers were over, and at night she never left the drawing room to attend our brief evening prayers in the hall.

If it had not been that it had casually come out in one of our careless talks that she had been baptised, I should have doubted her being a Christian. Religion was a subject on which I had never heard her speak a word. If I had known of the world better, this particular neglect or antipathy would not have so much surprised me.

The precautions of nervous people are infectious, and persons of a like temperament are pretty sure, after a time, to imitate them. I had adopted Carmilla's habit of locking her bed-room door, having taken into my head all her whimsical alarms about midnight invaders, and prowling assassins. I had also adopted her precaution of making a brief search through her room, to satisfy herself that no lurking assassin or robber was "ensconced."

These wise measures taken, I got into my bed and fell asleep. A light was burning in my room. This was an old habit, of very early date, and which nothing could have tempted me to dispense with.

Thus fortified I might take my rest in peace. But dreams come through stone walls, light up dark rooms, or darken light ones, and their persons make their exits and their entrances as they please, and laugh at locksmiths.

I had a dream that night that was the beginning of a very strange agony.

I cannot call it a nightmare, for I was quite conscious of being asleep. But I was equally conscious of being in my room, and lying in bed, precisely as I actually was. I saw, or fancied I saw, the room and its furniture just as I had seen it last, except that it was very dark, and I saw something moving round the foot of the bed, which at first I could not accurately distinguish. But I soon saw that it was a sooty-black animal that resembled a monstrous cat. It appeared to me about four or five feet long, for it measured fully the length of the hearth-rug as it passed over it; and it continued to-ing and fro-ing with the lithe sinister restlessness of a beast in a cage. I could not cry out, although as you may suppose, I was terrified. Its pace was growing faster, and the room rapidly darker and darker, and at length so dark that I could no longer see any-thing of it but its eyes. I felt it spring lightly on the bed. The two broad eyes approached my face, and suddenly I felt a stinging pain as if two large needles darted, an inch or two apart, deep into my breast. I waked with a scream. The room was lighted by the candle that burnt there all through the night, and I saw a female figure standing at the foot of the bed, a little at the right side. It was in a dark loose dress, and its hair was down and covered its shoulders. A block of stone could not have been more still. There was not the slightest stir of respiration. As I stared at it, the figure appeared to have changed its place, and was now nearer the door; then, close to it, the door opened, and it passed out.

I was now relieved, and able to breathe and move. My first thought was that Carmilla had been playing me a trick, and that I had forgotten to secure my door. I hastened to it, and found it locked as usual on the inside. I was afraid to open it—I was hor-rified. I sprang into my bed and covered my head up in the bed-clothes, and lay there more dead than alive till morning.

I saw a female figure standing at the foot of the bed.

CHAPTER VII
Descending

It would be vain my attempting to tell you the horror with which, even now, I recall the occurrence of that night. It was no such transitory terror as a dream leaves behind it. It seemed to deepen by time, and communicated itself to the room and the very furniture that had encompassed the apparition.

I could not bear the next day to be alone for a moment. I should have told papa, but for two opposite reasons. At one time I thought he would laugh at my story, and I could not bear its being treated as a jest; and at another, I thought he might fancy that I had been attacked by the mysterious complaint which had invaded our neighbourhood. I had myself no misgivings of the kind, and as he had been rather an invalid for some time, I was afraid of alarming him.

I was comfortable enough with my good-natured companions, Madame Perrodon, and the vivacious Mademoiselle Lafontaine. They both perceived that I was out of spirits and nervous, and at length I told them what lay so heavy at my heart.

Mademoiselle laughed, but I fancied that Madame Perrodon looked anxious.

"By-the-by," said Mademoiselle, laughing, "the long lime tree walk, behind Carmilla's bedroom window, is haunted!"

"Nonsense!" exclaimed Madame, who probably thought the theme rather inopportune, "and who tells that story, my dear?"

"Martin says that he came up twice, when the old yard-gate was being repaired before sunrise, and twice saw the same female figure walking down the lime tree avenue."

"So he well might, as long as they have cows to milk in the river fields," said Madame.

"I daresay; but Martin chooses to be frightened, and never did I see fool *more* frightened."

"You must not say a word about it to Carmilla, because she can see down that walk from her room window," I interposed, "and she is, if possible, a greater coward than I."

Carmilla came down rather later than usual that day.

"I was so frightened last night," she said, so soon as we were together, "and I am sure I should have seen something dreadful if it had not been for that charm I bought from the poor little hunchback whom I called such hard names. I had a dream of something black coming round my bed, and I awoke in a perfect horror, and

I really thought, for some seconds, I saw a dark figure near the chimney piece, but I felt under my pillow for my charm, and the moment my fingers touched it, the figure disappeared, and I felt quite certain, only that I had it by me, that something frightful would have made its appearance, and, perhaps, throttled me, as it did those poor people we heard of."

"Well, listen to me," I began, and recounted my adventure, at the recital of which she appeared horrified.

"And had you the charm near you?" she asked, earnestly.

"No, I had dropped it into a china vase in the drawing-room, but I shall certainly take it with me to-night, as you have so much faith in it."

At this distance of time I cannot tell you, or even understand, how I overcame my horror so effectually as to lie alone in my room that night. I remember distinctly that I pinned the charm to my pillow. I fell asleep almost immediately, and slept even more soundly than usual all night.

Next night I passed as well. My sleep was delightfully deep and dreamless. But I wakened with a sense of lassitude and melancholy, which, however, did not exceed a degree that was almost luxurious.

"Well, I told you so," said Carmilla, when I described my quiet sleep, "I had such delightful sleep myself last night; I pinned the charm to the breast of my nightdress. It was too far away the night before. I am quite sure it was all fancy, except the dreams. I used to think that evil spirits made dreams, but our doctor told me it is no such thing. Only a fever passing by, or some other malady, as they often do, he said, knocks at the door, and not being able to get in, passes on, with that alarm."

"And what do you think the charm is?" said I.

"It has been fumigated or immersed in some drug, and is an antidote against the malaria," she answered.

"Then it acts only on the body?"

"Certainly; you don't suppose that evil spirits are frightened by bits of ribbon, or the perfumes of a druggist's shop? No, these complaints, wandering in the air, begin by trying the nerves, and so infect the brain; but before they can seize upon you, the antidote repels them. That I am sure is what the charm has done for us. It is nothing magical, it is simply natural."

I should have been happier if I could quite have agreed with Carmilla, but I did my best, and the impression was a little losing its force.

For some nights I slept profoundly; but still every morning I felt the same lassitude, and a languor weighed upon me all day. I felt myself a changed girl. A strange melancholy was stealing over me, a melancholy that I would not have interrupted. Dim thoughts of death began to open, and an idea that I was slowly sinking took gentle, and, somehow, not unwelcome possession of me. If it was sad, the tone of mind which this induced was also sweet. Whatever it might be, my soul acquiesced in it.

I would not admit that I was ill, I would not consent to tell my papa, or to have the doctor sent for.

Carmilla became more devoted to me than ever, and her strange paroxysms of languid adoration more frequent. She used to gloat on me with increasing ardour the more my strength and spirits waned. This always shocked me like a momentary glare of insanity.

Without knowing it, I was now in a pretty advanced stage of the strangest illness under which mortal ever suffered. There was an unaccountable fascination in its earlier symptoms that more than reconciled me to the incapacitating effect of that stage of the malady. This fascination increased for a time, until it reached a certain point, when gradually a sense of the horrible mingled itself with it, deepening, as you shall hear, until it discoloured and perverted the whole state of my life.

The first change I experienced was rather agreeable. It was very near the turning point from which began the descent of Avernus.

Certain vague and strange sensations visited me in my sleep. The prevailing one was of that pleasant, peculiar cold thrill which we feel in bathing, when we move against the current of a river. This was soon accompanied by dreams that seemed interminable, and were so vague that I could never recollect their scenery and persons, or any one connected portion of their action. But they left an awful impression, and a sense of exhaustion, as if I had passed through a long period of great mental exertion and danger. After all these dreams there remained on waking a remembrance of having been in a place very nearly dark, and of having spoken to people whom I could not see; and especially of one clear voice, of a female's, very deep, that spoke as if at a distance, slowly, and producing always the same sensation of indescribable solemnity and fear. Sometimes there came a sensation as if a hand was drawn softly along my cheek and neck. Sometimes it was as if warm lips kissed me, and longer and more lovingly as they reached my throat, but there the caress fixed itself. My heart beat faster, my breathing rose and fell rapidly and full drawn; a sobbing, that rose into a sense of strangulation, supervened, and turned into a dreadful convulsion, in which my senses left me, and I became unconscious.

It was now three weeks since the commencement of this unaccountable state. My sufferings had, during the last week, told upon my appearance. I had grown pale, my eyes were dilated and darkened underneath, and the languor which I had long felt began to display itself in my countenance.

My father asked me often whether I was ill; but, with an obstinacy which now seems to me unaccountable, I persisted in assuring him that I was quite well.

In a sense this was true. I had no pain, I could complain of no bodily derangement. My complaint seemed to be one of the imagination, or the nerves, and, horrible as my sufferings were, I kept them, with a morbid reserve, very nearly to myself.

It could not be that terrible complaint which the peasants call the oupire, for I had now been suffering for three weeks, and they were seldom ill for much more than three days, when death put an end to their miseries.

Carmilla complained of dreams and feverish sensations, but by no means of so alarming a kind as mine. I say that mine were extremely alarming. Had I been capable of comprehending my condition, I would have invoked aid and advice on my knees. The narcotic of an unsuspected influence was acting upon me, and my perceptions were benumbed.

I am going to tell you now of a dream that led immediately to an odd discovery.

One night, instead of the voice I was accustomed to hear in the dark, I heard one, sweet and tender, and at the same time terrible, which said, "Your mother warns you to beware of the assassin." At the same time a light unexpectedly sprang up, and I saw Carmilla, standing, near the foot of my bed, in her white nightdress, bathed, from her chin to her feet, in one great stain of blood.

I wakened with a shriek, possessed with the one idea that Carmilla was being murdered. I remember springing from my bed, and my next recollection is that of standing on the lobby, crying for help.

Madame and Mademoiselle came scurrying out of their rooms in alarm; a lamp burned always on the lobby, and seeing me, they soon learned the cause of my terror.

I insisted on our knocking at Carmilla's door. Our knocking was unanswered. It soon became a pounding and an uproar. We shrieked her name, but all was vain.

We all grew frightened, for the door was locked. We hurried back, in panic, to my room. There we rang the bell long and furiously. If my father's room had been at that side of the house, we would have called him up at once to our aid. But, alas! he was quite out of hearing, and to reach him involved an excursion for which we none of us had courage.

Servants, however, soon came running up the stairs; I had got on my dressing-gown and slippers meanwhile, and my companions were already similarly furnished. Recognizing the voices of the servants on the lobby, we sallied out together; and having renewed, as fruitlessly, our summons at Carmilla's door, I ordered the men to force the lock. They did so, and we stood, holding our lights aloft, in the doorway, and so stared into the room.

We called her by name; but there was still no reply. We looked round the room. Everything was undisturbed. It was exactly in the state in which I left it on bidding her good night. But Carmilla was gone.

CHAPTER VIII

Search

At sight of the room, perfectly undisturbed except for our violent entrance, we began to cool a little, and soon recovered our senses sufficiently to dismiss the men. It had struck Mademoiselle that possibly Carmilla had been wakened by the uproar at her door, and in her first panic had jumped from her bed, and hid herself in a press, or behind a curtain, from which she could not, of course, emerge until the majordomo and his myrmidons had withdrawn. We now recommenced our search, and began to call her by name again.

It was all to no purpose. Our perplexity and agitation increased. We examined the windows, but they were secured. I implored of Carmilla, if she had concealed herself, to play this cruel trick no longer—to come out, and to end our anxieties. It was all useless. I was by this time convinced that she was not in the room, nor in the dressing-room, the door of which was still locked on this side. She could not have passed it. I was utterly puzzled. Had Carmilla discovered one of those secret passages which the old housekeeper said were known to exist in the schloss, although the tradition of their exact situation had been lost? A little time would, no doubt, explain all—utterly perplexed as, for the present, we were.

It was past four o'clock, and I preferred passing the remaining hours of darkness in Madame's room. Daylight brought no solution of the difficulty.

The whole household, with my father at its head, was in a state of agitation next morning. Every part of the château was searched. The grounds were explored. Not a trace of the missing lady could be discovered. The stream was about to be dragged; my father was in distraction; what a tale to have to tell the poor girl's mother on her return. I, too, was almost beside myself, though my grief was quite of a different kind.

The morning was passed in alarm and excitement. It was now one o'clock, and still no tidings. I ran up to Carmilla's room, and found her standing at her dressing-table. I was astounded. I could not believe my eyes. She beckoned me to her with her pretty finger, in silence. Her face expressed extreme fear.

I ran to her in an ecstasy of joy; I kissed and embraced her again and again. I ran to the bell and rang it vehemently, to bring others to the spot, who might at once relieve my father's anxiety.

"Dear Carmilla, what has become of you all this time? We have been in agonies of anxiety about you," I exclaimed. "Where have you been? How did you come back?"

"Last night has been a night of wonders," she said.

"For mercy's sake, explain all you can."

"It was past two last night," she said, "when I went to sleep as usual in my bed, with my doors locked, that of the dressing room, and that opening upon the gallery. My sleep was uninterrupted, and, so far as I know, dreamless; but I awoke just now on the sofa in the dressing-room there, and I found the door between the rooms open, and the other door forced. How could all this have happened without my being wakened? It must have been accompanied with a great deal of noise, and I am particularly easily wakened; and how could I have been carried out of my bed without my sleep having been interrupted, I whom the slightest stir startles?"

By this time, Madame, Mademoiselle, my father, and a number of the servants were in the room. Carmilla, was, of course, overwhelmed with inquiries, congratulations, and welcomes. She had but one story to tell, and seemed the least able of all the party to suggest any way of accounting for what had happened.

My father took a turn up and down the room, thinking. I saw Carmilla's eye follow him for a moment with a sly, dark glance.

When my father had sent the servants away, Mademoiselle having gone in search of a little bottle of valerian and sal-volatile, and there being no one in the room with Carmilla except my father,

Madame, and myself, he came to her thoughtfully, took her hand very kindly, led her to the sofa, and sat down beside her.

"Will you forgive me, my dear, if I risk a conjecture, and ask a question?"

"Who can have a better right?" she said. "Ask what you please, and I will tell you everything. But my story is simply one of bewilderment and darkness. I know absolutely nothing. Put any question you please. But you know, of course, the limitations mamma has placed me under."

"Perfectly, my dear child. I need not approach the topics on which she desires our silence. Now, the marvel of last night consists in your having been removed from your bed and your room without being wakened, and this removal having occurred apparently while the windows were still secured, and the two doors locked upon the inside. I will tell you my theory, and first ask you a question."

Carmilla was leaning on her hand dejectedly; Madame and I were listening breathlessly.

"Now, my question is this. Have you ever been suspected of walking in your sleep?"

"Never since I was very young indeed."

"But you did walk in your sleep when you were very young?"

"Yes; I know I did. I have been told so often by my old nurse."

My father smiled and nodded.

"Well, what has happened is this. You got up in your sleep, unlocked the door, not leaving the key, as usual, in the lock, but taking it out and locking it on the outside; you again took the key out, and carried it away with you to some one of the five-and-twenty rooms on this floor, or perhaps upstairs or downstairs. There are so many rooms and closets, so much heavy furniture, and such accumulations of lumber, that it would require a week to search this old house thoroughly. Do you see, now, what I mean?"

"I do, but not all," she answered.

"And how, papa, do you account for her finding herself on the sofa in the dressing-room, which we had searched so carefully?"

"She came there after you had searched it, still in her sleep, and at last awoke spontaneously, and was as much surprised to find herself where she was as any one else. I wish all mysteries were as easily and innocently explained as yours, Carmilla," he said, laughing. "And so we may congratulate ourselves on the certainty that the most natural explanation of the occurrence is one that involves no drugging, no tampering with locks, no burglars, or poisoners, or witches—nothing that need alarm Carmilla, or any one else, for our safety."

Carmilla was looking charmingly. Nothing could be more beautiful than her tints. Her beauty was, I think, enhanced by that graceful languor that was peculiar to her. I think my father was silently contrasting her looks with mine, for he said:—

"I wish my poor Laura was looking more like herself;" and he sighed.

So our alarms were happily ended, and Carmilla restored to her friends.

CHAPTER IX

The Doctor

As Carmilla would not hear of an attendant sleeping in her room, my father arranged that a servant should sleep outside her door, so that she could not attempt to make another such excursion without being arrested at her own door.

That night passed quickly; and next morning early, the doctor, whom my father had sent for without telling me a word about it, arrived to see me.

Madame accompanied me to the library; and there the grave little doctor, with white hair and spectacles, whom I mentioned before, was waiting to receive me.

I told him my story, and as I proceeded he grew graver and graver.

We were standing, he and I, in the recess of one of the windows, facing one another. When my statement was over, he leaned with his shoulders against the wall, and with his eyes fixed on me earnestly, with an interest in which was a dash of horror.

After a minute's reflection, he asked Madame if he could see my father.

He was sent for accordingly, and as he entered, smiling, he said:

"I dare say, doctor, you are going to tell me that I am an old fool for having brought you here; I hope I am."

But his smile faded into shadow as the doctor, with a very grave face, beckoned him to him.

He and the doctor talked for some time in the same recess where

I had just conferred with the physician. It seemed an earnest and argumentative conversation. The room is very large, and I and Madame stood together, burning with curiosity, at the further end. Not a word could we hear, however, for they spoke in a very low tone, and the deep recess of the window quite concealed the doctor from view, and very nearly my father, whose foot, arm, and shoulder only could we see: and the voices were, I suppose, all the less audible for the sort of closet which the thick wall and window formed.

After a time my father's face looked into the room; it was pale, thoughtful, and, I fancied, agitated.

"Laura, dear, come here for a moment. Madame, we shan't trouble you, the doctor says, at present."

Accordingly I approached, for the first time a little alarmed; for, although I felt very weak, I did not feel ill; and strength, one always fancies, is a thing that may be picked up when we please.

My father held out his hand to me as I drew near, but he was looking at the doctor, and he said:

"It certainly *is* very odd; I don't understand it quite. Laura, come here, dear; now attend to Doctor Spielsberg, and recollect yourself."

"You mentioned a sensation like that of two needles piercing the skin, somewhere about your neck, on the night when you experienced your first horrible dream. Is there still any soreness?"

"None at all," I answered.

"Can you indicate with your finger about the point at which you think this occurred?"

"Very little below my throat—*here*," I answered.

I wore a morning dress, which covered the place I pointed to.

"Now you can satisfy yourself," said the doctor. "You won't mind your papa's lowering your dress a very little. It is necessary, to detect a symptom of the complaint under which you have been suffering."

I acquiesced. It was only an inch or two below the edge of my collar.

"God bless me!—so it is," exclaimed my father, growing pale.

"You see it now with your own eyes," said the doctor, with a gloomy triumph.

"What is it?" I exclaimed, beginning to be frightened.

"Nothing, my dear young lady, but a small blue spot, about the size of the tip of your little finger; and now," he continued, turning to papa, "the question is what is the best to be done?"

"Is there any danger?" I urged, in great trepidation.

"I trust not, my dear," answered the doctor. "I don't see why you should not recover. I don't see why you should not begin *immediately* to get better. That is the point at which the sense of strangulation begins?"

"Yes," I answered.

"And—recollect as well as you can—the same point was a kind of centre of that thrill which you described just now like the current of a cold stream running against you?"

"It may have been; I think it was."

"Ay, you see?" he added, turning to my father. "Shall I say a word to Madame?"

"Certainly," said my father.

He called Madame to him, and said:

"I find my young friend here far from well. It won't be of any great consequence, I hope; but it will be necessary that some steps be taken, which I will explain by-and-by; but in the meantime, Madame, you will be so good as not to let Miss Laura be alone for one moment. That is the only direction I need give for the present. It is indispensable."

"We may rely upon your kindness, Madame, I know," added my father.

Madame satisfied him eagerly.

"And you, dear Laura, I know you will observe the doctor's direction."

"I shall have to ask your opinion upon another patient, whose symptoms slightly resemble those of my daughter, that have just been detailed to you—very much milder in degree, but I believe quite of the same sort. She is a young lady—our guest; but as you say you will be passing this way again this evening, you can't do better than take your supper here, and you can then see her. She does not come down till the afternoon."

"I thank you," said the doctor. "I shall be with you, then, at about seven this evening."

And then they repeated their directions to me and to Madame, and with this parting charge my father left us, and walked out with the doctor; and I saw them pacing together up and down between the road and the moat, on the grassy platform in front of the castle, evidently absorbed in earnest conversation.

The doctor did not return. I saw him mount his horse there, take his leave, and ride away eastward through the forest. Nearly at the same time I saw the man arrive from Dranfeld with the letters, and dismount and hand the bag to my father.

In the meantime, Madame and I were both busy, lost in conjecture as to the reasons of the singular and earnest direction which the doctor and my father had concurred in imposing. Madame, as she afterwards told me, was afraid the doctor apprehended a sudden seizure, and that, without prompt assistance, I might either lose my life in a fit, or at least be seriously hurt.

This interpretation did not strike me; and I fancied, perhaps luckily for my nerves, that the arrangement was prescribed simply to secure a companion, who would prevent my taking too much exercise, or eating unripe fruit, or doing any of the fifty foolish thing to which young people are supposed to be prone.

About half-an-hour after my father came in—he had a letter in his hand—and said:

"This letter has been delayed; it is from General Spielsdorf. He might have been here yesterday, he may not come till to-morrow, or he may be here to-day."

He put the open letter into my hand; but he did not look pleased, as he used when a guest, especially one so much loved as the General, was coming. On the contrary, he looked as if he wished him at the bottom of the Red Sea. There was plainly something on his mind which he did not choose to divulge.

"Papa, darling, will you tell me this?" said I, suddenly laying my hand on his arm, and looking, I am sure, imploringly in his face.

"Perhaps," he answered, smoothing my hair caressingly over my eyes.

"Does the doctor think me very ill?"

"No, dear; he thinks, if right steps are taken, you will be quite well again, at least on the high road to a complete recovery, in a day or two," he answered, a little drily. "I wish our good friend, the General, had chosen any other time; that is, I wish you had been perfectly well to receive him."

"But do tell me papa," I insisted, *what* does he think is the matter with me?"

"Nothing; you must not plague me with questions," he answered, with more irritation than I ever remember him to have displayed before; and seeing that I looked wounded, I suppose, he kissed me, and added, "You shall know all about it in a day or two; that is, all that *I* know. In the meantime, you are not to trouble your head about it."

He turned and left the room, but came back before I had done wondering and puzzling over the oddity of all this; it was merely to say that he was going to Karnstein, and had ordered the carriage to be ready at twelve, and that I and Madame should accompany him; he was going to see the priest who lived near those picturesque grounds, upon business, and as Carmilla had never seen them, she could follow, when she came down, with Mademoiselle, who would bring materials for what you call a pic-nic, which might be laid for us in the ruined castle.

At twelve o'clock, accordingly, I was ready, and not long after, my father, Madame and I set out upon our projected drive. Passing the drawbridge we turn to the right, and follow the road over the steep Gothic bridge, westward, to reach the deserted village and ruined castle of Karnstein.

No sylvan drive can be fancied prettier. The ground breaks into gentle hills and hollows, all clothed with beautiful wood, totally destitute of the comparative formality which artificial planting and early culture and pruning impart.

The irregularities of the ground often lead the road out of its course, and cause it to wind beautifully round the sides of broken hollows and the steeper sides of the hills, among varieties of ground almost inexhaustible.

Turning one of these points, we suddenly encountered our old friend, the General, riding towards us, attended by a mounted servant. His portmanteaus were following in a hired waggon, such as we term a cart.

The General dismounted as we pulled up, and, after the usual greetings, was easily persuaded to accept the vacant seat in the carriage, and send his horse on with his servant to the schloss.

CHAPTER X

Bereaved

It was about ten months since we had last seen him; but that time had sufficed to make an alteration of years in his appearance. He had grown thinner; something of gloom and anxiety had taken the place of that cordial serenity which used to characterise his features. His dark blue eyes, always penetrating, now gleamed with a sterner light from under his shaggy grey eyebrows. It was not such a change as grief alone usually induces, and angrier passions seemed to have had their share in bringing it about.

We had not long resumed our drive, when the General began to talk, with his usual soldierly directness, of the bereavement, as he termed it, which he had sustained in the death of his beloved niece and ward; and he then broke out in a tone of intense bitterness and fury, inveighing against the "hellish arts" to which she had fallen a victim, and expressing with more exasperation than piety, his wonder that Heaven should tolerate so monstrous an indulgence of the lusts and malignity of hell.

My father, who saw at once that something very extraordinary had befallen, asked him, if not too painful to him, to detail the circumstances which he thought justified the strong terms in which he expressed himself.

"I should tell you all with pleasure," said the General, "but you would not believe me."

"Why should I not?" he asked.

"Because," he answered testily, "you believe in nothing but what consists with your own prejudices and illusions. I remember when I was like you, but I have learned better."

"Try me," said my father; "I am not such a dogmatist as you suppose. Besides which, I very well know that you generally require proof for what you believe and am, therefore, very strongly predisposed to respect your conclusions."

"You are right in supposing that I have not been led lightly into a belief in the marvellous—for what I have experienced *is* marvellous—and I have been forced by extraordinary evidence to credit that which ran counter, diametrically, to all my theories. I have been made the dupe of a preternatural conspiracy."

Notwithstanding his profession of confidence in the General's penetration, I saw my father, at this point, glance at the General, with, as I thought, a marked suspicion of his sanity.

The General did not see it, luckily. He was looking gloomily and curiously into the glades and vistas of the woods that were opening before us.

"You are going to the Ruins of Karnstein?" he said. "Yes, it is a lucky coincidence; do you know I was going to ask you to bring me there to inspect them. I have a special object in exploring. There is a ruined chapel, ain't there, with a great many tombs of that extinct family?"

"So there are—highly interesting," said my father, "I hope you are thinking of claiming the title and estates?"

My father said this gaily, but the General did not recollect the laugh, or even smile, which courtesy exacts for a friend's joke; on the contrary, he looked grave and even fierce, ruminating on a matter that stirred his anger and horrror.

"Something very different," he said, gruffly. "I mean to unearth some of those fine people. I hope by God's blessing, to accomplish a pious sacrilege here, which will relieve our earth of certain monsters, and enable honest people to sleep in their beds without being assailed by murderers. I have strange things to tell you, my dear friend, such as I myself would have scouted as incredible a few months since."

My father looked at him again, but this time not with a glance of suspicion—with an eye, rather, of keen intelligence and alarm.

"The house of Karnstein," he said, "has been long extinct: a hundred years at least. My dear wife was maternally descended from the Karnsteins. But the name and title have long ceased to exist. The castle is a ruin; the very village is deserted; it is fifty years since the smoke of a chimney was seen there; not a roof left."

"Quite true. I have heard a great deal about that since I last saw you; a great deal that will astonish you. But I had better relate everything in the order in which it occurred," said the General. "You saw my dear ward—my child, I may call her. No creature could have been more beautiful, and only three months ago none more blooming."

"Yes, poor thing! when I saw her last she certainly was quite lovely," said my father. "I was grieved and shocked more than I can tell you, my dear friend; I knew what a blow it was to you."

He took the General's hand, and they exchanged a kind pressure. Tears gathered in the old soldier's eyes. He did not seek to conceal them. He said:

"We have been very old friends; I knew you would feel for me, childless as I am. She had become an object of very dear interest to me, and repaid my care by an affection that cheered my home and made my life happy. That is all gone. The years that remain to me on earth may not be very long; but by God's mercy I hope to accomplish a service to mankind before I die, and to subserve the vengeance of Heaven upon the fiends who have murdered my poor child in the spring of her hopes and beauty!"

"You said, just now, that you intended relating everything as it occurred," said my father. "Pray do; I assure you that it is not mere curiosity that prompts me."

By this time we had reached the point at which the Drunstall road, by which the General had come, diverges from the road which we were travelling to Karnstein.

"How far is it to the ruins?" inquired the General, looking anxiously forward.

"About half a league," answered my father. "Pray let us hear the story you were so good as to promise."

CHAPTER XI

The Story

"With all my heart," said the General, with an effort; and after a pause in which to arrange his subject, he commenced one of the strangest narratives I ever heard.

"My dear child was looking forward with great pleasure to the visit you had been so good as to arrange for her to your charming daughter." Here he made me a gallant but melancholy bow. "In the meantime we had an invitation to my old friend the Count Carlsfeld, whose schloss is about six leagues to the other side of Karnstein. It was to attend the series of fêtes which, you remember, were given by him in honor of his illustrious visitor, the Grand Duke Charles."

"Yes; and very splendid, I believe they were," said my father.

"Princely! But then his hospitalities are quite regal. He has Aladdin's lamp. The night from which my sorrow dates was devoted to a magnificent masquerade. The grounds were thrown open, the trees hung with coloured lamps. There was such a display of fireworks as Paris itself had never witnessed. And such music—music, you know, is my weakness—such ravishing music! The finest instrumental band, perhaps, in the world, and the finest singers who could be collected from all the great operas in Europe. As you wandered through those fantastically illuminated grounds, the moon-lighted château throwing a rosy light from its long rows of windows, you would suddenly hear these ravishing voices stealing from the silence of some grove, or rising from boats upon the lake. I felt myself, as I looked and listened, carried back into the romance and poetry of my early youth.

"When the fireworks were ended, and the ball beginning, we returned to the noble suite of rooms that were thrown open to the dancers. A masked ball, you know, is a beautiful sight; but so brilliant a spectacle of the kind I never saw before.

"It was a very aristocratic assembly. I saw myself almost the only 'nobody' present.

"My dear child was looking quite beautiful. She wore no mask. Her excitement and delight added an unspeakable charm to her features, always lovely. I remarked a young lady, dressed magnificently, but wearing a mask, who appeared to me to be observing my ward with extraordinary interest. I had seen her, earlier in the evening, in the great hall, and again, for a few minutes, walking near us, on the terrace under the castle windows, similarly employed. A lady, also masked, richly and gravely dressed, and with stately air, like a person of rank, accompanied her as a chaperon. Had the young lady not worn a mask, I could of course, have been much more certain upon the question whether she was really watching my poor darling. I am now well assured that she was.

"We were in one of the *salons*. My poor dear child had been dancing, and was resting a little in one of the chairs near the door; I was standing near. The two ladies I have mentioned had approached, and the younger took the chair next my ward; while her companion stood beside me, and for a little time addressed herself, in a low tone, to her charge.

"Availing herself of the privilege of her mask, she turned to me, and in the tone of an old friend, and calling me by my name, opened a conversation with me, which piqued my curiosity a good deal. She referred to many scenes where she had met me—at Court, and at distinguished houses. She alluded to little incidents which I had long ceased to think of, but which, I found, had only lain in abeyance in my memory, for they instantly started into life at her touch.

"I became more and more curious to ascertain who she was, every moment. She parried my attempts to discover very adroitly and pleasantly. The knowledge she showed of many passages in my life seemed to me all but unaccountable; and she appeared to take a not unnatural pleasure in foiling my curiosity, and in seeing me flounder, in my eager perplexity, from one conjecture to another.

"In the meantime the young lady, whom her mother called by the odd name of Millarca, when she once or twice addressed her, had, with the same ease and grace, got into conversation with my ward.

"She introduced herself by saying that her mother was a very old acquaintance of mine. She spoke of the agreeable audacity which a mask rendered practicable; she talked like a friend; she admired her dress, and insinuated very prettily her admiration of her beauty. She amused her with laughing criticisms upon the people who crowded the ballroom, and laughed at my poor child's fun. She was very witty and lively when she pleased, and after a time they had grown very good friends, and the young stranger lowered her mask, displaying a remarkably beautiful face. I had never seen it before, neither had my dear child. But though it was new to us, the features were so engaging, as well as lovely, that it was impossible not to feel the attraction powerfully. My poor girl did so. I never saw anyone more taken with another at first sight, unless, indeed, it was the stranger herself, who seemed quite to have lost her heart to her.

"In the meantime, availing myself of the licence of a masquerade, I put not a few questions to the elder lady.

" 'You have puzzled me utterly,' I said, laughing. 'Is that not enough? won't you, now, consent to stand on equal terms, and do me the kindness to remove your mask?'

" 'Can any request be more unreasonable?' she replied. 'Ask a lady to yield an advantage! Beside, how do you know you should recognize me? Years make changes.'

" 'As you see,' I said, with a bow, and, I suppose, a rather melancholy little laugh.

" 'As philosophers tell us,' she said; 'and how do you know that a sight of my face would help you?'

" 'I should take chance for that,' I answered. 'It is vain trying to make yourself out an old woman; your figure betrays you.'

" 'Years, nevertheless, have passed since I saw you, rather since you saw me, for that is what I am considering. Millarca, there, is my daughter; I cannot then be young, even in the opinion of people whom time has taught to be indulgent, and I may not like to be compared with what you remember me. You have no mask to remove. You can offer me nothing in exchange.'

" 'My petition is to your pity, to remove it.'

" 'And mine to yours, to let it stay where it is,' she replied.

" 'Well, then, at least you will tell me whether you are French or German; you speak both languages so perfectly.'

" 'I don't think I shall tell you that, General; you intend a surprise, and are meditating the particular point of attack.'

" 'At all events, you won't deny this,' I said, 'that being honoured by your permission to converse, I ought to know how to address you. Shall I say Madame la Comtesse?'

"She laughed, and she would, no doubt, have met me with another evasion—if, indeed, I can treat any occurrence in an interview every circumstance of which was pre-arranged, as I now believe, with the profoundest cunning, as liable to be modified by accident.

" 'As to that,' she began; but she was interrupted, almost as she opened her lips, by a gentleman, dressed in black, who looked particularly elegant and distinguished, with this drawback, that his face was the most deadly pale I ever saw, except in death. He was in no masquerade—in the plain evening dress of a gentleman; and he said, without a smile, but with a courtly and unusually low bow:—

"Will Madame la Comtesse permit me to say a very few words which may interest her?'

"The lady turned quickly to him, and touched her lip in token of silence; she then said to me, 'Keep my place for me, General; I shall return when I have said a few words.'

"And with this injunction, playfully given, she walked a little aside with the gentleman in black, and talked for some minutes, apparently very earnestly. They then walked away slowly together in the crowd, and I lost them for some minutes.

"I spent the interval in cudgelling my brains for conjecture as to the identity of the lady who seemed to remember me so kindly, and I was thinking of turning about and joining in the conversation between my pretty ward and the Countess's daughter, and trying whether, by the time she returned, I might not have a surprise in store for her, by having her name, title, château, and estates at my fingers' ends. But at this moment she returned, accompanied by the pale man in black, who said:

" 'I shall return and inform Madame la Comtesse when her carriage is at the door.'

"He withdrew with a bow."

CHAPTER XII

A Petition

" 'Then we are to lose Madame la Comtesse, but I hope only for a few hours,' I said, with a low bow.

" 'It may be that only, or it may be a few weeks. It was very unlucky his speaking to me just now as he did. Do you now know me?"

"I assured her I did not.

" 'You shall know me,' she said, 'but not at present. We are older and better friends than, perhaps, you suspect. I cannot yet declare myself. I shall in three weeks pass your beautiful schloss about which I have been making enquiries. I shall then look in upon you for an hour or two, and renew a friendship which I never think of without a thousand pleasant recollections. This moment a piece of news has reached me like a thunderbolt. I must set out now, and travel by a devious route, nearly a hundred miles, with all the dispatch I can possibly make. My perplexities multiply. I am only deterred by the compulsory reserve I practise as to my name from making a very singular request of you. My poor child has not quite recovered her strength. Her horse fell with her, at a hunt which she had ridden out to witness, her nerves have not yet recovered the shock, and our physician says that she must on no account exert herself for some time to come. We came here, in consequence, by very easy stages—hardly six leagues a day. I must now travel day and night, on a mission of life and death—a mission the critical and momentous nature of which I shall be able to explain to you when we meet, as I hope we shall, in a few weeks, without the necessity of any concealment.'

"She went on to make her petition, and it was in the tone of a person from whom such a request amounted to conferring, rather than seeking a favour. This was only in manner, and, as it seemed, quite unconsciously. Than the terms in which it was expressed, nothing could be more deprecatory. It was simply that I would consent to take charge of her daughter during her absence.

"This was, all things considered, a strange, not to say, an audacious request. She in some sort disarmed me, by stating and admitting everything that could be urged against it, and throwing herself entirely upon my chivalry. At the same moment, by a fatality that seems to have predetermined all that happened, my poor child came to my side, and, in an undertone, besought me to invite her new friend, Millarca, to pay us a visit. She had just been sounding her, and thought, if her mamma would allow her, she would like it extremely.

"At another time I should have told her to wait a little, until, at least, we knew who they were. But I had not a moment to think in. The two ladies assailed me together, and I must confess the refined and beautiful face of the young lady, about which there was something extremely engaging, as well as the elegance and fire of high birth, determined me; and quite overpowered, I submitted, and undertook, too easily, the care of the young lady, whom her mother called Millarca.

"The Countess beckoned to her daughter, who listened with grave attention while she told her, in general terms, how suddenly and peremptorily she had been summoned, and also of the arrangement she had made for her under my care, adding that I was one of her earliest and most valued friends.

"I made, of course, such speeches as the case seemed to call for, and found myself, on reflection, in a position which I did not half like.

"The gentleman in black returned, and very ceremoniously conducted the lady from the room.

"The demeanour of this gentleman was such as to impress me with the conviction that the Countess was a lady of very much more importance than her modest title alone might have led me to assume.

"Her last charge to me was that no attempt was to be made to learn more about her than I might have already guessed, until her return. Our distinguished host, whose guest she was, knew her reasons.

" 'But here,' she said, 'neither I nor my daughter could safely remain more than a day. I removed my mask imprudently for a moment, about an hour ago, and, too late, I fancied you saw me. So I have resolved to seek an opportunity of talking a little to you, Had I found that you *had* seen me, I should have thrown myself on your high sense of honour to keep my secret for some weeks. As it is, I am satisfied that you did not see me; but if you now *suspect,* or, on reflection, *should* suspect, who I am, I commit myself, in like manner, entirely to your honour. My daughter will observe the same secresy, and I well know that you will, from time to time, remind her, lest she should thoughtlessly disclose it.'

"She whispered a few words to her daughter, kissed her hurriedly twice, and went away, accompanied by the pale gentleman in black, and disappeared in the crowd.

" 'In the next room,' said Millarca, 'there is a window that looks upon the hall door. I should like to see the last of mamma, and to kiss my hand to her.'

"We assented, of course, and accompanied her to the window. We looked out, and saw a handsome old-fashioned carriage, with a troop of couriers and footmen. We saw the slim figure of the pale gentleman in black, as he held a thick velvet cloak, and placed it about her shoulders and threw the hood over her head. She nodded to him, and just touched his hand with hers. He bowed low repeatedly as the door closed, and the carriage began to move.

" 'She is gone,' said Millarca with a sigh.

" 'She is gone,' I repeated to myself, for the first time—in the hurried moments that had elapsed since my consent—reflecting upon the folly of my act.

" 'She did not look up,' said the young lady, plaintively.

" 'The Countess had taken off her mask, perhaps, and did not care to show her face,' I said; 'and she could not know that you were in the window.'

"She sighed and looked in my face. She was so beautiful that I relented. I was sorry I had for a moment repented of my hospitality, and I determined to make her amends for the unavowed churlishness of my reception.

"The young lady, replacing her mask, joined my ward in persuading me to return to the grounds, where the concert was soon to be renewed. We did so, and walked up and down the terrace that lies under the castle windows. Millarca became very intimate with us, and amused us with lively descriptions and stories of most of the great people whom we saw upon the terrace. I liked her more and more every minute. Her gossip, without being ill-natured, was extremely diverting to me, who had been so long out of the great world. I thought what life she would give to our sometimes lonely evenings at home.

"This ball was not over until the morning sun had almost reached the horizon. It pleased the Grand Duke to dance till then, so loyal people could not go away, or think of bed.

"We had just got through a crowded saloon, when my ward asked me what had become of Millarca. I thought she had been by her side, and she fancied she was by mine. The fact was, we had lost her.

"All my efforts to find her were in vain. I feared that she had mistaken, in the confusion of the momentary separation from us, other people for her new friends, and had, possibly, pursued and lost them in the extensive grounds which were thrown open to us.

"Now, in its full force, I recognized a new folly in my having undertaken the charge of a young lady without so much as knowing her name; and fettered as I was by promises, of the reasons for imposing which I knew nothing, I could not even point my inquiries by saying that the missing young lady was the daughter of the Countess who had taken her departure a few hours before.

"Morning broke. It was clear daylight before I gave up my search. It was not till near two o'clock next day that we heard anything of my missing charge.

"At about that time a servant knocked at my niece's door, to say that he had been earnestly requested by a young lady, who appeared to be in great distress, to make out where she could find the General Baron Spielsdorf and the young lady, his daughter, in whose charge she had been left by her mother.

"There could be no doubt, notwithstanding the slight inaccuracy, that our young friend had turned up; and so she had. Would to Heaven we had lost her!

"She told my poor child a story to account for her having failed to recover us for so long. Very late, she said, she had got into the housekeeper's bedroom in despair of finding us, and had then fallen into a deep sleep which, long as it was, had hardly sufficed to recruit her strength after the fatigues of the ball.

"That day Millarca came home with us. I was only too happy, after all, to have secured so charming a companion for my dear girl.

CHAPTER XIII

The Wood-Man

"There soon, however, appeared some drawbacks. In the first place, Millarca complained of extreme languor—the weakness that remained after her late illness—and she never emerged from her room till the afternoon was pretty far advanced. In the next place, it was accidentally discovered, although she always locked her door on the inside, and never disturbed the key from its place, till she admitted the maid to assist at her toilet, that she was undoubtedly sometimes absent from her room in the very early morning, and at various times later in the day, before she wished it to be understood that she was stirring. She was repeatedly seen from the windows of the schloss, in the first faint grey of the morning, walking through the trees, in an easterly direction, and looking like a person in a trance. This convinced me that she walked in her sleep. But this hypothesis did not solve the puzzle. How did she pass out from her room, leaving the door locked on the inside. How did she escape from the house without unbarring door or window?

"In the midst of my perplexities, an anxiety of far more urgent kind presented itself.

"My dear child began to lose her looks and health, and that in a manner so mysterious, and even horrible, that I became thoroughly frightened.

"She was at first visited by appalling dreams; then, as she fancied, by a spectre, sometimes resembling Millarca, sometimes in the shape of a beast, indistinctly seen, walking round the foot of her bed, from side to side. Lastly came sensations. One, not unpleasant, but very peculiar, she said, resembled the flow of an icy stream against her breast. At a later time, she felt something like a pair of large needles pierce her, a little below the throat, with a very sharp pain. A few nights after, followed a gradual and convulsive sense of strangulation; then came unconsciousness."

I could hear distinctly every word the kind old General was saying, because by this time we were driving upon the short grass that
spreads on either side of the road as you approach the roofless
village which had not shown the smoke of a chimney for more
than half a century.

You may guess how strangely I felt as I heard my own symptoms
so exactly described in those which had been experienced by the
poor girl who, but for the catastrophe which followed, would have
been at that moment a visitor at my father's château. You may
suppose, also, how I felt as I heard him detail habits and mysterious peculiarities which were, in fact, those of our beautiful guest,
Carmilla!

A vista opened in the forest; we were on a sudden under the
chimneys and gables of the ruined village, and the towers and
battlements of the dismantled castle, round which gigantic trees
are grouped, overhung us from a slight eminence.

In a frightened dream I got down from the carriage, and in
silence, for we had each abundant matter for thinking; we soon
mounted the ascent, and were among the spacious chambers,
winding stairs, and dark corridors of the castle.

"And this was once the palatial residence of the Karnsteins!"
said the old General at length, as from a great window he looked
out across the village, and saw the wide, undulating expanse of
forest. "It was a bad family, and here its blood-stained annals were
written," he continued. "It is hard that they should, after death,
continue to plague the human race with their atrocious lusts. That
is the chapel of the Karnsteins, down there."

He pointed down to the grey walls of the Gothic building, partly
visible through the foliage, a little way down the steep. "And I
hear the axe of a woodman," he added, "busy among the trees that
surround it; he possibly may give us the information of which I
am in search, and point out the grave of Mircalla, Countess of
Karnstein. These rustics preserve the local traditions of great families, whose stories die out among the rich and titled so soon as
the families themselves become extinct."

"We have a portrait, at home, of of Mircalla, the Countess Karnstein; should you like to see it?" asked my father.

"Time enough," dear friend, replied the General. "I believe
that I have seen the original; and one motive which has led me to
you earlier that I at first intended, was to explore the chapel which
we are now approaching."

"What! see the Countess Mircalla," exclaimed my father;
"why, she has been dead more than a century!"

"Not so dead as you fancy, I am told," answered the General.

"I confess, General, you puzzle me utterly," replied my father, looking at him, I fancied, for a moment with a return of the suspicion I detected before. But although there was anger and detestation, at times, in the old General's manner, there was nothing flighty.

"There remains to me," he said, as we passed under the heavy arch of the Gothic church—for its dimensions would have justified its being so styled—"but one object which can interest me during the few years that remain to me on earth, and that is to wreak on her the vengeance which, I thank God, may still be accomplished by a mortal arm."

"What vengeance can you mean?" asked my father, in increasing amazement.

"I mean, to decapitate the monster," he answered, with a fierce flush, and a stamp that echoed mournfully through the hollow ruin, and his clenched hand was at the same moment raised, as if it grasped the handle of an axe, while he shook it ferociously in the air.

"What!" exclaimed my father, more than ever bewildered.

"To strike her head off."

"Cut her head off!"

"Aye, with a hatchet, with a spade, or with anything that can cleave through her murderous throat. You shall hear," he answered, trembling with rage. And hurrying forward he said:

"That beam will answer for a seat; your dear child is fatigued; let her be seated, and I will, in a few sentences, close my dreadful story."

The squared block of wood, which lay on the grass-grown pavement of the chapel, formed a bench on which I was very glad to seat myself, and in the meantime the General called to the woodman, who had been removing some boughs which leaned upon the old walls; and, axe in hand, the hardy old fellow stood before us.

He could not tell us anything of these monuments; but there was an old man, he said, a ranger of this forest, at present sojourning in the house of the priest, about two miles away, who could point out every monument of the old Karnstein family; and, for a trifle, he undertook to bring back with him, if we would lend him one of our horses, in little more than half-an-hour.

"Have you been long employed about this forest?" asked my father of the old man.

"I have been a woodman here," he answered in his *patois*, "under the forester, all my days; so has my father before me, and so on, as many generations as I can count up. I could show you the very house in the village here, in which my ancestors lived."

"How came the village to be deserted?" asked the General.

"It was troubled by *revenants,* sir; several were tracked to their graves, there detected by the usual tests, and extinguished in the usual way, by decapitation, by the stake, and by burning; but not until many of the villagers were killed.

"But after all these proceedings according to law," he continued —"so many graves opened, and so many vampires deprived of their horrible animation—the village was not relieved. But a Moravian nobleman, who happened to be travelling this way, heard how matters were, and being skilled—as many people are in his country—in such affairs, he offered to deliver the village from its tormentor. He did so thus: There being a bright moon that night, he ascended, shortly after sunset, the tower of the chapel here, from whence he could distinctly see the churchyard beneath him; you can see it from that window. From this point he watched until he saw the vampire come out of his grave, and place near it the linen clothes in which he had been folded, and glide away towards the village to plague its inhabitants.

"The stranger, having seen all this, came down from the steeple, took the linen wrappings of the vampire, and carried them up to the top of the tower, which he again mounted. When the vampire returned from his prowlings and missed his clothes, he cried furiously to the Moravian, whom he saw at the summit of the tower, and who, in reply, beckoned him to ascend and take them. Whereupon the vampire, accepting his invitation, began to climb the steeple, and so soon as he had reached the battlements, the Moravian, with a stroke of his sword, clove his skull in twain, hurling him down to the churchyard, whither, descending by the winding stairs, the stranger followed and cut his head off, and next day delivered it and the body to the villagers, who duly impaled and burnt them.

"This Moravian nobleman had the authority from the then head of the family to remove the tomb of Mircalla, Countess Karnstein, which he did effectually, so that in a little while its site was quite forgotten."

"Can you point out where it stood?" asked the General, eagerly.

The forester shook his head and smiled.

"Not a living soul could tell you that now," he said; "besides, they say her body was removed; but no one is sure of that either."

Having thus spoken, as time pressed, he dropped his axe and departed, leaving us to hear the remainder of the General's strange story.

CHAPTER XIV
The Meeting

"My beloved child," he resumed, "was now growing rapidly worse. The physician who attended her had failed to produce the slightest impression upon her disease, for such I then supposed it to be. He saw my alarm, and suggested a consultation. I called in an abler physician, from Gratz. Several days elapsed before he arrived. He was a good and pious, as well as a learned man. Having seen my poor ward together, they withdrew to my library to confer and discuss. I, from the adjoining room, where I awaited their summons, heard these two gentlemen's voices raised in something sharper than a strictly philosophical discussion. I knocked at the door and entered. I found the old physician from Gratz maintaining his theory. His rival was combating it with undisguised ridicule, accompanied with bursts of laughter. This unseemly manifestation subsided and the altercation ended on my entrance.

" 'Sir,' said my first physician, 'my learned brother seems to think that you want a conjuror, and not a doctor.'

" 'Pardon me,' said the old physician from Gratz, looking displeased, 'I shall state my own view of the case in my own way another time. I grieve, Monsieur le Général, that by my skill and science I can be of no use. Before I go I shall do myself the honour to suggest something to you.'

"He seemed thoughtful, and sat down at a table, and began to write. Profoundly disappointed, I made my bow, and as I turned to go, the other doctor pointed over his shoulder to his companion who was writing, and then, with a shrug, significantly touched his forehead.

"This consultation, then, left me precisely where I was. I walked out into the grounds, all but distracted. The doctor from Gratz, in ten or fifteen minutes, overtook me. He apologised for having followed me, but said that he could not conscientiously take his leave without a few words more. He told me that he could not be mistaken; no natural disease exhibited the same symptoms; and that death was already very near. There remained, however, a day, or possibly two, of life. If the fatal seizure were at once arrested, with great care and skill her strength might possibly return. But all hung now upon the confines of the irrevocable. One more assault might extinguish the last spark of vitality which is, every moment, ready to die.

" 'And what is the nature of the seizure you speak of?' I entreated.

" 'I have stated all fully in this note, which I place in your hands, upon the distinct condition that you send for the nearest clergyman, and open my letter in his presence, and on no account read it till he is with you; you would despise it else, and it is a matter of life and death. Should the priest fail you, then, indeed, you may read it.'

"He asked me, before taking his leave finally, whether I would wish to see a man curiously learned upon the very subject, which, after I had read his letter, would probably interest me above all others, and he urged me earnestly to invite him to visit him there; and so took his leave.

"The ecclesiastic was absent, and I read the letter by myself. At another time, or in another case, it might have excited my ridicule. But into what quackeries will not people rush for a last chance, where all accustomed means have failed, and the life of a beloved object is at stake?

"Nothing, you will say, could be more absurd than the learned man's letter. It was monstrous enough to have consigned him to a madhouse. He said that the patient was suffering from the visits of a vampire! The punctures which she described as having occurred near the throat, were, he insisted, the insertion of those two long, thin, and sharp teeth which, it is well known, are peculiar to vampires; and there could be no doubt, he added, as to the well defined presence of the small livid mark which all concurred in describing as that induced by the demon's lips, and every symptom described by the sufferer was in exact conformity with those recorded in every case of a similar visitation.

"Being myself wholly sceptical as to the exisence of any such portent as the vampire, the supernatural theory of the good doctor furnished, in my opinion, but another instance of learning and intelligence oddly associated with some one hallucination. I was so miserable, however, that, rather than try nothing, I acted upon the instructions of the letter.

"I concealed myself in the dark dressing-room, that opened upon the poor patient's room, in which a candle was burning, and watched there until she was fast asleep. I stood at the door, peeping through the small crevice, my sword laid on the table beside me, as my directions prescribed, until, a little after one, I saw a large black object, very ill-defined, crawl, as it seemed to me, over the foot of the bed, and swiftly spread itself up to the poor girl's throat, where it swelled, in a moment, into a great, palpitating mass.

"For a few moments I had stood petrified. I now sprang forward, with my sword in my hand. The black creature suddenly contracted toward the foot of the bed, glided over it, and, standing on the floor about a yard below the foot of the bed, with a glare of skulking ferocity and horror fixed on me, I saw Millarca. Speculating I know not what, I struck at her instantly with my sword; but I saw her standing near the door, unscathed. Horrified, I pursued, and struck again. She was gone! and my sword flew to shivers against the door.

"I can't describe to you all that passed on that horrible night. The whole house was up and stirring. The spectre Millarca was gone. But her victim was sinking fast, and before the morning dawned, she died."

The old General was agitated. We did not speak to him. My father walked to some little distance, and began reading the inscriptions on the tombstones; and thus occupied, he strolled into the door of a side chapel to prosecute his researches. The General leaned against the wall, dried his eyes, and sighed heavily. I was relieved on hearing the voices of Carmilla and Madame, who were at that moment approaching. The voices died away.

In this solitude, having just listened to so strange a story, connected, as it was, with the great and titled dead, whose monuments were moulding among the dust and ivy round us, and every incident of which bore so awfully upon my own mysterious case—in this haunted spot, darkened by the towering foliage that rose on every side, dense and high above its noiseless walls—a horror began to steal over me, and my heart sank as I thought that my friends were, after all, now about to enter and disturb this triste and ominous scene.

The old General's eyes were fixed on the ground, as he leaned with his hand upon the basement of a shattered monument.

Under a narrow, arched doorway, surmounted by one of those demoniacal grotesques in which the cynical and ghastly fancy of old Gothic carving delights, I saw very gladly the beautiful face and figure of Carmilla enter the shadowy chapel.

I was just about to rise and speak, and nodded smiling, in answer to her peculiarly engaging smile; when with a cry, the old man by my side caught up the woodman's hatchet, and started forward. On seeing him a brutalised change came over her features. It was an instantaneous and horrible transformation, as she made a crouching step backwards. Before I could utter a scream, he struck at her with all his force, but she dived under his blow, and unscathed, caught him in her tiny grasp by the wrist. He struggled for a moment to release his arm, but his hand opened, the axe fell to the ground, and the girl was gone.

"I now sprang forward, with my sword in my hand."

He staggered against the wall. His grey hair stood upon his head, and a moisture shone over his face, as if he were at the point of death.

The frightful scene had passed in a moment. The first thing I recollect after, is Madame standing before me, and impatiently repeating again and again, the question, "Where is Mademoiselle Carmilla?"

I answered at length, "I don't know—I can't tell—she went there," and I pointed to the door through which Madame had just entered; "only a minute or two since."

"But I have been standing there, in the passage, ever since Mademoiselle Carmilla entered; and she did not return."

She then began to call "Carmilla" through every door and passage and from the windows, but no answer came.

"She called herself Carmilla?" asked the General, still agitated.

"Carmilla, yes," I answered.

"Aye," he said, "that is Millarca. That is the same person who long ago was called Mircalla, Countess Karnstein. Depart from this accursed ground, my poor child, as quickly as you can. Drive to the clergyman's house, and stay there till we come. Begone! May you never behold Carmilla more; you will not find her here."

CHAPTER XV

Ordeal and Execution

As he spoke one of the strangest looking men I ever beheld, entered the chapel at the door through which Carmilla had made her entrance and her exit. He was tall, narrow-chested, stooping, with high shoulders, and dressed in black. His face was brown and dried in with deep furrows; he wore an oddly-shaped hat with a broad leaf. His hair, long and grizzled, hung on his shoulders. He wore a pair of gold spectacles, and walked slowly, with an odd shambling gait, with his face sometimes turned up to the sky, and sometimes bowed down toward the ground, seemed to wear a perpetual smile; his long thin arms were swinging, and his lank hands, in old black gloves ever so much too wide for them, waving and gesticulating in utter abstraction.

"The very man!" exclaimed the General, advancing with manifest delight. "My dear Baron, how happy I am to see you, I had no hope of meeting you so soon." He signed to my father, who had by this time returned, and leading the fantastic old gentleman, whom he called the Baron, to meet him. He introduced him formally, and they at once entered into earnest conversation. The stranger took a roll of paper from his pocket, and spread it on the worn surface of a tomb that stood by. He had a pencil case in his fingers, with which he traced imaginary lines from point to point on the paper, which from their often glancing from it, together, at certain points of the building, I concluded to be a plan of the chapel. He accompanied, what I may term his lecture, with occasional readings from a dirty little book, whose yellow leaves were closely written over.

They sauntered together down the side aisle, opposite to the spot where I was standing, conversing as they went; then they begun measuring distances by paces, and finally they all stood together, facing a piece of the side-wall, which they began to examine with great minuteness; pulling off the ivy that clung over it, and rapping the plaster with the ends of their sticks, scraping here, and knocking there. At length they ascertained the existence of a broad marble tablet, with letters carved in relief upon it.

With the assistance of the woodman, who soon returned, a monumental inscription, and carved escutcheon, were disclosed. They proved to be of those of the long lost monument of Mircalla, Countess Karnstein.

The old General, though not I fear given to the praying mood, raised his hands and eyes to heaven, in mute thanksgiving for some moments.

"To-morrow," I heard him say; "the commissioner will be here, and the Inquisition will be held according to law."

Then turning to the old man with the gold spectacles, whom I have described, he shook him warmly by both hands and said:

"Baron, how can I thank you? How can we all thank you? You wil have delivered this region from a plague that has scourged its inhabitants for more than a century. The horrible enemy, thank God, is at last tracked."

My father led the stranger aside, and the General followed. I knew that he had led them out of hearing, that he might relate my case, and I saw them glance often quickly at me, as the discussion proceeded.

My father came to me, kissed me again and again, and leading me from the chapel said:

"It is time to return, but before we go home, we must add to our party the good priest, who lives but a little way from this; and persuade him to accompany us to the schloss."

In this quest we were successful: and I was glad, being unspeakably fatigued when we reached home. But my satisfaction was changed to dismay, on discovering that there were no tidings of Carmilla. Of the scene that had occurred in the ruined chapel, no explanation was offered to me, and it was clear that it was a secret which my father for the present determined to keep from me.

The sinister absence of Carmilla made the remembrance of the scene more horrible to me. The arrangements for that night were singular. Two servants and Madame were to sit up in my room that night; and the ecclesiastic with my father kept watch in the adjoining dressing-room.

The priest had performed certain solemn rites that night, the purport of which I did not understand any more than I comprehended the reason of this extraordinary precaution taken for my safety during sleep.

I saw all clearly a few days later.

The disappearance of Carmilla was followed by the discontinuance of my nightly sufferings.

You have heard, no doubt, of the appalling superstition that prevails in Upper and Lower Styria, in Moravia, Silesia, in Turkish Servia, in Poland, even in Russia; the superstition, so we must call it, of the vampire.

If human testimony, taken with every care and solemnity, judicially, before commissions innumerable, each consisting of many members, all chosen for integrity and intelligence, and constituting reports more voluminous perhaps that exist upon any one other class of cases, is worth anything, it is difficult to deny, or even to doubt the existence of such a phenomenon as the vampire.

For my part I have heard no theory by which to explain what I myself have witnessed and experienced, other than that supplied by the ancient and well-attested belief of the country.

The next day the formal proceedings took place in the Chapel of Karnstein. The grave of the Countess Mircalla was opened; and the General and my father recognized each his perfidious and beautiful guest, in the face now disclosed to view. The features, though a hundred and fifty years had passed since her funeral, were tinted with the warmth of life. Her eyes were open; no cadaverous smell exhaled from the coffin. The two medical men, one officially present, the other on the part of the promoter of the inquiry, attested the marvellous fact, that there was a faint, but appreciable respiration, and a corresponding action of the heart. The limbs were perfectly flexible, the flesh elastic; and the leaden coffin floated with blood, in which to a depth of seven inches, the body lay immersed. Here then, were all the admitted signs and proofs of vampirism. The body, therefore, in accordance with the ancient practice, was raised, and a sharp stake driven through the heart of the vampire, who uttered a piercing shriek at the moment, in all respects such as might escape from a living person in the last agony. Then the head was struck off, and a torrent of blood flowed from the severed neck. The body and head were next placed on a pile of wood, and reduced to ashes, which were thrown upon the river and borne away, and that territory has never since been plagued by the visits of a vampire.

My father has a copy of the report of the Imperial Commission, with the signatures of all who were present at these proceedings, attached in verification of the statement. It is from this official paper that I have summarized my account of this last shocking scene.

CHAPTER XVI

Conclusion

I write all this you suppose with composure. But far from it; I cannot think of it without agitation. Nothing but your earnest desire so repeatedly expressed, could have induced me to sit down to a task that has unstrung my nerves for months to come, and re-induced a shadow of the unspeakable horror which years after my deliverance continued to make my days and nights dreadful, and solitude insupportably terrific.

Let me add a word or two about that quaint Baron Vordenburg, to whose curious lore we were indebted for the discovery of the Countess Mircalla's grave.

He had taken up his abode in Gratz, where, living upon a mere pittance, which was all that remained to him of the once princely estates of his family, in Upper Styria, he devoted himself to the minute and laborious investigation of the marvellously authenticated tradition of vampirism. He had at his fingers' ends all the great and little works upon the subject. "Magia Posthuma," "Phlegon de Mirabilibus," " Augustinus de curâ pro Mortuis,"

"Philosophicæ et Christianæ Cogitationes de Vampiris," by John
Christofer Harenberg; and a thousand others, among which I remember only a few of those which he lent to my father. He had
a voluminous digest of all the judicial cases, from which he had
extracted a system of principles that appear to govern—some always, and others occasionally only—the condition of the vampire.
I may mention, in passing, that the deadly pallor attributed to
that sort of *revenants*, is a mere melodramatic fiction. They present, in the grave, and when they show themselves in human society, the appearance of healthy life. When disclosed to light in
their coffins, they exhibit all the symptoms that are enumerated
as those which proved the vampire life of the long-dead Countess
Karnstein.

How they escape from their graves and return to them for certain hours every day, without displacing the clay or leaving any
trace of disturbance in the state of the coffin or the cerements, has
always been admitted to be utterly inexplicable. The amphibious
existence of the vampire is sustained by daily renewed slumber in
the grave. Its horrible lust for living blood supplies the vigour of
its waking existence. The vampire is prone to be fascinated with an
engrossing vehemence, resembling the passion of love, by particular persons. In pursuit of these it will exercise inexhaustible patience and stratagem, for access to a particular object may be obstructed in a hundred ways. It will never desist until it has satiated
its passion, and drained the very life of its coveted victim. But it
will, in these cases, husband and protract its murderous enjoyment with the refinement of an epicure, and heighten it by the
gradual approaches of an artful courtship. In these cases it seems
to yearn for something like sympathy and consent. In ordinary
ones it goes direct to its object, overpowers with violence, and
strangles and exhausts often at a single feast.

The vampire is, apparently, subject, in certain situations, to
special conditions. In the particular instance of which I have given
you a relation, Mircalla seemed to be limited to a name which,
if not her real one, should at least reproduce, without the omis-
sion or addition of a single letter, those, as we say, anagrammat-
ically, which compose it. *Carmilla* did this; so did *Millarca*.

My father related to the Baron Vordenburg, who remained
with us for two or three weeks after the expulsion of Carmilla, the
story about the Moravian nobleman and the vampire at Karnstein
churchyard, and then he asked the Baron how he had discovered
the exact position of the long-concealed tomb of the Countess Millarca? The Baron's grotesque features puckered up into a myste-

rious smile; he looked down, still smiling, on his worn spectacle-case and fumbled with it. Then looking up, he said:

"I have many journals, and other papers, written by that remarkable man; the most curious among them is one treating of the visit of which you speak, to Karnstein. The tradition, of course, discolours and distorts a little. He might have been termed a Moravian nobleman, for he had changed his abode to that territory, and was, beside, a noble. But he was, in truth, a native of Upper Styria. It is enough to say that in very early youth he had been a passionate and favoured lover of the beautiful Mircalla, Countess Karnstein. Her early death plunged him into inconsolable grief. It is the nature of vampires to increase and multiply, but according to an ascertained and ghostly law.

"Assume, at starting, a territory perfectly free from that pest. How does it begin, and how does it multiply itself? I will tell you. A person, more or less wicked, puts an end to himself. A suicide, under certain circumstances, becomes a vampire. That spectre visits living people in their slumbers; *they* die, and almost invariably, in the grave, develope into vampires. This happened in the case of the beautiful Mircalla, who was haunted by one of those demons. My ancestor, Vordenburg, whose title I still bear, soon discovered this, and in the course of the studies to which he devoted himself, learned a great deal more.

"Among other things, he concluded that suspicion of vampirism would probably fall, sooner or later, upon the dead Countess, who in life had been his idol. He conceived a horror, be she what she might, of her remains being profaned by the outrage of a posthumous execution. He has left a curious paper to prove that the vampire, on its expulsion from its amphibious existence, is projected into a far more horrible life; and he resolved to save his once beloved Mircalla from this.

"He adopted the stratagem of a journey here, a pretended removal of her remains, and a real obliteration of her monument. When age had stolen upon him, and from the vale of years he looked back on the scenes he was leaving, he considered, in a different spirit, what he had done; and a horror took possession of him. He made the tracings and notes which have guided me to the very spot, and drew up a confession of the deception that he had practised. If he had intended any further action in this matter, death prevented him; and the hand of a remote descendant has, too late for many, directed the pursuit to the lair of the beast."

We talked a little more, and among other things he said was this:

"One sign of the vampire is the power of the hand. The slender hand of Mircalla closed like a vice of steel on the General's wrist when he raised the hatchet to strike. But its power is not confined to its grasp; it leaves a numbness in the limb it seizes, which is slowly, if ever, recovered from."

The following Spring my father took me a tour through Italy. We remained away for more than a year. It was long before the terror of recent events subsided; and to this hour the image of Carmilla returns to memory with ambiguous alternations—sometimes the playful, languid, beautiful girl; sometimes the writhing fiend I saw in the ruined church; and often from a reverie I have started, fancying I heard the light step of Carmilla at the drawing-room door.

The Fortunes of
Sir Robert Ardagh

*Being a Second Extract from the Papers of
the Late Father Purcell*

The earth hath bubbles as the water hath—.
And these are of them.

In the south of Ireland, and on the borders of the county of
Limerick, there lies a district of two or three miles in length, which
is rendered interesting by the fact that it is one of the very few
spots throughout this country, in which some fragments of abor-
iginal wood have found a refuge. It has little or none of the lordly
character of the American forests; for the axe has felled its oldest
and its grandest trees; but in the close wood which survives, live
all the wild and pleasing peculiarities of nature—its complete
irregularity—its vistas, in whose perspective the quiet cattle are
peacefully browsing—its refreshing glades, where the grey rocks
arise from amid the nodding fern—the silvery shafts of the old
birch trees—the knotted trunks of the hoary oak—the grotesque
but graceful branches, which never shed their honours under the
tyrant pruning hook— the soft green sward—the chequered light
and shade—the wild luxuriant weeds—its lichen and its moss—all,
all are beautiful alike in the green freshness of spring, or in the
sadness and sear of autumn—their beauty is of that kind which
makes the heart full with joy—appealing to the affections with a
power which belongs to nature only. This wood runs up, from
below the base, to the ridge of a long line of irregular hills, having
perhaps in primitive times, formed but the skirting of some mighty
forest which occupied the level below.

But now, alas, whither have we drifted?—whither has the tide of
civilization borne us?—it has passed over a land unprepared for it
—it has left nakedness behind it—we have lost our forests, but our

marauders remain—we have destroyed all that is picturesque, while we have retained everything that is revolting in barbarism. Through the midst of this woodland, there runs a deep gulley or glen; where the stillness of the scene is broken in upon by the brawling of a mountain stream, which, however, in the winter season, swells into a rapid and formidable torrent.

There is one point at which the glen becomes extremely deep and narrow, the sides descend to the depth of some hundred feet, and are so steep as to be nearly perpendicular. The wild trees which have taken root in the crannies and chasms of the rock, have so intersected and entangled, that one can with difficulty catch a glimpse of the stream, which wheels, flashes, and foams below, as if exulting in the surrounding silence and solitude.

This spot was not unwisely chosen, as a point of no ordinary strength, for the erection of a massive square tower or keep, one side of which rises as if in continuation of the precipitous cliff on which it is based. Originally, the only mode of ingress was by a narrow portal, in the very wall which overtopped the precipice; opening upon a ledge of rock which afforded a precarious pathway, cautiously intersected, however, by a deep trench cut with great labour in the living rock: so that, in its original state, and before the introduction of artillery into the art of war, this tower might have been pronounced, and that not presumptuously, almost impregnable.

The progress of improvement, and the increasing security of the times had, however, tempted its successive proprietors, if not to adorn, at least to enlarge their premises, and at about the middle of the last century, when the castle was last inhabited, the original square tower formed but a small part of the edifice.

The castle, and a wide tract of the surrounding country had from time immemorial, belonged to a family, which, for distinctness, we shall call by the name of Ardagh; and, owing to the associations which, in Ireland, almost always attach to scenes which have long witnessed alike, the exercise of stern feudal authority, and of that savage hospitality which distinguished the good old times, this building has become the subject and the scene of many wild and extraordinary traditions. One of them I have been enabled, by a personal acquaintance with an eye-witness of the events, to trace to its origin; and yet it is hard to say, whether the events which I am about to record, appear more strange or improbable, as seen through the distorting medium of tradition, or in the appalling dimness of uncertainty, which surrounds the reality.

Tradition says that, sometime in the last century, Sir Robert

Ardagh, a young man, and the last heir of that family, went abroad and served in foreign armies, and that having acquired considerable honour and emolument, he settled at Castle Ardagh, the building we have just now attempted to describe. He was what the country people call a *dark* man; that is, he was considered morose, reserved, and ill-tempered; and as it was supposed from the utter solitude of his life, was upon no terms of cordiality with the other members of his family.

The only occasion upon which he broke through the solitary monotony of his life, was during the continuance of the racing season, and immediately subsequent to it; at which time he was to be seen among the busiest upon the course, betting deeply and unhesitatingly, and invariably with success. Sir Robert was, however, too well-known as a man of honour, and of too high a family to be suspected of any unfair dealing. He was, moreover, a soldier, and a man of an intrepid as well as of a haughty character, and no one cared to hazard a surmise, the consequences of which would be felt most probably by its originator only. Gossip, however, was not silent—it was remarked that Sir Robert never appeared at the race ground, which was the only place of public resort which he frequented, except in company with a certain strange looking person, who was never seen elsewhere, or under other circumstances. It was remarked, too, that this man, whose relation to Sir Robert was never distinctly ascertained, was the only person to whom he seemed to speak unnecessarily; it was observed, that while with the country gentry he exchanged no further communication than what was unavoidable in arranging his sporting transactions, with this person he would converse earnestly and frequently. Tradition asserts, that to enhance the curiosity which this unaccountable and exclusive preference excited, the stranger possessed some striking and unpleasant peculiarities of person and of garb—she does not say, however, what these were—but they, in conjunction with Sir Robert's secluded habits, and extraordinary run of luck—a success which was supposed to result from the suggestions and immediate advice of the unknown—were sufficient to warrant report in pronouncing that there was something *queer* in the wind, and in surmising that Sir Robert was playing a fearful and a hazardous game, and that in short, his strange companion was little better than the devil himself.

Years, however, rolled quietly away, and nothing novel occurred in the arrangements of Castle Ardagh, excepting that Sir Robert parted with his odd companion, but as nobody could tell whence he came, so nobody could say whither he had gone. Sir Robert's habits, however, underwent no consequent change; he continued regularly to frequent the race meetings, without mixing at all in the convivialities of the gentry, and immediately afterwards to relapse into the secluded monotony of his ordinary life.

It was said that he had accumulated vast sums of money—and, as his bets were always successful, and always large, such must have been the case. He did not suffer the acquisition of wealth, however, to influence his hospitality or his housekeeping—he neither purchased land, nor extended his establishment; and his mode of enjoying his money must have been altogether that of the miser—consisting, merely, in the pleasure of touching and telling his gold, and in the consciousness of wealth. Sir Robert's temper, so far from improving, became more than ever gloomy and morose. He sometimes carried the indulgence of his evil dispositions to such a height, that it bordered upon insanity. During these paroxysms, he would neither eat, drink, nor sleep. On such occasions he insisted on perfect privacy, even from the intrusion of his most trusted servants;—his voice was frequently heard, sometimes in earnest supplication, sometimes raised as if in loud and angry altercation, with some unknown visitant—sometimes he would, for hours together, walk to and fro, throughout the long oak wainscotted apartment, which he generally occupied, with wild gesticulations and agitated pace, in the manner of one who has been roused to a state of unnatural excitement, by some sudden and appalling intimation.

These paroxysms of apparent lunacy were so frightful, that during their continuance, even his oldest and most faithful domestics dared not approach him; consequently, his hours of agony were never intruded upon, and the mysterious causes of his sufferings appeared likely to remain hidden for ever. On one occasion, a fit of this kind continued for an unusual time—the ordinary term of their duration, about two days, had been long past—and the old servant, who generally waited upon Sir Robert, after these visitations, having in vain listened for the well-known tinkle of his master's hand-bell, began to feel extremely anxious; he feared that his master might have died from sheer exhaustion, or perhaps put an end to his own existence, during his miserable depression. These fears at length became so strong, that having in vain urged some of his brother-servants to accompany him, he determined to go up alone, and himself see whether any accident had befallen Sir Robert. He traversed the several passages which conducted from the new to the more ancient parts of the mansion; and having arrived in the old hall of the castle, the utter silence of the hour, for it was very late in the night, the idea of the nature of the enterprise in which he was engaging himself, a sensation of remoteness from anything like human companionship, but more than all the vivid but undefined anticipation of something horrible, came upon him with such oppressive weight, that he hesitated as to whither he should proceed. Real uneasiness, however, respecting the fate of his master, for whom he felt that kind of attachment, which the force of habitual intercourse, not unfrequently engenders respecting objects not in themselves amiable —and also a latent unwillingness to expose his weakness to the ridicule of his fellow-servants, combined to overcome his reluctance; and he had just placed his foot upon the first step of the staircase, which conducted to his master's chamber, when his attention was arrested by a low but distinct knocking at the halldoor. Not, perhaps, very sorry at finding thus an excuse even for deferring his intended expedition, he placed the candle upon a stone block which lay in the hall, and approached the door, uncertain whether his ears had not deceived him. This doubt was justified by the circumstance, that the hall entrance had been for nearly fifty years disused as a mode of ingress to the castle. The situation of this gate also, which we have endeavoured to describe, opening upon a narrow ledge of rock which overhangs a perilous cliff, rendered it at all times, but particularly at night, a dangerous entrance; this shelving platform of rock, which formed the only avenue to the door, was divided, as I have already stated, by a broad chasm, the planks across which had long disappeared by decay or otherwise, so that it seemed at least highly improbable that any man could have found his way across the passage in safety to the door—more particularly, on a night like that, of singular darkness. The old man, therefore, listened attentively, to ascertain whether the first application should be followed by another; he had not long to wait; the same low but singularly distinct knocking was repeated; so low that it seemed as if the applicant had employed no harder or heavier instrument than his hand, and yet despite the immense thickness of the door, so very distinct, that he could not mistake the sound. It was repeated a third time, without any increase of loudness; and the old man obeying an impulse for which to his dying hour, he could never account, proceeded to remove, one by one, the three great oaken bars which secured the door. Time and damp had effectually corroded the iron chambers of the lock, so that it afforded little resistance. With some effort, as he believed, assisted from without, the old servant succeeded in opening the door; and a low, square-built figure, apparently that of a man wrapped in a large black cloak, entered the hall. The servant could not see much of this visitant with any distinctness; his dress appeared foreign, the skirt of his ample cloak was thrown over one shoulder; he wore a large felt hat, with a very heavy leaf, from under which escaped what appeared to be a mass of long sooty-black hair;—his feet were cased in heavy ridingboots. Such were the few particulars which the servant had time and light to observe. The stranger desired him to let his master know instantly that a friend had come, by appointment, to settle some business with him. The servant hesitated, but a slight motion on the part of his visitor, as if to possess himself of the candle, determined him; so taking it in his hand, he ascended the castle stairs, leaving his guest in the hall.

On reaching the apartment which opened upon the oak-chamber, he was surprised to observe the door of that room partly open, and the room itself lit up. He paused, but there was no sound— he looked in, and saw Sir Robert—his head, and the upper part of his body, reclining on a table, upon which burned a lamp; his arms were stretched forward on either side, and perfectly motionless; it appeared that having been sitting at the table, he had thus sunk forward, either dead or in a swoon. There was no sound of breathing; all was silent, except the sharp ticking of a watch, which lay beside the lamp. The servant coughed twice or thrice, but with no effect—his fears now almost amounted to certainty, and he was approaching the table on which his master partly lay—to satisfy himself of his death—when Sir Robert slowly raised his head, and throwing himself back in his chair, fixed his eyes in a ghastly and uncertain gaze upon his attendant. At length he said, slowly and painfully, as if he dreaded the answer—

"In God's name, what are you?"

"Sir," said the servant, "a strange gentleman wants to see you below."

At this intimation, Sir Robert, starting on his legs, and tossing his arms wildly upwards, uttered a shriek of such appalling and despairing terror, that it was almost too fearful for human endurance; and long after the sound had ceased, it seemed to the terrified imagination of the old servant, to roll through the deserted passages in bursts of unnatural laughter. After a few moments, Sir Robert said—

"Can't you send him away? Why does he come so soon? Oh God! oh God! let him leave me for an hour—a little time. I can't see him now—try to get him away. You see I can't go down now—I have not strength. Oh God! oh God! let him come back in an hour—it is not long to wait. He cannot lose any thing by it—nothing, nothing, nothing. Tell him that—say any thing to him."

The servant went down. In his own words, he did not feel the stairs under him, till he got to the hall. The figure stood exactly as he had left it. He delivered his master's message as coherently as he could. The stranger replied in a careless tone—

"If Sir Robert will not come down to me, I must go up to him."

The man returned, and to his surprise he found his master much more composed in manner. He listened to the message; and though the cold perspiration stood in drops upon his forehead, faster than he could wipe it away, his manner had lost the dreadful agitation which had marked it before. He rose feebly, and casting a last look of agony behind him, passed from the room to the lobby, where he signed to his attendant not to follow him. The man moved as far as the head of the staircase, from whence he had a tolerably distinct view of the hall, which was imperfectly lighted by the candle he had left there.

He saw his master reel, rather than walk down the stairs, clinging all the way to the banisters. He walked on as if about to sink every moment from weakness. The figure advanced as if to meet him, and in passing struck down the light. The servant could see no more; but there was a sound of struggling, renewed at intervals with silent but fearful energy. It was evident, however, that the parties were approaching the door, for he heard the solid oak sound twice or thrice, as the feet of the combatants, in shuffling hither and thither over the floor, struck upon it. After a slight pause he heard the door thrown open, with such violence that the leaf struck the sidewall of the hall, and it was so dark without that this was made known in no other way than by the sound. The struggle was renewed with an agony and intenseness of energy, that betrayed itself in deep-drawn gasps. One desperate effort, which terminated in the breaking of some part of the door, producing a sound as if the door-post was wrenched from its position, was followed by another wrestle, evidently upon the narrow ledge which ran outside the door, overtopping the precipice. This seemed as fruitless as the rest, for it was followed by a crashing sound as if some heavy body had fallen over, and was rushing down the precipice, through the light boughs that crossed near the top. All then became still as the grave, except the moan of the night wind that sighed up the wooded glen.

The old servant had not nerve to return through the hall, and to him that night seemed all but endless; but morning at length came, and with it the disclosure of the events of the night. Near the door, upon the ground, lay Sir Robert's sword-belt, which had given way in the scuffle. A huge splinter from the massive door-post had been wrenched off, by an almost superhuman effort—one which nothing but the gripe of a despairing man could have severed—and on the rock outside were left the marks of the slipping and sliding of feet.

At the foot of the precipice, not immediately under the castle, but dragged some way up the glen, were found the remains of Sir Robert, with hardly a vestige of a limb or feature left distinguishable. The right hand, however was uninjured, and in its fingers was clutched, with the fixedness of death, a long lock of coarse sooty hair—the only direct circumstantial evidence of the presence of a second person. So says tradition.

This story, as I have mentioned, was current among the dealers in such lore; but the original facts are so dissimilar in all but the name of the principal person mentioned, Sir Robert Ardagh, and the fact that his death was accompanied with circumstances of extraordinary mystery, that the two narratives are totally irreconcileable, (even allowing the utmost for the exaggerating influence of tradition,) except by supposing report to have combined and blended together the fabulous histories of several distinct heroes of the family of Ardagh. However this may be, I shall lay before the reader a distinct recital of the events from which the foregoing tradition arose. With respect to these there can be no mistake; they are authenticated as fully as any thing can be by human testimony; and I state them principally upon the evidence of a lady who herself bore a prominent part in the strange events which she related, and which I now record as being among the few well-attested tales of the marvellous, which it has been my fate to hear. I shall, as far as I am able, arrange in one combined narrative, the evidence of several distinct persons, who were eye-witnesses of what they related, and with the truth of whose testimony I am solemnly and deeply impressed.

Sir Robert Ardagh was the heir and representative of the family whose name he bore; but owing to the prodigality of his father, the estates descended to him in a very impaired condition. Urged by the restless spirit of youth, or more probably by a feeling of pride, which could not submit to witness, in the paternal mansion, what he considered a humiliating alteration in the style and hospitality which up to that time had distinguished his family, Sir Robert left Ireland and went abroad. How he occupied himself, or what countries he visited during his absence, was never known, nor did he afterwards make any allusion, or encourage any inquiries touching his foreign sojourn. He left Ireland in the year 1742, being then just of age, and was not heard of until the year 1760—about eighteen years afterwards—at which time he returned. His personal appearance was, as might have been expected, very greatly altered, more altered, indeed, than the time of his absence might have warranted one in supposing likely. But to counterbalance the unfavourable change which time had wrought in his form and features, he had acquired all the advantages of polish of manner, and refinement of taste, which foreign travel is supposed to bestow. But what was truly surprising was, that it soon became evident that Sir Robert was very wealthy—wealthy to an extraordinary and unaccountable degree; and this fact was made manifest, not only by his expensive style of living, but by his proceeding to disembarrass his property, and to purchase extensive estates in addition. Moreover, there could be nothing deceptive in these appearances, for he paid ready money for every thing, from the most important purchase to the most trifling.

Sir Robert was a remarkably agreeable man, and possessing the combined advantages of birth and property, he was, as a matter of course, gladly received into the highest society which the metropolis then commanded. It was thus that he became acquainted with the two beautiful Miss F——ds, then among the brightest ornaments of the highest circles of Dublin fashion. Their family was in more than one direction allied to nobility; and Lady D——, their elder sister by many years, and some time married to a once well-known nobleman, was now their protectress. These considerations, besides the fact that the young ladies were what is usually termed heiresses, though not to a very great amount, secured to them a high position in the best society which Ireland then produced. The two young ladies differed strongly, alike in appearance and in character. The elder of the two, Emily, was generally considered the handsomer—for her beauty was of that impressive kind which never failed to strike even at the first glance, possessing all the advantages of a fine person, and of a commanding carriage. The beauty of her features strikingly assorted in character with that of her figure and deportment. Her hair was raven black and richly luxuriant, beautifully contrasting with the even, perfect whiteness of her forehead—her finely pencilled brows were black as the ringlets that clustered near them—and her eyes, full, lustrous, and animated, possessed all the power and brilliancy of the black, with more than their softness and variety of expression. She was not, however, merely the tragedy queen. When she smiled, and that was not unfrequently, the dimpling of cheek and chin, the laughing display of the small and beautiful teeth—but more than all, the roguish archness of her deep, bright eye, shewed that nature had not neglected in her the lighter and the softer characteristics of woman.

Her younger sister Mary was, as I believe not unfrequently occurs in the case of sisters, quite in the opposite style of beauty. She was light-haired, had more colour, had nearly equal grace, with much more liveliness of manner. Her eyes were of that dark grey which poets so much admire—full of expression and vivacity. She was altogether a very beautiful and animated girl—though as unlike her sister as the presence of those two qualities would permit her to be. Their dissimilarity did not stop here—it was deeper than mere appearance—the character of their minds differed almost as strikingly as did their complexion. The fair-haired beauty had a large proportion of that softness and pliability of temper which physiognomists assign as the characteristics of such complexions. She was much more the creature of impulse than of feeling, and consequently more the victim of extrinsic circumstances than was her sister. Emily, on the contrary, possessed considerable firmness and decision. She was less excitable, but when excited, her feelings were more intense and enduring. She wanted much of the gaiety, but with it the volatility of her younger sister. Her opinions were adopted, and her friendships formed more reflectively, and her affections seemed to move, as it were, more slowly, but more determinedly. This firmness of character did not amount to any thing masculine, and did not at all impair the feminine grace of her manners.

Sir Robert Ardagh was for a long time apparently equally attentive to the two sisters, and many were the conjectures and the surmises as to which would be the lady of the choice. At length, however, these doubts were determined; he proposed for and was accepted by the dark beauty, Emily T——d.

The bridals were celebrated in a manner becoming the wealth and connections of the parties; and Sir Robert and Lady Ardagh left Dublin to pass the honeymoon at the family mansion, Castle Ardagh, which had lately been fitted up in a style bordering upon magnificent. Whether in compliance with the wishes of his lady, or owing to some whim of his own, his habits were henceforward strikingly altered, and from having moved among the gayest if not the most profligate of the votaries of fashion, he suddenly settled down into a quiet, domestic, country gentleman, and seldom, if ever, visited the capital, and then his sojourns were brief as the nature of his business would permit.

Lady Ardagh, however, did not suffer from this change further than in being secluded from general society; for Sir Robert's wealth, and the hospitality which he had established in the family mansion, commanded that of such of his lady's friends and relatives as had leisure or inclination to visit the castle; and as the style of living was very handsome, and its internal resources of amusement considerable, few invitations from Sir Robert or his lady were neglected.

Many years passed quietly away, during which Sir Robert's and Lady Ardagh's hopes of issue were several times disappointed. In the lapse of all this time there occurred but one event worth recording. Sir Robert had brought with him from abroad a valet, who sometimes professed himself to be a Frenchman; at others an Italian; and at others again a German. He spoke all these languages with equal fluency, and seemed to take a kind of pleasure in puzzling the sagacity and balking the curiosity of such of the visitors at the castle as at any time happened to enter into conversation with him, or who, struck by his singularities, became inquisitive respecting his country and origin. Sir Robert called him by the French name, JACQUE; and among the lower orders he was familiarly known by the title of "Jack the devil," an appellation which originated in a supposed malignity of disposition, and a real reluctance to mix in the society of those who were believed to be his equals. This morose reserve, coupled with the mystery which enveloped all about him, rendered him an object of suspicion and inquiry to his fellow-servants, amongst whom it was whispered that this man in secret governed the actions of Sir Robert with a despotic dictation, and that as if to indemnify himself for his public and apparent servitude and self-denial, he in private exacted a degree of respectful homage from his so-called master, totally inconsistent with the relation generally supposed to exist between them.

This man's personal appearance was, to say the least of it, extremely odd; he was low in stature; and this defect was enhanced by a distortion of the spine, so considerable as almost to amount to a hunch; his features, too, had all that sharpness and sickliness of hue which generally accompany deformity; he wore his hair, which was black as soot, in heavy neglected ringlets about his shoulders, and always without powder—a peculiarity in those days. There was something unpleasant, too, in the circumstance that he never raised his eyes so as to meet those of another; this fact was often cited as a proof of his being SOMETHING NOT QUITE RIGHT, and said to result not from the timidity which is supposed in most cases to induce this habit, but from a consciousness that his eye possessed a power, which, if exhibited, would betray a supernatural origin. Once, and once only, had he violated this sinister observance: it was on the occasion of Sir Robert's hopes having been most bitterly disappointed; his lady, after a severe and dangerous confinement, gave birth to a dead child. Immediately after the intelligence had been made known, a servant, having upon some business, passed outside the gate of the castle yard, was met by Jacque, who, contrary to his wont, accosted him, observing, "so, after all the pother, the son and heir is still-born." This remark was accompanied by a chuckling laugh, only, the only approach to merriment which he was ever known to exhibit. The servant, who was really disappointed, having hoped for holy-day times, feasting and debauchery with impunity during the rejoicings which would have accompanied a christening, turned tartly upon the little valet, telling him that he should let Sir Robert know how he had received the tidings which should have filled any faithful servant with sorrow; and having once broken the ice, he was proceeding with increasing fluency, when his harangue was cut short and his temerity punished, by the little man's raising his head and treating him to a scowl so fearful, half demoniac, half insane, that it haunted his imagination in nightmares and nervous tremours for months after.

To this man Lady Ardagh had, at first sight, conceived an antipathy amounting to horror, a mixture of loathing and dread so very powerful that she had made it a particular and urgent request to Sir Robert, that he would dismiss him, offering herself, from that property which Sir Robert had, by the marriage settlements, left at her own disposal, to provide handsomely for him, provided only she might be relieved from the continual anxiety and discomfort which the fear of encountering him induced.

Sir Robert, however, would not hear of it; the request seemed at first to agitate and distress him; but when still urged in defiance of his peremptory refusal, he burst into a violent fit of fury; he spoke darkly of great sacrifices which he had made, and threatened that if the request were at any time renewed he would leave both her and the country for ever. This was, however, a solitary instance of violence; his general conduct towards Lady Ardagh, though at no time bordering upon the uxorious, was certainly kind and respectful, and he was more than repaid in the fervent attachment which she bore him in return.

Some short time after this strange interview between Sir Robert and Lady Ardagh; one night after the family had retired to bed, and when everything had been quiet for some time, the bell of

Sir Robert's dressing-room rang suddenly and violently; the ring-ing was repeated again and again at still shorter intervals, and with increasing violence, as if the person who pulled the bell was agi-tated by the presence of some terrifying and imminent danger. A servant named Donovan was the first to answer it; he threw on his clothes, and hurried to the room with haste proportioned to the urgency of the call.

Sir Robert had selected for his private room an apartment, re-mote from the bed-chambers of the castle, most of which lay in the more modern parts of the mansion, and secured at its entrance by a double door; as the servant opened the first of these, Sir Robert's bell again sounded with a longer and louder peal; the inner door resisted his efforts to open it; but after a few violent struggles, not having been perfectly secured or owing to the inadequancy of the bolt itself, it gave way, and the servant rushed into the apartment, advancing several paces before he could recover himself. As he entered, he heard Sir Robert's voice exclaiming loudly "wait with-out, do not come in yet;" but the prohibition came too late. Near a low truckle-bed, upon which Sir Robert sometimes slept, for he was a whimsical man, in a large arm chair, sate, or rather lounged, the form of the valet, Jacque; his arms folded, and his heels stretched forward on the floor so as fully to exhibit his misshapen legs, his head thrown back, and his eyes fixed upon his master with a look of indescribable defiance and derision, while, as if to add to the strange insolence of his attitude and expression, he had placed upon his head the black cloth cap which it was his habit to wear.

Sir Robert was standing before him at the distance of several yards in a posture expressive of despair, terror, and what might be called an agony of humility. He waved his hand twice or thrice, as if to dismiss the servant, who, however, remained fixed on the spot where he had first stood; and then, as if forgetting every thing but the agony within him, he pressed his clenched hands on his cold damp brow, and dashed away the heavy drops that gathered chill and thickly there. Jacque broke the silence.

"Donovan," said he, "shake up that drone and drunkard, Carl-ton; tell him that his master directs that the travelling carriage shall be at the door within half an hour."

The servant paused as if in doubt as to what he should do; but his scruples were resolved by Sir Robert's saying hurriedly, "Go, go, do whatever he directs; his commands are mine, tell Carlton the same."

The servant hurried to obey, and in about half an hour the

carriage was at the door, and Jacque having directed the coachman to drive to B——n, a small town at about the distance of twelve miles, the nearest point, however, at which post horses could be obtained, stept into the vehicle which accordingly quitted the castle immediately.

Although it was a fine moonlight night, the carriage made its way but slowly, and after the lapse of two hours, the travellers had arrived at a point about eight miles from the castle, at which the road strikes through a desolate and heathy flat, sloping up, distantly at either side into bleak undulatory hills, in whose monotonous sweep the imagination beholds the heaving of some dark sluggish sea, arrested in its first commotion by some preternatural power; it is a gloomy and divested spot; there is neither tree nor habitation near it; its monotony is unbroken, except by here and there the grey front of a rock peering above the heath, and the effect is rendered yet more dreary and spectral by the exaggerated and misty shadows which the moon casts along the sloping sides of the hills. When they had gained about the centre of this tract, Carlton, the coachman, was surprised to see a figure standing, at some distance in advance, immediately beside the road, and still more so when, on coming up, he observed that it was no other than the person whom he believed to be at that moment quietly seated in the carriage; the coachman drew up, and nodding to him, the little valet exclaimed, "Carlton, I have got the start of you, the roads are heavy, so I shall even take care of myself the rest of the way; do you make your way back as best you can; and I shall follow my own nose;" so saying he chucked a purse into the lap of the coachman, and turning off at a right angle with the road he began to move rapidly away in the direction of the dark ridge, that lowered in the distance. The servant watched him until he was lost in the shadowy haze of night; and neither he nor any of the inmates of the castle saw Jacque again. His disappearance, as might have been expected, did not cause any regret among the servants and dependants at the castle; and Lady Ardagh did not attempt to conceal her delight; but with Sir Robert matters were different; for two or three days subsequent to this event, he confined himself to his room; and when he did return to his ordinary occupations, it was with a gloomy indifference which showed that he did so more from habit than from any interest he felt in them; he appeared from that moment unaccountably and strikingly changed, and thenceforward walked through life as a thing from which he could derive neither profit nor pleasure. His temper, however, so far from growing wayward or morose, became, though gloomy, very, almost unnaturally, placid and cold; but his spirits totally failed, and he became silent and abstracted.

These sombre habits of mind, as might have been anticipated, very materially affected the gay housekeeping of the castle; and the dark and melancholy spirit of its master, seemed to have communicated itself to the very domestics, almost to the very walls of the mansion. Several years rolled on in this way, and the sounds of mirth and wassail had long been strangers to the castle, when Sir Robert requested his lady, to her great astonishment, to invite some twenty or thirty of their friends to spend the Christmas, which was fast approaching, at the castle. Lady Ardagh gladly complied, and her sister Mary, who still continued unmarried, and Lady D—— were of course included in the invitations. Lady Ardagh had requested her sisters to set forward as early as possible, in order that she might enjoy a little of their society before the arrival of the other guests; and in compliance with this request they left Dublin almost immediately upon receiving the invitation, a little more than a week before the arrival of the festival which was to be the period at which the whole party were to muster.

For expedition's sake it was arranged that they should post, while Lady D——'s groom was to follow with her horses; she taking with herself her own maid and one male servant. They left the city when the day was considerably spent, and consequently made but three stages in the first day; upon the second, at about eight in the evening, they had reached the town of K——k, distant about fifteen miles from Castle Ardagh. Here owing to Miss F——d's great fatigue, she having been for a considerable time in a very delicate state of health, it was determined to put up for the night. They, accordingly, took possession of the best sitting room which the inn commanded, and Lady D—— remained in it to direct and urge the preparations for some refreshment, which the fatigues of the day had rendered necessary, while her younger sister retired to her bed-chamber to rest there for a little time, as the parlour commanded no such luxury as a sofa.

Miss F——d was, as I have already stated, at this time, in very delicate health; and upon this occasion the exhaustion of fatigue, and the dreary badness of the weather, combined to depress her spirits. Lady D—— had not been left long to herself, when the door communicating with the passage was abruptly opened, and her sister Mary entered in a state of great agitation; she sate down pale and trembling upon one of the chairs, and it was not until a copious flood of tears had relieved her, that she became sufficiently calm to relate the cause of her excitement and distress. It was simply this. Almost immediately upon lying down upon the bed she sank into a feverish and unrefreshing slumber; images of all grotesque shapes and startling colours flitted before her sleeping fancy with all the rapidity and variety of the changes in a kaleidoscope. At length, as she described it, a mist seemed to interpose itself between her sight and the ever-shifting scenery which sported before her imagination, and out of this cloudy shadow, gradually emerged a figure whose back seemed turned towards the sleeper; it was that of a lady, who, in perfect silence, was expressing as far as pantomimic gesture could, by wringing her hands, and throwing her head from side to side, in the manner of one who is exhausted by the over indulgence, by the very sickness and impatience of grief, the extremity of misery. For a long time she sought in vain to catch a glimpse of the face of the apparition, who thus seemed to stir and live before her. But at length the figure seemed to move with an air of authority, as if about to give directions to some inferior, and in doing so, it turned its head so as to display, with a ghastly distinctness, the features of Lady Ardagh, pale as death, with her dark hair all dishevelled, and her eyes dim and sunken with weeping. The revulsion of feeling which Miss F——d experienced at this disclosure—for up to that point she had contemplated the appearance rather with a sense of curiosity and of interest, than of any thing deeper—was so horrible, that the shock awoke her perfectly. She sat up in the bed, and looked fearfully around the room, which was imperfectly lighted by a single candle burning dimly, as if she almost expected to see the reality of her dreadful vision lurking in some corner of the chamber. Her fears were, however, verified, though not in the way she expected; yet in a manner sufficiently horrible—for she had hardly time to breathe and to collect her thoughts, when she heard, or thought she heard, the voice of her sister, Lady Ardagh, sometimes sobbing violently, and sometimes almost shrieking as if in terror, and calling upon her and Lady D——, with the most imploring earnestness of despair, for God's sake to lose no time in coming to her. All this was so horribly distinct, that it seemed as if the mourner was standing within a few yards of the spot where Miss F——d lay. She sprang from the bed, and leaving the candle in the room behind her, she made her way in the dark through the passage, the voice still following her, until as she arrived at the door of the sitting-room it seemed to die away in low sobbing.

As soon as Miss F——d was tolerably recovered, she declared

her determination to proceed directly, and without further loss of time to Castle Ardagh. It was not without much difficulty that Lady D—— at length prevailed upon her to consent to remain where they then were, until morning should arrive, when it was to be expected that the young lady would be much refreshed by at least remaining quiet for the night, even though sleep were out of the question. Lady D—— was convinced, from the nervous and feverish symptoms which her sister exhibited, that she had already done too much, and was more than ever satified of the necessity of prosecuting the journey no further upon that day. After some time she persuaded her sister to return to her room, where she remained with her until she had gone to bed, and appeared comparatively composed. Lady D—— then returned to the parlour, and not finding herself sleepy, she remained sitting by the fire. Her solitude was a second time broken in upon, by the entrance of her sister, who now appeared, if possible, more agitated than before. She said that Lady D—— had not long left the room, when she was roused by a repetition of the same wailing and lamentations, accompanied by the wildest and most agonized supplications that no time should be lost in coming to Castle Ardagh, and all in her sister's voice, and uttered at the same proximity as before. This time the voice had followed her to the very door of the sitting room, and until she closed it, seemed to pour forth its cries and sobs at the very threshold.

Miss F——d now most positively declared that nothing should prevent her proceeding instantly to the castle, adding that if Lady D—— would not accompany her, she would go on by herself. Superstitious feelings are at all times more or less contagious, and the last century afforded a soil much more congenial to their growth than the present. Lady D—— was so far affected by her sister's terrors, that she became, at least, uneasy; and seeing that her sister was immoveably determined upon setting forward immediately, she consented to accompany her forthwith. After a slight delay, fresh horses were procured, and the two ladies and their attendants renewed their journey, with strong injunctions to the driver to quicken their rate of travelling as much as possible, and promises of reward in case of his doing so.

Roads were then in a much worse condition throughout the south, even than they now are; and the fifteen miles which modern posting would have passed in little more than an hour and a half, were not completed even with every possible exertion in twice the time. Miss F——d had been nervously restless during the journey. Her head had been out at the carriage window every minute; and as they approached the entrance to the castle demesne, which lay about a mile from the building, her anxiety began to communicate itself to her sister. The postillion had just dismounted, and was endeavouring to open the gate—at that time a necessary trouble; for in the middle of the last century, porter's lodges were not common in the south of Ireland, and locks and keys almost unknown. He had just succeeded in rolling back the heavy oaken gate, so as to admit the vehicle, when a mounted servant rode rapidly down the avenue, and drawing up at the carriage, asked of the postillion who the party were; and on hearing, he rode round to the carriage window, and handed in a note which Lady D—— received. By the assistance of one of the coach-lamps they succeeded in deciphering it. It was scrawled in great agitation, and ran thus—

My Dear Sister—my dear Sisters both,—In God's name lose no time, I am frightened and miserable; I cannot explain all till you come. I am too much terrified to write coherently; but understand me—hasten—do not waste a minute. I am afraid you will come too late.   E. A.

The servant could tell nothing more than that the castle was in great confusion, and that Lady Ardagh had been crying bitterly all the night. Sir Robert was perfectly well. Altogether at a loss as to the cause of Lady Ardagh's great distress, they urged their way up the steep and broken avenue which wound through the crowding trees, whose wild and grotesque branches, now stript and naked by the blasts of winter, stretched drearily across the road. As the carriage drew up in the area before the door, the anxiety of the ladies almost amounted to sickness; and scarcely waiting for the assistance of their attendant, they sprang to the ground, and in an instant stood at the castle door. From within were distinctly audible the sounds of lamentation and weeping, and the suppressed hum of voices as if of those endeavouring to soothe the mourner. The door was speedily opened, and when the ladies entered, the first object which met their view was their sister, Lady Ardagh, sitting on a form in the hall, weeping and wringing her hands in deep agony. Beside her stood two old, withered crones, who were each endeavouring in their own way to administer consolation, without even knowing or caring what the subject of her grief might be.

Immediately on Lady Ardagh's seeing her sisters, she started up, fell on their necks, and kissed them again and again without speaking, and then taking them each by a hand, still weeping bitterly, she led them into a small room adjoining the hall, in which burned a light, and having closed the door, she sat down between them. After thanking them for the haste they had made, she proceeded to tell them, in words incoherent from agitation, that Sir Robert had in private, and in the most solemn manner, told her that he should die upon that night, and that he had occupied himself during the evening in giving minute directions respecting the arrangements of his funeral. Lady D—— here suggested the possibility of his labouring under the hallucinations of a fever; but to this Lady Ardagh quickly replied,

"Oh! no, no! would to God I could think it. Oh! no, no! wait till you have seen him. There is a frightful calmness about all he says and does; and his directions are all so clear, and his mind so perfectly collected, it is impossible, quite impossible;" and she wept yet more bitterly.

At that moment Sir Robert's voice was heard in issuing some directions, as he came down stairs; and Lady Ardagh exclaimed, hurriedly—

"Go now and see him yourself; he is in the hall."

Lady D—— accordingly went out into the hall, where Sir Robert met her; and saluting her with kind politeness, he said, after a pause—

"You are come upon a melancholy mission—the house is in great confusion, and some of its inmates in considerable grief." He took her hand, and looking fixedly in her face, continued— "I shall not live to see tomorrow's sun shine."

"You are ill, sir, I have no doubt," replied she; "but I am very certain we shall see you much better to-morrow, and still better the day following."

"I am *not* ill, sister," replied he: "Feel my temples, they are cool; lay your finger to my pulse, its throb is slow and temperate. I never was more perfectly in health, and yet do I know that ere three hours be past, I shall be no more."

"Sir, sir," said she, a good deal startled, but wishing to conceal the impression which the calm solemnity of his manner had, in her own despite, made upon her, "Sir, you should not jest; you should not even speak lightly upon such subjects. You trifle with what is sacred—you are sporting with the best affections of your wife——"

"Stay, my good lady," said he; "if when this clock shall strike the hour of three, I shall be anything but a helpless clod, then upbraid me. Pray return now to your sister. Lady Ardagh is, indeed, much to be pitied; but what is past cannot now be helped. I have now a few papers to arrange, and some to destroy. I shall see you and Lady Ardagh before my death; try to compose her—her sufferings distress me much; but what is past cannot now be mended."

Thus saying he went up stairs, and Lady D—— returned to the room where her sisters were sitting.

"Well," exclaimed Lady Ardagh, as she re-entered, "is it not so? —do you still doubt?—do you think there is any hope?"

Lady D—— was silent.

"Oh! none, none, none," continued she; "I see, I see you are convinced," and she wrung her hands in bitter agony.

"My dear sister," said Lady D——, "there is, no doubt, something strange in all that has appeared in this matter; but still I cannot but hope that there may be something deceptive in all the apparent calmness of Sir Robert. I still must believe that some latent fever has affected his mind, as that owing to the state of nervous depression into which he has been sinking, some trivial occurrence has been converted, in his disordered imagination, into an augury foreboding his immediate dissolution."

In such suggestions, unsatisfactory even to those who originated them, and doubly so to her whom they were intended to comfort, more than two hours passed; and Lady D—— was beginning to hope that the fated term might elapse without the occurrence of any tragical event, when Sir Robert entered the room. On coming in, he placed his finger with a warning gesture upon his lips, as if to enjoin silence; and then having successively pressed the hands of his two sisters-in-law, he stooped over the almost lifeless form of his lady, and twice pressed her cold, pale forehead with his lips, and then passed motionlessly out of the room.

Lady D—— followed to the door, saw him take a candle in the hall, and walk deliberately up the stairs. Stimulated by a feeling of horrible curiosity, she continued to follow him at a distance. She saw him enter his own private room, and heard him close and lock the door after him. Continuing to follow him as far as she could, she placed herself at the door of the chamber, as noiselessly as possible; where after a little time, she was joined by her two sisters, Lady Ardagh and Miss F——d. In breathless silence they listened to what should pass within. They distinctly heard Sir Robert pacing up and down the room for some time; and then, after a pause, a sound as if some one had thrown himself heavily upon the bed. At this moment Lady D——, forgetting that the door had been secured within, turned the handle for the purpose of entering; some one from the inside, close to the door, said, "Hush! hush!" The same lady, now much alarmed, knocked violently at the door—there was no answer. She knocked again more violently, with no further success. Lady Ardagh, now uttering a piercing shriek, sank in a swoon upon the floor. Three or four servants, alarmed by the noise, now hurried up stairs, and Lady Ardagh was carried apparently lifeless to her own chamber. They then, after having knocked long and loudly in vain, applied themselves to forcing an entrance into Sir Robert's room. After resisting some violent efforts, the door at length gave way, and all entered the room nearly together. There was a single candle burning upon a table at the far end of the apartment; and stretched upon the bed lay Sir Robert Ardagh. He was a corpse—the eyes were open—no convulsion had passed over the features, or distorted the limbs—it seemed as if the soul had sped from the body without a struggle to remain there. On touching the body it was found to be cold as clay —all lingering of the vital heat had left it. They closed the ghastly eyes of the corpse, and leaving it to the care of those who seem to consider it a privilege of their age and sex to gloat over the revolting spectacle of death in all its stages, they returned to Lady Ardagh, now a widow. The party assembled at the castle, but the atmosphere was tainted with death. Grief there was not much, but awe and panic were expressed in every face. The guests talked in whispers, and the servants walked on tiptoe, as if afraid of the very noise of their own footsteps.

The funeral was conducted almost with splendour. The body having been conveyed, in compliance with Sir Robert's last directions, to Dublin, was there laid within the ancient walls of Saint Audoen's Church—where I have read the epitaph, telling the age and titles of the departed dust. Neither painted escutcheon, nor marble slab, have served to rescue from oblivion the story of the dead, whose very name will ere long moulder from their tracery—

Et sunt sua fata sepulchris.*

The events which I have recorded are not imaginary. They are FACTS; and there lives one whose authority none would venture to question, who could vindicate the accuracy of every statement which I have set down, and that, too, with all the circumstantiality of an eye witness.†

---

* This prophesy has since been realised; for the aisle in which Sir Robert's remains were laid, has been suffered to fall completely to decay; and the tomb which marked his grave, and other monuments more curious, form now one indistinguishable mass of rubbish.

† This paper, from a memorandum, I find to have been written in 1803. The lady to whom allusion is made, I believe to be Miss Mary F——d. She never married, and survived both her sisters, living to a very advanced age.

An Account of Some Strange Disturbances in Aungier Street

It is not worth telling, this story of mine—at least, not worth writing. Told, indeed, as I have sometimes been called upon to tell it, to a circle of intelligent and eager faces, lighted up by a good after-dinner fire on a winter's evening, with a cold wind rising and wailing outside, and all snug and cosy within, it has gone off—though I say it, who should not—indifferent well. But it is a venture to do as you would have me. Pen, ink, and paper are cold vehicles for the marvellous, and a "reader" decidedly a more critical animal than a "listener." If, however, you can induce your friends to read it after nightfall, and when the fireside talk has run for a while on thrilling tales of shapeless terror; in short, if you will secure me the *mollia tempora fandi,* I will go to my work, and say my say, with better heart. Well, then, these conditions presupposed, I shall waste no more words, but tell you simply how it all happened.

My cousin (Tom Ludlow) and I studied medicine together. I think he would have succeeded, had he stuck to the profession; but he preferred the Church, poor fellow, and died early, a sacrifice to contagion, contracted in the noble discharge of his duties. For my present purpose, I say enough of his character when I mention that he was of a sedate but frank and cheerful nature; very exact in his observance of truth, and not by any means like myself—of an excitable or nervous temperament.

My Uncle Ludlow—Tom's father—while we were attending lectures, purchased three or four old houses in Aungier Street, one of which was unoccupied. *He* resided in the country, and Tom proposed that we should take up our abode in the untenanted house, so long as it should continue unlet; a move which would accomplish the double end of settling us nearer alike to our lecture-rooms and to our amusements, and of relieving us from the weekly charge of rent for our lodgings.

Our furniture was very scant—our whole equipage remarkably modest and primitive; and, in short, our arrangements pretty nearly as simple as those of a bivouac. Our new plan was, therefore, executed almost as soon as conceived. The front drawing-room was our sitting-room. I had the bedroom over it, and Tom the back bedroom on the same floor, which nothing could have induced me to occupy.

The house, to begin with, was a very old one. It had been, I believe, newly fronted about fifty years before; but with this exception, it had nothing modern about it. The agent who bought it and looked into the titles for my uncle, told me that it was sold, along with much other forfeited property, at Chichester House, I think, in 1702; and had belonged to Sir Thomas Hacket, who was Lord Mayor of Dublin in James II.'s time. How old it was *then*, I can't say; but, at all events, it had seen years and changes enough to have contracted all that mysterious and saddened air, at once exciting and depressing, which belongs to most old mansions.

There had been very little done in the way of modernising details; and, perhaps, it was better so; for there was something queer and by-gone in the very walls and ceilings—in the shape of doors and windows—in the odd diagonal site of the chimney-pieces —in the beams and ponderous cornices—not to mention the singular solidity of all the woodwork, from the banisters to the window-frames, which hopelessly defied disguise, and would have emphatically proclaimed their antiquity through any conceivable amount of modern finery and varnish.

An effort had, indeed, been made, to the extent of papering the drawing-rooms; but somehow, the paper looked raw and out of keeping; and the old woman, who kept a little dirt-pie of a shop in the lane, and whose daughter— a girl of two and fifty—was our solitary handmaid, coming in at sunrise, and chastely receding again as soon as she had made all ready for tea in our state apartment;—this woman, I say, remembered it, when old Judge Horrocks (who, having earned the reputation of a particularly "hanging judge," ended by hanging himself, as the coroner's jury found, under an impulse of "temporary insanity," with a child's skipping-rope, over the massive old bannisters) resided there, entertaining good company, with fine venison and rare old port. In those halcyon days, the drawing-rooms were hung with gilded leather, and, I dare say, cut a good figure, for they were really spacious rooms.

The bedrooms were wainscoted, but the front one was not gloomy; and in it the cosiness of antiquity quite overcame its sombre associations. But the back bedroom, with its two queerly-placed melancholy windows, staring vacantly at the foot of the bed, and with the shadowy recess to be found in most old houses in Dublin, like a large ghostly closet, which, from congeniality of temperament, had amalgamated with the bedchamber, and dissolved the partition. At night-time, this "alcove"—as our "maid" was wont to call it—had, in my eyes, a specially sinister and suggestive character. Tom's distant and solitary candle glimmered vainly into its darkness. *There* it was always overlooking him—always itself impenetrable. But this was only part of the effect. The whole room was, I can't tell how, repulsive to me. There was, I suppose, in its proportions and features, a latent discord—a certain mysterious and indescribable relation, which jarred indistinctly upon some secret sense of the fitting and the safe, and raised indefinable suspicions and apprehensions of the imagination. On the whole, as I began by saying, nothing could have induced me to pass a night alone in it.

I had never pretended to conceal from poor Tom my superstitious weakness; and he, on the other hand, most unaffectedly ridiculed my tremors. The sceptic was, however, destined to receive a lesson, as you shall hear.

We had not been very long in occupation of our respective dormitories, when I began to complain of uneasy nights and disturbed sleep. I was, I suppose, the more impatient under this annoyance, as I was usually a sound sleeper, and by no means prone to nightmares. It was now, however, my destiny, instead of enjoying my customary repose, every night to "sup full of horrors." After a preliminary course of disagreeable and frightful dreams, my troubles took a definite form, and the same vision, without an appreciable variation in a single detail, visited me at least (on an average) every second night in the week.

Now, this dream, nightmare, or infernal illusion—which you please—of which I was the miserable sport, was on this wise:—

I saw, or thought I saw, with the most abominable distinctness, although at the time in profound darkness, every article of furniture and accidental arrangement of the chamber in which I lay. This, as you know, is incidental to ordinary nightmare. Well, while in this clairvoyant condition, which seemed but the lighting up of the theatre in which was to be exhibited the monotonous tableau of horror, which made my nights insupportable, my attention invariably became, I know not why, fixed upon the windows opposite the foot of my bed; and, uniformly with the same effect, a sense of dreadful anticipation always took slow but sure possession of me. I became somehow conscious of a sort of horrid but undefined preparation going forward in some unknown quarter, and by some unknown agency, for my torment; and, after an interval, which always seemed to me of the same length, a picture suddenly flew up to the window, where it remained fixed, as if by an electrical attraction, and my discipline of horror then commenced, to last perhaps for hours. The picture thus mysteriously glued to the window-panes, was the portrait of an old man, in a crimson flowered silk dressing-gown, the folds of which I could now describe, with a countenance embodying a strange mixture of intellect, sensuality, and power, but withal sinister and full of malignant omen. His nose was hooked, like the beak of a vulture; his eyes large, grey, and prominent, and lighted up with a more than mortal cruelty and coldness. These features were surmounted by a crimson velvet cap, the hair that peeped from under which was white with age, while the eyebrows retained their original blackness. Well I remember every line, hue, and shadow of that stony countenance, and well I may! The gaze of this hellish visage was fixed upon me, and mine returned it with the inexplicable fascination of nightmare, for what appeared to me to be hours of agony. At last—

The cock he crew, away then flew

the fiend who had enslaved me through the awful watches of the night; and, harassed and nervous, I rose to the duties of the day.

I had—I can't say exactly why, but it may have been from the exquisite anguish and profound impressions of unearthly horror, with which this strange phantasmagoria was associated—an insurmountable antipathy to describing the exact nature of my nightly troubles to my friend and comrade. Generally, however, I told him that I was haunted by abominable dreams; and, true to the imputed materialism of medicine, we put our heads together to dispel my horrors, not by exorcism, but by a tonic.

I will do this tonic justice, and frankly admit that the accursed portrait began to intermit its visits under its influence. What of that? Was this singular apparition—as full of character as of terror —therefore the creature of my fancy, or the invention of my poor stomach? Was it, in short, *subjective* (to borrow the technical slang of the day) and not the palpable aggression and intrusion of an external agent? That, good friend, as we will both admit, by no means follows. The evil spirit, who enthralled my senses in the

shape of that portrait, may have been just as near me, just as
energetic, just as malignant, though I saw him not. What means
the whole moral code of revealed religion regarding the due keeping of our own bodies, soberness, temperance, etc.? here is an
obvious connexion between the material and the invisible; the
healthy tone of the system, and its unimpaired energy, may, for
aught we can tell, guard us against influences which would otherwise render life itself terrific. The mesmerist and the electro-biol-
ogist will fail upon an average with nine patients out of ten—so
may the evil spirit. Special conditions of the corporeal system are
indispensable to the production of certain spiritual phenomena.
The operation succeeds sometimes—sometimes fails—that is all.

I found afterwards that my would-be sceptical companion had
his troubles too. But of these I knew nothing yet. One night, for a
wonder, I was sleeping soundly, when I was roused by a step on
the lobby outside my room, followed by the loud clang of what
turned out to be a large brass candlestick, flung with all his force
by poor Tom Ludlow over the banisters, and rattling with a rebound down the second flight of stairs; and almost concurrently
with this, Tom burst open my door, and bounced into my room
backwards, in a state of extraordinary agitation.

I had jumped out of bed and clutched him by the arm before
I had any distinct idea of my own whereabouts. There we were—
in our shirts—standing before the open door—staring through the
great old banister opposite, at the lobby window, through which
the sickly light of a clouded moon was gleaming.

"What's the matter, Tom? What's the matter with you? What
the devil's the matter with you, Tom?" I demanded shaking him
with nervous impatience.

He took a long breath before he answered me, and then it was
not very coherently.

"It's nothing, nothing at all—did I speak?—what did I say?
where's the candle, Richard? It's dark; I—I had a candle!"

"Yes, dark enough," I said; "but what's the matter?—what is it?
—why don't you speak, Tom?—have you lost your wits?—what is
the matter?"

"The matter?—oh, it is all over. It must have been a dream—
nothing at all but a dream—don't you think so? It could not be
anything more than a dream."

"Of course," said I, feeling uncommonly nervous, "it was a
dream."

"I thought," he said, "there was a man in my room, and—and
I jumped out of bed; and—and—where's the candle?"

"In your room, most likely," I said, "shall I go and bring it?"
"No; stay here—don't go; it's no matter—don't, I tell you; it
was all a dream. Bolt the door, Dick; I'll stay here with you—I feel
nervous. So, Dick, like a good fellow, light your candle and open
the window—I am in a *shocking state.*"

I did as he asked me, and robing himself like Granuaile in one
of my blankets, he seated himself close beside my bed.

Every body knows how contagious is fear of all sorts, but more
especially that particular kind of fear under which poor Tom was
at that moment labouring. I would not have heard, nor I believe
would he have recapitulated, just at that moment, for half the
world, the details of the hideous vision which had so unmanned
him.

"Don't mind telling me anything about your nonsensical dream,
Tom," said I, affecting contempt, really in a panic; "let us talk
about something else; but it is quite plain that this dirty old house
disagrees with us both, and hang me if I stay here any longer, to be
pestered with indigestion and—and—bad nights, so we may as
well look out for lodgings—don't you think so?—at once."

Tom agreed, and, after an interval, said—

"I have been thinking, Richard, that it is a long time since I
saw my father, and I have made up my mind to go down to-morrow
and return in a day or two, and you can take rooms for us in the
meantime."

I fancied that this resolution, obviously the result of the vision
which had so profoundly scared him, would probably vanish next
morning with the damps and shadows of night. But I was mistaken.
Off went Tom at peep of day to the country, having agreed that so
soon as I had secured suitable lodgings, I was to recall him by letter
from his visit to my Uncle Ludlow.

Now, anxious as I was to change my quarters, it so happened,
owing to a series of petty procrastinations and accidents, that
nearly a week elapsed before my bargain was made and my letter
of recall on the wing to Tom; and, in the meantime, a trifling
adventure or two had occurred to your humble servant, which,
absurd as they now appear, diminished by distance, did certainly
at the time serve to whet my appetite for change considerably.

A night or two after the departure of my comrade, I was sitting
by my bedroom fire, the door locked, and the ingredients of a
tumbler of hot whisky-punch upon the crazy spider-table; for, as
the best mode of keeping the

> Black spirits and white,
> Blue spirits and grey,

with which I was environed, at bay, I had adopted the practice recommended by the wisdom of my ancestors, and "kept my spirits up by pouring spirits down." I had thrown aside my volume of Anatomy, and was treating myself by way of a tonic, preparatory to my punch and bed, to half-a-dozen pages of the *Spectator,* when I heard a step on the flight of stairs descending from the attics. It was two o'clock, and the streets were as silent as a churchyard—the sounds were, therefore, perfectly distinct. There was a slow, heavy tread, characterised by the emphasis and deliberation of age, descending by the narrow staircase from above; and, what made the sound more singular, it was plain that the feet which produced it were perfectly bare, measuring the descent with something between a pound and a flop, very ugly to hear.

I knew quite well that my attendant had gone away many hours before, and that nobody but myself had any business in the house. It was quite plain also that the person who was coming down stairs had no intention whatever of concealing his movements; but, on the contrary, appeared disposed to make even more noise, and proceed more deliberately, than was at all necessary. When the step reached the foot of the stairs outside my room, it seemed to stop; and I expected every moment to see my door open spontaneously, and give admission to the original of my detested portrait. I was, however, relieved in a few seconds by hearing the descent renewed, just in the same manner, upon the staircase leading down to the drawing-rooms, and thence, after another pause, down the next flight, and so on to the hall, whence I heard no more.

Now, by the time the sound had ceased, I was wound up, as they say, to a very unpleasant pitch of excitement. I listened, but there was not a stir. I screwed up my courage to a decisive experiment— opened my door, and in a stentorian voice bawled over the banisters, "Who's there?" There was no answer but the ringing of my own voice through the empty old house,—no renewal of the movement; nothing, in short, to give my unpleasant sensations a definite direction. There is, I think, something most disagreeably disenchanting in the sound of one's own voice under such circumstances, exerted in solitude, and in vain. It redoubled my sense of isolation, and my misgivings increased on perceiving that the door, which I certainly thought I had left open, was closed behind me; in a vague alarm, lest my retreat should be cut off, I got again into my room as quickly as I could, where I remained in a state of imaginary blockade, and very uncomfortable indeed, till morning.

Next night brought no return of my barefooted fellow-lodger; but the night following, being in my bed, and in the dark—somewhere, I suppose, about the same hour as before, I distinctly heard the old fellow again descending from the garrets.

This time I had had my punch, and the *morale* of the garrison was consequently excellent. I jumped out of bed, clutched the poker as I passed the expiring fire, and in a moment was upon the lobby. The sound had ceased by this time—the dark and chill were discouraging; and, guess my horror, when I saw, or thought I saw, a black monster, whether in the shape of a man or a bear I could not say, standing, with its back to the wall, on the lobby, facing me, with a pair of great greenish eyes shining dimly out. Now, I must be frank, and confess that the cupboard which displayed our plates and cups stood just there, though at the moment I did not recollect it. At the same time I must honestly say, that making every allowance for an excited imagination, I never could satisfy myself that I was made the dupe of my own fancy in this matter; for this apparition, after one or two shiftings of shape, as if in the act of incipient transformation, began, as it seemed on second thoughts, to advance upon me in its original form. From an instinct of terror rather than of courage, I hurled the poker, with all my force, at its head; and to the music of a horrid crash made my way into my room, and double-locked the door. Then, in a minute more, I heard the horrid bare feet walk down the stairs, till the sound ceased in the hall, as on the former occasion.

If the apparition of the night before was an ocular delusion of my fancy sporting with the dark outlines of our cupboard, and if its horrid eyes were nothing but a pair of inverted teacups, I had, at all events, the satisaction of having launched the poker with admirable effect, and in true "fancy" phrase, "knocked its two daylights into one," as the commingled fragments of my tea-service testified. I did my best to gather comfort and courage from these evidences; but it would not do. And then what could I say of those horrid bare feet, and the regular tramp, tramp, tramp, which measured the distance of the entire staircase through the solitude of my haunted dwelling, and at an hour when no good influence was stirring? Confound it!—the whole affair was abominable. I was out of spirits, and dreaded the approach of night.

It came, ushered ominously in with a thunder-storm and dull torrents of depressing rain. Earlier than usual the streets grew silent; and by twelve o'clock nothing but the comfortless pattering of the rain was to be heard.

I made myself as snug as I could. I lighted *two* candles instead of one. I forswore bed, and held myself in readiness for a sally, candle in hand; for, *coûte qui coûte,* I was resolved to *see* the being, if visible at all, who troubled the nightly stillness of my mansion. I was fidgetty and nervous and tried in vain to interest myself with my books. I walked up and down my room, whistling in turn martial and hilarious music, and listening ever and anon for the dreaded noise. I sate down and stared at the square label on the solemn and reserved-looking black bottle, until "FLANAGAN & Co's BEST OLD MALT WHISKY" grew into a sort of subdued accompaniment to all the fantastic and horrible speculations which chased one another through my brain.

Silence, meanwhile, grew more silent, and darkness darker. I listened in vain for the rumble of a vehicle, or the dull clamour of a distant row. There was nothing but the sound of a rising wind, which had succeeded the thunder-storm that had travelled over the Dublin mountains quite out of hearing. In the middle of this great city I began to feel myself alone with nature, and Heaven knows what beside. My courage was ebbing. Punch, however, which makes beasts of so many, made a man of me again—just in time to hear with tolerable nerve and firmness the lumpy, flabby, naked feet deliberately descending the stairs again.

I took a candle, not without a tremour. As I crossed the floor I tried to extemporise a prayer, but stopped short to listen, and never finished it. The steps continued. I confess I hesitated for some seconds at the door before I took heart of grace and opened it. When I peeped out the lobby was perfectly empty—there was no monster standing on the staircase; and as the detested sound ceased, I was reassured enough to venture forward nearly to the banisters. Horror of horrors! within a stair or two beneath the spot where I stood the unearthly tread smote the floor. My eye caught something in motion; it was about the size of Goliah's foot—it was grey, heavy, and flapped with a dead weight from one step to another. As I am alive, it was the most monstrous grey rat I ever beheld or imagined.

Shakespeare says—"Some men there are cannot abide a gaping pig, and some that are mad if they behold a cat." I went well-nigh out of my wits when I beheld this *rat;* for, laugh at me as you may, it fixed upon me, I thought, a perfectly human expression of malice; and, as it shuffled about and looked up into my face almost from between my feet, I saw, I could swear it—I felt it then, and know it now, the infernal gaze and the accursed countenance of my old friend in the portrait, transfused into the visage of the bloated vermin before me.

I bounced into my room again with a feeling of loathing and horror I cannot describe, and locked and bolted my door as if a

lion had been at the other side. D—n him or *it;* curse the portrait and its original! I felt in my soul that the rat—yes, the *rat,*
the RAT I had just seen, was that evil being in masquerade, and
rambling through the house upon some infernal night lark.

Next morning I was early trudging through the miry streets;
and, among other transactions, posted a peremptory note recalling
Tom. On my return, however, I found a note from my absent
"chum," announcing his intended return next day. I was doubly
rejoiced at this, because I had succeeded in getting rooms; and
because the change of scene and return of my comrade were
rendered specially pleasant by the last night's half ridiculous half
horrible adventure.

I slept extemporaneously in my new quarters in Digges' Street
that night, and next morning returned for breakfast to the haunted
mansion, where I was certain Tom would call immediately on his
arrival.

I was quite right—he came; and almost his first question referred to the primary object of our change of residence.

"Thank God," he said with genuine fervour, on hearing that all
was arranged. "On *your* account I am delighted. As to myself, I
assure you that no earthly consideration could have induced me
ever again to pass a night in this disastrous old house."

"Confound the house!" I ejaculated, with a genuine mixture of
fear and detestation, "we have not had a pleasant hour since we
came to live here"; and so I went on, and related incidentally my
adventure with the plethoric old rat.

"Well, if that were *all,*" said my cousin, affecting to make light
of the matter, "I don't think I should have minded it very much."

"Ay, but its eye—its countenance, my dear Tom," urged I; "if
you had seen *that,* you would have felt it might be *anything* but
what it seemed."

"I inclined to think the best conjurer in such a case would be an
able-bodied cat," he said, with a provoking chuckle.

"But let us hear your own adventure," I said tartly.

At this challenge he looked uneasily round him. I had poked up
a very unpleasant recollection.

"You shall hear it, Dick; I'll tell it to you," he said. "Begad, sir,
I should feel quite queer, though, telling it *here,* though we are
too strong a body for ghosts to meddle with just now."

Though he spoke this like a joke, I think it was serious calculation. Our Hebe was in a corner of the room, packing our cracked
delft tea and dinner-services in a basket. She soon suspended opera-
tions, and with mouth and eyes wide open became an absorbed

listener. Tom's experiences were told nearly in these words:—

"I saw it three times, Dick—three distinct times; and I am perfectly certain it meant me some infernal harm. I was, I say, in danger—in *extreme* danger; for, if nothing else had happened, my reason would most certainly have failed me, unless I had escaped so soon. Thank God. I *did* escape.

"The first night of this hateful disturbance, I was lying in the attitude of sleep, in that lumbering old bed. I hate to think of it. I was really wide awake, though I had put out my candle, and was lying as quietly as if I had been asleep; and although accidentally restless, my thoughts were running in a cheerful and agreeable channel.

"I think it must have been two o'clock at least when I thought I heard a sound in that—that odious dark recess at the far end of the bedroom. It was as if someone was drawing a piece of cord slowly along the floor, lifting it up, and dropping it softly down again in coils. I sate up once or twice in my bed, but could see nothing, so I concluded it must be mice in the wainscot. I felt no emotion graver than curiosity, and after a few minutes ceased to observe it.

"While lying in this state, strange to say; without at first a suspicion of anything supernatural, on a sudden I saw an old man, rather stout and square, in a sort of roan-red dressing-gown, and with a black cap on his head, moving stiffly and slowly in a diagonal direction, from the recess, across the floor of the bedroom, passing my bed at the foot, and entering the lumber-closet at the left. He had something under his arm; his head hung a little at one side; and, merciful God! when I saw his face."

Tom stopped for a while, and then said—

"That awful countenance, which living or dying I never can forget, disclosed what he was. Without turning to the right or left, he passed beside me, and entered the closet by the bed's head.

"While this fearful and indescribable type of death and guilt was passing, I felt that I had no more power to speak or stir than if I had been myself a corpse. For hours after it had disappeared, I was too terrified and weak to move. As soon as daylight came, I took courage, and examined the room, and especially the course which the frightful intruder had seemed to take, but there was not a vestige to indicate anybody's having passed there; no sign of any disturbing agency visible among the lumber that strewed the floor of the closet.

"I now began to recover a little. I was fagged and exhausted, and at last, overpowered by a feverish sleep. I came down late; and finding you out of spirits, on account of your dreams about the portrait, whose *original* I am now certain disclosed himself to me, I did not care to talk about the infernal vision. In fact, I was trying to persuade myself that the whole thing was an illusion, and I did not like to revive in their intensity the hated impressions of the past night—or to risk the constancy of my scepticism, by recounting the tale of my sufferings.

"It required some nerve, I can tell you, to go to my haunted chamber next night, and lie down quietly in the same bed," continued Tom. "I did so with a degree of trepidation, which, I am not ashamed to say, a very little matter would have sufficed to stimulate to downright panic. This night, however, passed off quietly enough, as also the next; and so too did two or three more. I grew more confident, and began to fancy that I believed in the theories of spectral illusions, with which I had at first vainly tried to impose upon my convictions.

"The apparition had been, indeed, altogether anomalous. It had crossed the room without any recognition of my presence: I had not disturbed *it*, and *it* had no mission to *me*. What, then, was the imaginable use of its crossing the room in a visible shape at all? Of course it might have *been* in the closet instead of *going* there, as easily as it introduced itself into the recess without entering the chamber in a shape discernible by the senses. Besides, how the deuce *had* I seen it? It was a dark night; I had no candle; there was no fire; and yet I saw it as distinctly, in colouring and outline, as ever I beheld human form! A cataleptic dream would explain it all; and I was determined that a dream it should be.

"One of the most remarkable phenomena connected with the practice of mendacity is the vast number of deliberate lies we tell ourselves, whom, of all persons, we can least expect to deceive. In all this, I need hardly tell you, Dick, I was simply lying to myself, and did not believe one word of the wretched humbug. Yet I went on, as men will do, like persevering charlatans and impostors, who tire people into credulity by the mere force of reiteration; so I hoped to win myself over at last to a comfortable scepticism about the ghost.

"He had not appeared a second time—that certainly was a comfort; and what, after all, did I care for him, and his queer old toggery and strange looks? Not a fig! I was nothing the worse for having seen him, and a good story the better. So I tumbled into bed, put out my candle, and, cheered by a loud drunken quarrel in the back lane, went fast asleep.

"From this deep slumber I awoke with a start. I knew I had had a horrible dream; but what it was I could not remember. My heart was thumping furiously; I felt bewildered and feverish; I sate up in the bed and looked about the room. A broad flood of moonlight came in through the curtainless window; everything was as I had last seen it; and though the domestic squabble in the back lane was, unhappily for me, allayed, I yet could hear a pleasant fellow singing, on his way home, the then popular comic ditty called, 'Murphy Delany.' Taking advantage of this diversion I lay down again, with my face towards the fireplace, and closing my eyes, did my best to think of nothing else but the song, which was every moment growing fainter in the distance:—

> 'Twas Murphy Delany, so funny and frisky,
> Stept into a shebeen shop to get his skin full;
> He reeled out again pretty well lined with whiskey,
> As fresh as a shamrock, as blind as a bull.

"The singer, whose condition I dare say resembled that of his hero, was soon too far off to regale my ears any more; and as his music died away, I myself sank into a doze, neither sound nor refreshing. Somehow the song had got into my head, and I went meandering on through the adventures of my respectable fellow-countryman, who, on emerging from the 'shebeen shop,' fell into a river, from which he was fished up to be 'sat upon' by a coroner's jury, who having learned from a 'horse-doctor' that he was 'dead as a door-nail, so there was an end,' returned their verdict accordingly, just as he returned to his senses, when an angry altercation and a pitched battle between the body and the coroner winds up the lay with due spirit and pleasantry.

"Through this ballad I continued with a weary monotony to plod, down to the very last line, and then da capo, and so on, in my uncomfortable half-sleep, for how long, I can't conjecture. I found myself at last, however, muttering, 'dead as a door-nail, so there was an end'; and something like another voice within me, seemed to say, very faintly, but sharply, 'dead! dead! dead! and may the Lord have mercy on your soul!' and instantaneously I was wide awake, and staring right before me from the pillow.

"Now—will you believe it, Dick?—I saw the same accursed figure standing full front, and gazing at me with its stony and fiendish countenance, not two yards from the bedside."

Tom stopped here, and wiped the perspiration from his face. I felt very queer. The girl was as pale as Tom; and, assembled as we were in the very scene of these adventures, we were all, I dare say, equally grateful for the clear daylight and the resuming bustle out of doors.

"For about three seconds only I saw it plainly; then it grew indistinct; but, for a long time, there was something like a column of dark vapour where it had been standing, between me and the wall; and I felt sure that he was still there. After a good while, this appearance went too. I took my clothes downstairs to the hall, and dressed there, with the door half open; then went out into the street, and walked about the town till morning, when I came back, in a miserable state of nervousness and exhaustion. I was such a fool, Dick, as to be ashamed to tell you how I came to be so upset. I thought you would laugh at me; especially as I had always talked philosophy, and treated *your* ghosts with contempt. I concluded you would give me no quarter; and so kept my tale of horror to myself.

"Now, Dick, you will hardly believe me, when I assure you, that for many nights after this last experience, I did not go to my room at all. I used to sit up for a while in the drawing-room after you had gone up to your bed; and then steal down softly to the hall-door, let myself out, and sit in the 'Robin Hood' tavern until the last guest went off; and then I got through the night like a sentry, pacing the streets till morning.

"For more than a week I never slept in bed. I sometimes had a snooze on a form in the 'Robin Hood,' and sometimes a nap in a chair during the day; but regular sleep I had absolutely none.

"I was quite resolved that we should get into another house; but I could not bring myself to tell you the reason, and I somehow put it off from day to day, although my life was, during every hour of this procrastination, rendered as miserable as that of a felon with the constables on his track. I was growing absolutely ill from this wretched mode of life.

"One afternoon I determined to enjoy an hour's sleep upon your bed. I hated mine; so that I had never, except in a stealthy visit every day to unmake it, lest Martha should discover the secret of my nightly absence, entered the ill-omened chamber.

"As ill-luck would have it, you had locked your bedroom, and taken away the key. I went into my own to unsettle the bedclothes, as usual, and give the bed the appearance of having been slept in. Now, a variety of circumstances concurred to bring about the dreadful scene through which I was that night to pass. In the first place, I was literally overpowered with fatigue, and longing for sleep; in the next place, the effect of this extreme exhaustion upon my nerves resembled that of a narcotic, and rendered me less susceptible than, perhaps, I should in any other condition have been, of the exciting fears which had become habitual to me. Then again, a little bit of the window was open, a pleasant freshness pervaded the room, and, to crown all, the cheerful sun of day was making the room quite pleasant. What was to prevent my enjoying an hour's nap *here?* The whole air was resonant with the cheerful hum of life, and the broad matter-of-fact light of day filled every corner of the room.

"I yielded—stifling my qualms—to the almost overpowering temptation; and merely throwing off my coat, and loosening my cravat, I lay down, limiting myself to *half*-an-hour's doze in the unwonted enjoyment of a feather bed, a coverlet, and a bolster.

"It was horribly insidious; and the demon, no doubt, marked my infatuated preparations. Dolt that I was, I fancied, with mind and body worn out for want of sleep, and an arrear of a full week's rest to my credit, that such measure as *half*-an-hour's sleep, in such a situation, was possible. My sleep was death-like, long, and dreamless.

"Without a start or fearful sensation of any kind, I waked gently, but completely. It was, as you have good reason to remember, long past midnight—I believe, about two o'clock. When sleep has been deep and long enough to satisfy nature thoroughly, one often wakens in this way, suddenly, tranquilly, and completely.

"There was a figure seated in that lumbering, old sofa-chair, near the fireplace. Its back was rather towards me, but I could not be mistaken; it turned slowly round, and, merciful heavens! there was the stony face, with its infernal lineaments of malignity and despair, gloating on me. There was now no doubt as to its consciousness of my presence, and the hellish malice with which it was animated, for it arose, and drew close to the bedside. There was a rope about its neck, and the other end, coiled up, it held stiffly in its hand.

"My good angel nerved me for this horrible crisis. I remained for some seconds transfixed by the gaze of this tremendous phantom. He came close to the bed, and appeared on the point of mounting upon it. The next instant I was upon the floor at the far side, and in a moment more was, I don't know how, upon the lobby.

"But the spell was not yet broken; the valley of the shadow of death was not yet traversed. The abhorred phantom was before me there; it was standing near the banisters, stooping a little, and with one end of the rope round its own neck, was poising a noose at the other, as if to throw over mine; and while engaged in this baleful pantomime, it wore a smile so sensual, so unspeakably dreadful, that my senses were nearly overpowered. I saw and remember nothing more, until I found myself in your room.

"I had a wonderful escape, Dick—there is no disputing *that*—an escape for which, while I live, I shall bless the mercy of heaven. No one can conceive or imagine what it is for flesh and blood to stand in the presence of such a thing, but one who has had the terrific experience. Dick, Dick, a shadow has passed over me—a chill has crossed my blood and marrow, and I will never be the same again—never, Dick—never!"

Our handmaid, a mature girl of two-and-fifty, as I have said, stayed her hand, as Tom's story proceeded, and by little and little drew near to us, with open mouth, and her brows contracted over her little, beady black eyes, till stealing a glance over her shoulder now and then, she established herself close behind us. During the relation, she had made various earnest comments, in an undertone; but these and her ejaculations, for the sake of brevity and simplicity. I have omitted in my narration.

"It's often I heard tell of it," she now said, "but I never believed it rightly till now—though, indeed, why should not I? Does not my mother, down there in the lane, know quare stories, God bless us, beyant telling about it? But you ought not to have slept in the back bedroom. She was loath to let me be going in and out of that room even in the day time, let alone for any Christian to spend the night in it; for sure she says it was his own bedroom."

"*Whose* own bedroom?" we asked, in a breath.

"Why, *his*—the ould Judge's—Judge Horrock's, to be sure, God rest his sowl"; and she looked fearfully round.

"Amen!" I muttered. "But did he die there?"

"Die there! No, not quite *there*," she said. "Shure, was not it over the banisters he hung himself, the ould sinner, God be merciful to us all? and was not it in the alcove they found the handles of the skipping-rope cut off, and the knife where he was settling the cord, God bless us, to hang himself with? It was his housekeeper's daughter owned the rope, my mother often told me, and the child never throve after, and used to be starting up out of her sleep, and screeching in the night time, wid dhrames and frights that cum an her; and they said how it was the speerit of the ould Judge that was tormentin' her; and she used to be roaring and yelling out to hould back the big ould fellow with the crooked neck; and then she'd screech 'Oh, the master! the master! he's stampin' at me, and beckoning to me! Mother, darling, don't let me go!' And so the poor crathure died at last, and the docthers

said it was wather on the brain, for it was all they could say."
"How long ago was all this?" I asked.
"Oh, then, how would I know?" she answered. "But it must be
a wondherful long time ago, for the housekeeper was an ould
woman, with a pipe in her mouth, and not a tooth left, and better
nor eighty years ould when my mother was first married; and they
said she was a rale buxom, fine-dressed woman when the ould
Judge come to his end; an', indeed, my mother's not far from
eighty years ould herself this day; and what made it worse for the
unnatural ould villain, God rest his soul, to frighten the little girl
out of the world the way he did, was what was mostly thought and
believed by every one. My mother says how the poor little crathure
was his own child; for he was by all accounts an ould villain every
way, an' the hangin'est judge that ever was known in Ireland's
ground."
"From what you said about the danger of sleeping in that bedroom," said I, "I suppose there were stories about the ghost having
appeared there to others."
"Well, there *was* things said—quare things, surely," she answered, as it seemed, with some reluctance. "And why would not
there? Sure was it not up in that same room he slept for more than
twenty years? and was it not in the *alcove* he got the rope ready
that done his own business at last, the way he done many a betther
man's in his lifetime?—and was not the body lying in the same
bed after death, and put in the coffin there, too, and carried out to
his grave from it in Pether's churchyard, after the coroner was
done? But there was quare stories—my mother has them all—
about how one Nicholas Spaight got into trouble on the head
of it."
"And what did they say of this Nicholas Spaight?" I asked.
"Oh, for that matther, it's soon told," she answered.
And she certainly did relate a very strange story, which so
piqued my curiosity, that I took occasion to visit the ancient lady,
her mother, from whom I learned many very curious particulars.
Indeed, I am tempted to tell the tale, but my fingers are weary,
and I must defer it. But if you wish to hear it another time, I shall
do my best.
When we had heard the strange tale I have *not* told you, we put
one or two further questions to her about the alleged spectral
visitations, to which the house had, ever since the death of the
wicked old Judge, been subjected.
"No one ever had luck in it," she told us. "There was always
cross accidents, sudden deaths, and short times in it. The first that

tuck it was a family—I forget their name—but at any rate there was two young ladies and their papa. He was about sixty, and a stout healthy gentleman as you'd wish to see at that age. Well, he slept in that unlucky back bedroom; and, God between us an' harm! sure enough he was found dead one morning, half out of the bed, with his head as black as a sloe, and swelled like a puddin', hanging down near the floor. It was a fit, they said. He was as dead as a mackerel, and so *he* could not say what it was; but the ould people was all sure that it was nothing at all but the ould Judge, God bless us! that frightened him out of his senses and his life together.

"Some time after there was a rich old maiden lady took the house. I don't know which room *she* slept in, but she lived alone; and at any rate, one morning, the servants going down early to their work, found her sitting on the passage-stairs, shivering and talkin' to herself, quite mad; and never a word more could any of *them* or her friends get from her ever afterwards but, 'Don't ask me to go, for I promised to wait for him.' They never made out from her who it was she meant by *him,* but of course those that knew all about the ould house were at no loss for the meaning of all that happened to her.

"Then afterwards, when the house was let out in lodgings, there was Micky Byrne that took the same room, with his wife and three little children; and sure I heard Mrs. Byrne myself telling how the children used to be lifted up in the bed at night, she could not see by what mains; and how they were starting and screeching every hour, just all as one as the housekeeper's little girl that died, till at last one night poor Micky had a dhrop in him, the way he used now and again; and what do you think in the middle of the night he thought he heard a noise on the stairs, and being in liquor, nothing less id do him but out he must go himself to see what was wrong. Well, after that, all she ever heard of him was himself sayin', 'Oh, God!' and a tumble that shook the very house; and there, sure enough, he was lying on the lower stairs, under the lobby, with his neck smashed double undher him, where he was flung over the banisters."

Then the handmaiden added—

"I'll go down to the lane, and send up Joe Gavvey to pack up the rest of the taythings, and bring all the things across to your new lodgings."

And so we all sallied out together, each of us breathing more freely, I have no doubt, as we crossed that ill-omened threshold for the last time.

Now, I may add thus much, in compliance with the immemorial usage of the realm of fiction, which sees the hero not only through his adventures, but fairly out of the world. You must have perceived that what the flesh, blood, and bone hero of romance proper is to the regular compounder of fiction, this old house of brick, wood, and mortar is to the humble recorder of this true tale. I, therefore, relate, as in duty bound, the catastrophe which ultimately befell it, which was simply this—that about two years subsequently to my story it was taken by a quack doctor, who called himself Baron Duhlstoerf, and filled the parlour windows with bottles of indescribable horrors preserved in brandy, and the newspapers with the usual grandiloquent and mendacious advertisements. This gentleman among his virtues did not reckon sobriety, and one night, being overcome with much wine, he set fire to his bed curtains, partially burned himself, and totally consumed the house. It was afterwards rebuilt, and for a time an undertaker established himself in the premises.

I have now told you my own and Tom's adventures, together with some valuable collateral particulars; and having acquitted myself of my engagement, I wish you a very good night, and pleasant dreams.

The Dead Sexton

The sunsets were red, the nights were long, and the weather pleasantly frosty; and Christmas, the glorious herald of the New Year, was at hand, when an event—still recounted by winter firesides, with a horror made delightful by the mellowing influence of years—occurred in the beautiful little town of Golden Friars, and signalized, as the scene of its catastrophe, the old inn known throughout a wide region of the Northumbrian counties as the George and Dragon.

Toby Crooke, the sexton, was lying dead in the old coach-house in the inn yard. The body had been discovered, only half an hour before this story begins, under strange circumstances, and in a place where it might have lain the better part of a week undisturbed; and a dreadful suspicion astounded the village of Golden Friars.

A wintry sunset was glaring through a gorge of the western mountains, turning into fire the twigs of the leafless elms, and all the tiny blades of grass on the green by which the quaint little town is surrounded. It is built of light, grey stone, with steep gables and slender chimneys rising with airy lightness from the level sward by the margin of the beautiful lake, and backed by the grand amphitheatre of the fells at the other side, whose snowy peaks show faintly against the sky, tinged with the vaporous red of the western light. As you descend towards the margin of the lake, and see Golden Friars, its taper chimneys and slender gables, its curious old inn and gorgeous sign, and over all the graceful tower and spire of the ancient church, at this hour or by moonlight, in the solemn grandeur and stillness of the natural scenery that surrounds it, it stands before you like a fairy town.

Toby Crooke, the lank sexton, now fifty or upwards, had passed an hour or two with some village cronies, over a solemn pot of purl, in the kitchen of that cosy hostelry, the night before. He generally turned in there at about seven o'clock, and heard the news. This contented him: for he talked little, and looked always surly.

Many things are now raked up and talked over about him.

In early youth, he had been a bit of a scamp. He broke his indentures, and ran away from his master, the tanner of Bryemere; he had got into fifty bad scrapes and out again; and, just as the little world of Golden Friars had come to the conclusion that it would be well for all parties—except, perhaps, himself—and a happy riddance for his afflicted mother, if he were sunk, with a gross of quart pots about his neck, in the bottom of the lake in which the grey gables, the elms, and the towering fells of Golden Friars are mirrored, he suddenly returned, a reformed man at the ripe age of forty.

For twelve years he had disappeared, and no one knew what had become of him. Then, suddenly, as I say, he reappeared at Golden Friars—a very black and silent man, sedate and orderly. His mother was dead and buried; but the "prodigal son" was received good-naturedly. The good vicar, Doctor Jenner, reported to his wife:

"His hard heart has been softened, dear Dolly. I saw him dry his eyes, poor fellow, at the sermon yesterday."

"I don't wonder, Hugh darling. I know the part—'There is joy in Heaven.' I am sure it was—wasn't it? It was quite beautiful. I almost cried myself."

The Vicar laughed gently, and stooped over her chair and kissed her, and patted her cheek fondly.

"You think too well of your old man's sermons," he said. "I preach, you see, Dolly, very much to the *poor*. If *they* understand me, I am pretty sure everyone else must; and I think that my simple style goes more home to both feelings and conscience——"

"You ought to have told me of his crying before. You *are* so eloquent," exclaimed Dolly Jenner. "No one preaches like my man. I have never heard such sermons."

Not many, we may be sure; for the good lady had not heard more than six from any other divine for the last twenty years.

The personages of Golden Friars talked Toby Crooke over on his return. Doctor Lincote said:

"He must have led a hard life; he had *dried in* so, and got a good deal of hard muscle; and he rather fancied he had been soldiering—he stood like a soldier; and the mark over his right eye looked like a gunshot."

People might wonder how he could have survived a gunshot over the eye; but was not Lincote a doctor—and an army doctor to boot—when he was young; and who, in Golden Friars, could dispute with him on points of surgery? And I believe the truth is, that this mark had been really made by a pistol bullet.

Mr. Jarlcot, the attorney, would "go bail" he had picked up some sense in his travels; and honest Turnbull, the host of the George and Dragon, said heartily:

"We must look out something for him to put his hand to. *Now's* the time to make a man of him."

The end of it was that he became, among other things, the sexton of Golden Friars.

He was a punctual sexton. He meddled with no other person's business; but he was a silent man, and by no means popular. He was reserved in company; and he used to walk alone by the shore of the lake, while other fellows played at fives or skittles; and when he visited the kitchen of the George, he had his liquor to himself, and in the midst of the general talk was a saturnine listener. There was something sinister in this man's face; and when things went wrong with him, he could look dangerous enough.

There were whispered stories in Golden Friars about Toby Crooke. Nobody could say how they got there. Nothing is more mysterious than the spread of rumour. It is like a vial poured on the air. It travels, like an epidemic, on the sightless currents of the atmosphere, or by the laws of a telluric influence equally intangible. These stories treated, though darkly, of the long period of his absence from his native village; but they took no well-defined shape, and no one could refer them to any authentic source.

The Vicar's charity was of the kind that thinketh no evil; and in such cases he always insisted on proof. Crooke was, of course, undisturbed in his office.

On the evening before the tragedy came to light—trifles are always remembered after the catastrophe—a boy, returning along the margin of the mere, passed him by seated on a prostrate trunk of a tree, under the "bield" of a rock, counting silver money. His lean body and limbs were bent together, his knees were up to his chin, and his long fingers were telling the coins over hurriedly in the hollow of his other hand. He glanced at the boy, as the old English saying is, like "the devil looking over Lincoln." But a black and sour look from Mr. Crooke, who never had a smile for a child nor a greeting for a wayfarer, was nothing strange.

Toby Crooke lived in the grey stone house, cold and narrow, that stands near the church porch, with the window of its staircase looking out into the churchyard, where so much of his labour, for many a day, had been expended. The greater part of this house was untenanted.

The old woman who was in charge of it slept in a settle-bed, among broken stools, old sacks, rotten chests and other rattle-traps, in the small room at the rear of the house, floored with tiles.

At what time of the night she could not tell, she awoke, and saw a man, with his hat on, in her room. He had a candle in his hand, which he shaded with his coat from her eye; his back was towards her, and he was rummaging in the drawer in which she usually kept her money.

Having got her quarter's pension of two pounds that day, however, she had placed it, folded in a rag, in the corner of her tea caddy, and locked it up in the "eat-malison" or cupboard.

She was frightened when she saw the figure in her room, and she could not tell whether her visitor might not have made his entrance from the contiguous churchyard. So, sitting bolt upright in her bed, her grey hair almost lifting her kerchief off her head, and all over in "a fit o' t' creepins," as she expressed it, she demanded:

"In God's name, what want ye thar?"

"Whar's the peppermint ye used to hev by ye, woman? I'm bad wi' an inward pain."

"It's all gane a month sin'," she answered; and offered to make him a "het" drink if he'd get to his room.

But he said:

"Never mind, I'll try a mouthful o' gin."

And, turning on his heel, he left her.

In the morning the sexton was gone. Not only in his lodging was there no account of him, but, when inquiry began to be extended, nowhere in the village of Golden Friars could he be found.

Still he might have gone off, on business of his own, to some distant village, before the town was stirring; and the sexton had no near kindred to trouble their heads about him. People, therefore, were willing to wait, and take his return ultimately for granted.

At three o'clock the good Vicar, standing at his hall door, looking across the lake towards the noble fells that rise, steep and furrowed, from that beautiful mere, saw two men approaching across the green, in a straight line, from a boat that was moored at the water's edge. They were carrying between them something which, though not very large, seemed ponderous.

"Ye'll ken this, sir," said one of the boatmen as they set down, almost at his feet, a small church bell, such as in old-fashioned chimes yields the treble notes.

"This won't be less nor five stean. I ween it's fra' the church steeple yon."

"What! one of our church bells?" ejaculated the Vicar—for a moment lost in horrible amazment. "Oh, no!—no, that can't possibly be! Where did you find it?"

He had found the boat, in the morning, moored about fifty yards from her moorings where he had left it the night before, and could not think how that came to pass; and now, as he and his partner were about to take their oars, they discovered this bell in the bottom of the boat, under a bit of canvas, also the sexton's pick and spade—"tom-spey'ad," they termed that peculiar, broad-bladed implement.

"Very extraordinary! We must try whether there is a bell missing from the tower," said the Vicar, getting into a fuss. "Has Crooke come back yet? Does anyone know where he is?"

The sexton had not yet turned up.

"That's odd—that's provoking," said the Vicar. "However, my key will let us in. Place the bell in the hall while I get it; and then we can see what all this means."

To the church, accordingly, they went, the Vicar leading the way, with his own key in his hand. He turned it in the lock, and stood in the shadow of the ground porch, and shut the door.

A sack, half full, lay on the ground, with open mouth, a piece of cord lying beside it. Something clanked within it as one of the men shoved it aside with his clumsy shoe.

The Vicar opened the church door and peeped in. The dusky glow from the western sky, entering through a narrow window, illuminated the shafts and arches, the old oak carvings, and the discoloured monuments, with the melancholy glare of a dying fire.

The Vicar withdrew his head and closed the door. The gloom of the porch was deeper than ever as, stooping, he entered the narrow door that opened at the foot of the winding stair that leads to the first loft; from which a rude ladder-stair of wood, some five and twenty feet in height, mounts through a trap to the ringers' loft.

Up the narrow stairs the Vicar climbed, followed by his attendants, to the first loft. It was very dark: a narrow bow-slit in the thick wall admitted the only light they had to guide them. The ivy leaves, seen from the deep shadow, flashed and flickered redly, and the sparrows twittered among them.

"Will one of you be so good as to go up and count the bells, and see if they are all right?" said the Vicar. "There should be—"

"Agoy! what's that?" exclaimed one of the men, recoiling from the foot of the ladder.

"By Jen!" ejaculated the other, in equal surprise.

"Good gracious!" gasped the Vicar, who, seeing indistinctly a dark mass lying on the floor, had stooped to examine it, and placed his hand upon a cold, dead face.

The men drew the body into the streak of light that traversed the floor.

It was the corpse of Toby Crooke! There was a frightful scar across his forehead.

The alarm was given. Doctor Lincote, and Mr. Jarlcot, and Turnbull, of the George and Dragon, were on the spot immediately; and many curious and horrified spectators of minor importance.

The first thing ascertained was that the man must have been many hours dead. The next was that his skull was fractured, across the forehead, by an awful blow. The next was that his neck was broken.

His hat was found on the floor, where he had probably laid it, with his handkerchief in it.

The mystery now began to clear a little; for a bell—one of the chime hung in the tower—was found where it had rolled to, against the wall, with blood and hair on the rim of it, which corresponded with the grizzly fracture across the front of his head.

The sack that lay in the vestibule was examined, and found to contain all the church plate; a silver salver that had disappeared, about a month before, from Dr. Lincote's store of valuables; the Vicar's gold pencil-case, which he thought he had forgot in the vestry book; silver spoons, and various other contributions, levied from time to time off a dozen different households, the mysterious disappearance of which spoils had, of late years, begun to make the honest little community uncomfortable. Two bells had been taken down from the chime; and now the shrewd part of the assemblage, putting things together, began to comprehend the nefarious plans of the sexton, who lay mangled and dead on the floor of the tower, where only two days ago he had tolled the holy bell to call the good Christians of Golden Friars to worship.

The body was carried into the yard of the George and Dragon and laid in the old coach-house; and the townsfolk came grouping in to have a peep at the corpse, and stood round, looking darkly, and talking as low as if they were in a church.

The Vicar, in gaiters and slightly shovel hat, stood erect, as one

in a little circle of notables—the doctor, the attorney, Sir Geoffrey
Mardykes, who happened to be in the town, and Turnbull, the
host—in the centre of the paved yard, they having made an
inspection of the body, at which troops of the village stragglers,
to-ing and fro-ing, were gaping and frowning as they whispered
their horrible conjectures.

"What d'ye think o' that?" said Tom Scales, the old hostler of
the George, looking pale, with a stern, faint smile on his lips, as he
and Dick Linklin sauntered out of the coach-house together.

"The deaul will hev his ain noo," answered Dick, in his friend's
ear. "T' sexton's got a craigthraw like he gav' the lass over the
clints of Scarsdale; ye mind what the ald soger telt us when he hid
his face in the kitchen of the George here? By Jen! I'll ne'er forget
that story."

"I ween 'twas all true enough," replied the hostler; "and the
sizzup he gav' the sleepin' man wi' t' poker across the forehead.
See whar the edge o' t' bell took him, and smashed his ain, the
self-same lids. By ma sang, I wonder the deaul did na carry awa'
his corpse i' the night, as he did wi' Tam Lunder's at Mooltern
Mill."

"Hout, man, who ever sid t' deaul inside o' a church?"

"The corpse is ill-faur'd enew to scare Satan himsel', for that
matter; though it's true what you say. Ay, ye're reet tul a trippet,
thar; for Beelzebub dar'n't show his snout inside the church, not
the length o' the black o' my nail."

While this discussion was going on, the gentlefolk who were
talking the matter over in the centre of the yard had dispatched a
message for the coroner all the way to the town of Hextan.

The last tint of sunset was fading from the sky by this time; so,
of course, there was no thought of an inquest earlier than next day.

In the meantime it was horribly clear that the sexton had
intended to rob the church of its plate, and had lost his life in the
attempt to carry the second bell, as we have seen, down the worn
ladder of the tower. He had tumbled backwards and broken his
neck upon the floor of the loft; and the heavy bell, in its fall,
descended with its edge across his forehead.

Never was a man more completely killed by a double catastrophe, in a moment.

The bells and the contents of the sack, it was surmised, he
meant to have conveyed across the lake that night, and with the
help of his spade and pick to have buried them in Clousted Forest,
and returned, after an absence of but a few hours—as he easily
might—before morning, unmissed and unobserved. He would no

It was the corpse of Toby Crooke!

doubt, having secured his booty, have made such arrangements as would have made it appear that the church had been broken into. He would, of course, have taken all measures to divert suspicion from himself, and have watched a suitable opportunity to repossess himself of the buried treasure and dispose of it in safety.

And now came out, into sharp relief, all the stories that had, one way or other, stolen after him into the town. Old Mrs. Pullen fainted when she saw him, and told Doctor Lincote, after, that she thought he was the highwayman who fired the shot that killed the coachman the night they were robbed on Hounslow Heath. There were the stories also told by the wayfaring old soldier with the wooden leg, and fifty others, up to this more than half disregarded, but which now seized on the popular belief with a startling grasp.

The fleeting light soon expired, and twilight was succeeded by the early night.

The inn yard gradually became quiet; and the dead sexton lay alone, in the dark, on his back, locked up in the old coach-house, the key of which was safe in the pocket of Tom Scales, the trusty old hostler of the George.

It was about eight o'clock, and the hostler, standing alone on the road in the front of the open door of the George and Dragon, had just smoked his pipe out. A bright moon hung in the frosty sky. The fells rose from the opposite edge of the lake like phantom mountains. The air was stirless. Through the boughs and sprays of the leafless elms no sigh or motion, however hushed, was audible. Not a ripple glimmered on the lake, which at one point only reflected the brilliant moon from its dark blue expanse like burnished steel. The road that runs by the inn door, along the margin of the lake, shone dazzlingly white.

White as ghosts, among the dark holly and juniper, stood the tall piers of the Vicar's gate, and their great stone balls, like heads, overlooking the same road, a few hundred yards up the lake, to the left. The early little town of Golden Friars was quiet by this time. Except for the townsfolk who were now collected in the kitchen of the inn itself, no inhabitant was now outside his own threshold.

Tom Scales was thinking of turning in. He was beginning to fell a little queer. He was thinking of the sexton, and could not get the fixed features of the dead man out of his head, when he heard the sharp though distant ring of a horse's hoof upon the frozen road. Tom's instinct apprized him of the approach of a guest to the George and Dragon. His experienced ear told him that the horseman was approaching by the Dardale road, which, after crossing that wide and dismal moss, passes the southern fells by Dunner Cleugh and finally enters the town of Golden Friars by joining the Mardykes-road, at the edge of the lake, close to the gate of the Vicar's house.

A clump of tall trees stood at this point; but the moon shone full upon the road and cast their shadow backward.

The hoofs were plainly coming at a gallop, with a hollow rattle. The horseman was a long time in appearing. Tom wondered how he had heard the sound—so sharply frosty as the air was—so very far away.

He was right in his guess. The visitor was coming over the mountainous road from Dardale Moss; and he now saw a horseman, who must have turned the corner of the Vicar's house at the moment when his eye was wearied; for when he saw him for the first time he was advancing, in the hazy moonlight, like the shadow of a cavalier, at a gallop, upon the level strip of road that skirts the margin of the mere, between the George and the Vicar's piers.

The hostler had not long to wonder why the rider pushed his beast at so furious a pace, and how he came to have heard him, as he now calculated, at least three miles away. A very few moments sufficed to bring horse and rider to the inn door.

It was a powerful black horse, something like the great Irish hunter that figured a hundred years ago, and would carry sixteen stone with ease across country. It would have made a grand charger. Not a hair turned. It snorted, it pawed, it arched its neck; then threw back its ears and down its head, and looked ready to lash, and then to rear; and seemed impatient to be off again, and incapable of standing quiet for a moment.

The rider got down

As light as shadow falls.

But he was a tall, sinewy figure. He wore a cape or short mantle, a cocked hat, and a pair of jack-boots, such as held their ground in some primitive corners of England almost to the close of the last century.

"Take him, lad," said he to old Scales. "You need not walk or wisp him—he never sweats or tires. Give him his oats, and let him take his own time to eat them. House!" cried the stranger—in the old-fashioned form of summons which still lingered, at that time, in out-of-the-way places—in a deep and piercing voice.

As Tom Scales led the horse away to the stables it turned its head towards its master with a short, shill neigh.

"About *your* business, old gentleman—we must not go too fast," the stranger cried back again to his horse, with a laugh as harsh and piercing; and he strode into the house.

The hostler led this horse into the inn yard. In passing, it sidled up to the coach-house gate, within which lay the dead sexton—snorted, pawed and lowered its head suddenly, with ear close to the plank, as if listening for a sound from within; then uttered again the same short, piercing neigh.

The hostler was chilled at this mysterious coquetry with the dead. He liked the brute less and less every minute.

In the meantime, its master had proceeded.

"I'll go to the inn kitchen," he said, in his startling bass, to the drawer who met him in the passage.

And on he went, as if he had known the place all his days: not seeming to hurry himself—stepping leisurely, the servant thought —but gliding on at such a rate, nevertheless, that he had passed his guide and was in the kitchen of the George before the drawer had got much more than half-way to it.

A roaring fire of dry wood, peat and coal lighted up this snug but spacious apartment—flashing on pots and pans, and dressers high-piled with pewter plates and dishes; and making the uncertain shadows of the long "hanks" of onions and many a flitch and ham, depending from the ceiling, dance on its glowing surface.

The doctor and the attorney, even Sir Geoffrey Mardykes, did not disdain on this occasion to take chairs and smoke their pipes by the kitchen fire, where they were in the thick of the gossip and discussion excited by the terrible event.

The tall stranger entered uninvited.

He looked like a gaunt, athletic Spaniard of forty, burned half black in the sun, with a bony, flattened nose. A pair of fierce black eyes were just visible under the edge of his hat; and his mouth seemed divided, beneath the moustache, by the deep scar of a hare-lip.

Sir Geoffrey Mardykes and the host of the George, aided by the doctor and the attorney, were discussing and arranging, for the third or fourth time, their theories about the death and the probable plans of Toby Crooke, when the stranger entered.

The new-comer lifted his hat, with a sort of smile, for a moment from his black head.

"What do you call this place, gentlemen?" asked the stranger.

"The town of Golden Friars, sir," answered the doctor politely.

"The George and Dragon, sir: Anthony Turnbull, at your service," answered mine host, with a solemn bow, at the same moment—so that the two voices went together, as if the doctor and the innkeeper were singing a catch.

"The George and the Dragon," repeated the horseman, expanding his long hands over the fire which he had approached. "Saint George, King George, the Dragon, the Devil: it is a very grand idol, that outside your door, sir. You catch all sorts of worshippers—courtiers, fanatics, scamps: all's fish, eh? Everybody welcome, provided he drinks like one. Suppose you brew a bowl or two of punch. I'll stand it. How many are we? *Here*—count, and let us have enough. Gentlemen, I mean to spend the night here, and my horse is in the stable. What holiday, fun, or fair has got so many pleasant faces together? When I last called here—for, now I bethink me, I have seen the place before—you all looked sad. It was on a Sunday, that dismalest of holidays; and it would have been positively melancholy only that your sexton—that saint upon earth—Mr. Crooke, was here." He was looking round, over his shoulder, and added: "Ha! don't I see him there?"

Frightened a good deal were some of the company. All gaped in the direction in which, with a nod, he turned his eyes.

"He's *not* thar—he *can't* be thar—we *see* he's not thar," said Turnbull, as dogmatically as old Joe Willet might have delivered himself—for he did not care that the George should earn the reputation of a haunted house. "He's met an accident, sir: he's dead—he's elsewhere—and therefore can't be here."

Upon this the company entertained the stranger with the narrative—which they made easy by a division of labour, two or three generally speaking at a time, and no one being permitted to finish a second sentence without finding himself corrected and supplanted.

"The man's in Heaven, so sure as you're not," said the traveller so soon as the story was ended. "What! he was fiddling with the church bell, was he, and d——d for that—eh? Landlord, get us some drink. A sexton d——d for pulling down a church bell he has been pulling at for ten years!"

"You came, sir, by the Dardale-road, I believe?" said the doctor (village folk are curious). "A dismal moss is Dardale Moss, sir; and a bleak clim' up the fells on t'other side."

"I say 'Yes' to all—from Dardale Moss, as black as pitch and as rotten as the grave, up that zigzag wall you call a road, that looks like chalk in the moonlight, through Dunner Cleugh, as dark as a coal-pit, and down here to the George and the Dragon, where you have a roaring fire, wise men, good punch—here it is—and a

corpse in your coach-house. Where the carcase is, there will the
eagles be gathered together. Come, landlord, ladle out the nectar.
Drink, gentlemen—drink, all. Brew another bowl at the bar. How
divinely it stinks of alcohol! I hope you like it, gentlemen: it smells
all over of spices, like a mummy. Drink, friends. Ladle, landlord.
Drink, all. Serve it out."

The guest fumbled in his pocket, and produced three guineas,
which he slipped into Turnbull's fat palm.

"Let punch flow till that's out. I'm an old friend of the house.
I call here, back and forward. I know you well, Turnbull, though
you don't recognize me."

"You have the advantage of me, sir," said Mr. Turnbull, looking
hard on that dark and sinister countenance—which, or the like of
which, he could have sworn he had never seen before in his life.
But he liked the weight and colour of his guineas, as he dropped
them into his pocket. "I hope you will find yourself comfortable
while you stay."

"You have given me a bedroom?"

"Yes, sir—the cedar chamber."

"I know it—the very thing. No—no punch for me. By and by,
perhaps."

The talk went on, but the stranger had grown silent. He had
seated himself on an oak bench by the fire, towards which he extended his feet and hands with seeming enjoyment; his cocked hat
being, however, a little over his face.

Gradually the company began to thin. Sir Geoffrey Mardykes
was the first to go; then some of the humbler townsfolk. The last
bowl of punch was on its last legs. The stranger walked into the
passage and said to the drawer:

"Fetch me a lantern. I must see my nag. Light it—hey! That
will do. No—you need not come."

The gaunt traveller took it from the man's hand and strode
along the passage to the door of the stableyard, which he opened
and passed out.

Tom Scales, standing on the pavement, was looking through the
stable window at the horses when the stranger plucked his shirt-
sleeve. With an inward shock the hostler found himself alone in
presence of the very person he had been thinking of.

"I say—they tell me you have something to look at in there"—
he pointed with his thumb at the old coach-house door. "Let us
have a peep."

Tom Scales happened to be at that moment in a state of mind
highly favourable to anyone in search of a submissive instrument.

He was in great perplexity, and even perturbation. He suffered the
stranger to lead him to the coach-house gate.

"You must come in and hold the lantern," said he. "I'll pay you
handsomely."

The old hostler applied his key and removed the padlock.

"What are you afraid of? Step in and throw the light on his
face," said the stranger grimly. "Throw open the lantern: stand
there. Stoop over him a little—he won't bite you. Steady, or you
may pass the night with him!"

In the meantime the company at the George had dispersed; and,
shortly after, Anthony Turnbull—who, like a good landlord, was
always last in bed, and first up, in his house—was taking, alone,
his last look round the kitchen before making his final visit to the
stable-yard, when Tom Scales tottered into the kitchen, looking
like death, his hair standing upright; and he sat down on an oak
chair, all in a tremble, wiped his forehead with his hand, and,
instead of speaking, heaved a great sigh or two.

It was not till after he had swallowed a dram of brandy that he
found his voice, and said:

"We've the deaul himsel' in t' house! By Jen! ye'd best send fo
t' sir" (the clergyman). "Happen he'll tak him in hand wi' holy
writ, and send him elsewhidder deftly. Lord atween us and harm!
I'm a sinfu' man. I tell ye, Mr. Turnbull, I dar'n't stop in t' George
to-night under the same roof wi' him."

"Ye mean the ra-beyoned, black-feyaced lad, wi' the brocken
neb? Why, that's a gentleman wi' a pocket ful o' guineas, man, and
a horse worth fifty pounds!"

"That horse is no better nor his rider. The nags that were in the
stable wi' him, they all tuk the creepins, and sweated like rain
down a thack. I tuk them all out o' that, away from him, into the
hack-stable, and I thocht I cud never get them past him. But that's
not all. When I was keekin inta t' winda at the nags, he comes
behint me and claps his claw on ma shouther, and he gars me gang
wi' him, and open the aad coach-house door, and haad the cannle
for him, till he pearked into the deed man't feyace; and, as God's
my judge, I sid the corpse open its eyes and wark its mouth, like a
man smoorin' and strivin' to talk. I cudna move or say a word,
though I felt my hair rising on my heed; but at lang-last I gev a
yelloch, and say I, 'La! what is that?' And he himsel' looked round
on me, like the devil he is; and, wi' a skirl o' a laugh, he strikes the
lantern out o' my hand. When I cum to myself we were outside
the coach-house door. The moon was shinin' in, ad I cud see the

corpse stretched on the table whar we left it; and he kicked the door to wi' a purr o' his foot. 'Lock it,' says he; and so I did. And here's the key for ye—tak it yoursel', sir. He offer'd me money: he said he'd mak me a rich man if I'd sell him the corpse, and help him awa' wi' it."

"Hout, man! What cud he want o' t' corpse? He's not doctor, to do a' that lids. He was takin' a rise out o' ye, lad," said Turnbull.

"Na, na—he wants the corpse. There's summat you a' me can't tell he wants to do wi' 't; and he'd liefer get it wi' sin and thievin', and the damage of my soul. He's one of them freytens a boo or a dobbies off Dardale Moss, that's always astir wi' the like after nightfall; unless—Lord save us!—he be the deaul himsel.' "

"Whar is he noo?" asked the landlord, who was growing uncomfortable.

"He spang'd up the back stair to his room. I wonder you didn't hear him trampin' like a wild horse; and he clapt his door that the house shook again—but Lord knows whar he is noo. Let us gang awa's up to the Vicar's, and gan him come down, and talk wi' him."

"Hoity toity, man—you're too easy scared," said the landlord, pale enough by this time. " 'Twould be a fine thing, truly, to send abroad that the house was haunted by the deaul himsel'! Why, 'twould be the ruin o' the George. You're sure ye locked the door on the corpse?"

"Aye, sir—sartain."

"Come wi' me, Tom—we'll gi' a last look round the yard."

So, side by side, with many a jealous look right and left, and over their shoulders, they went in silence. On entering the old-fashioned quadrangle, surrounded by stables and other offices—built in the antique cagework fashion—they stopped for a while under the shadow of the inn gable, and looked round the yard, and listened. All was silent—nothing stirring.

The stable lantern was lighted; and with it in his hand Tony Turnbull, holding Tom Scales by the shoulder, advanced. He hauled Tom after him for a step or two; then stood still and shoved him before him for a step or two more; and thus cautiously—as a pair of skirmishers under fire—they approached the coach-house door.

"There, ye see—all safe," whispered Tom, pointing to the lock, which hung—distinct in the moonlight—in its place. "Cum back, I say!"

"Cum on, say I!" retorted the landlord valorously. "It would never do to allow any tricks to be played with the chap in there" —he pointed to the coachhouse door.

"The coroner here in the morning, and never a corpse to sit on!"
He unlocked the padlock with these words, having handed the
lantern to Tom. "Here, keck in, Tom," he continued; "ye hev the
lantern—and see if all's as ye left it."

"Not me—na, not for the George and a' that's in it!" said Tom,
with a shudder, sternly, as he took a step backward.

"What the—what are ye afraid on? Gi' me the lantern—it is all
one: I will."

And cautiously, little by little, he opened the door; and, holding
the lantern over his head in the narrow slit, he peeped in—
frowning and pale—with one eye, as if he expected something to
fly in his face. He closed the door without speaking, and locked it
again.

"As safe as a thief in a mill," he whispered with a nod to his
companion. And at that moment a harsh laugh overhead broke
the silence startlingly, and set all the poultry in the yard gabbling.

"Thar he be!" said Tom, clutching the landlord's arm—"in the
winda—see!"

The window of the cedar-room, up two pair of stairs, was open;
and in the shadow a darker outline was visible of a man, with his
elbows on the window-stone, looking down upon them.

"Look at his eyes—like two live coals!" gasped Tom.

The landlord could not see all this so sharply, being confused,
and not so long-sighted as Tom.

"Time, sir," called Tony Turnbull, turning cold as he thought
he saw a pair of eyes shining down redly at him—"time for honest
folk to be in their beds, and asleep!"

"As sound as your sexton!" said the jeering voice from above.

"Come out of this," whispered the landlord fiercely to his hostler,
plucking him hard by the sleeve.

They got into the house, and shut the door.

"I wish we were shot of him," said the landlord, with something
like a groan, as he leaned against the wall of the passage. "I'll sit
up, anyhow—and, Tom, you'll sit wi' me. Cum into the gun-room.
No one shall steal the dead man out of my yard while I can draw
a trigger."

The gun-room in the George is about twelve feet square. It
projects into the stable-yard and commands a full view of the old
coach-house; and, through a narrow side window, a flanking view
of the back door of the inn, through which the yard is reached.

Tony Turnbull took down the blunderbuss—which was the
great ordnance of the house—and loaded it with a stiff charge of
pistol bullets.

He put on a great-coat which hung there, and was his covering when he went out at night, to shoot wild ducks. Tom made himself comfortable likewise. They then sat down at the window, which was open, looking into the yard, the opposite side of which was white in the brilliant moonlight.

The landlord laid the blunderbuss across his knees, and stared into the yard. His comrade stared also. The door of the gun-room was locked; so they felt tolerably secure.

An hour passed; nothing had occurred. Another. The clock struck one. The shadows had shifted a little; but still the moon shone full on the old coach-house, and the stable where the guest's horse stood.

Turnbull thought he heard a step on the back-stair. Tom was watching the back-door through the side window, with eyes glazing with the intensity of his stare. Anthony Turnbull, holding his breath, listened at the room door. It was a false alarm.

When he came back to the window looking into the yard:

"Hish! Look thar!" said he in a vehement whisper.

From the shadow at the left they saw the figure of the gaunt horseman, in short cloak and jack-boots, emerge. He pushed open the stable door, and led out his powerful black horse. He walked it across the front of the building till he reached the old coach-house door; and there, with its bridle on its neck, he left it standing, while he stalked to the yard gate; and, dealing it a kick with his heel, it sprang back with the rebound, shaking from top to bottom, and stood open. The stranger returned to the side of his horse; and the door which secured the corpse of the dead sexton seemed to swing slowly open of itself as he entered, and returned with the corpse in his arms, and swung it across the shoulders of the horse, and instantly sprang into the saddle.

"Fire!" shouted Tom, and bang went the blunderbuss with a stunning crack. A thousand sparrows' wings winnowed through the air from the thick ivy. The watch-dog yelled a furious bark. There was a strange ring and whistle in the air. The blunderbuss had burst to shivers right down to the very breech. The recoil rolled the inn-keeper upon his back on the floor, and Tom Scales was flung against the side of the recess of the window, which had saved him from a tumble as violent. In this position they heard the searing laugh of the departing horseman, and saw him ride out of the gate with his ghastly burden.

Perhaps some of my readers, like myself, have heard this story told by Roger Turnbull, now host of the George and Dragon, the grandson of the very Tony who then swayed the spigot and keys of that inn, in the identical kitchen of which the fiend treated so many of the neighbours to punch.

What infernal object was subserved by the possession of the dead villain's body, I have not learned. But a very curious story, in which a vampire resuscitation of Crooke the sexton figures, may throw a light upon this part of the tale.

The result of Turnbull's shot at the disappearing fiend certainly justifies old Andrew Moreton's dictum, which is thus expressed in his curious "History of Apparitions": "I warn rash brands who, pretending not to fear the devil, are for using the ordinary violences with him, which affect one man from another—or with an apparition, in which they may be sure to receive some mischief. I knew one fired a gun at an apparition and the gun burst in a hundred pieces in his hand; another struck at an apparition with a sword, and broke his sword in pieces and wounded his hand grievously; and 'tis next to madness for anyone to go that way to work with any spirit, be it angel or be it devil."

Ghost Stories of the
Tiled House

I

Old Sally always attended her young mistress while she prepared for bed—not that Lilias required help, for she had the spirit of neatness and a joyous, gentle alacrity, and only troubled the good old creature enough to prevent her thinking herself grown old and useless.

Sally, in her quiet way, was garrulous, and she had all sorts of old-world tales of wonder and adventure, to which Lilias often went pleasantly to sleep; for there was no danger while old Sally sat knitting there by the fire, and the sound of the rector's mounting upon his chairs, as was his wont, and taking down and putting up his books in the study beneath, though muffled and faint, gave evidence that that good and loving influence was awake and busy.

Old Sally was telling her young mistress, who sometimes listened with a smile, and sometimes lost a good five minutes together of her gentle prattle, how the young gentleman, Mr. Mervyn, had taken that awful old haunted habitation, the Tiled House "beyant at Ballyfermot," and was going to stay there, and wondered no one had told him of the mysterious dangers of that desolate mansion.

It stood by a lonely bend of the narrow road. Lilias had often looked up the short, straight, grass-grown avenue with an awful curiosity at the old house which she had learned in childhood to fear as the abode of shadowy tenants and unearthly dangers.

"There are people, Sally, now-a-days, who call themselves free-thinkers, and don't believe in any thing—even in ghosts," said Lilias.

"A then the place he's stopping in now, Miss Lilly, 'ill soon cure him of freethinking, if the half they say about it's true," answered Sally.

"But I don't say, mind, *he*'s a freethinker, for I don't know any thing of Mr. Mervyn; but if he be not, he must be very brave, or very good, indeed. I know, Sally, I should be horribly afraid, indeed, to sleep in it myself," answered Lilias, with a cosey little shudder, as the aërial image of the old house for a moment stood before her, with its peculiar malign, scared, and skulking aspect, as if it had drawn back in shame and guilt among the melancholy old elms and tall hemlock and nettles.

"And now, Sally, I'm safe in bed. Stir the fire, my old darling." For although it was the first week in May, the night was frosty. "And tell me all about the Tiled House again, and frighten me out of my wits."

So good old Sally, whose faith in such matters was a religion, went off over the well-known ground in a gentle little amble— sometimes subsiding into a walk as she approached some special horror, and pulling up altogether—that is to say, suspending her knitting, and looking with a mysterious nod at her young mistress in the four-poster, or lowering her voice to a sort of whisper when the crisis came.

So she told her how when the neighbours hired the orchard that ran up to the windows at the back of the house, the dogs they kept then used to howl so wildly and wolfishly all night among the trees, and prowl under the walls of the house so dejectedly, that they were fain to open the door and let them in at last; and, indeed, small need there was there for dogs; for no one, young or old, dared go near the orchard after night-fall. No, the golden pippins that peeped so splendid through the leaves in the western rays of evening, and made the mouths of the Ballyfermot schoolboys water, glowed undisturbed in the morning sunbeams, and secure in the mysterious tutelage of the night, smiled coyly on their predatory longings. And this was no fanciful reserve and avoid- ance. Mick Daly, when he had the orchard, used to sleep in the loft over the kitchen; and he swore that within five or six weeks, while he lodged there, he twice saw the same thing, and that was a lady in a hood and a loose dress, her head drooping, and her finger on her lip, walking in silence among the crooked stems, with a little child by the hand, who ran smiling and skipping beside her. And the Widow Cresswell once met them at night-fall on the path through the orchard to the back-door, and she did not know what it was until she saw the men looking at one another as she told it.

"It's often she told it to me," said old Sally; "and how she came on them all of a sudden at the turn of the path, just by the thick clump of alder trees; and how she stopped, thinking it was some

lady that had a right to be there; and how they went by as swift as
the shadow of a cloud, though she only seemed to be walking slow
enough, and the little child pulling by her arm, this way and that
way, and took no notice of her, nor even raised her head, though
she stopped and curtsied. And old Clinton, don't you remember
old Clinton, Miss Lilly?"

"I think I do, the old man who limped, and wore the odd black
wig?"

"Yes, indeed, acushla, so he did. See how well she remembers?
That was by a kick of one of the earl's horses—he was groom then,"
resumed Sally. "He used to be troubled with hearing the very
sounds his master used to make to bring him and old Oliver to the
door, when he came back late. It was only on very dark nights
when there was no moon. They used to hear, all on a sudden, the
whimpering and scraping of dogs at the hall-door, and the sound
of the whistle, and the light stroke across the window with the
lash of the whip, just like as if the earl himself—may his poor
soul find rest—was there. First the wind 'id stop, like you'd be
holding your breath, then came these sounds they knew so well,
and when they made no sign of stirring or opening the door, the
wind 'id begin again with such a hoo-hoo-o-o-high, you'd think it
was laughing, and crying, and hooting, all at once."

Here old Sally resumed her knitting, suspended for a moment,
as if she were listening to the wind outside the haunted precincts
of the Tiled House, and she took up her parable again.

"The very night he met his death in London, old Oliver, the
butler, was listening to Clinton—for Clinton was a scholar—
reading the letter that came to him through the post that day,
telling him to get things ready, for his troubles were nearly over,
and he expected to be with them again in a few days, and maybe
almost as soon as the letter; and sure enough, while he was reading,
there came a frightful rattle to the window, like some one all in a
tremble, trying to shake it open, and the earl's voice, as they both
conceited, cries from outside, 'Let me in, let me in, let me in!'
'It's him,' says the butler. ' 'Tis so, bedad,' says Clinton, and they
both looked at the windy, and at one another—and then back
again—overjoyed and frightened all at onst. Old Oliver was bad
with the rheumatiz in his knee, and went lame like. So away goes
Clinton to the hall-door, and he calls, who's there? and no answer.
Maybe, says Clinton, to himself, 'tis what he's rid round to the
back-door; so to the back-door with him, and there he shouts again
—and no answer, and not a sound outside—and he began to feel
quare, and to the hall-door with him back again. 'Who's there?

do you hear, who's there?' he shouts, and receiving no answer still. 'I'll open the door at any rate,' says he, 'maybe it's what he's made his escape,' for they knew all about his troubles, 'and wants to get in without noise,' so praying all the time—for his mind misgave him, it might not be all right—he shifts the bars and unlocks the door; but neither man, woman, nor child, nor horse, nor any living shape, was standing there, only something or another slipt into the house close by his leg; it might be a dog, or something that way, he could not tell, for he only seen it for a moment with the corner of his eye, and it went in just like as if it belonged to the place. He could not see which way it went, up or down, but the house was never a happy one, or a quiet house after; and Clinton bangs the hall-door, and he took a sort of a turn and a thrembling, and back with him to Oliver, the butler, looking as white as the blank leaf of his master's letter that was fluttering between his finger and thumb. 'What is it? *what* is it?' says the butler, catching his crutch like a waypon, fastening his eyes on Clinton's white face, and growing almost as pale himself. 'The master's dead,' says Clinton —and so he was, signs on it.

"After the turn she got by what she seen in the orchard, when she came to know the truth of what it was, Jinny Cresswell, you may be sure, did not stay there any longer than she could help; and she began to take notice of things she did not mind before— such as when she went into the big bed-room over the hall that the lord used to sleep in, whenever she went in at one door the other door used to be pulled to very quick, as if some one avoiding her was getting out in haste; but the thing that frightened her most was just this– that sometimes she used to find a long, straight mark from the head to the foot of her bed, as if 'twas made by something heavy lying there, and the place where it was used to feel warm, as if—whoever it was—they only left it as she came into the room.

"But the worst of all was poor Kitty Halpin, the young woman that died of what she seen. Her mother said it was how she was kept awake all the night with the walking about of some one in the next room, tumbling about boxes and pulling open drawers and talking and sighing to himself, and she, poor thing, wishing to go to sleep and wondering who it could be, when in he comes, a fine man, in a sort of loose silk morning-dress an' no wig, but a velvet cap on, and to the windy with him quiet and aisy, and she makes a turn in the bed to let him know there was some one there, thinking he'd go away, but instead of that, over he comes to the side of the bed, looking very bad, and says something to her—but his speech was thick and queer, like a dummy's that 'id be trying to spake—and she grew very frightened, and says she, 'I ask your honour's pardon, sir, but I can't hear you right,' and with that he stretches up his neck high out of his cravat, turning his face up towards the ceiling, and—grace between us and harm!—his throat was cut across like another mouth, wide open, laughing at her; she seen no more, but dropped in a dead faint in the bed, and back to her mother with her in the morning, and she never swallied bit or sup more, only she just sat by the fire holding her mother's hand, crying and trembling, and peepin' over her shoulder, and starting with every sound, till she took the fever and died, poor thing, not five weeks after."—

And so on, and on, and on flowed the stream of old Sally's narrative, while Lilias dropped into dreamless sleep, and then the story-teller stole away to her own tidy bed-room and innocent slumbers.

II

I'm sure she believed every word she related, for old Sally was veracious. But all this was worth just so much as such talk commonly is—marvels, fabulæ, what our ancestors call winter's tales —which gathered details from every narrator and dilated in the act of narration. Still it was not quite for nothing that the house was held to be haunted. Under all this smoke there smouldered just a little spark of truth—an authenticated mystery, for the solution of which some of my readers may possibly suggest a theory, though I confess I can't.

Miss Rebecca Chattesworth, in a letter dated late in the autumn of 1753, gives a minute and curious relation of occurrences in the Tiled House, which, it is plain, although at starting she protests against all such fooleries, she has heard with a peculiar sort of interest, and relates it certainly with an awful sort of particularity.

I was for printing the entire letter, which is really very singular as well as characteristic. But my publisher meets me with his *veto;* and I believe he is right. The worthy old lady's letter *is*, perhaps, too long; and I must rest content with a few hungry notes of its tenor.

That year, and somewhere about the 24th October, there broke out a strange dispute between Mr. Alderman Harper, of High-street, Dublin, and my Lord Castlemallard, who, in virtue of his cousinship to the young heir's mother, had undertaken for him the management of the tiny estate on which the Tiled or Tyled House—for I find it spelt both ways—stood.

This Alderman Harper had agreed for a lease of the house for his daughter, who was married to a gentleman named Prosser. He furnished it and put up hangings, and otherwise went to considerable expense. Mr. and Mrs. Prosser came there some time in June, and after having parted with a good many servants in the interval, she made up her mind that she could not live in the house, and her father waited on Lord Castlemallard and told him plainly that he would not take out the lease because the house was subjected to annoyances which he could not explain. In plain terms, he said it was haunted, and that no servants would live there more than a few weeks, and that after what his son-in-law's family had suffered there, not only should he be excused from taking a lease of it, but that the house itself ought to be pulled down as a nuisance and the habitual haunt of something worse than human malefactors.

Lord Castlemallard filed a bill in the Equity side of Exchequer to compel Mr. Alderman Harper to perform his contract, by taking out the lease. But the alderman drew an answer, supported by no less than seven long affidavits, copies of all which were furnished to his lordship, and with the desired effect; for rather than compel him to place them upon the file of the court, his lordship struck, and consented to release him.

I am sorry the cause did not proceed at least far enough to place upon the records of the court the very authentic and unaccountable story which Miss Rebecca relates.

The annoyances described did not begin till the end of August, when, one evening, Mrs. Prosser, quite alone, was sitting in the twilight at the back parlour window, which was open, looking out into the orchard, and plainly saw a hand stealthily placed upon the stone window-sill outside, as if by some one beneath the window, at her right side, intending to climb up. There was nothing but the hand, which was rather short, but handsomely formed, and white and plump, laid on the edge of the window-sill; and it was not a very young hand, but one aged, somewhere above forty, as she conjectured. It was only a few weeks before that the horrible robbery at Clondalkin had taken place, and the lady fancied that the hand was that of one of the miscreants who was now about to scale the windows of the Tiled House. She uttered a loud scream and an ejaculation of terror, and at the same moment the hand was quietly withdrawn.

Search was made in the orchard, but there were no indications of any person's having been under the window, beneath which, ranged along the wall, stood a great column of flower-pots, which it seemed must have prevented any one's coming within reach of it.

The same night there came a hasty tapping, every now and then, at the window of the kitchen. The women grew frightened, and the servant-man, taking fire-arms with him, opened the back-door, but discovered nothing. As he shut it, however, he said "a thump came on it," and a pressure as of somebody striving to force his way in, which frightened *him;* and though the tapping went on upon the kitchen window-panes, he made no further explorations.

About six o'clock on Saturday evening, the cook, "an honest, sober woman, now aged nigh sixty years," being alone in the kitchen, saw, on looking up, it is supposed, the same fat but aristocratic-looking hand laid with its palm against the glass, near the side of the window, and this time moving slowly up and down, pressed all the while against the glass, as if feeling carefully for some inequality in its surface. She cried out, and said something like a prayer, on seeing it. But it was not withdrawn for several seconds after.

After this, for a great many nights, there came at first a low, and afterwards an angry rapping, as it seemed with a set of clenched knuckles, at the back-door. And the servant-man would not open it, but called to know who was there; and there came no answer, only a sound as if the palm of the hand was placed against it, and drawn slowly from side to side, with a sort of soft, groping motion.

All this time, sitting in the back parlour, which, for the time, they used as a drawing-room, Mr. and Mrs. Prosser were disturbed by rappings at the window, sometimes very low and furtive, like a clandestine signal, and at others sudden and so loud as to threaten the breaking of the pane.

This was all at the back of the house, which looked upon the orchard, as you know. But on a Tuesday night, at about half-past nine, there came precisely the same rapping at the hall-door, and went on, to the great annoyance of the master and terror of his wife, at intervals, for nearly two hours.

After this, for several days and nights, they had no annoyance whatsoever, and began to think that the nuisance had expended itself. But on the night of the 13th September, Jane Easterbrook, an English maid, having gone into the pantry for the small silver bowl in which her mistress's posset was served, happening to look up at the little window of only four panes, observed through an auger-hole which was drilled through the window-frame, for the admission of a bolt to secure the shutter, a white pudgy finger— first the tip, and then the two first joints introduced, and turned about this way and that, crooked against the inside, as if in search of a fastening which its owner designed to push aside. When the maid got back into the kitchen, we are told "she fell into 'a swounde,' and was all the next day very weak."

Mr. Prosser being, I've heard, a hard-headed and conceited sort of fellow, scouted the ghost, and sneered at the fears of his family. He was privately of opinion that the whole affair was a practical joke or a fraud, and waited an opportunity of catching the rogue *flagrante delicto*. He did not long keep this theory to himself, but let it out by degrees with no stint of oaths and threats, believing that some domestic traitor held the thread of the conspiracy.

Indeed it was time something were done; for not only his servants, but good Mrs. Prosser herself, had grown to look unhappy and anxious, and kept at home from the hour of sunset, and would not venture about the house after night-fall, except in couples.

The knocking had ceased for about a week; and one night, Mrs. Prosser being in the nursery, her husband, who was in the parlour, heard it begin very softly at the hall-door. The air was quite still, which favoured his hearing distinctly. This was the first time there had been any disturbance at that side of the house, and the character of the summons also was changed.

Mr. Prosser, leaving the parlour door open, it seems, went quietly into the hall. The sound was that of beating on the outside of the stout door, softly and regularly, "with the flat of the hand." He was going to open it suddenly, but changed his mind; and went back very quietly, and on to the head of the kitchen stair, where was "a strong closet" over the pantry, in which he kept his "fire-arms, swords, and canes."

Here he called his man-servant, whom he believed to be honest; and with a pair of loaded pistols in his own coat-pockets, and giving another pair to him, he went as lightly as he could, followed by the man, and with a stout walking-cane in his hand, forward to the door.

Every thing went as Mr. Prosser wished. The besieger of his house, so far from taking fright at their approach, grew more impatient; and the sort of patting which had roused his attention at first, assumed the rhythm and emphasis of a series of double-knocks.

Mr. Prosser, angry, opened the door with his right arm across, cane in hand. Looking, he saw nothing; but his arm was jerked up oddly, as it might be with the hollow of a hand, and something passed under it, with a kind of gentle squeeze. The servant neither saw nor felt any thing, and did not know why his master looked back so hastily, and shut the door with so sudden a slam.

From that time, Mr. Prosser discontinued his angry talk and

swearing about it, and seemed nearly as averse from the subject as the rest of his family. He grew, in fact, very uncomfortable, feeling an inward persuasion that when, in answer to the summons, he had opened the hall-door, he had actually given admission to the besieger.

He said nothing to Mrs. Prosser, but went up earlier to his bedroom, where "he read a while in his Bible, and said his prayers:" I hope the particular relation of this circumstance does not indicate its singularity. He lay awake a good while, it appears; and as he supposed, about a quarter past twelve, he heard the soft palm of a hand patting on the outside of the bedroom door, and then brushed slowly along it.

Up bounced Mr. Prosser, very much frightened, and locked the door, crying, "Who's there?" but receiving no answer but the same brushing sound of a soft hand drawn over the panels, which he knew only too well.

In the morning the housemaid was terrified by the impression of a hand in the dust of the "little parlour" table, where they had been unpacking delft and other things the day before. The print of the naked foot in the sea-sand did not frighten Robinson Crusoe half so much. They were by this time all nervous, and some of them half crazed, about the hand.

Mr. Prosser went to examine the mark, and made light of it, but, as he swore afterwards, rather to quiet his servants than from any comfortable feeling about it in his own mind; however, he had them all, one by one, into the room, and made each place his or her hand, palm downward, on the same table, thus taking a similar impression from every person in the house, including himself and his wife; and his "affidavit" deposed that the formation of the hand so impressed differed altogether from those of the living inhabitants of the house, and corresponded exactly with that of the hand seen by Mrs. Prosser and by the cook.

Whoever or whatever the owner of that hand might be, they all felt this subtle demonstration to mean that it was declared he was no longer out of doors, but had established himself in the house.

And now Mrs. Prosser began to be troubled with strange and horrible dreams, some of which, as set out in detail, in Aunt Rebecca's long letter, are really very appalling nightmares. But one night, as Mr. Prosser closed his bedchamber door, he was struck somewhat by the utter silence of the room, there being no sound of breathing, which seemed unaccountable to him, as he knew his wife was in bed, and his ears were particularly sharp.

There was a candle burning on a small table at the foot of the bed, besides the one he held in one hand, a heavy leger connected with his father-in-law's business being under his arm. He drew the curtain at the side of the bed, and saw Mrs. Prosser lying, as for a few seconds he mortally feared, dead, her face being motionless, white, and covered with a cold dew; and on the pillow, close beside her head, and just within the curtains, was the same white, fattish hand, the wrist resting on the pillow, and the fingers extended towards her temple with a slow, wavy motion.

Mr. Prosser, with a horrified jerk, pitched the leger right at the curtains behind which the owner of the hand might be supposed to stand. The hand was instantaneously and smoothly snatched away, the curtains made a great wave, and Mr. Prosser got round the bed in time to see the closet-door, which was at the other side, drawn close by the same white, puffy hand, as he believed.

He drew the door open with a fling, and stared in; but the closet was empty, except for the clothes hanging from the pegs on the wall, and the dressing-table and looking-glass facing the windows. He shut it sharply, and locked it, and felt for a minute, he says, "as if he were like to lose his wits;" then, ringing at the bell, he brought the servants, and with much ado they recovered Mrs. Prosser from a sort of "trance," in which, he says, from her looks, she seemed to have suffered "the pains of death;" and Aunt Rebecca adds, "from what she told me of her visions, with her own lips, he might have added 'and of hell also.' "

But the occurrence which seems to have determined the crisis was the strange sickness of their eldest child, a little girl aged between two and three years. It lay awake, seemingly in paroxysms of terror, and the doctors who were called in set down the symptoms to incipient water on the brain. Mrs. Prosser used to sit up with the nurse, by the nursery fire, much troubled in mind about the condition of her child.

Its bed was placed sideways along the wall, with its head against the door of a press or cupboard, which, however, did not shut quite close. There was a little valance, about a foot deep, round the top of the child's bed, and this descended within some ten or twelve inches of the pillow on which it lay.

They observed that the little creature was quieter whenever they took it up and held it on their laps. They had just replaced it, as it seemed to have grown quite sleepy and tranquil, but it was not five minutes in its bed when it began to scream in one of its frenzies of terror; at the same moment the nurse for the first time detected, and Mrs. Prosser equally plainly saw, following the direction of her eyes, the real cause of the child's sufferings.

Protruding through the aperture of the press, and shrouded in the shade of the valance, they plainly saw the white fat hand, palm downwards, presented towards the head of the child. The mother uttered a scream, and snatched the child from its little bed, and she and the nurse ran down to the lady's sleeping-room, where Mr. Prosser was in bed, shutting the door as they entered; and they had hardly done so, when a gentle tap came to it from the outside.

There is a great deal more, but this will suffice. The singularity of the narrative seems to me to be this, that it describes the ghost of a hand, and no more. The person to whom that hand belonged never once appeared; nor was it a hand separated from a body, but only a hand so manifested and introduced, that its owner was always, by some crafty accident, hidden from view.

In the year 1819, at a college breakfast, I met a Mr. Prosser—a thin, grave, but rather chatty old gentleman, with very white hair, drawn back into a pigtail—and he told us all, with a concise particularity, a story of his cousin, James Prosser, who, when an infant, had slept for some time in what his mother said was a haunted nursery in an old house near Chapelizod, and who, whenever he was ill, over-fatigued, or in anywise feverish, suffered all through his life, as he had done from a time he could scarce remember, from a vision of a certain gentleman, fat and pale, every curl of whose wig, every button and fold of whose laced clothes, and every feature and line of whose sensual, malignant*, and unwholesome face, was as minutely engraven upon his memory as the dress and lineaments of his father's portrait, which hung before him every day at breakfast, dinner, and supper.

Mr. Prosser mentioned this as an instance of a curiously monotonous, individualized, and persistent nightmare, and hinted the extreme horror and anxiety with which his cousin, of whom he spoke in the past tense as "poor Jemmie," was at any time induced to mention it.

I hope the reader will pardon me for loitering so long in the Tiled House, but this sort of lore has always had a charm for me; and people, you know, especially old people, will talk of what most interests themselves, too often forgetting that others may have had more than enough of it.

*"Benignant" in the text.—E.B.

The White Cat of
Drumgunniol

There is a famous story of a white cat, with which we all become acquainted in the nursery. I am going to tell a story of a white cat very different from the amiable and enchanted princess who took that disguise for a season. The white cat of which I speak was a more sinister animal.

The traveller from Limerick toward Dublin, after passing the hills of Killaloe upon the left, as Keeper Mountain rises high in view, finds himself gradually hemmed in, up the right, by a range of lower hills. An undulating plain that dips gradually to a lower level than that of the road interposes, and some scattered hedgerows relieve its somewhat wild and melancholy character.

One of the few human habitations that send up their films of turf-smoke from that lonely plain, is the loosely-thatched, earth-built dwelling of a "strong farmer," as the more prosperous of the tenant-farming classes are termed in Munster. It stands in a clump of trees near the edge of a wandering stream, about half-way between the mountains and the Dublin road, and had been for generations tenanted by people named Donovan.

In a distant place, desirous of studying some Irish records which had fallen into my hands, and inquiring for a teacher capable of instructing me in the Irish language, a Mr. Donovan, dreamy, harmless, and learned, was recommended to me for the purpose.

I found that he had been educated as a Sizar in Trinity College, Dublin. He now supported himself by teaching, and the special direction of my studies, I suppose, flattered his national partialities, for he unbosomed himself of much of his long-reserved thoughts, and recollections about his country and his early days. It was he who told me this story, and I mean to repeat it, as nearly as I can, in his own words.

I have myself seen the old farm-house, with its orchard of huge

mossgrown apple trees. I have looked round on the peculiar landscape; the roofless, ivied tower, that two hundred years before had
afforded a refuge from raid and rapparee, and which still occupies
its old place in the angle of the haggard; the bush-grown "liss,"
that scarcely a hundred and fifty steps away records the labours of
a bygone race; the dark and towering outline of old Keeper in the
background; and the lonely range of furze and heath-clad hills that
form a nearer barrier, with many a line of grey rock and clump of
dwarf oak or birch. The pervading sense of loneliness made it a
scene not unsuited for a wild and unearthly story. And I could
quite fancy how, seen in the grey of a wintry morning, shrouded
far and wide in snow, or in the melancholy glory of an autumnal
sunset, or in the chill splendour of a moonlight night, it might
have helped to tone a dreamy mind like honest Dan Donovan's to
superstition and a proneness to the illusions of fancy. It is certain,
however, that I never anywhere met with a more simple-minded
creature, or one on whose good faith I could more entirely rely.

When I was a boy, said he, living at home at Drumgunniol, I
used to take my Goldsmith's *Roman History* in my hand and go
down to my favourite seat, the flat stone, sheltered by a hawthorn
tree beside the little lough, a large and deep pool, such as I have
heard called a tarn in England. It lay in the gentle hollow of a
field that is overhung toward the north by the old orchard, and
being a deserted place was favourable to my studious quietude.

One day reading here, as usual, I wearied at last, and began to
look about me, thinking of the heroic scenes I had just been
reading of. I was as wide awake as I am at this moment, and I saw
a woman appear at the corner of the orchard and walk down the
slope. She wore a long, light grey dress, so long that it seemed to
sweep the grass behind her, and so singular was her appearance in
a part of the world where female attire is so inflexibly fixed by
custom, that I could not take my eyes off her. Her course lay
diagonally from corner to corner of the field, which was a large
one, and she pursued it without swerving.

When she came near I could see that her feet were bare, and
that she seemed to be looking steadfastly upon some remote object
for guidance. Her route would have crossed me—had the tarn not
interposed—about ten or twelve yards below the point at which I
was sitting. But instead of arresting her course at the margin of the
lough, as I had expected, she went on without seeming conscious
of its existence, and I saw her, as plainly as I see you, sir, walk
across the surface of the water, and pass, without seeming to see
me, at about the distance I had calculated.

I was ready to faint from sheer terror. I was only thirteen years old then, and I remember every particular as if it had happened this hour.

The figure passed through the gap at the far corner of the field, and there I lost sight of it. I had hardly strength to walk home, and was so nervous, and ultimately so ill, that for three weeks I was confined to the house, and could not bear to be alone for a moment. I never entered that field again, such was the horror with which from that moment every object in it was clothed. Even at this distance of time I should not like to pass through it.

This apparition I connected with a mysterious event; and, also, with a singular liability, that has for nearly eight years distinguished, or rather afflicted, our family. It is no fancy. Everybody in that part of the country knows all about it. Everybody connected what I had seen with it.

I will tell it all to you as well as I can.

When I was about fourteen years old—that is about a year after the sight I had seen in the lough field—we were one night expecting my father home from the fair of Killaloe. My mother sat up to welcome him home, and I with her, for I liked nothing better than such a vigil. My brothers and sisters, and the farm servants, except the men who were driving home the cattle from the fair, were asleep in their beds. My mother and I were sitting in the chimney corner chatting together, and watching my father's supper, which was kept hot over the fire. We knew that he would return before the men who were driving home the cattle, for he was riding, and told us that he would only wait to see them fairly on the road, and then push homeward.

At length we heard his voice and the knocking of his loaded whip at the door, and my mother let him in. I don't think I ever saw my father drunk, which is more than most men of my age, from the same part of the country, could say of theirs. But he could drink his glass of whisky as well as another, and he usually came home from fair or market a little merry and mellow, and with a jolly flush in his cheeks.

To-night he looked sunken, pale and sad. He entered with the saddle and bridle in his hand, and he dropped them against the wall, near the door, and put his arms round his wife's neck, and kissed her kindly.

"Welcome home, Meehal," said she, kissing him heartily.

"God bless you, mavourneen," he answered.

And hugging her again, he turned to me, who was plucking him by the hand, jealous of his notice. I was little, and light of my age, and he lifted me up in his arms, and kissed me, and my arms being about his neck, he said to my mother:

"Draw the bolt, acuishla."

She did so, and setting me down very dejectedly, he walked to the fire and sat down on a stool, and stretched his feet toward the glowing turf, leaning with his hands on his knees.

"Rouse up, Mick, darlin'," said my mother, who was growing anxious, "and tell me how did the cattle sell, and did everything go lucky at the fair, or is there anything wrong with the landlord, or what in the world is it that ails you, Mick, jewel?"

"Nothin', Molly. The cows sould well, thank God, and there's nothin' fell out between me an' the landlord, an' everything's the same way. There's no fault to find anywhere."

"Well, then, Mickey, since so it is, turn round to your hot supper, and ate it, and tell us is there anything new."

"I got my supper, Molly, on the way, and I can't ate a bit," he answered.

"Got your supper on the way, an' you knowin' 'twas waiting for you at home, an' your wife sittin' up an' all!" cried my mother, reproachfully.

"You're takin' a wrong meanin' out of what I say," said my father. "There's something happened that leaves me that I can't ate a mouthful, and I'll not be dark with you, Molly, for, maybe, it ain't very long I have to be here, an' I'll tell you what it was. It's what I've seen, the white cat."

"The Lord between us and harm!" exclaimed my mother, in a moment as pale and as chap-fallen as my father; and then, trying to rally, with a laugh, she said: "Ha! 'tis only funnin' me you are. Sure a white rabbit was snared a Sunday last, in Grady's wood; an' Teigue seen a big white rat in the haggard yesterday."

" 'Twas neither rat nor rabbit was in it. Don't ye think but I'd know a rat or a rabbit from a big white cat, with green eyes as big as halfpennies, and its back riz up like a bridge, trottin' on and across me, and ready, if I dar' stop, to rub its sides against my shins, and maybe to make a jump and seize my throat, if that it's a cat, at all, an' not something worse?"

As he ended his description in a low tone, looking straight at the fire, my father drew his big hand across his forehead once or twice, his face being damp and shining with the moisture of fear, and he sighed, or rather groaned, heavily.

My mother had relapsed into panic, and was praying again in her fear. I, too, was terribly frightened, and on the point of crying, for I knew all about the white cat.

Clapping my father on the shoulder, by way of encouragement, my mother leaned over him, kissing him, and at last began to cry. He was wringing her hands in his, and seemed in great trouble.

"There was nothin' came into the house with me?" he asked, in a very low tone, turning to me.

"There was nothin', father," I said, "but the saddle and bridle that was in your hand."

"Nothin' white kem in at the doore wid me," he repeated.

"Nothin' at all," I answered.

"So best," said my father, and making the sign of the cross, he began mumbling to himself, and I knew he was saying his prayers.

Waiting for a while, to give him time for this exercise, my mother asked him where he first saw it.

"When I was riding up the bohereen,"—the Irish term meaning a little road, such as leads up to a farm-house—"I bethought myself that the men was on the road with the cattle, and no one to look to the horse barrin' myself, so I thought I might as well leave him in the crooked field below, an' I tuck him there, he bein' cool, and not a hair turned, for I rode him aisy all the way. It was when I turned, after lettin' him go—the saddle and bridle bein' in my hand—that I saw it, pushin' out o' the long grass at the side o' the path, an' it walked across it, in front of me, an' then back again, before me, the same way, an' sometimes at one side, an' then at the other, lookin' at me wid them shinin' eyes; and I consayed I heard it growlin' as it kep' beside me—as close as ever you see—till I kem up to the doore, here, an' knocked an' called, as ye heerd me."

Now, what was it, in so simple an incident, that agitated my father, my mother, myself, and finally, every member of this rustic household, with a terrible foreboding? It was this that we, one and all, believed that my father had received, in thus encountering the white cat, a warning of his approaching death.

The omen had never failed hitherto. It did not fail now. In a week after my father took the fever that was going, and before a month he was dead.

My honest friend, Dan Donovan, paused here; I could perceive that he was praying, for his lips were busy, and I concluded that it was for the repose of that departed soul.

In a little while he resumed.

It is eighty years now since that omen first attached to my family. Eighty years? Ay, is it. Ninety is nearer the mark. And I have spoken to many old people, in those earlier times, who had a distinct recollection of everything connected with it.

It happened in this way.

My grand-uncle, Connor Donovan, had the old farm of Drumgunniol in his day. He was richer than ever my father was, or my father's father either, for he took a short lease of Balraghan, and made money of it. But money won't soften a hard heart, and I'm afraid my grand-uncle was a cruel man—a profligate man he was, surely, and that is mostly a cruel man at heart. He drank his share, too, and cursed and swore, when he was vexed, more than was good for his soul, I'm afraid.

At that time there was a beautiful girl of the Colemans, up in the mountains, not far from Capper Cullen. I'm told that there are no Colemans there now at all, and that family has passed away. The famine years made great changes.

Ellen Coleman was her name. The Colemans were not rich. But, being such a beauty, she might have made a good match. Worse than she did for herself, poor thing, she could not.

Con Donovan—my grand-uncle, God forgive him!—sometimes in his rambles saw her at fairs or patterns, and he fell in love with her, as who might not?

He used her ill. He promised her marriage, and persuaded her to come away with him; and, after all, he broke his word. It was just the old story. He tired of her, and he wanted to push himself in the world; and he married a girl of the Collopys, that had a great fortune—twenty-four cows, seventy sheep, and a hundred and twenty goats.

He married this Mary Collopy, and grew richer than before; and Ellen Coleman died broken-hearted. But that did not trouble the strong farmer much.

He would have liked to have children, but he had none, and this was the only cross he had to bear, for everything else went much as he wished.

One night he was returning from the fair of Nenagh. A shallow stream at that time crossed the road—they have thrown a bridge over it, I am told, some time since—and its channel was often dry in summer weather. When it was so, as it passes close by the old farm-house of Drumgunniol, without a great deal of winding, it makes a sort of road, which people then used as a short cut to reach the house by. Into this dry channel, as there was plenty of light from the moon, my grand-uncle turned his horse, and when he had reached the two ash-trees at the meering of the farm he turned his horse short into the river-field, intending to ride through the gap at the other end, under the oak-tree, and so he would have been within a few hundred yards of his door.

As he approached the "gap" he saw, or thought he saw, with a slow motion, gliding along the ground toward the same point, and now and then with a soft bound, a white object, which he described as being no bigger than his hat, but what it was he could not see, as it moved along the hedge and disappeared at the point to which he was himself tending.

When he reached the gap the horse stopped short. He urged and coaxed it in vain. He got down to lead it through, but it recoiled, snorted, and fell into a wild trembling fit. He mounted it again. But its terror continued, and it obstinately resisted his caresses and his whip. It was bright moonlight, and my grand-uncle was chafed by the horse's resistance, and, seeing nothing to account for it, and being so near home, what little patience he possessed forsook him, and, plying his whip and spur in earnest, he broke into oaths and curses.

All on a sudden the horse sprang through, and Con Donovan, as he passed under the broad branch of the oak, saw clearly a woman standing on the bank beside him, her arm extended, with the hand of which, as he flew by, she struck him a blow upon the shoulders. It threw him forward upon the neck of the horse, which, in wild terror, reached the door at a gallop, and stood there quivering and steaming all over.

Less alive than dead, my grand-uncle got in. He told his story, at least, so much as he chose. His wife did not quite know what to think. But that something very bad had happened she could not doubt. He was very faint and ill, and begged that the priest should be sent for forthwith. When they were getting him to his bed they saw distinctly the marks of five fingerpoints on the flesh of his shoulder, where the spectral blow had fallen. These singular marks —which they said resembled in tint the hue of a body struck by lightning—remained imprinted on his flesh, and were buried with him.

When he had recovered sufficiently to talk with the people about him—speaking, like a man at his last hour, from a burdened heart, and troubled conscience—he repeated his story, but said he did not see, or, at all events, know, the face of the figure that stood in the gap. No one believed him. He told more about it to the priest than to others. He certainly had a secret to tell. He might as well have divulged it frankly, for the neighbours all knew well enough that it was the face of dead Ellen Coleman that he had seen.

From that moment my grand-uncle never raised his head. He was a scared, silent, broken-spirited man. It was early summer then, and at the fall of the leaf in the same year he died.

Of course there was a wake, such as beseemed a strong farmer so rich as he. For some reason the arrangements of this ceremonial were a little different from the usual routine.

The usual practice is to place the body in the great room, or kitchen, as it is called, of the house. In this particular case there was, as I told you, for some reason, an unusual arrangement. The body was placed in a small room that opened upon the greater one. The door of this, during the wake, stood open. There were candles about the bed, and pipes and tobacco on the table, and stools for such guests as chose to enter, the door standing open for their reception.

The body, having been laid out, was left alone, in this smaller room, during the preparations for the wake. After nightfall one of the women, approaching the bed to get a chair which she had left near it, rushed from the room with a scream, and, having recovered her speech at the further end of the "kitchen," and surrounded by a gaping audience, she said, at last:

"May I never sin, if his face bain't riz up again the back o' the bed, and he starin' down to the doore, wid eyes as big as pewter plates, that id be shinin' in the moon!"

"Arra, woman! Is it cracked you are?" said one of the farm boys as they are termed, being men of any age you please.

"Agh, Molly, don't be talkin', woman! 'Tis what ye consayted it, goin' into the dark room, out o' the light. Why didn't ye take a candle in your fingers, ye aumadhaun?" said one of her female companions.

"Candle, or no candle; I seen it," insisted Molly. "An' what's more, I could a'most tak' my oath I seen his arum, too, stretchin' out o' the bed along the flure, three times as long as it should be, to take hould o' me be the fut."

"Nansinse, ye fool, what id he want o' yer fut?" exclaimed one scornfully.

"Gi' me the candle, some o' yez—in the name o' God," said old Sal Doolan, that was straight and lean, and a woman that could pray like a priest almost.

"Give her a candle," agreed all.

But whatever they might say, there wasn't one among them that did not look pale and stern enough as they followed Mrs. Doolan, who was praying as fast as her lips could patter, and leading the van with a tallow candle, held like a taper, in her fingers.

The door was half open, as the panic-stricken girl had left it; and holding the candle on high the better to examine the room, she made a step or so into it.

If my grand-uncle's hand had been stretched along the floor, in the unnatural way described, he had drawn it back again under the sheet that covered him. And tall Mrs. Doolan was in no danger of tripping over his arm as she entered. But she had not gone more than a step or two with her candle aloft, when, with a drowning face, she suddenly stopped short, staring at the bed which was now fully in view.

"Lord, bless us, Mrs. Doolan, ma'am, come back," said the woman next her, who had fast hold of her dress, or her 'coat,' as they call it, and drawing her backwards with a frightened pluck, while a general recoil among her followers betokened the alarm which her hesitation had inspired.

"Whisht, will yez?" said the leader, peremptorily, "I can't hear my own ears wid the noise ye're makin', an' which iv yez let the cat in here, an' whose cat is it?" she asked, peering suspiciously at a white cat that was sitting on the breast of the corpse.

"Put it away, will yez?" she resumed, with horror at the profanation. "Many a corpse as I sthretched and crossed in the bed, the likes o' that I never seen yet. The man o' the house, wid a brute baste like that mounted on him, like a phooka, Lord forgi' me for namin' the like in this room. Dhrive it away, some o' yez! out o' that, this minute, I tell ye."

Each repeated the order, but no one seemed inclined to execute it. They were crossing themselves, and whispering their conjectures and misgivings as to the nature of the beast, which was no cat of that house, nor one that they had ever seen before. On a sudden, the white cat placed itself on the pillow over the head of the body, and having from that place glared for a time at them over the features of the corpse, it crept softly along the body towards them, growling low and fiercely as it drew near.

Out of the room they bounced, in dreadful confusion, shutting the door fast after them, and not for a good while did the hardiest. venture to peep in again.

The white cat was sitting in its old place, on the dead man's breast, but this time it crept quietly down the side of the bed, and disappeared under it, the sheet which was spread like a coverlet, and hung down nearly to the floor, concealing it from view.

Praying, crossing themselves, and not forgetting a sprinkling of holy water, they peeped, and finally searched, poking spades, "wattles," pitchforks and such implements under the bed. But the cat was not to be found, and they concluded that it had made its escape among their feet as they stood near the threshold. So they secured the door carefully, with hasp and padlock.

But when the door was opened next morning they found the

white cat sitting, as if it had never been disturbed, upon the breast of the dead man.

Again occurred very nearly the same scene with a like result, only that some said they saw the cat afterwards lurking under a big box in a corner of the outer-room, where my grand-uncle kept his leases and papers, and his prayer-book and beads.

Mrs. Doolan heard it growling at her heels wherever she went; and although she could not see it, she could hear it spring on the back of her chair when she sat down, and growl in her ear, so that she would bounce up with a scream and a prayer, fancying that it was on the point of taking her by the throat.

And the priest's boy, looking round the corner, under the branches of the old orchard, saw a white cat sitting under the little window of the room where my grand-uncle was laid out and look-ing up at the four small panes of glass as a cat will watch a bird.

The end of it was that the cat was found on the corpse again, when the room was visited, and do what they might, whenever the body was left alone, the cat was found again in the same ill-omened contiguity with the dead man. And this continued, to the scandal and fear of the neighbourhood, until the door was opened finally for the wake.

My grand-uncle being dead, and, with all due solemnities, buried, I have done with him. But not quite yet with the white cat. No banshee ever yet was more inalienably attached to a family than this ominous apparition is to mine. But there is this differ-ence. The banshee seems to be animated with an affectionate sympathy with the bereaved family to whom it is hereditarily at-tached, whereas this thing has about it a suspicion of malice. It is the messenger simply of death. And its taking the shape of a cat —the coldest, and they say, the most vindictive of brutes—is in-dicative of the spirit of its visit.

When my grandfather's death was near, although he seemed quite well at the time, it appeared not exactly, but very nearly in the same way in which I told you it showed itself to my father.

The day before my Uncle Teigue was killed by the bursting of his gun, it appeared to him in the evening, at twilight, by the lough, in the field where I saw the woman who walked across the water, as I told you. My uncle was washing the barrel of his gun in the lough. The grass is short there, and there is no cover near it. He did not know how it approached but the first he saw of it, the white cat was walking close round his feet, in the twilight, with an angry twist of its tail, and a green glare in its eyes, and do what he would, it continued walking round and round him, in larger or smaller circles, till he reached the orchard, and there he lost it.

My poor Aunt Peg—she married one of the O'Brians, near Oolah—came to Drumgunniol to go to the funeral of a cousin who died about a mile away. She died herself, poor woman, only a month after.

Coming from the wake, at two or three o'clock in the morning, as she got over the stile into the farm of Drumgunniol, she saw the white cat at her side, and it kept close beside her, she ready to faint all the time, till she reached the door of the house, where it made a spring up into the white-thorn tree that grows close by, and so it parted from her. And my little brother Jim saw it also, just three weeks before he died. Every member of our family who dies, or takes his death-sickness, at Drumgunniol, is sure to see the white cat, and no one of us who sees it need hope for long life after.

An Authentic Narrative of a Haunted House

[The Editor of the UNIVERSITY MAGAZINE submits the following very remarkable statement, with every detail of which he has been for some years acquainted, upon the ground that it affords the most authentic and ample relation of a series of marvellous phenoma, in nowise connected with what is technically termed "spiritualism," which he has anywhere met with. All the persons—and there are many of them living—upon whose separate evidence some parts, and upon whose united testimony others, of this most singular recital depend, are, in their several walks of life, respectable, and such as would in any matter of judicial investigation be deemed wholly unexceptionable witnesses. There is not as incident here recorded which would not have been distinctly deposed to on oath had any necessity existed, by the persons who severally, and some of them in great fear, related their own distinct experiences. The Editor begs most pointedly to meet in limine the suspicion, that he is elaborating a trick, or vouching for another ghost of Mrs. Veal. As a mere story the narrative is valueless: its sole claim to attention is its absolute truth. For the good faith of its relator he pledges his own and the character of this Magazine. With the Editor's concurrence, the name of the watering-place, and some special circumstances in no essential way bearing upon the peculiar character of the story, but which might have indicated the locality, and possibly annoyed persons interested in house property there, have been suppressed by the narrator. Not the slightest liberty has been taken with the narrative, which is presented precisely in the terms in which the writer of it, who employs throughout the first person, would, if need were, fix it in the form of an affidavit.]

Within the last eight years—the precise date I purposely omit

419

—I was ordered by my physician, my health being in an unsatisfactory state, to change my residence to one upon the sea-coast; and accordingly, I took a house for a year in a fashionable watering-place, at a moderate distance from the city in which I had previously resided, and connected with it by a railway.

Winter was setting in when my removal thither was decided upon; but there was nothing whatever dismal or depressing in the change. The house I had taken was to all appearance, and in point of convenience, too, quite a modern one. It formed one in a cheerful row, with small gardens in front, facing the sea, and commanding sea air and sea views in perfection. In the rear it had coach-house and stable, and between them and the house a considerable grass-plot, with some flower-beds, interposed.

Our family consisted of my wife and myself, with three children, the eldest about nine years old, she and the next in age being girls; and the youngest, between six and seven, a boy. To these were added six servants, whom, although for certain reasons I decline giving their real names, I shall indicate, for the sake of clearness, by arbitrary ones. There was a nurse, Mrs. Southerland; a nursery-maid, Ellen Page; the cook, Mrs. Greenwood; and the housemaid, Ellen Faith; a butler, whom I shall call Smith, and his son, James, about two-and-twenty.

We came out to take possession at about seven o'clock in the evening; every thing was comfortable and cheery; good fires lighted, the rooms neat and airy, and a general air of preparation and comfort, highly conducive to good spirits and pleasant anticipations.

The sitting-rooms were large and cheerful, and they and the bed-rooms more than ordinarily lofty, the kitchen and servants' rooms, on the same level, were well and comfortably furnished, and had, like the rest of the house, an air of recent painting and fitting up, and a completely modern character, which imparted a very cheerful air of cleanliness and convenience.

There had been just enough of the fuss of settling agreeably to occupy us, and to give a pleasant turn to our thoughts after we had retired to our rooms. Being an invalid, I had a small bed to myself —resigning the four-poster to my wife. The candle was extinguished, but a night-light was burning. I was coming up stairs, and she, already in bed, had just dismissed her maid, when we were both startled by a wild scream from her room; I found her in a state of the extremest agitation and terror. She insisted that she had seen an unnaturally tall figure come beside her bed and stand there. The light was too faint to enable her to define any thing respecting this apparition, beyond the fact of her having most distinctly seen such a shape, colourless from the insufficiency of the light to disclose more than its dark outline.

We both endeavoured to re-assure her. The room once more looked so cheerful in the candlelight, that we were quite uninfluenced by the contagion of her terrors. The movements and voices of the servants down stairs still getting things into their places and completing our comfortable arrangements, had also their effect in steeling us against any such influence, and we set the whole thing down as a dream, or an imperfectly-seen outline of the bed-curtains. When, however, we were alone, my wife reiterated, still in great agitation, her clear assertion that she had most positively seen, being at the time as completely awake as ever she was, precisely what she had described to us. And in this conviction she continued perfectly firm.

A day or two after this, it came out that our servants were under an apprehension that, somehow or other, thieves had established a secret mode of access to the lower part of the house. The butler, Smith, had seen an ill-looking woman in his room on the first night of our arrival; and he and other servants constantly saw, for many days subsequently, glimpses of a retreating figure, which corresponded with that so seen by him, passing through a passage which led to a back area in which were some coal-vaults.

This figure was seen always in the act of retreating, its back turned, generally getting round the corner of the passage into the area, in a stealthy and hurried way, and, when closely followed, imperfectly seen again entering one of the coal-vaults, and when pursued into it, nowhere to be found.

The idea of any thing supernatural in the matter had, strange to say, not yet entered the mind of any one of the servants. They had heard some stories of smugglers having secret passages into houses, and using their means of access for purposes of pillage, or with a view to frighten superstitious people out of houses which they needed for their own objects, and a suspicion of similar practices here, caused them extreme uneasiness. The apparent anxiety also manifested by this retreating figure to escape observation, and her always appearing to make her egress at the same point, favoured this romantic hypothesis. The men, however, made a most careful examination of the back area, and of the coal-vaults, with a view to discover some mode of egress, but entirely without success. On the contrary, the result was, so far as it went, subversive of the theory; solid masonry met them on every hand.

I called the man, Smith, up, to hear from his own lips the particulars of what he had seen; and certainly his report was very curious. I give it as literally as my memory enables me:—

His son slept in the same room, and was sound asleep; but he lay awake, as men sometimes will on a change of bed, and having many things on his mind. He was lying with his face towards the wall, but observing a light and some little stir in the room, he turned round in his bed, and saw the figure of a woman, squalid, and ragged in dress; her figure rather low and broad; as well as I recollect, she had something—either a cloak or shawl—on, and wore a bonnet. Her back was turned, and she appeared to be searching or rummaging for something on the floor, and, without appearing to observe him, she turned in doing so towards him. The light, which was more like the intense glow of a coal, as he described it, being of a deep red colour, proceeded from the hollow of her hand, which she held beside her head, and he saw her perfectly distinctly. She appeared middle-aged, was deeply pitted with the smallpox, and blind of one eye. His phrase in describing her general appearance was, that she was "a miserable, poor-looking creature."

He was under the impression that she must be the woman who had been left by the proprietor in charge of the house, and who had that evening, after having given up the keys, remained for some little time with the female servants. He coughed, therefore, to apprize her of his presence, and turned again towards the wall. When he again looked round she and the light were gone; and odd as was her method of lighting herself in her search, the circumstances excited neither uneasiness nor curiosity in his mind, until he discovered next morning that the woman in question had left the house long before he had gone to his bed.

I examined the man very closely as to the appearance of the person who had visited him, and the result was what I have described. It struck me as an odd thing, that even then, considering how prone to superstition persons in his rank of life usually are, he did not seem to suspect any thing supernatural in the occurrence; and, on the contrary, was thoroughly persuaded that his visitant was a living person, who had got into the house by some hidden entrance.

On Sunday, on his return from his place of worship, he told me that, when the service was ended, and the congregation making their way slowly out, he saw the very woman in the crowd, and kept his eye upon her for several minutes, but such was the crush, that all his efforts to reach her were unavailing, and when he got into the open street she was gone. He was quite positive as to his having distinctly seen her, however, for several minutes, and scouted the possibility of any mistake as to identity; and fully impressed with the substantial and living reality of his visitant, he was very much provoked at her having escaped him. He made inquiries also in the neighbourhood, but could procure no information, nor hear of any other persons having seen any woman corresponding with his visitant.

The cook and the housemaid occupied a bed-room on the kitchen floor. It had whitewashed walls, and they were actually terrified by the appearance of the shadow of a woman passing and repassing across the side wall opposite to their beds. They suspected that this had been going on much longer than they were aware, for its presence was discovered by a sort of accident, its movements happening to take a direction in distinct contrariety to theirs.

This shadow always moved upon one particular wall, returning after short intervals, and causing them extreme terror. They placed the candle, as the most obvious specific, so close to the infested wall, that the flame all but touched it; and believed for some time that they had effectually got rid of this annoyance; but one night, notwithstanding this arrangement of the light, the shadow returned, passing and repassing, as heretofore, upon the same wall, although their only candle was burning within an inch of it, and it was obvious that no substance capable of casting such a shadow could have interposed; and, indeed, as they described it, the shadow seemed to have no sort of relation to the position of the light, and appeared, as I have said, in manifest defiance of the laws of optics.

I ought to mention that the housemaid was a particularly fearless sort of person, as well as a very honest one; and her companion, the cook, a scrupulously religious woman, and both agreed in every particular in their relation of what occurred.

Meanwhile, the nursery was not without its annoyances, though as yet of a comparatively trivial kind. Sometimes, at night, the handle of the door was turned hurriedly as if by a person trying to come in, and at others a knocking was made at it. These sounds occurred after the children had settled to sleep, and while the nurse still remained awake. Whenever she called to know "who is there," the sounds ceased; but several times, and particularly at first, she was under the impression that they were caused by her mistress, who had come to see the children, and thus impressed she had got up and opened the door, expecting to see her, but discovering only darkness, and receiving no answer to her inquiries.

With respect to this nurse, I must mention that I believe no more perfectly trustworthy servant was ever employed in her capacity; and, in addition to her integrity, she was remarkably gifted with sound common sense.

One morning, I think about three or four weeks after our arrival, I was sitting at the parlour window which looked to the front, when I saw the little iron door which admitted into the small garden that lay between the window where I was sitting and the public road, pushed open by a woman who so exactly answered the description given by Smith of the woman who had visited his room on the night of his arrival as instantaneously to impress me with the conviction that she must be the identical person. She was a square, short woman, dressed in soiled and tattered clothes, scarred and pitted with small-pox, and blind of an eye. She stepped hurriedly into the little enclosure, and peered from a distance of a few yards into the room where I was sitting. I felt that now was the moment to clear the matter up; but there was something stealthy in the manner and look of the woman which convinced me that I must not appear to notice her until her retreat was fairly cut off. Unfortunately, I was suffering from a lame foot, and could not reach the bell as quickly as I wished. I made all the haste I could, and rang violently to bring up the servant Smith. In the short interval that intervened, I observed the woman from the window, who having in a leisurely way, and with a kind of scrutiny, looked along the front windows of the house, passed quickly out again, closing the gate after her, and followed a lady who was walking along the footpath at a quick pace, as if with the intention of begging from her. The moment the man entered I told him— "the blind woman you described to me has this instant followed a lady in that direction, try to overtake her." He was, if possible, more eager than I in the chase, but returned in a short time after a vain pursuit, very hot, and utterly disappointed. And, thereafter, we saw her face no more.

All this time, and up to the period of our leaving the house, which was not for two or three months later, there occurred at intervals the only phenomenon in the entire series having any resemblance to what we hear described of "Spiritualism." This was a knocking, like a soft hammering with a wooden mallet, as it seemed in the timbers between the bedroom ceilings and the roof. It had this special peculiarity, that it was always rythmical, and, I think, invariably, the emphasis upon the last stroke. It would sound rapidly "one, two, three, *four*—one, two, three, *four*;" or "one, two, *three*—one, two, *three*," and sometimes "one, *two*—

one, *two*," &c., and this, with intervals and resumptions, monotonously for hours at a time.

At first this caused my wife, who was a good deal confined to her bed, much annoyance; and we sent to our neighbours to inquire if any hammering or carpentering was going on in their houses, but were informed that nothing of the sort was taking place. I have myself heard it frequently, always in the same inaccessible part of the house, and with the same monotonous emphasis. One odd thing about it was, that on my wife's calling out, as she used to do when it became more than usually troublesome, "stop that noise," it was invariably arrested for a longer or shorter time.

Of course none of these occurrences were ever mentioned in hearing of the children. They would have been, no doubt, like most children, greatly terrified had they heard any thing of the matter, and known that their elders were unable to account for what was passing; and their fears would have made them wretched and troublesome.

They used to play for some hours every day in the back garden —the house forming one end of this oblong inclosure, the stable and coach-house the other, and two parallel walls of considerable height the sides. Here, as it afforded a perfectly safe playground, they were frequently left quite to themselves; and in talking over their days' adventures, as children will, they happened to mention a woman, or rather the woman, for they had long grown familiar with her appearance, whom they used to see in the garden while they were at play. They assumed that she came in and went out at the stable door, but they never actually saw her enter or depart. They merely saw a figure—that of a very poor woman, soiled and ragged—near the stable wall, stooping over the ground, and apparently grubbing in the loose clay in search of something. She did not disturb, or appear to observe them; and they left her in undisturbed possession of her nook of ground. When seen it was always in the same spot, and similarly occupied; and the description they gave of her general appearance—for they never saw her face—corresponded with that of the one-eyed woman whom Smith, and subsequently as it seemed, I had seen.

The other man, James, who looked after a mare which I had purchased for the purpose of riding exercise, had, like every one else in the house, his little trouble to report, though it was not much. The stall in which, as the most comfortable, it was decided to place her, she peremptorily declined to enter. Though a very docile and gentle little animal, there was no getting her into it. She would snort and rear, and, in fact, do or suffer any thing rather than set her hoof in it. He was fain, therefore, to place her in another. And on several occasions he found her there, exhibiting all the equine symptoms of extreme fear. Like the rest of us, however, this man was not troubled in the particular case with any superstitious qualms. The mare had evidently been frightened; and he was puzzled to find out how, or by whom, for the stable was well-secured, and had, I am nearly certain, a lock-up yard outside.

One morning I was greeted with the intelligence that robbers had certainly got into the house in the night; and that one of them had actually been seen in the nursery. The witness, I found, was my eldest child, then, as I have said, about nine years of age. Having awoke in the night, and lain awake for some time in her bed, she heard the handle of the door turn, and a person whom she distinctly saw—for it was a light night, and the window-shutters unclosed—but whom she had never seen before, stepped in on tiptoe, and with an appearance of great caution. He was a rather small man, with a very red face; he wore an oddly cut frock coat, the collar of which stood up, and trousers, rough and wide, like those of a sailor, turned up at the ankles, and either short boots or clumsy shoes, covered with mud. This man listened beside the nurse's bed, which stood next the door, as if to satisfy himself that she was sleeping soundly; and having done so for some seconds, he began to move cautiously in a diagonal line, across the room to the chimney-piece, where he stood for a while, and so resumed his tiptoe walk, skirting the wall, until he reached a chest of drawers, some of which were open, and into which he looked, and began to rummage in a hurried way, as the child supposed, making search for something worth taking away. He then passed on to the window, where was a dressing-table, at which he also stopped, turning over the things upon it, and standing for some time at the window as if looking out, and then resuming his walk by the side wall opposite to that by which he had moved up to the window, he returned in the same way toward the nurse's bed, so as to reach it at the foot. With its side to the end wall, in which was the door, was placed the little bed in which lay my eldest child, who watched his proceedings with the extremest terror. As he drew near she instinctively moved herself in the bed, with her head and shoulders to the wall, drawing up her feet; but he passed by without appearing to observe, or, at least, to care for her presence. Immediately after the nurse turned in her bed as if about to waken; and when the child, who had drawn the clothes about her head, again ventured to peep out, the man was gone.

The child had no idea of her having seen any thing more

formidable than a thief. With the prowling, cautious, and noiseless manner of proceeding common to such marauders, the air and movements of the man whom she had seen entirely corresponded. And on hearing her perfectly distinct and consistent account, I could myself arrive at no other conclusion than that a stranger had actually got into the house. I had, therefore, in the first instance, a most careful examination made to discover any traces of an entrance having been made by any window into the house. The doors had been found barred and locked as usual; but no sign of any thing of the sort was discernible. I then had the various articles—plate, wearing apparel, books, &c., counted; and after having conned over and reckoned up every thing, it became quite clear that nothing whatever had been removed from the house, nor was there the slightest indication of any thing having been so much as disturbed there. I must here state that this child was remarkably clear, intelligent, and observant; and that her description of the man, and of all that had occurred, was most exact, and as detailed as the want of perfect light rendered possible.

I felt assured that an entrance had actually been effected into the house, though for what purpose was not easily to be conjectured. The man, Smith, was equally confident upon this point; and his theory was that the object was simply to frighten us out of the house by making us believe it haunted; and he was more than ever anxious and on the alert to discover the conspirators. It often since appeared to me odd. Every year, indeed, more odd, as this cumulative case of the marvellous becomes to my mind more and more inexplicable—that underlying my sense of mystery and puzzle, was all along the quiet assumption that all these occurrences were one way or another referable to natural causes. I could not account for them, indeed, myself; but during the whole period I inhabited that house, I never once felt, though much alone, and often up very late at night, any of those tremors and thrills which every one has at times experienced when situation and the hour are favourable. Except the cook and housemaid, who were plagued with the shadow I mentioned crossing and recrossing upon the bedroom wall, we all, without exception, experienced the same strange sense of security, and regarded these phenomena rather with a perplexed sort of interest and curiosity, than with any more unpleasant sensations.

The knockings which I have mentioned at the nursery door, preceded generally by the sound of a step on the lobby, meanwhile continued. At that time (for my wife, like myself, was an invalid) two eminent physicians, who came out occasionally by rail, were attending us. These gentlemen were at first only amused, but ultimately interested, and very much puzzled by the occurrences which we described. One of them, at last, recommended that a candle should be kept burning upon the lobby. It was in fact a recurrence to an old woman's recipe against ghosts—of course it might be serviceable, too, against impostors; at all events, seeming, as I have said, very much interested and puzzled, he advised it, and it was tried. We fancied that it was successful; for there was an interval of quiet for, I think, three or four nights. But after that, the noises—the footsteps on the lobby—the knocking at the door, and the turning of the handle recommenced in full force, notwithstanding the light upon the table outside; and these particular phenomena became only more perplexing than ever.

The alarm of robbers and smugglers gradually subsided after a week or two; but we were again to hear news from the nursery. Our second little girl, then between seven and eight years of age, saw in the night time—she alone being awake—a young woman, with black, or very dark hair, which hung loose, and with a black cloak on, standing near the middle of the floor, opposite the hearthstone, and fronting the foot of her bed. She appeared quite unobservant of the children and nurse sleeping in the room. She was very pale, and looked, the child said, both "sorry and frightened," and with something very peculiar and terrible about her eyes, which made the child conclude that she was dead. She was looking, not at, but in the direction of the child's bed, and there was a dark streak across her throat, like a scar with blood upon it. This figure was not motionless; but once or twice turned slowly, and without appearing to be conscious of the presence of the child, or the other occupants of the room, like a person in vacancy or abstraction. There was on this occasion a night-light burning in the chamber; and the child saw, or thought she saw, all these particulars with the most perfect distinctness. She got her head under the bedclothes; and although a good many years have passed since then, she cannot recall the spectacle without feelings of peculiar horror.

One day, when the children were playing in the back garden, I asked them to point out to me the spot where they were accustomed to see the woman who occasionally showed herself as I have described, near the stable wall. There was no division of opinion as to this precise point, which they indicated in the most distinct and confident way. I suggested that, perhaps, something might be hidden there in the ground; and advised them digging a hole there with their little spades, to try for it. Accordingly, to work they went, and by my return in the evening they had grubbed up a piece of a jawbone, with several teeth in it. The bone was very much decayed, and ready to crumble to pieces, but the teeth were quite sound. I could not tell whether they were human grinders; but I showed the fossil to one of the physicians I have mentioned, who came out the next evening, and he pronounced them human teeth. The same conclusion was come to a day or two later by the other medical man. It appears to me now, on reviewing the whole matter, almost unaccountable that, with such evidence before me, I should not have got in a labourer, and had the spot effectually dug and searched. I can only say, that so it was. I was quite satisfied of the moral truth of every word that had been related to me, and which I have here set down with scrupulous accuracy. But I experienced an apathy, for which neither then nor afterwards did I quite know how to account. I had a vague, but immovable impression that the whole affair was referable to natural agencies. It was not until some time after we had left the house, which, by-the-by, we afterwards found had had the reputation of being haunted before we had come to live in it, that on reconsideration I discovered the serious difficulty of accounting satisfactorily for all that had occurred upon ordinary principles. A great deal we might arbitrarily set down to imagination. But even in so doing there was, *in limine*, the oddity, not to say improbability, of so many different persons having nearly simultaneously suffered from different spectral and other illusions during the short period for which we had occupied that house, who never before, nor so far as we learned, afterwards were troubled by any fears or fancies of the sort. There were other things, too, not to be so accounted for. The odd knockings in the roof I frequently heard myself.

There were also, which I before forgot to mention, in the daytime, rappings at the doors of the sitting-rooms, which constantly deceived us; and it was not till our "come in" was unanswered, and the hall or passage outside the door was discovered to be empty, that we learned that whatever else caused them, human hands did not. All the persons who reported having seen the different persons or appearances here described by me, were just as confident of having literally and distinctly seen them, as I was of having seen the hard-featured woman with the blind eye, so remarkably corresponding with Smith's description.

About a week after the discovery of the teeth, which were found, I think, about two feet under the ground, a friend, much advanced in years, and who remembered the town in which we had now taken up our abode, for a very long time, happened to pay us a visit. He good-humouredly pooh-poohed the whole thing; but at the same time was evidently curious about it. "We might construct a sort of story," said I (I am giving, of course, the substance and purport, not the exact words, of our dialogue), "and assign to each of the three figures who appeared their respective parts in some dreadful tragedy enacted in this house. The male figure represents the murderer; the ill-looking, one-eyed woman his accomplice, who, we will suppose, buried the body where she is now so often seen grubbing in the earth, and where the human teeth and jaw-bone have so lately been disinterred; and the young woman with dishevelled tresses, and black cloak, and the bloody scar across her throat, their victim. A difficulty, however, which I cannot get over, exists in the cheerfulness, the great publicity, and the evident very recent date of the house." "Why, as to that," said he, "the house is *not* modern; it and those beside it formed an old government store, altered and fitted up recently as you see. I remember it well in my young days, fifty years ago, before the town had grown out in this direction, and a more entirely lonely spot, or one more fitted for the commission of a secret crime, could not have been imagined."

I have nothing to add, for very soon after this my physician pronounced a longer stay unnecessary for my health, and we took our departure for another place of abode. I may add, that although I have resided for considerable periods in many other houses, I never experienced any annoyances of a similar kind elsewhere; neither have I made (stupid dog! you will say), any inquiries respecting either the antecedents or subsequent history of the house in which we made so disturbed a sojourn. I was content with what I knew, and have here related as clearly as I could, and I think it a very pretty puzzle as it stands.

[Thus ends the statement, which we abandon to the ingenuity of our readers, having ourselves no satisfactory explanation to suggest; and simply repeating the assurance with which we prefaced it, namely, that we can vouch for the perfect good faith and the accuracy of the narrator.—E. D. U. M.]

Sir Dominick's Bargain

A Legend of Dunoran

In the early autumn of the year 1838, business called me to the south of Ireland. The weather was delightful, the scenery and people were new to me, and sending my luggage on by the mail-coach route in charge of a servant, I hired a serviceable nag at a posting-house, and, full of the curiosity of an explorer, I commenced a leisurely journey of five-and-twenty miles on horseback, by sequestered cross-roads, to my place of destination. By bog and hill, by plain and ruined castle, and many a winding stream, my picturesque road led me.

I had started late, and having made little more than half my journey, I was thinking of making a short halt at the next convenient place, and letting my horse have a rest and a feed, and making some provision also for the comforts of his rider.

It was about four o'clock when the road, ascending a gradual steep, found a passage through a rocky gorge between the abrupt termination of a range of mountain to my left and a rocky hill, that rose dark and sudden at my right. Below me lay a little thatched village, under a long line of gigantic beech-trees, through the boughs of which the lowly chimneys sent up their thin turf-smoke. To my left, stretched away for miles, ascending the mountain range I have mentioned, a wild park, through whose sward and ferns the rock broke, time-worn and lichen-stained. This park was studded with straggling wood, which thickened to something like a forest, behind and beyond the little village I was approaching, clothing the irregular ascent of the hillsides with beautiful, and in some places discoloured foliage.

As you descend, the road winds slightly, with the grey park-wall, built of loose stone, and mantled here and there with ivy, at its left, and crosses a shallow ford; and as I approached the village, through breaks in the woodlands, I caught glimpses of the long front of an old ruined house, placed among the trees, about half-way up the picturesque mountain-side.

The solitude and melancholy of this ruin piqued my curiosity, and when I had reached the rude thatched public-house, with the sign of St. Columbkill, with robes, mitre, and crozier, displayed over its lintel, having seen to my horse and made a good meal myself on a rasher and eggs, I began to think again of the wooded park and the ruinous house, and resolved on a ramble of half an hour among its sylvan solitudes.

The name of the place, I found, was Dunoran; and beside the gate a stile admitted to the grounds, through which, with a pensive enjoyment, I began to saunter towards the dilapidated mansion.

A long grass-grown road, with many turns and windings, led up to the old house, under the shadow of the wood.

The road, as it approached the house, skirted the edge of a precipitous glen, clothed with hazel, dwarf-oak, and thorn, and the silent house stood with its wide-open hall-door facing this dark ravine, the further edge of which was crowned with towering forest; and great trees stood about the house and its deserted court-yard and stables.

I walked in and looked about me, through passages overgrown with nettles and weeds; from room to room with ceilings rotted, and here and there a great beam dark and worn, with tendrils of ivy trailing over it. The tall walls with rotten plaster were stained and mouldy, and in some rooms the remains of decayed wain-scoting crazily swung to and fro. The almost sashless windows were darkened also with ivy, and about the tall chimneys the jackdaws were wheeling, while from the huge trees that overhung the glen in sombre masses at the other side, the rooks kept up a ceaseless cawing.

As I walked through these melancholy passages—peeping only into some of the rooms, for the flooring was quite gone in the middle, and bowed down toward the centre, and the house was very nearly un-roofed, a state of things which made the exploration a little critical—I began to wonder why so grand a house, in the midst of scenery so picturesque, had been permitted to go to decay; I dreamed of the hospitalities of which it had long ago been the rallying place, and I thought what a scene of Redgauntlet revelries it might disclose at midnight.

The great staircase was of oak, which had stood the weather wonderfully, and I sat down upon its steps, musing vaguely on the transitoriness of all things under the sun.

Except for the hoarse and distant clamour of the rooks, hardly audible where I sat, no sound broke the profound stillness of the spot. Such a sense of solitude I have seldom experienced before. The air was stirless, there was not even the rustle of a withered leaf along the passage. It was oppressive. The tall trees that stood close about the building darkened it, and added something of awe to the melancholy of the scene.

In this mood I heard, with an unpleasant surprise, close to me, a voice that was drawling, and, I fancied, sneering, repeat the words: "Food for worms, dead and rotten; God over all."

There was a small window in the wall, here very thick, which had been built up, and in the dark recess of this, deep in the shadow, I now saw a sharp-featured man, sitting with his feet dangling. His keen eyes were fixed on me, and he was smiling cynically, and before I had well recovered my surprise, he repeated the distich:

> If death was a thing that money could buy,
> The rich they would live, and the poor they would die.

"It was a grand house in its day, sir," he continued, "Dunoran House, and the Sarsfields. Sir Dominick Sarsfield was the last of the old stock. He lost his life not six foot away from where you are sitting."

As he thus spoke he let himself down, with a little jump, on to the ground.

He was a dark-faced, sharp-featured, little hunchback, and had a walking-stick in his hand, with the end of which he pointed to a rusty stain in the plaster of the wall.

"Do you mind that mark, sir?" he asked.

"Yes," I said, standing up, and looking at it, with a curious anticipation of something worth hearing.

"That's about seven or eight feet from the ground, sir, and you'll not guess what it is."

"I dare say not," said I, "unless it is a stain from the weather."

" 'Tis nothing so lucky, sir," he answered, with the same cynical smile and a wag of his head, still pointing at the mark with his stick. "That's a splash of brains and blood. It's there this hundhred years; and it will never leave it while the wall stands."

"He was murdered, then?"

"Worse than that, sir," he answered.

"He killed himself, perhaps?"

"Worse than that, itself, this cross between us and harm! I'm oulder than I look, sir; you wouldn't guess my years."

He became silent, and looked at me, evidently inviting a guess.

"Well, I should guess you to be about five-and-fifty."

He laughed, and took a pinch of snuff, and said:

"I'm that, your honour, and something to the back of it. I was seventy last Candlemas. You would not a' thought that, to look at me."

"Upon my word I should not; I can hardly believe it even now. Still, you don't remember Sir Dominick Sarsfield's death?" I said, glancing up at the ominous stain on the wall.

"No, sir, that was a long while before I was born. But my grandfather was butler here long ago, and many a time I heard tell how Sir Dominick came by his death. There was no masther in the great house ever sinst that happened. But there was two sarvants in care of it, and my aunt was one o' them; and she kep' me here wid her till I was nine year old, and she was lavin' the place to go to Dublin; and from that time it was let to go down. The wind sthript the roof, and the rain rotted the timber, and little by little, in sixty years' time, it kem to what you see. But I have a likin' for it still, for the sake of ould times; and I never come this way but I take a look in. I don't think it's many more times I'll be turnin' to see the ould place, for I'll be undher the sod myself before long."

"You'll outlive younger people," I said.

And, quitting that trite subject, I ran on:

"I don't wonder that you like this old place; it is a beautiful spot, such noble trees."

"I wish ye seen the glin when the nuts is ripe; they're the sweetest nuts in all Ireland, I think," he rejoined, with a practical sense of the picturesque. "You'd fill your pockets while you'd be lookin' about you."

"These are very fine old woods," I remarked. "I have not seen any in Ireland I thought so beautiful."

"Eiah! your honour, the woods about here is nothing to what they wor. Al the mountains along here was wood when my father was a gossoon, and Murroa Wood was the grandest of them all. All oak mostly, and all cut down as bare as the road. Not one left here that's fit to compare with them. Which way did your honour come hither—from Limerick?"

"No. Killaloe."

"Well, then, you passed the ground where Murroa Wood was in former times. You kem undher Lisnavourra, the steep knob of a hill about a mile above the village here. 'Twas near that Murroa Wood was, and 'twas there Sir Dominick Sarsfield first met the devil, the Lord between us and harm, and a bad meeting it was for him and his."

I had become interested in the adventure which had occurred in the very scenery which had so greatly attracted me, and my new acquaintance, the little hunchback, was easily entreated to tell me the story, and spoke thus, so soon as we had each resumed his seat:

"It was a fine estate when Sir Dominick came into it; and grand doings there was entirely, feasting and fiddling, free quarters for all the pipers in the counthry round, and a welcome for every one that liked to come. There was wine, by the hogshead, for the quality; and potteen enough to set a town a-fire, and beer and cidher enough to float a navy, for the boys and girls, and the likes o' me. It was kep' up the best part of a month, till the weather broke, and the rain spoilt the sod for the moneen jigs, and the fair of Allybally Killudeen comin' on they wor obliged to give over their divarsion, and attind to the pigs.

But Sir Dominick was only beginnin' when they wor lavin' off. There was no way of gettin' rid of his money and estates he did not try—what with drinkin', dicin', racin', cards, and all soarts, it was not many years before the estates wor in debt, and Sir Dominick a distressed man. He showed a bold front to the world as long as he could; and then he sould off his dogs, and most of his horses, and gev out he was going to thravel in France, and the like; and so off with him for awhile; and no one in these parts heard tale or tidings of him for two or three years. Till at last quite unexpected, one night there comes a rapping at the big kitchen window. It was past ten o'clock, and old Connor Hanlon, the butler, my grand-father, was sittin' by the fire alone, warming his shins over it. There was keen east wind blowing along the mountains that night, and whistling cowld enough, through the tops of the trees, and soundin' lonesome through the long chimneys.

(And the story-teller glanced up at the nearest stack visible from his seat.)

So he wasn't quite sure of the knockin' at the window, and up he gets, and sees his master's face.

My grandfather was glad to see him safe, for it was a long time since there was any news of him; but he was sorry, too, for it was a changed place and only himself and old Juggy Broadrick in charge of the house, and a man in the stables, and it was a poor thing to see him comin' back to his own like that.

He shook Con by the hand, and says he:

"I came here to say a word to you. I left my horse with Dick in the stable; I may want him again before morning, or I may never want him."

And with that he turns into the big kitchen, and draws a stool, and sits down to take an air of the fire.

"Sit down, Connor, opposite me, and listen to what I tell you, and don't be afeard to say what you think."

He spoke all the time lookin' into the fire, with his hands stretched over it, and a tired man he looked.

"An' why should I be afeard, Masther Dominick?" says my grandfather. "Yourself was a good masther to me, and so was your father, rest his sould, before you, and I'll say the truth, and dar' the devil, and more than that, for any Sarsfield of Dunoran, much less yourself, and a good right I'd have."

"It's all over with me, Con," says Sir Dominick.

"Heaven forbid!" says my grandfather.

" 'Tis past praying for," says Sir Dominick. "The last guinea's gone; the ould place will follow it. It must be sold, and I'm come here, I don't know why, like a ghost to have a last look round me, and go off in the dark again."

And with that he tould him to be sure, in case he should hear of his death, to give the oak box, in the closet off his room, to his cousin, Pat Sarsfield, in Dublin, and the sword and pistols his grandfather carried in Aughrim, and two or three thrifling things of the kind.

And says he, "Con, they say if the divil gives you money over-night, you'll find nothing but a bagful of pebbles, and chips, and nutshells, in the morning. If I thought he played fair, I'm in the humour to make a bargain with him to-night."

"Lord forbid!" says my grandfather, standing up, with a start, and crossing himself.

"They say the country's full of men, listin' sogers for the King o' France. If I light on one o' them, I'll not refuse his offer. How contrary things goes! How long is it since me an Captain Waller fought the jewel at New Castle?"

"Six years, Masther Dominick, and ye broke his thigh with the bullet the first shot."

"I did, Con," says he, "and I wish, instead, he had shot me through the heart. Have you any whisky?"

My grandfather took it out of the buffet, and the masther pours out some into a bowl, and drank it off.

"I'll go out and have a look at my horse," says he, standing up. There was sort of a stare in his eyes, as he pulled his riding-cloak about him, as if there was something bad in his thoughts.

"Sure, I won't be a minute running out myself to the stable, and looking after the horse for you myself," says my grandfather.

"I'm not goin' to the stable," says Sir Dominick; "I may as well tell you, for I see you found it out already—I'm goin' across the deer-park; if I come back you'll see me in an hour's time. But, anyhow, you'd better not follow me, for if you do I'll shoot you, and that 'id be a bad ending to our friendship."

And with that he walks down this passage here, and turns the key in the side door at that end of it, and out wid him on the sod into the moonlight and the cowld wind; and my grandfather seen him walkin' hard towards the park-wall, and then he comes in and closes the door with a heavy heart.

Sir Dominick stopped to think when he got to the middle of the deer-park, for he had not made up his mind, when he left the house, and the whisky did not clear his head, only it gev him courage.

He did not feel the cowld wind now, nor fear death, nor think much of anything but the shame and fall of the old family.

And he made up his mind, if no better thought came to him between that and there, so soon as he came to Murroa Wood, he'd hang himself from one of the oak branches with his cravat.

It was a bright moonlight night, there was just a bit of a cloud driving across the moon now and then, but, only for that, as light a'most as day.

Down he goes, right for the wood of Murroa. It seemed to him every step he took was as long as three, and it was no time till he was among the big oak-trees with their roots spreading from one to another, and their branches stretching overhead like the timbers of a naked roof, and the moon shining down through them, and casting their shadows thick and twist abroad on the ground as black as my shoe.

He was sobering a bit by this time, and he slacked his pace, and he thought 'twould be better to list in the French king's army, and thry what that might do for him, for he knew a man might take his own life any time, but it would puzzle him to take it back again when he liked.

Just as he made up his mind not to make away with himself, what should he hear but a step clinkin' along the dry ground under the trees, and soon he sees a grand gentleman right before him comin' up to meet him.

He was a handsome young man like himself, and he wore a cocked-hat with gold-lace round it, such as officers wears on their coats, and he had on a dress the same as French officers wore in them times.

He stopped opposite Sir Dominick, and he cum to a standstill also.

The two gentlemen took off their hats to one another, and says the stranger:

"I am recruiting, sir," says he, "for my sovereign, and you'll find my money won't turn into pebbles, chips, and nutshells, by to-morrow."

At the same time he pulls out a big purse full of gold.

The minute he set eyes on that gentleman, Sir Dominick had his own opinion of him; and at those words he felt the very hair standing up on his head.

"Don't be afraid," says he, "the money won't burn you. If it proves honest gold, and if it prospers with you, I'm willing to make a bargain. This is the last day of February," says he; "I'll serve you seven years, and at the end of that time you shall serve me, and I'll come for you when the seven years is over, when the clock turns the minute between February and March; and the first of March ye'll come away with me, or never. You'll not find me a bad master, any more than a bad servant. I love my own; and I command all the pleasures and the glory of the world. The bargain dates from this day, and the lease is out at midnight on the last day I told you; and in the year"—he told him the year, it was easy reckoned, but I forget it—"and if you'd rather wait," he says, "for eight months and twenty eight days, before you sign the writin', you may, if you meet me here. But I can't do a great deal for you in the mean time; and if you don't sign then, all you get from me, up to that time, will vanish away, and you'll be just as you are to-night, and ready to hang yourself on the first tree you meet."

Well, the end of it was, Sir Dominick chose to wait, and he came back to the house with a big bag full of money, as round as your hat a'most.

My grandfather was glad enough, you may be sure, to see the master safe and sound again so soon. Into the kitchen he bangs again, and swings the bag o' money on the table; and he stands up straight, and heaves up his shoulders like a man that has just got shut of a load; and he looks at the bag, and my grandfather looks at him, and from him to it, and back again. Sir Dominick looked as white as a sheet, and says he:

"I don't know, Con, what's in it; it's the heaviest load I ever carried."

He seemed shy of openin' the bag; and he made my grandfather heap up a roaring fire of turf and wood, and then, at last, he opens it, and, sure enough, 'twas stuffed full o' golden guineas, bright and new, as if they were only that minute out o' the Mint.

Sir Dominick made my grandfather sit at his elbow while he counted every guinea in the bag.

When he was done countin', and it wasn't far from daylight when that time came, Sir Dominick made my grandfather swear not to tell a word about it. And a close secret it was for many a day after.

When the eight months and twenty-eight days were pretty near spent and ended, Sir Dominick returned to the house here with a troubled mind, in doubt what was best to be done, and no one alive but my grandfather knew anything about the matter, and he not half what had happened.

As the day drew near, towards the end of October, Sir Dominick grew only more and more troubled in mind.

One time he made up his mind to have no more to say to such things, nor to speak again with the like of them he met with in the wood of Murroa. Then, again, his heart failed him when he thought of his debts, and he not knowing where to turn. Then, only a week before the day, everything began to go wrong with him. One man wrote from London to say that Sir Dominick paid three thousand pounds to the wrong man, and must pay it over again; another demanded a debt he never heard of before; and another, in Dublin, denied the payment of a thundherin' big bill, and Sir Dominick could nowhere find the receipt, and so on, wid fifty other things as bad.

Well, by the time the night of the 28th of October came round, he was a'most ready to lose his senses with all the demands that was risin' up again him on all sides, and nothing to meet them but the help of the one dhreadful friend he had to depind on at night in the oak-wood down there below.

So there was nothing for it but to go through with the business that was begun already, and about the same hour as he went last, he takes off the little crucifix he wore round his neck, for he was a Catholic, and his gospel, and his bit o' the thrue cross that he had in a locket, for since he took the money from the Evil One he was growin' frightful in himself, and got all he could to guard him from the power of the devil. But to-night, for his life, he daren't take them with him. So he gives them into my grandfather's hands without a word, only he looked as white as a sheet o' paper; and he takes his hat and sword, and telling my grandfather to watch for him, away he goes, to try what would come of it.

It was a fine still night, and the moon—not so bright, though, now as the first time—was shinin' over heath and rock, and down on the lonesome oak-wood below him.

His heart beat thick as he drew near it. There was not a sound, not even the distant bark of a dog from the village behind him. There was not a lonesomer spot in the country round, and if it wasn't for his debts and losses that was drivin' him on half mad, in spite of his fears for his soul and his hopes of paradise, and all his good angel was whisperin' in his ear, he would a' turned back, and sent for his clargy, and made his confession and his penance, and changed his ways, and led a good life, for he was frightened enough to have done a great dale.

Softer and slower he stept as he got, once more, in undher the big branches of the oak-threes; and when he got in a bit, near where he met with the bad spirit before, he stopped and looked round him, and felt himself, every bit, turning as cowld as a dead man, and you may be sure he did not feel much betther when he seen the same man steppin' from behind the big tree that was touchin' his elbow a'most.

"You found the money good," says he, "but it was not enough. No matter, you shall have enough and to spare. I'll see after your luck, and I'll give you a hint whenever it can serve you; and any time you want to see me you have only to come down here, and call my face to mind, and wish me present. You shan't owe a shilling by the end of the year, and you shall never miss the right card, the best throw, and the winning horse. Are you willing?"

The young gentleman's voice almost stuck in his throat, and his hair was rising on his head, but he did get out a word or two to signify that he consented; and with that the Evil One handed him a needle, and bid him give him three drops of blood from his arm; and he took them in the cup of an acorn, and gave him a pen, and bid him write some words that he repeated, and that Sir Dominick did not understand, on two thin slips of parchment. He took one himself and the other he sunk in Sir Dominick's arm at the place where he drew the blood, and he closed the flesh over it. And that's as true as you're sittin' there!

Well, Sir Dominick went home. He was a frightened man, and well he might be. But in a little time he began to grow aisier in his mind. Anyhow, he got out of debt very quick, and money came tumbling in to make him richer, and everything he took in hand prospered, and he never made a wager, or played a game, but he won; and for all that, there was not a poor man on the estate that was not happier than Sir Dominick.

So he took again to his old ways; for, when the money came back, all came back, and there were hounds and horses, and wine galore, and no end of company, and grand doin's, and divarsion, up here at the great house. And some said Sir Dominick was thinkin' of gettin' married; and more said he wasn't. But, anyhow, there was somethin' troublin' him more than common, and so one night, unknownst to all, away he goes to the lonesome oak-wood. It was something, maybe, my grandfather thought was troublin' him about a beautiful young lady he was jealous of, and mad in love with her. But that was only guess.

Well, when Sir Dominick got into the wood this time, he grew more in dread than ever; and he was on the point of turnin' and lavin' the place, when who should he see, close beside him, but my gentleman, seated on a big stone undher one of the trees. In place of looking the fine young gentleman in goold lace and grand clothes he appeared before, he was now in rags, he looked twice the size he had been, and his face smutted with soot, and he had a murtherin' big steel hammer, as heavy as a half-hundred, with a handle a yard long, across his knees. It was so dark under the tree, he did not see him quite clear for some time.

He stood up, and he looked awful tall entirely. And what passed between them in that discourse my grandfather never heered. But Sir Dominick was as black as night afterwards, and hadn't a laugh for anything nor a word a'most for any one, and he only grew worse and worse, and darker and darker. And now this thing, whatever it was, used to come to him of its own accord, whether he wanted it or no; sometimes in one shape, and sometimes in another, in lonesome places, and sometimes at his side by night when he'd be ridin' home alone, until at last he lost heart altogether and sent for the priest.

The priest was with him a long time, and when he heered the whole story, he rode off all the way for the bishop, and the bishop came here to the great house next day, and he gev Sir Dominick a good advice. He toult him he must give over dicin', and swearin,' and drinkin', and all bad company, and live a vartuous steady life until the seven years' bargain was out, and if the divil didn't come for him the minute afther the stroke of twelve the first morning of the month of March, he was safe out of the bargain. There was not more than eight or ten months to run now before the seven years wor out, and he lived all the time according to the bishop's advice, as strict as if he was "in retreat."

Well, you may guess he felt quare enough when the mornin' of the 28th of February came.

The priest came up by appointment, and Sir Dominick and his raverence wor together in the room you see there, and kep' up their prayers together till the clock struck twelve, and a good hour after, and not a sign of a disturbance, nor nothing came near them, and the priest slep' that night in the house in the room next Sir Dominick's, and all went over as comfortable as could be, and they shook hands and kissed like two comrades after winning a battle.

So, now, Sir Dominick thought he might as well have a pleasant evening, after all his fastin' and praying; and he sent round to half a dozen of the neighbouring gentlemen to come and dine with him, and his raverence stayed and dined also, and a roarin' bowl o' punch they had, and no end o' wine, and the swearin' and dice, and cards and guineas changing hands, and songs and stories, that wouldn't do any one good to hear, and the priest slipped away, when he seen the turn things was takin', and it was not far from the stroke of twelve when Sir Dominick, sitting at the head of his table, swears, "this is the best first of March I ever sat down with my friends."

"It ain't the first o' March," says Mr. Hiffernan of Ballyvoreen. He was a scholard, and always kep' an almanack.

"What is it, then?" says Sir Dominick, startin' up, and dhroppin' the ladle into the bowl, and starin' at him as if he had two heads.

" 'Tis the twenty-ninth of February, leap year," says he. And just as they were talkin', the clock strikes twelve; and my grandfather, who was half asleep in a chair by the fire in the hall, openin' his eyes, sees a short square fellow with a cloak on, and long black hair bushin' out from under his hat, standin' just there where you see the bit o' light shinin' again' the wall.

(My hunchbacked friend pointed with his stick to a little patch of red sunset light that relieved the deepening shadow of the passage.)

"Tell your master," says he, in an awful voice, like the growl of a baist, "that I'm here by appointment, and expect him down-stairs this minute."

Up goes my grandfather, by these very steps you are sittin' on.

"Tell him I can't come down yet," says Sir Dominick, and he turns to the company in the room; and says he with a cold sweat shinin' on his face, "for God's sake, gentlemen, will any of you jump from the window and bring the priest here?" One looked at another and no one knew what to make of it, and in the mean time, up comes my grandfather again, and says he, tremblin', "He says, sir, unless you go down to him, he'll come up to you."

"I don't understand this, gentlemen, I'll see what it means," says Sir Dominick, trying to put a face on it, and walkin' out o' the room like a man through the press-room, with the hangman waitin' for him outside. Down the stairs he comes, and two or three of the gentlemen peeping over the banisters, to see. My grandfather was walking six or eight steps behind him, and he seen the stranger take a stride out to meet Sir Dominick, and catch him up in his arms, and whirl his head against the wall, and wi' that the hall-doore flies open, and out goes the candles, and the turf and wood-ashes flyin' with the wind out o' the hall-fire, ran in a drift o' sparks along the floore by his feet.

Downs runs the gintlemen. Bang goes the hall-doore. Some comes runnin' up, and more runnin' down, with lights. It was all over with Sir Dominick. They lifted up the corpse, and put its shoulders again' the wall; but there was not a gasp left in him. He was cowld and stiffenin' already.

Pat Donovan was comin' up to the great house late that night and after he passed the little brook, that the carriage track up to the house crosses, and about fifty steps to this side of it, his dog, that was by his side, makes a sudden wheel, and springs over the wall, and sets up a yowlin' inside you'd hear a mile away; and that minute two men passed him by in silence, goin' down from the house, one of them short and square, and the other like Sir Dominick in shape, but there was little light under the trees where he was, and they looked only like shadows; and as they passed him by he could not hear the sound of their feet and he drew back to the wall frightened; and when he got up to the great house, he found all in confusion, and the master's body, with the head smashed to pieces, lying just on *that spot*.

The narrator stood up and indicated with the point of his stick the exact site of the body, and, as I looked, the shadow deepened, the red stain of sunlight vanished from the wall, and the sun had gone down behind the distant hill of New Castle, leaving the haunted scene in the deep grey of darkening twilight.

So I and the story-teller parted, not without good wishes on both sides, and a little "tip," which seemed not unwelcome, from me.

It was dusk and the moon up by the time I reached the village, remounted my nag, and looked my last on the scene of the terrible legend of Dunoran.

Ultor De Lacy

A Legend of Cappercullen

CHAPTER I

The Jacobite's Legacy

In my youth I heard a great many Irish family traditions, more or
less of a supernatural character, some of them very peculiar, and
all, to a child at least, highly interesting. One of these I will now
relate, though the translation to cold type from oral narrative,
with all the aids of animated human voice and countenance, and
the appropriate *mise-en-scène* of the old-fashioned parlour fireside
and its listening circle of excited faces, and, outside, the wintry
blast and the moan of leafless boughs, with the occasional rattle
of the clumsy old window-frame behind shutter and curtain, as the
blast swept by, is at best a trying one.

About midway up the romantic glen of Cappercullen, near the
point where the counties of Limerick, Clare, and Tipperary con-
verge, upon the then sequestered and forest-bound range of the
Slieve-Felim hills, there stood, in the reigns of the two earliest
Georges, the picturesque and massive remains of one of the finest
of the Anglo-Irish castles of Munster—perhaps of Ireland.

It crowned the precipitous edge of the wooded glen, itself half-
buried among the wild forest that covered that long and solitary
range. There was no human habitation within a circle of many
miles, except the half-dozen hovels and the small thatched chapel
composing the little village of Murroa, which lay at the foot of the
glen among the straggling skirts of the noble forest.

Its remoteness and difficulty of access saved it from demolition.
It was worth nobody's while to pull down and remove the ponderous and clumsy oak, much less the masonry or flagged roofing of
the pile. Whatever would pay the cost of removal had been long
since carried away. The rest was abandoned to time—the destroyer.

444

The hereditary owners of this noble building and of a wide territory in the contiguous counties I have named, were English— the De Lacys—long naturalized in Ireland. They had acquired at least this portion of their estate in the reign of Henry VIII, and held it, with some vicissitudes, down to the establishment of the revolution in Ireland, when they suffered attainder, and, like other great families of that period, underwent a final eclipse.

The De Lacy of that day retired to France, and held a brief command in the Irish Brigade, interrupted by sickness. He retired, became a poor hanger-on of the Court of St. Germains, and died early in the eighteenth century—as well as I remember, 1705— leaving an only son, hardly twelve years old, called by the strange but significant name of Ultor.

At this point commences the marvellous ingredient of my tale.

When his father was dying, he had him to his bedside, with no one by except his confessor; and having told him, first, that on reaching the age of twenty-one, he was to lay claim to a certain small estate in the county of Clare, in Ireland, in right of his mother—the title-deeds of which he gave him—and next, having enjoined him not to marry before the age of thirty, on the ground that earlier marriages destroyed the spirit and the power of enter- prise, and would incapacitate him from the accomplishment of his destiny—the restoration of his family—he then went on to open to the child a matter which so terrified him that he cried lamen- tably, trembling all over, clinging to the priest's gown with one hand and to his father's cold wrist with the other, and imploring him, with screams of horror, to desist from his communication.

But the priest, impressed, no doubt, himself, with its necessity, compelled him to listen. And then his father showed him a small picture, from which also the child turned with shrieks, until similarly constrained to look. They did not let him go until he had carefully conned the features, and was able to tell them, from memory, the colour of the eyes and hair, and the fashion and hues of the dress. Then his father gave him a black box containing this portrait, which was a full-length miniature, about nine inches long, painted very finely in oils, as smooth as enamel, and folded above it a sheet of paper, written over in a careful and very legible hand.

The deeds and this black box constituted the most important legacy bequeathed to his only child by the ruined Jacobite, and he deposited them in the hands of the priest, in trust, till his boy, Ultor, should have attained to an age to understand their value, and to keep them securely.

When this scene was ended, the dying exile's mind, I suppose, was relieved, for he spoke cheerily, and said he believed he would recover; and they soothed the crying child, and his father kissed him, and gave him a little silver coin to buy fruit with; and so they sent him off with another boy for a walk, and when he came back his father was dead.

He remained in France under the care of this ecclesiastic until he had attained the age of twenty-one, when he repaired to Ireland, and his title being unaffected by his father's attainder, he easily made good his claim to the small estate in the county of Clare.

There he settled, making a dismal and solitary tour now and then of the vast territories which had once been his father's, and nursing those gloomy and impatient thoughts which befitted the enterprises to which he was devoted.

Occasionally he visited Paris, that common centre of English, Irish, and Scottish disaffection; and there, when a little past thirty, he married the daughter of another ruined Irish house. His bride returned with him to the melancholy seclusion of their Munster residence, where she bore him in succession two daughters—Alice, the elder, dark-eyed and dark-haired, grave and sensible—Una, four years younger, with large blue eyes and long and beautiful golden hair.

Their poor mother was, I believe, naturally a lighthearted, sociable, high-spirited little creature; and her gay and childish nature pined in the isolation and gloom of her lot. At all events she died young, and the children were left to the sole care of their melancholy and embittered father. In process of time the girls grew up, tradition says, beautiful. The elder was designed for a convent, the younger her father hoped to mate as nobly as her high blood and splendid beauty seemed to promise, if only the great game on which he had resolved to stake all succeeded.

CHAPTER II

The Fairies in the Castle

The Rebellion of '45 came, and Ultor de Lacy was one of the few Irishmen implicated treasonably in that daring and romantic insurrection. Of course there were warrants out against him, but he was not to be found. The young ladies, indeed, remained as heretofore in their father's lonely house in Clare; but whether he had crossed the water or was still in Ireland was for some time unknown, even to them. In due course he was attainted, and his little estate forfeited. It was a miserable catastrophe—a tremendous and beggarly waking up from a life-long dream of returning principality.

In due course the officers of the crown came down to take possession, and it behoved the young ladies to flit. Happily for them the ecclesiastic I have mentioned was not quite so confident as their father, of his winning back the magnificent patrimony of his ancestors; and by his advice the daughters had been secured twenty pounds a year each, under the marriage settlement of their parents, which was all that stood between this proud house and literal destitution.

Late one evening, as some little boys from the village were returning from a ramble through the dark and devious glen of Cappercullen, with their pockets laden with nuts and "frahans," to their amazement and even terror they saw a light streaming redly from the narrow window of one of the towers overhanging the precipice among the ivy and the lofty branches, across the glen, already dim in the shadows of the deepening night.

"Look—look—look—'tis the Phooka's tower!" was the general cry, in the vernacular Irish, and a universal scamper commenced.

The bed of the glen, strewn with great fragments of rock, among which rose the tall stems of ancient trees, and overgrown with a tangled copse, was at the best no favourable ground for a run. Now it was dark; and, terrible work breaking through brambles and hazels and tumbling over rocks. Little Shaeen Mull Ryan, the last of the panic rout, screaming to his mates to wait for him— saw a whitish figure emerge from the thicket at the base of the stone flight of steps that descended the side of the glen, close by the castle-wall, intercepting his flight, and a discordant male voice shrieked—

"I have you!"

At the same time the boy, with a cry of terror, tripped and tumbled; and felt himself roughly caught by the arm, and hauled to his feet with a shake.

A wild yell from the child, and a volley of terror and entreaty followed.

"Who is it, Larry; what's the matter?" cried a voice, high in air, from the turret window. The words floated down through the trees, clear and sweet as the low notes of a flute.

"Only a child, my lady; a boy."

"Is he hurt?"

"Are you hurted?" demanded the whitish man, who held him
fast, and repeated the question in Irish; but the child only kept
blubbering and crying for mercy, with his hands clasped, and
trying to drop on his knees.

Larry's strong old hand held him up. He *was* hurt, and bleeding
from over his eye.

"Just a trifle hurted, my lady!"

"Bring him up here."

Shaeen Mull Ryan gave himself over. He was among "the good
people," who he knew would keep him prisoner for ever and a day.
There was no good in resisting. He grew bewildered, and yielded
himself passively to his fate, and emerged from the glen on the
platform above; his captor's knotted old hand still on his arm, and
looked round on the tall mysterious trees, and the gray front of
the castle, revealed in the imperfect moonlight, as upon the scenery
of a dream.

The old man who, with thin wiry legs, walked by his side, in a
dingy white coat, and blue facings, and great pewter buttons, with
his silver gray hair escaping from under his battered three-cocked
hat; and his shrewd puckered resolute face, in which the boy could
read no promise of sympathy, showing so white and phantom-like
in the moonlight, was, as he thought, the incarnate ideal of a fairy.

This figure led him in silence under the great arched gateway,
and across the grass-grown court, to the door in the far angle of the
building; and so, in the dark, round and round, up a stone screw
stair, and with a short turn into a large room, with a fire of turf
and wood, burning on its long unused hearth, over which hung a
pot, and about it an old woman with a great wooden spoon was
busy. An iron candlestick supported their solitary candle; and
about the floor of the room, as well as on the table and chairs, lay
a litter of all sorts of things; piles of old faded hangings, boxes,
trunks, clothes, pewter-plates, and cups; and I know not what
more.

But what instantly engaged the fearful gaze of the boy were the
figures of two ladies; red drugget cloaks they had on, like the
peasant girls of Munster and Connaught, and the rest of their dress
was pretty much in keeping. But they had the grand air, the refined
expression and beauty, and above all, the serene air of command
that belong to people of a higher rank.

The elder, with black hair and full brown eyes, sat writing at the deal table on which the candle stood, and raised her dark gaze to the boy as he came in. The other, with her hood thrown back, beautiful and *riant*, with a flood of wavy golden hair, and great blue eyes, and with something kind, and arch, and strange in her countenance, struck him as the most wonderful beauty he could have imagined.

They questioned the man in a language strange to the child. It was not English, for he had a smattering of that, and the man's story seemed to amuse them. The two young ladies exchanged a glance, and smiled mysteriously. He was more convinced than ever that he was among the good people. The younger stepped gaily forward and said—

"Do you know who *I* am, my little man? Well, I'm the fairy Una, and this is my palace; and that fairy you see there (pointing to the dark lady, who was looking out something in a box), is my sister and family physician, the Lady Graveairs; and these (glancing at the old man and woman), are some of my courtiers; and I'm considering now what I shall do with *you*, whether I shall send you to-night to Lough Guir, riding on a rush, to make my compliments to the Earl of Desmond in his enchanted castle; or, straight to your bed, two thousand miles under ground, among the gnomes; or to prison in that little corner of the moon you see through the window —with the man-in-the-moon for your gaoler, for thrice three hundred years and a day! There, don't cry. You only see how serious a thing it is for you, little boys, to come so near my castle. Now, for this once, I'll let you go. But, henceforward, any boys I, or my people, may find within half a mile round my castle, shall belong to me for life, and never behold their home or their people more."

And she sang a little air and chased mystically half a dozen steps before him, holding out her cloak with her pretty fingers, and courtesying very low, to his indescribable alarm.

Then, with a little laugh, she said—

"My little man, we must mend your head."

And so they washed his scratch, and the elder one applied a plaister to it. And she of the great blue eyes took out of her pocket a little French box of bon-bons and emptied it into his hand, and she said—

"You need not be afraid to eat these—they are very good—and I'll send my fairy, Blanc-et-bleu, to set you free. Take him (she addressed Larry), and let him go, with a solemn charge."

The elder, with a grave and affectionate smile, said, looking on the fairy—

"Brave, dear, wild Una! nothing can ever quell your gaiety of heart."

And Una kissed her merrily on the cheek.

So the oak door of the room again opened, and Shaeen, with his conductor, descended the stair. He walked with the scared boy in grim silence near half way down the wild hill-side toward Murroa, and then he stopped, and said in Irish—

"You never saw the fairies before, my fine fellow, and 'tisn't often those who once set eyes on us return to tell it. Whoever comes nearer, night or day, than this stone," and he tapped it with the end of his cane, "will never see his home again, for we'll keep him till the day of judgment; goodnight, little gossoon—and away with you."

So these young ladies, Alice and Una, with two old servants, by their father's direction, had taken up their abode in a portion of that side of the old castle which overhung the glen; and with the furniture and hangings they had removed from their late residence, and with the aid of glass in the casements and some other indispensable repairs, and a thorough airing, they made the rooms they had selected just habitable, as a rude and temporary shelter.

CHAPTER III

The Priest's Adventures in the Glen

At first, of course, they saw or heard little of their father. In general, however, they knew that his plan was to procure some employment in France, and to remove them there. Their present strange abode was only an adventure and an episode, and they believed that any day they might receive instructions to commence their journey.

After a little while the pursuit relaxed. The government, I believe, did not care, provided he did not obtrude himself, what became of him, or where he concealed himself. At all events, the local authorities showed no disposition to hunt him down. The young ladies' charges on the little forfeited property were paid without any dispute, and no vexatious inquiries were raised as to what had become of the furniture and other personal property which had been carried away from the forfeited house.

The haunted reputation of the castle—for in those days, in matters of the marvellous, the oldest were children—secured the little family in the seclusion they coveted. Once, or sometimes twice a week, old Laurence, with a shaggy little pony, made a secret expedition to the city of Limerick, starting before dawn, and returning under the cover of the night, with his purchases. There was beside an occasional sly moonlit visit from the old parish priest, and a midnight mass in the old castle for the little outlawed congregation.

As the alarm and inquiry subsided, their father made them, now and then, a brief and stealthy visit. At first these were but of a night's duration, and with great precaution; but gradually they were extended and less guarded. Still he was, as the phrase is in Munster, "on his keeping." He had firearms always by his bed, and had arranged places of concealment in the castle in the event of a surprise. But no attempt nor any disposition to molest him appearing, he grew more at ease, if not more cheerful.

It came, at last, that he would sometimes stay so long as two whole months at a time, and then depart as suddenly and mysteriously as he came. I suppose he had always some promising plot on hand, and his head full of ingenious treason, and lived on the sickly and exciting dietary of hope deferred.

Was there a poetical justice in this, that the little *ménage* thus secretly established, in the solitary and timeworn pile, should have themselves experienced, but from causes not so easily explicable, those very supernatural perturbations which they had themselves essayed to inspire?

The interruption of the old priest's secret visits was the earliest consequence of the mysterious interference which now began to display itself. One night, having left his cob in care of his old sacristan in the little village, he trudged on foot along the winding pathway, among the gray rocks and ferns that threaded the glen, intending a ghostly visit to the fair recluses of the castle, and he lost his way in this strange fashion.

There was moonlight, indeed, but it was little more than quarter-moon, and a long train of funereal clouds were sailing slowly across the sky—so that, faint and wan as it was, the light seldom shone full out, and was often hidden for a minute or two altogether. When he reached the point in the glen where the castle-stairs were wont to be, he could see nothing of them, and above, no trace of the castle-towers. So, puzzled somewhat, he pursued his way up the ravine, wondering how his walk had become so unusually protracted and fatiguing.

At last, sure enough, he saw the castle as plain as could be, and a lonely streak of candle-light issuing from the tower, just as usual, when his visit was expected. But he could not find the stair; and had to clamber among the rocks and copse-wood the best way he could. But when he emerged at top, there was nothing but the bare heath. Then the clouds stole over the moon again, and he moved along with hesitation and difficulty, and once more he saw the outline of the castle against the sky, quite sharp and clear. But this time it proved to be a great battlemented mass of cloud on the horizon. In a few minutes more he was quite close, all of a sudden, to the great front, rising gray and dim in the feeble light, and not till he could have struck it with his good oak "wattle" did he discover it to be only one of those wild, gray frontages of living rock that rise here and there in picturesque tiers along the slopes of those solitary mountains. And so, till dawn, pursuing this mirage of the castle, through pools and among ravines, he wore out a night of miserable misadventure and fatigue.

Another night, riding up the glen, so far as the level way at bottom would allow, and intending to make his nag fast at his customary tree, he heard on a sudden a horrid shriek at top of the steep rocks above his head, and something—a gigantic human form, it seemed—came tumbling and bounding headlong down through the rocks, and fell with a fearful impetus just before his horse's hoofs and there lay like a huge palpitating carcass. The horse was scared, as, indeed, was his rider, too, and more so when this apparently lifeless thing sprang up to his legs, and throwing his arms apart to bar their further progress, advanced his white and gigantic face towards them. Then the horse started about, with a snort of terror, nearly unseating the priest, and broke away into a furious and uncontrollable gallop.

I need not recount all the strange and various misadventures which the honest priest sustained in his endeavours to visit the castle, and its isolated tenants. They were enough to wear out his resolution, and frighten him into submission. And so at last these spiritual visits quite ceased; and fearing to awaken inquiry and suspicion, he thought it only prudent to abstain from attempting them in the daytime.

So the young ladies of the castle were more alone than ever. Their father, whose visits were frequently of long duration, had of late ceased altogether to speak of their contemplated departure for France, grew angry at any allusion to it, and they feared, had abandoned the plan altogether.

CHAPTER IV

The Light in the Bell Tower

Shortly after the discontinuance of the priest's visits, old Laurence, one night, to his surprise, saw light issuing from a window in the Bell Tower. It was at first only a tremulous red ray, visible only for a few minutes, which seemed to pass from the room, through whose window it escaped upon the courtyard of the castle, and so to lose itself. This tower and casement were in the angle of the building, exactly confronting that in which the little outlawed family had taken up their quarters.

The whole family were troubled at the appearance of this dull red ray from the chamber in the Bell Tower. Nobody knew what to make of it. But Laurence, who had campaigned in Italy with his old master, the young ladies' grandfather—"the heavens be his bed this night!"—was resolved to see it out, and took his great horse-pistols with him, and ascended to the corridor leading to the tower. But his search was vain.

This light left a sense of great uneasiness among the inmates, and most certainly it was not pleasant to suspect the establishment of an independent and possibly dangerous lodger or even colony, within the walls of the same old building.

The light very soon appeared again, steadier and somewhat brighter, in the same chamber. Again old Laurence buckled on his armour, swearing ominously to himself, and this time bent in earnest upon conflict. The young ladies watched in thrilling suspense from the great window in *their* stronghold, looking diagonally across the court. But as Laurence, who had entered the massive range of buildings opposite, might be supposed to be approaching the chamber from which this ill-omened glare proceeded, it steadily waned, finally disappearing altogether, just a few seconds before his voice was heard shouting from the arched window to know which way the light had gone.

This lighting up of the great chamber of the Bell Tower grew at last to be of frequent and almost continual recurrence. It was, there, long ago, in times of trouble and danger, that the De Lacys of those evil days used to sit in feudal judgment upon captive adversaries, and, as tradition alleged, often gave them no more time for shrift and prayer, than it needed to mount to the battlement of the turret over-head, from which they were forthwith hung by the necks, for a caveat and admonition to all evil disposed persons viewing the same from the country beneath.

Old Laurence observed these mysterious glimmerings with an evil and an anxious eye, and many and various were the stratagems he tried, but in vain, to surprise the audacious intruders. It is, however, I believe, a fact that no phenomenon, no matter how startling at first, if prosecuted with tolerable regularity, and unattended with any new circumstances of terror, will very long continue to excite alarm or even wonder.

So the family came to acquiesce in this mysterious light. No harm accompanied it. Old Laurence, as he smoked his lonely pipe in the grass-grown courtyard, would cast a disturbed glance at it, as it softly glowed out through the darking aperture, and mutter a prayer or an oath. But he had given over the chase as a hopeless business. And Peggy Sullivan, the old dame of all work, when, by chance, for she never willingly looked toward the haunted quarter, she caught the faint reflection of its dull effulgence with the corner of her eye, would sign herself with the cross or fumble at her beads, and deeper furrows would gather in her forehead, and her face grow ashen and perturbed. And this was not mended by the levity with which the young ladies, with whom the spectre had lost his influence, familiarity, as usual, breeding contempt, had come to talk, and even to jest, about it.

CHAPTER V

The Man with the Claret Mark

But as the former excitement flagged, old Peggy Sullivan produced a new one; for she solemnly avowed that she had seen a thin-faced man, with an ugly red mark all over the side of his cheek, looking out of the same window, just at sunset, before the young ladies returned from their evening walk.

This sounded in their ears like an old woman's dream, but still it was an excitement, jocular in the morning, and just, perhaps, a little fearful as night overspread the vast and desolate building, but still, not wholly unpleasant. This little flicker of credulity suddenly, however, blazed up into the full light of conviction.

Old Laurence, who was not given to dreaming, and had a cool, hard head, and an eye like a hawk, saw the same figure, just about the same hour, when the last level gleam of sunset was tinting the summits of the towers and the tops of the tall trees that surrounded them.

He had just entered the court from the great gate, when he heard all at once the hard peculiar twitter of alarm which sparrows make when a cat or a hawk invades their safety, rising all round from the thick ivy that overclimbed the wall on his left, and raising his eyes listlessly, he saw, with a sort of shock, a thin, ungainly man, standing with his legs crossed, in the recess of the window from which the light was wont to issue, leaning with his elbows on the stone mullion, and looking down with a sort of sickly sneer, his hollow yellow cheeks being deeply stained on one side with what is called a "claret-mark."

"I have you at last, you villain!" cried Larry, in a strange rage and panic: "drop down out of that on the grass here, and give yourself up, or I'll shoot you."

The threat was backed with an oath, and he drew from his coat pocket the long holster pistol he was wont to carry, and covered his man cleverly.

"I give you while I count ten—one-two-three-four. If you draw back, I'll fire, mind; five-six—you'd better be lively—seven-eight-nine—one chance more; will you come down? Then take it—ten!"

Bang went the pistol. The sinister stranger was hardly fifteen feet removed from him, and Larry was a dead shot. But this time he made a scandalous miss, for the shot knocked a little white dust from the stone wall a full yard at one side; and the fellow never shifted his negligent posture or qualified his sardonic smile during the procedure.

Larry was mortified and angry.

"You'll not get off this time, my tulip!" he said with a grin, exchanging the smoking weapon for the loaded pistol in reserve.

"What are you pistolling, Larry?" said a familiar voice close by his elbow, and he saw his master, accompanied by a handsome young man in a cloak.

"That villain, your honour, in the window, there."

"Why there's nobody there, Larry," said De Lacy, with a laugh, though that was no common indulgence with him.

As Larry gazed, the figure somehow dissolved and broke up without receding. A hanging tuft of yellow and red ivy nodded queerly in place of the face, some broken and discoloured masonry in perspective took up the outline and colouring of the arms and figure, and two imperfect red and yellow lichen streaks carried on the curved tracing of the long spindle shanks. Larry blessed himself, and drew his hand across his damp forehead, over his bewildered eyes, and could not speak for a minute. It was all some devilish trick; he could take his oath he saw every feature in the fellow's face, the lace and buttons of his cloak and doublet, and even his long finger nails and thin yellow fingers that overhung the cross-shaft of the window, where there was now nothing but a rusty stain left.

The young gentleman who had arrived with De Lacy, stayed that night and shared with great apparent relish the homely fare of the family. He was a gay and gallant Frenchman, and the beauty of the younger lady, and her pleasantry and spirit, seemed to make his hours pass but too swiftly, and the moment of parting sad.

When he had departed early in the morning, Ultor De Lacy had a long talk with his elder daughter, while the younger was busy with her early dairy task, for among their retainers this *proles generosa* reckoned a "kind" little Kerry cow.

He told her that he had visited France since he had been last at Cappercullen, and how good and gracious their sovereign had been, and how he had arranged a noble alliance for her sister Una. The young gentleman was of high blood, and though not rich, had, nevertheless, his acres and his *nom de terre*, besides a captain's rank in the army. He was, in short, the very gentleman with whom they had parted only that morning. On what special business he was now in Ireland there was no necessity that he should speak; but being here he had brought him hither to present him to his daughter, and found that the impression she had made was quite what was desirable.

"You, you know, dear Alice, are promised to a conventual life. Had it been otherwise—"

He hesitated for a moment.

"You are right, dear father," she said, kissing his hand, "I *am* so promised, and no earthly tie or allurement has power to draw me from that holy engagement."

"Well," he said, returning her caress, "I do not mean to urge you upon that point. It must not, however, be until Una's marriage has taken place. That cannot be, for many good reasons, sooner than this time twelve months; we shall then exchange this strange and barbarous abode for Paris, where are many eligible convents, in which are entertained as sisters some of the noblest ladies of France; and there, too, in Una's marriage will be continued, though not the name, at all events the blood, the lineage, and the title which, so sure as justice ultimately governs the course of human events, will be again established, powerful and honoured in this country, the scene of their ancient glory and transitory misfortunes. Meanwhile, we must not mention this engagement to Una. Here she runs no risk of being sought or won; but the mere knowledge that her hand was absolutely pledged, might excite a capricious opposition and repining such as neither I nor you would like to see; therefore be secret."

The same evening he took Alice with him for a ramble round the castle wall, while they talked of grave matters, and he as usual allowed her a dim and doubtful view of some of those cloud-built castles in which he habitually dwelt, and among which his jaded hopes revived.

They were walking upon a pleasant short sward of darkest green, on one side overhung by the gray castle walls, and on the other by the forest trees that here and there closely approached it, when precisely as they turned the angle of the Bell Tower, they were encountered by a person walking directly towards them. The sight of a stranger, with the exception of the one visitor introduced by her father, was in this place so absolutely unprecedented, that Alice was amazed and affrighted to such a degree that for a moment she stood stock-still.

But there was more in this apparition to excite unpleasant emotions, than the mere circumstance of its unexpectedness. The figure was very strange, being that of a tall, lean, ungainly man, dressed in a dingy suit, somewhat of a Spanish fashion, with a brown laced cloak, and faded red stockings. He had long lank legs, long arms, hands, and fingers, and a very long sickly face, with a drooping nose, and a sly, sarcastic leer, and a great purplish stain over-spreading more than half of one cheek.

As he strode past, he touched his cap with his thin, discoloured fingers, and an ugly side glance, and disappeared round the corner. The eyes of father and daughter followed him in silence.

Ultor De Lacy seemed first absolutely terror-stricken, and then suddenly inflamed with ungovernable fury. He dropped his cane on the ground, drew his rapier, and, without wasting a thought on his daughter, pursued.

He just had a glimpse of the retreating figure as it disappeared round the far angle. The plume, and the lank hair, the point of the rapier-scabbard, the flutter of the skirt of the cloak, and one red stocking and heel; and this was the last he saw of him.

When Alice reached his side, his drawn sword still in his hand, he was in a state of abject agitation.

"Thank Heaven, he's gone!" she exclaimed.

"He's gone," echoed Ultor, with a strange glare.

"And you are safe," she added, clasping his hand.

He sighed a great sigh.

"And you don't think he's coming back?"

"He!—who?"

"The stranger who passed us but now. Do you know him, father?"

"Yes—and—no, child—I know him not—and yet I know him too well. Would to heaven we could leave this accursed haunt tonight. Cursed be the stupid malice that first provoked this horrible feud, which no sacrifice and misery can appease, and no exorcism can quell or even suspend. The wretch has come from afar with a sure instinct to devour my last hope—to dog us into our last retreat—and to blast with his triumph the very dust and ruins of our house. What ails that stupid priest that he has given over his visits? Are *my* children to be left without mass or confession—the sacraments which *guard* as well as save—because he once loses his way in a mist, or mistakes a streak of foam in the brook for a dead man's face? D——n him!"

"See, Alice, if he won't come," he resumed, "you must only *write* your confession to him in full—you and Una. Laurence is trusty, and will carry it—and we'll get the bishop's—or, if need be, the Pope's leave for him to give you absolution. I'll move heaven and earth, but you *shall* have the sacraments, poor children!—and see him. I've been a wild fellow in my youth, and never pretended to sanctity; but I know there's but one safe way—and—and—keep you each a bit of this— (he opened a small silver box) —about you while you stay here—fold and sew it up reverently in a bit of the old psaltery parchment and wear it next your hearts—'tis a fragment of the consecrated wafer—and will help, with the saints' protection, to guard you from harm—and be strict in fasts, and constant in prayer—*I* can do nothing—nor devise any help. The curse has fallen, indeed, on me and mine."

And Alice, saw, in silence, the tears of despair roll down his pale and agitated face.

This adventure was also a secret, and Una was to hear nothing of it.

CHAPTER VI

Voices

Now Una, nobody knew why, began to lose spirit, and to grow

pale. Her fun and frolic were quite gone! Even her songs ceased.
She was silent with her sister, and loved solitude better. She said
she was well, and quite happy, and could in no wise be got to
account for the lamentable change that had stolen over her. She
had grown odd too, and obstinate in trifles; and strangely reserved
and cold.

Alice was very unhappy in consequence. What was the cause of
this estrangement—had she offended her, and how? But Una had
never before borne resentment for an hour. What could have
altered her entire nature so? Could it be the shadow and chill of
coming insanity?

Once or twice, when her sister urged her with tears and en-
treaties to disclose the secret of her changed spirits and demeanour,
she seemed to listen with a sort of silent wonder and suspicion,
and then she looked for a moment full upon her, and seemed on
the very point of revealing all. But the earnest dilated gaze stole
downward to the floor, and subsided into an odd wily smile, and
she began to whisper to herself, and the smile and the whisper
were both a mystery to Alice.

She and Alice slept in the same bedroom—a chamber in a
projecting tower—which on their arrival, when poor Una was so
merry, they had hung round with old tapestry, and decorated
fantastically according to their skill and frolic. One night, as they
went to bed, Una said, as if speaking to herself—

" 'Tis my last night in this room—I shall sleep no more with
Alice."

"And what has poor Alice done, Una, to deserve your strange
unkindness?"

Una looked on her curiously, and half frightened, and then the
odd smile stole over her face like a gleam of moonlight.

"My poor Alice, what have you to do with it?" she whispered.

"And why do you talk of sleeping no more with me?" said Alice.

"Why? Alice dear—no why—no reason—only a knowledge that
it must be so, or Una will die."

"Die, Una darling!—what can you mean?"

"Yes, sweet Alice, die, indeed. We must all die some time, you
know, or—or undergo a change; and my time is near—*very* near—
unless I sleep apart from you."

"Indeed, Una, sweetheart, I think you *are* ill, but not near
death."

"Una knows what you think, wise Alice—but she's not mad—
on the contrary, she's wiser than other folks."

"She's sadder and stranger too," said Alice, tenderly.

"Knowledge is sorrow," answered Una, and she looked across the room through her golden hair which she was combing—and through the window, beyond which lay the tops of the great trees, and the still foliage of the glen in the misty moonlight.

" 'Tis enough, Alice dear; it must be so. The bed must move hence, or Una's bed will be low enough ere long. See, it shan't be far though, only into that small room."

She pointed to an inner room or closet opening from that in which they lay. The walls of the building were hugely thick, and there were double doors of oak between the chambers, and Alice thought, with a sigh, how completely separated they were going to be.

However she offered no opposition. The change was made, and the girls for the first time since childhood lay in separate chambers. A few nights afterwards Alice awoke late in the night from a dreadful dream, in which the sinister figure which she and her father had encountered in their ramble round the castle walls, bore a principal part.

When she awoke there were still in her ears the sounds which had mingled in her dream. They were the notes of a deep, ringing, bass voice rising from the glen beneath the castle walls—something between humming and singing—listlessly unequal and intermittent, like the melody of a man whiling away the hours over his work. While she was wondering at this unwonted minstrelsy, there came a silence, and—could she believe her ears?—it certainly was Una's clear low contralto—softly singing a bar or two from the window. Then once more silence—and then again the strange manly voice, faintly chaunting from the leafy abyss.

With a strange wild feeling of suspicion and terror, Alice glided to the window. The moon who sees so many things, and keeps all secrets, with her cold impenetrable smile, was high in the sky. But Alice saw the red flicker of a candle from Una's window, and, she thought, the shadow of her head against the deep side wall of its recess. Then this was gone, and there were no more sights or sounds that night.

As they sate at breakfast, the small birds were singing merrily from among the sun-tipped foliage.

"I love this music," said Alice, unusually pale and sad; "it comes with the pleasant light of morning. I remember, Una, when *you* used to sing, like those gay birds, in the fresh beams of the morning; that was in the old time, when Una kept no secret from poor Alice."

"And Una knows what her sage Alice means; but there are other

birds, silent all day long, and, they say, the sweetest too, that love
to sing by *night* alone."

So things went on—the elder girl pained and melancholy—the
younger silent, changed, and unaccountable.

A little while after this, very late one night, on awaking, Alice
heard a conversation being carried on in her sister's room. There
seemed to be no disguise about it. She could not distinguish the
words, indeed, the walls being some six feet thick, and two great
oak doors intercepting. But Una's clear voice, and the deep bell-
like tones of the unknown, made up the dialogue.

Alice sprung from her bed, threw her clothes about her, and
tried to enter her sister's room; but the inner door was bolted.
The voices ceased to speak as she knocked, and Una opened it, and
stood before her in her nightdress, candle in hand.

"Una—Una, darling, as you hope for peace, tell me who is
here?" cried frightened Alice, with her trembling arms about her
neck.

Una drew back, with her large innocent blue eyes fixed full
upon her.

"Come in, Alice," she said, coldly.

And in came Alice, with a fearful glance around. There was no
hiding place there; a chair, a table, a little bedstead, and two or
three pegs in the wall to hang clothes on; a narrow window, with
two iron bars across; no hearth or chimney—nothing but bare
walls.

Alice looked round in amazement, and her eyes glanced with
painful inquiry into those of her sister. Una smiled one of her
peculiar sidelong smiles, and said—

"Strange dreams! I've been dreaming—so has Alice. She hears
and sees Una's dreams, and wonders—and well she may."

And she kissed her sister's cheek with a cold kiss, and lay down
in her little bed, her slender hand under her head, and spoke no
more.

Alice, not knowing what to think, went back to hers.

About this time Ultor De Lacy returned. He heard his elder
daughter's strange narrative with marked uneasiness, and his
agitation seemed to grow rather than subside. He enjoined her,
however, not to mention it to the old servant, nor in presence of
anybody she might chance to see, but only to him and to the priest,
if he could be persuaded to resume his duty and return. The trial,
however, such as it was, could not endure very long; matters had
turned out favourably. The union of his younger daughter might

be accomplished within a few months, and in eight or nine weeks they should be on their way to Paris.

A night or two after her father's arrival, Alice, in the dead of the night, heard the well-known strange deep voice speaking softly, as it seemed, close to her own window on the outside; and Una's voice, clear and tender, spoke in answer. She hurried to her own casement, and pushed it open, kneeling in the deep embrasure, and looking with a stealthy and affrighted gaze towards her sister's window. As she crossed the floor the voices subsided, and she saw a light withdrawn from within. The moonbeams slanted bright and clear on the whole side of the castle overlooking the glen, and she plainly beheld the shadow of a man projected on the wall as on a screen.

This black shadow recalled with a horrid thrill the outline and fashion of the figure in the Spanish dress. There were the cap and mantle, the rapier, the long thin limbs and sinister angularity. It was so thrown obliquely that the hands reached to the window-sill, and the feet stretched and stretched, longer and longer as she looked, toward the ground, and disappeared in the general darkness; and the rest, with a sudden flicker, shot downwards, as shadows will on the sudden movement of a light, and was lost in one gigantic leap down the castle wall.

"I do not know whether I dream or wake when I hear and see these sights; but I will ask my father to sit up with me, and we *two* surely cannot be mistaken. May the holy saints keep and guard us!" And in her terror she buried her head under the bed-clothes, and whispered her prayers for an hour.

CHAPTER VII

Una's Love

"I have been with Father Denis," said De Lacy, next day, "and he will come to-morrow; and, thank Heaven! you may both make your confession and hear mass, and my mind will be at rest; and you'll find poor Una happier and more like herself."

But 'tween cup and lip there's many a slip. The priest was not destined to hear poor Una's shrift. When she bid her sister good-night she looked on her with her large, cold, wild eyes, till something of her old human affections seemed to gather there, and they slowly filled with tears, which dropped one after the other on her homely dress as she gazed in her sister's face.

Alice, delighted, sprang up, and clasped her arms about her neck. "My own darling treasure, 'tis all over; you love your poor Alice again, and will be happier than ever."

But while she held her in her embrace Una's eyes were turned towards the window, and her lips apart, and Alice felt instinctively that her thoughts were already far away.

"Hark!—listen!—hush!" and Una, with her delighted gaze fixed, as if she saw far away beyond the castle wall, the trees, the glen, and the night's dark curtain, held her hand raised near her ear, and waved her head slightly in time, as it seemed, to music that reached not Alice's ear, and smiled her strange pleased smile, and then the smile slowly faded away, leaving that sly suspicious light behind it which somehow scared her sister with an uncertain sense of danger; and she sang in tones so sweet and low that it seemed but a reverie of a song, recalling, as Alice fancied, the strain to which she had just listened in that strange ecstasy, the plaintive and beautiful Irish ballad, "Shule, shule, shule, aroon," the midnight summons of the outlawed Irish soldier to his darling to follow him.

Alice had slept little the night before. She was now overpowered with fatigue; and leaving her candle burning by her bedside, she fell into a deep sleep. From this she awoke suddenly, and completely, as will sometimes happen without any apparent cause, and she saw Una come into the room. She had a little purse of embroidery—her own work—in her hand; and she stole lightly to the bedside, with her peculiar oblique smile, and evidently thinking that her sister was asleep.

Alice was thrilled with a strange terror, and did not speak or move; and her sister slipped her hand softly under her bolster, and withdrew it. Then Una stood for while by the hearth, and stretched her hand up to the mantelpiece, from which she took a little bit of chalk, and Alice thought she saw her place it in the fingers of a long yellow hand that was stealthily introduced from her own chamber-door to receive it; and Una paused in the dark recess of the door, and smiled over her shoulder toward her sister, and then glided into her room, closing the doors.

Almost freezing with terror, Alice rose and glided after her, and stood in her chamber, screaming—

"Una, Una, in heaven's name what troubles you?"

But Una seemed to have been sound asleep in her bed, and raised herself with a start, and looking upon her with a peevish surprise, said—

"What does Alice seek here?"

"You were in my room, Una, dear; you seem disturbed and troubled."

"Dreams, Alice. My dreams crossing your brain; only dreams— dreams. Get you to bed, and sleep."

And to bed she went, but *not* to sleep. She lay awake more than an hour; and then Una emerged once more from her room. This time she was fully dressed, and had her cloak and thick shoes on, as their rattle on the floor plainly discovered. She had a little bundle tied up in a handkerchief in her hand, and her hood was drawn about her head; and thus equipped, as it seemed, for a journey, she came and stood at the foot of Alice's bed, and stared on her with a look so soulless and terrible that her senses almost forsook her. Then she turned and went back into her own chamber.

She may have returned; but Alice thought not—at least she did not see her. But she lay in great excitement and perturbation; and was terrified, about an hour later, by a knock at her chamber door —not that opening into Una's room, but upon the little passage from the stone screw staircase. She sprang from her bed; but the door was secured on the inside, and she felt relieved. The knock was repeated, and she heard some one laughing softly on the out- side.

The morning came at last; that dreadful night was over. But Una! Where was Una?

Alice never saw her more. On the head of her empty bed were traced in chalk the words—Ultor De Lacy, Ultor O'Donnell. And Alice found beneath her own pillow the little purse of embroidery she had seen in Una's hand. It was her little parting token, and bore the simple legend—"Una's love!"

De Lacy's rage and horror were boundless. He charged the priest, in frantic language, with having exposed his child, by his coward- ice and neglect, to the machinations of the Fiend, and raved and blasphemed like a man demented.

It is said that he procured a solemn exorcism to be performed, in the hope of disenthralling and recovering his daughter. Several times, it is alleged, she was seen by the old servants. Once on a sweet summer morning, in the window of the tower, she was perceived combing her beautiful golden tresses, and holding a little mirror in her hand; and first, when she saw herself discovered, she looked affrighted, and then smiled, her slanting, cunning smile.

Sometimes, too, in the glen, by moonlight, it was said belated villagers had met her, always startled first, and then smiling, generally singing snatches of old Irish ballads, that seemed to bear a sort of dim resemblance to her melancholy fate. The apparition has long ceased. But it is said that now and again, perhaps once in two or three years, late on a summer night, you may hear—but faint and far away in the recesses of the glen—the sweet, sad notes of Una's voice, singing those plaintive melodies. This, too, of course, in time will cease, and all be forgotten.

CHAPTER VIII

Sister Agnes and the Portrait

When Ultor De Lacy died, his daughter Alice found among his effects a small box, containing a portrait such as I have described. When she looked on it, she recoiled in horror. There, in the plenitude of its sinister peculiarities, was faithfully portrayed the phantom which lived with a vivid and horrible accuracy in her remembrance. Folded in the same box was a brief narrative, stating that, "A.D. 1601, in the month of December, Walter De Lacy, of Cappercullen, made many prisoners at the ford of Ownhey, or Abington, of Irish and Spanish soldiers, flying from the great overthrow of the rebel powers at Kinsale, and among the number one Roderic O'Donnell, an arch traitor, and near kinsman to that other O'Donnell who led the rebels; who, claiming kindred through his mother to De Lacy, sued for his life with instant and miserable entreaty, and offered great ransom, but was by De Lacy, through great zeal for the queen, as some thought, cruelly put to death. When he went to the tower-top, where was the gallows, finding himself in extremity, and no hope of mercy, he swore that though he could work them no evil before his death, yet that he would devote himself thereafter to blast the greatness of the De Lacys, and never leave them till his work was done. He hath been seen often since, and always for that family perniciously, insomuch that it hath been the custom to show to young children of that lineage the picture of the said O'Donnell, in little, taken among his few valuables, to prevent their being misled by him unawares, so that he should not have his will, who by devilish wiles and hell-born cunning, hath steadfastly sought the ruin of that ancient house, and especially to leave that *stemma generosum* destitute of issue for the transmission of their pure blood and worshipful name."

Old Miss Croker, of Ross House, who was near seventy in the year 1821, when she related this story to me, had seen and conversed with Alice De Lacy, a professed nun, under the name of Sister Agnes, in a religious house in King-street, in Dublin, founded by the famous Duchess of Tyrconnell, and had the narrative from her own lips. I thought the tale worth preserving, and have no more to say.

Sources

"Green Tea" and "The Familiar" have been reprinted from *In a Glass Darkly* (London, 1886); names have been added in "The Familiar" from the almost identical text of "The Watcher" from *The Watcher and Other Weird Stories* (London, 1894), to replace initials and blanks. "Squire Toby's Will" has been reprinted from *Madam Crowl's Ghost* (London, 1923), edited by Montague Rhodes James. "Schalken the Painter" follows the text revised by LeFanu for *Ghost Stories and Tales of Mystery* (Dublin & London, 1851), rather than the earlier, more frequently met text of *The Purcell Papers*. "Madam Crowl's Ghost" has been reprinted from *Chronicles of Golden Friars* (London, 1871), for the first time with the lead-in passage. "The Haunted Baronet" follows the text of *Chronicles of Golden Friars*. "Mr. Justice Harbottle" follows the text of "The Haunted House in Westminster," *Belgravia*, 1872, rather than that of *In a Glass Darkly*, which adds a series introduction. "Carmilla" follows the text of *In a Glass Darkly*, and "The Fortunes of Sir Robert Ardagh" and "An Account of Some Strange Disturbances in Aungier Street" have been reprinted from the *Dublin University Magazine*, respectively 1838 and 1853. "The Dead Sexton" has been reprinted from the Christmas number, 1871, of *Once a Week*. The fragment which we have titled "Ghost Stories of the Tiled House" has been reprinted from the serial publication of "The House by the Churchyard" (Chapters VIII and IX) in the *Dublin University Magazine*, 1861. Chapter IX has been anthologized by Montague Summers (*The Supernatural Omnibus*) under the title "An Authentic Narrative of the Ghost of a Hand." "The White Cat of Drumgunniol" has been reprinted from *Madam Crowl's Ghost*, as has "Sir Dominick's Bargain." "Ultor De Lacy" and "An Authentic Narrative of a Haunted House" first appeared in the *Dublin University Magazine*, 1861 and 1862, respectively.

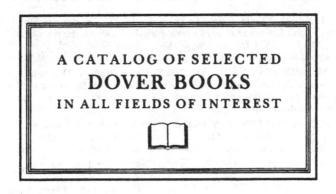

A CATALOG OF SELECTED

DOVER BOOKS

IN ALL FIELDS OF INTEREST

A CATALOG OF SELECTED DOVER
BOOKS IN ALL FIELDS OF INTEREST

100 BEST-LOVED POEMS, Edited by Philip Smith. "The Passionate Shepherd to His Love," "Shall I compare thee to a summer's day?" "Death, be not proud," "The Raven," "The Road Not Taken," plus works by Blake, Wordsworth, Byron, Shelley, Keats, many others. 96pp. 5³⁄₁₆ x 8¼. 0-486-28553-7

100 SMALL HOUSES OF THE THIRTIES, Brown-Blodgett Company. Exterior photographs and floor plans for 100 charming structures. Illustrations of models accompanied by descriptions of interiors, color schemes, closet space, and other amenities. 200 illustrations. 112pp. 8⅜ x 11. 0-486-44131-8

1000 TURN-OF-THE-CENTURY HOUSES: With Illustrations and Floor Plans, Herbert C. Chivers. Reproduced from a rare edition, this showcase of homes ranges from cottages and bungalows to sprawling mansions. Each house is meticulously illustrated and accompanied by complete floor plans. 256pp. 9⅜ x 12¼.
0-486-45596-3

101 GREAT AMERICAN POEMS, Edited by The American Poetry & Literacy Project. Rich treasury of verse from the 19th and 20th centuries includes works by Edgar Allan Poe, Robert Frost, Walt Whitman, Langston Hughes, Emily Dickinson, T. S. Eliot, other notables. 96pp. 5³⁄₁₆ x 8¼. 0-486-40158-8

101 GREAT SAMURAI PRINTS, Utagawa Kuniyoshi. Kuniyoshi was a master of the warrior woodblock print — and these 18th-century illustrations represent the pinnacle of his craft. Full-color portraits of renowned Japanese samurais pulse with movement, passion, and remarkably fine detail. 112pp. 8⅜ x 11. 0-486-46523-3

ABC OF BALLET, Janet Grosser. Clearly worded, abundantly illustrated little guide defines basic ballet-related terms: arabesque, battement, pas de chat, relevé, sissonne, many others. Pronunciation guide included. Excellent primer. 48pp. 4³⁄₁₆ x 5¾.
0-486-40871-X

ACCESSORIES OF DRESS: An Illustrated Encyclopedia, Katherine Lester and Bess Viola Oerke. Illustrations of hats, veils, wigs, cravats, shawls, shoes, gloves, and other accessories enhance an engaging commentary that reveals the humor and charm of the many-sided story of accessorized apparel. 644 figures and 59 plates. 608pp. 6⅛ x 9¼.
0-486-43378-1

ADVENTURES OF HUCKLEBERRY FINN, Mark Twain. Join Huck and Jim as their boyhood adventures along the Mississippi River lead them into a world of excitement, danger, and self-discovery. Humorous narrative, lyrical descriptions of the Mississippi valley, and memorable characters. 224pp. 5³⁄₁₆ x 8¼. 0-486-28061-6

ALICE STARMORE'S BOOK OF FAIR ISLE KNITTING, Alice Starmore. A noted designer from the region of Scotland's Fair Isle explores the history and techniques of this distinctive, stranded-color knitting style and provides copious illustrated instructions for 14 original knitwear designs. 208pp. 8⅜ x 10⅞. 0-486-47218-3

Browse over 9,000 books at www.doverpublications.com

ALICE'S ADVENTURES IN WONDERLAND, Lewis Carroll. Beloved classic about a little girl lost in a topsy-turvy land and her encounters with the White Rabbit, March Hare, Mad Hatter, Cheshire Cat, and other delightfully improbable characters. 42 illustrations by Sir John Tenniel. 96pp. 5³⁄₁₆ x 8¼.   0-486-27543-4

AMERICA'S LIGHTHOUSES: An Illustrated History, Francis Ross Holland. Profusely illustrated fact-filled survey of American lighthouses since 1716. Over 200 stations — East, Gulf, and West coasts, Great Lakes, Hawaii, Alaska, Puerto Rico, the Virgin Islands, and the Mississippi and St. Lawrence Rivers. 240pp. 8 x 10¾.
   0-486-25576-X

AN ENCYCLOPEDIA OF THE VIOLIN, Alberto Bachmann. Translated by Frederick H. Martens. Introduction by Eugene Ysaye. First published in 1925, this renowned reference remains unsurpassed as a source of essential information, from construction and evolution to repertoire and technique. Includes a glossary and 73 illustrations. 496pp. 6½ x 9¼.   0-486-46618-3

ANIMALS: 1,419 Copyright-Free Illustrations of Mammals, Birds, Fish, Insects, etc., Selected by Jim Harter. Selected for its visual impact and ease of use, this outstanding collection of wood engravings presents over 1,000 species of animals in extremely lifelike poses. Includes mammals, birds, reptiles, amphibians, fish, insects, and other invertebrates. 284pp. 9 x 12.   0-486-23766-4

THE ANNALS, Tacitus. Translated by Alfred John Church and William Jackson Brodribb. This vital chronicle of Imperial Rome, written by the era's great historian, spans A.D. 14-68 and paints incisive psychological portraits of major figures, from Tiberius to Nero. 416pp. 5³⁄₁₆ x 8¼.   0-486-45236-0

ANTIGONE, Sophocles. Filled with passionate speeches and sensitive probing of moral and philosophical issues, this powerful and often-performed Greek drama reveals the grim fate that befalls the children of Oedipus. Footnotes. 64pp. 5³⁄₁₆ x 8 ¼.   0-486-27804-2

ART DECO DECORATIVE PATTERNS IN FULL COLOR, Christian Stoll. Reprinted from a rare 1910 portfolio, 160 sensuous and exotic images depict a breathtaking array of florals, geometrics, and abstracts — all elegant in their stark simplicity. 64pp. 8⅜ x 11.   0-486-44862-2

THE ARTHUR RACKHAM TREASURY: 86 Full-Color Illustrations, Arthur Rackham. Selected and Edited by Jeff A. Menges. A stunning treasury of 86 full-page plates span the famed English artist's career, from *Rip Van Winkle* (1905) to masterworks such as *Undine*, *A Midsummer Night's Dream*, and *Wind in the Willows* (1939). 96pp. 8⅜ x 11.   0-486-44685-9

THE AUTHENTIC GILBERT & SULLIVAN SONGBOOK, W. S. Gilbert and A. S. Sullivan. The most comprehensive collection available, this songbook includes selections from every one of Gilbert and Sullivan's light operas. Ninety-two numbers are presented uncut and unedited, and in their original keys. 410pp. 9 x 12.
   0-486-23482-7

THE AWAKENING, Kate Chopin. First published in 1899, this controversial novel of a New Orleans wife's search for love outside a stifling marriage shocked readers. Today, it remains a first-rate narrative with superb characterization. New introductory Note. 128pp. 5³⁄₁₆ x 8¼.   0-486-27786-0

BASIC DRAWING, Louis Priscilla. Beginning with perspective, this commonsense manual progresses to the figure in movement, light and shade, anatomy, drapery, composition, trees and landscape, and outdoor sketching. Black-and-white illustrations throughout. 128pp. 8⅜ x 11.   0-486-45815-6

Browse over 9,000 books at www.doverpublications.com

THE BATTLES THAT CHANGED HISTORY, Fletcher Pratt. Historian profiles 16 crucial conflicts, ancient to modern, that changed the course of Western civilization. Gripping accounts of battles led by Alexander the Great, Joan of Arc, Ulysses S. Grant, other commanders. 27 maps. 352pp. 5⅜ x 8½. 0-486-41129-X

BEETHOVEN'S LETTERS, Ludwig van Beethoven. Edited by Dr. A. C. Kalischer. Features 457 letters to fellow musicians, friends, greats, patrons, and literary men. Reveals musical thoughts, quirks of personality, insights, and daily events. Includes 15 plates. 410pp. 5⅜ x 8½. 0-486-22769-3

BERNICE BOBS HER HAIR AND OTHER STORIES, F. Scott Fitzgerald. This brilliant anthology includes 6 of Fitzgerald's most popular stories: "The Diamond as Big as the Ritz," the title tale, "The Offshore Pirate," "The Ice Palace," "The Jelly Bean," and "May Day." 176pp. 5⅜ x 8½. 0-486-47049-0

BESLER'S BOOK OF FLOWERS AND PLANTS: 73 Full-Color Plates from Hortus Eystettensis, 1613, Basilius Besler. Here is a selection of magnificent plates from the Hortus Eystettensis, which vividly illustrated and identified the plants, flowers, and trees that thrived in the legendary German garden at Eichstätt. 80pp. 8⅜ x 11. 0-486-46005-3

THE BOOK OF KELLS, Edited by Blanche Cirker. Painstakingly reproduced from a rare facsimile edition, this volume contains full-page decorations, portraits, illustrations, plus a sampling of textual leaves with exquisite calligraphy and ornamentation. 32 full-color illustrations. 32pp. 9⅜ x 12¼. 0-486-24345-1

THE BOOK OF THE CROSSBOW: With an Additional Section on Catapults and Other Siege Engines, Ralph Payne-Gallwey. Fascinating study traces history and use of crossbow as military and sporting weapon, from Middle Ages to modern times. Also covers related weapons: balistas, catapults, Turkish bows, more. Over 240 illustrations. 400pp. 7¼ x 10¼. 0-486-28720-3

THE BUNGALOW BOOK: Floor Plans and Photos of 112 Houses, 1910, Henry L. Wilson. Here are 112 of the most popular and economic blueprints of the early 20th century — plus an illustration or photograph of each completed house. A wonderful time capsule that still offers a wealth of valuable insights. 160pp. 8⅜ x 11. 0-486-45104-6

THE CALL OF THE WILD, Jack London. A classic novel of adventure, drawn from London's own experiences as a Klondike adventurer, relating the story of a heroic dog caught in the brutal life of the Alaska Gold Rush. Note. 64pp. 5³⁄₁₆ x 8¼. 0-486-26472-6

CANDIDE, Voltaire. Edited by Francois-Marie Arouet. One of the world's great satires since its first publication in 1759. Witty, caustic skewering of romance, science, philosophy, religion, government — nearly all human ideals and institutions. 112pp. 5³⁄₁₆ x 8¼. 0-486-26689-3

CELEBRATED IN THEIR TIME: Photographic Portraits from the George Grantham Bain Collection, Edited by Amy Pastan. With an Introduction by Michael Carlebach. Remarkable portrait gallery features 112 rare images of Albert Einstein, Charlie Chaplin, the Wright Brothers, Henry Ford, and other luminaries from the worlds of politics, art, entertainment, and industry. 128pp. 8⅜ x 11. 0-486-46754-6

CHARIOTS FOR APOLLO: The NASA History of Manned Lunar Spacecraft to 1969, Courtney G. Brooks, James M. Grimwood, and Loyd S. Swenson, Jr. This illustrated history by a trio of experts is the definitive reference on the Apollo spacecraft and lunar modules. It traces the vehicles' design, development, and operation in space. More than 100 photographs and illustrations. 576pp. 6¾ x 9¼. 0-486-46756-2

Browse over 9,000 books at www.doverpublications.com

A CHRISTMAS CAROL, Charles Dickens. This engrossing tale relates Ebenezer Scrooge's ghostly journeys through Christmases past, present, and future and his ultimate transformation from a harsh and grasping old miser to a charitable and compassionate human being. 80pp. 5³⁄₁₆ x 8¼. 0-486-26865-9

COMMON SENSE, Thomas Paine. First published in January of 1776, this highly influential landmark document clearly and persuasively argued for American separation from Great Britain and paved the way for the Declaration of Independence. 64pp. 5³⁄₁₆ x 8¼. 0-486-29602-4

THE COMPLETE SHORT STORIES OF OSCAR WILDE, Oscar Wilde. Complete texts of "The Happy Prince and Other Tales," "A House of Pomegranates," "Lord Arthur Savile's Crime and Other Stories," "Poems in Prose," and "The Portrait of Mr. W. H." 208pp. 5³⁄₁₆ x 8¼. 0-486-45216-6

COMPLETE SONNETS, William Shakespeare. Over 150 exquisite poems deal with love, friendship, the tyranny of time, beauty's evanescence, death, and other themes in language of remarkable power, precision, and beauty. Glossary of archaic terms. 80pp. 5³⁄₁₆ x 8¼. 0-486-26686-9

THE COUNT OF MONTE CRISTO: Abridged Edition, Alexandre Dumas. Falsely accused of treason, Edmond Dantès is imprisoned in the bleak Chateau d'If. After a hair-raising escape, he launches an elaborate plot to extract a bitter revenge against those who betrayed him. 448pp. 5³⁄₁₆ x 8¼. 0-486-45643-9

CRAFTSMAN BUNGALOWS: Designs from the Pacific Northwest, Yoho & Merritt. This reprint of a rare catalog, showcasing the charming simplicity and cozy style of Craftsman bungalows, is filled with photos of completed homes, plus floor plans and estimated costs. An indispensable resource for architects, historians, and illustrators. 112pp. 10 x 7. 0-486-46875-5

CRAFTSMAN BUNGALOWS: 59 Homes from "The Craftsman," Edited by Gustav Stickley. Best and most attractive designs from Arts and Crafts Movement publication — 1903–1916 — includes sketches, photographs of homes, floor plans, descriptive text. 128pp. 8¼ x 11. 0-486-25829-7

CRIME AND PUNISHMENT, Fyodor Dostoyevsky. Translated by Constance Garnett. Supreme masterpiece tells the story of Raskolnikov, a student tormented by his own thoughts after he murders an old woman. Overwhelmed by guilt and terror, he confesses and goes to prison. 480pp. 5³⁄₁₆ x 8¼. 0-486-41587-2

THE DECLARATION OF INDEPENDENCE AND OTHER GREAT DOCUMENTS OF AMERICAN HISTORY: 1775-1865, Edited by John Grafton. Thirteen compelling and influential documents: Henry's "Give Me Liberty or Give Me Death," Declaration of Independence, The Constitution, Washington's First Inaugural Address, The Monroe Doctrine, The Emancipation Proclamation, Gettysburg Address, more. 64pp. 5³⁄₁₆ x 8¼. 0-486-41124-9

THE DESERT AND THE SOWN: Travels in Palestine and Syria, Gertrude Bell. "The female Lawrence of Arabia," Gertrude Bell wrote captivating, perceptive accounts of her travels in the Middle East. This intriguing narrative, accompanied by 160 photos, traces her 1905 sojourn in Lebanon, Syria, and Palestine. 368pp. 5⅜ x 8½. 0-486-46876-3

A DOLL'S HOUSE, Henrik Ibsen. Ibsen's best-known play displays his genius for realistic prose drama. An expression of women's rights, the play climaxes when the central character, Nora, rejects a smothering marriage and life in "a doll's house." 80pp. 5³⁄₁₆ x 8¼. 0-486-27062-9

DOOMED SHIPS: Great Ocean Liner Disasters, William H. Miller, Jr. Nearly 200 photographs, many from private collections, highlight tales of some of the vessels whose pleasure cruises ended in catastrophe: the *Morro Castle, Normandie, Andrea Doria, Europa,* and many others. 128pp. 8⅜ x 11¼. 0-486-45366-9

THE DORÉ BIBLE ILLUSTRATIONS, Gustave Doré. Detailed plates from the Bible: the Creation scenes, Adam and Eve, horrifying visions of the Flood, the battle sequences with their monumental crowds, depictions of the life of Jesus, 241 plates in all. 241pp. 9 x 12. 0-486-23004-X

DRAWING DRAPERY FROM HEAD TO TOE, Cliff Young. Expert guidance on how to draw shirts, pants, skirts, gloves, hats, and coats on the human figure, including folds in relation to the body, pull and crush, action folds, creases, more. Over 200 drawings. 48pp. 8¼ x 11. 0-486-45591-2

DUBLINERS, James Joyce. A fine and accessible introduction to the work of one of the 20th century's most influential writers, this collection features 15 tales, including a masterpiece of the short-story genre, "The Dead." 160pp. 5³⁄₁₆ x 8¼. 0-486-26870-5

EASY-TO-MAKE POP-UPS, Joan Irvine. Illustrated by Barbara Reid. Dozens of wonderful ideas for three-dimensional paper fun — from holiday greeting cards with moving parts to a pop-up menagerie. Easy-to-follow, illustrated instructions for more than 30 projects. 299 black-and-white illustrations. 96pp. 8⅜ x 11. 0-486-44622-0

EASY-TO-MAKE STORYBOOK DOLLS: A "Novel" Approach to Cloth Dollmaking, Sherralyn St. Clair. Favorite fictional characters come alive in this unique beginner's dollmaking guide. Includes patterns for Pollyanna, Dorothy from *The Wonderful Wizard of Oz,* Mary of *The Secret Garden,* plus easy-to-follow instructions, 263 black-and-white illustrations, and an 8-page color insert. 112pp. 8¼ x 11. 0-486-47360-0

EINSTEIN'S ESSAYS IN SCIENCE, Albert Einstein. Speeches and essays in accessible, everyday language profile influential physicists such as Niels Bohr and Isaac Newton. They also explore areas of physics to which the author made major contributions. 128pp. 5 x 8. 0-486-47011-3

EL DORADO: Further Adventures of the Scarlet Pimpernel, Baroness Orczy. A popular sequel to *The Scarlet Pimpernel,* this suspenseful story recounts the Pimpernel's attempts to rescue the Dauphin from imprisonment during the French Revolution. An irresistible blend of intrigue, period detail, and vibrant characterizations. 352pp. 5³⁄₁₆ x 8¼. 0-486-44026-5

ELEGANT SMALL HOMES OF THE TWENTIES: 99 Designs from a Competition, Chicago Tribune. Nearly 100 designs for five- and six-room houses feature New England and Southern colonials, Normandy cottages, stately Italianate dwellings, and other fascinating snapshots of American domestic architecture of the 1920s. 112pp. 9 x 12. 0-486-46910-7

THE ELEMENTS OF STYLE: The Original Edition, William Strunk, Jr. This is the book that generations of writers have relied upon for timeless advice on grammar, diction, syntax, and other essentials. In concise terms, it identifies the principal requirements of proper style and common errors. 64pp. 5⅜ x 8½. 0-486-44798-7

THE ELUSIVE PIMPERNEL, Baroness Orczy. Robespierre's revolutionaries find their wicked schemes thwarted by the heroic Pimpernel — Sir Percival Blakeney. In this thrilling sequel, Chauvelin devises a plot to eliminate the Pimpernel and his wife. 272pp. 5³⁄₁₆ x 8¼. 0-486-45464-9

AN ENCYCLOPEDIA OF BATTLES: Accounts of Over 1,560 Battles from 1479 B.C. to the Present, David Eggenberger. Essential details of every major battle in recorded history from the first battle of Megiddo in 1479 B.C. to Grenada in 1984. List of battle maps. 99 illustrations. 544pp. 6½ x 9¼. 0-486-24913-1

ENCYCLOPEDIA OF EMBROIDERY STITCHES, INCLUDING CREWEL, Marion Nichols. Precise explanations and instructions, clearly illustrated, on how to work chain, back, cross, knotted, woven stitches, and many more — 178 in all, including Cable Outline, Whipped Satin, and Eyelet Buttonhole. Over 1400 illustrations. 219pp. 8⅜ x 11¼. 0-486-22929-7

ENTER JEEVES: 15 Early Stories, P. G. Wodehouse. Splendid collection contains first 8 stories featuring Bertie Wooster, the deliciously dim aristocrat and Jeeves, his brainy, imperturbable manservant. Also, the complete Reggie Pepper (Bertie's prototype) series. 288pp. 5⅜ x 8½. 0-486-29717-9

ERIC SLOANE'S AMERICA: Paintings in Oil, Michael Wigley. With a Foreword by Mimi Sloane. Eric Sloane's evocative oils of America's landscape and material culture shimmer with immense historical and nostalgic appeal. This original hardcover collection gathers nearly a hundred of his finest paintings, with subjects ranging from New England to the American Southwest. 128pp. 10⅝ x 9. 0-486-46525-X

ETHAN FROME, Edith Wharton. Classic story of wasted lives, set against a bleak New England background. Superbly delineated characters in a hauntingly grim tale of thwarted love. Considered by many to be Wharton's masterpiece. 96pp. 5³⁄₁₆ x 8 ¼. 0-486-26690-7

THE EVERLASTING MAN, G. K. Chesterton. Chesterton's view of Christianity — as a blend of philosophy and mythology, satisfying intellect and spirit — applies to his brilliant book, which appeals to readers' heads as well as their hearts. 288pp. 5⅜ x 8½. 0-486-46036-3

THE FIELD AND FOREST HANDY BOOK, Daniel Beard. Written by a co-founder of the Boy Scouts, this appealing guide offers illustrated instructions for building kites, birdhouses, boats, igloos, and other fun projects, plus numerous helpful tips for campers. 448pp. 5³⁄₁₆ x 8¼. 0-486-46191-2

FINDING YOUR WAY WITHOUT MAP OR COMPASS, Harold Gatty. Useful, instructive manual shows would-be explorers, hikers, bikers, scouts, sailors, and survivalists how to find their way outdoors by observing animals, weather patterns, shifting sands, and other elements of nature. 288pp. 5⅜ x 8½. 0-486-40613-X

FIRST FRENCH READER: A Beginner's Dual-Language Book, Edited and Translated by Stanley Appelbaum. This anthology introduces 50 legendary writers — Voltaire, Balzac, Baudelaire, Proust, more — through passages from *The Red and the Black, Les Misérables, Madame Bovary,* and other classics. Original French text plus English translation on facing pages. 240pp. 5⅜ x 8½. 0-486-46178-5

FIRST GERMAN READER: A Beginner's Dual-Language Book, Edited by Harry Steinhauer. Specially chosen for their power to evoke German life and culture, these short, simple readings include poems, stories, essays, and anecdotes by Goethe, Hesse, Heine, Schiller, and others. 224pp. 5⅜ x 8½. 0-486-46179-3

FIRST SPANISH READER: A Beginner's Dual-Language Book, Angel Flores. Delightful stories, other material based on works of Don Juan Manuel, Luis Taboada, Ricardo Palma, other noted writers. Complete faithful English translations on facing pages. Exercises. 176pp. 5⅜ x 8½. 0-486-25810-6

FIVE ACRES AND INDEPENDENCE, Maurice G. Kains. Great back-to-the-land classic explains basics of self-sufficient farming. The one book to get. 95 illustrations. 397pp. 5⅜ x 8½. 0-486-20974-1

FLAGG'S SMALL HOUSES: Their Economic Design and Construction, 1922, Ernest Flagg. Although most famous for his skyscrapers, Flagg was also a proponent of the well-designed single-family dwelling. His classic treatise features innovations that save space, materials, and cost. 526 illustrations. 160pp. 9⅜ x 12¼. 0-486-45197-6

FLATLAND: A Romance of Many Dimensions, Edwin A. Abbott. Classic of science (and mathematical) fiction — charmingly illustrated by the author — describes the adventures of A. Square, a resident of Flatland, in Spaceland (three dimensions), Lineland (one dimension), and Pointland (no dimensions). 96pp. 5³⁄₁₆ x 8¼. 0-486-27263-X

FRANKENSTEIN, Mary Shelley. The story of Victor Frankenstein's monstrous creation and the havoc it caused has enthralled generations of readers and inspired countless writers of horror and suspense. With the author's own 1831 introduction. 176pp. 5³⁄₁₆ x 8¼. 0-486-28211-2

THE GARGOYLE BOOK: 572 Examples from Gothic Architecture, Lester Burbank Bridaham. Dispelling the conventional wisdom that French Gothic architectural flourishes were born of despair or gloom, Bridaham reveals the whimsical nature of these creations and the ingenious artisans who made them. 572 illustrations. 224pp. 8⅜ x 11. 0-486-44754-5

THE GIFT OF THE MAGI AND OTHER SHORT STORIES, O. Henry. Sixteen captivating stories by one of America's most popular storytellers. Included are such classics as "The Gift of the Magi," "The Last Leaf," and "The Ransom of Red Chief." Publisher's Note. 96pp. 5³⁄₁₆ x 8¼. 0-486-27061-0

THE GOETHE TREASURY: Selected Prose and Poetry, Johann Wolfgang von Goethe. Edited, Selected, and with an Introduction by Thomas Mann. In addition to his lyric poetry, Goethe wrote travel sketches, autobiographical studies, essays, letters, and proverbs in rhyme and prose. This collection presents outstanding examples from each genre. 368pp. 5⅜ x 8½. 0-486-44780-4

GREAT EXPECTATIONS, Charles Dickens. Orphaned Pip is apprenticed to the dirty work of the forge but dreams of becoming a gentleman — and one day finds himself in possession of "great expectations." Dickens' finest novel. 400pp. 5³⁄₁₆ x 8¼. 0-486-41586-4

GREAT WRITERS ON THE ART OF FICTION: From Mark Twain to Joyce Carol Oates, Edited by James Daley. An indispensable source of advice and inspiration, this anthology features essays by Henry James, Kate Chopin, Willa Cather, Sinclair Lewis, Jack London, Raymond Chandler, Raymond Carver, Eudora Welty, and Kurt Vonnegut, Jr. 192pp. 5⅜ x 8½. 0-486-45128-3

HAMLET, William Shakespeare. The quintessential Shakespearean tragedy, whose highly charged confrontations and anguished soliloquies probe depths of human feeling rarely sounded in any art. Reprinted from an authoritative British edition complete with illuminating footnotes. 128pp. 5³⁄₁₆ x 8¼. 0-486-27278-8

THE HAUNTED HOUSE, Charles Dickens. A Yuletide gathering in an eerie country retreat provides the backdrop for Dickens and his friends — including Elizabeth Gaskell and Wilkie Collins — who take turns spinning supernatural yarns. 144pp. 5⅜ x 8½. 0-486-46309-5

HEART OF DARKNESS, Joseph Conrad. Dark allegory of a journey up the Congo River and the narrator's encounter with the mysterious Mr. Kurtz. Masterly blend of adventure, character study, psychological penetration. For many, Conrad's finest, most enigmatic story. 80pp. 5³⁄₁₆ x 8¼. 0-486-26464-5

HENSON AT THE NORTH POLE, Matthew A. Henson. This thrilling memoir by the heroic African-American who was Peary's companion through two decades of Arctic exploration recounts a tale of danger, courage, and determination. "Fascinating and exciting." — *Commonweal*. 128pp. 5⅜ x 8½. 0-486-45472-X

HISTORIC COSTUMES AND HOW TO MAKE THEM, Mary Fernald and E. Shenton. Practical, informative guidebook shows how to create everything from short tunics worn by Saxon men in the fifth century to a lady's bustle dress of the late 1800s. 81 illustrations. 176pp. 5⅜ x 8½. 0-486-44906-8

THE HOUND OF THE BASKERVILLES, Arthur Conan Doyle. A deadly curse in the form of a legendary ferocious beast continues to claim its victims from the Baskerville family until Holmes and Watson intervene. Often called the best detective story ever written. 128pp. 5³⁄₁₆ x 8¼. 0-486-28214-7

THE HOUSE BEHIND THE CEDARS, Charles W. Chesnutt. Originally published in 1900, this groundbreaking novel by a distinguished African-American author recounts the drama of a brother and sister who "pass for white" during the dangerous days of Reconstruction. 208pp. 5⅜ x 8½. 0-486-46144-0

THE HUMAN FIGURE IN MOTION, Eadweard Muybridge. The 4,789 photographs in this definitive selection show the human figure — models almost all undraped — engaged in over 160 different types of action: running, climbing stairs, etc. 390pp. 7⅞ x 10⅝. 0-486-20204-6

THE IMPORTANCE OF BEING EARNEST, Oscar Wilde. Wilde's witty and buoyant comedy of manners, filled with some of literature's most famous epigrams, reprinted from an authoritative British edition. Considered Wilde's most perfect work. 64pp. 5³⁄₁₆ x 8¼. 0-486-26478-5

THE INFERNO, Dante Alighieri. Translated and with notes by Henry Wadsworth Longfellow. The first stop on Dante's famous journey from Hell to Purgatory to Paradise, this 14th-century allegorical poem blends vivid and shocking imagery with graceful lyricism. Translated by the beloved 19th-century poet, Henry Wadsworth Longfellow. 256pp. 5³⁄₁₆ x 8¼. 0-486-44288-8

JANE EYRE, Charlotte Brontë. Written in 1847, *Jane Eyre* tells the tale of an orphan girl's progress from the custody of cruel relatives to an oppressive boarding school and its culmination in a troubled career as a governess. 448pp. 5³⁄₁₆ x 8¼. 0-486-42449-9

JAPANESE WOODBLOCK FLOWER PRINTS, Tanigami Kônan. Extraordinary collection of Japanese woodblock prints by a well-known artist features 120 plates in brilliant color. Realistic images from a rare edition include daffodils, tulips, and other familiar and unusual flowers. 128pp. 11 x 8¼. 0-486-46442-3

JEWELRY MAKING AND DESIGN, Augustus F. Rose and Antonio Cirino. Professional secrets of jewelry making are revealed in a thorough, practical guide. Over 200 illustrations. 306pp. 5⅜ x 8½. 0-486-21750-7

JULIUS CAESAR, William Shakespeare. Great tragedy based on Plutarch's account of the lives of Brutus, Julius Caesar and Mark Antony. Evil plotting, ringing oratory, high tragedy with Shakespeare's incomparable insight, dramatic power. Explanatory footnotes. 96pp. 5³⁄₁₆ x 8¼. 0-486-26876-4

Browse over 9,000 books at www.doverpublications.com

THE JUNGLE, Upton Sinclair. 1906 bestseller shockingly reveals intolerable labor practices and working conditions in the Chicago stockyards as it tells the grim story of a Slavic family that emigrates to America full of optimism but soon faces despair. 320pp. 5³⁄₁₆ x 8¼. 0-486-41923-1

THE KINGDOM OF GOD IS WITHIN YOU, Leo Tolstoy. The soul-searching book that inspired Gandhi to embrace the concept of passive resistance, Tolstoy's 1894 polemic clearly outlines a radical, well-reasoned revision of traditional Christian thinking. 352pp. 5³⁄₁₆ x 8¼. 0-486-45138-0

THE LADY OR THE TIGER?: and Other Logic Puzzles, Raymond M. Smullyan. Created by a renowned puzzle master, these whimsically themed challenges involve paradoxes about probability, time, and change; metapuzzles; and self-referentiality. Nineteen chapters advance in difficulty from relatively simple to highly complex. 1982 edition. 240pp. 5⅜ x 8½. 0-486-47027-X

LEAVES OF GRASS: The Original 1855 Edition, Walt Whitman. Whitman's immortal collection includes some of the greatest poems of modern times, including his masterpiece, "Song of Myself." Shattering standard conventions, it stands as an unabashed celebration of body and nature. 128pp. 5³⁄₁₆ x 8¼. 0-486-45676-5

LES MISÉRABLES, Victor Hugo. Translated by Charles E. Wilbour. Abridged by James K. Robinson. A convict's heroic struggle for justice and redemption plays out against a fiery backdrop of the Napoleonic wars. This edition features the excellent original translation and a sensitive abridgment. 304pp. 6⅛ x 9¼. 0-486-45789-3

LILITH: A Romance, George MacDonald. In this novel by the father of fantasy literature, a man travels through time to meet Adam and Eve and to explore humanity's fall from grace and ultimate redemption. 240pp. 5⅜ x 8½. 0-486-46818-6

THE LOST LANGUAGE OF SYMBOLISM, Harold Bayley. This remarkable book reveals the hidden meaning behind familiar images and words, from the origins of Santa Claus to the fleur-de-lys, drawing from mythology, folklore, religious texts, and fairy tales. 1,418 illustrations. 784pp. 5⅜ x 8½. 0-486-44787-1

MACBETH, William Shakespeare. A Scottish nobleman murders the king in order to succeed to the throne. Tortured by his conscience and fearful of discovery, he becomes tangled in a web of treachery and deceit that ultimately spells his doom. 96pp. 5³⁄₁₆ x 8¼. 0-486-27802-6

MAKING AUTHENTIC CRAFTSMAN FURNITURE: Instructions and Plans for 62 Projects, Gustav Stickley. Make authentic reproductions of handsome, functional, durable furniture: tables, chairs, wall cabinets, desks, a hall tree, and more. Construction plans with drawings, schematics, dimensions, and lumber specs reprinted from 1900s *The Craftsman* magazine. 128pp. 8⅛ x 11. 0-486-25000-8

MATHEMATICS FOR THE NONMATHEMATICIAN, Morris Kline. Erudite and entertaining overview follows development of mathematics from ancient Greeks to present. Topics include logic and mathematics, the fundamental concept, differential calculus, probability theory, much more. Exercises and problems. 641pp. 5⅜ x 8½. 0-486-24823-2

MEMOIRS OF AN ARABIAN PRINCESS FROM ZANZIBAR, Emily Ruete. This 19th-century autobiography offers a rare inside look at the society surrounding a sultan's palace. A real-life princess in exile recalls her vanished world of harems, slave trading, and court intrigues. 288pp. 5⅜ x 8½. 0-486-47121-7

Browse over 9,000 books at www.doverpublications.com

THE METAMORPHOSIS AND OTHER STORIES, Franz Kafka. Excellent new English translations of title story (considered by many critics Kafka's most perfect work), plus "The Judgment," "In the Penal Colony," "A Country Doctor," and "A Report to an Academy." Note. 96pp. 5³⁄₁₆ x 8¼. 0-486-29030-1

MICROSCOPIC ART FORMS FROM THE PLANT WORLD, R. Anheisser. From undulating curves to complex geometrics, a world of fascinating images abound in this classic, illustrated survey of microscopic plants. Features 400 detailed illustrations of nature's minute but magnificent handiwork. The accompanying CD-ROM includes all of the images in the book. 128pp. 9 x 9. 0-486-46013-4

A MIDSUMMER NIGHT'S DREAM, William Shakespeare. Among the most popular of Shakespeare's comedies, this enchanting play humorously celebrates the vagaries of love as it focuses upon the intertwined romances of several pairs of lovers. Explanatory footnotes. 80pp. 5³⁄₁₆ x 8¼. 0-486-27067-X

THE MONEY CHANGERS, Upton Sinclair. Originally published in 1908, this cautionary novel from the author of *The Jungle* explores corruption within the American system as a group of power brokers joins forces for personal gain, triggering a crash on Wall Street. 192pp. 5⅜ x 8½. 0-486-46917-4

THE MOST POPULAR HOMES OF THE TWENTIES, William A. Radford. With a New Introduction by Daniel D. Reiff. Based on a rare 1925 catalog, this architectural showcase features floor plans, construction details, and photos of 26 homes, plus articles on entrances, porches, garages, and more. 250 illustrations, 21 color plates. 176pp. 8⅜ x 11. 0-486-47028-8

MY 66 YEARS IN THE BIG LEAGUES, Connie Mack. With a New Introduction by Rich Westcott. A Founding Father of modern baseball, Mack holds the record for most wins — and losses — by a major league manager. Enhanced by 70 photographs, his warmhearted autobiography is populated by many legends of the game. 288pp. 5⅜ x 8½. 0-486-47184-5

NARRATIVE OF THE LIFE OF FREDERICK DOUGLASS, Frederick Douglass. Douglass's graphic depictions of slavery, harrowing escape to freedom, and life as a newspaper editor, eloquent orator, and impassioned abolitionist. 96pp. 5³⁄₁₆ x 8¼. 0-486-28499-9

THE NIGHTLESS CITY: Geisha and Courtesan Life in Old Tokyo, J. E. de Becker. This unsurpassed study from 100 years ago ventured into Tokyo's red-light district to survey geisha and courtesan life and offer meticulous descriptions of training, dress, social hierarchy, and erotic practices. 49 black-and-white illustrations; 2 maps. 496pp. 5⅜ x 8½. 0-486-45563-7

THE ODYSSEY, Homer. Excellent prose translation of ancient epic recounts adventures of the homeward-bound Odysseus. Fantastic cast of gods, giants, cannibals, sirens, other supernatural creatures — true classic of Western literature. 256pp. 5³⁄₁₆ x 8¼. 0-486-40654-7

OEDIPUS REX, Sophocles. Landmark of Western drama concerns the catastrophe that ensues when King Oedipus discovers he has inadvertently killed his father and married his mother. Masterly construction, dramatic irony. Explanatory footnotes. 64pp. 5³⁄₁₆ x 8¼. 0-486-26877-2

ONCE UPON A TIME: The Way America Was, Eric Sloane. Nostalgic text and drawings brim with gentle philosophies and descriptions of how we used to live — self-sufficiently — on the land, in homes, and among the things built by hand. 44 line illustrations. 64pp. 8⅜ x 11. 0-486-44411-2

Browse over 9,000 books at www.doverpublications.com